Praise for
STEPHEN KING
and the #1 *New York Times* bestseller
THE INSTITUTE

"*The Institute* is another winner: creepy and touching and horrifyingly believable, all at once . . . a major work . . . an intimate picture of horror."

—*The Boston Globe*

"With *The Institute*, King leans into the theme of 'great events' happening with the smallest of decisions as well as the world-changing power of togetherness. And in that case, it's a frequent lesson he extols that never gets old."

—*USA Today*

"This is King at his best, scaring the heck out of readers by making them wonder what else the government may be doing under cover of science."

—*The St. Louis Post-Dispatch*

"A tale delineating a troubling separation between children and the adult world . . . vibrant . . . nuanced webs of action and consequence . . . comprise this engaging narrative."

—*Los Angeles Review of Books*

"A horror story, but not in the traditional Stephen King supernatural sense. Its realism results in a deeper terror . . . an entirely original story that can only come from the mind of a master teller like King."

—*The Florida Times-Union*

The air is soft, medium moist
~~Even~~ A breeze cools yet caresses
Your skin until it lays on you ~~to~~
a warm blanket tickling a little
as you stir, back to sleep

STEPHEN KING

THE
INSTITUTE
A NOVEL

POCKET BOOKS

New York London Toronto Sydney New Delhi

Pocket Books
An Imprint of Simon & Schuster, Inc.
1230 Avenue of the Americas
New York, NY 10020

This Pocket Books paperback edition July 2021

POCKET and colophon are registered trademarks of Simon & Schuster, Inc.

For information about special discounts for bulk purchases, please contact Simon & Schuster Special Sales at 1-866-506-1949 or business@simonandschuster.com.

The Simon & Schuster Speakers Bureau can bring authors to your live event. For more information or to book an event, contact the Simon & Schuster Speakers Bureau at 1-866-248-3049 or visit our website at www.simonspeakers.com.

Manufactured in the United States of America

10 9 8 7 6 5 4 3 2 1

ISBN 978-1-9821-1057-4
ISBN 978-1-9821-1059-8 (ebook)

For my grandsons:
Ethan, Aidan, and Ryan

And Samson called unto the LORD, and said, O Lord God, remember me, I pray thee, and strengthen me, I pray thee, only this once, O God, that I may be at once avenged of the Philistines . . .

And Samson took hold of the two middle pillars upon which the house stood, and on which it was borne up, of the one with his right hand, and of the other with his left.

And Samson said, Let me die with the Philistines. And he bowed himself with all his might; and the house fell upon the lords, and upon all the people that were therein. So the dead which he slew at his death were more than they which he slew in his life.

Judges, Chapter 16

But whoso shall offend one of these little ones . . . it were better for him that a millstone were hanged about his neck, and that he were drowned in the depth of the sea.

Matthew, Chapter 18

According to the National Center for Missing and Exploited Children, roughly 800,000 children are reported missing each year in the United States.
Most are found.
Thousands are not.

THE NIGHT KNOCKER

1

Half an hour after Tim Jamieson's Delta flight was scheduled to leave Tampa for the bright lights and tall buildings of New York, it was still parked at the gate. When a Delta agent and a blond woman with a security badge hanging around her neck entered the cabin, there were unhappy, premonitory murmurings from the packed residents of economy class.

"May I have your attention, please!" the Delta guy called.

"How long's the delay gonna be?" someone asked. "Don't sugarcoat it."

"The delay should be short, and the captain wants to assure you all that your flight will arrive approximately on time. We have a federal officer who needs to board, however, so we'll need someone to give up his or her seat."

A collective groan went up, and Tim saw several people unlimber their cell phones in case of trouble. There had been trouble in these situations before.

"Delta Air Lines is authorized to offer a free ticket to New York on the next outbound flight, which will be tomorrow morning at 6:45 AM—"

Another groan went up. Someone said, "Just shoot me."

The functionary continued, undeterred. "You'll be given a hotel voucher for tonight, plus four hundred dollars. It's a good deal, folks. Who wants it?"

He had no takers. The security blond said nothing, only surveyed the crowded economy-class cabin with all-seeing but somehow lifeless eyes.

"Eight hundred," the Delta guy said. "Plus the hotel voucher and the complimentary ticket."

"Guy sounds like a quiz show host," grunted a man in the row ahead of Tim's.

There were still no takers.

"Fourteen hundred?"

And still none. Tim found this interesting but not entirely surprising. It wasn't just because a six forty-five flight meant getting up before God, either. Most of his fellow economy-class passengers were family groups headed home after visiting various Florida attractions, couples sporting beachy-keen sunburns, and beefy, red-faced, pissed-off-looking guys who probably had business in the Big Apple worth considerably more than fourteen hundred bucks.

Someone far in the back called, "Throw in a Mustang convertible and a trip to Aruba for two, and you can have both our seats!" This sally provoked laughter. It didn't sound terribly friendly.

The gate agent looked at the blond with the badge, but if he hoped for help there, he got none. She just continued her survey, nothing moving but her eyes. He sighed and said, "Sixteen hundred."

Tim Jamieson suddenly decided he wanted to get the fuck off this plane and hitchhike north. Although such an idea had never so much as crossed his mind before this moment, he found he could imagine himself doing it, and with absolute clarity. There he was, standing on Highway 301 somewhere in the middle of Hernando County with his thumb out. It was hot, the lovebugs were swarming, there was a billboard advertising some slip-and-fall attorney, "Take It on the Run" was blaring from a boombox sitting on the concrete-block step of a nearby trailer where a shirtless man was washing his car, and eventually some Farmer John would come along and give him a ride in a pickup truck with stake sides, melons in the back, and a magnetic Jesus on the dashboard. The best part wouldn't even be the cash money in his pocket. The best part would be standing out there by himself, miles from this sardine can with its warring smells of perfume, sweat, and hair spray.

The second-best part, however, would be squeezing the government tit for a few dollars more.

He stood up to his perfectly normal height (five-ten and a fraction), pushed his glasses up on his nose, and raised his hand. "Make it two thousand, sir, plus a cash refund of my ticket, and the seat is yours."

2

The voucher turned out to be for a cheesedog hotel located near the end of Tampa International's most heavily used runway. Tim fell asleep to the sound of airplanes, awoke to more of the same, and went down to ingest a hardboiled egg and two rubber pancakes from the complimentary breakfast buffet. Although far from a gourmet treat, Tim ate heartily, then went back to his room to wait for nine o'clock, when the banks opened.

He cashed his windfall with no trouble, because the bank knew he was coming and the check had been approved in advance; he had no intention of waiting around in the cheesedog hotel for it to clear. He took his two thousand in fifties and twenties, folded it into his left front pocket, reclaimed his duffel bag from the bank's security guard, and called an Uber to take him to Ellenton. There he paid the driver, strolled to the nearest 301-N sign, and stuck out his thumb. Fifteen minutes later he was picked up by an old guy in a Case gimme cap. There were no melons in the back of his pickup, and no stake sides, but otherwise it pretty much conformed to his vision of the previous night.

"Where you headed, friend?" the old guy asked.

"Well," Tim said, "New York, eventually. I guess."

The old guy spat a ribbon of tobacco juice out the window. "Now why would any man in his right mind want to go there?" He pronounced it *raht mahnd*.

"I don't know," Tim said, although he did; an old service buddy had told him there was plenty of private security work in the Big Apple, including some for companies that would give more weight to his experience than to the Rube Goldberg fuckup that had ended his career in Florida policing. "I'm just hoping to get to Georgia tonight. Maybe I'll like that better."

"Now you're talking," the old guy said. "Georgia ain't bad, specially if you like peaches. They gi' me the backdoor trots. You don't mind some music, do you?"

"Not at all."

"Got to warn you, I play it loud. I'm a little on the deef side."

"I'm just happy to be riding."

It was Waylon Jennings instead of REO Speed-

wagon, but that was okay with Tim. Waylon was followed by Shooter Jennings and Marty Stuart. The two
men in the mud-streaked Dodge Ram listened and
watched the highway roll. Seventy miles up the line,
the old guy pulled over, gave Tim a tip of his Case cap,
and wished him a real fahn day.

Tim didn't make Georgia that night—he spent it in
another cheesedog motel next to a roadside stand selling orange juice—but he got there the following day.
In the town of Brunswick (where a certain kind of tasty
stew had been invented), he took two weeks' work in
a recycling plant, doing it with no more forethought
than he had put into deciding to give up his seat on
the Delta flight out of Tampa. He didn't need the
money, but it seemed to Tim that he needed the time.
He was in transition, and that didn't happen over-
night. Also, there was a bowling alley with a Denny's
right next door. Hard to beat a combo like that.

3

With his pay from the recycling plant added to his
airline windfall, Tim was standing on the Brunswick
ramp of I-95 North and feeling pretty well-heeled for
a rambling man. He stood there for over an hour in the
sun, and was thinking of giving up and going back
to Denny's for a cold glass of sweet tea when a Volvo
station wagon pulled over. The back was filled with
cartons. The elderly woman behind the wheel powered
down the passenger side window and peered at him
through thick glasses. "Although not large, you look
well-muscled," she said. "You are not a rapist or a psy-
chotic, are you?"

"No, ma'am," Tim told her, thinking: But what else *would* I say?

"Of course you would say that, wouldn't you? Are you going as far as South Carolina? Your duffel bag suggests that you are."

A car swept around her Volvo and sped up the ramp, horn blaring. She took no notice, only kept her serene gaze fixed on Tim.

"Yes, ma'am. All the way to New York."

"I'll take you to South Carolina—not far into that benighted state, but a little way—if you'll help me out a bit in return. One hand washes the other, if you see what I mean."

"You scratch my back and I scratch yours," Tim said, grinning.

"There will be no scratching of any kind, but you may get in."

Tim did so. Her name was Marjorie Kellerman, and she ran the Brunswick library. She also belonged to something called the Southeastern Library Association. Which, she said, had no money because "Trump and his cronies took it all back. They understand culture no more than a donkey understands algebra."

Sixty-five miles north, still in Georgia, she stopped at a pokey little library in the town of Pooler. Tim unloaded the cartons of books and dollied them inside. He dollied another dozen or so cartons out to the Volvo. These, Marjorie Kellerman told him, were bound to the Yemassee Public Library, about forty miles further north, across the South Carolina state line. But not long after passing Hardeeville, their progress came to a stop. Cars and trucks were stacked up in both lanes, and more quickly filled in behind them.

"Oh, I hate it when this happens," Marjorie said,

"and it always seems to in South Carolina, where they're too cheap to widen the highway. There's been a wreck somewhere up ahead, and with only two lanes, nobody can get by. I'll be here half the day. Mr. Jamieson, you may be excused from further duty. If I were you, I would exit my vehicle, walk back to the Hardeeville exit, and try your luck on Highway 17."

"What about all those cartons of books?"

"Oh, I'll find another strong back to help me unload," she said, and smiled at him. "To tell you the truth, I saw you standing there in the hot sun and just decided to live a little dangerously."

"Well, if you're sure." The traffic clog was making him feel claustrophobic. The way he'd felt stuck halfway back in economy class of the Delta flight, in fact. "If you're not, I'll hang in. It's not like I'm racing a deadline or anything."

"I'm sure," she said. "It's been a pleasure meeting you, Mr. Jamieson."

"Likewise, Ms. Kellerman."

"Do you need monetary assistance? I can spare ten dollars, if you do."

He was touched and surprised—not for the first time—by the ordinary kindness and generosity of ordinary folks, especially those without much to spare. America was still a good place, no matter how much some (including himself, from time to time) might disagree. "No, I'm fine. Thank you for the offer."

He shook her hand, got out, and walked back along the I-95 breakdown lane to the Hardeeville exit. When a ride was not immediately forthcoming on US 17, he strolled a couple of miles to where it joined State Road 92. Here a sign pointed toward the town of Du-Pray. By then it was late afternoon, and Tim decided he had better find a motel in which to spend the night. It would undoubtedly be another of the cheesedog variety, but the alternatives—sleeping outside and getting eaten alive by skeeters or in some farmer's barn—were even less appealing. And so he set out for DuPray.

Great events turn on small hinges.

4

An hour later he was sitting on a rock at the edge of the two-lane, waiting for a seemingly endless freight train to cross the road. It was headed in the direction of DuPray at a stately thirty miles an hour: boxcars, autoracks (most loaded with wrecks rather than new vehicles), tankers, flatcars, and gondolas loaded with God knew what evil substances that might, in the event of a derailment, catch the piney woods afire or afflict the DuPray populace with noxious or even fatal fumes. At last came an orange caboose where a man in bib overalls sat in a lawn chair, reading a paperback and smoking a cigarette. He looked up from his book and tipped Tim a wave. Tim tipped one right back.

The town was two miles further on, built around the intersection of SR 92 (now called Main Street) and two other streets. DuPray seemed to have largely escaped the chain stores that had taken over the bigger towns; there was a Western Auto, but it was closed down, the windows soaped over. Tim noted a grocery store, a drug store, a mercantile that appeared to sell a little bit of everything, and a couple of beauty salons. There was also a movie theater with FOR SALE OR RENT on the marquee, an auto supply store that fancied itself the DuPray Speed Shop, and a restaurant called Bev's

Eatery. There were three churches, one Methodist, two off-brand, all of the come-to-Jesus variety. There were no more than two dozen cars and farm trucks scattered along the slant-parking spaces that lined the business district. The sidewalks were nearly deserted.

Three blocks up, after yet another church, he spied the DuPray Motel. Beyond it, where Main Street presumably reverted to SR 92, there was another rail crossing, a depot, and a row of metal roofs glittering in the sun. Beyond these structures, the piney woods closed in again. All in all, it looked to Tim like a town out of a country ballad, one of those nostalgia pieces sung by Alan Jackson or George Strait. The motel sign was old and rusty, suggesting the place might be as closed-down as the movie theater, but since the afternoon was now ebbing away and it appeared to be the only game in town when it came to shelter, Tim headed for it.

Halfway there, after the DuPray Town Office, he came to a brick building with ladders of ivy climbing the sides. On the neatly mowed lawn was a sign proclaiming this the Fairlee County Sheriff's Department. Tim thought it must be a poor-ass county indeed, if this town was its seat.

Two cruisers were parked in front, one of them a newish sedan, the other an elderly, mud-splashed 4Runner with a bubble light on the dash. Tim looked toward the entrance—the almost unconscious glance of a drifter with quite a lot of cash money in his pocket—walked on a few steps, then turned back for a closer look at the notice boards flanking the double doors. At one of the notices in particular. Thinking he must have read it wrong but wanting to make sure.

Not in this day and age, he thought. Can't be.

But it was. Next to a poster reading IF YOU THOUGHT MARIJUANA IS LEGAL IN SOUTH CAROLINA, **THINK AGAIN**, was one that read simply NIGHT KNOCKER WANTED. APPLY WITHIN.

Wow, he thought. Talk about a blast from the past.

He turned toward the rusty motel sign and paused again, thinking about that help-wanted sign. Just then one of the police station doors opened and a lanky cop came out, settling his cap on his red hair. The latening sun twinkled on his badge. He took in Tim's workboots, dusty jeans, and blue chambray shirt. His eyes dwelled for a moment on the duffel bag slung over Tim's shoulder before moving to his face. "Can I help you, sir?"

The same impulse that had made him stand up on the plane swept over him now. "Probably not, but who knows?"

5

The redheaded cop was Deputy Taggart Faraday. He escorted Tim inside, where the familiar smells of bleach and ammonia cakes wafted into the office from the four-cell holding area in the back. After introducing Tim to Veronica Gibson, the middle-aged deputy working dispatch this afternoon, Faraday asked to see Tim's driver's license and at least one other piece of identification. What Tim produced in addition to his DL was his Sarasota Police ID, making no attempt to hide the fact that it had expired nine months before. Nevertheless, the attitudes of the deputies changed slightly when they saw it.

"You're not a resident of Fairlee County," Ronnie Gibson said.

"No," Tim agreed. "Not at all. But I could be if I got the night knocker job."

"Doesn't pay much," Faraday said, "and in any case it's not up to me. Sheriff Ashworth hires and fires."

Ronnie Gibson said, "Our last night knocker retired and moved down to Georgia. Ed Whitlock. He got ALS, that Lou Gehrig's thing. Nice man. Tough break. But he's got people down there to take care of him."

"It's always the nice ones who get hit with the shit," Tag Faraday said. "Give him a form, Ronnie." Then, to Tim: "We're a small outfit here, Mr. Jamieson, crew of seven and two of them part-time. All the taxpayers can afford. Sheriff John's currently out on patrol. If he's not in by five, five-thirty at the latest, he's gone home to supper and won't be in until tomorrow."

"I'll be here tonight in any case. Assuming the motel's open, that is."

"Oh, I think Norbert's got a few rooms," Ronnie Gibson said. She exchanged a glance with the redhead and they both laughed.

"I'm guessing it might not be a four-star establishment."

"No comment on that," Gibson said, "but I'd check the sheets for those little red bugs before you lie down, if I was you. Why'd you leave Sarasota PD, Mr. Jamieson? You're young to retire, I'd say."

"That's a matter I'll discuss with your chief, assuming he grants me an interview."

The two officers exchanged another, longer look, then Tag Faraday said, "Go on and give the man an application, Ronnie. Nice to meet you, sir. Welcome to

DuPray. Act right and we'll get along fine." With that he departed, leaving the alternative to good behavior open to interpretation. Through the barred window, Tim saw the 4Runner back out of its spot and roll off down DuPray's short main street.

The form was on a clipboard. Tim sat down in one of the three chairs against the lefthand wall, placed his duffel between his feet, and began filling it out.

Night knocker, he thought. I will be goddamned.

6

Sheriff Ashworth—Sheriff John to most of the towns-folk as well as to his deputies, Tim discovered—was a big-bellied slow walker. He had basset hound jowls and a lot of white hair. There was a ketchup stain on his uniform shirt. He wore a Glock on his hip and a ruby ring on one pinkie. His accent was strong, his attitude was good-ole-boy friendly, but his eyes, deep in their fatty sockets, were smart and inquisitive. He could have been typecast in one of those southern-cliché movies like *Walking Tall*, if not for the fact that he was black. And something else: a framed certificate of graduation from the FBI's National Academy in Quantico hung on the wall next to the official portrait of President Trump. That was not the sort of thing you got by mailing in cereal boxtops.

"All right, then," Sheriff John said, rocking back in his office chair. "I haven't got long. Marcella hates it when I'm late for dinner. Unless there's some sort of crisis, accourse."

"Understood."

"So let's get right to the good part. Why'd you

leave Sarasota PD and what are you doing here? South Cah'lina doesn't have too many beaten tracks, and Du-Pray idn't exactly on any of them."

Ashworth probably wouldn't be on the phone to Sarasota tonight, but he would be in the morning, so there was no point in gilding the lily. Not that Tim wanted to. If he didn't get the night knocker job, he would spend the night in DuPray and move on in the morning, continuing his stop-and-start progress to New York, a journey he now understood to be a necessary hiatus between what had happened one day late last year at Sarasota's Westfield Mall and whatever might happen next. All that aside, honesty was the best policy, if only because lies—especially in an age when almost all information was available to anyone with a keyboard and a Wi-Fi connection—usually came back to haunt the liar.

"I was given a choice between resignation and dismissal. I chose resignation. No one was happy about it, least of all me—I liked my job and I liked the Gulf Coast—but it was the best solution. This way I get a little money, nothing like a full pension, but better than nothing. I split it with my ex-wife."

"Cause? And make it simple so I can get to my dinner while it's still hot."

"This won't take long. At the end of my shift one day last November, I swung into the Westfield Mall to buy a pair of shoes. Had to go to a wedding. I was still in uniform, okay?"

"Okay."

"I was coming out of the Shoe Depot when a woman ran up and said a teenager was waving a gun around up by the movie theater. So I went up there, double-time."

"Did you draw your weapon?"

"No sir, not then. The kid with the gun was maybe fourteen, and I ascertained that he was either drunk or high. He had another kid down and was kicking him. He was also pointing the gun at him."

"Sounds like that Cleveland deal. The cop who shot the black kid who was waving a pellet gun."

"That was in my mind when I approached, but the cop who shot Tamir Rice swore he thought the kid was waving a real gun around. I was pretty sure the one I saw wasn't real, but I couldn't be *completely* sure. Maybe you know why."

Sheriff John Ashworth seemed to have forgotten about dinner. "Because your subject was pointing it at the kid he had on the floor. No sense pointing a fake gun at someone. Unless, I s'pose, the kid on the ground didn't know that."

"The perp said later he was *shaking* it at the kid, not pointing it. Saying 'It's mine, motherfucker, you don't take what's mine.' I didn't see that. To me he looked like he was pointing it. I yelled at him to drop the weapon and put his hands up. He either didn't hear me or didn't pay any attention. He just went on kicking and pointing. Or shaking, if that's what he was doing. In any case, I drew my sidearm." He paused. "If it makes any difference, these kids were white."

"Not to me, it doesn't. Kids were fighting. One was down and getting hurt. The other had what might or might not have been a real gun. So did you shoot him? Tell me it didn't come to that."

"No one got shot. But . . . you know how people will gather around to watch a fistfight, but tend to scatter once a weapon comes out?"

"Sure. If they've got any sense, they run like hell."

"That happened, except for a few people who stayed even then."

"The ones filming it with their phones."

Tim nodded. "Four or five wannabe Spielbergs. Anyway, I pointed my gun at the ceiling and fired what was supposed to be a warning shot. It might have been a bad decision, but in that moment it seemed like the right one. The only one. There are hanging lights in that part of the mall. The bullet hit one of them and it came down dead-center on a lookie-loo's head. The kid with the gun dropped it, and as soon as it hit the floor, I knew for sure it wasn't real because it bounced. Turned out to be a plastic squirt gun made to look like a .45 auto. The kid who was on the floor getting kicked had some bruises and a few cuts, nothing that looked like it would need stitches, but the bystander was unconscious and stayed that way for three hours. Concussion. According to his lawyer he's got amnesia and blinding headaches."

"Sued the department?"

"Yes. It'll go on for awhile, but he'll end up getting something."

Sheriff John considered. "If he hung around to film the altercation, he may not get all that much, no matter how bad his headaches are. I suppose the department landed you with reckless discharge of a weapon."

They had, and it would be nice, Tim thought, if we could leave it at that. But they couldn't. Sheriff John might look like an African-American version of Boss Hogg in *The Dukes of Hazzard*, but he was no dummy. He was clearly sympathetic to Tim's situation—almost any cop would be—but he'd still check. Better he got the rest of the story from Tim himself.

"Before I went into the shoe store, I went into

Beachcombers and had a couple of drinks. The responding officers who took the kid into custody smelled it on my breath and gave me the test. I blew oh-six, under the legal limit but not good considering I had just fired my sidearm and put a man in the hospital."

"You ordinarily a drinking man, Mr. Jamieson?"

"Quite a lot in the six months or so after my divorce, but that was two years ago. Not now." Which is, of course, what I *would* say, he thought.

"Uh-huh, uh-huh, now let's see if I got this right." The sheriff stuck up a fat index finger. "You were off duty, which means if you'd been out of uniform, that woman never would have run up to you in the first place."

"Probably not, but I would have heard the commotion and gone to the scene anyway. A cop is never really off duty. As I'm sure you know."

"Uh-huh, uh-huh, but would you have had your gun?"

"No, it would have been locked in my car."

Ashworth popped a second finger for that point, then added a third. "The kid had what was probably a fake gun, but it could have been real. You couldn't be sure, one way or the other."

"Yes."

Here came finger number four. "Your warning shot struck a light, not only bringing it down but bringing it down on an innocent bystander's head. If, that is, you can call an asshole filming with a cell phone an innocent bystander."

Tim nodded.

Up popped the sheriff's thumb. "And before this altercation occurred, you just happened to have ingested two alcoholic drinks."

"Yes. And while I was in uniform."

"Not a good decision, not a good . . . what do they call it . . . *optic*, but I'd still have to say you had one insane run of bad luck." Sheriff John drummed his fingers on the edge of his desk. The ruby pinkie ring punctuated each roll with a small click. "I think your story is too outrageous not to be true, but I believe I'll call your previous place of employment and check it for myself. If for no other reason than to hear the story again and marvel anew."

Tim smiled. "I reported to Bernadette DiPino. She's the Sarasota Chief of Police. And you better get home to dinner, or your wife is going to be mad."

"Uh-huh, uh-huh, you let me worry about Marcy." The sheriff leaned forward over his stomach. His eyes were brighter than ever. "If I Breathalyzed you right now, Mr. Jamieson, what would you blow?"

"Go ahead and find out."

"Don't believe I will. Don't believe I need to." He leaned back; his office chair uttered another longsuffering squall. "Why would you want the job of night knocker in a pissant little burg like this? It only pays a hundred dollars a week, and while it doesn't amount to much in the way of trouble Sunday to Thursday, it can be an aggravation on Friday and Saturday nights. The strip club in Penley closed down last year, but there are several ginmills and juke joints in the immediate area."

"My grandfather was a night knocker in Hibbing, Minnesota. The town where Bob Dylan grew up? This was after he retired from the State Police. He was the reason I wanted to be a cop when I was growing up. I saw the sign, and just thought . . ." Tim shrugged. What *had* he thought? Pretty much the same thing as when he'd taken the job in the recycling plant. A whole lot of nothing much. It occurred to him that he might be, mentally speaking, at least, in sort of a hard place.

"Following in your grandpop's footsteps, uh-huh." Sheriff John clasped his hands over his considerable belly and stared at Tim—those bright, inquisitive eyes deep in their pockets of fat. "Consider yourself retired, is that the deal? Just looking for something to while away the idle hours? A little young for that, wouldn't you say?"

"Retired from the police, yes. That's over. A friend said he could get me security work in New York, and I wanted a change of scene. Maybe I don't have to go to New York to get one." He guessed what he really wanted was a change of heart. The night knocker job might not accomplish that, but then again it might.

"Divorced, you say?"

"Yes."

"Kids?"

"No. She wanted them, I didn't. Didn't feel I was ready."

Sheriff John looked down at Tim's application. "It says here you're forty-two. In most cases—probably not all—if you're not ready by then . . ."

He trailed off, waiting in best cop fashion for Tim to fill the silence. Tim didn't.

"You may be headed to New York eventually, Mr. Jamieson, but right now you're just drifting. That fair to say?"

Tim thought it over and agreed it *was* fair.

"If I give you this job, how do I know you won't take a notion to just drift on out of here two weeks or a month from now? DuPray idn't the most interesting place on earth, or even in South Cah'lina. What I'm asking, sir, is how do I know you're dependable?"

"I'll stick around. Always assuming you feel like I'm doing the job, that is. If you decide I'm not, you'll can me. If I should decide to move on, I'll give you plenty of notice. That's a promise."

"Job's not enough to live on."

Tim shrugged. "I'll find something else if I need to. You want to tell me I'd be the only guy around here working two jobs to make ends meet? And I've got a little put by to get started on."

Sheriff John sat where he was for a little while, thinking it over, then got to his feet. He did it with surprising agility for such a heavy man. "You come around tomorrow morning and we'll see what we're gonna do about this. Around ten would be about right."

Which will give you plenty of time to talk to Sarasota PD, Tim thought, and see if my story checks out. Also to discover if there are other smudges on my record.

He stood himself and stuck out his hand. Sheriff John's grip was a good strong one. "Where will you be staying tonight, Mr. Jamieson?"

"That motel down the way, if there's a vacant room."

"Oh, Norbert'll have plenty of vacant rooms," the sheriff said, "and I doubt if he'll try to sell you any of the herb. You've still got a little of the cop look about you, seems to me. If you don't have a problem digesting fried food, Bev's down the street is open until seven. I'm partial to the liver and onions, myself."

"Thanks. And thanks for talking to me."

"Not at all. Interesting conversation. And when you check in at the DuPray, tell Norbert Sheriff John said to give you one of the good rooms."

"I'll do that."

"But I'd still take a look for bugs before you climb into the rack."

Tim smiled. "I already got that advice."

7

Dinner at Bev's Eatery was chicken-fried steak, green beans, and peach cobbler to follow. Not bad. The room he was assigned at the DuPray Motel was a different matter. It made the ones Tim had stayed in during his ramble north look like palaces. The air conditioner in the window rattled busily, but didn't cool things off much. The rusty shower head dripped, and there seemed to be no way to stop it. (He finally put a towel under it to muffle the clockwork sound.) The shade on the bedside lamp was burned in a couple of places. The room's one picture—an unsettling composition depicting a sailing ship crewed entirely by grinning and possibly homicidal black men—hung crooked. Tim straightened it, but it immediately fell crooked again.

There was a lawn chair outside. The seat sagged and the legs were as rusty as the defective shower head, but it held him. He sat there with his legs stretched out, slapping at bugs and watching the sun burn its orange furnace light through the trees. Looking at it made him feel happy and melancholy at the same time. Another nearly endless freight appeared around quarter past eight, rolling across the state road and past the warehouses on the outskirts of town.

"That damn Georgia Southern's always late."

Tim looked around and beheld the proprietor and sole evening employee of this fine establishment. He was rail thin. A paisley vest hung off his top half. He wore his khakis high-water, the better to display his white socks and elderly Converse sneakers. His vaguely ratlike face was framed by a vintage Beatle haircut.

"Do tell," Tim said.

"Doesn't matter," Norbert said, shrugging. "The even' train always goes right through. The midnight train *most* always does unless it's got diesel to unload or fresh fruit n vegimals for the grocery. There's a junction down yonder." He crossed his index fingers to demonstrate. "The one line goes to Atlanta, Birmin'am, Huntsville, places like 'at. T'other comes up from Jacksonville and goes on to Charleston, Wilmington, Newport News, places like 'at. It's the day freights that mostly stop. Y'all thinkin about warehouse work? They usually a man or two short over there. Got to have a strong back, though. Not for me."

Tim looked at him. Norbert shuffled his sneakers and gave a grin that exposed what Tim thought of as gone-country teeth. They were there, but looked as if they might be gone soon.

"Where's your car?"

Tim just kept looking.

"Are you a cop?"

"Just now I'm a man watching the sun go down through the trees," Tim said, "and I would as soon do it alone."

"Say nummore, say nummore," Norbert said, and beat a retreat, pausing only for a single narrow, assessing glance over his shoulder.

The freight eventually passed. The red crossing lights quit. The barriers swung up. The two or three vehicles that had been waiting started their engines and got moving. Tim watched the sun go from orange to red as it sank—*red sky at night, sailor's delight*, his night knocker gramp would have said. He watched the shadows of the pines lengthen across SR 92 and join together. He was quite sure he wasn't going to get the night knocker job, and maybe that was for the best. DuPray felt far from everything, not just a sidetrack but a damn near no-track. If not for those four warehouses, the town probably wouldn't exist. And what was the *point* of their existence? To store TVs from some northern port like Wilmington or Norfolk, so they could eventually be shipped on to Atlanta or Marietta? To store boxes of computer supplies shipped from Atlanta so they could eventually be loaded up again and shipped to Wilmington or Norfolk or Jacksonville? To store fertilizer or dangerous chemicals, because in this part of the United States there was no law against it? Around and around it went, and what was round *had* no point, any fool knew that.

He went inside, locked his door (stupid; the thing was so flimsy a single kick would stave it in), shucked down to his underwear, and lay on the bed, which was saggy but bugless (as far as he had been able to ascertain, at least). He put his hands behind his head and stared at the picture of the grinning black men manning the frigate or whatever the hell you called a ship like that. Where were they going? Were they pirates? They looked like pirates to him. Whatever they were, it would eventually come to loading and unloading at the next port of call. Maybe everything did. And everyone. Not long ago he had unloaded himself from a Delta flight bound for New York. After that he had loaded cans and bottles into a sorting machine. Today he had loaded books for a nice lady librarian at one place and unloaded them at another. He was only here because I-95 had loaded up with cars and trucks waiting for the wreckers to come and haul away some unfortunate's crashed car. Probably after an ambulance had loaded up the driver and unloaded him at the nearest hospital.

But a night knocker doesn't load or unload, Tim thought. He just walks and knocks. That is, Grandpa would have said, the beauty part.

He fell asleep, waking only at midnight, when another freight went rumbling through. He used the bathroom and, before going back to bed, took down the crooked picture and leaned the crew of grinning black men facing the wall.

Damn thing gave him the willies.

8

When the phone in his room rang the next morning, Tim was showered and sitting in the lawn chair again, watching the shadows that had covered the road at sunset melt back the other way. It was Sheriff John. He didn't waste time.

"Didn't think your Chief would be in this early, so I looked you up online, Mr. Jamieson. Seems like you failed to note a couple of things on your application. Didn't bring them up in our conversation, either. You got a lifesaving commendation in 2017, and nabbed Sarasota PD's Sworn Officer of the Year in 2018. Did you just forget?"

"No," Tim said. "I applied for the job on the spur of the moment. If I'd had more time to think, I'd have put those things down."

"Tell me about the alligator. I grew up on the edge

of Little Pee Dee Swamp, and I love a good gator story."

"It's not a very good one, because it wasn't a very big gator. And I didn't save the kid's life, but the story does have its funny side."

"Let's hear it."

"Call came in from the Highlands, which is a private golf course. I was the closest officer. The kid was up a tree near one of the water hazards. He was eleven, twelve, something like that, and yelling his head off. The gator was down below."

"Sounds like Little Black Sambo," Sheriff John said. "Only as I recollect, there were tigers instead of a gator in that story, and if it was a private golf course, I bet the kid up that tree wadn't black."

"No, and the gator was more asleep than awake," Tim said. "Just a five-footer. Six at most. I borrowed a five-iron from the kid's father—he was the one who put me in for the commendation—and whacked him a couple of times."

"Whacked the gator, I'm thinking, not the dad."

Tim laughed. "Right. The gator went back to the water hazard, the kid climbed down, and that was it." He paused. "Except I got on the evening news. Waving a golf club. The newscaster joked about how I 'drove' it off. Golf humor, you know."

"Uh-huh, uh-huh, and the Officer of the Year thing?"

"Well," Tim said, "I always showed up on time, never called in sick, and they had to give it to somebody."

There was silence for several moments on the other end of the line. Then Sheriff John said, "I don't know if you call that becomin modesty or low self-esteem, but I don't much care for the sound of it either way. I know that's a lot to put out there on short acquaintance, but I'm a man who speaks his mind. I shoot from the lip, some folks say. My wife, for one."

Tim looked at the road, looked at the railroad tracks, looked at the retreating shadows. Spared a glance for the town water tower, looming like a robot invader in a science fiction movie. It was going to be another hot day, he judged. He judged something else, as well. He could have this job or lose it right here and now. It all depended on what he said next. The question was, did he really want it, or had it just been a whim born of a family story about Grandpa Tom?

"Mr. Jamieson? Are you still there?"

"I earned that award. There were other cops it could have gone to, I worked with some fine officers, but yeah, I earned it. I didn't bring a whole lot with me when I left Sarasota—meant to have the rest shipped if I caught on to something in New York—but I brought the citation. It's in my duffel. I'll show you, if you want."

"I do," Sheriff John said, "but not because I don't believe you. I'd just like to see it. You're ridiculously overqualified for the job of night knocker, but if you really want it, you start at eleven tonight. Eleven to six, that's the deal."

"I want it," Tim said.

"All right."

"Just like that?"

"I'm also a man who trusts his instincts, and I'm hiring a night knocker, not a Brinks guard, so yeah, just like that. No need to come in at ten. You catch a little more sleep and drop by around noon. Officer Gullickson will give you the rundown. Won't take long. It ain't rocket science, as they say, although you're apt to see some road rockets on Main Street Saturday nights after the bars close."

"All right. And thank you."

"Let's see how thankful you are after your first weekend. One more thing. You are not a sheriff's deputy, and you are not authorized to carry a firearm. You run into a situation you can't handle, or you consider dangerous, you radio back to the house. We good on that?"

"Yes."

"We better be, Mr. Jamieson. If I find out you're packing a gun, you'll be packing your bags."

"Understood."

"Then get some rest. You're about to become a creature of the night."

Like Count Dracula, Tim thought. He hung up, put the DO NOT DISTURB sign on the door, drew the thin and dispirited curtain over the window, set his phone, and went back to sleep.

9

Deputy Wendy Gullickson, one of the Sheriff's Department part-timers, was ten years younger than Ronnie Gibson and a knockout, even with her blond hair pulled back in a bun so tight it seemed to scream. Tim made no attempt to charm her; it was clear her charm shield was up and fully powered. He wondered briefly if she'd had someone else in mind for the night knocker job, maybe a brother or a boyfriend.

She gave him a map of DuPray's not-much-to-it business district, a handheld belt radio, and a time clock that also went on his belt. There were no batteries, Deputy Gullickson explained; he wound it up at the start of each shift.

"I bet this was state of the art back in 1946," Tim said. "It's actually sort of cool. Retro."

She didn't smile. "You punch your clock at Fromie's Small Engine Sales and Service, and again at the rail depot at the west end of Main. That's one-point-six miles each way. Ed Whitlock used to make four circuits each shift."

Which came to almost thirteen miles. "I won't need Weight Watchers, that's for sure."

Still no smile. "Ronnie Gibson and I will work out a schedule. You'll have two nights a week off, probably Mondays and Tuesdays. The town's pretty quiet after the weekend, but sometimes we may have to shift you. If you stick around, that is."

Tim folded his hands in his lap and regarded her with a half-smile. "Do you have a problem with me, Deputy Gullickson? If you do, speak up now or hold your peace."

Her complexion was Nordic fair, and there was no hiding the flush when it rose in her cheeks. It only added to her good looks, but he supposed she hated it, just the same.

"I don't know if I do or not. Only time will tell. We're a good crew. Small but good. We all pull together. You're just some guy who walked in off the street and landed a job. People in town joke about the night knocker, and Ed was a real good sport about all the ribbing, but it's important, especially in a town with a policing force as small as ours."

"An ounce of prevention is worth a pound of cure," Tim said. "My grandpa used to say that. He was a night knocker, Officer Gullickson. That's why I applied for the job."

Maybe she thawed a little at that. "As for the time clock, I agree that it's archaic. All I can say is get used to it. Night knocker is an analog job in a digital age. At least in DuPray, it is."

10

Tim discovered what she meant soon enough. He was basically a beat cop circa 1954, only without a gun or even a nightstick. He had no power to arrest. A few of the larger town businesses were equipped with security devices, but most of the smaller shops had no such technology. At places like DuPray Mercantile and Oberg's Drug, he checked to make sure the green security lights were burning and there was no sign of intruders. For the smaller ones, he shook doorknobs and doorhandles, peered through the glass, and gave the traditional triple knock. Occasionally this brought a response—a wave or a few words—but mostly it didn't, which was fine. He made a chalk mark and moved on. He followed the same procedure on his return trip, this time erasing the marks as he went. The process reminded him of an old Irish joke: *If you get there first, Paddy, chalk a mark on the door. If I get there first, I'll rub it out.* There seemed no practical reason for the marks; it was simply tradition, perhaps dating all the way back, through a long chain of night knockers, to reconstruction days.

Thanks to one of the part-time deputies, Tim found a decent place to stay. George Burkett told him that his mother had a small furnished apartment over her garage and she'd rent it to him cheap if he was interested. "Only two rooms, but pretty nice. My brother lived there a couple of years before he moved down to Florida. Caught on at that Universal theme park in Orlando. Makes a decent wage."

"Good for him."

"Yeah, but the prices they charge for things in Florida . . . whoo, out of sight. Got to warn you, Tim, if you take the place, you can't play music loud late at night. Mom don't like music. She didn't even like Floyd's banjo, which he could play like a house on fire. They used to argue about it something awful."

"George, I'm rarely home at night."

Officer Burkett—mid-twenties, goodhearted and cheerful, not overburdened with native intelligence—brightened at this. "Right, forgot about that. Anyway, there's a little Carrier up there, not much, but it keeps the place cool enough so you can sleep—Floyd could, at least. You indrested?"

Tim was, and although the window-shaker unit really wasn't up to much, the bed was comfortable, the living room was cozy, and the shower didn't drip. The kitchen was nothing but a microwave and a hotplate, but he was taking most of his meals at Bev's Eatery anyway, so that was all right. And the rent couldn't be beat: seventy a week. George had described his mother as something of a dragon, but Mrs. Burkett turned out to be a good old soul with a southern drawl so thick he could only understand half of what she said. Sometimes she left a piece of cornbread or a slice of cake wrapped in waxed paper outside his door. It was like having a Dixie elf for a landlady.

Norbert Hollister, the rat-faced motel owner, had been right about DuPray Storage & Warehousing; they were chronically short-staffed and always hiring. Tim guessed that in places where the work was manual labor recompensed by the smallest per-hour wage allowed by law (in South Carolina, that came to seven and a quarter an hour), high turnover was typical. He went to see the foreman, Val Jarrett, who was willing to put him on for three hours a day, starting at eight in the morning. That gave Tim time to get cleaned up and eat a meal after he finished his night knocker shift. And so, in addition to his nocturnal duties, he once more found himself loading and unloading.

The way of the world, he told himself. The way of the world. And just for now.

11

As his time in the little southern town passed, Tim Jamieson fell into a soothing routine. He had no intention of staying in DuPray for the rest of his life, but he could see himself still hanging around at Christmas (perhaps putting up a tiny artificial tree in his tiny over-the-garage apartment), maybe even until next summer. It was no cultural oasis, and he understood why the kids were mostly wild to escape its mono-chrome boringness, but Tim luxuriated in it. He was sure that would change in time, but for now it was okay.

Up at six in the evening; dinner at Bev's, sometimes alone, sometimes with one of the deputies; night knocker tours for the next seven hours; breakfast at Bev's; running a forklift at DuPray Storage & Ware-housing until eleven; a sandwich and a Coke or sweet tea for lunch in the shade of the rail depot; back to Mrs.

Burkett's; sleep until six. On his days off, he sometimes slept for twelve hours at a stretch. He read legal thrillers by John Grisham and the entire Song of Ice and Fire series. He was a big fan of Tyrion Lannister. Tim knew there was a TV show based on the Martin books, but felt no need to watch it; his imagination provided all the dragons he needed.

As a cop, he had become familiar with Sarasota's night side, as different from that vacation town's surf-and-sun days as Mr. Hyde was from Dr. Jekyll. The night side was often disgusting and sometimes dangerous, and although he had never sunk to using that odious cop slang for dead addicts and abused prostitutes—NHI, no humans involved—ten years on the force had made him cynical. Sometimes he brought those feelings home (try *often*, he told himself when he was willing to be honest), and they had become part of the acid that had eaten away at his marriage. Those feelings were also, he supposed, one of the reasons he had remained so closed off to the idea of having a kid. There was too much bad stuff out there. Too many things that could go wrong. An alligator on a golf course was the very least of it.

When he took the night knocker job, he would not have believed that a township of fifty-four hundred (much of it in the outlying rural areas) could have a night side, but DuPray did, and Tim discovered he liked it. The people he met on the night side were actually the best part of the job.

There was Mrs. Goolsby, with whom he exchanged waves and quiet hellos on most nights as he started his first tour. She sat out on her porch glider, moving gently back and forth, sipping from a cup that might have contained whiskey, soda pop, or chamomile tea.

Sometimes she was still there on his second return swing. It was Frank Potter, one of the deputies with whom he sometimes ate dinner at Bev's, who told him that Mrs. G. had lost her husband the year before. Wendell Goolsby's big rig had slid off the side of a Wisconsin highway during a blizzard.

"She ain't fifty yet, but Wen n Addie were married a long, long time, just the same," Frank said. "Got hitched back when neither of em was old enough to vote or buy a legal drink. Like that Chuck Berry song, the one about the teenage wedding. That kind of hook-up usually doesn't last long, but theirs did."

Tim also made the acquaintance of Orphan Annie, a homeless woman who many nights slept on an air mattress in the alley running between the sheriff's office and the DuPray Mercantile. She also had a little tent in a field behind the rail depot, and when it rained, she slept there.

"Annie Ledoux is her real name," Bill Wicklow said when Tim asked. Bill was the oldest of the DuPray deputies, a part-timer who seemed to know everyone in town. "She's been sleepin back in that alley for years. Prefers it to the tent."

"What does she do when the weather turns cold?" Tim asked.

"Goes up to Yemassee. Ronnie Gibson takes her most times. They're related somehow, third cousins or something. There's a homeless shelter there. Annie says she doesn't use it unless she has to, on account of it's full of crazy people. I tell her look who's talkin, girlfriend."

Tim checked her alley hideaway once a night, and visited her tent one day after his warehouse shift, mostly out of simple curiosity. Planted in the dirt out front were three flags on bamboo poles: a stars and stripes, a stars and bars, and one Tim didn't recognize.

"That's the flag of Guiana," she said when he asked. "Found it in the trash barrel behind the Zoney's. Pretty, ennit?"

She was sitting in an easy chair covered with clear plastic and knitting a scarf that looked long enough for one of George R. R. Martin's giants. She was friendly enough, exhibiting no sign of what one of Tim's fellow Sarasota officers had named "homeless paranoid syndrome," but she was a fan of late-night talk radio on WMDK, and her conversation sometimes wandered off into strange byroads that had to do with flying saucers, walk-ins, and demonic possession.

One night when he found her reclining on her air mattress in the alley, listening to her little radio, he asked her why she stayed there when she had a tent that looked to be in tip-top condition. Orphan Annie—perhaps sixty, perhaps eighty—looked at him as though he were mad. "Back here I'm close to the po-lice. You know what's behind the depot and them warehouses, Mr. J.?"

"Woods, I guess."

"Woods and bog. Miles of slash and muck and deadfalls that go on all the way to Georgia. There's *critters* out there, and some bad human beings, too. When it's pissing down and I have to stay in my tent, I tell myself nothing's likely to come out in a rainstorm, but I still don't sleep good. I got a knife and I keep it handy, but I don't think it'd be much help against some swamp rat hopped up on crank."

Annie was thin to the point of emaciation, and Tim took to bringing her small treats from Bev's before punching in for his short shift of loading and unloading at the warehouse complex. Sometimes it was a bag of boiled peanuts or Mac's Cracklins, sometimes a moon pie or a cherry tart. Once it was a jar of Wickles that she grabbed and held between her scrawny breasts, laughing with pleasure.

"Wickies! I ain't had a Wicky since Hector was a pup! Why are you so good to me, Mr. J.?"

"I don't know," Tim said. "I guess I just like you, Annie. Can I try one of those?"

She held out the jar. "Sure. You got to open it, anyway, my hands too sore with the arthritis." She held them out, displaying fingers so badly twisted that they looked like pieces of driftwood. "I can still knit n sew, but Lord knows how much longer that'll keep up."

He opened the jar, winced a little at the strong smell of vinegar, and fished out one of the pickle chips. It was dripping with something that could have been formaldehyde, for all he knew.

"Gi'me back, gi'me back!"

He handed her the jar and ate the Wickle. "Jesus, Annie, my mouth may never unpucker."

She laughed, displaying her few remaining teeth. "They best with bread n butter n a nice cold RC. Or a beer, but I don't drink that anymore."

"What's that you're knitting? Is it a scarf?"

"The Lord shall not come in His own raiment," Annie said. "You go on now, Mr. J., and do your duty. Watch out for men in black cars. George Allman on the radio talks about them all the time. You know where *they* come from, don't you?" She cocked a knowing glance at him. She might have been joking. Or not. With Orphan Annie it was hard to tell.

Corbett Denton was another denizen of DuPray's night side. He was the town barber, and known locally as Drummer, for some teenage exploit no one seemed exactly clear on, only that it had resulted in a month's suspension from the regional high school. He might have been wild in his salad days, but those were far behind him. Drummer was now in his late fifties or early sixties, overweight, balding, and afflicted with insomnia. When he couldn't sleep, he sat on the stoop of his shop and watched DuPray's empty main drag. Empty, that was, except for Tim. They exchanged the desultory conversational gambits of mere acquaintances—the weather, baseball, the town's annual Summer Sidewalk Sale—but one night Denton said something that put Tim on yellow alert.

"You know, Jamieson, this life we think we're living isn't real. It's just a shadow play, and I for one will be glad when the lights go out on it. In the dark, all the shadows disappear."

Tim sat down on the stoop under the barber pole, its endless spiral now stilled for the night. He took off his glasses, polished them on his shirt, put them back on. "Permission to speak freely?"

Drummer Denton flicked his cigarette into the gutter, where it splashed brief sparks. "Go right ahead. Between midnight and four, everyone should have permission to speak freely. That's my opinion, at least."

"You sound like a man suffering from depression."

Drummer laughed. "Call you Sherlock Holmes."

"You ought to go see Doc Roper. There are pills that will brighten your attitude. My ex takes them. Although getting rid of me probably brightened her attitude more." He smiled to show this was a joke, but Drummer Denton didn't smile back, just got to his feet.

"I know about those pills, Jamieson. They're like

booze and pot. Probably like the ecstasy the kids take nowadays when they go to their raves, or whatever they call them. Those things make you believe for awhile that all of this is real. That it matters. But it's not and it doesn't."

"Come on," Tim said softly. "That's no way to be."

"In my opinion, it's the only way to be," the barber said, and walked toward the stairs leading to his apartment above the barber shop. His gait was slow and lumbering.

Tim looked after him, disquieted. He thought Drummer Denton was one of those fellows who might decide some rainy night to kill himself. Maybe take his dog with him, if he had one. Like some old Egyptian pharaoh. He considered talking to Sheriff John about it, then thought of Wendy Gullickson, who still hadn't unbent much. The last thing he wanted was for her or any of the other deputies to think he was getting above himself. He was no longer law enforcement, just the town's night knocker. Best to let it go.

But Drummer Denton never quite left his mind.

12

On his rounds one night near the end of June, he spotted two boys walking west down Main Street with knapsacks on their backs and lunchboxes in their hands. They might have been headed off to school, had it not been two in the morning. These nocturnal promenaders turned out to be the Bilson twins. They were pissed at their parents, who had refused to take them to the Dunning Agricultural Fair because their report cards had been unacceptable.

"We got mostly Cs and din't fail nothing," Robert Bilson said, "and we got promoted. What's so bad about that?"

"It ain't right," Roland Bilson chimed in. "We're going to be at the fair first thing in the morning and get jobs. We heard they always need roundabouts."

Tim thought about telling the boy the correct word was *roustabouts*, then decided that was beside the point. "Kids, I hate to pop your balloon, but you're what? Eleven?"

"Twelve!" they chorused.

"Okay, twelve. Keep your voices down, people are sleeping. No one is going to hire you on at that fair. What they're going to do is slam you in the Dollar Jail on whatever excuse they've got for a midway and keep you there until your parents show up. Until they do, folks are going to come by and gawk at you. Some may throw peanuts or pork rinds."

The Bilson twins stared at him with dismay (and perhaps some relief).

"Here's what you do," Tim said. "You go on back home right now, and I'll walk behind you, just to make sure you don't change your collective mind."

"What's a collective mind?" Robert asked.

"A thing twins are reputed to have, at least according to folklore. Did you use the door or go out a window?"

"Window," Roland said.

"Okay, that's how you go back in. If you're lucky, your folks will never know you were out."

Robert: "You won't tell them?"

"Not unless I see you try it again," Tim said. "Then I'll not only tell them what you did, I'll tell them about how you sassed me when I caught you."

Roland, shocked: "We didn't do no such thing!"

"I'll lie," Tim said. "I'm good at it."

He followed them, and watched as Robert Bilson made a step with his hands to help Roland into the open window. Tim then did Robert the same favor. He waited to see if a light would go on somewhere, signaling imminent discovery of the would-be runaways, and when none did, he resumed his rounds.

13

There were more people out and about on Friday and Saturday nights, at least until midnight or one in the morning. Courting couples, mostly. After that there might be an invasion of what Sheriff John called the road rockets, young men in souped-up cars or trucks who went blasting down DuPray's empty main street at sixty or seventy miles an hour, racing side by side and waking people up with the ornery blat of their glasspack mufflers. Sometimes a deputy or an SP trooper would run one of them down and write him up (or jail him if he blew .09), but even with four Du-Pray officers on duty during weekend nights, arrests were relatively rare. Mostly they got away with it.

Tim went to see Orphan Annie. He found her sitting outside her tent, knitting slippers. Arthritis or not, her fingers moved like lightning. He asked if she'd like to make twenty dollars. Annie said a little money always came in handy, but it would depend on what the job was. He told her, and she cackled.

"Happy to do it, Mr. J. If you throw in a couple of bottles of Wickles, that is."

Annie, whose motto seemed to be "go big or go

home," made him a banner thirty feet long and seven feet wide. Tim attached it to a steel roller he made himself, welding together pieces of pipe in the shop of Fromie's Small Engine Sales and Service. After explaining to Sheriff John what he wanted to do and receiving permission to give it a try, Tim and Tag Faraday hung the roller on a cable above Main Street's three-way intersection, anchoring the cable to the false fronts of Oberg's Drug on one side and the defunct movie theater on the other.

On Friday and Saturday nights, around the time the bars closed, Tim yanked a cord that unfurled the banner like a window shade. On either side, Annie had drawn an old-fashioned flash camera. The message beneath read **SLOW DOWN, IDIOT! WE ARE PHOTOGRAPHING YOUR LICENSE PLATE!**

They were doing no such thing, of course (although Tim did note down tag numbers when he had time to make them out), but Annie's banner actually seemed to work. It wasn't perfect, but what in life was?

In early July, Sheriff John called Tim into his office. Tim asked if he was in trouble.

"Just the opposite," Sheriff John said. "You're doing a good job. That banner thing sounded crazy to me, but I have to admit that I was wrong and you were right. It was never the midnight drag races that bothered me, anyway, nor the folks complaining that we were too lazy to put a stop to it. The same people, mind you, who vote down a law enforcement payroll increase year after year. What bothers me are the messes we have to clean up when one of those stampeders hits a tree or a telephone pole. Dead is bad, but the ones who are never the same after one night of stupid hooraw . . . I sometimes think they're worse. But June was okay this year. Better than okay. Maybe it was just an exception to the general rule, but I don't think so. I think it's the banner. You tell Annie she might have saved some lives with that one, and she can sleep in one of the back cells any night she wants once it's cold weather."

"I'll do that," Tim said. "As long as you keep a stock of Wickles, she'll be there plenty."

Sheriff John leaned back. His chair groaned more despairingly than ever. "When I said you were overqualified for the night knocker job, I didn't know the half of it. We're going to miss you when you move on to New York."

"I'm in no hurry," Tim said.

14

The only business in town that stayed open twenty-four hours a day was the Zoney's Go-Mart out by the warehouse complex. In addition to beer, soda, and chips, Zoney's sold an off-brand gasoline called Zoney Juice. Two handsome Somali brothers, Absimil and Gutaale Dobira, alternated on the night shift from midnight to eight. On a dog-hot night in mid-July, as Tim was chalking and knocking his way up the west end of Main, he heard a bang from the vicinity of Zoney's. It wasn't especially loud, but Tim knew a gunshot when he heard one. It was followed by a yell of either pain or anger, and the sound of breaking glass.

Tim broke into a run, time clock banging against his thigh, hand automatically feeling for the butt of a gun that was no longer there. He saw a car parked at the pumps, and as he approached the convenience store, two young men came charging out, one of them with a handful of something that was probably cash. Tim dropped to one knee, watching as they got into the car and roared away, tires sending up puffs of blue smoke from the oil- and grease-stained tarmac.

He pulled his walkie from his belt. "Station, this is Tim. Who's there, come on back to me."

It was Wendy Gullickson, sounding sleepy and put-out. "What do you want, Tim?"

"There's been a two-eleven at Zoney's. A shot was fired."

That woke her up. "Jesus, a robbery? I'll be right th—"

"No, just listen to me. Two perpetrators, male, white, teens or twenties. Compact car. Might have been a Chevy Cruze, no way to tell the color under those gas station fluorescents, but late model, North Carolina plate, starts WTB-9, couldn't make out the last three digits. Get it out there to whoever's on patrol and the State Police before you do *anything* else!"

"What—"

He clicked off, re-holstered the walkie, and sprinted for the Zoney's. The glass front of the counter was trashed and the register was open. One of the Dobira brothers lay on his side in a growing pool of blood. He was gasping for breath, each inhale ending in a whistle. Tim knelt beside him. "Gotta turn you on your back, Mr. Dobira."

"Please don't . . . hurts . . ."

Tim was sure it did, but he needed to look at the damage. The bullet had gone in high on the right side of Dobira's blue Zoney's smock, which was now a muddy purple with blood. More was spilling from his mouth, soaking his goatee. When he coughed, he sprayed Tim's face and glasses with fine droplets.

Tim grabbed his walkie again, and was relieved that Gullickson hadn't left her post. "Need an ambulance, Wendy. Fast as they can make it from Dunning. One of the Dobira brothers is down, looks like the bullet clipped his lung."

She acknowledged, then started to ask a question. Tim cut her off again, dropped his walkie on the floor, and pulled off the tee-shirt he was wearing. He pressed it against the hole in Dobira's chest. "Can you hold that for a few seconds, Mr. Dobira?"

"Hard . . . to breathe."

"I'm sure it is. Hold it. It'll help."

Dobira pressed the wadded-up shirt to his chest. Tim didn't think he'd be able to hold it for long, and he couldn't expect an ambulance for at least twenty minutes. Even that would be a miracle.

Gas-n-go convenience stores were heavy on snacks but light on first aid supplies. There was Vaseline, however. Tim grabbed a jar, and from the next aisle a box of Huggies. He tore it open as he ran back to the man on the floor. He removed the tee-shirt, now sodden with blood, gently pulled up the equally sodden blue smock, and began to unbutton the shirt Dobira wore beneath.

"No, no, no," Dobira moaned. "Hurts, you don't touch, please."

"Got to." Tim heard an engine approaching. Blue jackpot lights started to spark and dance in the shards of broken glass. He didn't look around. "Hang on, Mr. Dobira."

He hooked a glob of Vaseline out of the jar and packed it into the wound. Dobira cried out in pain, then looked at Tim with wide eyes. "Can breathe . . . a little better."

"This is just a temporary patch, but if your breathing's better, your lung probably didn't collapse." At least not entirely, Tim thought.

Sheriff John came in and took a knee next to Tim. He was wearing a pajama top the size of a mainsail over his uniform pants, and his hair was every whichway.

"You got here quick," Tim said.

"I was up. Couldn't sleep, so I was making myself a sandwich when Wendy called. Sir, are you Gutaale or Absimil?"

"Absimil, sir." He was still wheezing, but his voice was stronger. Tim took one of the disposable diapers, still folded up, and pressed it against the wound. "Oh, that is painful."

"Was it a through-and-through, or is it still in there?" Sheriff John asked.

"I don't know, and I don't want to turn him over again to find out. He's relatively stable, so we gotta just wait for the ambulance."

Tim's walkie crackled. Sheriff John plucked it gingerly from the litter of broken glass. It was Wendy. "Tim? Bill Wicklow spotted those guys out on Deep Meadow Road and lit them up."

"It's John, Wendy. Tell Bill to show caution. They're armed."

"They're down, is what they are." She might have been sleepy before, but Wendy was wide awake now, and sounding satisfied. "They tried to run and ditched their car. One's got a broken arm, the other one's cuffed to the bull bars on Bill's ride. State Police are en route. Tell Tim he was right about it being a Cruze. How's Dobira?"

"He'll be fine," Sheriff John said. Tim wasn't entirely sure of that, but he understood that the sheriff had been talking to the wounded man as well as Deputy Gullickson.

"I gave them the money from the register," Dobira said. "It is what we are told to do." He sounded ashamed, even so. *Deeply* ashamed.

"That was the right thing," Tim said.

"The one with the gun shot me, anyway. Then the other one broke in the counter. To take . . ." More coughing.

"Hush, now," Sheriff John said.

"To take the lottery tickets," Absimil Dobira said. "The ones you scratch off. We must have them back. Until bought, they are the property of . . ." He coughed weakly. "Of the state of South Carolina."

Sheriff John said, "Be quiet, Mr. Dobira. Stop worrying about those damn scratchers and save your strength."

Mr. Dobira closed his eyes.

15

The next day, while Tim was eating his lunch on the porch of the rail depot, Sheriff John pulled up in his personal vehicle. He mounted the steps and looked at the sagging seat of the other available chair. "Think that'll hold me?"

"Only one way to find out," Tim said.

Sheriff John sat down gingerly. "Hospital says Dobira's going to be okay. His brother's with him—Gutaale—and he says he's seen those two dirtbags before. Couple of times."

"Dey wuz casin da joint," Tim said.

"No doubt. I sent Tag Faraday over to take both brothers' statements. Tag's the best I've got, which I probably didn't need to tell you."

"Gibson and Burkett aren't bad."

Sheriff John sighed. "No, but neither of them would have moved as fast or as decisively as you did last night. And poor Wendy probably just would have stood there gawking, if she didn't faint dead away."

"She's good on dispatch," Tim said. "Made for the job. Just my opinion, you know."

"Uh-huh, uh-huh, and a whiz at clerical—reorganized all our files last year, plus got everything on flash drives—but on the road, she's damn near useless. She loves being on the team, though. How would *you* like to be on the team, Tim?"

"I didn't think you could afford another cop's salary. Did you all at once get a payroll increase?"

"Don't I wish. But Bill Wicklow's turning in his badge at the end of the year. I was thinking maybe you and him could swap jobs. He walks and knocks, you put on a uniform and get to carry a gun again. I asked Bill. He says night knocking would suit him, at least for a while."

"Can I think about it?"

"I don't know why not." Sheriff John stood up. "End of the year's still five months away. But we'd be glad to have you."

"Does that include Deputy Gullickson?"

Sheriff John grinned. "Wendy's hard to win over, but you got a long way down that road last night."

"Really? And if I asked her out to dinner, what do you think she'd say?"

"I think she'd say yes, as long as it wasn't Bev's you were thinking of taking her to. Good-looking girl like her is going to expect the Roundup in Dunning, at the very least. Maybe that Mexican joint down in Hardeeville."

"Thanks for the tip."

"Not a problem. You think about that job."

"I will."

He did. And was still thinking of it when all hell broke loose on a hot night later that summer.

THE SMART KID

1

On a fine Minneapolis morning in April of that year—Tim Jamieson still months from his arrival in DuPray—Herbert and Eileen Ellis were being ushered into the office of Jim Greer, one of three guidance counselors at the Broderick School for Exceptional Children.

"Luke's not in trouble, is he?" Eileen asked when they were seated. "If he is, he hasn't said anything."

"Not at all," Greer said. He was in his thirties, with thinning brown hair and a studious face. He was wearing a sport shirt open at the collar and pressed jeans. "Look, you know how things work here, right? How things have to work, given the mental capacity of our students. They are graded but not *in* grades. They can't be. We have ten-year-olds with mild autism who are doing high school math but still reading at a third-grade level. We have kids who are fluent in as many as four languages but have trouble multiplying fractions. We teach them in all subjects, and we board ninety per cent of them—we have to, they come from all parts of the United States and a dozen or so from abroad—but we center our attention on their special talents, whatever those happen to be. That makes the traditional system, where kids advance from kindergarten to twelfth grade, pretty useless to us."

"We understand that," Herb said, "and we know Luke's a smart kid. That's why he's here." What he didn't add (certainly Greer knew it) was that they never could have afforded the school's astronomical fees. Herb was the foreman in a plant that made boxes; Eileen was a grammar school teacher. Luke was one of the Brod's few day students, and one of the school's *very* few scholarship students.

"Smart? Not exactly."

Greer looked down at an open folder on his otherwise pristine desk, and Eileen had a sudden premonition: either they were going to be asked to withdraw their son, or his scholarship was going to be canceled—which would make withdrawal a necessity. Yearly tuition fees at the Brod were forty thousand dollars a year, give or take, roughly the same as Harvard. Greer was going to tell them it had all been a mistake, that Luke wasn't as bright as they had all believed. He was just an ordinary kid who read far above his level and seemed to remember it all. Eileen knew from her own reading that eidetic memory was not exactly uncommon in young children; somewhere between ten and fifteen per cent of all normal kids possessed the ability to remember almost everything. The catch was that the talent usually disappeared when children became adolescents, and Luke was nearing that point.

Greer smiled. "Let me give it to you straight. We pride ourselves on teaching exceptional children, but we've never had a student at the Broderick quite like Luke. One of our emeritus teachers—Mr. Flint, now in his eighties—took it on himself to give Luke a tutorial on the history of the Balkans, a complicated subject, but one that casts great light on the current geopolitical situation. So Flint says, anyway. After the first week, he came to me and said that his experience with your son must have been like the experience of the Jewish elders, when Jesus not only taught them but rebuked them, saying it wasn't what went into their mouths that made them unclean, but what came out of them."

"I'm lost," Herb said.

"So was Billy Flint. That's my point."

Greer leaned forward.

"Understand me now. Luke absorbed two semesters' worth of extremely difficult postgraduate work in a single week, and drew many of the conclusions Flint had intended to make once the proper historical groundwork had been laid. On some of those conclusions Luke argued, and very convincingly, that they were 'received wisdom rather than original thought.' Although, Flint added, he did so very politely. Almost apologetically."

"I'm not sure how to respond to that," Herb said. "Luke doesn't talk much about his school work, because he says we wouldn't understand."

"Which is pretty much true," Eileen said. "I might have known something about the binomial theorem once, but that was a long time ago."

Herb said, "When Luke comes home, he's like any other kid. Once his homework's done, and his chores, he boots up the Xbox or shoots hoops in the driveway with his friend Rolf. He still watches *SpongeBob SquarePants*." He considered, then added, "Although usually with a book in his lap."

Yes, Eileen thought. Just lately, *Principles of Sociology*. Before that, William James. Before that, the AA Big Book, and before that, the complete works of Cormac McCarthy. He read the way free-range cows graze, moving to wherever the grass is greenest. That was a thing her husband chose to ignore, because the strangeness of it frightened him. It frightened her as well, which was probably one reason why she knew nothing of Luke's tutorial on Balkan history. He hadn't told her because she hadn't asked.

"We have prodigies here," Greer said. "In fact, I'd rate well over fifty per cent of the Brod's student body as prodigies. But they are limited. Luke is different, because Luke is *global*. It isn't one thing; it's everything. I don't think he'll ever play professional baseball or basketball—"

"If he takes after my side of the family, he'll be too short for pro basketball." Herb was smiling. "Unless he's the next Spud Webb, that is."

"Hush," Eileen said.

"But he plays with enthusiasm," Greer continued. "He enjoys it, doesn't consider it wasted time. He's no klutz on the athletic field. He gets along fine with his mates. He's not introverted or emotionally dysfunctional in any way. Luke is your basic moderately cool American kid wearing rock band tees and his cap around backward. He might not be that cool in an ordinary school—the daily trudge might drive him crazy—but I think even there he'd be okay; he'd just pursue his studies on his own." He added hastily: "Not that you'd want to road-test that."

"No, we're happy with him here," Eileen said. "Very. And we know he's a good kid. We love him like crazy."

"And he loves you. I've had several conversations with Luke, and he makes that crystal clear. To find a child this brilliant is extremely rare. To find one who's also well-adjusted and well-grounded—who sees the outward world as well as the one inside his own head—is even rarer."

"If nothing's wrong, why are we here?" Herb asked. "Not that I mind hearing you sing my kid's praises, don't get that idea. And by the way, I can still beat his ass at HORSE, although he's got a decent hook shot."

Greer leaned back in his chair. The smile disappeared. "You're here because we're reaching the end of what we can do for Luke, and he knows it. He's expressed an interest in doing rather unique college work. He would like to major in engineering at the Massachusetts Institute of Technology in Cambridge, and in English at Emerson, across the river in Boston."

"What?" Eileen asked. "At the *same time?*"

"Yes."

"What about the SATs?" It was all Eileen could think of to say.

"He'll take them next month, in May. At North Community High. And he'll knock the roof off those tests."

I'll have to pack him a lunch, she thought. She had heard the cafeteria food at North Comm was awful.

After a moment of stunned silence, Herb said, "Mr. Greer, our boy is *twelve.* In fact, he just turned twelve last month. He may have the inside dope on Serbia, but he won't even be able to raise a mustache for another three years. You . . . this . . ."

"I understand how you feel, and we wouldn't be having this conversation if my colleagues in guidance and the rest of the faculty didn't believe he was academically, socially, and emotionally capable of doing the work. And yes, at *both* campuses."

Eileen said, "I'm not sending a twelve-year-old halfway across the country to live among college kids old enough to drink and go to the clubs. If he had relatives he could stay with, that might be different, but . . ."

Greer was nodding along with her. "I understand, couldn't agree more, and Luke knows he's not ready to be on his own, even in a supervised environment. He's very clear-headed about that. Yet he's becoming frustrated and unhappy with his current situation, because he's hungry to learn. Famished, in fact. I don't know what fabulous gadgetry is in his head—none of us do, probably old Flint came closest when he talked about Jesus teaching the elders—but when I try to visualize it, I think of a huge, gleaming machine that's running at only two per cent of its capacity. Five per cent at the very most. But because this is a *human* machine, he feels . . . hungry."

"Frustrated and unhappy?" Herb said. "Huh. We don't see that side of him."

I do, Eileen thought. Not all the time, but sometimes. Yes. That's when the plates rattle or the doors shut by themselves.

She thought of Greer's huge, gleaming machine, something big enough to fill three or even four buildings the size of warehouses, and working at doing what, exactly? No more than making paper cups or stamping out aluminum fast food trays. They owed him more, but did they owe him this?

"What about the University of Minnesota?" she asked. "Or Concordia, in St. Paul? If he went to one of those places, he could live at home."

Greer sighed. "You might as well consider taking him out of the Brod and putting him in an ordinary high school. We're talking about a boy for whom the IQ scale is useless. He knows where he wants to go. He knows what he needs."

"I don't know what we can do about it," Eileen said. "He might be able to get scholarships to those places, but we *work* here. And we're far from rich."

"Well now, let's talk about that," Greer said.

2

When Herb and Eileen returned to the school that afternoon, Luke was jiving around in front of the pick-up lane with four other kids, two boys and two girls. They were laughing and talking animatedly. To Eileen they looked like kids anywhere, the girls in skirts and leggings, their bosoms just beginning to bloom, Luke and his friend Rolf in baggy cords—this year's fashion statement for young men—and t-tops. Rolf's read BEER IS FOR BEGINNERS. He had his cello in its quilted case and appeared to be pole-dancing around it as he held forth on something that might have been the spring dance or the Pythagorean theorem.

Luke saw his parents, paused long enough to dap Rolf, then grabbed his backpack and dove into the backseat of Eileen's 4Runner. "Both Ps," he said. "Excellent. To what do I owe this extraordinary honor?"

"Do you really want to go to school in Boston?" Herb asked.

Luke was not discomposed; he laughed and punched both fists in the air. "Yes! Can I?"

Like asking if he can spend Friday night at Rolf's

house, Eileen marveled. She thought of how Greer had expressed what their son had. He'd called it *global*, and that was the perfect word. Luke was a genius who had somehow not been distorted by his own outsized intellect; he had absolutely no compunctions about mounting his skateboard and riding his one-in-a-billion brain down a steep sidewalk, hellbent for election.

"Let's get some early supper and talk about it," she said.

"Rocket Pizza!" Luke exclaimed. "How about it? Assuming you took your Prilosec, Dad. Did you?"

"Oh, believe me, after today's meeting, I'm totally current on that."

3

They got a large pepperoni and Luke demolished half all by himself, along with three glasses of Coke from the jumbo pitcher, leaving his parents to marvel at the kid's digestive tract and bladder as well as his mind. Luke explained that he had talked to Mr. Greer first because "I didn't want to freak you guys out. It was your basic exploratory conversation."

"Putting it out to see if the cat would take it," Herb said.

"Right. Running it up the flagpole to see who'd salute it. Sticking it on the five-fifteen to see if it gets off at Edina. Throwing it against the wall to see how much—"

"Enough. He explained how we might be able to come with you."

"You have to," Luke said earnestly. "I'm too young to be without my exalted and revered mater and pater.

Also . . ." He looked at them from across the ruins of the pizza. "I couldn't work. I'd miss you guys too much."

Eileen instructed her eyes not to fill, but of course they did. Herb handed her a napkin. She said, "Mr. Greer . . . um . . . laid out a scenario, I guess you might say . . . where we could possibly . . . well . . ."

"Relo," Luke said. "Who wants this last piece?"

"All yours," Herb said. "May you not die before you get a chance to do this crazy matriculation thing."

"*Ménage à college*," Luke said, and laughed. "He talked to you about rich alumni, didn't he?"

Eileen put down the napkin. "Jesus, Lukey, you discussed your parents' financial options with your guidance counselor? Who are the grownups in this conversation? I'm starting to feel confused about that."

"Calm down, *mamacita*, it just stands to reason. Although my first thought was the endowment fund. The Brod has a huge one, they could pay for you to relocate out of that and never feel the pinch, but the trustees would never okay it, even though it makes logical sense."

"It does?" Herb asked.

"Oh yeah." Luke chewed enthusiastically, swallowed, and slurped Coke. "I'm an investment. A stock with good growth potential. Invest the nickels and reap the dollars, right? It's how America works. The trustees could see that far, no prob, but they can't break out of the cognitive box they're in."

"Cognitive box," his father said.

"Yeah, you know. A box built as a result of the ancestral dialectic. It might even be tribal, although it's kind of hilarious to think of a tribe of trustees. They go, 'If we do this for him, we might have to do it for another kid.' That's the box. It's, like, handed down."

"Received wisdom," Eileen said.

"You nailed it, Mom. The trustees'll kick it to the wealthy alumni, the ones who made *mucho* megabucks thinking outside the box but still love the ol' Broderick blue and white. Mr. Greer will be the point man. At least I hope he will. The deal is, they help me now and I help the school later on, when I'm rich and famous. I don't actually care about being either of those things, I'm middle-class to the bone, but I might get rich anyway, as a side effect. Always assuming I don't contract some gross disease or get killed in a terrorist attack or something."

"Don't say things that invite sorrow," Eileen said, and made the sign of the cross over the littered table.

"Superstition, Mom," Luke said indulgently.

"Humor me. And wipe your mouth. Pizza sauce. Looks like your gums are bleeding."

Luke wiped his mouth.

Herb said, "According to Mr. Greer, certain interested parties might indeed fund a relocation move, and fund *us* for as long as sixteen months."

"Did he tell you that the same people who'd front you might be able to help find you a new job?" Luke's eyes were sparkling. "A better one? Because one of the school's alumni is Douglas Finkel. He happens to own American Paper Products, and that's close to your sweet spot. Your hot zone. Where the rubber meets the r—"

"Finkel's name actually came up," Herb said. "Just in a speculative way."

"Also . . ." Luke turned to his mother, eyes bright. "Boston is a buyer's market right now when it comes to teachers. Average starting salary for someone with your experience goes sixty-five thou."

"Son, how do you know these things?" Herb asked.

Luke shrugged. "Wikipedia, to start with. Then I trace down the major sources cited in the Wikipedia articles. It's basically a question of keeping current with the environment. My environment is the Broderick School. I knew all of the trustees; the big money alumni I had to look up."

Eileen reached across the table, took what remained of the last pizza slice out of her son's hand, and put it back on the tin tray with the bits of leftover crust. "Lukey, even if this could happen, wouldn't you miss your friends?"

His eyes clouded. "Yeah. Especially Rolf. Maya, too. Although we can't officially ask girls to the spring dance, unofficially she's my date. So yeah. *But.*"

They waited. Their son, always verbal and often verbose, now seemed to struggle. He started, stopped, started again, and stopped again. "I don't know how to say it. I don't know if I *can* say it."

"Try," Herb said. "We'll have plenty of important discussions in the future, but this one is the most important to date. So try."

At the front of the restaurant, Richie Rocket put in his hourly appearance and began dancing to "Mambo Number 5." Eileen watched as the silver space-suited figure beckoned to the nearby tables with his gloved hands. Several little kids joined him, boogying to the music and laughing while their parents looked on, snapped pictures, and applauded. Not so long ago—five short years—Lukey had been one of those kids. Now they were talking about impossible changes. She didn't know how such a child as Luke had come from a couple like them, ordinary people with ordinary aspirations and expectations, and sometimes she wished for different. Sometimes she actively hated the role into which they had been cast, but she had never hated Lukey, and never would. He was her baby, her one and only.

"Luke?" Herb said. Speaking very quietly. "Son?"

"It's just what comes next," Luke said. He raised his head and looked directly at them, his eyes lighted with a brilliance his parents rarely saw. He hid that brilliance from them because he knew it frightened them in a way a few rattling plates never could. "Don't you see? *It's what comes next.* I want to go there . . . and learn . . . and then move on. Those schools are like the Brod. Not the goal, only stepping stones *to* the goal."

"What goal, honey?" Eileen asked.

"*I don't know.* There's so much I want to learn, and figure out. I've got this thing inside my head . . . it reaches . . . and sometimes it's satisfied, but mostly it isn't. Sometimes I feel so small . . . so damn stupid . . ."

"Honey, no. Stupid's the last thing you are." She reached for his hand, but he drew away, shaking his head. The tin pizza pan shivered on the table. The pieces of crust jittered.

"There's an abyss, okay? Sometimes I dream about it. It goes down forever, and it's full of all the things I don't know. I don't know how an abyss can be full— it's an oxymoron—but it is. It makes me feel small and stupid. But there's a bridge over it, and I want to walk on it. I want to stand in the middle of it, and raise my hands . . ."

They watched, fascinated and a little afraid, as Luke raised his hands to the sides of his narrow, intense face. The pizza pan was now not just shivering but rattling. Like the plates sometimes did in the cupboards.

". . . and all those things in the darkness will come floating up. *I know it*."

The pizza pan skated across the table and banged on the floor. Herb and Eileen barely noticed. Such things happened around Luke when he was upset. Not often, but sometimes. They were used to it.

"I understand," Herb said.

"Bullshit he does," Eileen said. "Neither of us do. But you should go ahead and start the paperwork. Take the SATs. You can do those things and still change your mind. If you don't change it, if you stay committed . . ." She looked at Herb, who nodded. "We'll try to make it happen."

Luke grinned, then picked up the pizza pan. He looked at Richie Rocket. "I used to dance with him like that when I was little."

"Yes," Eileen said. She needed to use the napkin again. "You sure did."

"You know what they say about the abyss, don't you?" Herb asked.

Luke shook his head, either because it was the rare thing he didn't know, or because he didn't want to spoil his father's punchline.

"When you stare into it, it stares back at you."

"You bet it does," Luke said. "Hey, can we get dessert?"

4

With the essay included, the SAT test lasted four hours, but there was a merciful break in the middle. Luke sat on a bench in the high school's lobby, munching the sandwiches his mother had packed for him and wishing for a book. He had brought *Naked Lunch*, but one of the proctors appropriated it (along with his phone and everyone else's), telling Luke it would be returned to him later. The guy also riffled through the pages, looking either for dirty pictures or a crib sheet or two.

While he was eating his Snackimals, he became aware of several other test-takers standing around him. Big boys and girls, high school juniors and seniors.

"Kid," one of them asked, "what the hell are you doing here?"

"Taking the test," Luke said. "Same as you."

They considered this. One of the girls said, "Are you a genius? Like in a movie?"

"No," Luke said, smiling, "but I *did* stay at a Holiday Inn Express last night."

They laughed, which was good. One of the boys held up his palm, and Luke slapped him five. "Where are you going? What school?"

"MIT, if I get in," Luke said. Which was disingenuous; he had already been granted provisional admission to both schools of his choice, contingent on doing well today. Which wasn't going to be much of a problem. So far, the test had been a breeze. It was the kids surrounding him that he found intimidating. In the fall, he would be in classes filled with kids like these, kids much older and about twice his size, and of course they would all be looking at him. He had discussed this with Mr. Greer, saying he'd probably seem like a freak to them.

"It's what *you* feel like that matters," Mr. Greer said. "Try to keep that in mind. And if you need counseling—just someone to talk to about your feelings—for God's sake, get it. And you can always text me."

One of the girls—a pretty redhead—asked him if he'd gotten the hotel question in the math section.

"The one about Aaron?" Luke asked. "Yeah, pretty sure I did."

"What did you say was the right choice, can you remember?"

The question had been how to figure how much some dude named Aaron would have to pay for his motel room for x number of nights if the rate was $99.95 per night, plus 8% tax, plus an additional one-time charge of five bucks, and of course Luke remembered because it was a slightly nasty question. The answer wasn't a number, it was an equation.

"It was B. Look." He took out his pen and wrote on his lunch bag: $1.08(99.95x) + 5$.

"Are you sure?" she asked. "I had A." She bent, took Luke's bag—he caught a whiff of her perfume, lilac, delicious—and wrote: $(99.95 + 0.08x) + 5$.

"Excellent equation," Luke said, "but that's how the people who make these tests screw you at the drive-thru." He tapped her equation. "Yours only reflects a one-night stay. It also doesn't account for the room tax."

She groaned.

"It's okay," Luke said. "You probably got the rest of them."

"Maybe you're wrong and she's right," one of the boys said. It was the one who'd slapped Luke five.

She shook her head. "The kid's right. I forgot how to calculate the fucking tax. I suck."

Luke watched her walk away, her head drooping. One of the boys went after her and put an arm around her waist. Luke envied him.

One of the others, a tall drink of water wearing designer glasses, sat down next to Luke. "Is it weird?" he asked. "Being you, I mean?"

Luke considered this. "Sometimes," he said. "Usually it's just, you know, life."

One of the proctors leaned out and rang a hand bell. "Let's go, kids."

Luke got up with some relief and tossed his lunch sack in a trash barrel by the door to the gym. He looked at the pretty redhead a final time, and as he went in, the barrel shimmied three inches to the left.

5

The second half of the test was as easy as the first, and he thought he did a passable job on the essay. Kept it short, anyway. When he left the school he saw the pretty redhead, sitting on a bench by herself and crying. Luke wondered if she'd bricked the test, and if so, how badly—just not-gonna-get-your-first-choice badly, or stuck-with-community-college badly. He wondered what it was like to have a brain that didn't seem to know all the answers. He wondered if he should go over there and try to comfort her. He wondered if she'd accept comfort from a kid who was still your basic pipsqueak. She'd probably tell him to make like an amoeba and split. He even wondered about the way the trashcan had moved—that stuff was eerie. It came to him (and with the force of a revelation) that life was basically one long SAT test, and instead of four or five choices, you got dozens. Including shit like *some of the time* and *maybe so, maybe not*.

His mom was waving. He waved back and ran to

the car. When he was in and belted up, she asked him how he thought he'd done.

"Aced it," Luke said. He gave her his sunniest grin, but he couldn't stop thinking about the redhead. The crying was bad, but the way her head drooped when he pointed out the mistake in her equation—like a flower in a dry spell—had somehow been worse.

He told himself not to think about it, but of course you couldn't do that. *Try not to think of a polar bear,* Fyodor Dostoyevsky once said, *and you will see the cursed thing come to mind every minute.*

"Mom?"

"What?"

"Do you think memory is a blessing or a curse?"

She didn't have to think about it; God only knew what *she* was remembering. "Both, dear."

6

At 2 AM on a morning in June, while Tim Jamieson was night-knocking his way up DuPray's main street, a black SUV turned onto Wildersmoot Drive in one of the suburbs on the north side of Minneapolis. It was a crazy name for a street; Luke and his friend Rolf called it Wildersmooch Drive, partly because it made the name even crazier and partly because they both longed to smooch a girl, and wildly.

Inside the SUV were a man and two women. He was Denny; they were Michelle and Robin. Denny was driving. Halfway along the curving, silent street, he shut off the lights, coasted to the curb, and killed the engine. "You're sure this one isn't TP, right? Because I didn't bring my tinfoil hat."

"Ha ha," Robin said, perfectly flat. She was sitting in the backseat.

"He's just your average TK," Michelle said. "Nothing to get your undies in a bunch about. Let's get this thing going."

Denny opened the console between the two front seats and took out a cell phone that looked like a refugee from the nineties: blocky rectangular body and short stubby antenna. He handed it to Michelle. While she punched in a number, he opened the console's false bottom and took out thin latex gloves, two Glock Model 37s, and an aerosol can which, according to the label, contained Glade air freshener. He handed back one of the guns to Robin, kept one for himself, and passed the aerosol can to Michelle.

"Here we go, big team, here we go," he chanted as he gloved up. "Ruby Red, Ruby Red, that's what I said."

"Quit the high school shit," Michelle said. Then, into the phone, crooked against her shoulder so she could put on her own gloves: "Symonds, do you copy?"

"Copy," Symonds said.

"This is Ruby Red. We're here. Go on and kill the system."

She waited, listening to Jerry Symonds on the other end of the call. In the Ellis home, where Luke and his parents slept, the DeWalt alarm consoles in the front hall and the kitchen went dark. Michelle got the go-ahead and gave her teammates a thumbs-up. "Okay. All set."

Robin slung the go-bag, which looked like a medium-sized ladies' purse, over her shoulder. No interior lights went on when they exited the SUV, which had Minnesota State Patrol plates. They walked single file between the Ellis house and the Destin house next door (where Rolf was also sleeping, perchance to dream of smooching wildly) and entered through the kitchen, Robin first because she had the key.

They paused by the stove. From the go-bag, Robin brought out two compact silencers and three sets of lightweight goggles on elastic straps. The goggles gave their faces an insectile look, but rendered the shadowy kitchen bright. Denny and Robin screwed on the silencers. Michelle led the way through the family room into the front hall, then to the stairs.

They moved slowly but with a fair amount of confidence along the upstairs hall. There was a rug runner to muffle their steps. Denny and Robin stopped outside the first closed door. Michelle continued to the second. She looked back at her partners and tucked the aerosol under her arm so she could raise both hands with the fingers spread: *give me ten seconds*. Robin nodded and returned a thumbs-up.

Michelle opened the door and entered Luke's bedroom. The hinges squeaked faintly. The shape in the bed (nothing showing but a tuft of hair) stirred a little, then settled. At two in the morning the kid should have been dead to the world, in the deepest part of his night's sleep, but he clearly wasn't. Maybe genius kids didn't sleep the same as regular ones, who knew? Certainly not Michelle Robertson. There were two posters on the walls, both daylight-visible viewed through the goggles. One was of a skateboarder in full flight, knees bent, arms outstretched, wrists cocked. The other was of the Ramones, a punk group Michelle had listened to way back in middle school. She thought they were all dead now, gone to that great Rockaway Beach in the sky.

She crossed the room, keeping mental count as she did so: Four . . . five . . .

On six, her hip struck the kid's bureau. There was a trophy of some kind on it, and it fell over. The noise it made wasn't loud, but the kid rolled onto his back and opened his eyes. "Mom?"

"Sure," Michelle said. "Whatever you want."

She saw the beginnings of alarm in the boy's eyes, saw him open his mouth to say something else. She held her breath and triggered the aerosol can two inches from his face. He went out like a light. They always did, and there was never a hangover when they woke up six or eight hours later. Better living through chemistry, Michelle thought, and counted seven . . . eight . . . nine.

On ten, Denny and Robin entered Herb and Eileen's room. The first thing they saw was a problem: the woman wasn't in bed. The door to the bathroom was open, casting a trapezoid of light on the floor. It was too bright for the goggles. They stripped them off and dropped them. The floor in here was polished hardwood, and the double clack was clearly audible in the silent room.

"Herb?" Low, from the bathroom. "Did you knock over your water glass?"

Robin advanced to the bed, taking her Glock from the waistband of her slacks at the small of her back while Denny walked to the bathroom door, making no attempt to muffle his footfalls. It was too late for that. He stood beside it, gun raised to the side of his face.

The pillow on the woman's side was still indented from the weight of her head. Robin put it over the man's face and fired into it. The Glock made a low coughing sound, no more than that, and discharged a little brown smut onto the pillow from its vents.

Eileen came out of the bathroom, looking worried. "Herb? Are you all r—"

She saw Denny. He seized her by the throat, put the Glock to her temple, and pulled the trigger. There was another of those low coughing sounds. She slid to the floor.

Meanwhile, Herb Ellis's feet were kicking aimlessly, making the coverlet he and his late wife had been sleeping under puff and billow. Robin fired twice more into the pillow, the second shot a bark instead of a cough, the third one even louder.

Denny took the pillow away. "What, did you see *The Godfather* too many times? Jesus, Robin, his head's halfway gone. What's an undertaker supposed to do with that?"

"I got it done, that's what matters." The fact was, she didn't like to look at them when she shot them, the way the light went out of them.

"You need to man up, girl. That third one was loud. Come on."

They picked up the goggles and went down to the boy's room. Denny hoisted Luke into his arms—no problem there, the kid didn't weigh more than ninety pounds—and gave his chin a jerk for the women to go ahead of him. They left the way they had come, through the kitchen. There were no lights on in the adjacent house (even the third shot hadn't been *that* loud), and no soundtrack except for the crickets and a faraway siren, maybe all the way over in St. Paul.

Michelle led the way between the two houses, checked the street, and motioned for the others to come ahead. This was the part Denny Williams hated. If some guy with insomnia looked out and saw three people on his neighbor's lawn at two in the morning, that would be suspicious. If one of them was carrying what looked like a body, that would be *very* suspicious.

But Wildersmoot Drive—named after some long-gone Twin Cities bigwig—was fast asleep. Robin opened the SUV's curbside back door, got in, and held out her arms. Denny handed the boy in and she pulled Luke against her, his head lolling on her shoulder. She fumbled for her seatbelt.

"Uck, he's drooling," she said.

"Yes, unconscious people do that," Michelle said, and closed the rear door. She got in the shotgun seat and Denny slid back behind the wheel. Michelle stowed the guns and the aerosol as Denny cruised slowly away from the Ellis house. As they approached the first intersection, Denny put the headlights back on.

"Make the call," he said.

Michelle punched in the same number. "This is Ruby Red. We have the package, Jerry. Airport ETA in twenty-five minutes. Wake up the system."

In the Ellis home, the alarms came back on. When the police finally arrived, they would find two dead, one gone, the kid the most logical suspect. He was said to be brilliant, after all, and those were the ones that tended to be a little wonky, weren't they? A little unstable? They'd ask him when they found him, and finding him was only a matter of time. Kids could run, but even the brilliant ones couldn't hide.

Not for long.

7

Luke woke up remembering a dream he'd had—not exactly a nightmare, but definitely of the not-so-nice variety. Some strange woman in his room, leaning over his bed with her blond hair hanging around the sides of her face. *Sure, whatever you want*, she'd said. Like a chick in one of the porno clips he and Rolf sometimes watched.

He sat up, looked around, and at first thought this was another dream. It was his room—same blue wallpaper, same posters, same bureau with his Little League trophy on it—but where was the window? His window looking out at Rolf's house was gone.

He shut his eyes tight, then sprang them open. No change; the windowless room remained windowless. He considered pinching himself, but that was such a cliché. He popped his fingers against his cheek instead. Everything stayed the same.

Luke got out of bed. His clothes were on the chair, where his mom had put them the night before—underwear, socks, and tee-shirt on the seat, jeans folded over the back. He put them on slowly, looking at where the window should have been, then sat down to put on his sneakers. His initials were on the sides, **LE**, and that was right, but the middle horizontal stroke of the **E** was too long, he was sure of it.

He turned them over, looking for street grit, and saw none. Now he was completely sure. These were not his sneaks. The laces were wrong, too. They were too clean. Nevertheless, they fit perfectly.

He went to the wall and laid his hands against it, pressing, feeling for the window underneath the wallpaper. It wasn't there.

He asked himself if maybe he'd gone crazy, just snapped, like a kid in a scary movie written and directed by M. Night Shyamalan. Weren't kids with high-functioning minds supposed to be prone to breakdowns? But he wasn't crazy. He was as sane as he'd been last night when he went to sleep. In a movie, the crazy kid would *think* he was sane—that would be the Shyamalan twist—but according to the psychology books Luke had read, most crazy people understood they were crazy. He wasn't.

As a little kid (five as opposed to twelve), he'd gone through a craze of collecting political buttons. His dad had been happy to help him build his collection, because most of the buttons were really cheap on eBay. Luke had been especially fascinated (for reasons he could not explain, even to himself) with the buttons of presidential candidates who had lost. The fever had eventually passed, and most of the buttons were probably stored in the attic crawlspace or in the cellar, but he had saved one as a kind of good-luck talisman. It had a blue plane on it, surrounded by the words WINGS FOR WILLKIE. Wendell Willkie ran for president against Franklin Roosevelt in 1940 but lost badly, winning only ten states for a total of eighty-two electoral votes.

Luke had put the button in the cup of his Little League trophy. He fished for it now and came up with nothing.

Next, he went to the poster showing Tony Hawk on his Birdhouse deck. It looked right, but it wasn't. The small rip on the lefthand side was gone.

Not his sneakers, not his poster, Willkie button gone.

Not his room.

Something began to flutter in his chest, and he took several deep breaths to try and quiet it. He went to the door and grasped the knob, sure he would find himself locked in.

He wasn't, but the hallway beyond the door was nothing like the upstairs hallway in the house where he had lived his twelve-plus years. It was cinderblock instead of wood paneling, the blocks painted a pale industrial green. Opposite the door was a poster showing three kids about Luke's age, running through a meadow of high grass. One was frozen in mid-leap. They were either lunatics or deliriously happy. The message at the bottom seemed to suggest the latter. JUST ANOTHER DAY IN PARADISE, it read.

Luke stepped out. To his right, the corridor ended in institutional double doors, the kind with pushbars. To his left, about ten feet in front of another set of those institutional doors, a girl was sitting on the floor. She was wearing bellbottoms and a shirt with puffy sleeves. She was black. And although she looked to be Luke's own age, give or take, she seemed to be smoking a cigarette.

8

Mrs. Sigsby sat behind her desk, looking at her computer. She was wearing a tailored DVF business suit that did not disguise her beyond-lean build. Her gray hair was perfectly groomed. Dr. Hendricks stood at her shoulder. Good morning, Scarecrow, he thought, but would never say.

"Well," Mrs. Sigsby said, "there he is. Our newest arrival. Lucas Ellis. Got a ride on a Gulfstream for the first and only time and doesn't even know it. By all accounts, he's quite the prodigy."

"He won't be for long," Dr. Hendricks said, and

laughed his trademark laugh, first exhaled, then inhaled, a kind of hee-haw. Along with his protruding
front teeth and extreme height—he was six-seven—it
accounted for the techs' nickname for him: Donkey
Kong.

She turned and gave him a hard look. "These are
our charges. Cheap jokes are not appreciated, Dan."

"Sorry." He felt like adding, *But who are you kidding,
Siggers?*

To say such a thing would be impolitic, and really,
the question was rhetorical at best. He knew she wasn't
kidding anyone, least of all herself. Siggers was like
that unknown Nazi buffoon who thought it would be a
terrific idea to put *Arbeit macht frei*, work sets you free,
over the entrance to Auschwitz.

Mrs. Sigsby held up the new boy's intake form.
Hendricks had placed a circular pink sticky in the
upper righthand corner. "Are you learning *anything*
from your pinks, Dan? Anything at all?"

"You know we are. You've seen the results."

"Yes, but anything of proven value?"

Before the good doctor could reply, Rosalind popped
her head in. "I've got paperwork for you, Mrs. Sigsby.
We've got five more coming in. I know they were on
your spreadsheet, but they're ahead of schedule."

Mrs. Sigsby looked pleased. "All five today? I must
be living correctly."

Hendricks (aka Donkey Kong) thought, You
couldn't bear to say *living right*, could you? You might
split a seam somewhere.

"Only *two* today," Rosalind said. "Tonight, actually.
From Emerald team. Three tomorrow, from Opal. Four
are TK. One is TP, and he's a catch. Ninety-three nano-
grams BDNF."

"Avery Dixon, correct?" Mrs. Sigsby said. "From Salt Lake City."

"Orem," Rosalind corrected.

"A Mormon from Orem," Dr. Hendricks said, and gave his hee-haw laugh.

He's a catch, all right, Mrs. Sigsby thought. There will be no pink sticker on Dixon's form. He's too valuable for that. Minimal injections, no risking seizures, no near-drowning experiences. Not with a BDNF over 90.

"Excellent news. Really excellent. Bring in the files and put them on my desk. You also emailed them?"

"Of course." Rosalind smiled. Email was the way the world wagged, but they both knew Mrs. Sigsby preferred paper to pixels; she was old-school that way. "I'll bring them ASAP."

"Coffee, please, and also ASAP."

Mrs. Sigsby turned to Dr. Hendricks. All that height, and he's still carrying a front porch, she thought. As a doctor he should know how dangerous that is, especially for a man that tall, where the vascular system has to work harder to begin with. But no one is quite as good at ignoring the medical realities as a medical man.

Neither Mrs. Sigsby nor Hendricks was TP, but at that moment they were sharing a single thought: how much easier all this would be if there was liking instead of mutual detestation.

Once they had the room to themselves again, Mrs. Sigsby leaned back to look at the doctor looming over her. "I agree that young Master Ellis's intelligence doesn't matter to our work at the Institute. He could just as well have an IQ of 75. It is, however, why we took him a bit early. He had been accepted at not one but two class-A schools—MIT and Emerson."

Hendricks blinked. "At *twelve*?"

"Indeed. The murder of his parents and his subsequent disappearance is going to be news, but not *big* news outside the Twin Cities, although it may ripple the Internet for a week or so. It would have been much bigger news if he'd made an academic splash in Boston before he dropped from sight. Kids like him have a way of getting on the TV news, usually the golly-gosh segments. And what do I always say, Doctor?"

"That in our business, no news is good news."

"Right. In a perfect world, we would have let this one go. We still get our fair share of TKs." She tapped the pink circle on the intake form. "As this indicates, his BDNF isn't even all that high. Only . . ."

She didn't have to finish. Certain commodities were getting rarer. Elephant tusks. Tiger pelts. Rhino horns. Rare metals. Even oil. Now you could add these special children, whose extraordinary qualities had nothing to do with their IQs. Five more coming in this week, including the Dixon boy. A very good haul, but two years ago they might have had thirty.

"Oh, look," Mrs. Sigsby said. On the screen of her computer, their new arrival was approaching the most senior resident of Front Half. "He's about to meet the too-smart-for-her-own-good Benson. She'll give him the scoop, or some version of it."

"Still in Front Half," Hendricks said. "We ought to make her the goddam official greeter."

Mrs. Sigsby offered her most glacial smile. "Better her than you, Doc."

Hendricks looked down and thought of saying, *From this vantage point, I can see how fast your hair is thinning, Siggers. It's all part of your low-level but long-running anorexia. Your scalp is as pink as an albino rabbit's eye.*

There were lots of things he thought of saying to her, the grammar-perfect no-tits chief administrator of the Institute, but he never did. It would have been unwise.

9

The cinderblock hallway was lined with doors and more posters. The girl was sitting under one showing a black boy and a white girl with their foreheads together, grinning like fools. The caption beneath said I CHOOSE TO BE HAPPY!

"You like that one?" the black girl said. On closer inspection, the cigarette dangling from her mouth turned out to be of the candy variety. "I'd change it to I CHOOSE TO BE CRAPPY, but they might take away my pen. Sometimes they let shit slide, but sometimes they don't. The problem is that you can never tell which way things are going to tip."

"Where am I?" Luke asked. "What is this place?" He felt like crying. He guessed it was mostly the disorientation.

"Welcome to the Institute," she said.

"Are we still in Minneapolis?"

She laughed. "Not hardly. And not in Kansas anymore, Toto. We're in Maine. Way up in the williwags. At least according to Maureen, we are."

"In *Maine*?" He shook his head, as if he had taken a blow to the temple. "Are you sure?"

"Yup. You're looking mighty white, white boy. I think you should sit down before you fall down."

He sat, bracing himself with one hand as he did so, because his legs didn't exactly flex. It was more like a collapse.

"I was home," he said. "I was home, and then I woke up here. In a room that looks like my room, but isn't."

"I know," she said. "Shock, innit?" She wriggled her hand into the pocket of her pants and brought out a box. On it was a picture of a cowboy spinning a lariat. ROUND-UP CANDY CIGARETTES, it said. SMOKE JUST LIKE DADDY! "Want one? A little sugar might help your state of mind. It always helps mine."

Luke took the box and flipped up the lid. There were six cigarettes left inside, each one with a red tip that he guessed was supposed to be the coal. He took one, stuck it between his lips, then bit it in half. Sweetness flooded his mouth.

"Don't ever do that with a real cigarette," she said. "You wouldn't like the taste half so well."

"I didn't know they still sold stuff like this," he said.

"They don't sell this kind, for sure," she said. "Smoke just like Daddy? Are you kiddin me? Got to be an antique. But they got some weird shit in the canteen. Including *real* cigarettes, if you can believe that. All straights, Luckies and Chesterfields and Camels, like in those old flicks on Turner Classic Movies. I'm tempted to try, but man, they take a *lot* of tokens."

"Real cigarettes? You don't mean for kids?"

"Kids be the whole population here. Not that there are many in Front Half just now. Maureen says we may have more coming. I don't know where she gets her info, but it's usually good."

"Cigarettes for kids? What is this? Pleasure Island?" Not that he felt very pleasurable just now.

That cracked her up. "Like in *Pinocchio*! Good one!"

She held up her hand. Luke slapped her five and felt a little better. Hard telling why.

"What's your name? I can't just keep calling you white boy. It's, like, racial profiling."

"Luke Ellis. What's yours?"

"Kalisha Benson." She raised a finger. "Now pay attention, Luke. You can call me Kalisha, or you can call me Sha. Just don't call me Sport."

"Why not?" Still trying to get his bearings, still not succeeding. Not even close. He ate the other half of his cigarette, the one with the fake ember on the tip.

"Cause that's what Hendricks and his fellow dipsticks say when they give you the shots or do their tests. 'I'm gonna stick a needle in your arm and it'll hurt, but be a good sport. I'm gonna take a throat culture, which will make you gag like a fuckin maggot, but be a good sport. We're gonna dip you in the tank, but just hold your breath and be a good sport.' *That's* why you can't call me Sport."

Luke hardly paid attention to the stuff about the tests, although he would consider it later. He was back on *fuckin*. He had heard it from plenty of boys (he and Rolf said it a lot when they were out), and he had heard it from the pretty redhead who might have bricked the SATs, but never from a girl his own age. He supposed that meant he had led a sheltered life.

She put her hand on his knee, which gave him a bit of a tingle, and looked at him earnestly. "But my advice is go on and be a good sport no matter how much it sucks, no matter what they stick down your throat or up your butt. The tank I don't really know about, I never had that one myself, only heard about it, but I know as long as they're testing you, you stay in Front Half. I don't know what goes on in Back Half, and I don't want to know. All I *do* know is that Back Half's like the Roach Motel—kids check in, but they don't check out. Not back to here, anyway."

He looked back the way he had come. There were lots of motivational posters, and there were also lots of doors, eight or so on either side. "How many kids are here?"

"Five, counting you and me. Front Half's never jammed, but right now it's like a ghost town. Kids come and go."

"Talking of Michelangelo," Luke muttered.

"Huh?"

"Nothing. What—"

One of the double doors at the near end of the corridor opened, and a woman in a brown dress appeared, her back to them. She was holding the door with her butt while she struggled with something. Kalisha was up in a flash. "Hey, Maureen, hey, girl, hold on, let us help."

Since it was *us* instead of *me*, Luke got up and went after Kalisha. When he got closer, he saw the brown dress was actually a kind of uniform, like a maid might wear in a swanky hotel—medium swanky, anyway, it wasn't gussied up with ruffles or anything. She was trying to drag a laundry basket over the metal strip between this hallway and the big room beyond, which looked like a lounge—there were tables and chairs and windows letting in bright sunlight. There was also a TV that looked the size of a movie screen. Kalisha opened the other door to make more room. Luke took hold of the laundry basket (DANDUX printed on the side) and helped the woman pull it into what he was starting to think of as the dormitory corridor. There were sheets and towels inside.

"Thank you, son," she said. She was pretty old, with a fair amount of gray in her hair, and she looked tired. The tag over her sloping left breast said MAUREEN. She looked him over. "You're new. Luke, right?"

"Luke Ellis. How did you know?"

"Got it on my day sheet." She pulled a folded piece of paper halfway out of her skirt pocket, then pushed it back in.

Luke offered his hand, as he had been taught. "Pleased to meet you."

Maureen shook it. She seemed nice enough, so he guessed he *was* pleased to meet her. But he wasn't pleased to be here; he was scared and worried about his parents as well as himself. They'd have missed him by now. He didn't think they'd want to believe he'd run away, but when they found his bedroom empty, what other conclusion could they draw? The police would be looking for him soon, if they weren't already, but if Kalisha was right, they'd be looking a long way from here.

Maureen's palm was warm and dry. "I'm Maureen Alvorson. Housekeeping and all-around handy gal. I'll be keeping your room nice for you."

"And don't make a lot of extra work for her," Kalisha said, giving him a forbidding look.

Maureen smiled. "You're a peach, Kalisha. This one don't look like he's gonna be messy, not like that Nicky. He's like Pigpen in the Peanuts comics. Is he in his room now? I don't see him out in the playground with George and Iris."

"You know Nicky," Kalisha said. "If he's up before one in the afternoon, he calls it an early day."

"Then I'll just do the others, but the docs want him at one. If he's not up, they'll get him up. Pleased to meet you, Luke." And she went on her way, now pushing her basket instead of tugging it.

"Come on," Kalisha said, taking Luke's hand. Worried about his parents or not, he got another of those tingles.

She tugged him into the lounge area. He wanted to scope the place out, especially the vending machines (real cigarettes, was that possible?), but as soon as the door was closed behind them, Kalisha was up in his face. She looked serious, almost fierce.

"I don't know how long you'll be here—don't know how much longer *I* will be, for that matter—but while you are, be cool to Maureen, hear? This place is staffed with some mean-ass shitheads, but she's not one of them. She's *nice*. And she's got problems."

"What kind of problems?" He asked mostly to be polite. He was looking out the window, at what had to be the playground. There were two kids there, a boy and a girl, maybe his own age, maybe a little older.

"She thinks she might be sick for one, but she doesn't want to go to the doctor because she can't *afford* to be sick. She only makes about forty grand a year, and she's got, like, twice that much in bills. Maybe more. Her husband ran them up, then ran out. And it keeps piling up, okay? The interest."

"The vig," Luke said. "That's what my dad calls it. Short for *vigorish*. From the Ukrainian word for profits or winnings. It's a hoodlum term, and Dad says the credit card companies are basically hoods. Based on the compounding interest they charge, he's got a . . ."

"Got what? A point?"

"Yeah." He stopped looking at the kids outside—George and Iris, presumably—and turned to Kalisha.

"She told you all that? To a kid? You must be an ace at intrapersonal relationships."

Kalisha looked surprised, then laughed. It was a big one, which she delivered with her hands on her hips and her head thrown back. It made her look like a woman instead of a kid. "Interpersonal relationships! You got some mouth on you, Lukey!"

"In*tra*, not in*ter*," he said. "Unless you're, like, meeting with a whole group. Giving them credit counseling, or something." He paused. "That's, um, a joke." And a lame one at that. A nerd joke.

She regarded him appraisingly, up and down and then up again, producing another of those not unpleasant tingles. "Just how smart are you?"

He shrugged, a bit embarrassed. He ordinarily didn't show off—it was the worst way in the world to win friends and influence people—but he was upset, confused, worried, and (might as well admit it) scared shitless. It was getting harder and harder not to label this experience with the word *kidnapping*. He was a kid, after all, he had been napping, and if Kalisha was telling the truth, he had awakened thousands of miles from his home. Would his parents have let him go without an argument, or an actual fight? Unlikely. Whatever had happened to him, he hoped they had stayed asleep while it was going on.

"Pretty goddam smart, would be my guess. Are you TP or TK? I'm thinking TK."

"I don't know what you're talking about."

Except maybe he did. He thought of the way the plates sometimes rattled in the cupboards, how his bedroom door would sometimes open or close on its own, and how the pan had jittered at Rocket Pizza.

Also the way the trashcan had moved by itself the day of the SAT test.

"TP is telepathy. TK is—"

"Telekinesis."

She smiled and pointed a finger at him. "You really are a smart kid. Telekinesis, right. You're either one or the other, supposedly no one's both—that's what the techs say, at least. I'm a TP." She said this last with some pride.

"You read minds," Luke said. "Sure. Every day and twice on Sunday."

"How do you think I know about Maureen? She'd never tell *anyone* here about her probs, she's not that kind of person. And I don't know any of the details, just the general outline." She considered. "There's something about a baby, too. Which is weird. I asked her once if she had kids, and she said she didn't."

Kalisha shrugged.

"I've always been able to do it—off and on, not all the time—but it ain't like being a superhero. If it was, I'd bust out of here."

"You're serious about this?"

"Yes, and here's your first test. First of many. I'm thinking of a number between one and fifty. What's my number?"

"No idea."

"True? Not faking?"

"Absolutely not faking." He walked to the door on the far side of the room. Outside, the boy was shooting hoops and the girl was bouncing on a trampoline— nothing fancy, just seat-drops and the occasional twist. Neither of them looked like they were having a good time; they looked like they were just *passing* time. "Those kids are George and Iris?"

"Yup." She joined him. "George Iles and Iris Stanhope. They're both TKs. TPs are rarer. Hey, smart kid, is that a word, or do you say *more rare?*"

"Either is okay, but I'd go with *more rare. Rarer* sounds like you're trying to start an outboard motor."

She thought this over for a few seconds, then laughed and pointed that finger at him again. "Good one."

"Can we go out?"

"Sure. Playground door is never locked. Not that you'll want to stay long, the bugs are pretty fierce out here in the boondocks. There'll be Deet in your bathroom medicine cabinet. You should use it, and I mean really slather it on. Maureen says the bug situation will get better once the dragonflies hatch out, but I haven't seen any yet."

"Are they nice kids?"

"George and Iris? Sure, I guess so. I mean, it's not like we're besties, or anything. I've only known George for a week. Iris got here . . . mmm . . . ten days ago, I think. About that, anyway. After me, Nick's been here the longest. Nick Wilholm. Don't look forward to meaningful relationships in Front Half, smart kid. Like I said, they come and go. And don't *any* of them talk of Michelangelo."

"How long have you been here, Kalisha?"

"Almost a month. I'm an old-timer."

"Then will you tell me what's going on?" He nodded to the kids outside. "Will they?"

"We'll tell you what we know, and what the orderlies and techs tell us, but I got an idea that most of it's lies. George feels the same. Iris, now . . ." Kalisha laughed. "She's like Agent Mulder on that *X-Files* show. *She* wants to believe."

"Believe what?"

The look she gave him—both wise and sad—again made her look more like a grownup than a kid. "That this is just a little detour on the great highway of life, and everything's going to come out all right in the end, like on *Scooby-Doo*."

"Where are your folks? How did you get here?"

The adult look disappeared. "Don't want to talk about that stuff now."

"Okay." Maybe he didn't want to, either. At least not quite yet.

"And when you meet Nicky, don't worry if he goes off on a rant. It's how he blows off steam, and some of his rants are . . ." She considered. "Entertaining."

"If you say so. Will you do me a favor?"

"Sure, if I can."

"Stop calling me smart kid. My name is Luke. Use it, okay?"

"I can do that."

He reached for the door, but she put her hand on his wrist.

"One more thing before we go out. Turn around, Luke."

He did. She was maybe an inch taller. He didn't know she was going to kiss him until she did it, a full-on lip-lock. She even put her tongue between his lips for a second or two, and that produced not just a tingle but a full-on jolt, like sticking a finger in a live socket. His first real kiss, and a wildersmooch for sure. Rolf, he thought (so far as he *could* think in the immediate aftermath), would be so jealous.

She pulled away, looking satisfied. "It's not true love or anything, don't get that idea. I'm not sure it's even a favor, but it might be. I was in quarantine the first week I was here. No shots for dots."

She pointed to a poster on the wall next to the candy machine. It showed a boy in a chair, pointing joyously at a bunch of colored dots on a white wall. A smiling doctor (white coat, stethoscope around his neck) was standing with a hand on the boy's shoulder. Above the picture it said SHOTS FOR DOTS! And below: THE QUICKER YOU SEE EM, THE QUICKER YOU'RE BACK HOME!

"What the hell does that mean?"

"Never mind right now. My folks were full-on anti-vaxxers, and two days after I landed in Front Half, I came down with chicken pox. Cough, high fever, big ugly red spots, the whole nine yards. I guess I'm over it, since I'm out and about and they're testing me again, but maybe I'm still a little bit contagious. If you're lucky, you'll get the pox and spend a couple of weeks drinking juice and watching TV instead of getting needles and MRIs."

The girl spotted them and waved. Kalisha waved back, and before Luke could say anything else, she pushed open the door. "Come on. Wipe that dopey look off your face and meet the Fockers."

SHOTS FOR DOTS

1

Outside the door of the Institute's canteen and TV lounge area, Kalisha put an arm around Luke's shoulders and pulled him close to her. He thought—hoped, really—she meant to kiss him again, but she whispered in his ear instead. Her lips tickled his skin and gave him goosebumps. "Talk about anything you want, only don't say anything about Maureen, okay? We think they only listen sometimes, but it's better to be careful. I don't want to get her in trouble."

Maureen, okay, the housekeeping lady, but who were *they*? Luke had never felt so lost, not even as a four-year-old, when he had gotten separated from his mother for fifteen endless minutes in the Mall of America.

Meanwhile, just as Kalisha had predicted, the bugs found him. Little black ones that circled his head in clouds.

Most of the playground was surfaced in fine gravel. The hoop area, where the kid named George continued to shoot baskets, was hot-topped, and the trampoline was surrounded with some kind of spongy stuff to cushion the fall if someone jumped wrong and went boinking off the side. There was a shuffle-board court, a badminton set-up, a ropes course, and a cluster of brightly colored cylinders that little kids could assemble into a tunnel—not that there were any kids here little enough to use it. There were also swings, teeter-totters, and a slide. A long green cabinet flanked by picnic tables was marked with signs reading **GAMES AND EQUIPMENT** and **PLEASE RETURN WHAT YOU TOOK OUT.**

The playground was surrounded by a chainlink fence at least ten feet high, and Luke saw cameras peering down at two of the corners. They were dusty, as if they hadn't been cleaned in a while. Beyond the fence there was nothing but forest, mostly pines. Judging by their thickness, Luke put their age at eighty years, give or take. The formula—given in *Trees of North America*, which he had read one Saturday afternoon when he was ten or so—was pretty simple. There was no need to read the rings. You just estimated the circumference of one of the trees, divided by pi to get the diameter, then multiplied by the average growth factor for North American pines, which was 4.5. Easy enough to figure, and so was the corollary deduction: these trees hadn't been logged for quite a long time, maybe a couple of generations. Whatever the Institute was, it was in the middle of an old-growth forest, which meant in the middle of no-where. As for the playground itself, his first thought was that if there was ever a prison exercise yard for kids between the ages of six and sixteen, it would look exactly like this.

The girl—Iris—saw them and waved. She double-bounced on the trampoline, her ponytail flying, then took a final leap off the side and landed on the springy stuff with her legs spread and her knees flexed. "Sha! Who you got there?"

"This is Luke Ellis," Kalisha said. "New this morning."

"Hey, Luke." Iris walked over and offered her hand. She was a skinny girl, taller than Kalisha by a couple of inches. She had a pleasant, pretty face, her cheeks and forehead shiny with what Luke supposed was a mixture of sweat and bug-dope. "Iris Stanhope."

Luke shook with her, aware that the bugs—minges were what they were called in Minnesota, he had no idea what they were called here—had begun to sample him. "Not pleased to be here, but I guess pleased to meet you."

"I'm from Abilene, Texas. What about you?"

"Minneapolis. That's in—"

"I know where it is," Iris said. "Land of a billion lakes, or some shit like that."

"George!" Kalisha shouted. "Where's your manners, young man? Come on over here!"

"Sure, but wait. This is important." George toed the foul line at the edge of the blacktop, held the basketball to his chest, and began speaking in a low, tension-filled voice. "Okay, folks, after seven hard-fought games, this is what it comes down to. Double overtime, Wizards trail the Celtics by one point, and George Iles, just in off the bench, has a chance to win this thing from the foul line. If he makes one, the Wizards tie it up yet again. If he makes both, he'll go down in history, probably get his picture in the Basketball Hall of Fame, maybe win a Tesla convertible—"

"That would have to be a custom job," Luke said. "Tesla doesn't make a convertible, at least not yet."

George paid no attention. "Nobody ever expected

Iles to be in this position, least of all Iles. An eerie silence has fallen over the Capital One Arena . . ."

"And then somebody farts!" Iris shouted. She put her tongue between her lips and blew a long, bubbly honk. "A real trumpet blast! Smelly, too!"

"Iles takes a deep breath . . . he bounces the ball twice, which is his trademark . . ."

"In addition to a motor mouth, George has a very active fantasy life," Iris told Luke. "You get used to it."

George glanced toward the three of them. "Iles casts an angry look at a lone Celtics fan razzing him from center court . . . it's a girl who looks stupid as well as amazingly ugly . . ."

Iris blew another raspberry.

"Now Iles faces the basket . . . Iles shoots . . ."

Air ball.

"Jesus, George," Kalisha said, "that was horrible. Either tie the fucking game or lose it, so we can talk. This kid doesn't know what happened to him."

"Like we *do*," Iris said.

George flexed his knees and shot. The ball rolled around the rim . . . thought it over . . . and fell away.

"*Celtics win, Celtics win!*" Iris yelled. She did a cheerleader jump and shook invisible pompoms. "Now come over here and say hello to the new kid."

George came over, waving away bugs as he did so. He was short and stocky, and Luke thought his fantasies were the only place he would ever play pro basketball. His eyes were a pale blue that reminded Luke of the Paul Newman and Steve McQueen movies he and Rolf liked to watch on TCM. Thinking about that, the two of them sprawled in front of the TV and eating popcorn, made him feel sick.

"Yo, kid. What's your name?"

"Luke Ellis."

"I'm George Iles, but you probably knew that from these girls. I'm a god to them."

Kalisha held her head. Iris flipped him the bird.

"A *love* god."

"But Adonis, not Cupid," Luke said, getting into it a little. Trying, anyway. "Adonis is the god of desire and beauty."

"If you say so. How do you like the place so far? Sucks, doesn't it?"

"What *is* it? Kalisha calls it the Institute, but what does that mean?"

"Might as well call it Mrs. Sigsby's Home for Wayward Psychic Children," Iris said, and spit.

This wasn't like coming in halfway through a movie; it was like coming in halfway through the third season of a TV show. One with a complicated plot.

"Who's Mrs. Sigsby?"

"The queen bitch," George said. "You'll meet her, and my advice is don't sass her. She does not like to be sassed."

"Are you TP or TK?" Iris asked.

"TK, I suppose." Actually it was a lot more than a supposition. "Sometimes things move around me, and since I don't believe in poltergeists, I'm probably doing it. But that can't be enough to . . ." He trailed off. *Can't be enough to land me here* was what he was thinking. But he *was* here.

"TK-positive?" George asked. He headed for one of the picnic tables. Luke followed, trailed by the two girls. He could calculate the rough age of the forest that surrounded them, he knew the names of a hundred different bacteria, he could fill these kids in on

Hemingway, Faulkner, or Voltaire, but he had still never felt more behind the curve.

"I have no idea what that means."

Kalisha said, "Pos is what *they* call kids like me and George. The techs and caretakers and doctors. We're not supposed to know it—"

"But we do," Iris finished. "It's what you call an open secret. TK- and TP-positives can do it when they want to, at least some of the time. The rest of us can't. For me, things only move when I'm pissed off, or really happy, or just startled. Then it's involuntary, like sneezing. So I'm just average. They call average TKs and TPs pinks."

"Why?" Luke asked.

"Because if you're just regular, there's a little pink dot on the papers in your folder. We're not supposed to see what's in our folders, either, but I saw in mine one day. Sometimes they're careless."

"You want to watch your step, or they are apt to get careless all over your ass," Kalisha said.

Iris said, "Pinks get more tests and more shots. I got the tank. It sucked, but not majorly."

"What's the—"

George gave Luke no chance to finish his question. "I'm TK-pos, no pink in my folder. Zero pink for this kid."

"You've seen your folder?" Luke asked.

"Don't need to. I'm awesome. Watch this."

There was no swami-like concentration, the kid just stood there, but an extraordinary thing happened. (It seemed extraordinary to Luke, at least, although neither of the girls seemed particularly impressed.) The cloud of minges circling George's head blew backward, forming a kind of cometary tail, as if they had been struck by a gust of strong wind. Only there *was* no wind.

"See?" he said. "TK-pos in action. Only it doesn't last long."

True enough. The minges were already back, circling him and only kept off by the bug-dope he was wearing.

"That second shot you took at the basket," Luke said. "Could you have made it go in?"

George shook his head, looking regretful.

"I wish they'd bring in a really powerful TK-pos," Iris said. Her meet-the-new-kid excitement had collapsed. She looked tired and scared and older than her age, which Luke put at around fifteen. "One who could teleport us the fuck *out* of here." She sat down on one of the picnic table's benches and put a hand over her eyes.

Kalisha sat down and put an arm around her. "No, come on, it's going to be okay."

"No it isn't," Iris said. "Look at this, I'm a pincushion!" She held out her arms. There were two Band-Aids on the left one, and three on the right. Then she gave her eyes a brisk rub and put on what Luke supposed was her game face. "So, new kid—can *you* move things around on purpose?"

Luke had never talked about the mind-over-matter stuff—also known as psychokinesis—except with his parents. His mom said it would freak people out if they knew. His dad said it was the least important thing about him. Luke agreed with both points, but these kids weren't freaked, and in this place it *was* important. That was clear.

"No. I can't even wiggle my ears."

They laughed, and Luke relaxed. The place was strange and scary, but at least these kids seemed okay.

"Once in a while things move around, that's all. Dishes, or silverware. Sometimes a door will shut by itself. Once or twice my study lamp turned on. It's never anything big. Hell, I wasn't completely sure I was doing it. I thought maybe drafts . . . or deep earth tremors . . ."

They were all looking at him with wise eyes.

"Okay," he said. "I knew. My folks did, too. But it was never a big deal."

Maybe it would have been, he thought, except for being freakishly smart, the kid accepted to not one but two colleges at the age of twelve. Suppose you had a seven-year-old who could play the piano like Van Cliburn. Would anyone care if that kid could also do a few simple card tricks? Or wiggle his ears? This was a thing he couldn't say to George, Iris, and Kalisha, though. It would sound like boasting.

"You're right, it's *not* a big deal!" Kalisha said vehemently. "That's what's so fucked up about it! We're not the Justice League or the X-Men!"

"Have we been kidnapped?" Praying for them to laugh. Praying for one of them to say *of course not*.

"Well, duh," George said.

"Because you can make bugs go away for a second or two? Because . . ." He thought of the pan falling off the table at Rocket Pizza. "Because every now and then I walk into a room and the door closes behind me?"

"Well," George said, "if they were grabbing people for their good looks, Iris and Sha wouldn't be here."

"Dinkleballs," Kalisha said.

George smiled. "An extremely sophisticated return. Right up there with bite my wiener."

"Sometimes I can't wait for you to go to Back

Half," Iris said. "God will probably strike me dead for that, but—"

"Wait," Luke said. "Just *wait*. Start from the beginning."

"This *is* the beginning, chum," said a voice from behind them. "Unfortunately, it's also probably the end."

2

Luke guessed the newcomer's age as sixteen, but later found out he was two years high. Nicky Wilholm was tall and blue-eyed, with a head of unkempt hair that was blacker than black and cried out for a double dose of shampoo. He was wearing a wrinkled button-up shirt over a pair of wrinkled shorts, his white athletic socks were at half-mast, and his sneakers were dirty. Luke remembered Maureen saying he was like Pigpen in the Peanuts comic strips.

The others were looking at him with wary respect, and Luke instantly got that. Kalisha, Iris, and George were no more happy to be here than Luke was himself, but they were trying to keep it positive; except for the moment when Iris had wavered, they gave off a slightly goofy making-the-best-of-it vibe. That wasn't the case with this guy. Nicky didn't look angry now, but it was clear he had been in the not-too-distant past. There was a healing cut on his swollen lower lip, the fading remains of a black eye, and a fresh bruise on one cheek.

A brawler, then. Luke had seen a few in his time, there were even a couple at the Broderick School. He and Rolf steered clear of them, but if this place was the prison Luke was beginning to suspect it was, there would be no way to steer clear of Nicky Wilholm. But the other three didn't seem to be afraid of him, and that was a good sign. Nicky might be pissed off at whatever purpose lay behind that bland Institute name, but with his mates he just seemed intense. Focused. Still, those marks on his face suggested unpleasant possibilities, especially if he wasn't a brawler by nature. Suppose they had been put there by an adult? A schoolteacher doing something like that, not just at the Brod but almost anywhere, would get canned, probably sued, and maybe arrested.

He thought of Kalisha saying *Not in Kansas anymore, Toto*.

"I'm Luke Ellis." He held out his hand, not sure what to expect.

Nicky ignored it and opened the green equipment cabinet. "You play chess, Ellis? These other three suck at it. Donna Gibson could give me at least a half-assed game, but she went to Back Half three days ago."

"And we will see her no more," George said dolefully.

"I play," Luke said, "but I don't feel like it now. I want to know where I am and what goes on here."

Nick brought out a chess board and a box with the armies inside. He set the pieces up rapidly, peering through the hair that had fallen across his eyes rather than brushing it back. "You're in the Institute. Somewhere in the wilds of Maine. Not even a town, just map coordinates. TR-110. Sha picked that up from a bunch of people. So did Donna, and so did Pete Littlejohn. He's another TP that's gone to Back Half."

"Seems like Petey's been gone forever, but it was only last week," Kalisha said wistfully. "Remember all those zits? And how his glasses kept sliding down?"

Nicky paid no attention. "The zookeepers don't try to hide it or deny it. Why would they, when they work on TP kids day in and day out? And they don't worry about the stuff they do want to keep secret, because not even Sha can go deep, and she's pretty good."

"I can score ninety per cent on the Rhine cards most days," Kalisha said. Not boasting, just matter-of-fact. "And I could tell you your grandmother's name if you put it in the front of your mind, but the front is as far as I can go."

My grandmother's name is Rebecca, Luke thought.

"Rebecca," Kalisha said, and when she saw Luke's expression of surprise, she burst into a fit of the giggles that made her look like the child she had been not so long ago.

"You've got the white guys," Nicky said. "I always play black."

"Nick's our honorary outlaw," George said.

"With the marks to prove it," Kalisha said. "Does him no good, but he can't seem to help it. His room is a mess, another act of childish rebellion that just makes more work for Maureen."

Nicky turned to the black girl, unsmiling. "If Maureen was really the saint you think she is, she'd get us out of here. Or blow the whistle to the nearest police."

Kalisha shook her head. "Get real. If you work here, you're a part of it. Good or bad."

"Nasty or nice," George added. He looked solemn.

"Besides, the nearest police force is probably a bunch of Deputy Dogs and Hiram Hoehandles miles from here," Iris said. "Since you seem to've nominated yourself Head Explainer, Nick, why don't you really fill the kid in? Jeepers, don't you remember how weird it is to wake up here in what looks like your own room?"

Nick sat back and crossed his arms. Luke happened to see how Kalisha was looking at him, and thought that if she ever kissed Nicky, it wouldn't be just to pass on a case of the chicken pox.

"Okay, Ellis, I'll tell you what we know. Or what we think we know. It won't take long. Ladies, feel free to chime in. George, keep your mouth shut if you feel a bullshit attack coming on."

"Thanks a lot," George said. "And after I let you drive my Porsche."

"Kalisha's been here the longest," Nicky said. "Because of the chicken pox. How many kids have you seen during that time, Sha?"

She considered. "Probably twenty-five. Maybe a few more."

Nicky nodded. "They—*we*—come from everywhere. Sha's from Ohio, Iris is from Texas, George is from Glory Hole, Montana—"

"I'm from Billings," George said. "A perfectly respectable town."

"First off, they tag us like we were migrating birds or goddam buffalo." Nicky brushed his hair back and folded his earlobe forward, showing a circlet of bright metal half the size of a dime. "They examine us, they test us, they give us shots for dots, then they examine us again and do more tests. Pinks get more shots and more tests."

"I got the tank," Iris said again.

"Whoopee for you," Nick said. "If we're pos, they make us do stupid pet tricks. I myself happen to be TK-pos, but George the motormouth there is quite a bit better at it than I am. And there was one kid here, can't remember his name, who was even better than George."

"Bobby Washington," Kalisha said. "Little black kid, maybe nine. He could push your plate right off the table. Been gone . . . what, Nicky? Two weeks?"

"A little less," Nicky said. "If it was two weeks, it would have been before I came."

"He was there one night at dinner," Kalisha said, "and gone to Back Half the next day. Poof. Now you see him, now you don't. I'll probably be next. I think they're about done with all their tests."

"Same here," Nicky said sourly. "They'll probably be glad to be rid of me."

"Strike the probably on that one," George said.

"They give us shots," Iris said. "Some of them hurt, some of them don't, some of them do stuff to you, some don't. I spiked a fever after one of them, and had the most godawful headache. I was thinking maybe I caught Sha's chicken pox, but it was gone after a day. They keep shooting you up until you see the dots and hear the hum."

"You got off easy," Kalisha told her. "A couple of kids . . . there was that one named Morty . . . can't remember his last name . . ."

"The nose-picker," Iris said. "The one who used to hang with Bobby Washington. I can't remember Morty's last name, either. He went to Back Half like two days after I got here."

"Except maybe he didn't," Kalisha said. "He wasn't here long at all, and he broke out in spots after one of those shots. He told me so in the canteen. He said his heart was still beating like crazy, too. I think maybe he got really sick." She paused. "Maybe he even died."

George was looking at her with big-eyed dismay. "Cynicism and teenage angst is fine, but tell me you don't really believe that."

"Well, I sure don't *want* to," Kalisha said.

"Shut up, all of you," Nicky said. He leaned forward over the board, staring at Luke. "They kidnap us, yes. Because we have psychic powers, yes. How do they find us? Don't know. But it's got to be a big operation, because this place is big. It's a fucking *compound*. They've got doctors, technicians, ones who call themselves caretakers . . . it's like a small hospital stuck out here in the woods."

"And security," Kalisha said.

"Yeah. The guy in charge of that is a big bald fuck. Stackhouse is his name."

"This is crazy," Luke said. "In America?"

"This isn't America, it's the Kingdom of the Institute. When we go to the caff for lunch, Ellis, look out the windows. You'll see a lot more trees, but if you look hard, you'll also see another building. Green cinderblock, just like this one. Blends in with the trees, I guess. Anyway, that's Back Half. Where the kids go when all the tests and shots are done."

"What happens there?"

It was Kalisha who answered. "We don't know."

It was on the tip of Luke's tongue to ask if Maureen knew, then remembered what Kalisha had whispered in his ear: *They listen.*

"We know what they tell us," Iris said. "They say—"

"They say everything is going to be *alllll RIGHT*!"

Nicky shouted this so loudly and so suddenly that Luke recoiled and almost fell off the picnic bench. The black-haired boy got to his feet and stood looking up into the dusty lens of one of the cameras. Luke remembered something else Kalisha had said: *When you meet Nicky, don't worry if he goes off on a rant. It's how he blows off steam.*

"They're like missionaries selling Jesus to a bunch of Indians who are so . . . so . . ."

"Naïve?" Luke ventured.

"Right! That!" Nicky was still staring up at the camera. "A bunch of Indians who are so naïve they'll believe *anything*, that if they give up their land for a handful of beads and fucking flea-ridden blankets, they'll go to heaven and meet all their dead relatives and be happy forever! That's us, a bunch of Indians naïve enough to believe anything that sounds good, that sounds like a *happy . . . fucking . . . ENDING*!"

He whirled back to them, hair flying, eyes burning, hands clenched into fists. Luke saw healing cuts on his knuckles. He doubted if Nicky had given as good as he'd gotten—he was only a kid, after all—but it seemed he had at least given somebody *something*.

"Do you think Bobby Washington had any doubts that his trials were over when they took him to Back Half? Or Pete Littlejohn? Jesus Christ, if brains were black powder, those two couldn't have blown their noses."

He turned to the dirty overhead camera again. That he had nothing else upon which to vent his rage rendered it a touch ludicrous, but Luke admired him just the same. He had not accepted the situation.

"Listen up, you guys! You can beat the shit out of me, and you can take me to Back Half, but I'll fight you every step of the way! *Nick Wilholm doesn't trade for beads and blankets!*"

He sat down, breathing hard. Then he smiled, displaying dimples and white teeth and good-humored eyes. The sullen, brooding persona was gone as if it had never been there. Luke had no attraction to guys, but when he saw that smile, he could understand why

Kalisha and Iris were looking at Nicky as if he were the lead singer in a boy band.

"I should probably be on their team instead of cooped up here like a chicken in a pen. I could sell this place better than Sigsby and Hendricks and the other docs. I have *conviction*."

"You certainly do," Luke said, "but I'm not entirely sure what you were getting at."

"Yeah, kinda went off on a sidetrack there, Nicky," George said.

Nicky crossed his arms again. "Before I whup your ass at chess, new kid, let me review the situation. They bring us here. They test us. They shoot us full of God knows what, and test us some more. Some kids get the tank, all kids get the weird eye test that makes you feel like you're going to pass out. We have rooms that look like our rooms at home, which is probably supposed to provide some kind of, I don't know, soothing for our tender emotions."

"Psychological acclimation," Luke said. "I guess that makes sense."

"There's good food in the caff. We actually order off a menu, limited though it may be. Room doors aren't locked, so if you can't sleep, you can wander down there and pick up a midnight snack. They leave out cookies, nuts, apples, stuff like that. Or you can go to the canteen. The machines there take tokens, of which I have none, because only good little girls and boys get tokens, and I am not a good little boy. My idea of what to do with a Boy Scout is to drop him on his pointy little—"

"Come back," Kalisha said sharply. "Stop the shit."

"Gotcha." Nick flashed her that killer smile, then returned his attention to Luke. "There's plenty of incentive to be good and get tokens. There are snacks and sodas in the canteen, an extremely wide variety."

"Cracker Jacks," George said dreamily. "Ho Hos."

"There are also cigarettes, wine coolers, and the hard stuff."

Iris: "There's a sign that says PLEASE DRINK RE-SPONSIBLY. With kids as young as ten pushing the buttons for Boone's Farm Blue Hawaiian and Mike's Hard Lemonade, how hilarious is that?"

"You've got to be kidding," Luke said, but Kalisha and George were nodding.

"You can get buzzed, but you can't get falling-down drunk," Nicky said. "Nobody has enough tokens for that."

"True," Kalisha said, "but we do have kids who stay buzzed as much as they can."

"Maintenance drinkers, you mean? Ten- and eleven-year-old maintenance drinkers?" Luke still couldn't believe it. "You're not serious."

"I am. There are kids who do whatever they're told just so they can use the booze dispenser every day. I haven't been here long enough to, like, make a study of it, but you hear stories from kids who were here before you."

"Also," Iris said, "we have plenty of kids who are working on a good tobacco habit."

It was ludicrous, but Luke supposed it also made a crazy kind of sense. He thought of the Roman satirist, Juvenal, who had said that if you gave the people bread and circuses, they'd be happy and not cause any trouble. He guessed the same might be true of booze and cigarettes, especially if you offered them to scared and unhappy kids who were locked up. "That stuff doesn't interfere with their tests?"

"Since we don't know what the tests are, it's hard to say," George told him. "All they seem to want is for you to see the dots and hear the hum."

"What dots? What hum?"

"You'll find out," George said. "That part's not so bad. It's getting there that's the bitch. I hate getting shots."

Nicky said, "Three weeks, give or take. That's how long most kids stay in Front Half. At least Sha thinks so, and she's been here the longest. Then we go to Back Half. After that—this is the story—we get debriefed and our memories of this place are wiped somehow." He unfolded his arms and raised his hands to the sky, fingers spread. "And after *that*, chilluns, we go to heaven! Washed clean, except maybe for a pack-a-day habit! Hallelujah!"

"Back home to our parents is what he means," Iris said quietly.

"Where we'll be welcomed with open arms," Nicky said. "No questions asked, just welcome home and let's all go out to Chuck E. Cheese to celebrate. Does that sound realistic to you, Ellis?"

It didn't.

"But our parents *are* alive, right?" Luke didn't know how it sounded to the others, but to him his voice sounded very small.

None of them answered, only looked at him. And really, that was answer enough.

3

There was a knock at Mrs. Sigsby's office door. She invited the visitor in without taking her eyes from her computer monitor. The man who entered was almost as tall as Dr. Hendricks, but ten years younger and in far better shape—broad-shouldered and muscled out. His skull was smooth, shaved, and gleaming. He wore jeans and a blue workshirt, the sleeves rolled up to display his admirable biceps. There was a holster on one hip with a short metal rod sticking up.

"The Ruby Red group's here, if you want to talk to them about the Ellis operation."

"Anything urgent or out of the ordinary on that, Trevor?"

"No, ma'am, not really, and if I'm intruding, I can come back later."

"You're fine, just give me a minute. Our residents are giving the new boy a backgrounder. Come and watch. The mixture of myth and observation is rather amusing. Like something out of *Lord of the Flies*."

Trevor Stackhouse came around the desk. He saw Wilholm—a troublesome little shit if ever there was one—on one side of a chessboard that was all set up and ready to go. The new intake was sitting on the other side. The girls were standing by, most of their attention fixed, as usual, on Wilholm—handsome, sullen, rebellious, a latter-day James Dean. He would be gone soon; Stackhouse couldn't wait for Hendricks to sign off on him.

"How many people work here in all, do you think?" the new boy was asking.

Iris and Kalisha (also known as the Chicken Pox Chick) looked at each other. It was Iris who answered. "Fifty? I think at least that many. There's the doctors . . . techs and caretakers . . . the cafeteria staff . . . um . . ."

"Two or three janitors," Wilholm said, "and the

housekeepers. Just Maureen right now, because there's only the five of us, but when there's more kids, they add another couple of housekeepers. They might come over from Back Half, not sure about that."

"With that many people, how can they keep the place a secret?" Ellis asked. "For one thing, where do they even park their *cars*?"

"Interesting," Stackhouse said. "I don't think anyone ever asked that before."

Mrs. Sigsby nodded. "This one's very smart, and not just book-smart, it looks like. Now hush. I want to hear this."

". . . must stay," Luke was saying. "You see the logic? Like a tour of duty. Which would mean this is actually a government installation. Like one of those black sites, where they take terrorists to interrogate them."

"Plus the old bag-over-the-head water cure," Wilholm said. "I never heard of them doing that to any of the kids here, but I wouldn't put it past them."

"They've got the tank," Iris said. "That's their water cure. They put a cap on you and duck you under and take notes. It's actually better than the shots." She paused. "At least it was for me."

"They must swap out the employees in groups," Ellis said. Mrs. Sigsby thought he was talking more to himself than the others. I bet he does that a lot, she thought. "It's the only way it would work."

Stackhouse was nodding. "Good deductions. Damn good. What is he, twelve?"

"Read your report, Trevor." She pushed a button on her computer and the screen saver appeared: a picture of her twin daughters in their double stroller, taken years before they acquired breasts, smart mouths, and bad boyfriends. Also a bad drug habit, in Judy's case. "Ruby Red's been debriefed?"

"By me personally. And when the cops check the kid's computer, they are going to find he's been looking at some stories about kids who kill their parents. Not a lot, just two or three."

"Standard operating procedure, in other words."

"Yes, ma'am. If it ain't broke, don't fix it." Stackhouse gave her a grin she thought almost as charming as Wilholm's when he turned it on at full wattage. Not quite, though. Their Nicky was a true babe magnet. For now, at least. "Do you want to see the team, or just the operation report? Denny Williams is writing it, so it should be fairly readable."

"If it all went smoothly, just the report. I'll have Rosalind get it to me."

"Fine. What about Alvorson? Any intel from her lately?"

"Do you mean are Wilholm and Kalisha canoodling yet?" Sigsby raised an eyebrow. "Is that germane to your security mission, Trevor?"

"I could give Shit One if those two are canoodling. In fact, I'm rooting for them to go ahead and lose their virginity, assuming they still have it, while they've got a chance. But from time to time Alvorson does pick up things that are germane to my mission. Like her conversation with the Washington boy."

Maureen Alvorson, the housekeeper who actually seemed to like and sympathize with the Institute's young subjects, was in reality a stool pigeon. (Given the little bits of tittle-tattle she brought in, Mrs. Sigsby thought *spy* too grand a term.) Neither Kalisha nor any of the other TPs had tipped to this, because Maureen was extremely good at keeping her way of making a little extra money far below the surface.

What made her especially valuable was the carefully planted idea that certain areas of the Institute—the south corner of the caff and a small area near the vending machines in the canteen, to name just a couple— were audio surveillance dead zones. Those were the places where Alvorson gleaned the kids' secrets. Most were paltry things, but sometimes there was a nugget of gold in the dross. The Washington boy, for instance, who had confided to Maureen that he was thinking about committing suicide.

"Nothing lately," Sigsby said. "I'll inform you if she passes on something I feel would be of interest to you, Trevor."

"Okay. I was just asking."

"Understood. Now please go. I have work to do."

4

"Fuck this shit," Nicky said, sitting down at the bench again. He finally brushed the hair out of his eyes. "The ding-dong's gonna go pretty soon, and I gotta get an eye test and look at the white wall after lunch. Let's see what you got, Ellis. Make a move."

Luke had never felt less like playing chess. He had a thousand other questions—mostly about shots for dots—but maybe this wasn't the time. There was such a thing as information overload, after all. He moved his king's pawn two squares. Nicky countered. Luke responded with his king's bishop, threatening Nicky's king's bishop's pawn. After a moment's hesitation,

Nicky moved his queen out four diagonal squares, and that pretty much sealed the deal. Luke moved his own queen, waited for Nicky to make some move that didn't matter one way or the other, then slid his queen down next to Nicky's king, nice and cozy.

Nicky frowned at the board. "Checkmate? In four moves? Are you serious?"

Luke shrugged. "It's called Scholar's Mate, and it only works if you're playing white. Next time you'll see it coming and counter. Best way is to move your queen's pawn forward two or your king's pawn forward one."

"If I do that, can you still beat me?"

"Maybe." The diplomatic answer. The real one was *of course*.

"Holy joe." Nicky was still studying the board. "That's fucking slick. Who taught you?"

"I read some books."

Nicky looked up, seeming to really see Luke for the first time, and asked Kalisha's question. "How smart *are* you, kid?"

"Smart enough to beat you," Iris said, which saved Luke having to answer.

At that moment, a soft two-note chime went off: the ding-dong.

"Let's go to lunch," Kalisha said. "I'm starving. Come on, Luke. Loser puts the game away."

Nicky pointed a finger gun at her and mouthed *bang bang*, but he was smiling as he did it. Luke got up and followed the girls. At the door to the lounge area, George caught up with him and grabbed his arm. Luke knew from his sociology reading (as well as from personal experience) that kids in a group had a tendency to fall into certain easily recognizable pigeon-holes. If Nicky Wilholm was this group's rebel, then George Iles was its class clown. Only now he looked as serious as a heart attack. He spoke low and fast.

"Nick's cool, I like him and the girls are crazy about him, probably you'll like him, too, and that's okay, but don't make him a role model. He won't accept that we're stuck here, but we are, so pick your battles. The dots, for instance. When you seem em, say so. When you don't, say that. Don't lie. *They know.*"

Nicky caught up with them. "Whatcha talkin about, Georgie Boy?"

"He wanted to know where babies come from," Luke said. "I told him to ask you."

"Oh Jesus, another fucking comedian. Just what this place needs." Nicky grabbed Luke by the neck and pretended to strangle him, which Luke hoped was a sign of liking. Maybe even respect. "Come on, let's eat."

5

What his new friends called the canteen was part of the lounge, across from the big TV. Luke wanted a close look at the vending machines, but the others were moving briskly and he still didn't get the chance. He did, however, note the sign Iris had mentioned: PLEASE DRINK RESPONSIBLY. So maybe they hadn't been just yanking his chain about the booze.

Not Kansas and not Pleasure Island, he thought. It's Wonderland. Someone came into my room in the middle of the night and pushed me down the rabbit hole.

The caff wasn't as big as the one at the Broderick School, but almost. The fact that the five of them were

the only diners made it seem even bigger. Most of the
tables were fourtops, but there were a couple of larger
ones in the middle. One of these had been set with five
places. A woman in a pink smock top and matching
pink trousers came over and filled their water glasses.
Like Maureen, she was wearing a nametag. Hers said
NORMA.

"How are you, my chickens?" she asked.

"Oh, we're plucking right along," George said
brightly. "How about you?"

"Doing fine," Norma said.

"Don't have a Get Out of Jail Free card on you, by
any chance?"

Norma gave him a cruise-control smile and went
back through the swinging door that presumably led
to the kitchen.

"Why do I bother?" George said. "My best lines are
wasted in here. Wasted, I tell you."

He reached for the stack of menus in the center of
the table and handed them around. At the top was
the day's date. Below that was STARTERS (buffalo
wings or tomato bisque), ENTREES (bison burger or
American chop suey), and FINISHERS (apple pie à la
mode or something called Magic Custard Cake). Half
a dozen soft drinks were listed.

"You can get milk, but they don't bother putting it
on the menu," Kalisha said. "Most kids don't want it
unless they have cereal for breakfast."

"Is the food really good?" Luke asked. The prosaic
nature of the question—as if they were maybe at a San-
dals resort where the meals were included—brought
back his sense of unreality and dislocation.

"Yes," Iris said. "Sometimes they weigh us. I've put
on four pounds."

"Fattening us up for the kill," Nicky said. "Like Hansel and Gretel."

"On Friday nights and Sunday noons there are buffets," Kalisha said. "All you can eat."

"Like Hansel and fucking Gretel," Nicky repeated. He made a half-turn, looking up at a camera in the corner. "Come on back, Norma. I think we're ready."

She returned at once, which only increased Luke's sense of unreality. But when his wings and chop suey came, he ate heartily. He was in a strange place, he was afraid for himself and terrified about what might have happened to his parents, but he was also twelve.

A growing boy.

6

They must have been watching, whoever *they* were, because Luke had barely finished the last bite of his custard cake before a woman dressed in another of those pink quasi-uniforms appeared at his side. GLADYS, her name badge said. "Luke? Come with me, please."

He looked at the other four. Kalisha and Iris wouldn't meet his gaze. Nicky was looking at Gladys, arms once more folded across his chest and wearing a faint smile. "Why don't you come back later, honey? Like around Christmas. I'll kick you under the mistletoe."

She paid no attention. "Luke? Please?"

George was the only one looking directly at him, and what Luke saw on his face made him think of what he'd said before they came in from the playground: *Pick your battles*. He got up. "See you guys later. I guess."

Kalisha mouthed soundless words at him: *Shots for dots*.

Gladys was small and pretty, but for all Luke knew, she was a black belt who could throw him over her shoulder if he gave her any trouble. Even if she wasn't, *they* were watching, and he had no doubt reinforcements would show up in a hurry. There was something else, as well, and it was powerful. He had been raised to be polite and obey his elders. Even in this situation, those were hard habits to break.

Gladys led him past the bank of windows Nicky had mentioned. Luke looked out and yes, there was another building out there. He could barely see it through the screening trees, but it was there, all right. Back Half.

He looked over his shoulder before leaving the caff, hoping for some reassurance—a wave, or even a smile from Kalisha would do. There was no wave, and no one was smiling. They were looking at him the way they had in the playground, when he had asked if their parents were alive. Maybe they didn't know about that, not for sure, but they knew where he was going now. Whatever it was, they had already been through it.

7

"Gosh, what a pretty day, huh?" Gladys said as she led him along the cinderblock corridor and past his room. The corridor continued down another wing—more doors, more rooms—but they turned left, into an annex that appeared to be your basic elevator lobby.

Luke, ordinarily quite good at make-nice conversation, said nothing. He was pretty sure it was what Nicky would do in this situation.

"The bugs, though . . . ooh!" She waved away invisible insects, and laughed. "You'll want to wear plenty of bug-dope, at least until July."

"When the dragonflies hatch out."

"Yes! Exactly!" She trilled a laugh.

"Where are we going?"

"You'll see." She waggled her eyebrows, as to say *don't spoil the surprise.*

The elevator doors opened. Two men in blue shirts and pants got off. One was JOE, the other HADAD. They both carried iPads.

"Hi, guys," Gladys said brightly.

"Hey, girl," Hadad said. "How's it going?"

"Fine," Gladys chirped.

"How about you, Luke?" Joe asked. "Adjusting okay?"

Luke said nothing.

"Silent treatment, huh?" Hadad was grinning. "That's okay for now. Later, maybe not so much. Here's the thing, Luke—treat us right and we'll treat you right."

"Go along to get along," Joe added. "Words of wisdom. See you later, Gladys?"

"You bet. You owe me a drink."

"If you say so."

The men went on their way. Gladys escorted Luke into the elevator. There were no numbers and no buttons. She said, "B," then produced a card from her pants pocket and waved it at a sensor. The doors shut. The car descended, but not far.

"B," crooned a soft female voice from overhead. "This is B."

Gladys waved her card again. The doors opened on a wide hall lit with translucent ceiling panels. Soft music played, what Luke thought of as supermarket music. A few people were moving about, some pushing trolleys with equipment on them, one carrying a wire basket that might have contained blood samples. The doors were marked with numbers, each prefixed with the letter B.

A big operation, Nicky had said. *A compound*. That had to be right, because if there was an underground B-Level, it stood to reason there must be a C-Level. Maybe even a D and E. You'd say it almost had to be a government installation, Luke thought, but how could they keep an operation this big a secret? Not only is it illegal and unconstitutional, it involves kidnapping children.

They passed an open door, and inside Luke saw what appeared to be a break room. There were tables and vending machines (no sign reading PLEASE DRINK RESPONSIBLY, though). Three people were sitting at one of the tables, a man and two women. They were dressed in regular clothes, jeans and button-up shirts, and drinking coffee. One of the women, the blondish one, seemed familiar. At first he didn't know why, then he thought of a voice saying *Sure, whatever you want*. It was the last thing he remembered before waking up here.

"You," he said, and pointed at her. "It was you."

The woman said nothing, and her face said nothing. But she looked at him. She was still looking when Gladys closed the door.

"She was the one," Luke said. "I know she was."

"Just a little further," Gladys said. "It won't take long, then you can go back to your room. You'd probably like to rest. First days can be exhausting."

"Did you hear me? She was the one who came into my room. She sprayed something in my face."

No answer, just the smile again. Luke found it a little creepier each time Gladys flashed it.

They reached a door marked B-31. "Behave and you'll get five tokens," she said. She reached into her other pocket and brought out a handful of metal circles that looked like quarters, only with an embossed triangle on either side. "See? Got them right here."

She knocked a knuckle on the door. The blue-clad man who opened it was TONY. He was tall and blond, handsome except for one slightly squinted eye. Luke thought he looked like a villain in a James Bond movie, maybe the suave ski instructor who turned out to be an assassin.

"Hey, pretty lady." He kissed Gladys on the cheek. "And you've got Luke. Hi, Luke." He stuck out his hand. Luke, channeling Nicky Wilholm, didn't shake it. Tony laughed as though this were a particularly good joke. "Come in, come in."

The invitation was just for him, it seemed. Gladys gave him a little push on the shoulder and closed the door. What Luke saw in the middle of the room was alarming. It looked like a dentist's chair. Except he'd never seen one that had straps on the arms.

"Sit down, champ," Tony said. Not sport, Luke thought, but close.

Tony went to a counter, opened a drawer beneath, and rummaged in it. He was whistling. When he turned around, he had something that looked like a small soldering gun in one hand. He seemed surprised to see Luke still standing inside the door. Tony grinned. "Sit down, I said."

"What are you going to do with that? Tattoo me?" He thought of Jews getting numbers tattooed on their arms when they entered the camps at Auschwitz and

Bergen-Belsen. That should have been a totally ridiculous idea, but . . .

Tony looked surprised, then laughed. "Gosh, no. I'm just going to chip your earlobe. It's like getting pierced for an earring. No big deal, and all our guests get em."

"I'm no guest," Luke said, backing up. "I'm a prisoner. And you're not putting anything in my ear."

"I am, though," Tony said, still grinning. Still looking like the guy who would help little kids on the bunny slopes before trying to kill James Bond with a poison dart. "Look, it's no more than a pinch. So make it easy on both of us. Sit in the chair, it'll be over in seven seconds. Gladys will give you a bunch of tokens when you leave. Make it hard and you still get the chip, but no tokens. What do you say?"

"I'm not sitting in that chair." Luke felt trembly all over, but his voice sounded strong enough.

Tony sighed. He set the chip insertion gadget carefully on the counter, walked to where Luke stood, and put his hands on his hips. Now he looked solemn, almost sorrowful. "Are you sure?"

"Yes."

His ears were ringing from the open-handed slap almost before he was aware Tony's right hand had left his hip. Luke staggered back a step and stared at the big man with wide, stunned eyes. His father had paddled him once (gently) for playing with matches when he was four or five, but he had never been slapped in the face before. His cheek was burning, and he still couldn't believe it had happened.

"That hurt a lot more than an earlobe pinch," Tony said. The grin was gone. "Want another? Happy to oblige. You kids who think you own the world. Man oh man."

For the first time, Luke noticed there was a small blue bruise on Tony's chin, and a small cut on his left jaw. He thought of the fresh bruise on Nicky Wilholm's face. He wished he had the guts to do the same, but he didn't. The truth was, he didn't know how to fight. If he tried, Tony would probably slap him all over the room.

"You ready to get in the chair?"

Luke got in the chair.

"Are you going to behave, or do I need the straps?"

"I'll behave."

He did, and Tony was right. The earlobe pinch wasn't as bad as the slap, possibly because he was ready for it, possibly because it felt like a medical procedure rather than an assault. When it was done, Tony went to a sterilizer and produced a hypodermic needle. "Round two, champ."

"What's in that?" Luke asked.

"None of your beeswax."

"If it's going into me, it *is* my beeswax."

Tony sighed. "Straps or no straps? Your choice."

He thought of George saying *pick your battles*. "No straps."

"Good lad. Just a little sting and done."

It was more than a little sting. Not agony, but a pretty big sting, just the same. Luke's arm went hot all the way down to his wrist, as if he had a fever in that one part of him, then it felt normal again.

Tony put on a Band-Aid Clear Spot, then swiveled the chair so it faced a white wall. "Now close your eyes."

Luke closed them.

"Do you hear anything?"

"Like what?"

"Stop asking questions and answer mine. Do you *hear* anything?"

"Be quiet and let me listen."

Tony was quiet. Luke listened.

"Someone walked by out there in the hall. And someone laughed. I think it was Gladys."

"Nothing else?"

"No."

"Okay, you're doing good. Now I want you to count to twenty, then open your eyes."

Luke counted and opened.

"What do you see?"

"The wall."

"Nothing else?"

Luke thought Tony almost had to be talking about the dots. *When you see em, say so*, George had told him. *When you don't, say that. Don't lie. They know.*

"Nothing else."

"Sure?"

"Yes."

Tony slapped him on the back, making Luke jump. "Okay, champ, we're done here. I'll give you some ice for that ear. You have yourself a great day."

8

Gladys was waiting for him when Tony showed him out of Room B-31. She was smiling her cheerful professional hostess smile. "How did you do, Luke?"

Tony answered for him. "He did fine. Good kid."

"It's what we specialize in," Gladys almost sang. "Have a good day, Tony."

"You too, Glad."

She led Luke back to the elevator, chattering away merrily. He had no idea what she was talking about. His arm only hurt a little, but he was holding the cold-pack to his ear, which throbbed. The slap had been worse than either. For all kinds of reasons.

Gladys escorted him to his room along the industrial green corridor, past the poster Kalisha had been sitting under, past the one reading JUST ANOTHER DAY IN PARADISE, and finally to the room that looked like his room but wasn't.

"Free time!" she cried, as if conferring a prize of great worth. Right now the prospect of being alone did feel like sort of a prize. "He gave you a shot, right?"

"Yes."

"If your arm starts to hurt, or if you feel faint, tell me or one of the other caretakers, okay?"

"Okay."

He opened the door, but before he could go in, Gladys grabbed him by the shoulder and turned him around. She was still smiling the hostess smile, but her fingers were steely, pressing into his flesh. Not quite hard enough to hurt, but hard enough to let him know they could hurt.

"No tokens, I'm afraid," she said. "I didn't need to discuss it with Tony. That mark on your cheek tells me all I need to know."

Luke wanted to say *I don't want any of your shitty tokens*, but kept silent. It wasn't a slap he was afraid of; he was afraid that the sound of his own voice—weak, unsteady, bewildered, the voice of a six-year-old— would cause him to break down in front of her.

"Let me give you some advice," she said. Not smiling now. "You need to realize that you are here to serve, Luke. That means you have to grow up fast. It means being realistic. Things will happen to you here. Some of them will not be so nice. You can be a good sport about them and get tokens, or you can be a bad sport and get none. Those things will happen either way, so which should you choose? It shouldn't be hard to figure out."

Luke made no reply. Her smile came back nevertheless, the hostess smile that said *oh yes, sir, I'll show you to your table right away*.

"You'll be back home before the summer is over, and it will be like none of this happened. If you remember it at all, it will be like a dream. But while it's *not* a dream, why not make your stay a happy one?" She relaxed her grip and gave him a gentle push. "You should rest a bit, I think. Lie down. Did you see the dots?"

"No."

"You will."

She closed the door, very gently. Luke sleepwalked across the room to the bed that wasn't his bed. He lay down, put his head on the pillow that wasn't his pillow, and stared at the blank wall where there was no window. No dots, either—whatever they were. He thought: I want my mom. Oh God, I want my mom so bad.

That broke him. He dropped the cold-pack, cupped his hands over his eyes, and began crying. Were they watching him? Or listening to his sobs? It didn't matter. He was past caring. He was still crying when he fell asleep.

9

He woke up feeling better—cleaned out, somehow. He saw two things had been added to his room while he was at lunch, and then meeting his wonderful new friends Gladys and Tony. There was a laptop on the desk. It was a Mac, like his, but an older model. The other addition was a small TV on a stand in the corner.

He went to the computer first and powered it up, feeling another deep pang of homesickness at the familiar Macintosh chime. Instead of a password prompt, he got a blue screen with this message: SHOW CAMERA ONE TOKEN TO OPEN. Luke banged the return key a couple of times, knowing it would do no good.

"You fucking thing."

Then, in spite of how horrible and surreal all this was, he had to laugh. It was harsh and brief, but genuine. Had he felt a certain sense of superiority—maybe even contempt—at the idea of kids scrounging for tokens so they could buy wine coolers or cigarettes? Sure he had. Had he thought *I'd never do that*? Sure he had. When Luke thought of kids who drank and smoked (which was rarely; he had more important things to consider), what came to mind were Goth losers who listened to Pantera and drew lopsided devil horns on their denim jackets, losers so dumb that they mistook wrapping themselves in the chains of addiction as an act of rebellion. He couldn't imagine doing either, but here he was, staring at a blank blue laptop screen and hitting the return key like a rat in a Skinner box banging the lever for a piece of kibble or a few grains of cocaine.

He closed the laptop and grabbed the remote off the top of the television. He fully expected another blue screen and another message telling him he needed a token or tokens to operate it, but instead he got Steve Harvey interviewing David Hasselhoff about the Hoff's bucket list. The audience was laughing it up at the Hoff's funny answers.

Pushing the guide button on the remote produced a DirecTV menu similar to the one at home, but as with the room and the laptop, not quite the same. Although there was a wide selection of movies and sports programs, there were no network or news channels. Luke turned the set off, replaced the remote on top, and looked around.

Other than the one leading to the corridor, there were two doors. One opened on a closet. There were jeans, tee-shirts (no effort had been made to exactly copy the ones he had at home, which was sort of a relief), a couple of button-up shirts, two pairs of sneakers, and one pair of slippers. There were no hard shoes.

The other door opened on a small, spandy-clean bathroom. There were a couple of toothbrushes, still in their cases, on the washbasin, next to a fresh tube of Crest. In the well-stocked medicine cabinet he found mouthwash, a bottle of children's Tylenol, with just four pills inside, deodorant, roll-on Deet bugspray, Band-Aids, and several other items, some more useful than others. The only thing that might be considered even remotely dangerous was a pair of nail clippers.

He swung the medicine cabinet closed and looked at himself. His hair was crazied up, and there were dark circles (beat-off circles, Rolf would have called them) under his eyes. He looked both older and younger, which was weird. He peered at his tender right earlobe and saw one of those tiny metal circles embedded in the slightly reddened skin. He had no doubt that somewhere on B-Level—or C, or D—there was a computer tech who could now track his every movement. Was perhaps tracking him now. Lucas David Ellis, who had been planning to matriculate at MIT and Emerson, had been reduced to a blinking dot on a computer screen.

Luke returned to his room (*the* room, he told himself, it's *the* room, not *my* room), looked around, and realized a dismaying thing. No books. Not a single one. That was as bad as no computer. Maybe worse. He went to the dresser and opened the drawers one by one, thinking he might at least find a Bible or a Book of Mormon, like they sometimes had in hotel rooms. He discovered only neat stacks of underwear and socks.

What did that leave? Steve Harvey interviewing David Hasselhoff? Reruns of *America's Funniest Home Videos?*

No. No way.

He left the room, thinking Kalisha or one of the other kids might be around. He found Maureen Alvorson instead, trundling her Dandux laundry basket slowly down the corridor. It was heaped with folded sheets and towels. She looked more tired than ever and sounded out of breath.

"Hello, Ms. Alvorson. Can I push that for you?"

"That would be kind," she said with a smile. "We've got five newbies coming in, two tonight and three tomorrow, and I've got to get the rooms ready. They're down thataway." She pointed in the opposite direction from the lounge and the playground.

He pushed the basket slowly, because she was walking slowly. "I don't suppose you know how I could earn a token, do you, Ms. Alvorson? I need one to unlock the computer in my room."

"Can you make a bed, if I stand by and give you instructions?"

"Sure. I make my bed at home."

"With hospital corners?"

"Well . . . no."

"Never mind, I'll show you. Make five beds for me, and I'll give you three tokes. It's all I've got in my pocket. They keep me short."

"Three would be great."

"All right, but enough with the Miz Alvorson. You call me Maureen, or just Mo. Same as the other kids."

"I can do that," Luke said.

They went past the elevator annex and into the hallway beyond. It was lined with more inspirational posters. There was also an ice machine, like in a motel hallway, and it didn't appear to take tokens. Just past it, Maureen put a hand on Luke's arm. He stopped pushing the basket and looked at her enquiringly.

When she spoke, it was just above a whisper. "You got chipped, I see, but you didn't get any tokens."

"Well . . ."

"You can talk, as long as you keep your voice down. There's half a dozen places in Front Half where their damn microphones don't reach, dead zones, and I know all of them. This is one, right by this ice machine."

"Okay . . ."

"Who did your chip and put that mark on your face? Was it Tony?"

Luke's eyes began to burn, and he didn't quite trust himself to speak, whether it was safe or not. He just nodded.

"He's one of the mean ones," Maureen said. "Zeke is another. So is Gladys, even though she smiles a lot. There are plenty of people working here who like pushing kids around, but those are three of the worst."

"Tony slapped me," Luke whispered. "Hard."

She ruffled his hair. It was the kind of thing ladies did to babies and little kids, but Luke didn't mind. It was being touched with kindness, and right now that meant a lot. Right now that meant everything.

"Do what he says," Maureen said. "Don't argue with him, that's my best advice. There's people you can argue with here, you can even argue with Mrs. Sigsby, much good it will do you, but Tony and Zeke are two bad bumblebees. Gladys, too. They *sting*."

She started down the corridor again, but Luke caught her by the sleeve of her brown uniform and tugged her back to the safe area. "I think Nicky hit Tony," he whispered. "He had a cut and a mousy eye."

Maureen smiled, showing teeth that looked long overdue for dental work. "Good for Nick," she said. "Tony probably paid him back double, but still . . . good. Now come on. With you to help me, we can get these rooms ready in a jiff."

The first one they visited had posters of Tommy Pickles and Zuko—Nickelodeon characters—on the walls, and a platoon of G.I. Joe action figures on the bureau. Luke recognized several of them right off the bat, having gone through his own G.I. Joe phase not all that long ago. The wallpaper featured happy clowns with balloons.

"Holy crap," Luke said. "This is a little kid's room."

She gave Luke an amused glance, as if to say *You're not exactly Methuselah*. "That's right. His name is Avery Dixon, and 'cording to my sheet, he's just ten. Let's get to work. I bet I only have to show you how to do a hospital corner once. You look like a kid who catches on quick."

10

Back in his room, Luke held one of his tokens up to the laptop's camera. He felt a little stupid doing it, but the computer opened at once, first showing a blue screen with a message on it reading **WELCOME BACK DONNA!** Luke frowned, then smiled a little. At some point before his arrival, this computer had belonged (or been on loan, anyway) to someone named Donna. The welcome screen hadn't been changed yet. Someone had slipped up. Just a tiny slip, but where there was one, there might be others.

The welcome message disappeared and a standard desktop photo appeared: a deserted beach under a dawn sky. The info strip at the bottom of the screen was like the one on his computer at home, with one glaring (but at this point unsurprising) difference: no little email postage stamp. There were, however, icons for two Internet providers. This surprised him, but it was a nice surprise. He opened Firefox and typed *AOL log-in*. The blue screen came back, this time with a pulsing red circle in the middle. A soft computer voice said, "I'm sorry, Dave, I'm afraid I can't do that."

For a moment Luke thought it was another slip-up—first Donna, then Dave—before realizing it was the voice of HAL 9000 from *2001: A Space Odyssey*. Not a goof, just geek humor, and under the circumstances, as funny as a rubber crutch.

He googled *Herbert Ellis* and got HAL again. Luke considered, then googled the Orpheum Theatre on Hennepin, not because he was planning to see a show there (or anywhere in the immediate future, it seemed), but because he wanted to know what information he *could* access. There had to be at least some stuff, or else why give him the connection at all?

The Orf, as his parents called it, seemed to be one of the sites approved for "guests" of the Institute. He was informed that *Hamilton* was coming back ("By Popular Demand!"), and Patton Oswalt would be there next month ("Your Sides Will Split!"). He tried googling the Broderick School and got their website, no problem. He tried Mr. Greer, his guidance counselor, and got HAL. He was beginning to understand Dr. Dave Bowman's frustration in the movie.

He started to close down, then reconsidered and typed *Maine State Police* into the search field. His finger hovered over the execute button, almost pressed it, then withdrew. He'd get HAL's meaningless apology, but Luke doubted if things would end with that. Very likely an alarm would go off on one of the lower levels. Not likely, surely. *They* might forget to change a kid's name on the computer's welcome screen, but they wouldn't forget an alert program if an Institute kid tried to contact the authorities. There would be punishment. Probably worse than a slap to the face. The computer that used to belong to someone named Donna was useless.

Luke sat back and crossed his arms on his narrow chest. He thought of Maureen, and the friendly way she'd ruffled his hair. Only a small, absent-minded gesture of kindness, but that (and the tokens) had taken some of the curse off Tony's slap. Had Kalisha said the woman was forty thousand dollars in debt? No, more like twice that.

Partly because of the friendly way Maureen had touched him and partly just to pass the time, Luke googled *I am overwhelmed with debt please help*. The computer immediately gave him access to all sorts of information on that subject, including a number of companies that declared clearing those pesky bills would be as easy as pie; all the back-to-the-wall debtor needed to do was make one phone call. Luke doubted it, but he supposed some folks wouldn't; it was how they got in over their heads in the first place.

Maureen Alvorson wasn't one of those people, though, at least according to Kalisha. She said Maureen's husband had run up the big bills before taking off. Maybe that was true and maybe it wasn't, but either way, there would be solutions to the problem. There always were; finding them was what learning was all about. Maybe the computer wasn't useless, after all.

Luke went to the sources that looked the most reliable, and was soon deep in the subjects of debt and debt repayment. The old hunger to *know* came over him. To learn a new thing. To isolate and understand the central issues. As always, each piece of information led to three more (or six, or twelve), and eventually a coherent picture began to emerge. A kind of terrain map. The most interesting concept—the linchpin to which all the others were attached—was simple but staggering (to Luke, at least). Debt was a *commodity*. It was bought and sold, and at some point it had become the center of not just the American economy, but of the world's. And yet it did not really exist. It wasn't a concrete thing like gas or gold or diamonds; it was only an idea. A promise to pay.

When his computer's IM chime rang, he shook his head like a boy emerging from a vivid dream. According to the computer's clock, it was almost 5 PM. He clicked on the balloon icon at the bottom of the machine and read this:

Mrs. Sigsby: Hello, Luke, I run this joint, and I'd like to see you.

He considered this, then typed.

Luke: Do I have any choice?

The reply came at once:

Mrs. Sigsby: No. ☺

"Take your smiley and stick it up your—"

There was a knock at the door. He went to it, expecting Gladys, but this time it was Hadad, one of the guys from the elevator.

"Want to take a walk, big boy?"

Luke sighed. "Give me a second. I have to put on my sneakers."

"No problem-o."

Hadad led him to a door past the elevator and used a key card to unlock it. They walked the short distance to the administration building together, waving away the bugs.

11

Mrs. Sigsby reminded Luke of his father's oldest sibling. Like Aunt Rhoda, this woman was skinny, with barely a hint of hips or breasts. Only there were smile lines around Aunt Rhoda's mouth, and always warmth in her eyes. She was a hugger. Luke thought there would be no hugs from the woman standing beside her desk in a plum-colored suit and matching heels. There might be smiles, but they would be the facial equivalent of three-dollar bills. In Mrs. Sigsby's eyes he saw careful assessment and nothing else. Nothing at all.

"Thank you, Hadad, I'll take it from here."

The orderly—Luke supposed that was what Hadad was—gave a respectful nod and left the office.

"Let's start with something obvious," she said. "We are alone. I spend ten minutes or so alone with every new intake soon after their arrival. Some of them, disoriented and angry, have tried to attack me. I bear them no ill will for that. Why would I, for goodness' sake? Our oldest intakes are sixteen, and the average age is eleven years and six months. Children, in other words, and children have poor impulse control at the best of times. I see such aggressive behavior as a teachable moment . . . and I teach them. Will I need to teach you, Luke?"

"Not about that," Luke said. He wondered if Nicky was one of those who had tried to lay hands on this trim little woman. Maybe he would ask later.

"Good. Have a seat, please."

Luke took the chair in front of her desk, leaning forward with his hands clasped tightly between his knees. Mrs. Sigsby sat opposite, her gaze that of a headmistress who would brook no nonsense. Who would treat nonsense harshly. Luke had never met a merciless adult, but he thought he might be facing one now. It was a frightening idea, and his first impulse was to reject it as ridiculous. He quashed it. Better to believe he had merely led a sheltered life. Better—safer—to believe she was what he thought she was, unless and until she proved different. This was a bad situation; that much was beyond doubt. Fooling himself might be the worst mistake he could make.

"You have made friends, Luke. That's good, a good start. You will meet others during your time in Front Half. Two of them, a boy named Avery Dixon and a girl named Helen Simms, have just arrived. They're sleeping now, but you'll make their acquaintance soon, Helen perhaps before lights-out at ten. Avery may sleep through the night. He's quite young, and is sure to be in an emotional state when he does wake up. I hope you will take him under your wing, as I'm sure Kalisha, Iris, and George will. Perhaps even Nick, although one never knows exactly how Nick will react. Including Nick himself, I should think. Helping Avery acclimate to his new situation will earn you tokens, which as you already know are the primary medium of exchange here at the Institute. That is entirely up to you, but we will be watching."

I know you will, Luke thought. *And listening. Except in the few places where you can't. Assuming Maureen's right about that.*

"Your friends have given you a certain amount of information, some of it accurate, some of it wildly inaccurate. What I tell you now is *completely* accurate, so listen carefully." She leaned forward, hands flat on her desk, her eyes locked on his. "Are your ears open, Luke? Because I do not, as the saying goes, chew my cabbage twice."

"Yes."

"Yes what?" Snapping it at him, although her face remained as calm as ever.

"Ears open. Mind attentive."

"Excellent. You will spend a certain amount of time in Front Half. It might be ten days; it might be two weeks; it might be as long as a month, although very few of our conscripts stay that long."

"Conscripts? Are you saying I've been drafted?"

She gave a brisk nod. "I'm saying exactly that.

There's a war going on, and you have been called upon to serve your country."

"Why? Because every now and then I can move a glass or a book without touching it? That's stu—"

"Shut your mouth!"

Almost as shocked by this as he had been by Tony's roundhouse slap, Luke did.

"When I talk, you listen. You don't interrupt. Are we clear?"

Not trusting his voice, Luke only nodded.

"This is not an arms race but a *mind* race, and if we lose, the consequences would be more than dire; they would be unimaginable. You may only be twelve, but you are a soldier in an undeclared war. The same is true of Kalisha and the others. Do you like it? Of course not. Draftees never do, and draftees sometimes need to be taught that there are consequences for not following orders. I believe you've already had one lesson in that regard. If you're as bright as your records say you are, perhaps you won't need another. If you do, however, you'll get it. This is not your home. This is not your school. You will not simply be given an extra *chore* or sent to the *principal's office* or given *detention*; you will be *punished*. Clear?"

"Yes." Tokens for good boys and girls, face-slaps for those who were bad. Or worse. The concept was chilling but simple.

"You will be given a number of injections. You will be given a number of tests. Your physical and mental condition will be monitored. You will eventually graduate to what we call Back Half, and there you will be given certain services to perform. Your stay in Back Half may last as long as six months, although the average length of active service is only six weeks. Then your memories will be wiped, and you will be sent home to your parents."

"They're alive? My parents are alive?"

She laughed, the sound surprisingly merry. "Of course they're alive. We're not murderers, Luke."

"I want to talk to them, then. Let me talk to them and I'll do whatever you want." The words were out before he realized what a rash promise this was.

"No, Luke. We still don't have a clear understanding." She sat back. Hands once more flat on her desk. "This is not a negotiation. You will do whatever we want, regardless. Believe me on that, and spare yourself a lot of pain. You will have no contact with the outside world during your time at the Institute, and that includes your parents. You will obey all orders. You will comply with all protocols. Yet you will not, with perhaps a few exceptions, find the orders arduous or the protocols onerous. Your time will pass quickly, and when you leave us, when you wake up in your own bedroom one fine morning, none of this will have happened. The sad part—*I* think so, anyway—is that you won't even know you had the great privilege of serving your country."

"I don't see how it's possible," Luke said. Speaking more to himself than to her, which was his way when something—a physics problem, a painting by Manet, the short- and long-term implications of debt—had completely engaged his attention. "So many people know me. The school . . . the people my folks work with . . . my friends . . . you can't wipe *all* their memories."

She didn't laugh, but she smiled. "I think you might be very surprised at what we can do. We're finished here." She stood, came around the desk, and held out her hand. "It's been a pleasure to meet you."

Luke also stood, but he didn't take her hand.

"Shake my hand, Luke."

Part of him wanted to, old habits were hard to break, but he kept his hand at his side.

"Shake it, or you'll wish you did. I won't tell you again."

He saw she absolutely meant it, so he shook her hand. She held it. Although she didn't squeeze, he could tell her hand was very strong. Her eyes stared into his. "I may see you, as another saying goes, around the campus, but hopefully this will be your only visit to my office. If you are called in here again, our conversation will be less pleasant. Do you understand?"

"Yes."

"Good. I know this is a dark time for you, but if you do as you're told, you'll come out into the sunshine. Trust me on that. Now go."

He left, once more feeling like a boy in a dream, or Alice down the rabbit hole. Hadad was chatting with Mrs. Sigsby's secretary or assistant or whatever she was, and waiting for him. "I'll take you back to your room. Close at my side, right? No running for the trees."

They went out, started across to the residence building, and then Luke stopped as a wave of dizziness came over him. "Wait," he said. "Hold on."

He bent down, grasping his knees. For a moment colored lights swarmed in front of his eyes.

"You going to pass out?" Hadad asked. "What do you think?"

"No," Luke said, "but give me a few more seconds."

"Sure. You got a shot, right?"

"Yes."

Hadad nodded. "It hits some kids that way. Delayed reaction."

Luke expected to be asked if he saw spots or dots, but Hadad just waited, whistling through his teeth and waving at the swarming noseeums.

Luke thought about Mrs. Sigsby's cold gray eyes, and her flat refusal to tell him how a place like this could possibly exist without some form of . . . what would be the correct term? Extreme rendition, maybe. It was as if she were daring him to do the math.

Do as you're told, you'll come out into the sunshine. Trust me on that.

He was only twelve, and understood that his experience of the world was limited, but one thing he was quite sure of: when someone said *trust me*, they were usually lying through their teeth.

"Feeling better? Ready to go, my son?"

"Yes." Luke straightened up. "But I'm not your son."

Hadad grinned; a gold tooth flashed. "For now you are. You're a son of the Institute, Luke. Might as well relax and get used to it."

12

Once they were inside the residence building, Hadad called the elevator, said "Seeya later, alligator," and stepped in. Luke started back to his room and saw Nicky Wilholm sitting on the floor opposite the ice machine, eating a peanut butter cup. Above him was a poster showing two cartoon chipmunks with comic-strip word balloons coming from their grinning mouths. The one on the left was saying, "Live the life you love!" The other was saying, "Love the life you live!" Luke stared at this, bemused.

"What do you call a poster like that in a place like this, smart kid?" Nicky asked. "Irony, sarcasm, or bullshit?"

"All three," Luke said, and sat down beside him.

Nicky held out the Reese's package. "Want the other one?"

Luke did. He said thanks, stripped off the crinkly paper the candy sat in, and ate the peanut butter cup in three quick bites.

Nicky watched him, amused. "Had your first shot, didn't you? They make you crave sugar. You may not want much for supper, but you'll eat dessert. Guaranteed. Seen any dots yet?"

"No." Then he remembered bending over and grasping his knees while he waited for the dizziness to pass. "Maybe. What are they?"

"The techs call em the Stasi Lights. They're part of the prep. I've only had a few shots and hardly any weird tests, because I'm a TK-pos. Same as George, and Sha's TP-pos. You get more if you're just ordinary." He considered. "Well, none of us are ordinary or we wouldn't be here, but you know what I mean."

"Are they trying to up our ability?"

Nicky shrugged.

"What are they prepping us for?"

"Whatever goes on in Back Half. How'd it go with the queen bitch? Did she give you the speech about serving your country?"

"She said I'd been conscripted. I feel more like I got press-ganged. Back in the seventeenth and eighteenth centuries, see, when captains needed men to crew their ships—"

"I know what press gangs were, Lukey. I did go to school, you know. And you're not wrong." He got up. "Come on, let's go out to the playground. You can give me another chess lesson."

"I think I just want to lie down," Luke said.

"You do look kinda pale. But the candy helped, right? Admit it."

"It did," Luke agreed. "What did you do to get a token?"

"Nothing. Maureen slipped me one before she went off-shift. Kalisha's right about her." Nicky said this almost grudgingly. "If there's one good person in this palace of shit, it's her."

They had arrived at Luke's door. Nicky held up a fist, and Luke bumped it with his own.

"See you when the ding-dong goes, smart kid. In the meantime, keep your pecker up."

MAUREEN AND AVERY

1

Luke slipped into a nap crowded with unpleasant dream fragments, only waking when the ding-dong went for supper. He was glad to hear it. Nicky had been wrong; he did want to eat, and he was hungry for company as well as food. Nevertheless, he stopped in the canteen to verify that the others hadn't just been pulling his leg. They hadn't been. Next to the snack machine was a fully stocked vintage cigarette dispenser, the lighted square on top showing a man and woman in fancy dress smoking on a balcony and laughing. Next to this was a coin-op dispensing adult beverages in small bottles—what some of the booze-inclined kids at the Brod called "airline nips." You could get a pack of cigarettes for eight tokens; a small bottle of Leroux Blackberry Wine for five. On the other side of the room was a bright red Coke cooler.

Hands grabbed him from behind and lifted him off his feet. Luke yelled in surprise, and Nicky laughed in his ear.

"If you wet your pants, you must take a chance and dance to France!"

"Put me down!"

Nicky swung him back and forth instead. "Lukey-tiddy-ooky-del-Lukey! Tee-legged, toe-legged, bow-legged Lukey!"

He set Luke down, spun him around, raised his hands, and began to boogaloo to the Muzak drifting from the overhead speakers. Behind him, Kalisha and Iris were looking on with identical *boys will be boys* expressions. "Wanna fight, Lukey? Tee-legged, toe-legged, bow-legged Lukey?"

"Stick your nose up my ass and fight for air," Luke said, and began to laugh. The word for Nicky, he thought, whether in a good mood or a bad one, was *alive*.

"Nice one," George said, pushing his way between the two girls. "I'm saving that for later use."

"Just make sure I get the credit," Luke said.

Nicky quit dancing. "I'm starvin, Marvin. Come on, let's eat."

Luke lifted the top of the Coke dispenser. "Soft drinks are free, I take it. You just pay for booze, smokes, and snacks."

"You take it right," Kalisha said.

"And, uh . . ." He pointed at the snack machine. Most of the goodies could be had for a single toke, but the one he was pointing at was a six-token buy. "Is that . . ."

"Are you asking if Hi Boy Brownies are what you think they are?" Iris asked. "I never had one myself, but I'm pretty sure they are."

"Yessum," George said. "I got off, but I also got a rash. I'm allergic. Come on, let's eat."

They sat at the same table. NORMA had been replaced by SHERRY. Luke ordered breaded mushrooms, chopped steak with salad, and something going under the alias of Vanilla Cream Brulay. There might be smart people in this sinister wonderland—certainly Mrs. Sigsby hadn't seemed like a dummy—but whoever made out the menus was perhaps not one of them. Or was that intellectual snobbery on his part?

Luke decided he didn't care.

They talked a bit about their schools before they had been torn out of their normal lives—regular schools, so far as Luke could tell, not special ones for smart kids—and about their favorite TV programs and movies. All good until Iris raised a hand to brush at one freckled cheek, and Luke realized she was crying. Not much, just a little, but yeah, those were tears.

"No shots today, but I had that damned ass-temp," she said. When she saw Luke's puzzled expression, she smiled, which caused another tear to roll down her cheek. "They take our temperature rectally."

The others were nodding. "No idea why," George said, "but it's humiliating."

"It's also nineteenth century," Kalisha said. "They must have some kind of reason, but . . ." She shrugged.

"Who wants coffee?" Nick asked. "I'll get it if you—"

"Hey."

From the doorway. They turned and saw a girl wearing jeans and a sleeveless top. Her hair, short and spiky, was green on one side and bluish-purple on the other. In spite of this punk 'do, she looked like a fairy-tale child lost in the woods. Luke guessed she was about his age.

"Where am I? Do any of you know what this place is?"

"Come on over, Sunshine," Nicky said, and flashed his dazzling smile. "Drag up a rock. Sample the cuisine."

"I'm not hungry," the newcomer said. "Just tell me one thing. Who do I have to blow to get out of here?"

That was how they met Helen Simms.

2

After they ate, they went out to the playground (Luke did not neglect to slather himself with bug-dope) and filled Helen in. It turned out that she was a TK, and like George and Nicky, she was a pos. She proved this by knocking over several pieces on the chessboard when Nicky set them up.

"Not just pos but *awesome* pos," George said. "Let me try that." He managed to knock over a pawn, and he made the black king rock a bit on its base, but that was all. He sat back and blew out his cheeks. "Okay, you win, Helen."

"I think we're all losers," she said. "That's what I think."

Luke asked her if she was worried about her parents.

"Not especially. My father's an alcoholic. My mother divorced him when I was six and married— surprise!—another alcoholic. She must have figured if you can't beat em, join em, because now she's an alkie, too. I miss my brother, though. Do you think he's all right?"

"Sure," Iris said, without much conviction, and then wandered away to the trampoline and began to bounce. Doing that so soon after a meal would have made Luke feel whoopsy, but Iris hadn't eaten much.

"Let me get this straight," Helen said. "You don't know why we're here, except it maybe has something to do with psychic abilities that wouldn't even pass an *America's Got Talent* audition."

"Wouldn't even get us on *Little Big Shots*," George said.

"They test us until we see dots, but you don't know why."

"Right," Kalisha said.

"Then they put us in this other place, Back Half, but you don't know what goes on there."

"Yup," Nicky said. "Can you play chess, or just knock over the pieces?"

She ignored him. "And when they're done with us, we get some sci-fi memory wipe and live happily ever after."

"That's the story," Luke said.

She considered, then said, "It sounds like hell."

"Well," Kalisha said, "I guess that's why God gave us wine coolers and Hi Boy Brownies."

Luke had had enough. He was going to cry again pretty soon; he could feel it coming on like a thunderstorm. Doing that in company might be okay for Iris, who was a girl, but he had an idea (surely outdated but all the same powerful) about how boys were supposed to behave. In a word, like Nicky.

He went back to his room, closed the door, and lay down on his bed with an arm over his eyes. Then, for no reason, he thought of Richie Rocket in his silver space suit, dancing as enthusiastically as Nicky Wilholm had before dinner, and how the little kids danced with him, laughing like crazy and singing along to "Mambo Number 5." As though nothing could go wrong, as if their lives would always be filled with innocent fun.

The tears came, because he was afraid and angry, but

mostly because he was homesick. He had never understood what that word meant until now. This wasn't
summer camp, and it wasn't a field trip. This was a
nightmare, and all he wanted was for it to be over. He
wanted to wake up. And because he couldn't, he fell
asleep with his narrow chest still hitching with a few
final sobs.

3

More bad dreams.

He awoke with a start from one in which a headless
black dog had been chasing him down Wildersmoot
Drive. For a single wonderful moment he thought the
whole *thing* had been a dream, and he was back in his
real room. Then he looked at the pajamas that weren't
his pajamas and at the wall where there should have
been a window. He used the bathroom, and then, because he was no longer sleepy, powered up the laptop.
He thought he might need another token to make it
work, but he didn't. Maybe it was on a twenty-four-
hour cycle, or—if he was lucky—forty-eight. According to the strip at the top, it was quarter past three in
the morning. A long time until dawn, then, and what
he got for first taking a nap and then falling asleep so
early in the evening.

He thought about going to YouTube and watching some of the vintage cartoons, stuff like Popeye
that had always had him and Rolf rolling around on
the floor, yelling "Where's me spinach?" and "Uck-
uck-uck!" But he had an idea they would only bring
the homesickness back, and raving. So what did that
leave? Going back to bed, where he'd lie awake until

daylight? Wandering the empty halls? A visit to the playground? He could do that, he remembered Kalisha saying the playground was never locked, but it would be too spooky.

"Then why don't you think, asshole?"

He spoke in a low voice, but jumped at the sound anyway, even half-raised a hand as if to cover his mouth. He got up and walked around the room, bare feet slapping and pajama bottoms flapping. It was a good question. Why *didn't* he think? Wasn't that what he was supposed to be good at? Lucas Ellis, the smart kid. The boy genius. Loves Popeye the Sailor Man, loves Call of Duty, loves shooting hoops in the backyard, but also has a working grasp of written French, although he still needs subtitles when he looks at French movies on Netflix, because they all talk so fast, and the idioms are crazy. *Boire comme un trou*, for instance. Why drink like a hole when drink like a fish makes much more sense? He can fill a blackboard with math equations, he can reel off all the elements in the periodic table, he can list every vice president going back to George Washington's, he can give you a reasonable explanation of why attaining light speed is never going to happen outside of the movies.

So why is he just sitting here and feeling sorry for himself?

What else *can* I do?

Luke decided to take that as a real question instead of an expression of despair. Escape was probably impossible, but what about learning?

He tried googling the *New York Times*, and wasn't surprised to get HAL 9000; no news for Institute kids. The question was, could he find a way around the prohibition? A back door? Maybe.

Let's see, he thought. Let's just see. He opened Firefox and typed in #!cloakofGriffin!#.

Griffin was H. G. Wells's invisible man, and this site, which Luke had learned about a year ago, was a way to get around parental controls—not the dark web, exactly, but next door to it. Luke had used it, not because he wanted to visit porn sites on the Brod's computers (although he and Rolf had done just that on a couple of occasions), or watch ISIS beheadings, but simply because the concept was cool and simple and he wanted to find out if it worked. It had at home and at school, but would it here? There was only one way to find out, so he banged the return key.

The Institue's Wi-Fi munched awhile—it was slow—and then, just when Luke was starting to think it was a lost cause, took him to Griffin. At the top of the screen was Wells's invisible man, head wrapped in bandages, badass goggles covering his eyes. Below this was a question that was also an invitation: WHICH LANGUAGE DO YOU WANT TRANSLATED? The list was a long one, from Assyrian to Zulu. The beauty of the site was it didn't matter which language you picked; the important thing was what got recorded in the search history. Once upon a time, a secret passage beneath parental controls had been available on Google, but the sages of Mountain View had shut it down. Hence, the Cloak of Griffin.

Luke picked German at random, and got ENTER PASSWORD. Calling on what his dad sometimes called his weird memory, Luke typed in #x49ger194GbL4. The computer munched a little more, then announced PASSWORD ACCEPTED.

He typed in *New York Times* and hit enter. This time the computer thought even longer, but eventually the *Times* came up. Today's issue, and in English, but from this point forward, the computer's search history would note nothing but a series of German words and English translations. Maybe a small victory, maybe a large one. For the moment, Luke didn't even care. It was a win, and that was enough.

How soon would his captors realize what he was doing? Camouflaging the computer's search history would mean nothing if they could do live look-ins. They'd see the newspaper and shut him down. Never mind the *Times* with its headline about Trump and North Korea; he ought to check the *Star Trib* before that could happen, see if there was anything about his parents. But before he could do that, the screaming started out in the hall.

"Help! Help! Help! Somebody help me! SOMEBODY HELP ME, I'M LOST!"

4

The screamer was a little boy in *Star Wars* pajamas, hammering on doors with small fists that went up and down like pistons. Ten? Avery Dixon looked six, seven at most. The crotch and one leg of his pajama pants were wet and sticking to him.

"Help me, I WANT TO GO HOME!"

Luke glanced around, expecting to see someone— maybe several someones—coming on the run, but the hall remained empty. Later, he would realize that in the Institute, a kid screaming to go home was par for the course. For the moment, Luke just wanted to shut the kid up. He was freaked out, and he was freaking Luke out.

He went to him, knelt down, and took the boy by the shoulders. "Hey. Hey. Take it easy, kid."

The kid in question stared at Luke with white-ringed eyes, but Luke wasn't entirely sure the kid was seeing him. His hair was sweaty and sticking up. His face was wet with tears, and his upper lip gleamed with fresh snot.

"Where's Mumma? Where's Daddy?"

Only it wasn't *Daddy* but *DAAAAAADY*, like the whoop of an air raid siren. The kid began to stomp his feet. He brought his fists down on Luke's shoulders. Luke let him go, got up, and stepped back, watching with amazement as the kid fell to the floor and began to thrash.

Across from the poster proclaiming this JUST ANOTHER DAY IN PARADISE, a door opened and Kalisha emerged, wearing a tie-dyed tee-shirt and gigantic basketball shorts. She walked to Luke and stood looking down at the newcomer, her hands on her mostly nonexistent hips. Then she looked at Luke. "I've seen tantrums before, but this one takes the prize."

Another door opened and Helen Simms appeared, clad—sort of—in what Luke believed were called babydoll pajamas. *She* had hips, plus other interesting equipment.

"Put your eyes back in their sockets, Lukey," Kalisha said, "and help me out a little. Kid's buggin my head like to give me a migraine." She knelt, reached out for the dervish—whose words had now devolved into wordless howls—and pulled back when one of his fists struck her forearm. "Jesus, work with me here. Grab his hands."

Luke also knelt, made a tentative move to grab the new kid's hands, pulled back, then decided he didn't want to look like a wuss in front of the lately arrived vision in pink. He grabbed the little boy at the elbows and pressed his arms to the sides of his chest. He could actually feel the kid's heart, racing along at triple time.

Kalisha bent over him, put her hands on the sides of his face, and looked into his eyes. The kid stopped yelling. Now there was only the sound of his rapid breathing. He looked at Kalisha, fascinated, and Luke suddenly understood what she'd meant when she said the kid was bugging her head.

"He's TP, isn't he? Like you."

Kalisha nodded. "Only he's a lot stronger than me, or any of the other TPs that have been through here during my time. Come on, let's take him down to my room."

"Can I come?" Helen asked.

"Suit yourself, hon," Kalisha said. "I'm sure Lukey here appreciates the view."

Helen flushed. "Maybe I'll change first."

"Do what you want," Kalisha said, then to the kid: "What's your name?"

"Avery." His voice was hoarse from crying and yelling. "Avery Dixon."

"I'm Kalisha. You can call me Sha, if you want."

"Just don't call her Sport," Luke said.

5

Kalisha's room was more girly than Luke would have expected, given her tough talk. There was a pink spread on the bed, and frou-frou flounces on the pillows. A framed picture of Martin Luther King stared at them from the bureau.

She saw Luke looking at it, and laughed. "They try to make things the same as at home, but I guess someone thought the picture I used to have there was taking it a little too far, so they changed it."

"Who did it used to be?"

"Eldridge Cleaver. Ever heard of him?"

"Sure. *Soul on Ice*. I haven't read it, but I've been meaning to get around to it."

She raised her eyebrows. "Man, you are *wasted* here."

Still sniffling, Avery started to get up on her bed, but she grabbed him and pulled him back, gently but firmly.

"Nuh-uh, not in those wet pants." She made as if to take them off and Avery stepped back, hands crossed protectively over his crotch.

Kalisha looked at Luke and shrugged. He shrugged back, then squatted in front of Avery. "Which room are you in?"

Avery only shook his head.

"Did you leave the door open?"

This time the kid nodded.

"I'll get you some dry clothes," Luke said. "You stay here with Kalisha, okay?"

No shake and no nod this time. The boy only stared at him, exhausted and confused, but at least not doing his air raid imitation anymore.

"Go on," Kalisha said. "I think I can soothe him down."

Helen appeared at the door, now wearing jeans and buttoning up a sweater. "Is he any better?"

"A little," Luke said. He saw a patter of drops tending in the direction he and Maureen had gone to change the sheets.

"No sign of those other two boys," Helen said. "They must sleep like the dead."

"They do," Kalisha said. "You go on with Luke, New Girl. Avery and I are having a meeting of the minds here."

6

"The kid's name is Avery Dixon," Luke said as he and Helen Simms stood in an open door just past the ice machine, which was clattering away to itself. "He's ten. Doesn't look it, does he?"

She stared at him, eyes wide. "What are you, TP after all?"

"No." Surveying the poster of Tommy Pickles, and the G.I. Joes on the bureau. "I was here with Maureen. She's one of the housekeepers. I helped her change the bed. Other than that, the room was all ready for him."

Helen smirked. "So *that's* what you are—teacher's pet."

Luke thought of Tony slapping him across the face, and wondered if Helen would soon be getting the same treatment. "No, but Maureen's not like some of the others. Treat her right and she'll treat you right."

"How long have you been here, Luke?"

"I got here just before you."

"So how do you know who's nice and who isn't?"

"Maureen's okay, that's all I'm saying. Help me get him some clothes."

Helen grabbed some pants and underwear out of the dresser (not neglecting to snoop her way through the rest of the drawers), and they walked back to Kalisha's room. On the way, Helen asked if Luke had had any of the tests George had told her about. He said he hadn't, but showed her the chip in his ear.

"Don't fight it. I did, and got whacked."

She stopped dead. "Shut up!"

He turned his head to show her his cheek, where two of Tony's fingers had left faint bruises.

"No one's whacking *me*," Helen said.

"That's a theory you don't want to test."

She tossed her two-tone hair. "My ears are pierced already, so no big deal."

Kalisha was sitting on her bed with Avery beside her, his butt on a folded towel. She was stroking his sweaty hair. He was looking up at her dreamily, as if she were Princess Tiana. Helen tossed Luke the clothes. He wasn't expecting it and dropped the underpants, which were imprinted with pictures of Spider-Man in various dynamic poses.

"I have no interest in seeing that kid's teeny peenie. I'm going back to bed. Maybe when I wake up I'll be in my room, my *real* room, and all of this will just have been a dream."

"Good luck with that," Kalisha said.

Helen strode away. Luke picked up Avery's underwear just in time to mark the swing of her hips in the faded jeans.

"Yummy, huh?" Kalisha's voice was flat.

Luke brought her the clothes, feeling his cheeks heat. "I guess so, but she leaves something to be desired in the personality department."

He thought that might make her laugh—he liked her laugh—but she looked sad. "This place will knock the bitch out of her. Pretty soon she'll be scurrying and flinching every time she sees a guy in a blue top.

Just like the rest of us. Avery, you need to get dressed in these things. Me and Lukey will turn our backs."

They did so, staring out Kalisha's open door at the poster proclaiming this was paradise. From behind them came sniffling and rustling clothes. At last Avery said, "I'm dressed. You can turn around."

They did. Kalisha said, "Now take those wet pj pants into the bathroom and hang em over the side of the tub."

He went without argument, then shuffled back. "I did it, Sha." The fury was gone from his voice. Now he sounded timid and tired.

"Good f'you. Go on and get back on the bed. Lie down, it's okay."

Kalisha sat, dropped Avery's feet on her lap, then patted the bed next to her. Luke sat down and asked Avery if he was feeling better.

"I guess so."

"You *know* so," Kalisha said, and began to stroke the little boy's hair again. Luke had a sense—maybe bullshit, maybe not—that a lot was going on between them. Inside traffic.

"Go on, then," Kalisha said. "Tell him your joke if you have to, then go to fuckin sleep."

"You said a bad word."

"I guess I did. Tell him the joke."

Avery looked at Luke. "Okay. The big moron and the little moron were standing on a bridge, see? And the big moron fell off. Why didn't the little one?"

Luke considered telling Avery that people no longer talked about morons in polite society, but since it was clear that polite society did not exist here, he just said, "I give up."

"Because he was a little more on. Get it?"

"Sure. Why did the chicken cross the road?"

"To get to the other side?"

"No, because she was a dumb cluck. Now go to sleep."

Avery started to say something else—maybe another joke had come to mind—but Kalisha hushed him. She went on stroking his hair. Her lips were moving. Avery's eyes grew heavy. The lids went down, slowly rose, went down again, and rose even more slowly. Next time they stayed down.

"Were you just doing something?" Luke asked.

"Singing him a lullabye my mom used to sing me." She spoke barely above a whisper, but there was no mistaking the amazement and pleasure in her voice. "I couldn't carry a tune in a bucket, but when it's mind to mind, the melody doesn't seem to matter."

"I have an idea he's not exactly too intelligent," Luke said.

She gave him a long look that made his face heat up, as it had when she caught him staring at Helen's legs and busted him on it. "For you, the whole world must not seem exactly too intelligent."

"No, I'm not that way," Luke protested. "I just meant—"

"Ease up. I know what you meant, but it's not brains he's lacking. Not exactly. TP as strong as he's got might not be a good thing. When you don't know what people are thinking, you have to start early when it comes to . . . mmm . . ."

"Picking up cues?"

"Yeah, that. Ordinary people have to survive by looking at faces, and judging the tone of voice they're hearing as well as the words. It's like growing teeth, so you can chew something tough. This poor little shit is like Thumper in that Disney cartoon. Any teeth he's got aren't good for much more than grass. Does that make sense?"

Luke said it did.

Kalisha sighed. "The Institute's a bad place for a Thumper, but maybe it doesn't matter, since we all go to Back Half eventually."

"How much TP has he got—compared, say, to you?"

"A ton more. They have this thing they measure—BDNF. I saw it on Dr. Hendricks's laptop one time, and I think it's a big deal, maybe the biggest. You're the brainiac, do you know what that is?"

Luke didn't, but intended to find out. If they didn't take his computer away first, that was.

"Whatever it is, this kid's must be over the moon. I talked to him! It was real telepathy!"

"But you must have been around other TPs, even if it's rarer than TK. Maybe not in the outside world, but here, for sure."

"You don't get it. Maybe you can't. That's like listening to a stereo with the sound turned way down, or listening to people talk out on the patio while you're in the kitchen with the dishwasher running. Sometimes it's not there at all, just falls completely out of the mix. This was the real deal, like in a science fiction movie. You have to take care of him after I'm gone, Luke. He's a goddam Thumper, and it's no surprise he doesn't act his age. He's had an easy cruise up to now."

What resonated with Luke was *after I'm gone.* "You . . . has anyone said anything to you about going to Back Half? Maureen, maybe?"

"No one needs to. I didn't get a single one of their bullshit tests yesterday. No shots, either. That's a sure sign. Nick's going, too. George and Iris may be here a little longer."

She gently gripped the back of Luke's neck, producing another of those tingles.

"I'm gonna be your sister for a minute, Luke, your soul sister, so listen to me. If the only thing you like about Punk Rock Girl is how she wiggles when she walks, keep it that way. It's bad to get too involved with people here. It fucks you up when they go away, and they all do. But you need to take care of this one for as long as you can. When I think of Tony or Zeke or that bitch Winona hitting Avery, it makes me want to cry."

"I'll do what I can," Luke said, "but I hope you'll be here a lot longer. I'd miss you."

"Thanks, but that's exactly what I'm talking about."

They sat quiet for awhile. Luke supposed he would have to go soon, but he didn't want to yet. He wasn't ready to be alone.

"I think I can help Maureen." He spoke in a low voice, hardly moving his lips. "With those credit card bills. But I'd have to talk to her."

Her eyes opened wide at that and she smiled. "Really? That would be great." Now she put her lips to his ear, causing fresh shivers. He was afraid to look at his arms, in case they had broken out in goosebumps. "Make it soon. She's got her week off coming up in a day or two." Now she placed her hand, oh God, high up on his leg, territory Luke's mother did not even visit these days. "After she comes back, she's somewhere else for three weeks. You might see her in the halls, or in the break room, but that's all. She won't talk about it even where it's safe to talk, so it just about has to be Back Half."

She removed her lips from his ear and her hand

from his thigh, leaving Luke to wish fervently that she had other secrets to impart.

"Go on back to your room," she said, and the little gleam in her eye made him think she was not unaware of the effect she'd had on him. "Try to catch some winks."

7

He awoke from deep and dreamless sleep to loud knocking on his door. He sat up, looking around wildly, wondering if he had overslept on a school day.

The door opened, and a smiling face peered in at him. It was Gladys, the woman who'd taken him to get chipped. The one who had told him he was here to serve. "Peekaboo!" she trilled. "Rise and shine! You missed breakfast, but I brought you orange juice. You can drink it while we walk. It's fresh squeezed!"

Luke saw the green power light on his new laptop. It had gone to sleep, but if Gladys came in and pushed one of the keys to check on what he'd been surfing (he wouldn't put it past her), she would see H. G. Wells's invisible man with his wrapped head and dark glasses. She wouldn't know what it was, might think it was just some kind of sci-fi or mystery site, but she probably made reports. If so, they'd go to someone above her pay grade. Someone who was supposed to be curious.

"Can I have a minute to put on some pants?"

"Thirty seconds. Don't let this oj get warm, now." She gave him a roguish wink and closed the door.

Luke leaped from bed, put on his jeans, grabbed a tee-shirt, and woke up the laptop to check the time.

He was amazed to see it was nine o'clock. He *never* slept that late. For a moment he wondered if they'd put something in his food, but if that was the case, he wouldn't have awakened in the middle of the night.

It's shock, he thought. I'm still trying to process this thing—get my head around it.

He killed the computer, knowing any efforts he made to hide Mr. Griffin would mean nothing if they were monitoring his searches. And if they were mirroring his computer, they'd already know he'd found a way to access the *New York Times*. Of course if you started thinking that way, everything was futile. Which was probably exactly how the Minions of Sigsby wanted him to think—him and every other kid kept prisoner in here.

If they knew, they'd already have taken the computer away, he told himself. And if they were mirroring my box, wouldn't they know the wrong name is on the welcome screen?

That seemed to make sense, but maybe they were just giving him more rope. That was paranoid, but the *situation* was paranoid.

When Gladys opened the door again, he was sitting on the bed and putting on his sneakers. "Good job!" she cried, as if Luke were a three-year-old who had just managed to dress himself for the first time. Luke was liking her less and less, but when she gave him the juice, he gulped it down.

8

This time when she waved her card, she told the elevator to take them to C-Level. "Gosh, what a pretty day!" she exclaimed as the car began to descend. This seemed to be her standard conversation opener.

Luke glanced at her hands. "I see you're wearing a wedding ring. Do you have kids, Gladys?"

Her smile became cautious. "That's between me, myself, and I."

"I just wondered if you did, how you'd like them locked up in a place like this."

"C," said the soft female voice. "This is C."

No smile on Gladys's face as she escorted him out, holding his arm a little tighter than absolutely necessary.

"I also wondered how you live with yourself. Guess that's a little personal, huh?"

"Enough, Luke. I brought you juice. I didn't have to do that."

"And what would you say to your kids, if anyone found out what's going on here? If it got, you know, on the news. How would you explain it to them?"

She walked faster, almost hauling him along, but there was no anger on her face; if there had been, he would at least have had the dubious comfort of knowing he'd gotten through to her. But no. There was only blankness. It was a doll's face.

They stopped at C-17. The shelves were loaded with medical and computer equipment. There was a padded chair that looked like a movie theater seat, and behind it, mounted on a steel post, was something that looked like a projector. At least there were no straps on the arms of the chair.

A tech was waiting for them—ZEKE, according to the nametag on his blue top. Luke knew the name. Maureen had said he was one of the mean ones.

"Hey there, Luke," Zeke said. "Are you feeling serene?"

Unsure of how to reply, Luke shrugged.

"Not going to make trouble? That's what I'm getting at, sport."

"No. No trouble."

"Good to hear."

Zeke opened a bottle filled with blue liquid. There was a sharp whiff of alcohol, and Zeke produced a thermometer that looked at least a foot long. Surely not, but—

"Drop trou and bend over that chair, Luke. Forearms on the seat."

"Not with . . ."

Not with Gladys here, he meant to say, but the door to C-17 was closed. Gladys was gone. *Maybe to preserve my modesty*, Luke thought, *but probably because she had enough of my shit*. Which would have cheered him up if not for the glass rod which would soon, he felt sure, be exploring previously unplumbed depths of his anatomy. It looked like the kind of thermometer a vet might use to take a horse's temperature.

"Not with what?" He wagged the thermometer back and forth like a majorette's baton. "Not with this? Sorry, sport, gotta be. Orders from headquarters, you know."

"Wouldn't a fever strip be easier?" Luke said. "I bet you could get one at CVS for a buck and a half. Even less with your discount car—"

"Save your wise mouth for your friends. Drop trou and bend over the chair, or I'll do it for you. And you won't like it."

Luke walked slowly to the chair, unbuttoned his pants, slid them down, bent over.

"Oh yay, *there's* that full moon!" Zeke stood in front of him. He had the thermometer in one hand and a jar of Vaseline in the other. He dipped the thermometer into the jar and brought it out. A glob of jelly dangled from the end. To Luke it looked like the punchline of a dirty joke. "See? Plenty of lube. Won't hurt a bit. Just relax your cheeks, and remind yourself that as long as you don't feel *both* of my hands on you, your backside virginity remains intact."

He circled behind Luke, who stood bent over with his forearms on the seat of the chair and his butt pushed out. He could smell his sweat, strong and rank. He tried to remind himself that he wasn't the first kid to get this treatment in the Institute. It helped a little . . . but really, not all that much. The room was loaded with high-tech equipment, and this man was preparing to take his temperature in the lowest-tech way imaginable. Why?

To break me down, Luke thought. To make sure I understand that I'm a guinea pig, and when you have guinea pigs, you can get the data you want any old way you want. And maybe they don't even *want* this particular piece of data. Maybe it's just a way of saying *If we can stick this up your ass, what else can we stick up there?* Answer: *Anything we feel like.*

"Suspense is killing you, isn't it?" Zeke said from behind him, and the son of a bitch was laughing.

9

After the indignity of the thermometer, which seemed to go on for a long time, Zeke took his blood pressure, put an O2 monitor on his finger, and checked his height and weight. He looked down Luke's throat and up his nose. He noted down the results, humming as he did it. By then Gladys was back in the room, drinking from a coffee mug with daisies on it and smiling her fake smile.

"Time for a shot, Lukey-boy," Zeke said. "Not going to give me any trouble, are you?"

Luke shook his head. The only thing he wanted right now was to go back to his room and wipe the Vaseline out of his butt. He had nothing to be ashamed of, but he felt ashamed, anyway. Demeaned.

Zeke gave him an injection. There was no heat this time. This time there was nothing but a little pain, there and gone.

Zeke looked at his watch, lips moving as he counted off seconds. Luke did the same, only without moving his lips. He'd gotten to thirty when Zeke lowered his arm. "Any nausea?"

Luke shook his head.

"Got a metallic taste in your mouth?"

The only thing Luke could taste was the residue of the orange juice. "No."

"Okay, good. Now look at the wall. See any dots? Or maybe they look bigger, like circles."

Luke shook his head.

"You're telling the truth, sport, right?"

"Right. No dots. No circles."

Zeke looked into his eyes for several seconds (Luke thought of asking him if he saw any dots in there, and restrained himself). Then he straightened up, made a show of dusting his palms together, and turned to Gladys. "Go on, get him out of here. Dr. Evans will want him this afternoon for the eye thing." He gestured at the projector gadget. "Four PM."

Luke thought about asking what the eye thing was, but he didn't really care. He was hungry, that didn't seem to change no matter what they did to him (at least so far), but what he wanted more than food was to clean himself up. He felt—only the British word adequately described it—buggered.

"Now, that wasn't so bad, was it?" Gladys asked him as they rode up in the elevator. "A lot of fuss about nothing." Luke thought of asking her if she would have felt it was a lot of fuss about nothing if it had been *her* ass. Nicky might have said it, but he wasn't Nicky.

She gave him the fake smile he was finding ever more horrible. "You're learning to behave, and that's *wonderful*. Here's a token. In fact, take two. I'm feeling generous today."

He took them.

Later, standing in the shower with his head bent and water running through his hair, he cried some more. He was like Helen in at least one way; he wanted all this to be a dream. He would have given anything, maybe his very soul, if he could wake up to sunlight lying across his bed like a second coverlet and smell frying bacon downstairs. The tears finally dried up, and he began to feel something other than sorrow and loss—something harder. A kind of bedrock, previously unknown to him. It was a relief to know it was there.

This was no dream, it was really happening, and to get out of here no longer seemed enough. That hard thing wanted more. It wanted to expose the whole kidnapping, child-torturing bunch of them, from Mrs. Sigsby all the way down to Gladys with her plastic smiles and Zeke with his slimy rectal thermometer. To bring the Institute down on their heads, as Samson had brought the temple of Dagon down on the Philistines. He knew this was no more than the resentful, impotent fantasy of a twelve-year-old kid, but he wanted it, just the same, and if there was any way he could do it, he would.

As his father liked to say, it was good to have goals. They could bring you through tough times.

10

By the time he got to the caff, it was empty except for a janitor (FRED, his nametag said) mopping the floor. It was still too early for lunch, but there was a bowl of fruit—oranges, apples, grapes, and a couple of bananas—on a table at the front. Luke took an apple, then went out to the vending machines and used one of his tokens to get a bag of popcorn. Breakfast of champions, he thought. Mom would have a cow.

He took his food into the lounge area and looked out at the playground. George and Iris were sitting at one of the picnic tables, playing checkers. Avery was on the trampoline, taking mildly cautious bounces. There was no sign of Nicky or Helen.

"I think that's the worst food combo I ever saw," Kalisha said.

He jumped, spilling some of his popcorn out of the bag and onto the floor. "Jeepers, scare a person, why don't you?"

"Sorry." She squatted, picked up the few spilled pieces of popcorn, and tossed them into her mouth.

"Off the floor?" Luke asked. "I can't believe you did that."

"Five-second rule."

"According to the National Health Service—that's

in England—the five-second rule is a myth. Total bullshit."

"Does being a genius mean you have a mission to spoil everyone's illusions?"

"No, I just—"

She smiled and stood up. "Yankin your chain, Luke. The Chicken Pox Chick is just yankin your chain. You okay?"

"Yes."

"Did you get the rectal?"

"Yes. Let's not talk about it."

"Heard that. Want to play cribbage until lunch? If you don't know how to play, I can teach you."

"I know how, but I don't want to. Think I'll go back to my room for awhile."

"Consider your situation?"

"Something like that. See you at lunch."

"When the ding-dong goes," she said. "It's a date. Cheer up, little hero, and gimme five."

She raised her hand, and Luke saw something pinched between her thumb and index finger. He pressed his white palm to her brown one, and the folded scrap of paper passed from her hand to his.

"Seeya, boy." She headed for the playground.

Back in his room, Luke lay down on his bed, turned on his side to face the wall, and unfolded the square of paper. Kalisha's printing was tiny and very neat.

Meet Maureen by the ice machine near Avery's room ASAP. Flush this.

He crumpled the paper, went into the bathroom, and dropped the note into the bowl as he lowered his pants. He felt ridiculous doing this, like a kid playing spy; at the same time he didn't feel ridiculous at all. He would have loved to believe there was at least no surveillance in *la maison du chier*, but he didn't quite believe it.

The ice machine. Where Maureen had spoken to him yesterday. That was sort of interesting. According to Kalisha, there were several places in Front Half where the audio surveillance worked poorly or not at all, but Maureen seemed to favor that one. Maybe because there was no video surveillance there. Maybe it was where she felt safest, possibly because the ice machine was so noisy. And maybe he was judging on too little evidence.

He thought about going to the *Star Tribune* before meeting Maureen, and sat down at his computer. He even went as far as Mr. Griffin, but there he stopped. Did he *really* want to know? To perhaps find out these bastards, these *monsters*, were lying, and his parents were dead? Going to the *Trib* to check would be a little like a guy wagering his life's savings on one spin of the roulette wheel.

Not now, he decided. Maybe after the humiliation of the thermometer was a bit further behind him, but not now. If that made him a chickenshit, so be it. He turned off the computer and took a walk to the other wing. Maureen wasn't near the ice machine, but her laundry cart was parked halfway down what Luke now thought of as Avery's hallway, and he could hear her singing something about raindrops. He went to the sound of her voice and saw her putting on fresh sheets in a room decorated with WWF posters of hulking beefcakes in spandex shorts. They all looked mean enough to chew nails and spit out staples.

"Hey, Maureen, how are you?"

"Fine," she said. "Back aches a little, but I've got my Motrin."

"Want some help?"

"Thanks, but this is the last room, and I'm almost finished. Two girls, one boy. Expected soon. This is the boy's room." She gestured at the posters and laughed. "As if you didn't know."

"Well, I thought I'd get some ice, but there's no bucket in my room."

"They're stacked in a cubby next to the bin." She straightened up, put her hands in the small of her back, and grimaced. Luke heard her spine crackle. "Oh, that's lots better. I'll show you."

"Only if it's no trouble."

"No trouble at all. Come on. You can push my cart, if you want to."

As they went down the hall, Luke thought about his researches into Maureen's problem. One horrifying statistic in particular stuck out: Americans owed over twelve trillion dollars. Money spent but not earned, just promised. A paradox only an accountant could love. While much of that debt had to do with mortgages on homes and businesses, an appreciable amount led back to those little plastic rectangles everyone kept in their purses and wallets: the oxycodone of American consumers.

Maureen opened a little cabinet to the right of the ice machine. "Can you get one, and save me stooping down? Some inconsiderate somebody pushed every damned bucket all the way to the back."

Luke reached. As he did, he spoke in a low voice. "Kalisha told me about your problem with the credit cards. I think I know how to fix it, but a lot of it depends on your declared residence."

"My declared—"

"What state do you live in?"

"I . . ." She took a quick, furtive look around. "We're not supposed to tell any personal stuff to the residents. It would mean my job if anyone found out. *More* than my job. Can I trust you, Luke?"

"I'll keep my mouth shut."

"I live over in Vermont. Burlington. That's where I'm going on my outside week." Telling him that seemed to release something inside her, and although she kept the volume down, the words came spilling out. "The first thing I have to do when I get off work is delete a bunch of dunning calls from my phone. And when I get home, from the answering machine on *that* phone. You know, the landline. When the answer-machine is full, they leave letters—warnings, threats— in the mailbox or under the door. My car, they can repo that any time they want, it's a beater, but now they're talking about my *house*! It's paid off, and no thanks to *him*. I killed the mortgage with my signing bonus when I came to work here, that's *why* I came to work here, but they'll take it, and the what-do-you-call-it will be gone—"

"The equity," Luke said, whispering it.

"Right, that." Color had bloomed in her sallow cheeks, whether of shame or anger Luke didn't know. "And once they have the house, they'll want what's put away, and that money's not for me! Not for me, but they'll take it just the same. They say so."

"He ran up that much?" Luke was astonished. The guy must have been a spending machine.

"Yes!"

"Keep it down." He held the plastic bucket in one hand and opened the ice machine with the other. "Vermont is good. It's not a community property state."

"What's that mean?"

Something they don't want you to know about, Luke thought. There's so much they don't want you to know about. Once you're stuck on the flypaper, that's where they want you to stay. He grabbed the plastic scoop inside the door of the ice machine and pretended to be breaking up chunks of ice. "The cards he used, were they in his name or yours?"

"His, of course, but they're still dunning me because we're still legally married, and the account numbers are the same!"

Luke began filling the plastic ice bucket . . . very slowly. "They say they can do that, and it sounds plausible, but they can't. Not legally, not in Vermont. Not in most states. If he was using *his* cards and his signature was on the slips, that's *his* debt."

"They say it's ours! Both of ours!"

"They lie," Luke said grimly. "As for the calls you mentioned—do any of them come after eight o'clock at night?"

Her voice dropped to a fierce whisper. "Are you kidding? Sometimes they call at midnight! 'Pay up or the bank's going to take your house next week! You'll come back to find the locks changed and your furniture out on the lawn!' "

Luke had read about this, and worse. Debt collectors threatening to turn aged parents out of their nursing homes. Threatening to go after young adult children still trying to get some financial traction. Anything to get their percentage of the cash grab. "It's good you're away most of the time and those calls go to voicemail. They don't let you have your cell here?"

"No! God, no! It's locked in my car, in . . . well, not here. I changed my number once, and they got the new one. How could they do that?"

Easily, Luke thought. "Don't delete those calls. Save them. They'll be time-stamped. It's illegal for collection agencies to call clients—that's what they call people like you, clients—after eight o'clock at night."

He dumped the bucket and began to fill it again, even more slowly. Maureen was looking at him with amazement and dawning hope, but Luke hardly noticed. He was deep in the problem, tracing the lines back to the central point where those lines could be cut.

"You need a lawyer. Don't even think about going to one of the quick-buck companies that advertise on cable, they'll take you for everything they can and then put you into Chapter 7. You'll never get your credit rating back. You want a straight-arrow Vermont lawyer who specializes in debt relief, knows all about the Fair Debt Collection Practices Act, and hates those bloodsuckers. I'll do some research and get you a name."

"You can do that?"

"I'm pretty sure." If they didn't take his computer away first, that was. "The lawyer needs to find out which collection agencies are in charge of trying to get the money. The ones that are scaring you and calling in the middle of the night. The banks and credit card companies don't like to give the names of the stooges they use, but unless Fair Debt's repealed—and there are powerful people in Washington trying to do that—a good lawyer can force them to do it. The people phoning you step over the line all the time. They're a bunch of scumbags working in boiler rooms."

Not all that different from the scumbags working here, Luke thought.

"What are boiler—"

"Never mind." This was going on too long. "A good debt relief lawyer will go to the banks with your answering machine tapes and tell them they have two choices: forgive the debts or go to court, charged with illegal business practices. Banks hate going to court and having people find out they're hiring guys just one step away from leg-breakers in a Scorsese movie."

"You don't think I have to pay?" Maureen looked dazed.

He looked straight into her tired, too-pale face. "Did *you* do anything wrong?"

She shook her head. "But it's so *much*. He was furnishing his own place in Albany, buying stereos and computers and flatscreen TVs, he's got a dolly and he's buying her things, he likes casinos, and it's been going on for *years*. Stupid trusting me didn't know until it was too late."

"It's not too late, that's what—"

"Hi, Luke."

Luke jumped, turned, and saw Avery Dixon. "Hi. How was the trampoline?"

"Good. Then boring. Guess what? I had a shot, and I didn't even cry."

"Good for you."

"Want to watch TV up in the lounge until lunch? They have Nickelodeon, Iris said so. *SpongeBob* and *Rusty Rivets* and *The Loud House*."

"Not now," Luke said, "but you knock yourself out."

Avery studied the two of them a moment longer, then headed up the hall.

Once he was gone, Luke turned back to Maureen.

"It's not too late, that's what I'm saying. But you have to move fast. Meet me here tomorrow. I'll have a name for you. Somebody good. Somebody with a track record. I promise."

"This . . . son, this is too good to be true."

He liked her calling him son. It gave him a warm feeling. Stupid, maybe, but still true.

"It's not, though. What they're trying to do to you is too *bad* to be true. I really have to go. It's almost lunchtime."

"I won't forget this," she said, and squeezed his hand. "If you can—"

The doors banged open at the far end of the hall. Luke was suddenly sure he was going to see a couple of caretakers, a couple of the mean ones—Tony and Zeke, maybe—coming for him. They'd take him somewhere and question him about what he and Maureen had been talking about, and if he didn't tell right away, they'd use "enhanced interrogation techniques" until he spilled everything. He'd be in trouble, but Maureen's trouble might be even worse.

"Take it easy, Luke," she said. "It's just the new residents."

Three pink-clad caretakers came through the doors. They were pulling a train of gurneys. There were sleeping girls on the first two, both blond. On the third was a hulk of a red-haired boy. Presumably the WWF fan. All were asleep. As they rolled closer, Luke said, "Holy crow, I think those girls are twins! Identicals!"

"You're right. Their names are Gerda and Greta. Now go on and get something to eat. I need to help those fellas get the new ones situated."

11

Avery was sitting in one of the lounge chairs, swinging his feet and eating a Slim Jim as he watched the goings-ons in Bikini Bottom. "I got two tokens for not crying when I got my shot."

"Good."

"You can have the other one, if you want it."

"No, thanks. You keep it for later."

"Okay. *SpongeBob* is good, but I wish I could go home." Avery didn't sob or bawl or anything, but tears began to leak from the corners of his eyes.

"Yeah, me too. Squish over."

Avery squished over and Luke sat down next to him. It was a tight fit, but that was okay. Luke put an arm around Avery's shoulders and gave him a little hug. Avery responded by putting his head on Luke's shoulder, which touched him in a way he couldn't define and made him feel a little like crying himself.

"Guess what, Maureen has a kid," Avery said.

"Yeah? You think?"

"Sure. He was little but now he's big. Older even than Nicky."

"Uh-huh, okay."

"It's a secret." Avery didn't take his eyes from the screen, where Patrick was having an argument with Mr. Krabs. "She's saving money for him."

"Really? And you know this how?"

Avery looked at him. "I just do. Like I know your best friend is Rolf and you lived on Wildersmoochy Drive."

Luke gaped at him. "Jesus, Avery."

"Good, ain't I?"

And although there were still tears on his cheeks, Avery giggled.

12

After lunch, George proposed a game of three-on-three badminton: he, Nicky, and Helen against Luke, Kalisha, and Iris. George said Nicky's team could even have Avery as a bonus.

"He's not a bonus, he's a liability," Helen said, and waved at a cloud of minges surrounding her.

"What's a liability?" Avery asked.

"If you want to know, read my mind," Helen said. "Besides, badminton's for pussies who can't play tennis."

"Aren't *you* cheerful company," Kalisha said.

Helen, walking toward the picnic tables and games cabinet, hoisted a middle finger over her shoulder without looking back. And pumped it. Iris said it could be Nicky and George against Luke and Kalisha; she, Iris, would ump the sidelines. Avery said he would help. All finding this agreeable, the game began. The score was ten-all when the door to the lounge banged open and the new boy walked out, almost managing a straight line. He looked dazed from whatever drug had been in his system. He also looked pissed off. Luke put him at six feet and maybe sixteen years of age. He was carrying a considerable belly in front—a food gut that might become a beer gut in adulthood—but his sunburned arms were slabbed with muscle, and he had an awesome set of traps, maybe from lifting. His cheeks were spattered with freckles and acne. His eyes looked pink and irritated. His red hair was standing up in sleep-scruffy patches. They all stopped what they were doing to check him out.

Whispering without moving her lips, like a con in a prison yard, Kalisha said, "It's the Incredible Bulk."

The new kid stopped by the trampoline and surveyed the others. He spoke slowly, in spaced bursts, as if suspecting those he addressed were primitives with little grasp of English. His accent was southern. "*What* . . . the *fuck* . . . is *this?*"

Avery trotted over. "It's the Institute. Hi, I'm Avery. What's your n—"

The new kid put the heel of his hand against Avery's chin and shoved. It wasn't particularly hard, almost absent-minded, but Avery went sprawling on one of the cushions surrounding the trampoline, staring up at the new kid with an expression of shocked surprise. The new kid took no notice of him, or the badminton players, or Iris, or Helen, who had paused in the act of dealing herself a hand of solitaire. He seemed to be talking to himself.

"*What* . . . the *fuck* . . . is *this?*" He waved irritably at the bugs. Like Luke on his first visit to the playground, New Kid hadn't slathered on any repellent. The minges weren't just swarming; they were lighting on him and sampling his sweat.

"Aw, man," Nicky said. "You shouldn't have knocked the Avester over like that. He was trying to be nice."

New Kid at last paid some attention. He turned to Nick. "*Who* . . . the *fuck* . . . are *you?*"

"Nick Wilholm. Help Avery up."

"*What?*"

Nick looked patient. "You knocked him over, you help him up."

"I'll do it," Kalisha said, and hurried to the trampoline. She bent to take Avery's arm, and New Kid pushed *her.* She missed the springy stuff and sprawled on the gravel, scraping one knee.

Nick dropped his badminton racquet and walked over to New Kid. He put his hands on his hips. "Now you can help them both up. I'm sure you're disoriented as hell, but that's no excuse."

"What if I don't?"

Nicky smiled. "Then I'll fuck you up, fat boy."

Helen Simms was looking on with interest from the picnic table. George apparently decided to head for safer territory. He strolled toward the door to the lounge, giving New Kid a wide berth as he did so.

"Don't bother with him if he wants to be an asshole," Kalisha said to Nicky. "We're okay, Avery, aren't we?" She helped him to his feet and started backing away.

"Sure we are," Avery said, but tears were once more spilling down his chubby cheeks.

"Who you callin a asshole, bitch?"

Nick said, "Must be you, since you're the only asshole here." He took a step closer to New Kid. Luke was fascinated by the contrast. New Kid was a mallet; Nicky was a blade. "You need to apologize."

"Fuck you and fuck your apology," New Kid said. "I don't know what this place is, but I know I'm not staying. Now get out my face."

"You're not going anywhere," Nicky said. "You're here for the long haul, just like the rest of us." He smiled without showing his teeth.

"Stop it, both of you," Kalisha said. She had her arm

around Avery's shoulders, and Luke didn't have to be a mind reader to know what she was thinking, because he was thinking the same thing: New Kid outweighed Nicky by sixty pounds at least, probably more like eighty, and although New Kid was carrying plenty of table muscle in front, those arms were slabs.

"Last warning," New Kid said. "Move or I'll lay you t'fuck out."

George seemed to have changed his mind about going inside. Now he was strolling back toward New Kid, not behind him but to one side. It was Helen who was coming up behind him, not fast but with that nice little hip-sway Luke so admired. And a small smile of her own.

George's face contracted in a frown of concentration, lips pressing together and forehead furrowing. The minges that had been circling both boys suddenly drew together and gusted at New Kid's face as if on an invisible breath of wind. He raised a hand to his eyes, waving at them. Helen dropped to her knees behind him, and Nicky gave the redhead a shove. New Kid went sprawling, half on gravel and half on asphalt.

Helen leaped to her feet and pranced away, laughing and pointing. "Nookies on you, big boy, nookies on you, nookies *all over* you!"

With a roar of fury, New Kid began getting up. Before he could accomplish that, Nick stepped forward and kicked him in the thigh. Hard. New Kid screamed, clutched at his leg, and pulled his knees up to his chest.

"Jesus, stop it!" Iris cried. "Haven't we got enough trouble without this?"

The old Luke might have agreed; the new Luke—

the Institute Luke—did not. "He started it. And maybe he needed it."

"I'll get you!" New Kid sobbed. "I'll get all of you fucking dirty fighters!" His face had gone an alarming red-purple. Luke found himself wondering if an overweight sixteen-year-old could have a stroke, and found—appalling but true—that he did not care.

Nicky dropped to one knee. "You won't get shit," he said. "Right now you need to listen to me, fatso. We're not your problem. *They're* your problem."

Luke looked around and saw three caretakers standing shoulder to shoulder just outside the door of the lounge: Joe, Hadad, and Gladys. Hadad no longer looked friendly, and Gladys's plastic smile was gone. All three were holding black gadgets with wires sticking out of them. They weren't moving in yet, but they were ready to. Because you don't let the test animals hurt each other, Luke thought. That's one thing you don't do. The test animals are valuable.

Nicky said, "Help me with this bastard, Luke."

Luke took one of New Kid's arms and got it around his neck. Nick did the same with the other. The kid's skin was hot and oily with sweat. He was gasping for breath between clenched teeth. Together, Luke and Nicky hauled him to his feet.

"Nicky?" Joe called. "Everything all right? Shitstorm over?"

"All over," Nicky said.

"It better be," Hadad said. He and Gladys went back inside. Joe stood where he was, still holding his black gadget.

"We're totally okay," Kalisha said. "It wasn't a *real* shit-storm, just a little . . ."

"Disagreement," Helen said. "Call it a fart skirmish."

"He didn't mean anything bad," Iris said, "he was just upset." There was genuine kindness in her voice, which made Luke a little ashamed about feeling so happy when Nicky put his foot to the new kid's leg.

"I'm going to puke," New Kid announced.

"Not on the trampoline, you're not," Nicky said. "We use that thing. Come on, Luke. Help me get him over by the fence."

New Kid began to make *urk-urk* noises, his considerable belly heaving. Luke and Nicky walked him toward the fence between the playground and the woods. They got there just in time. New Kid put his head against the chainlink diamonds and spewed through them, giving up the last remains of whatever he'd eaten on the outside, when he had been Free Kid instead of New Kid.

"Eww," Helen said. "Somebody had creamed corn, how gross is that?"

"Any better?" Nicky asked.

New Kid nodded.

"Finished?"

New Kid shook his head and upchucked again, this time with less strength. "I think . . ." He cleared his throat, and more goo sprayed.

"Jesus," Nicky said, wiping his cheek. "Do you serve towels with your showers?"

"I think I'm gonna pass out."

"You're not," Luke said. He actually wasn't sure of this, but thought it best to stay positive. "Come over here in the shade."

They got him to the picnic table. Kalisha sat down beside him and told him to lower his head. He did so without argument.

"What's your name?" Nicky asked.

"Harry Cross." The fight had gone out of him. He sounded tired and humbled. "I'm from Selma. That's in Alabama. I don't know how I got here or what's happening nor *nuthin*."

"We can tell you some stuff," Luke said, "but you need to cut the shit. You need to get right. This place is bad enough without fighting among ourselves."

"And you need to apologize to Avery," George said. There was none of the class clown in him now. "That's how the getting right starts."

"That's okay," Avery said. "He didn't hurt me."

Kalisha took no notice. "Apologize."

Harry Cross looked up. He swabbed a hand across his flushed and homely face. "Sorry I knocked you over, kid." He looked around at the others. "Okay?"

"Half okay." Luke pointed at Kalisha. "Her, too."

Harry heaved a sigh. "Sorry, whatever your name is."

"It's Kalisha. If we get on more friendly terms, which don't seem too likely as of this moment, you can call me Sha."

"Just don't call her Sport," Luke said. George laughed and clapped him on the back.

"Whatever," Harry muttered. He wiped something else from his chin.

Nicky said, "Now that the excitement's over, why don't we finish the goddam badminton ga—".

"Hello, girls," Iris said. "Do you want to come over here?"

Luke looked around. Joe was gone. There were two little blond girls standing where he had been. They were holding hands and wearing identical expressions of dazed terror. Everything about them was identical except for their tee-shirts, one green and one red. Luke thought of Dr. Seuss: Thing One and Thing Two.

"Come on," Kalisha said. "It's all right. The trouble's over."

If only that were true, Luke thought.

13

At quarter of four that afternoon, Luke was in his room reading more about Vermont lawyers who specialized in the Fair Debt Collection Practices Act. So far, no one had asked him why he was so interested in this particular subject. Nobody had asked him about H. G. Wells's invisible man, either. Luke supposed he could devise some sort of test to discover if they were monitoring him—googling ways to commit suicide would probably work—and then decided doing that would be nuts. Why kick a sleeping dog? And since it didn't make a whole lot of difference to life as he was now living it, it was probably better not to know.

There came a brisk rap on the door. It opened before he could call come in. It was a caretaker. She was tall and dark haired, the nametag on her pink top proclaiming her PRISCILLA.

"The eye thing, right?" Luke asked, turning off his laptop.

"Right. Let's go." No smile, no chirpy good cheer. After Gladys, Luke found this a relief.

They went back to the elevator, then down to C-Level.

"How deep does this place go?" Luke asked.

Priscilla glanced at him. "None of your business."

"I was only making con—"

"Well, don't. Just shut up."

Luke shut up.

Back in good old Room C-17, Zeke had been replaced by a tech whose nametag said BRANDON. There were also two men in suits present, one with an iPad and one with a clipboard. No nametags for them, so Luke guessed they were doctors. One was extremely tall, with a gut that put Harry Cross's to shame. He stepped forward and held out his hand.

"Hello, Luke. I'm Dr. Hendricks, Chief of Medical Operations."

Luke simply looked at the outstretched hand, feeling no urge at all to take it. He was learning all sorts of new behaviors. It was interesting, in a rather horrible way.

Dr. Hendricks gave an odd sort of hee-hawing laugh, half exhaled and half inhaled. "That's all right, perfectly all right. This is Dr. Evans, in charge of Ophthalmology Operations." He did the exhale/inhale hee-haw again, so Luke surmised *Ophthalmology Operations* was doctor humor of some sort.

Dr. Evans, a small man with a fussy mustache, did not laugh at the joke, or even smile. Nor did he offer to shake hands. "So you're one of our new recruits. Welcome. Have a seat, please."

Luke did as he was told. Sitting in the chair was certainly better than being bent over it with his bare butt sticking out. Besides, he was pretty sure what this was. He'd had his eyes examined before. In films, the nerdy kid genius always wore thick glasses, but Luke's vision was 20/20, at least so far. He felt more or less at ease until Hendricks approached him with another hypo. His heart sank at the sight of it.

"Don't worry, just another quick prick." Hendricks hee-hawed again, showing buck teeth. "Lots of shots, just like in the Army."

"Sure, because I'm a conscript," Luke said.

"Correct, absolutely correct. Hold still."

Luke took the injection without protesting. There was no flash of heat, but then something else began happening. Something bad. As Priscilla bent to put on one of those Clear Spots, he started to choke. "I can't . . ." *Swallow*, was what he wanted to say, but he couldn't. His throat locked shut.

"You're okay," Hendricks said. "It will pass." That sounded good, but the other doctor was approaching with a tube, which he apparently meant to jam down Luke's throat if it became necessary. Hendricks put a hand on his shoulder. "Give him a few seconds."

Luke stared at them desperately, spit running down his chin, sure they would be the last faces he would see . . . and then his throat unlocked. He whooped in a great gasp of air.

"See?" Hendricks said. "All fine. Jim, no need to intubate."

"What . . . what did you do to me?"

"Nothing at all. You're fine."

Dr. Evans handed the plastic tube to Brandon and took Hendricks's place. He shone a light into Luke's eyes, then took a small ruler and measured the distance between them. "No corrective lenses?"

"I want to know what that was! I couldn't *breathe*! I couldn't *swallow*!"

"You're fine," Evans said. "Swallowing like a champ. Color going back to normal. Now do you or don't you wear corrective lenses?"

"I don't," Luke said.

"Good. Good for you. Look straight ahead, please."

Luke looked at the wall. The sensation of having forgotten how to breathe was gone. Brandon pulled down a white screen, then dimmed the lights.

"Keep looking straight ahead," Dr. Evans said. "If you look away once, Brandon is going to slap you. If you look away a second time, he'll shock you—low voltage but very painful. Do you understand?"

"Yes," Luke said. He swallowed. It was okay, his throat felt normal, but his heart was still double-timing. "Does the AMA know about this?"

"You need to shut up," Brandon said.

Shut up seems to be the default position around here, Luke thought. He told himself the worst was over, now it was just an eye test, other kids had been through this and they were fine, but he kept swallowing, verifying that yes, he could do it. They would project the eye chart, he would read it, and this would be over.

"Straight ahead," Evans almost crooned. "Eyes on the screen and nowhere else."

Music started—violins playing classical stuff. Meant to be soothing, Luke supposed.

"Priss, turn on the projector," Evans said.

Instead of an eye chart, a blue spot appeared in the middle of the screen, pulsing slightly, as if it had a heartbeat. A red spot showed up below it, making him think of HAL—"I'm sorry, Dave." Next came a green spot. The red and green spots pulsed in sync with the blue one, then all three began to flash off and on. Others began to appear, first one by one, then two by two, then by the dozens. Soon the screen was crowded with hundreds of flashing colored dots.

"At the screen," Evans crooned. "The *screeeen*. No-where else."

"So if I don't see them on my own, you project them? Kind of like priming the pump, or something? That doesn't—"

"Shut up." Priscilla this time.

Now the dots began to swirl. They chased each other madly, some seeming to spiral, some to flock, some forming circles that rose and fell and criss-crossed. The violins were speeding up, the light classical tune turning into something like hoedown music. The dots weren't just moving now, they had become a Times Square electronic billboard with its circuits fried and having a consequent nervous breakdown. Luke started to feel like *he* was having a breakdown. He thought of Harry Cross puking through the chainlink fence and knew he was going to do the same thing if he kept looking at those madly racing colored dots, and he didn't want to puke, it would end up in his lap, it—

Brandon slapped him, good and hard. The noise was like a small firecracker going off both close and far away. "Look at the screen, sport."

Something warm was running over his upper lip. Son of a bitch got my nose as well as my cheek, Luke thought, but it didn't seem important. Those swirling dots were getting into his head, invading his brain like encephalitis or meningitis. *Some* kind of itis, anyway.

"Okay, Priss, switch off," Evans said, but she must not have heard him, because the dots didn't go away. They bloomed and shriveled, each bloom bigger than the last: *bwoosh* out and *zip* back in, *bwoosh* and *zip*. They were going 3-D, coming off the screen, rushing toward him, rushing back, rushing forward, rushing—

He thought Brandon was saying something about Priscilla, but that had to be in his head, right? And was someone really screaming? If so, could it be him?

"Good boy, Luke, that's good, you're doing fine." Evans's voice, droning from far away. From a drone high in the stratosphere. Maybe from the other side of the moon.

More colored dots. They weren't just on the screen now, they were on the walls, swirling on the ceiling, all around him, inside him. It came to Luke, in the last few seconds before he passed out, that they were *replacing* his brain. He saw his hands fly up among the dots of light, saw them jigging and racing on his skin, became aware that he was thrashing from side to side in the chair.

He tried to say *I'm having a seizure, you're killing me*, but all that came out of his mouth was a wretched gargling sound. Then the dots were gone, he was falling out of the chair, he was falling into darkness, and that was a relief. Oh God, what a relief.

14

He was slapped out of unconsciousness. They weren't hard slaps, not like the one that had made his nose bleed (if that had indeed happened), but they weren't love-taps, either. He opened his eyes and found himself on the floor. It was a different room. Priscilla was down on one knee beside him. She was the one administering the slaps. Brandon and the two doctors stood by, watching. Hendricks still had his iPad, Evans his clipboard.

"He's awake," Priscilla said. "Can you stand up, Luke?"

Luke didn't know if he could or not. Four or five years ago, he'd come down with strep throat and run a high fever. He felt now as he had then, as if half of him had slipped out of his body and into the atmosphere. His mouth tasted foul, and the latest injection site itched like crazy. He could still feel his throat swelling shut, how horrible that had been.

Brandon didn't give Luke a chance to test his legs, simply grabbed his arm and hauled him to his feet. Luke stood there, swaying.

"What's your name?" Hendricks asked.

"Luke . . . Lucas . . . Ellis." The words seemed to come not from his mouth but from the detached half of him floating over his head. He was tired. His face throbbed from the repeated slaps, and his nose hurt. He raised a hand (it drifted up slowly, as if through water), rubbed the skin above his lip, and looked without surprise at the flakes of dried blood on his finger. "How long was I out?"

"Sit him down," Hendricks said.

Brandon took one of his arms, Priscilla the other. They led him to a chair (a plain kitchen chair with no straps, thank God). It was placed in front of a table. Evans was sitting behind it on another kitchen chair. He had a stack of cards in front of him. They were as big as paperback books and had plain blue backs.

"I want to go back to my room," Luke said. His voice still didn't seem to be coming from his mouth, but it was a little closer. Maybe. "I want to lie down. I'm sick."

"Your disorientation will pass," Hendricks said, "although it might be wise to skip supper. For now, I want you to pay attention to Dr. Evans. We have a little test for you. Once it's finished, you can go back to your room and . . . er . . . decompress."

Evans picked up the first card and looked at it. "What is it?"

"A card," Luke said.

"Save the jokes for your YouTube site," Priscilla said, and slapped him. It was a much harder slap than the ones she'd used to bring him around.

Luke's ear began to ring, but at least his head felt a little clearer. He looked at Priscilla and saw no hesitation. No regret. Zero empathy. Nothing. Luke realized he wasn't a child at all to her. She had made some crucial separation in her mind. He was a test subject. You made it do what you wanted, and if it didn't, you administered what the psychologists called negative reinforcement. And when the tests were over? You went down to the break room for coffee and Danish and talked about your own kids (who were real kids) or bitched about politics, sports, whatever.

But hadn't he known that already? He supposed so, only knowing a thing and having the truth of it redden your skin were two different things. Luke could see a time coming—and it wouldn't be long—when he would cringe every time someone raised an open hand to him, even if it was only to shake or give a high five.

Evans laid the card carefully aside, and took another from the stack. "How about this one, Luke?"

"I told you, I don't know! How can I know what—"

Priscilla slapped him again. The ringing was stronger now, and Luke began to cry. He couldn't help it. He had thought the Institute was a nightmare, but this was the real nightmare, being half out of his body and asked to say what was on cards he couldn't see and getting slapped when he said he didn't know.

"Try, Luke," Hendricks said into the ear that wasn't ringing.

"I want to go back to my room. I'm *tired*. And I feel sick."

Evans set the second card aside and picked up a third one. "What is it?"

"You've made a mistake," Luke said. "I'm TK, not TP. Maybe Kalisha could tell you what's on those cards, and I'm sure Avery could, *but I'm not TP!*"

Evans picked up a fourth. "What is it? No more slaps. Tell me, or this time Brandon will shock you with his zap-stick, and it will hurt. You probably won't have another seizure, but you might, so tell me, Luke, what is it?"

"The Brooklyn Bridge!" he shouted. "The Eiffel Tower! Brad Pitt in a tuxedo, a dog taking a shit, the Indy 500, *I don't know!*"

He waited for the zap-stick—some kind of Taser, he supposed. Maybe it would crackle, or maybe it would make a humming sound. Maybe it would make no sound at all and he'd just jerk and fall on the floor, twitching and drooling. Instead, Evans set the card aside and motioned Brandon to step away. Luke felt no relief.

He thought, I wish I was dead. Dead and out of this.

"Priscilla," Hendricks said, "take Luke back to his room."

"Yes, Doctor. Bran, help me with him as far as the elevator."

By the time they got him there, Luke felt reintegrated again, his mind slipping back into gear. Had they really turned off the projector? And he *still* kept seeing the dots?

"You made a mistake." Luke's mouth and throat were very dry. "I'm not what you people call a TP. You know that, right?"

"Whatever," Priscilla said indifferently. She turned to Brandon and with a real smile became a new person. "I'll see you later, right?"

Brandon grinned. "You bet." He turned to Luke, suddenly made a fist, and drove it at Luke's face. He stopped an inch short of Luke's nose, but Luke cringed and cried out. Brandon laughed heartily, and Priscilla gave him an indulgent boys-will-be-boys smile.

"Shake her easy, Luke," Brandon said, and headed off down the C-Level hall in a modified swagger, his holstered zap-stick bumping against his hip.

Back in the main corridor—what Luke now understood to be the residents' wing—the little girls, Gerda and Greta, were standing and watching with wide, frightened eyes. They were holding hands and clutching dolls as identical as they were. They reminded Luke of twins in some old horror movie.

Priscilla accompanied him to his door and walked away without saying anything. Luke went in, saw that no one had come to take away his laptop, and collapsed on his bed without even taking off his shoes. There he slept for the next five hours.

15

Mrs. Sigsby was waiting when Dr. Hendricks, aka Donkey Kong, entered the private suite adjacent to her office. She was perched on the small sofa. He handed her a file. "I know you worship hard copy, so here you are. Much good it will do you."

She didn't open it. "It can't do me good or harm, Dan. These are your tests, your secondary experiments, and they don't seem to be panning out."

He set his jaw stubbornly. "Agnes Jordan. William Gortsen. Veena Patel. Two or three others whose names now escape me. Donna something. We had positive results with all of them."

She sighed and primped at her thinning hair. Hendricks thought Siggers had a bird's face: a sharp nose instead of a beak, but the same avid little eyes. A bird's face with a bureaucrat's brain behind it. Hopeless, really. "And dozens of pinks with whom you had no results at all."

"Perhaps that's true, but think about it," he said, because what he wanted to say—*How can you be so stupid?*—would get him in a world of trouble. "If telepathy and telekinesis are linked, as my experiments suggest they are, there may be other psychic abilities, as well, latent and just waiting to be brought to the fore. What these kids can do, even the most talented ones, may only be the tip of the iceberg. Suppose psychic healing is a real possibility? Suppose a glioblastoma tumor like the one that killed John McCain could be cured simply by the power of thought? Suppose these abilities could be channeled to lengthen life, perhaps to a hundred and fifty years, even longer? What we're using them for doesn't have to be the end; it might only be the beginning!"

"I've heard all this before," Mrs. Sigsby said. "And read it in what you're pleased to call your mission statement."

But you don't understand, he thought. Neither does Stackhouse. Evans does, sort of, but not even he sees the vast potential. "It's not as though the Ellis boy or Iris Stanhope are especially valuable. We don't call them pinks for nothing." He made a *pish* sound, and waved his hand.

"That was truer twenty years ago than it is today," Mrs. Sigsby replied. "Even ten."

"But—"

"Enough, Dan. Did the Ellis boy show indications of TP, or didn't he?"

"No, but he continued to see the lights after the projector was turned off, which we believe is an indicator. A *strong* indicator. Then, unfortunately, he had a seizure. Which isn't uncommon, as you know."

She sighed. "I have no objection to you continuing your tests with the Stasi Lights, Dan, but you need to keep perspective here. Our main purpose is to prepare the residents for Back Half. That's the important thing, the main objective. Any side-effects are not of great concern. The management isn't interested in the psychic equivalent of Rogaine."

Hendricks recoiled as if she had struck at him. "A hypertension medicine that also proved able to grow hair on the skulls of bald suburbanites is hardly in the same league as a procedure that could change the course of human existence!"

"Perhaps not, and perhaps if your tests had caused more frequent results, I—and the people who pay our salaries—might be more excited. But all you have now are a few random hits."

He opened his mouth to protest, then closed it again when she gave him her most forbidding look.

"You can continue your tests for the time being, be content with that. You should be, considering that we have lost several children as a result of them."

"Pinks," he said, and made that dismissive *pish* sound again.

"You act as though they were a dime a dozen," she said. "Maybe once they were, but no more, Dan. No more. In the meantime, here's a file for you."

It was a red file. Stamped across it was RELOCA-TION.

16

When Luke walked into the lounge that evening, he found Kalisha sitting on the floor with her back against one of the big windows looking out on the playground. She was sipping from one of the small bottles of alcohol available for purchase in the snack machine.

"You drink that stuff?" he asked, sitting down beside her. In the playground, Avery and Helen were on the trampoline. She was apparently teaching him how to do a forward roll. Soon it would be too dark and they'd have to come in. Although never closed, the playground had no lights, and that discouraged most nighttime visits.

"First time. Used all my tokens. It's pretty horrible. Want some?" She held out the bottle, which contained a beverage called Twisted Tea.

"I'll pass. Sha, why didn't you tell me that light test was so bad?"

"Call me Kalisha. You're the only one who does, and I like it." Her voice was the tiniest bit slurred. She couldn't have drunk more than a few ounces of the alcoholic tea, but he supposed she wasn't used to it.

"All right. Kalisha. Why didn't you tell me?"

She shrugged. "They make you look at dancing colored lights until you get a little woozy. What's so bad about that?" *That* came out *tha*.

"Really? Is that all that happened to you?"

"Yes. Why? What happened to *you*?"

"They gave me a shot first, and I had a reaction. My throat closed up. I thought for a minute I was going to die."

"Huh. They gave me a shot before I had the test, but nothing happened. That does sound bad. I'm sorry, Lukey."

"That was only the first bad part. I passed out while I was looking at the lights. Had a seizure, I think." He had also wet his pants a little, but that was information he'd keep to himself. "When I woke up . . ." He paused, getting himself under control. He had no urge to cry in front of this pretty girl with her pretty brown eyes and curly black hair. "When I woke up, they slapped me around."

She sat up straight. "Say *what*?"

He nodded. "Then one of the docs . . . Evans, do you know him?"

"The one with the little 'stash." She wrinkled her nose and had another sip.

"Yeah, him. He had some cards and tried to get me to say what was on them. They were ESP cards. Pretty much had to be. You talked about them, remember?"

"Sure. They've tested those on me a dozen times. *Two* dozen. But they didn't after the lights. They just took me back to my room." She took another tiny sip. "They must have confused their paperwork, thought you were TP instead of TK."

"That's what I thought at first, and I told them, but they kept slapping me. Like they thought I was faking."

"Craziest thing I ever heard," she said. *Hurr* instead of *heard*.

"I think it happened because I'm not what you guys call a pos. I'm just ordinary. They call us ordinary kids pinks."

"Yeah. Pinks. That's right."

"What about the other kids? Did any of that stuff happen to them?"

"Never asked them. Sure you don't want some of this?"

Luke took the bottle and had a swallow, mostly so she wouldn't drink all of it. In his estimation, she'd had enough. It was just as horrible as he'd expected. He handed it back.

"Don't you want to know what I'm celebrating?"

"What?"

"Iris. Her memory. She's like you, nothing special, just a little TK. They came and took her an hour ago. And as George would say, we will see her no more."

She began to cry. Luke put his arms around her. He couldn't think what else to do. She put her head on his shoulder.

17

That night he went to the Mr. Griffin site again, typed in the *Star Trib* web address, and stared at it for almost three minutes before backing out without hitting enter. Coward, he thought. I'm a coward. If they're dead, I should find out. Only he didn't know how he could face that news without breaking down completely. Besides, what good would it do?

He typed in *Vermont debt lawyers* instead. He had already researched this, but told himself that double-checking his work was always a good idea. And it would pass the time.

Twenty minutes later he shut down and was debating whether to take a walk and see who was around (Kalisha would be his first choice, if she wasn't sleeping it off), when the colored spots came back. They swirled in front of his eyes and the world started to go away. To *pull* away, like a train leaving the station while he watched from the platform.

He put his head down on the closed laptop and took big slow breaths, telling himself to hold on, hold on, just hold on. Telling himself it would pass, not allowing himself to wonder what would happen if it didn't. At least he could swallow. Swallowing was fine, and eventually that sense of drifting away from himself—drifting into a universe of swirling lights—*did* pass. He didn't know how long it took, maybe only a minute or two, but it felt much longer.

He went into the bathroom and brushed his teeth, looking at himself in the mirror as he did it. They could know about the dots, probably *did* know about the dots, but not about the other. He had no idea what had been on the first card, or on the third one, but the second had been a boy on a bike and the fourth had been a small dog with a ball in its mouth. Black dog, red ball. It seemed he was TP after all.

Or was now.

He rinsed his mouth, turned off the lights, undressed in the dark, and laid down on his bed. Those lights had changed him. They knew that might happen, but weren't sure. He didn't know how he could be positive of that, but—

He was a test subject, maybe they all were, but low-level TPs and TKs—pinks—got extra tests. Why? Because they were less valuable? More expendable if things went wrong? There was no way to be sure, but Luke thought it was likely. The doctors believed the experiment with the cards had been a failure. That was good. These were bad people, and keeping secrets from bad people had to be good, right? But he had an idea the lights might have some purpose beyond growing the talents of the pinks, because stronger TPs and TKs, like Kalisha and George, also got them. What might that other purpose be?

He didn't know. He only knew that the dots were gone, and Iris was gone, and the dots might come back but Iris wouldn't. Iris had gone to Back Half and they would see her no more.

18

There were nine children at breakfast the following morning, but with Iris gone, there was little talk and no laughter. George Iles cracked no jokes. Helen Simms breakfasted on candy cigarettes. Harry Cross got a mountain of scrambled eggs from the buffet, and shoveled them in (along with bacon and home fries) without looking up from his plate, like a man doing work. The little girls, Greta and Gerda Wilcox, ate nothing until Gladys appeared, sunny smile and all, and coaxed a few bites into them. The twins seemed to cheer up at her attentions, even laughed a little. Luke thought of taking them aside later and telling them not to trust that smile, but it would frighten them, and what good would that do?

What good would that do had become another mantra, and he recognized it was a bad way to think, a step down the path to acceptance of this place. He didn't want to go there, no way did he want to go there, but logic was logic. If the little Gs were comforted by the attentions of the big G, maybe that was for the best, but when he thought about those girls getting the rectal thermometer . . . and the lights . . .

"What's up with you?" Nicky asked. "You look like you bit into a lemon."

"Nothing. Thinking about Iris."

"She's history, man."

Luke looked at him. "That's cold."

Nicky shrugged. "The truth often is. Want to go out and play HORSE?"

"No."

"Come on. I'll spot you the *H* and even let you have your ride at the end."

"I'll pass."

"Chicken?" Nicky asked it without rancor.

Luke shook his head. "It would just make me feel bad. I used to play it with my dad." He heard that *used to* and hated it.

"Okay, I hear that." He looked at Luke with an expression Luke could barely stand, especially coming from Nicky Wilholm. "Listen, man . . ."

"What?"

Nicky sighed. "Just I'll be out there if you change your mind."

Luke left the caff and wandered up his corridor—the JUST ANOTHER DAY IN PARADISE corridor— and then up the next one, which he now thought of as the Ice Machine Hallway. No sign of Maureen, so he kept going. He passed more motivational posters and more rooms, nine on each side. All the doors stood open, displaying unmade beds and walls that were bare of posters. This made them look like what they really were: jail cells for kids. He passed the elevator annex and kept walking past more rooms. Certain conclusions seemed inescapable. One was that once upon a time there had been a lot more "guests" in the Institute. Unless those in charge had been overly optimistic.

Luke eventually came to another lounge, where the janitor named Fred was running a buffer in big, lackadaisical sweeps. There were snack and drink machines here, but they were empty and unplugged. There was no playground outside, only a swatch of gravel, more chainlink with some benches beyond (presumably for staff members who wanted to take their breaks outside), and the low green admin building seventy yards or so further on. The lair of Mrs. Sigsby, who had told him he was here to serve.

"What are you doing?" Fred the janitor asked.

"Just walking around," Luke said. "Seeing the sights."

"There are no sights. Go back where you came from. Play with the other kids."

"What if I don't want to?" That sounded pathetic rather than defiant, and Luke wished he'd kept his mouth shut.

Fred was wearing a walkie-talkie on one hip and a zap-stick on the other. He touched the latter. "Go back. Won't tell you again."

"Okay. Have a nice day, Fred."

"Fuck your nice day." The buffer started up again.

Luke retreated, marveling at how quickly all his unquestioned assumptions about adults—that they were nice to you if you were nice to them, just for starters—had been blown up. He tried not to look into all those empty rooms as he passed them. They were spooky. How many kids had lived in them? What happened to them when they went to Back Half? And where were they now? Home?

"The fuck they are," he murmured, and wished his mom was around to hear him use that word and reprimand him for it. That he didn't have his father was bad. That he didn't have his mother was like a pulled tooth.

When he got to the Ice Machine Hallway, he saw Maureen's Dandux basket parked outside Avery's room. He poked his head in, and she gave him a smile as she smoothed down the coverlet on the Avester's bed. "All okay, Luke?"

A stupid question, but he knew she meant it well; just how he knew might have something or nothing to do with yesterday's light-show. Maureen's face looked paler today, the lines around her mouth deeper. Luke thought, This woman is not okay.

"Sure. How about you?"

"I'm fine." She was lying. This didn't feel like a hunch or an insight; it felt like a rock-solid fact. "Except this one—Avery—wet the bed last night." She sighed. "He's not the first and he won't be the last. Thankfully it didn't go through the mattress pad. You take care now, Luke. Have a fine day." She was looking directly at him, her eyes hopeful. Except it was what was behind them that was hopeful. He thought again, They changed me. I don't know how and I don't know how much, but yes, they changed me. Something new has been added. He was very glad he'd lied about the cards. And very glad they believed his lie. At least for now.

He made as if to leave the doorway, then turned back. "Think I'll get some more ice. They slapped me around some yesterday, and my face is sore."

"You do that, son. You do that."

Again, that *son* warmed him. Made him want to smile.

He got the bucket that was still in his room, dumped the meltwater into the bathroom basin, and took it back to the ice machine. Maureen was there, bent over with her bottom against the cinderblock wall, hands on her shins almost all the way down to her ankles. Luke hurried to her, but she waved him off. "Just stretching my back. Getting the kinks out."

Luke opened the door of the ice machine and got the scoop. He couldn't pass her a note, as Kalisha had passed one to him, because although he had a laptop, he had no paper and no pen. Not even a stub of a pencil. Maybe that was good. Notes were dangerous in here.

"Leah Fink, in Burlington," he murmured as he scooped ice. "Rudolph Davis, in Montpelier. Both have five stars on Legal Eagle. That's a consumer website. Can you remember the names?"

"Leah Fink, Rudolph Davis. Bless you, Luke."

Luke knew he should leave it at that, but he was curious. He had always been curious. So instead of going, he pounded at the ice, as if to break it up. It didn't need any breaking, but it made a nice loud sound. "Avery said the money you've got saved is for a kid. I know it's not any of my business—"

"The little Dixon boy's one of the mind-readers,

isn't he? And he must be a powerful one, bed-wetter or not. No pink dot on *his* intake."

"Yeah, he is." Luke went on stirring with the ice scoop.

"Well, he's right. It was a church adoption, right after my boy was born. I wanted to keep him, but pastor and my mother talked me out of it. The dog I married never wanted kids, so it was just the one I gave away. Do you really care about this, Luke?"

"Yeah." He did, but talking too long might be a bad idea. *They* might not be able to hear, but they could watch.

"When I started getting my back pains, it came to me that I had to know what became of him, and I found out. State says they're not supposed to tell where the babies go, but the church keeps adoption records going all the way back to 1950, and I got the computer password. Pastor keeps it right underneath the keyboard in the parsonage. My boy's just two towns over from where I live in Vermont. A senior in high school. He wants to go to college. I found that out, too. My son wants to go to college. That's what the money's for, not to pay off that dirty dog's bills."

She wiped her eyes with her sleeve, a quick and almost furtive gesture.

He closed the ice chest and straightened up. "Take care of your back, Maureen."

"I will."

But what if it was cancer? That was what she thought it was, he knew it.

She touched his shoulder as he turned away and leaned close. Her breath was bad. It was a sick person's breath. "He doesn't ever have to know where the money came from, my boy. But he needs to have it.

And Luke? Do what they say, now. *Everything* they say."
She hesitated. "And if you want to talk to anybody
about anything . . . do it here."

"I thought there were some other places where—"

"Do it here," she repeated, and rolled her basket
back the way she had come.

19

When he returned to the playground, Luke was surprised to see Nicky playing HORSE with Harry Cross.
They were laughing and bumping and ranking on
each other as if they had been friends since first grade.
Helen was sitting at the picnic table, playing double-
deck War with Avery. Luke sat down beside her and
asked who was winning.

"Hard to tell," Helen said. "Avery beat me last
time, but this one's a nail-biter."

"She thinks it's boring as shit, but she's being nice,"
Avery said. "Isn't that right, Helen?"

"Indeed it is, Little Kreskin, indeed it is. And after
this, we're moving on to Slap Jack. You won't like that
one because I slap *hard*."

Luke looked around, and felt a sudden stab of concern. It bloomed a squadron of ghostly dots in front of
his eyes, there and then gone. "Where's Kalisha? They
didn't—"

"No, no, they didn't take her anywhere. She's just
having a shower."

"Luke likes her," Avery announced. "He likes her
a *lot*."

"Avery?"

"What, Helen?"

"Some things are better not discussed."

"Why?"

"Because *Y*'s a crooked letter and can't be made straight." She looked away suddenly. She ran a hand through her tu-tone hair, perhaps to hide her trembling mouth. If so, it didn't work.

"What's wrong?" Luke asked.

"Why don't you just ask Little Kreskin? He sees all, he knows all."

"She got a thermometer jammed up her butt," Avery said.

"Oh," Luke said.

"Right," Helen said. "How fucking degrading is that?"

"Demeaning," Luke said.

"But also delightful and delicious," Helen said, and then they were both laughing. Helen did it with tears standing in her eyes, but laughing was laughing, and being able to do it in here was a treasure.

"I don't get it," Avery said. "How is getting a thermometer up your butt delightful and delicious?"

"It's delicious if you lick it when it comes out," Luke said, and then they were all howling.

Helen whacked the table, sending the cards flying. "Oh God I'm peeing myself, gross, don't look!" And she went running, almost knocking George over as he came outside, noshing a peanut butter cup.

"What's her deal?" George asked.

"Peed herself," Avery said matter-of-factly. "I peed my bed last night, so I can relate."

"Thank you for sharing that," Luke said, smiling. "Go over and play HORSE with Nicky and New Kid."

"Are you crazy? They're too big, and Harry already pushed me down once."

"Then go jump on the trampoline."

"I'm bored of it."

"Go jump on it, anyway. I want to talk to George."

"About the lights? What lights?"

The kid, Luke thought, was fucking eerie. "Go jump, Avester. Show me a couple of forward rolls."

"And try not to break your neck," George said. "But if you do, I'll sing 'You Are So Beautiful' at your funeral."

Avery looked at George fixedly for a moment or two, then said, "But you hate that song."

"Yes," George said. "Yes, I do. Saying what I did is called satire. Or maybe irony. I always get those two things mixed up. Go on, now. Put an egg in your shoe and beat it."

They watched him trudge to the trampoline.

"That kid is ten and except for the ESP shit acts like he's six," George said. "How fucked up is that?"

"Pretty fucked up. How old are you, George?"

"Thirteen," George said, sounding morose. "But these days I feel a hundred. Listen, Luke, they say our parents are okay. Do you believe that?"

It was a delicate question. At last Luke said, "Not . . . exactly."

"If you could find out for sure, would you?"

"I don't know."

"Not me," George said. "I've got enough on my plate already. Finding out they were . . . you know . . . that would break me. But I can't help wondering. Like all the time."

I could find out for you, Luke thought. *I could find*

out for both of us. He almost leaned forward and whispered it in George's ear. Then he thought of George saying he had enough on his plate already. "Listen, that eye thing—you had it?"

"Sure. Everyone has it. Just like everyone gets the thermometer up the ass, and the EEG and the EKG and the MRI and the XYZ and the blood tests and the reflex tests and all the other wonderful things you have in store, Lukey."

Luke thought about asking if George had gone on seeing the dots after the projector was off and decided not to. "Did you have a seizure? Because I did."

"Nah. They did sit me down at a table, and the asshole doc with the mustache did some card tricks."

"You mean asking you what was on them."

"Yeah, that's what I mean. I thought they were Rhine cards, pretty much had to be. I got tested on those a couple of years before I wound up in this charming hole of hell. This was after my parents figured out I really could move things around sometimes if I looked at them. Once they decided I wasn't faking it just to freak them out, or as one of my little jokes, they wanted to find out what else was going on with me, so they took me to Princeton, where there's this thing called Anomalies Research. Or was. I think they closed it down."

"Anomalies . . . are you serious?"

"Yeah. Sounds more scientific than Psychic Research, I guess. It was actually part of the Princeton engineering department, if you can believe that. A couple of grad students ran the Rhine cards on me, but I pretty much zeroed out. I wasn't even able to move much stuff around that day. Sometimes it's just like that." He shrugged. "They probably thought I was a faker, which was okey-doke with me. I mean, on a good day I can knock over a pile of blocks, just thinking about them, but that'll never get me chicks. You agree?"

As someone whose big trick was knocking a pizza pan off a restaurant table without touching it, Luke did. "So did they slap you around?"

"I did get one, and it was a real hummer," George said. "It was because I tried to make a joke. This bitch named Priscilla laid it on me."

"I met her. She's a bitch, all right."

A word his mother hated even more than *fuck*, and using it made Luke miss her all over again.

"And you didn't know what was on the cards."

George gave him an odd look. "I'm TK, not TP. The same as you. How could I?"

"I guess you couldn't."

"Since I'd had the Rhine cards at Princeton, I guessed cross, then star, then wavy lines. Priscilla told me to stop lying, so when Evans looked at the next one, I told him it was a photo of Priscilla's tits. *That's* when she slapped me. Then they let me go back to my room. Tell you the truth, they didn't seem all that interested. More like they were crossing *t*'s and dotting *i*'s."

"Maybe they didn't really expect anything," Luke said. "Maybe you were just a control subject."

George laughed. "Man, I can't control jackshit in here. What are you talking about?"

"Nothing. Never mind. Did they come back? The lights, I mean? Those colored dots?"

"No." George looked curious now. "Did they with you?"

"No." Luke was suddenly glad that Avery wasn't

here, and could only hope the little kid's brain radio was short-range. "Just . . . I *did* have a seizure . . . or thought I did . . . and I was afraid they *might* come back."

"I don't get the point of this place," George said, sounding more morose than ever. "It almost has to be a government installation, but . . . my mother bought this book, okay? Not long before they took me to Princeton. *Psychic Histories and Hoaxes*, it was called. I read it when she was done. There was a chapter on government experiments about the stuff we can do. The CIA ran some back in the nineteen-fifties. For telepathy, telekinesis, precognition, even levitation and teleportation. LSD was involved. They got some results, but nothing much." He leaned forward, blue eyes on Luke's green ones. "And that's us, man— nothing much. Are we supposed to achieve world domination for the United States by moving Saltine boxes—and only if they're empty—or flipping the pages of a book?"

"They could send Avery to Russia," Luke said. "He could tell them what Putin had for breakfast, and if he was wearing boxers or briefs."

That made George smile.

"About our parents—" Luke began, but then Kalisha came running out, asking who wanted to play dodgeball.

It turned out they all did.

20

There were no tests for Luke that day, except of his own intestinal fortitude, and that one he flunked again. Twice more he went to the *Star Tribune*, and twice more he backed out, although the second time he did peep at the headline, something about a guy running over a bunch of people with a truck to prove how religious he was. That was a terrible thing, but at least it was something that was going on beyond the Institute. The outside world was still there, and at least one thing had changed in here: the laptop's welcome screen now had his name instead of the departed Donna's.

He would have to look for information about his parents sooner or later. He knew that, and now understood perfectly that old saying about no news being good news.

The following day he was taken back down to C-Level, where a tech named Carlos took three ampules of blood, gave him a shot (no reaction), then had him go into a toilet cubicle and pee in a cup. After that, Carlos and a scowling orderly named Winona escorted him down to D-Level. Winona was reputed to be one of the mean ones, and Luke made no attempt to talk to her. They took him to a large room containing an MRI tube that must have cost megabucks.

It almost has to be a government installation, George had said. If so, what would John and Josie Q. Public think about how their tax dollars were being spent? Luke guessed that in a country where people squalled about Big Brother even if faced with some piddling requirement like having to wear a motorcycle helmet or get a license to carry a concealed weapon, the answer would be "not much."

A new tech was waiting for them, but before he and Carlos could insert Luke in the tube, Dr. Evans darted in, checked Luke's arm around the site of his latest shot, and pronounced him "fine as paint." Whatever that meant. He asked if Luke had experienced any more seizures or fainting spells.

"No."

"What about the colored lights? Any recurrence of those? Perhaps while exercising, perhaps while looking at your laptop computer, perhaps while straining at stool? That means—"

"I know what it means. No."

"Don't lie to me, Luke."

"I'm not." Wondering if the MRI would detect some change in his brain activity and *prove* him a liar.

"Okay, good." Not good, Luke thought. You're disappointed. Which makes me happy.

Evans scribbled something on his clipboard. "Carry on, lady and gentlemen, carry on!" And he darted out again, like a white rabbit late for a very important date.

The MRI tech—DAVE, his tag said—asked Luke if he was claustrophobic. "You probably know what that means, too."

"I'm not," Luke said. "The only thing I'm phobic about is being locked up."

Dave was an earnest-looking fellow, middle-aged, bespectacled, mostly bald. He looked like an accountant. Of course, so had Adolf Eichmann. "Just if you are . . . claustrophobic, I mean . . . I can give you a Valium. It's allowed."

"That's all right."

"You should have one, anyway," Carlos said. "You're gonna be in there a long time, on and off, and it makes the experience more pleasant. You might even sleep, although it's pretty loud. Bumps and bangs, you know."

Luke knew. He'd never actually been in an MRI tube, but he'd seen plenty of doctor shows. "I'll pass."

But after lunch (brought in by Gladys), he took the Valium, partly out of curiosity, mostly out of boredom. He'd had three stints in the MRI, and according to Dave, had three more to go. Luke didn't bother asking what they were testing for, looking for, or hoping to find. The answer would have been some form of *none of your beeswax*. He wasn't sure they knew themselves.

The Valium gave him a floaty, dreamy feeling, and during the last stint in the tube, he fell into a light doze in spite of the loud banging the machine made when it took its pictures. By the time Winona appeared to take him back to the residence level, the Valium had worn off and he just felt spaced out.

She reached into her pocket and brought out a handful of tokens. When she handed them to him, one fell to the floor and rolled.

"Pick that up, butterfingers."

He picked it up.

"You've had a long day," she said, and actually smiled. "Why don't you go get yourself something to drink? Kick back. Relax. I recommend the Harveys Bristol Cream."

She was middle-aged, plenty old enough to have a kid Luke's age. Maybe two. Would she have made a similar recommendation to them? Gee, you had a tough day at school, why not kick back and have a wine cooler before tackling your homework? He thought of saying that, the worst she'd probably do was slap him, but . . .

"What good would it do?"

"Huh?" She was frowning at him. "What good would *what* do?"

"Anything," he said. "Anything at all, Winnie." He didn't want Harveys Bristol Cream, or Twisted Tea, or even Stump Jump Grenache, a name John Keats might have been thinking of when he said something or other was "call'd as romantic as that westwards moon in yon waning ribbon of the night."

"You want to watch that wise mouth, Luke."

"I'll work on that."

He put the tokens in his pocket. He believed there were nine of them. He would give three to Avery, and three to each of the Wilcox twins. Enough for snacks, not enough for any of the other stuff. All he wanted for himself at the present moment was a big load of protein and carbs. He didn't care what was on tonight's menu for supper as long as there was a lot of it.

21

The next morning Joe and Hadad took him back down to C-Level, where he was told to drink a barium solution. Tony stood by with his zap-stick, ready to administer a jolt if Luke voiced any disagreement. Once he'd drained every drop, he was led to a cubicle the size of a bathroom stall in a turnpike rest area and X-rayed. That part went all right, but as he left the cubicle, he cramped up and doubled over.

"Don't you hurl on this floor," Tony said. "If you're going to do it, use the sink in the corner."

Too late. Luke's half-digested breakfast came up in a barium puree.

"Ah, shit. You are now going to mop that up, and when you're done, I want the floor to be so clean I can eat off it."

"I'll do it," Hadad said.

"The fuck you will." Tony didn't look at him or

raise his voice, but Hadad flinched just the same. "You can get the mop and the bucket. The rest is Luke's job."

Hadad got the cleaning stuff. Luke managed to fill the bucket at the sink in the corner of the room, but he was still having stomach cramps, and his arms were trembling too badly to lower it again without spilling the soapy water everywhere. Joe did that for him, whispering "Hang in there, kid" into Luke's ear.

"Just give him the mop," Tony said, and Luke understood—in the new way he had of understanding things—that old Tones was enjoying himself.

Luke swabbed and rinsed. Tony surveyed his work, pronounced it unacceptable, and told him to do it again. The cramps had let up, and this time he was able to lift and lower the bucket by himself. Hadad and Joe were sitting down and discussing the chances of the Yankees and the San Diego Padres, apparently their teams of choice. On the way back to the elevator, Hadad clapped him on the back and said, "You done good, Luke. Got some tokens for him, Joey? I'm all out."

Joe gave him four.

"What are these tests for?" Luke asked.

"Plenty of things," Hadad said. "Don't worry about it."

Which was, Luke thought, perhaps the stupidest piece of advice he'd ever been given. "Am I ever getting out of here?"

"Absolutely," Joe said. "You won't remember a thing about it, though."

He was lying. Again, it wasn't mind-reading, at least as Luke had always imagined it—hearing words in his mind (or seeing them, like on the crawl at the bottom of a cable news broadcast); it was just *knowing*, as undeniable as gravity or the irrationality of the square root of two.

"How many more tests will there be?"

"Oh, we'll keep you busy," Joe said.

"Just don't puke on a floor Tony Fizzale has to walk on," Hadad said, and laughed heartily.

22

A new housekeeper was vacuuming the floor of his room when Luke arrived. This woman—JOLENE, according to her nametag—was plump and in her twenties.

"Where's Maureen?" Luke asked, although he knew perfectly well. This was Maureen's off week, and when she came back, it might not be to his part of the Institute, at least not for awhile. He hoped she was in Vermont, getting her runaway husband's crap sorted out, but he would miss her . . . although he supposed he might see her in Back Half when it was his turn to go there.

"Mo-Mo's off making a movie with Johnny Depp," Jolene said. "One of those pirate things all the kids like. She's playing the Jolly Roger." She laughed, then said, "Why don't you get out of here while I finish up?"

"Because I want to lie down. I don't feel good."

"Oh, wah-wah-wah," Jolene said. "You kids are spoiled rotten. Have someone to clean your room, cook your meals, you got your own TV . . . you think I had a TV in my room when I was a kid? Or my own bathroom? I had three sisters and two brothers and we all fought over it."

"We also get to swallow barium and then puke it up. You think you'd like to try some?"

I sound more like Nicky every day, Luke thought, and hey, what's wrong with that? It's good to have positive role models.

Jolene turned to him and brandished the vacuum cleaner attachment. "You want to see how getting hit upside the head with this feels?"

Luke left. He walked slowly along the connecting residence corridors, pausing twice to lean against the wall when the cramps hit. At least they were lessening in frequency and intensity. Just before he got to the deserted lounge with its view of the administration building, he went into one of the empty rooms, laid down on the mattress, and went to sleep. He woke up for the first time not expecting to see Rolf Destin's house outside his bedroom window.

In Luke's opinion, that was a step in exactly the wrong direction.

23

The next morning he was given a shot, then hooked up to heart and blood pressure monitors, and made to run on a treadmill, monitored by Carlos and Dave. They sped the treadmill up until he was gasping for breath and in danger of tumbling off the end. The readings were mirrored on the little dashboard, and just before Carlos slowed him down, Luke saw the BPM readout was 170.

While he was sipping at a glass of orange juice and getting his breath back, a big bald guy came in and leaned against the wall, arms crossed. He was wearing a brown suit that looked expensive and a white shirt with no tie. His dark eyes surveyed Luke, all the way down from his red and sweaty face to his new sneakers. He said, "I'm told you show signs of slow adjustment, young man. Perhaps Nick Wilholm has something to do with that. He's not someone you should emulate. You know the meaning of that word, don't you? Emulate?"

"Yes."

"He is insolent and unpleasant to men and women who are only trying to do their jobs."

Luke said nothing. Always safest.

"Don't let his attitude rub off on you, that would be my advice. My *strong* advice. And keep your interactions with the service staff to a minimum."

Luke felt a stab of alarm at that, then realized the bald guy wasn't talking about Maureen. It was Fred the janitor he was talking about. Luke knew that perfectly well, although he had only talked to Fred once and had talked to Maureen several times.

"Also, stay out of the West Lounge and the empty rooms. If you want to sleep, do it in your own room. Make your stay as pleasant as possible."

"There's nothing pleasant about this place," Luke said.

"You're welcome to your opinion," the bald man said. "As I'm sure you've heard, they're like assholes, everybody's got one. But I think you're smart enough to know there's a big difference between nothing pleasant and something *un*pleasant. Keep it in mind."

He left.

"Who was that?" Luke asked.

"Stackhouse," Carlos said. "The Institute's security officer. You want to stay off his bad side."

Dave came at him with a needle. "Need to take a little more blood. Won't take a minute. Be a good sport about it, okay?"

24

After the treadmill and the latest blood draw, there were a couple of days of no tests, at least for Luke. He got a couple of shots—one of which made his whole arm itch fiercely for an hour—but that was all. The Wilcox twins began to adjust, especially after Harry Cross befriended them. He was a TK, and boasted that he could move lots of stuff, but Avery said that was a crock of shit. "He's got even less than you do, Luke."

Luke rolled his eyes. "Don't be *too* diplomatic, Avery, you'll strain yourself."

"What's *diplomatic* mean?"

"Spend a token and look it up on your computer."

"I'm sorry, Dave, I can't do that," Avery said in a surprisingly good imitation of HAL 9000's softly sinister voice, and began to giggle.

Harry was good to Greta and Gerda, that was undeniable. Every time he saw them, a big goofy grin spread over his face. He would squat down, spread his arms wide, and they would run to him.

"Don't suppose he's fiddling with them, do you?" Nicky asked one morning on the playground, watching as Harry monitored the Gs on the trampoline.

"Eww, gross," Helen said. "You've been watching too many Lifetime movies."

"Nope," Avery said. He was eating a Choco Pop and had grown a brown mustache. "He doesn't want to . . ." He put his small hands on his backside and bumped his hips. Watching this, Luke thought it was a good example of how telepathy was all wrong. You knew way too much, and way too soon.

"Eww," Helen said again, and covered her eyes. "Don't make me wish I was blind, Avester."

"He had cocker spaniels," Avery said. "Back home. Those girls are like his, you know, there's a word."

"Substitute," Luke said.

"Right, that."

"I don't know how Harry was with his dogs," Nicky said to Luke at lunch later that day, "but those little girls pretty much run him. It's like someone gave them a new doll. One with red hair and a big gut. Look at that."

The twins were sitting on either side of Harry and feeding him bites of meatloaf from their plates.

"I think it's sort of cute," Kalisha said.

Nicky smiled at her—the one that lit up his whole face (which today included a black eye some staff member had gifted him with). "You would, Sha."

She smiled back, and Luke felt a twinge of jealousy. Pretty stupid, under the circumstances . . . yet there it was.

25

The following day, Priscilla and Hadad escorted Luke down to the previously unvisited E-Level. There he was hooked up to an IV that Priscilla said would relax him a little. What it did was knock him cold. When he awoke, shivering and naked, his abdomen, right leg, and right side had been bandaged. Another doctor—RICHARDSON, according to the nametag on her white coat—was leaning over him. "How do you feel, Luke?"

"What did you do to me?" He tried to scream this but could only manage a choked growl. They had put something down his throat, as well. Probably some kind of breathing tube. Belatedly, he cupped his hands over his crotch.

"Just took a few samples." Dr. Richardson whipped off her paisley surgical cap, releasing a flood of dark hair. "We didn't take out one of your kidneys to sell on the black market, if that's what you're worried about. You'll have a little pain, especially between your ribs, but it will pass. In the meantime, take these." She handed him an unmarked brown bottle with a few pills inside.

She left. Zeke came in with his clothes. "Dress when you feel like you can do it without falling down." Zeke, always considerate, dropped the clothes on the floor.

Eventually Luke was able to pick them up and dress. Priscilla—this time with Gladys—escorted him back to the residence level. It had been daylight when they took him down, but it was dark now. Maybe late at night, he couldn't tell, his time sense was totally fucked.

"Can you walk down to your room by yourself?" Gladys asked. No big smile; maybe it didn't work the night shift.

"Yeah."

"Then go on. Take one of those pills. They're Oxy-contin. They work for the pain, and they also make you feel good. A bonus. You'll be fine in the morning."

He walked down the hall, reached for the doorknob of his room, then stopped. Someone was crying. The sound came from the vicinity of that stupid JUST ANOTHER DAY IN PARADISE poster, which meant it was probably coming from Kalisha's room. He debated for a moment, not wanting to know what the crying was about, definitely not feeling up to comforting anyone. Still, it was her, so he went down and knocked softly on the door. There was no answer, so he turned the knob and poked his head in. "Kalisha?"

She was lying on her back with one hand over her eyes. "Go away, Luke. I don't want you to see me like this."

He almost did as she asked, but it wasn't what she wanted. Instead of leaving, he went in and sat down beside her. "What's wrong?"

But he knew that, too. Just not the details.

26

The kids had been outside in the playground—all of them except Luke, who was down on E-Level, lying unconscious while Dr. Richardson cored out her samples. Two men emerged from the lounge. They were in red scrubs rather than the pink and blue ones the Front Half caretakers and techs wore, and there were no nametags on their shirts. The three old-timers—Kalisha, Nicky, and George—knew what that meant.

"I was sure they were coming for me," Kalisha told Luke. "I've been here the longest, and I haven't had any tests for at least ten days, even though I'm over the chicken pox. I haven't even had bloodwork, and you know how those fucking vampires like to take blood. But it was Nicky they came for. *Nicky!*"

The break in her voice as she said this made Luke

sad, because he was pretty crazy about Kalisha, but it didn't surprise him. Helen turned to him like a compass needle pointing to magnetic north whenever he came in sight; Iris had done the same; even the little Gs looked at him with open mouths and shining eyes when he passed. But Kalisha had been with him the longest, they were Institute vets, and roughly the same age. As a couple they were at least possible.

"He fought them," Kalisha said. "He fought them *hard*." She sat up so suddenly she almost knocked Luke off the bed. Her lips were drawn back from her teeth and her fists were clenched on her chest above her slight bosom.

"*I* should have fought them! We all should have!"

"But it happened too fast, didn't it?"

"He punched one of them high up—in the throat—and the other one zapped him in the hip. It must have numbed his leg, but he held onto one of the ropes on the ropes course to keep from falling down, and he kicked at that one with his good leg before the bastard could use his zap-stick again."

"Knocked it out of his hand," Luke said. He could see it, but saying so was a mistake, it suggested something he didn't want her to know, but Kalisha didn't seem to notice.

"That's right. But then the other one, the one he punched in the throat, he zapped Nicky in the side, and the goddam thing must have been turned all the way up, because I could hear the crackle, even though I was all the way over by the shuffleboard court. Nicky fell down, and they bent over him and zapped him some more, and he *jumped*, even though he was lying there unconscious he *jumped*, and Helen ran over, she was shouting 'You're killing him, you're killing him,' and one of them kicked her high up in the leg, and went *hai*, like some half-assed karate guy, and he laughed, and she fell down crying, and they picked Nicky up, and they carried him away. But before they got him through the lounge doors . . ."

She stopped. Luke waited. He knew what came next, it was one of his new hunches that was more than a hunch, but he had to let her say it. Because she couldn't know what he was now, none of them could know.

"He came around a little," she said. Tears were rolling down her cheeks. "Enough to see us. He smiled, and he waved. He *waved*. That's how brave he was."

"Yeah," Luke said, hearing *was* and not *is*. Thinking: And we'll see him no more.

She grabbed his neck and brought his face down to hers so unexpectedly and so hard that their foreheads bonked together. "Don't you say that!"

"I'm sorry," Luke said, wondering what else she might have seen in his mind. He hoped it wasn't much. He hoped she was too upset over the red-shirt guys taking Nicky away to Back Half. What she said next eased his mind on that score considerably.

"Did they take samples? They did, didn't they? You've got bandages."

"Yes."

"That black-haired bitch, right? Richardson. How many?"

"Three. One from my leg, one from my stomach, one between my ribs. That's the one that hurts the most."

She nodded. "They took one from my boob, like a biopsy. That really hurt. Only what if they're not taking out? What if they're putting in? They say they're taking samples, but they lie about everything!"

"You mean more trackers? Why would they, when they've got these?" He fingered the chip in his earlobe. It no longer hurt; now it was just a part of him.

"I don't know," she said miserably.

Luke reached into his pocket and brought out the bottle of pills. "They gave me these. Maybe you should take one. I think it would mellow you out. Help you to sleep."

"Oxys?"

He nodded.

She reached for the bottle, then drew her hand back. "Problem is, I don't want one, I don't even want two. I want all of them. But I think I should feel what I'm feeling. I think that's the right thing, don't you?"

"I don't know," Luke said, which was the truth. These were deep waters, and no matter how smart he was, he was only twelve.

"Go away, Luke. I need to be sad on my own now."

"Okay."

"I'll be better tomorrow. And if they take me next . . ."

"They won't." Knowing that was a stupid thing to say, maximo retardo. She was due. Overdue, really.

"*If* they do, be a friend to Avery. He needs a friend." She looked at him fixedly. "And so do you."

"Okay."

She tried on a smile. "You're a peach. C'mere." He leaned over, and she kissed him first on the cheek, then on the corner of his mouth. Her lips were salty. Luke didn't mind.

As he opened the door, she said, "It should have been me. Or George. Not Nicky. He was the one who never gave in to their bullshit. The one who never gave up." She raised her voice. *"Are you there? Are you listen-*

ing? I hope you are, because I hate you and I want you to know it! I HATE YOU!"

She fell back on her bed and began to sob. Luke thought about going back to her, but didn't. He had given all the comfort he could, and he was hurting himself, not just about Nicky but in the places where Dr. Richardson had stuck him. It didn't matter if the woman with the dark hair had taken tissue samples, or put something into his body (trackers made no sense, but he supposed it could have been some sort of experimental enzyme or vaccine), because none of their tests and injections seemed to make sense. He thought again of the concentration camps, and the horrible, nonsensical experiments that had been conducted there. Freezing people, burning people, giving them diseases.

He went back to his room, considered taking one or even two of the Oxy pills, didn't.

Thought about using Mr. Griffin to go to the *Star Tribune*, and didn't do that, either.

He thought about Nicky, the heartthrob of all the girls. Nicky, who had first put Harry Cross in his place and then made friends with him, which was far bolder than beating him up. Nicky, who had fought their tests, and fought the men from Back Half when they came to get him, the one who never gave up.

27

The next day Joe and Hadad took Luke and George Iles down to C-11, where they were left alone for awhile. When the two caretakers came back, now equipped with cups of coffee, Zeke was with them. He looked red-eyed and hungover. He fitted the two boys with rubber electrode caps, cinching the straps tight under their chins. After Zeke checked the readouts, the two boys took turns in a driving simulator. Dr. Evans came in and stood by with his trusty clipboard, making notes as Zeke called out various numbers that might (or might not) have had to do with reaction time. Luke drove through several traffic signals and caused a fair amount of carnage before he got the hang of it, but after that, the test was actually sort of fun—an Institute first.

When it was over, Dr. Richardson joined Dr. Evans. Today she was dressed in a three-piece skirt suit and heels. She looked ready for a high-powered business meeting. "On a scale of one to ten, how is your pain this morning, Luke?"

"A two," he said. "On a scale of one to ten, my desire to get the hell out of here is an eleven."

She chuckled as if he had made a mild joke, said goodbye to Dr. Evans (calling him Jim), and then left.

"So who won?" George asked Dr. Evans.

He smiled indulgently. "It's not that kind of test, George."

"Yeah, but who won?"

"You were both quite fast, once you got used to the simulator, which is what we expect with TKs. No more tests today, boys, isn't that nice? Hadad, Joe, please take these young men upstairs."

On the way to the elevator, George said, "I ran over I think six pedestrians before I got the knack. How many did you run over?"

"Only three, but I hit a schoolbus. There might have been casualties there."

"You wank. I totally missed the bus." The elevator

came, and the four of them stepped on. "Actually, I hit seven pedestrians. The last one was on purpose. I was pretending it was Zeke."

Joe and Hadad looked at each other and laughed. Luke liked them a little for that. He didn't want to, but he did.

When the two caretakers got back into the elevator, presumably headed down to the break room, Luke said, "After the dots, they tried you on the cards. A telepathy test."

"Right, I told you that."

"Have they *ever* tested you for TK? Asked you to turn on a lamp or maybe knock over a line of dominoes?"

George scratched his head. "Now that you mention it, no. But why would they, when they already know I can do stuff like that? On a good day, at least. What about you?"

"Nope. And I hear what you're saying, but it's still funny that they don't seem to care about testing the limits of what we've got."

"None of it makes any sense, Lukey-Loo. Starting with being here. Let's get some chow."

Most of the kids were eating lunch in the caff, but Kalisha and Avery were in the playground. They were sitting on the gravel with their backs against the chain-link fence, looking at each other. Luke told George to go on to lunch and went outside. The pretty black girl and the little white boy weren't talking . . . and yet they were. Luke knew that much, but not what the conversation was about.

He flashed back to the SATs, and the girl who'd asked him about the math equation having to do with some guy named Aaron and how much he would have to pay for a hotel room. That seemed to be in another life, but Luke clearly remembered not being able to understand how a problem so simple for him could be so hard for her. He understood it now. Whatever was going on between Kalisha and Avery over there by the fence was far beyond him.

Kalisha looked around and waved him away. "I'll talk to you later, Luke. Go on and eat."

"Okay," he said, but he didn't talk to her at lunch, because she skipped it. Later, after a heavy nap (he finally broke down and took one of the pain pills), he walked down the hallway toward the lounge and the playground and stopped at her door, which was standing open. The pink bedspread and the pillows with the frou-frou flounces were gone. So was the framed photo of Martin Luther King. Luke stood there, hand over his mouth, eyes wide, letting it sink in.

If she'd fought, as Nicky had, Luke thought the noise would have awakened him in spite of the pill. The other alternative, that she had gone with them willingly, was less palatable but—he had to admit this—more likely. Either way, the girl who had kissed him twice was gone.

He went back to his room and put his face in his pillow.

28

That night, Luke flashed one of his tokens at the laptop's camera to wake it up, then went to Mr. Griffin. That he still *could* go there was hopeful. Of course the shitheads running this place might know all about his back door, but what would be the point of that?

This led to a conclusion that seemed sturdy enough, at least to him: the Minions of Sigsby might catch him peering into the outside world eventually, in fact that was likely, but so far they hadn't. They weren't mirroring his computer. They're lax about some things, he thought. Maybe about a lot of things, and why wouldn't they be? They're not dealing with military prisoners, just a bunch of scared, disoriented kids.

Staging from the Mr. Griffin site, he accessed the *Star Tribune*. Today's headline had to do with the continuing fight over health care, which had been going on for years now. The familiar terror of what he might find beyond the front page set in, and he almost exited to the desktop screen. Then he could erase his recent history, shut down, go to bed. Maybe take another pill. What you didn't know wouldn't hurt you, that was another saying, and hadn't he been hurt enough for one day?

Then he thought of Nick. Would Nicky Wilholm have backed out, had he known about a back door like Mr. Griffin? Probably not, almost certainly not, only he wasn't brave like Nicky.

He remembered Winona handing him that bunch of tokens and how, when he dropped one, she called him butterfingers and told him to pick it up. He had, without so much as a peep of protest. Nicky wouldn't have done that, either. Luke could almost hear him saying *Pick it up yourself, Winnie*, and taking the hit that would follow. Maybe even hitting back.

But Luke Ellis wasn't that guy. Luke Ellis was your basic good boy, doing what he was told, whether it was chores at home or going out for band at school. He hated his goddam trumpet, every third note was a sourball, but he stuck with it because Mr. Greer said he needed at least one extracurricular activity that wasn't intramural sports. Luke Ellis was the guy who went out of his way to be social so people wouldn't think he was a weirdo as well as a brainiac. He checked all the correct interaction boxes and then went back to his books. Because there was an abyss, and books contained magical incantations to raise what was hidden there: all the great mysteries. For Luke, those mysteries mattered. Someday, in the future, he might write books of his own.

But here, the only future was Back Half. Here, the truth of existence was *What good would it do?*

"Fuck that," he whispered, and went to the *Star Trib*'s Local section with his heartbeat thudding in his ears and pulsing in the small wounds, already closing, beneath the bandages.

There was no need to hunt; as soon as he saw his own school photograph from last year, he knew everything there was to know. The headline was unnecessary, but he read it anyway:

SEARCH GOES ON FOR MISSING SON
OF SLAIN FALCON HEIGHTS COUPLE

The colored lights came back, swirling and pulsing. Luke squinted through them, turned off the laptop, got up on legs that didn't feel like his legs, and went to his bed in two trembling strides. There he lay in the mild glow of the bedside lamp, staring up at the ceiling. At last those nasty pop-art dots began to fade.

Slain Falcon Heights couple.

He felt as if a previously unsuspected trapdoor had opened in the middle of his mind, and only one thought—clear, hard, and strong—kept him from falling through it: they might be watching. He didn't believe they knew about the Mr. Griffin site, and his ability to use it to access the outside world. He didn't believe they knew the lights had caused some fundamental change in his brain, either; they thought the experiment had been a failure. So far, at least. Those were the things he had, and they might be valuable.

The Minions of Sigsby weren't omnipotent. His continuing ability to access Mr. Griffin proved it. The only kind of rebellion they expected from the residents was the kind that was right out front. Once that was scared or beaten or zapped out of them, they could even be left alone for short periods, the way Joe and Hadad had left him and George alone in C-11 while they got their coffee.

Slain.

That word was the trapdoor, and it would be so easy to fall in. From the very start Luke had been almost sure he was being lied to, but the *almost* part kept the trapdoor closed. It allowed some small hope. That bald headline ended hope. And since they were dead—*slain*—who would the most likely suspect be? The **MISSING SON**, of course. The police investigating the crime would know by now that he was a special child, a genius, and weren't geniuses supposed to be fragile? Apt to go off the rails?

Kalisha had screamed her defiance, but Luke wouldn't, no matter how much he wanted to. In his heart he could scream all he wanted, but not out loud. He didn't know if his secrets could do him any good, but he did know that there were cracks in the walls of what George Iles had so rightly called this hole of hell. If he could use his secrets—and his supposedly superior intelligence—as a crowbar, he might be able to widen one of those cracks. He didn't know if escape was possible, but should he find a way to do it, escape would only be the first step to a greater goal.

Bring it down on them, he thought. Like Samson after Delilah coaxed him into getting a haircut. Bring it down and crush them. Crush them all.

At some point he dropped into a thin sleep. He dreamed that he was home, and his mother and father were alive. This was a good dream. His father told him not to forget to take out the trashcans. His mother made pancakes and Luke drenched his in blackberry syrup. His dad ate one with peanut butter while watching the morning news on CBS—Gayle King and Norah O'Donnell, who was foxy—and then went to work after kissing Luke on the cheek and Eileen on the mouth. A good dream. Rolf's mother was taking the boys to school, and when she honked out front, Luke grabbed his backpack and ran to the door. "Hey, don't forget your lunch money!" his mom called, and handed it to him, only it wasn't money, it was tokens, and that was when he woke up and realized someone was in his room.

29

Luke couldn't see who it was, because at some point he must have turned off the bedside lamp, although he couldn't remember doing it. He could hear a soft shuffle of feet from near his desk, and his first thought was that one of the caretakers had come to take his laptop, because they had been monitoring him all along, and he'd been stupid to believe otherwise. Maximo retardo.

Rage filled him like poison. He did not get out of bed so much as spring from it, meaning to tackle whoever it was that had come into his room. Let the intruder slap, punch, or use his goddam zap-stick. Luke would get in at least a few good blows. They might not understand the real reason he was hitting, but that was all right; Luke would know.

Only it wasn't an adult. He collided with a small body and knocked it sprawling.

"Ow, Lukey, don't! Don't hurt me!"

Avery Dixon. The Avester.

Luke groped, picked him up, and led him over to the bed, where he turned on the lamp. Avery looked terrified.

"Jesus, what are you doing here?"

"I woke up and was scared. I can't go in with Sha, because they took her away. So I came here. Can I stay? Please?"

All of that was true, but it wasn't the whole truth. Luke understood this with a clarity that made the other "knowings" he'd had seem dim and tentative. Because Avery was a strong TP, much stronger than Kalisha, and right now Avery was . . . well . . . *broadcasting*.

"You can stay." But when Avery started to get into bed: "Nuh-uh, you need to go to the bathroom first. You're not peeing in my bed."

Avery didn't argue, and Luke soon heard urine splattering in the bowl. Quite a lot of it. When Avery came back, Luke turned off the light. Avery snuggled up. It was nice not to be alone. Wonderful, in fact.

In his ear, Avery whispered, "I'm sorry about your mumma and your daddy, Luke."

For a few moments Luke couldn't speak. When he

could, he whispered back, "Were you and Kalisha talking about me yesterday on the playground?"

"Yes. She told me to come. She said she would send you letters, and I would be the mailman. You can tell George and Helen, if you think it's safe."

But he wouldn't, because nothing here was safe. Not even thinking was safe. He replayed what he'd said when Kalisha was telling him about Nicky fighting the red caretakers from Back Half: *Knocked it out of his hand.* Meaning one of the zap-sticks. She hadn't asked Luke how he knew that, because she almost certainly knew already. Had he thought he could keep his new TP ability a secret from her? Maybe from the others, but not from Kalisha. And not from Avery.

"Look!" Avery whispered.

Luke could look at nothing, with the lamp off and no window to admit ambient light from outside, the room was completely dark, but he looked anyway, and thought he saw Kalisha.

"Is she all right?" Luke whispered.

"Yes. For now."

"Is Nicky there? Is he all right?"

"Yes," Avery whispered. "Iris, too. Only she gets headaches. Other kids do, too. Sha thinks they get them from the movies. And the dots."

"What movies?"

"I don't know, Sha hasn't seen any yet, but Nicky has. Iris, too. Kalisha says she thinks there are other kids—like maybe in the back half of Back Half—but only a few in the place where they are right now. Jimmy and Len. Also Donna."

I got Donna's computer, Luke thought. Inherited it.

"Bobby Washington was there at first, but now he's gone. Iris told Kalisha she saw him."

"I don't know those kids."

"Kalisha says Donna went to Back Half just a couple of days before you came. That's why you got her computer."

"You're eerie," Luke said.

Avery, who probably knew he was eerie, ignored this. "They get hurty shots. Shots and dots, dots and shots. Sha says she thinks bad things happen in Back Half. She says maybe you can do something. She says . . ."

He didn't finish, and didn't have to. Luke had a brief but blindingly clear image, surely sent from Kalisha Benson by way of Avery Dixon: a canary in a cage. The door swung open and the canary flew out.

"She says you're the only one who's smart enough."

"I will if I can," Luke said. "What else did she tell you?"

To this there was no answer. Avery had gone to sleep.

ESCAPE

1

Three weeks passed.

Luke ate. He slept, woke, ate again. He soon memo-
rized the menu, and joined the other kids in sarcastic
applause when something on it changed. Some days
there were tests. Some days there were shots. Some days
there were both. Some days there were neither. A few
shots made him sick. Most didn't. His throat never
closed up again, for which he was grateful. He hung
out in the playground. He watched TV, making friends
with Oprah, Ellen, Dr. Phil, Judge Judy. He watched
YouTube videos of cats looking at themselves in mirrors
and dogs that caught Frisbees. Sometimes he watched
alone, sometimes with some of the other kids. When
Harry came into his room, the twins came with him
and demanded cartoons. When Luke went to Harry's
room, the twins were almost always there. Harry didn't
care for cartoons. Harry was partial to wrestling, cage
fighting videos, and NASCAR pile-ups. His usual
greeting to Luke was "Watch this one." The twins were
coloring fools, the caretakers supplying endless stacks
of coloring books. Usually they stayed inside the lines,
but there was one day when they didn't, and laughed a

lot, and Luke deduced they were either drunk or high. When he asked Harry, Harry said they wanted to try it. He had the good grace to look ashamed, and when they vomited (in tandem, as they did everything), he had the good grace to look more ashamed. And he cleaned up the mess. One day Helen did a triple roll on the trampoline, laughed, bowed, then burst into tears and would not be consoled. When Luke tried, she hit him with her small fists, whap-whap-whap-whap. For awhile Luke beat all comers at chess, and when that got boring he found ways to lose, which was surprisingly hard for him.

He felt like he was sleeping even when he was awake. He felt his IQ declining, absolutely felt it, like water going down in a water cooler because someone had left the tap open. He marked off the time of this strange summer with the date strip on his computer. Other than YouTube vids, he only used his laptop— with one significant exception—to IM with George or Helen in their rooms. He never initiated those conversations, and kept them as brief as he could.

What the shit is wrong with you? Helen texted once.

Nothing, he texted back.

Why are we still in Front Half, do you think? George texted. Not that I am complaining.

Don't know, Luke texted, and signed off.

He discovered it wasn't hard to hide his grief from the caretakers, techs, and doctors; they were used to dealing with depressed children. Yet even in his deep unhappiness, he sometimes thought of the bright image Avery had projected: a canary flying from its cage.

His waking sleep of grief was sometimes pierced with brilliant slices of memory that always came unexpectedly: his father spraying him with the garden hose;

his father making a foul shot with his back turned to the hoop and Luke tackling him when it went in and both of them falling on the grass, laughing; his mother bringing a gigantic cupcake covered with flaming candles to the table on his twelfth birthday; his mother hugging him and saying *You're getting so big*; his mother and father dancing like crazy in the kitchen while Rihanna sang "Pon de Replay." These memories were beautiful, and they stung like nettles.

When he wasn't thinking of the *slain Falcon Heights couple*—dreaming of them—Luke thought of the cage he was in and the free bird he aspired to be. Those were the only times when his mind regained its former sharp focus. He noticed things that seemed to confirm his belief that the Institute was operating in an inertial glide, like a rocket that switches off its engines once escape velocity has been attained. The black-glass surveillance bulbs in the hallway ceilings, for instance. Most of them were dirty, as if they hadn't been cleaned in a long time. This was especially true in the deserted West Wing of the residence floor. The cameras inside the bulbs probably still worked, but the view they gave would be blurry at best. Even so, it seemed that no orders had come down for Fred and his fellow janitors—Mort, Connie, Jawed—to clean them, and that meant whoever was supposed to monitor the hallways didn't give much of a shit if the view had grown murky.

Luke went about his days with his head down, doing what he was told without argument, but when he wasn't zoned out in his room, he had become a little pitcher with big ears. Most of what he heard was useless, but he took it all in, anyway. Took it in and stored it away. Gossip, for instance. Like how Dr. Evans was always chasing after Dr. Richardson, trying to strike up conversations, too pussy-stunned (this phrase from caretaker Norma) to know Felicia Richardson wouldn't touch him with a ten-foot pole. Like how Joe and two other caretakers, Chad and Gary, sometimes used the tokens they didn't give away to get wine nips and those little bottles of hard lemonade from the canteen vending machine in the East Lounge. Sometimes they talked about their families, or about drinking at a bar called Outlaw Country, where there were bands. "If you want to call that music," Luke once overheard a caretaker named Sherry telling Fake Smile Gladys. This bar, known to the male techs and caretakers as The Cunt, was in a town called Dennison River Bend. Luke could get no clear fix on how far away this town was, but thought it must be within twenty-five miles, thirty at most, because they all seemed to go when they had time off.

Luke tucked away names when he heard them. Dr. Evans was James, Dr. Hendricks was Dan, Tony was Fizzale, Gladys was Hickson, Zeke was Ionidis. If he ever got out of here, if this canary ever flew from its cage, he hoped to have quite a list for when he testified against these assholes in a court of law. He realized that might only be a fantasy, but it kept him going.

Now that he was marching through the days like a good little boy, he was sometimes left alone on C-Level for short periods of time, always with the admonition to stay put. He would nod, give the technician time to depart on his errand, and then leave himself. There were plenty of cameras on the lower levels, and these were all kept nice and clean, but no alarms went off and no caretakers came charging down the hall waving their zap-sticks. Twice he was spotted walking around and brought back, once with a scolding and once with a perfunctory slap to the back of his neck.

On one of these expeditions (he always tried to look bored and aimless, a kid just passing the time before the next test or being allowed to go back to his room), Luke found a treasure. In the MRI room, which was empty that day, he spied one of the cards they used to operate the elevator lying half-hidden under a computer monitor. He walked past the table, picked it up, and slipped it in his pocket as he peered into the empty MRI tube. He almost expected the card to start yelling "Thief, thief" when he left the room (like the magic harp Jack the beanstalk boy stole from the giant), but nothing happened, then or later. Didn't they keep track of those cards? It seemed they did not. Or maybe it was expired, as useless as a hotel key card when the guest it had been computer-coded for checked out.

But when Luke tried the card in the elevator a day later, he was delighted to find it worked. When Dr. Richardson came across him a day later, peering into the D-Level room where the immersion tank was kept, he expected punishment—maybe a jolt from the zap-stick she kept holstered under the white coat she usually wore, maybe a beating from Tony or Zeke. Instead, she actually slipped him a token, for which he thanked her.

"I haven't had that one yet," Luke said, pointing to the tank. "Is it awful?"

"No, it's fun," she said, and Luke gave her a big grin, as if he actually believed her bullshit. "Now what are you doing down here?"

"Caught a ride with one of the caretakers. I don't know which one. He forgot his nametag, I guess."

"That's good," she said. "If you knew his name, I'd have to report him, and he'd get in trouble. After that? Paperwork, paperwork, paperwork." She rolled her eyes and Luke gave her a look that said *I sympathize*. She took him back to the elevator, asked him where he was supposed to be, and he told her B-Level. She rode up with him, asked him how his pain was, and he told her it was fine, all gone.

The card also took him to E-Level, where there was a lot of mechanical shit, but when he tried to go lower—there *was* a lower, he'd heard conversations about levels F and G—Miss Elevator Voice pleasantly informed him that access was denied. Which was okay. You learned by trying.

There were no paper tests in Front Half, but there were plenty of EEGs. Sometimes Dr. Evans did kids in bunches, but not always. Once, when Luke was being tested alone, Dr. Evans suddenly grimaced, put a hand to his stomach, and said he'd be right back. He told Luke not to touch anything and rushed out. To drop a load, Luke presumed.

He examined the computer screens, ran his fingers over a couple of keyboards, thought about messing with them a little, decided it would be a bad idea, and went to the door instead. He looked out just as the elevator opened and the big bald guy emerged, wearing the same expensive brown suit. Or maybe it was another one. For all Luke knew, Stackhouse had a whole closetful of expensive brown suits. He had a sheaf of papers in his hand. He started down the hall, shuffling through them, and Luke withdrew quickly. C-4, the room with the EEG and EKG machines, had a small equipment alcove lined with shelves full of various supplies. Luke went in there without knowing if hiding was an ordinary hunch, one of his new TP brainwaves, or plain old paranoia. In any case, he was just in time. Stackhouse poked his head in, glanced around, then left. Luke waited to be sure he wasn't going to come back, then resumed his seat next to the EEG machine.

Two or three minutes later, Evans hurried in with his white lab coat flying out behind him. His cheeks were flushed and his eyes were wide. He grabbed Luke by the shirt. "What did Stackhouse say when he saw you in here by yourself? Tell me!"

"He didn't say anything because he didn't see me. I was looking out the door for you, and when Mr. Stack-house got off the elevator, I went in there." He pointed at the equipment alcove, then looked up at Evans with wide, innocent eyes. "I didn't want to get you in any trouble."

"Good boy," Evans said, and clapped him on the back. "I had a call of nature, and I felt sure you could be trusted. Now let's get this test done, shall we? Then you can go upstairs and play with your friends."

Before calling Yolanda, another caretaker (last name: Freeman), to escort him back to A-Level, Evans gave Luke a dozen tokens and another hearty clap on the back. "Our little secret, right?"

"Right," Luke said.

He actually thinks I like him, Luke marveled. How does *that* fry your bacon? Wait'll I tell George.

2

Only he never did. There were two new kids at supper that evening, and one old one missing. George had been taken away, for all Luke knew while he himself was hiding from Stackhouse in the equipment alcove.

"He's with the others," Avery whispered to Luke that night as they lay in bed. "Sha says he's crying because he's scared. She told him that was normal. She told him they're all scared."

3

Two or three times on his expeditions, Luke stopped outside the B-Level lounge, where the conversations were interesting and illuminating. Staff used the room, but so did outside groups that sometimes arrived still carrying travel bags that had no airline luggage tickets on their handles. When they saw Luke—maybe getting a drink from the nearby water fountain, maybe pretending to read a poster on hygiene—most looked right through him, as if he were no more than part of the furniture. The people making up these groups had a hard look about them, and Luke became increasingly sure they were the Institute's hunter-gatherers. It made sense, because there were more kids in West Wing now. Once Luke overheard Joe telling Hadad—the two of them were goodbuddies—that the Institute was like the beachfront town in Long Island where he'd grown up. "Sometimes the tide's in," he said, "sometimes it's out."

"More often out these days," Hadad replied, and maybe it was true, but as that July wore on, it was definitely coming in.

Some of the outside groups were trios, some were

quartets. Luke associated them with the military, maybe only because the men all had short hair and the women wore theirs pulled tight to the skull and bunned in back. He heard an orderly refer to one of these groups as Emerald. A tech called another Ruby Red. This latter group was a trio, two women and a man. He knew that Ruby Red was the group that had come to Minneapolis to kill his parents and snatch him away. He tried for their names, listening with his mind as well as his ears, and got only one: the woman who had sprayed something in his face on his last night in Falcon Heights was Michelle. When she saw him in the hall, leaning over the drinking fountain, her eyes swept past him . . . then came back for a moment or two.

Michelle.

Another name to remember.

It didn't take long for Luke to get confirmation of his theory that these were the people tasked with bringing in fresh TPs and TKs. The Emerald group was in the break room, and as Luke stood outside, reading that poster on hygiene for the dozenth time, he heard one of the Emerald men saying they had to go back out to make a quick pickup in Missouri. The next day a bewildered fourteen-year-old girl named Frieda Brown joined their growing West Wing group.

"I don't belong here," she told Luke. "It's a mistake."

"Wouldn't that be nice," Luke replied, then told her how she could get tokens. He wasn't sure she was taking it in, but she'd catch on eventually. Everyone did.

4

No one seemed to mind Avery sleeping in Luke's room almost every night. He was the mailman, and to Luke he brought letters from Kalisha in Back Half, missives that came via telepathy rather than USPS. The fact of his parents' murder was still too fresh and hurtful for these letters to wake Luke from his half-dreaming state, but the news they contained was disturbing, all the same. It was also enlightening, although it was enlightenment Luke could have done without. In Front Half, kids were tested and punished for misbehavior; in Back Half they were being put to work. Used. And, it seemed, destroyed, little by little.

The movies brought on the headaches, and the headaches lasted longer and got worse after each one. George was fine when he arrived, just scared, according to Kalisha, but after four or five days of exposure to the dots, and the movies, and the hurty shots, he also began to have headaches.

The movies were in a small screening room with plushy comfortable seats. They started with old-time cartoons—sometimes Road Runner, sometimes Bugs Bunny, sometimes Goofy and Mickey. Then, after the warm-up, came the real show. Kalisha thought the films were short, half an hour at most, but it was hard to tell because she was woozy during and headachey afterward. They all were.

Her first two times in the screening room, the Back Half kids got a double feature. The star of the first one was a man with thinning red hair. He wore a black suit and drove a shiny black car. Avery tried to show this car to Luke, but Luke got only a vague image, maybe because that was all Kalisha could send. Still, he thought it must be a limousine or a Town Car, because Avery said the red-haired man's passengers always rode in the back. Also, the guy opened the doors for the passengers when they got in and out. On most days he had the same ones, mostly old white guys, but one was a younger guy with a scar on his cheek.

"Sha says he has regulars," Avery whispered as he and Luke lay in bed together. "She says it's Washington, D.C., because the man drives past the Capitol and the White House and sometimes she sees that big stone needle."

"The Washington Monument."

"Yeah, that."

Toward the end of this movie, the redhead swapped the black suit for regular clothes. They saw him riding a horse, then pushing a little girl on a swing, then eating ice cream with the little girl on a park bench. After that Dr. Hendricks came on the screen, holding up an unlit Fourth of July sparkler.

The second feature was of a man in what Kalisha called an Arab headdress, which probably meant a keffiyeh. He was in a street, then he was in an outdoor café drinking tea or coffee from a glass, then he was making a speech, then he was swinging a little boy by the hands. Once he was on television. The movie ended with Dr. Hendricks holding up the unlit sparkler.

The following morning, Sha and the others got a Sylvester and Tweety cartoon followed by fifteen or twenty minutes of the red-haired car driver. Then lunch in the Back Half cafeteria, where there were free cigarettes. That afternoon it was Porky Pig followed by the Arab. Each film ended with Dr. Hendricks and the unlit sparkler. That night they were given hurty shots and a fresh dose of the flashing lights. Then they were taken back to the screening room, where they watched twenty minutes of car crash movies. After each crash, Dr. Hendricks came on the screen, holding up the unlit sparkler.

Luke, grief-stricken but not stupid, began to understand. It was crazy, but no crazier than occasionally being able to know what was going on in other peoples' heads. Also, it explained a great deal.

"Kalisha says she thinks she blacked out and had a dream while the crashes were going on," Avery whispered in Luke's ear. "Only she's not sure it was a dream. She says the kids—her, Nicky, Iris, Donna, Len, some others—were standing in those dots with their arms around each other and their heads together. She says Dr. Hendricks was there, and this time he lit the sparkler, and that was scary. But as long as they stayed together, holding each other, their heads didn't ache no more. But she says maybe it *was* a dream, because she woke up in her room. The rooms in Back Half aren't like ours. They get locked up at night." Avery paused. "I don't want to talk about this anymore tonight, Lukey."

"Fine. Go to sleep."

Avery did, but Luke lay awake for a long time.

The next day, he finally used his laptop for something more than checking the date, IMing with Helen, or watching *BoJack Horseman*. He went to Mr. Griffin, and from Mr. Griffin to the *New York Times*, which informed him he could read ten free articles before he hit a pay wall. Luke didn't know exactly what he was looking for, but was sure he'd know it when he saw it. And he did. A headline on the front page of the July

15th issue read **REPRESENTATIVE BERKOWITZ SUCCUMBS TO INJURIES**.

Rather than reading the article, Luke went to the day before. This headline read **PRESIDENTIAL HOPEFUL MARK BERKOWITZ CRITICALLY INJURED IN CAR ACCIDENT**. There was a picture. Berkowitz, a US Representative from Ohio, had black hair and a scar on his cheek from a wound suffered in Afghanistan. Luke read the story quickly. It said that the Lincoln Town Car in which Berkowitz had been riding while on his way to a meeting with foreign dignitaries from Poland and Yugoslavia had veered out of control and hit a concrete bridge stanchion. The driver had been killed instantly; unnamed MedStar Hospital sources described Berkowitz's injuries as "extremely grave." The article didn't say if the driver was a redhead, but Luke knew he had been, and he was pretty sure that some guy in one of the Arab countries was going to die soon, if he hadn't already. Or maybe he was going to murder somebody important.

Luke's growing certainty that he and the other kids were being prepped for use as psychic drones—yes, even inoffensive Avery Dixon, who wouldn't say boo to a goose—began to rouse Luke, but it took the horror show with Harry Cross to bring him fully out of his sleep of grief.

5

The following evening there were fourteen or fifteen kids in the caff at dinner, some talking, some laughing, some of the new ones crying or shouting. In a way,

Luke thought, being in the Institute was like being in an old-time mental asylum where the crazy people were just kept and never cured.

Harry wasn't there at first, and he hadn't been at lunch. The big galoot wasn't much of a blip on Luke's radar, but he was hard to miss at meals because Gerda and Greta always sat with him, one on either side in their identical outfits, watching him with shining eyes as he blathered away about NASCAR, wrestling, his favorite shows, and life "down Selma." If someone told him to pipe down, the little Gs would turn killing looks on the interrupting someone.

This evening the Gs were eating on their own, and looking unhappy about it. They had saved Harry a seat between them, though, and when he came walking slowly in, belly swinging and glowing with sunburn, they rushed to him with shouts of greeting. For once he barely seemed to notice them. There was a vacant look in his eyes, and they didn't seem to be tracking together the way eyes are supposed to. His chin was shiny with drool, and there was a wet spot on the crotch of his pants. Conversation died. The newest arrivals looked puzzled and horrified; those who had been around long enough to get a run of tests threw worried glances at each other.

Luke and Helen exchanged a look. "He'll be okay," she said. "It's just worse for some kids than it is for—"

Avery was sitting beside her. Now he took one of her hands in both of his. He spoke with eerie calmness. "He's not okay. He'll never be okay."

Harry let out a cry, dropped to his knees, then hit the floor face-first. His nose and lips sprayed blood on the linoleum. He first began to shake, then to spasm, legs pulling up and shooting out in a Y shape, arms flailing. He started to make a growling noise—not like an animal but like an engine stuck in low gear and being revved too hard. He flopped onto his back, still growling and spraying bloody foam from between his blabbering lips. His teeth chomped up and down.

The little Gs began shrieking. As Gladys ran in from the hall and Norma from around the steam table, one of the twins knelt and tried to hug Harry. His big right hand rose, swung out, came whistling back. It struck her on the side of her face with terrible force, and sent her flying. Her head struck the wall with a thud. The other twin ran to her sister, screaming.

The cafeteria was in an uproar. Luke and Helen stayed seated, Helen with her arm around Avery's shoulders (more to comfort herself than the little boy, it seemed; Avery appeared unmoved), but many of the other kids were gathering around the seizing boy. Gladys shoved a couple of them away and snarled, "Get back, you idiots!" No big fake smile tonight for the big G.

Now more Institute personnel were appearing: Joe and Hadad, Chad, Carlos, a couple Luke didn't know, including one still in his civvies who must have just come on duty. Harry's body was rising and falling in galvanic leaps, as if the floor had been electrified. Chad and Carlos pinned his arms. Hadad zapped him in the solar plexus, and when that didn't stop the seizures, Joe hit him in the neck, the crackle of a zap-stick set on high audible even in the babble of confused voices. Harry went limp. His eyes bulged beneath half-closed lids. Foam drizzled from the corners of his mouth. The tip of his tongue protruded.

"He's all right, situation under control!" Hadad bellowed. "Go back to your tables! He's fine!"

The kids drew away, silent now, watching. Luke leaned over to Helen and spoke in a low voice. "I don't think he's breathing."

"Maybe he is and maybe he isn't," Helen said, "but look at that one." She pointed to the twin who had been driven to the wall. Luke saw that the little girl's eyes were glazed and her head looked all crooked on her neck. Blood was running down one of her cheeks and dripping onto the shoulder of her dress.

"*Wake up!*" the other twin was shouting, and began to shake her. Silverware flew from the tables in a storm; kids and caretakers ducked. "*Wake up, Harry didn't mean to hurt you, wake up, WAKE UP!*"

"Which one is which?" Luke asked Helen, but it was Avery who replied, and in that same eerily calm voice.

"The screamy one throwing the silverware is Gerda. The dead one is Greta."

"She's not dead," Helen said in a shocked voice. "She *can't* be."

Knives, forks, and spoons rose to the ceiling (I could never do anything like that, Luke thought) and then fell with a clatter.

"She is, though," Avery said matter-of-factly. "So is Harry." He stood up, holding one of Helen's hands and one of Luke's. "I liked Harry even if he did push me down. I'm not hungry anymore." He looked from one to the other. "And neither are you guys."

The three of them left unnoticed, giving the screaming twin and her dead sister a wide berth. Dr. Evans came striding up the hall from the elevator, looking harried and put out. Probably he was eating his dinner, Luke thought.

Behind them, Carlos was calling, "Everyone's fine,

you guys! Settle down and finish your dinner, everyone's just fine!"

"The dots killed him," Avery said. "Dr. Hendricks
and Dr. Evans never should have showed him the dots
even if he was a pink. Maybe his BDNF was still too
high. Or maybe it was something else, like a allergy."

"What's BDNF?" Helen asked.

"I don't know. I only know that if kids have a really
high one, they shouldn't get the big shots until Back
Half."

"What about you?" Helen asked, turning to Luke.

Luke shook his head. Kalisha mentioned it once,
and he had heard the initials bandied about on a couple
of his wandering expeditions. He'd thought about
googling BDNF, but was wary it might set off an
alarm.

"You've never had them, have you?" Luke asked
Avery. "The big shots? The special tests?"

"No. But I will. In Back Half." He looked at Luke
solemnly. "Dr. Evans might get in trouble for what he
did to Harry. I hope he does. I'm scared to death of the
lights. And the big shots. The *powerful* shots."

"Me too," Helen said. "The shots I've gotten already are bad enough."

Luke thought of telling Helen and Avery about the
shot that had made his throat close up, or the two that
had made him vomit (seeing those goddamned dots
each time he heaved), but it seemed like pretty small
beans compared to what had just happened to Harry.

"Make way, you guys," Joe said.

They stood against the wall near the poster saying
I CHOOSE TO BE HAPPY. Joe and Hadad passed
them with Harry Cross's body. Carlos had the little
girl with the broken neck. It lolled back and forth over

his arm, her hair hanging down. Luke, Helen, and Avery watched them until they got into the elevator, and Luke found himself wondering if the morgue was on E-Level or F.

"She looked like a doll," Luke heard himself say. "She looked like her own doll."

Avery, whose eerie, sybilline calm had actually been shock, began to cry.

"I'm going to my room," Helen said. She patted Luke on the shoulder and kissed Avery on the cheek. "See you guys tomorrow."

Only they didn't. The blue caretakers came for her in the night and they saw her no more.

6

Avery urinated, brushed his teeth, dressed in the pj's he now kept in Luke's room, and got into Luke's bed. Luke did his own bathroom business, got in with the Avester, and turned out the light. He put his forehead against Avery's and whispered, "I have to get out of here."

How?

Not a spoken word but one that briefly lit up in his mind and then faded away. Luke was getting a little better at catching these thoughts now, but he could only do it when Avery was close, and sometimes still couldn't do it at all. The dots—what Avery said were the Stasi Lights—had given him some TP, but not much. Just like his TK had never been much. His IQ might be over the moon, but in terms of psychic ability, he was a dope. *I could use some more,* he thought, and one of his grandfather's old sayings occurred to him:

wish in one hand, shit in the other, see which one fills up first.

"I don't know," Luke said. What he did know was that he had been here a long time—longer than Helen, and she was gone. They would come for him soon.

7

In the middle of the night, Avery shook Luke out of a dream about Greta Wilcox—Greta lying against the wall with her head all wrong on her neck. This was not a dream he was sorry to leave. The Avester was huddled up against him, all knees and sharp elbows, shivering like a dog caught in a thunderstorm. Luke turned on the bedside lamp. Avery's eyes were swimming with tears.

"What's wrong?" Luke asked. "Bad dream?"

"No. *They* woke me up."

"Who?" Luke looked around, but the room was empty and the door was shut.

"Sha. And Iris."

"You can hear Iris as well as Kalisha?" This was new.

"I couldn't before, but . . . they had the movies, then they had the dots, then they had the sparkler, then they had their group hug with their heads together, I told you about that—"

"Yes."

"Usually it's better afterward, the headaches go away for awhile, but Iris's came back as soon as the hug was over and it was so bad she started screaming and wouldn't stop." Avery's voice rose beyond its usual treble, wavering in a way that made Luke feel cold all over. " 'My head, my head, it's splitting open, oh my poor head, make it stop, somebody make it st—' "

Luke gave Avery a hard shake. "Lower your voice. They might be listening."

Avery took several deep breaths. "I wish you could hear me inside your head, like Sha. I could tell you everything then. Telling out loud is hard for me."

"Try."

"Sha and Nicky tried to comfort her, but they couldn't. She scratched at Sha and tried to punch Nicky. Then Dr. Hendricks came—he was still in his pajamas—and he called for the red guys. They were going to take Iris away."

"To the back half of Back Half?"

"I think so. But then she started to get better."

"Maybe they gave her a painkiller. Or a sedative."

"I don't think so. I think she just got better. Maybe Kalisha helped her?"

"Don't ask me," Luke said. "How would I know?"

But Avery wasn't listening. "There's a way to help, maybe. A way they can . . ." He trailed off. Luke thought he was going back to sleep. Then Avery stirred and said, "There's something really bad over there."

"It's all bad over there," Luke said. "The movies, the shots, the dots . . . all bad."

"Yeah, but it's something else. Something worse. Like . . . I dunno . . ."

Luke put his forehead against Avery's and listened as hard as he could. What he picked up was the sound of an airplane passing far overhead. "A sound? Kind of a droning sound?"

"Yes! But not like an airplane. More like a hive of bees. It's the hum. I think it comes from the back half of Back Half."

Avery shifted in the bed. In the light of the lamp, he no longer looked like a child; he looked like a worried old man. "The headaches get worse and worse and last longer and longer, because they won't stop making them look at the dots . . . you know, the lights . . . and they won't stop giving them the shots and making them watch the movies."

"And the sparkler," Luke said. "They have to look at that, because it's the trigger."

"What do you mean?"

"Nothing. Go to sleep."

"I don't think I can."

"Try."

Luke put his arms around Avery, and looked up at the ceiling. He was thinking of a bluesy old song his mother sometimes used to sing: *I was yours from the start, you took my heart. You got the best, so what the hell, come on, baby, take the rest.*

Luke was increasingly sure that was exactly what they were there for: To have the best taken away. They were weaponized here, and used there until they were emptied out. Then they went to the back half of Back Half, where they joined the drone . . . whatever *that* was.

Things like that don't happen, he told himself. Except people would say things like the Institute didn't happen, either, certainly not in America, and if they did, word would get out because you couldn't keep anything a secret these days; everyone blabbed. Yet here he was. Here *they* were. The thought of Harry Cross seizing and foaming at the mouth on the cafeteria floor was awful, the sight of that harmless little girl with her head on crooked and her glazed eyes staring at nothing was worse, but nothing he could think of was as terrible as minds subjected to constant assault until they finally became part of a hive drone. According to the Avester that had almost happened to Iris tonight, and it would soon happen to Nicky, heartthrob of all the girls, and wisecracking George.

And Kalisha.

Luke finally slept. When he woke, breakfast was long over and he was alone in the bed. Luke ran down the hall and burst into Avery's room, sure of what he would find, but the Avester's posters were still on the walls and his G.I. Joes were still on the bureau, this morning in a skirmish line.

Luke breathed a sigh of relief, then cringed when he was slapped across the back of the head. He turned and saw Winona (last name: Briggs). "Put on some clothes, young man. I'm not interested in seeing any male in his undies unless he's at least twenty-two and buffed out. You're not either one."

She waited for him to get going. Luke gave her the finger (okay, so he held it hidden against his chest instead of flashing it, but it still felt good) and returned to his room to dress. Far down the hall, where it met the next corridor, he saw a Dandux laundry basket. It could have belonged to Jolene or one of the other housekeepers who had appeared to help deal with the current influx of "guests," but he knew it was Maureen's. He could feel her. She was back.

8

When he saw her fifteen minutes later, Luke thought, This woman is sicker than ever.

She was cleaning out the twins' room, taking down

the posters of Disney princes and princesses and putting them carefully in a cardboard box. The little Gs' beds had already been stripped, the sheets piled in Maureen's basket with the other dirty laundry she had collected.

"Where's Gerda?" Luke asked. He also wondered where Greta and Harry were, not to mention any others who might have died as a result of their bullshit experiments. Was there perhaps a crematorium somewhere in this hole of hell? Maybe way down on F-Level? If so, it must have state-of-the-art filters, or he would have smelled the smoke of burning children.

"Ask me no questions and I'll tell you no lies. Get out of here, boy, and go about your business." Her voice was brisk and dry, dismissive, but all that was show. Even low-grade telepathy could be useful.

Luke got an apple from the bowl of fruit in the caff, and a pack of Round-Ups (SMOKE JUST LIKE DADDY) from one of the vending machines. The pack of candy cigarettes made him miss Kalisha, but it also made him feel close to her. He peeked out at the playground, where eight or ten kids were using the equipment—a full house, compared to when Luke himself had come in. Avery was sitting on one of the pads surrounding the trampoline, his head on his chest, his eyes closed, fast asleep. Luke wasn't surprised. Little shit had had a tough night.

Someone thumped his shoulder, hard but not in an unfriendly way. Luke turned and saw Stevie Whipple— one of the new kids. "Man, that was bad last night," Stevie said. "You know, the big redhead and that little girl."

"Tell me about it."

"Then this morning those guys in the red unis came and took that punk-rock girl to Back Half."

Luke looked at Stevie in silent dismay. "Helen?"

"Yeah, her. This place sucks," Stevie said, staring out at the playground. "I wish I had, like, jet-boots. I'd be gone so fast it'd make your head spin."

"Jet-boots and a bomb," Luke said.

"Huh?"

"Bomb the motherfucker, *then* fly away."

Stevie considered this, his moon face going slack, then laughed. "That's good. Yeah, bomb it flat and then jet-boot the hell outta here. Hey, you ain't got an extra token, do you? I get hungry this time of day and I ain't much on apples. I'm more of a Twix man. Or Funyuns. Funyuns are good."

Luke, who'd gotten many tokens while burnishing his good-boy image, gave Stevie Whipple three and told him to knock himself out.

9

Remembering the first time he'd set eyes on Kalisha, and perhaps to commemorate the occasion, Luke went inside, sat down next to the ice machine, and put one of the candy cigarettes in his mouth. He was on his second Round-Up when Maureen came trundling along with her basket, now filled with fresh sheets and pillowcases.

"How's your back?" Luke asked her.

"Worse than ever."

"Sorry. That sucks."

"I got my pills. They help." She leaned over and grasped her shins, which put her face near Luke's.

He whispered, "They took my friend Kalisha. Nicky and George. Helen, just today." Most of his friends were gone. And who had become the Institute's long-timer? Why, nobody but Luke Ellis.

"I know." She was also whispering. "I been in Back Half. We can't keep meeting here and talking, Luke. They'll get suspicious."

This seemed to make sense, but there was something odd about it, just the same. Like Joe and Hadad, Maureen talked to the kids all the time, and gave them tokens when she had them to give. And weren't there other places, dead zones, where the audio surveillance didn't work? Certainly Kalisha had thought so.

Maureen stood up and stretched, bracing her hands against the small of her back. She spoke in a normal voice now. "Are you just going to sit there all day?"

Luke sucked in the candy cigarette currently dangling from his lower lip, crunched it up, and got to his feet.

"Wait, here's a token." She pulled it from the pocket of her dress and handed it to him. "Use it for something tasty."

Luke ambled back to his room and sprawled on his bed. He curled up and unfolded the tight square of note-paper she had given him along with the token. Maureen's hand was shaky and old-fashioned, but that was only part of the reason it was hard to read. The writing was *small*. She had packed the whole sheet from side to side, top to bottom, all of one side and part of the other. It made Luke think of something Mr. Sirois had said in English class, about Ernest Hemingway's best short stories: *They are miracles of compression.* That was true of this communique. How many drafts had it taken her to boil down what she had to tell him to these essentials, written on one small piece of paper? He admired her brevity even as he began to

understand what Maureen had been doing. What she
was.

> Luke, <u>You have to get rid of this Note after you read
> it</u>. It is like God sent you to me as a Last Chance to
> atone for some of the Wrongs I have done. I talked
> to Leah Fink in Burlington. Everything you said
> was True and everything is going to be All Right
> w/ the money I owe. Not so All Right w/ me, as
> my back pain is what I feared. BUT now that the
> $$$ I put away is safe, I "cashed out." There is a
> way to get it to my Son, so he can go to College. He
> will never know it came from me & that is the way
> I want it. <u>I owe you so much!!</u> Luke you have to get
> out of here. You will go to Back Half soon. You are
> a "pink" and when they stop testing, you might only
> have 3 days. I have something to give you and much
> Important Things to tell you but dont know how, only
> Ice Machine is safe & we have been there Too Much. I
> dont care for me but dont want you to lose your Only
> Chance. I wish I hadnt done what I have done or had
> never seen this Place. I was thinking of the child I
> gave up but that is no Excuse. Too late now. I wish
> our Talk didnt have to be at Ice Machine but may
> have to risk it. PLEASE get rid of this note Luke
> and BE CAREFUL, not for me, my life will be over
> soon, but for you. THANK YOU FOR HELPING
> ME. Maureen A.

So Maureen was a snitch, listening to kids in places
that were supposed to be safe, then running to Sigsby
(or Stackhouse) with little bits of info given to her in
whispers. She might not be the only one, either; the
two friendly caretakers, Joe and Hadad, might also be

snitching. In June, Luke would have hated her for this, but now it was July, and he was much older.

He went into the bathroom and dropped Maureen's note into the john when he lowered his pants, just as he'd done with Kalisha's. That seemed like a hundred years ago.

10

That afternoon, Stevie Whipple got up a game of dodgeball. Most of the kids played, but Luke declined. He went to the games cabinet for the chessboard (in memory of Nicky) and replayed what many considered the best game ever, Yakov Estrin versus Hans Berliner, Copenhagen, 1965. Forty-two moves, a classic. He went back and forth, white-black, white-black, white-black, his memory doing the work while most of his mind remained on Maureen's note.

He hated the thought of Maureen snitching, but understood her reasons. There were other people here with at least some shreds of decency left, but working in a place like this destroyed your moral compass. They were damned, whether they knew it or not. Maureen might be, too. The only thing that mattered now was whether or not she really knew a way he might be able to get out of here. To do that she needed to give him information without arousing the suspicions of Mrs. Sigsby and that guy Stackhouse (first name: Trevor). There was also the corollary question of whether or not she could be trusted. Luke thought she could. Not just because he had helped her in her time of need, but because the note had a desperate quality, the feel of a woman who had decided to bet all her chips on one turn of the wheel. Besides, what choice did he have?

Avery was one of the dodgers running around inside the circle, and now someone bonked him right in the face with the ball. He sat down and began to cry. Stevie Whipple helped him to his feet and examined his nose. "No blood, you're okay. Why don't you go over there and sit with Luke?"

"Out of the game is what you mean," Avery said, still sniffling. "That's okay. I can still—"

"Avery!" Luke called. He held up a couple of tokens. "You want some peanut butter crackers and a Coke?"

Avery trotted over, smack in the face forgotten. "Sure!"

They went inside to the canteen. Avery dropped a token into the snack machine slot, and when he bent over to fish the package from the tray, Luke bent over with him and whispered in his ear. "You want to help me get out of here?"

Avery held up the package of Nabs. "Want one?" And in Luke's mind, the word lit up and faded: *How?*

"I'll just take one, you have the rest," Luke said, and sent back three words: *Tell you tonight.*

Two conversations going on, one aloud, one between their minds. And that was how it would work with Maureen.

He hoped.

11

After breakfast the next day, Gladys and Hadad took Luke down to the immersion tank. There they left him with Zeke and Dave.

Zeke Iōnidis said, "We do tests here, but it's also where we dunk bad boys and girls who don't tell the truth. Do you tell the truth, Luke?"

"Yes," Luke said.

"Have you got the telep?"

"The what?" Knowing perfectly well what Zeke the Freak meant.

"The telep. The TP. You got it?"

"No. I'm TK, remember? Move spoons and stuff?" He tried a smile. "Can't bend them, though. I've tried."

Zeke shook his head. "If you're TK and see the dots, you get the telep. You're TP and see the dots, you move the spoons. That's how it works."

You don't know how it works, Luke thought. None of you do. He remembered someone—maybe Kalisha, maybe George—telling him they'd know if he lied about seeing the dots. He guessed that was true, maybe the EEG readings showed them, but did they know this? They did not. Zeke was bluffing.

"I *have* seen the dots a couple of times, but I can't read minds."

"Hendricks and Evans think you can," Dave said.

"I really can't." He looked at them with his very best honest-to-God eyes.

"We're going to find out if that's the truth," Dave said. "Strip down, sport."

With no choice, Luke took off his clothes and stepped into the tank. It was about four feet deep and eight feet across. The water was cool and pleasant; so far, so good.

"I'm thinking of an animal," Zeke said. "What is it?"

It was a cat. Luke got no image, just the word, as big and bright as a Budweiser sign in a bar window.

"I don't know."

"Okay, sport, if that's how you want to play it. Take a deep breath, go under, and count to fifteen. Put a *howdy-do* between each number. One howdy-do, two howdy-do, three howdy-do, like that."

Luke did it. When he emerged, Dave (last name unknown, at least so far) asked him what animal *he* was thinking of. The word in his mind was KANGA-ROO.

"I don't know. I told you, I'm TK, not TP. And not even TK-pos."

"Down you go," Zeke said. "Thirty seconds, with a *howdy-do* between each number. I'll be timing you, sport."

The third dip was forty-five seconds, the fourth a full minute. He was questioned after each one. They switched from animals to the names of various care-takers: Gladys, Norma, Pete, Priscilla.

"I can't!" Luke shouted, wiping water from his eyes. "Don't you get that?"

"What I get is we're going to try for a minute and a quarter," Zeke said. "And while you're counting, think about how long you want to keep this up. It's in your hands, sport."

Luke tried to surface after he'd counted to sixty-seven. Zeke grabbed his head and pushed him back down. He came up at a minute-fifteen gasping for air, his heart pounding.

"What sports team am I thinking about?" Dave asked, and in his mind Luke saw a bright bar sign reading VIKINGS.

"I don't know!"

"Bullshit," Zeke said. "Let's go for a minute-thirty."

"No," Luke said, splashing back toward the center of the tank. He was trying not to panic. "I can't."

Zeke rolled his eyes. "Stop being a pussy. Abalone fishermen can go under for nine minutes. All I want is ninety *seconds.* Unless you tell your Uncle Dave here what his favorite sports team is."

"He's not my uncle and I can't do that. Now let me out." And because he couldn't help it: "Please."

Zeke unholstered his zap-stick and made a production of turning the dial up to max. "You want me to touch this to the water? I do that and you'll dance like Michael Jackson. Now get over here."

With no choice, Luke waded toward the edge of the immersion tank. *It's fun*, Richardson had said.

"One more chance," Zeke said. "What's he thinking of?"

Vikings, Minnesota Vikings, my hometown team.

"I don't know."

"Okay," Zeke said, sounding regretful. "USN *Luke* now submerging."

"Wait, give him a few secs to get ready," Dave said. He looked worried, and that worried Luke. "Flood your lungs with air, Luke. And try to be calm. When your body's on red alert, it uses more oxy."

Luke gasped in and out half a dozen times and submerged. Zeke's hand came down on his head and gripped his hair. Calm, calm, calm, Luke thought. Also, You fucker, Zeke, you fucker, I hate your sadistic guts.

He made the ninety seconds and came up gasping. Dave dried his face with a towel. "Stop this," he murmured in Luke's ear. "Just tell me what I'm thinking. This time it's a movie star."

MATT DAMON, the bar sign in Dave's head now said.

"I don't know." Luke began to cry, the tears running down his wet face.

Zeke said, "Fine. Let's go for a minute forty-five. One hundred and five big seconds, and don't forget to put a *howdy-do* between each one. We'll turn you into an abalone fisherman yet."

Luke hyperventilated again, but by the time he reached one hundred, counting in his head, he felt sure he was going to open his mouth and suck in water. They would haul him out, resuscitate him, and do it again. They would keep on until he either told them what they wanted to hear or drowned.

At last the hand on his head was gone. He surged up, gasping and coughing. They gave him time to recover, then Zeke said, "Never mind the animals and sports teams and the whatever. Just say it. Say 'I'm a telep, I'm TP,' and this stops."

"Okay! Okay, I'm a telep!"

"Great!" Zeke cried. "Progress! What number am I thinking of?"

The bright bar sign read 17.

"Six," Luke said.

Zeke made a game-show buzzer sound. "Sorry, it was seventeen. Two minutes this time."

"No! I can't! Please!"

Dave spoke quietly. "Last one, Luke."

Zeke gave his colleague a shoulder-shove almost hard enough to knock him off his feet. "Don't tell him what might not be true." He returned his attention to Luke. "I'll give you thirty seconds to get fully aerated, and then down you go. Olympic Diving Team, baby."

With no choice, Luke inhaled and exhaled rapidly,

but long before he could count to thirty in his head, Zeke's hand closed on his hair and shoved him down.

Luke opened his eyes and stared at the white side of the tank. The paint was scratched in a couple of places, maybe by the fingernails of other children subjected to this torture, which was reserved strictly for pinks. And why? It was pretty obvious. Because Hendricks and Evans thought the range of psychic talents could be expanded, and pinks were expendable.

Expand, expend, he thought. Expand, expend. Calm, calm, calm.

And although he tried his best to enter a Zenlike state, his lungs eventually demanded more air. His Zenlike state, which hadn't been very Zenlike to begin with, broke down when he thought that if he survived this he'd be forced to go two minutes and fifteen, then two minutes and thirty, then—

He began to thrash. Zeke held him down. He planted his feet and pushed, almost made it to the surface, but Zeke added his other hand and pushed him down again. The dots came back, flashing in front of his eyes, rushing toward him, pulling back, then rushing toward him again. They started to swirl around him like a carousel gone crazy. Luke thought, The Stasi Lights. I'm going to drown looking at the—

Zeke hauled him up by the hair. His white tunic was soaked. He looked fixedly at Luke. "I'm going to put you down again, Luke. Again and again and again. I'll put you down until you drown and then we'll resuscitate you and drown you again and resuscitate you again. Last chance: what number am I thinking of?"

"I don't . . ." Luke retched out water. ". . . know!"

That fixed gaze remained for perhaps five seconds. Luke met it, although his eyes were gushing tears.

Then Zeke said, "Fuck this and fuck you, sport. Dave, dry him off and send him back. I don't want to look at his little cunt face."

He left, slamming the door.

Luke floundered from the pool, staggered, almost fell. Dave steadied him, then handed him a towel. Luke dried himself and got back into his clothes as fast as he could. He didn't want to be anywhere near this man or this place, but even feeling half-dead, his curiosity remained. "Why is it so important? Why is it so important when it isn't even what we're here *for*?"

"How would you know what you're here for?" Dave asked.

"Because I'm not stupid, that's why."

"You want to keep your mouth shut, Luke," Dave said. "I like you, but that doesn't mean I want to listen to you run your mouth."

"Whatever the dots are for, it doesn't have anything to do with finding out if I can go both ways, TP as well as TK. What are you guys *doing*? Do you even kn—"

Dave slapped him, a big roundhouse that knocked Luke off his feet. Water puddled on the tile floor soaked into the seat of his jeans. "I'm not here to answer your questions." He bent toward Luke. "We know what we're doing, smartass! *We know exactly what we're doing!*" And, as he hauled Luke up: "We had a kid here last year who lasted three and a half minutes. He was a pain in the ass, but at least he had balls!"

12

Avery came to his room, concerned, and Luke told him to go away, he needed to be alone for awhile.

"It was bad, wasn't it?" Avery asked. "The tank. I'm sorry, Luke."

"Thanks. Now go away. We'll talk later."

"Okay."

Avery went, considerately closing the door behind him. Luke lay on his back, trying not to relive those endless minutes submerged in the tank and doing it anyway. He kept waiting for the lights to come back, bobbing and racing through his field of vision, turning circles and making dizzy whirlpools. When they didn't, he began to calm. One thought trumped all others, even his fear that the dots might come back . . . and stay this time.

Get out. I have to get out. And if I can't do that, I have to die before they take me to Back Half and take the rest of me.

13

The worst of the bugs had departed with June, so Dr. Hendricks met with Zeke Ionidis in front of the administration building, where there was a bench under a shady oak tree. Nearby was a flagpole, with the stars and stripes flapping lazily in a light summer breeze. Dr. Hendricks held Luke's folder on his lap.

"You're sure," he said to Zeke.

"Positive. I dunked the little bastard five or six times, I guess, each one fifteen seconds longer, just like you said. If he could read minds, he would have done it, and you can take that to the bank. A Navy SEAL couldn't stand up to that shit, let alone a kid not old enough to have more than six hairs on his balls."

Hendricks seemed ready to push it, then sighed and

shook his head. "All right. I can live with that. We've got plenty of pinks right now, and more due in. An embarrassment of riches. But it's still a disappointment. I had hopes for that boy."

He opened the file with its little pink dot in the upper righthand corner. He took a pen from his pocket and drew a diagonal line across the first page. "At least he's healthy. Evans gave him a clean bill. That idiot girl—Benson—didn't pass her chicken pox on to him."

"He wasn't vaccinated against that?" Zeke asked.

"He was, but she took pains to swap spit with him. And she had quite a serious case. Couldn't risk it. Nope. Better safe than sorry."

"So when does he go to Back Half?"

Hendricks smiled a little. "Can't wait to get rid of him, can you?"

"Actually, no," Zeke said. "The Benson girl might not have infected him with chicken pox, but Wilholm passed on his fuck-you germ."

"He goes as soon as I get a green light from Heckle and Jeckle."

Zeke pretended to shiver. "Those two. *Brrr*. Creepy."

Hendricks advanced no opinion on the Back Half doctors. "You're sure he's flat as far as telepathy goes?"

Zeke patted him on the shoulder. "Absolutely, Doc. Take it to the bank."

14

While Hendricks and Zeke were discussing his future, Luke was on his way to lunch. As well as terrorizing him, the immersion tank had left him ravenously hungry. When Stevie Whipple asked where he'd been and what was wrong, Luke just shook his head. He didn't want to talk about the tank. Not now, not ever. He supposed it was like being in a war. You got drafted, you went, but you didn't want to talk about what you'd seen, or what had happened to you there.

Full of the caff's version of fettuccini alfredo, he took a nap and awoke feeling marginally better. He went looking for Maureen and spied her in the formerly deserted East Wing. It seemed the Institute might soon be hosting more guests. He walked down to her and asked if she needed help. "Because I wouldn't mind earning some tokens," he said.

"No, I'm fine." To Luke she looked like she was ageing almost by the hour. Her face was dead pale. He wondered how long it would be before someone noticed her condition and made her stop working. He didn't like to think about what might become of her if that happened. Was there a retirement program for housekeepers who were also Institute snitches? He doubted it.

Her laundry basket was half filled with fresh linen, and Luke dropped his own note into it. He had written it on a memo sheet he'd stolen from the equipment alcove in C-4, along with a cheap ballpoint pen which he'd hidden under his mattress. Stamped on the barrel of the pen was DENNISON RIVER BEND REALTY. Maureen saw the folded note, covered it with a pillowcase, and gave him a slight nod. Luke went on his way.

That night in bed, he whispered to Avery for a long time before allowing the kid to go to sleep. There were two scripts, he told Avery, there had to be. He thought the Avester understood. Or maybe the right word was *hoped*.

Luke stayed awake a long time, listening to Avery's light snores and meditating on escape. The idea seemed simultaneously absurd and perfectly possible. There were those dusty surveillance bulbs, and all the times he had been left alone to wander, gathering in his little bits and bobs of information. There were the fake surveillance dead zones that Sigsby and her minions knew about, and the real one that they didn't (or so he hoped). In the end, it was a pretty simple equation. He had to try. The alternative was the Stasi Lights, the movies, the headaches, the sparkler that triggered whatever it triggered. And at the end of it all, the drone.

When they stop testing, you might only have 3 days.

15

The following afternoon, Trevor Stackhouse joined Mrs. Sigsby in her office. She was bent over an open file, reading and making notes. She raised a single finger without looking up. He went to her window, which looked out on the East Wing of the building they called the Residence Hall, as if the Institute really were a college campus, one that happened to be situated in the deep woods of northern Maine. He could see two or three kids milling around snack and soda machines that had just been restocked. There was no tobacco or alcohol available in that lounge, hadn't been since 2005. The East Wing was usually thinly populated or not populated at all, and when there were residents boarded there, they could get cigarettes and wine nips from the vending machines at the other end of the building. Some only sampled, but a surprising number—usually those who were the most depressed and terrified by the sudden catastrophic change in their lives—became addicted quickly. Those were the ones who gave the least trouble, because they didn't just want tokens, they needed them. Karl Marx had called religion the opiate of the people, but Stackhouse begged to differ. He thought Lucky Strikes and Boone's Farm (greatly favored by their female guests) did the job quite nicely.

"Okay," Mrs. Sigsby said, closing her file. "Ready for you, Trevor."

"Four more coming in tomorrow from Opal team," Stackhouse said. His hands were clasped behind his back and his feet were spread apart. Like a captain on the foredeck of his ship, Mrs. Sigsby thought. He was wearing one of his trademark brown suits, which she would have thought a terrible choice for midsummer, but he no doubt considered it part of his *image*. "We haven't had this many onboard since 2008."

He turned from the view, which really wasn't that interesting. Sometimes—often, even—he got very tired of children. He didn't know how teachers did it, especially without the freedom to whack the insolent and administer a splash of electricity to the rebellious, like the now departed Nicholas Wilholm.

Mrs. Sigsby said, "There was a time—long before yours and mine—when there were over a hundred children here. There was a *waiting list*."

"All right, there was a waiting list. Good to know. Now what did you call me here for? The Opal team is in place, and at least one of these pickups is going to be delicate. I'm flying out tonight. The kid's in a closely supervised environment."

"A rehab, you mean."

"That is correct." High-functioning TKs seemed to get along relatively well in society, but similarly high-functioning TPs had problems, and often turned to booze or drugs. They damped the torrent of input, Stackhouse supposed. "But she's worth it. Not up there with the Dixon boy—he's a powerhouse—but close. So tell me what's concerning you, and let me go about my business."

"Not a concern, just a heads-up. And don't hover behind me, it gives me the willies. Drag up a rock."

While he got the visitor's chair from the other side of her desk, Mrs. Sigsby opened a video file on her desktop and started it playing. It showed the snack machines outside the cafeteria. The picture was cloudy, it jittered every ten seconds or so, and was occasionally interrupted by static frizz. Mrs. Sigsby paused it during one of these.

"The first thing I want you to notice," she said, using the dry lecture-hall voice he had so come to dislike, "is the quality of this video. It's totally unacceptable. The same is true of at least half the surveillance cams. The one in that shitty little convenience store in the Bend is better than most of ours." Meaning Dennison River Bend, and it was true.

"I'll pass that on, but we both know the basic infrastructure of this place is shit. The last total renovation was forty years ago, when things in this country were different. A lot looser. As it stands, we have just two IT guys, and one of them is currently on leave. The computer equipment is outdated, and so are the generators. You *know* all this."

Mrs. Sigsby absolutely did. It wasn't lack of funds; it was their inability to bring in outside help. Your basic catch-22, in other words. The Institute had to stay airtight, and in the age of social media and hackers, that became ever more difficult. Even a whisper of what they were up to out here would be the kiss of death. For the vitally important work they did, yes, but also for the staff. It made hiring hard, it made resupply hard, and repairs were a nightmare.

"That fritzing is coming from kitchen equipment," he said. "Mixers, garbage disposals, the microwaves. I might be able to get something done about that."

"Perhaps you can even get something done about the bulbs in which the cameras are enclosed. Something low-tech. I believe it's called 'dusting.' We *do* have janitors."

Stackhouse looked at his watch.

"All right, Trevor. I can take a hint." She started the video again. Maureen Alvorson appeared with her cleaning basket. She was accompanied by two residents: Luke Ellis and Avery Dixon, the exceptional TP-pos who was now bunking in with Ellis most nights. The video might have been substandard, but the audio was good.

"We can talk here," Maureen told the boys. "There's a mic, but it hasn't worked for years. Just smile a lot, so if anyone looks at the video, they think you're buttering me up for tokens. Now what's on your minds? And keep it short."

There was a pause. The little boy scratched at his arms, pinched his nostrils, then looked at Luke. So Dixon was only along for the ride. This was Ellis's deal. Stackhouse wasn't surprised; Ellis was the smart one. The chess player.

"Well," Luke said, "it's about what happened in the cafeteria. To Harry and the little Gs. That's what's on our minds."

Maureen sighed and put down her basket. "I heard about it. It was too bad, but from what I hear, they're okay."

"Really? All three of them?"

Maureen paused. Avery was staring up at her anxiously, scratching his arms, pinching his nose, and generally looking like he needed to pee. She said finally, "Maybe not okay right *now*, at least not completely, I heard Dr. Evans say they were taken to the infirmary in Back Half. They have a fine one there."

"What else do they have—"

"Quiet." She raised a hand to Luke and looked around. The picture fritzed, but the sound stayed clear. "Don't you ask me about Back Half. I can't talk about that, except to say it's nice, nicer than Front Half, and after the boys and girls spend some time there, they go back home."

She had her arms around them when the video cleared. Holding them close. "Look at that," Stackhouse said admiringly. "Mother Courage. She's good."

"Hush," Mrs. Sigsby said.

Luke asked Maureen if she was absolutely *sure* Harry and Greta were alive. "Because they looked . . . well . . . dead."

"Yeah, all the kids are saying that," Avery agreed, and gave his nose a particularly vicious honk. "Harry spazzed out and stopped breathing. Greta's head looked all crooked and weird on her neck."

Maureen didn't rush ahead; Stackhouse could see her choosing her words. He thought she might have made a decent intelligence agent in a place where intelligence-gathering actually mattered. Meanwhile, both boys were looking up at her, waiting.

At last she said, "Of course I wasn't there, and I

know it must have been scary, but I have to think it looked much worse than it was." She stopped again, but after Avery gave his nose another comforting squeeze, she pushed on. "If the Cross boy had a seizure—I said *if*—they'll be giving him the correct medication. As for Greta, I was passing the break room and heard Dr. Evans tell Dr. Hendricks she's suffering from a sprained neck. They probably put her in a brace. Her sister must be with her. For comfort, you know."

"Okay," Luke said, sounding relieved. "As long as you're sure."

"As sure as I can be, that's all I can tell you, Luke. A fair amount of lying goes on in this place, but I was raised not to lie to folks, especially not to children. So all I can say is I'm as sure as I can be. Now why is it so important? Just because you're worried about your friends, or is there something more?"

Luke looked at Avery, who gave his nose an actual yank, then nodded.

Stackhouse rolled his eyes. "Jesus Christ, kid, if you have to pick it, go on and pick it. The foreplay is driving me crazy."

Mrs. Sigsby paused the video. "It's a self-comforting gesture, and better than grabbing his basket. I've had a fair number of crotch-grabbers in my time, girls as well as boys. Now be quiet. This is the interesting part."

"If I tell you something, will you promise to keep it to yourself?" Luke asked.

She thought this over while Avery continued to torture his poor schnozz. Then she nodded.

Luke lowered his voice. Mrs. Sigsby turned up the volume.

"Some of the kids are talking about going on a hunger strike. No more food until we can be sure the little Gs and Harry are all right."

Maureen lowered her own voice. "Which kids?"

"I don't exactly know," Luke said. "Some of the new ones."

"You tell them that would be a very bad idea. You're a smart boy, Luke, very smart, and I'm sure you know what the word *reprisals* means. You can explain it to Avery later." She looked fixedly at the younger boy, who withdrew from her arm and put a protective hand to his nose, as if he were afraid she meant to grab it herself, maybe even pull it off. "Now I have to go. I don't want you guys to get in trouble, and I don't want to get in trouble myself. If someone asks what we were talking about—"

"Coaxing you for chores to get more tokes," Avery said. "Got it."

"Good." She glanced up at the camera, started away, then turned back. "You'll be out of here soon, and back home. Until then, be smart. Don't rock the boat."

She grabbed a dust rag, gave the delivery tray of the booze-dispensing machine a quick wipe, then picked up her basket and left. Luke and Avery lingered a moment or two, then also went on their way. Mrs. Sigsby killed the video.

"Hunger strike," Stackhouse said, smiling. "That's a new one."

"Yes," Mrs. Sigsby agreed.

"The very idea fills me with terror." His smile widened into a grin. Siggers might disapprove, but he couldn't help it.

To his surprise, she actually laughed. When had he

last heard her do that? The correct answer might be never. "It does have its funny side. Growing children would make the world's worst hunger strikers. They're eating machines. But you're right, it's something new under the sun. Which of the new intakes do you think floated it?"

"Oh, come on. None of them. We've only got one kid smart enough to even know what a hunger strike *is*, and he's been here for almost a month."

"Yes," she agreed. "And I'll be glad when he's out of Front Half. Wilholm was an annoyance, but at least he was out front with his anger. Ellis, though . . . he's *sneaky*. I don't like sneaky children."

"How long until he's gone?"

"Sunday or Monday, if Hallas and James in Back Half agree. Which they will. Hendricks is pretty much through with him."

"Good. Will you address this hunger strike idea, or let it go? I'd suggest letting it go. It'll die a natural death, if it happens at all."

"I believe I'll address it. As you say, we've currently got a lot of residents, and it might be well to speak to them at least once en masse."

"If you do, Ellis is probably going to figure out Alvorson's a rat." Given the kid's IQ, there was no probably about it.

"Doesn't matter. He'll be gone in a few days, and his nose-tweaking little friend will follow soon after. Now about those surveillance cameras . . ."

"I'll write a memo to Andy Fellowes before I leave tonight, and we'll make them a priority as soon as I'm back." He leaned forward, hands clasped, his brown eyes fixed on her steel-gray ones. "In the meantime, lighten up. You'll give yourself an ulcer. Remind yourself at least once a day that we're dealing with kids, not hardened criminals."

Mrs. Sigsby made no reply, because she knew he was right. Even Luke Ellis, smart as he might be, was only a kid, and after he spent some time in Back Half, he'd still be a kid, but he wouldn't be smart at all.

16

When Mrs. Sigsby walked into the cafeteria that night, slim and erect in a crimson suit, gray blouse, and single strand of pearls, there was no need for her to tap a spoon against a glass and call for attention. All chatter ceased at once. Techs and caretakers drifted into the doorway giving on the West Lounge. Even the kitchen staff came out, gathering behind the salad bar.

"As most of you know," Mrs. Sigsby said in a pleasant, carrying voice, "there was an unfortunate incident here in the cafeteria two nights ago. There have been rumors and gossip that two children died in that incident. This is absolutely untrue. We do not kill children here in the Institute."

She surveyed them. They looked back, eyes wide, food forgotten.

"In case some of you were concentrating on your fruit cocktail and not paying attention, let me repeat my last statement: *we do not kill children*." She paused to let that sink in. "You did not ask to be here. We all understand that, but we do not apologize for it. You are here to serve not only your country, but the entire world. When your service is done, you will not be given medals. There will be no parades in your honor. You will not be aware of our heartfelt thanks, because before you leave, your memories of the Institute will be expunged. Wiped away, for those of you who don't know that word." Her eyes found Luke's for a moment and they said *But of course* you *know it*. "Please understand that you have those thanks, nonetheless. You will be tested in your time here, and some of the tests may be hard, but you will survive and rejoin your families. We have never lost a child."

She paused again, waiting for anyone to respond or object. Wilholm might have, but Wilholm was gone. Ellis didn't, because direct response wasn't his way. As a chess player, he preferred sneaky gambits to direct assault. Much good would it do him.

"Harold Cross had a brief seizure following the visual field and acuity test some of you, those who've had it, call 'the dots' or 'the lights.' He inadvertently struck Greta Wilcox, who was trying—admirably, I'm sure we all feel—to comfort him. She suffered a severely sprained neck, but is recovering. Her sister is with her. The Wilcox twins and Harold are to be sent home next week, and I'm sure we will send our good wishes with them."

Her eyes again sought Luke, sitting at a table against the far wall. His little friend was with him. Dixon's mouth was hanging agape, but at least he was leaving his nose alone for the time being.

"If anyone should contradict what I've just told you, you may be sure that person is lying, and his lies should be immediately reported to one of the caretakers or technicians. Is that understood?"

Silence, without even a nervous cough to break it.

"If it's understood, I would like you to say 'Yes, Mrs. Sigsby.'"

"Yes, Mrs. Sigsby," the kids responded.

She offered a thin smile. "I think you can do better."

"*Yes, Mrs. Sigsby!*"

"And now with real conviction."

"*YES, MRS. SIGSBY!*" This time even the kitchen staff, techs, and caretakers joined in.

"Good." Mrs. Sigsby smiled. "There's nothing like an affirmative shout to clear the lungs and the mind, is there? Now carry on with your meals." She turned to the white-coated kitchen staff. "And extra desserts before bedtime, assuming you can provide cake and ice cream, Chef Doug?"

Chef Doug made a circle with his thumb and forefinger. Someone began to clap. Others joined in. Mrs. Sigsby nodded right and left to acknowledge the applause as she left the room, walking with her head up and her hands swinging back and forth in tiny, precise arcs. A small smile, what Luke thought of as a Mona Lisa smile, curved the corners of her mouth. The white-coats parted to let her pass.

Still applauding, Avery leaned close to Luke and whispered, "She lied about *everything*."

Luke gave an almost imperceptible nod.

"That fucking bitch," Avery said.

Luke gave the same tiny nod and sent a brief mental message: *Keep clapping.*

17

That night Luke and Avery lay side by side in Luke's bed as the Institute wound down for another night.

Avery whispered, recounting everything Maureen told him each time he went to his nose, signaling her to send. Luke had been afraid Maureen might not understand the note he'd dropped into her basket (a little unconscious prejudice there, maybe based on the brown housekeeper's uni she wore, he'd have to work on that), but she had understood perfectly, and provided Avery with the step-by-step list. Luke thought the Avester could have been a little more subtle about the signals, but it seemed to have turned out okay. He had to hope it had. Supposing that were true, Luke's only real question was whether or not the first step could actually work. It was simple to the point of crudity.

The two boys lay on their backs, staring into the dark. Luke was going over the steps for the tenth time—or maybe the fifteenth—when Avery invaded his mind with three words that flashed on like a red neon, then faded out, leaving an afterimage.

Yes, Mrs. Sigsby.

Luke poked him.

Avery sniggered.

A few seconds later, the words came again, this time even brighter.

Yes, Mrs. Sigsby!

Luke gave him another poke, but he was smiling, and Avery probably knew it, dark or not. The smile was in his mind as well as on his mouth, and Luke thought he had a right to it. He might not be able to escape the Institute—he had to admit the odds were against—but today had been a good one. Hope was such a fine word, such a fine thing to feel.

YES, MRS. SIGSBY, YOU FUCKING BITCH!

"Stop, or I'll tickle you," Luke murmured.

"It worked, didn't it?" Avery whispered. "It really worked. Do you think you can really . . ."

"I don't know, I only know I'm going to try. Now shut up and go to sleep."

"I wish you could take me with you. I wish it *bad*."

"Me too," Luke said, and he meant it. It would be tough for Avery here on his own. He was more socially adjusted than the little Gs or Stevie Whipple, but nobody was ever going to crown him Mr. Personality.

"When you come back, bring about a thousand cops with you," Avery whispered. "And do it fast, before they take me to Back Half. Do it while we can still save Sha."

"I'll do what I can," Luke promised. "Now stop yelling in my head. That joke wears out fast."

"I wish you had more TP. And that it didn't hurt you to send. We could talk better."

"If wishes were horses, beggars would ride. For the last time, go to sleep."

Avery did, and Luke began to drift off himself. Maureen's first step was as clanky as the ice machine where they sometimes talked, but he had to admit that it tallied with all the things he'd already observed: dusty camera housings, baseboards where paint had chipped off years ago and had never been touched up, an elevator card carelessly left behind. He mused again on how this place was like a rocket with its engines off, still moving but now in an inertial glide.

18

The next day Winona escorted him down to C-Level, where he was given a quick once-over: blood pressure, heart rate, temperature, O2 level. When Luke asked what came next, Dave checked his clipboard, gave him a sunny grin—as if he had never knocked him to the floor—and said there was nothing on the schedule.

"You've got an off-day, Luke. Enjoy it." He raised his hand, palm out.

Luke grinned back and slapped him five, but it was Maureen's note he was thinking of: *When they stop testing, you might only have 3 days.*

"What about tomorrow?" he asked as they returned to the elevator.

"We'll let tomorrow take care of itself," Dave said. "It's the only way to be."

Maybe that was true for some, but it was no longer true for Luke. He wished for extra time to go over Maureen's plan—or to procrastinate, more like it—but he was afraid that his time was almost up.

Dodgeball had become a daily affair on the Institute's playground, almost a ritual, and nearly everyone joined in at least for awhile. Luke got in the circle and jostled around with the other dodgers for ten minutes or so before allowing himself to be hit. Instead of joining the throwers, he walked across the asphalt half-court, past Frieda Brown, who was standing by herself and taking foul shots. Luke thought she still had no real idea where she was. He sat down on the gravel with his back against the chainlink fence. At least the bug situation was a little better now. He dropped his hands and swept them idly back and forth at his sides, eyes on the dodgeball game.

"Want to shoot some?" Frieda asked.

"Maybe later," Luke said. He casually reached one hand behind him, felt for the bottom of the fence, and found that yes, Maureen was right; there was a gap where the ground slumped a bit. That slump might have been created by snowmelt in the early spring. Only an inch or two, but it was there. Nobody had bothered to fill it in. Luke's upturned hand rested on the exposed bottom of the fence, the wire tines pressing into his palm. He waggled his fingertips in the free air outside the Institute for a moment or two, then got up, dusted off his bottom, and asked Frieda if she wanted to play HORSE. She gave him an eager smile that said *Yes! Of course! Be my friend!*

It sort of broke his heart.

19

Luke had no tests the following day, either, and nobody even bothered taking his vitals. He helped Connie, one of the janitors, carry two mattresses from the elevator to a couple of rooms in the East Wing, got a single lousy token for his trouble (all the janitors were miserly when it came to handing out tokes), and on his way back to his room, he encountered Maureen standing by the ice machine, drinking from the bottle of water she always kept chilling in there. He asked if she needed any help.

"No, I'm fine." Then, lowering her voice: "Hendricks and Zeke were talking out front by the flagpole. I saw them. Have they been testing you?"

"No. Not for two days."

"That's what I thought. This is Friday. You might have until Saturday or Sunday, but I wouldn't take that chance." The mixture of worry and compassion he saw on her haggard face terrified him.

Tonight.

He didn't speak the word aloud, only mouthed it with a hand at the side of his face, scratching below his eye. She nodded.

"Maureen . . . do they know you have . . ." He couldn't finish, and didn't have to.

"They think it's sciatica." Her voice was barely a whisper. "Hendricks might have an idea, but he doesn't care. None of them do, as long as I can keep working. Go on now, Luke. I'll turn your room while you're at lunch. Look under your mattress when you go to bed. Good luck." She hesitated. "I wish I could hug you, son."

Luke felt his eyes fill up. He hurried away before she could see.

He ate a big lunch, although he wasn't particularly hungry. He would do the same at supper. He had a feeling that if this worked, he was going to need all the fuel he could take on.

That evening at dinner, he and Avery were joined by Frieda, who seemed to have imprinted on Luke. After, they went out to the playground. Luke declined to shoot more hoops with the girl, saying he would spot Avery for awhile on the trampoline.

One of those red neon words bloomed in Luke's mind as he watched the Avester jump up and down, doing lackadaisical seat-drops and tummy-bounces.

Tonight?

Luke shook his head. "But I need you to sleep in your own room. I'd like to get a full eight hours for once."

Avery slid off the trampoline and looked at Luke solemnly. "Don't tell me what isn't true because you think someone will see me looking sad and wonder why. I don't have to look sad." And he stretched his lips in a hopelessly counterfeit grin.

Okay. Just don't fuck up my chance, Avester.

Come back for me if you can. Please.

I will.

The dots were returning, bringing a vivid memory of the immersion tank. Luke thought it was the effort it took to consciously send his thoughts.

Avery looked at him a moment longer, then ran to the basketball hoop. "Want to play HORSE, Frieda?"

She looked down on him and gave him a smile. "Kid, I'd beat you like a drum."

"Spot me an *H* and an *O*, and we'll see about that."

They played as the light began to drain out of the day. Luke crossed the playground and looked back once as Avery—who Harry Cross had once called Luke's "little bitty buddy"—attempted a hook shot that missed everything. He thought Avery would come down to his room that night at least long enough to retrieve his toothbrush, but he didn't.

20

Luke played a few games of Slap Dash and 100 Balls on his laptop, then brushed his own teeth, undressed to his shorts, and got into bed. He turned off the lamp and reached under his mattress. He might have cut his fingers on the knife Maureen had left him (unlike the plastic ones they got in the caff, this felt like a paring knife with a real blade) if she hadn't wrapped it in a washcloth. There was something else as well, something he could identify by touch. God knew he'd used plenty of them before coming here. A flash drive. He leaned over in the dark and slipped both items into the pocket of his pants.

Then came waiting. For awhile kids ran up and

down the corridor, maybe playing tag, maybe just grab-assing around. This happened every night now that there were more kids. There were whoops and laughter, followed by exaggerated hushing sounds, followed by more laughter. They were blowing off steam. Blowing off *fear*. One of tonight's loudest whoopers was Stevie Whipple, and Luke deduced that Stevie had been into the wine or hard lemonade. There were no stern adults demanding silence; those in charge weren't interested in enforcing noise-abatement rules or imposing cur-fews.

Finally Luke's part of the residence floor settled down. Now there was just the sound of his own steadily beating heart and the turn of his thoughts as he went over Maureen's list for the final time.

Back to the trampoline once you're out, he reminded himself. Use the knife if you have to. Then a slight turn to the right.

If he got out.

He was relieved to find himself eighty per cent determined and only twenty per cent afraid. Even that much fear made no real sense, but Luke supposed it was natural. What drove the determination—what he absolutely *knew*—was simple and stark: this was his chance, the only one he'd have, and he intended to make the most of it.

When the corridor outside had been silent for what he judged to be half an hour, Luke got out of bed and grabbed his plastic ice bucket from on top of his TV. He had made up a story for the watchers—if, that was, anyone was actually watching the monitors at this hour, and not just sitting in some lower level surveil-lance room and playing solitaire.

This story was about a kid who goes to bed early,

then awakens for some reason, maybe a need to pee, maybe because of a nightmare. Anyway, the kid is still more asleep than awake, so he walks down the hall in his underwear. Cameras in dusty bulbs watch him as he goes to the ice machine for a refill. And when he returns with not just a bucket of ice but the scoop as well, they assume the kid's just too dozey to realize he still has it in his hand. He'll see it in the morning, lying on his desk or in the bathroom sink, and wonder how it got there.

In his room again, Luke put some ice in a glass, filled it from the bathroom tap, and drank half of it down. It was good. His mouth and throat were very dry. He left the scoop on the toilet tank and went back to bed. He tossed and turned. He muttered to himself. Maybe the kid in the story he was making up is missing his little bitty buddy. Maybe that's why he can't get back to sleep. And maybe nobody's watching or listening, but maybe somebody is, and that's the way he has to play it.

Finally he turned on the lamp again and got dressed. He went into the bathroom, where there was no surveillance (*probably* no surveillance) and stuck the scoop down the front of his pants, dropping his Twins teeshirt over it. If there *was* video in here, and if someone was monitoring it, he was probably cooked already. There was nothing he could do about that but push on to the next part of his story.

He left the room and went down the hall to the lounge. Stevie Whipple and some other kid, one of the newbies, were there, lying on the floor fast asleep. Half a dozen Fireball nips, all empty, were scattered around them. Those little bottles represented a lot of tokens. Stevie and his new friend would wake up with hangovers and empty pockets.

Luke stepped over Stevie and went into the caff. With only the salad bar fluorescents lit, the place was gloomy and a little spooky. He grabbed an apple from the never-empty bowl of fruit and took a bite as he wandered back into the lounge, hoping no one was watching, hoping that if someone was, they would understand the pantomime he was acting out, and buy it. The kid woke up. The kid got ice from the machine and had a nice cold glass of water, but after that he's more awake than ever, so he goes up to the caff for something to eat. Then the kid thinks, Hey, why not go out to the playground for awhile, get some fresh air. He wouldn't be the first one to do that; Kalisha said that she and Iris had gone out several times to look at the stars—they were incredibly bright out here with no light pollution to obscure them. Or sometimes, she said, kids used the playground at night to make out. He just hoped no one was out here stargazing or necking tonight.

There wasn't, and with no moon the playground was fairly dark, the various pieces of equipment only angular shadows. Without a buddy or two for company, little kids had a tendency to be afraid of the dark. Bigger kids, too, although most wouldn't admit it.

Luke strolled across the playground, waiting for one of the less familiar night caretakers to appear and ask him what he was doing out here with that scoop hidden under his shirt. Surely he wasn't thinking about escape, was he? Because that would be pretty darn wacky!

"Wacky," Luke murmured, and sat down with his back to the chainlink fence. "That's me, a real whack-job."

He waited to see if someone would come. No one

did. There was only the sound of crickets and the hoot of an owl. There was a camera, but was anybody really monitoring it? There was security, he knew that, but it was *sloppy* security. He knew that, too. Just how sloppy he would now find out.

He lifted his shirt and removed the scoop. In his imaginings of this part, he scooped behind his back with his right hand, maybe shifting over to his left when his arm got tired. In reality, this didn't work very well. He scraped the scoop against the bottom of the chainlink repeatedly, making a noise that sounded very loud in the stillness, and he couldn't see if he was making any progress.

This is crazy, he thought.

Throwing worry about the camera aside, Luke got on his knees and began to dig under the fence, flinging gravel to the right and the left. Time seemed to stretch out. He felt that hours were passing. Was anyone in that surveillance room he'd never seen (but could imagine vividly) starting to wonder why the kid with insomnia hadn't come back from the playground? Would he or she send someone to check? And say, what if that camera has a night-vision feature, Lukey? What about that?

He dug. He could feel sweat starting to oil his face, and the bugs working the night shift were homing in on it. He dug. He could smell his armpits. His heart had sped up to a gallop. He felt someone standing behind him, but when he looked over his shoulder, he saw only the gantry of the basketball post standing against the stars.

Now he had a trench under the bottom of the fence. Shallow, but he had come to the Institute skinny and had lost more weight since then. Maybe—

But when he lay down and tried to slide under, the fence stopped him. It wasn't even close.

Go back in. Go back in and get into bed before they find you and do something horrible to you for trying to get out of here.

But that wasn't an option, only cowardice. They *were* going to do something horrible to him: the movies, the headaches, the Stasi Lights . . . and finally, the drone.

He dug, gasping now, going back and forth, left and right. The gap between the bottom of the fence and the ground slowly deepened. So stupid of them to have left the surface unpaved on either side of the fence. So stupid not to have run an electrical charge, even a mild one, through the wire. But they hadn't, and here he was.

He lay down again, tried again to ease under, and again the bottom of the fence stopped him. But he was close. Luke got on his knees again and dug more, dug faster, left and right, back and forth, to and fro. There was a snapping sound when the scoop's handle finally let go. Luke tossed the handle aside and went on digging, feeling the edge of the scoop bite into his palms. When he paused to look at them, he saw they were bleeding.

Got to be this time. Got to be.

But he still couldn't . . . quite . . . fit.

And so back to work with the scoop. Left and right, starboard and larboard. Blood was dripping down his fingers, his hair was sweat-pasted to his forehead, mosquitoes sang in his ears. He put the scoop aside, lay down, and tried again to slide under the fence. The protruding tines pulled his shirt sideways, then bit into his skin, drawing more blood from his shoulder-blades. He kept going.

Halfway under, he stuck. He stared at the gravel, saw the way dust puffed up in tiny swirls below his nostrils as he panted. He had to go back, had to dig deeper yet—maybe only a little. Except when he tried to edge back into the playground, he discovered he couldn't go that way, either. Not just stuck, caught. He would still be here, trapped under this goddam fucking fence like a rabbit in a trap when the sun came up tomorrow morning.

The dots started to come back, red and green and purple, emerging from the bottom of the dug-up ground that was only an inch or two from his eyes. They rushed toward him, breaking apart, coming together, spinning and strobing. Claustrophobia squeezed his heart, squeezed his head. His hands throbbed and sang.

Luke reached out, hooked his fingers into the dirt, and pulled with everything he had. For a moment the dots filled not only his field of vision but his entire brain; he was lost in their light. Then the bottom of the fence seemed to rise a little. That might have been strictly imagination, but he didn't think so. He heard it creak.

Maybe thanks to the shots and the tank, I'm a TK-pos now, he thought. Just like George.

He decided it didn't matter. The only thing that mattered was that he had begun to move once more.

The dots subsided. If the bottom of the fence really had risen, it had come back down. Metal prongs scored not just his shoulderblades but his buttocks and thighs. There was an agonizing moment when he stopped again, the fence grasping him greedily, not wanting to let go, but when he turned his head and laid his cheek on the pebbly ground, he could see a bush. It might be in reach. He stretched, came up short, stretched some more, and grasped it. He pulled. The bush began to tear free, but before it could come entirely out of the ground, he was moving again, thrusting with his hips and pushing with his feet. A protruding fence tine gave him a goodbye kiss, drawing a hot line across one calf, and then he wriggled through to the far side of the fence.

He was out.

Luke swayed to his knees and cast a wild look back, sure he'd see all the lights coming on—not just in the lounge, but in the hallways and the cafeteria, and in their glow he would see running figures: caretakers with their zap-sticks unholstered and turned up to maximum power.

There was no one.

He got to his feet and began to run blindly, the vital next step—orientation—forgotten in his panic. He might have run into the woods and become lost there before reason reasserted itself, except for the sudden scorching pain in his left heel as he came down on a sharp rock and realized he had lost one of his sneakers in that final desperate lunge.

Luke returned to the fence, bent, retrieved it, and put it on. His back and buttocks only smarted, but that final cut into his calf had been deeper, and burned like a hot wire. His heartbeat slowed and clear thinking returned. *Once you're out, go level with the trampoline*, Avery had said, relaying the second of Maureen's steps. *Put your back to it, then turn right one medium-sized step. That's your direction. You only have a mile or so to go, and you don't need to keep in a perfectly straight line, what you're aiming for is pretty big, but try your best.* Later, in bed that night, Avery had said that maybe Luke could use the stars to guide him. He didn't know about that stuff himself.

All right, then. Time to go. But there was one other thing he had to do first.

He reached up to his right ear and felt the small circle embedded there. He remembered someone—maybe Iris, maybe Helen—saying the implant hadn't hurt her, because her ears were already pierced. Only pierced earrings unscrewed, Luke had seen his mother do it. This one was fixed in place.

Please God, don't let me have to use the knife.

Luke steeled himself, worked his nails under the curved upper edge of the tracker, and pulled. His earlobe stretched, and it hurt, hurt plenty, but the tracker remained fixed. He let go, took two deep breaths (memories of the immersion tank recurring as he did so), and pulled again. Harder. The pain was worse this time, but the tracker remained in place and time was passing. The west residence wing, looking strange from this unfamiliar angle, was still dark and quiet, but for how long?

He thought about pulling again, but that would only be postponing the inevitable. Maureen had known; it was why she left the paring knife. He took it from his pocket (being careful not to pull out the thumb drive as well) and held it in front of his eyes in the scant starlight. He felt for the sharp edge with the ball of his thumb, then reached across his body with his left hand and pulled down on his earlobe, stretching it as far as it would go, which was not very.

He hesitated, taking a moment to let himself really understand he was on the free side of the fence. The owl hooted again, a sleepy sound. He could see fireflies stitching the dark and even in this moment of extremity realized they were beautiful.

Do it fast, he told himself. Pretend you're slicing a piece of steak. And don't scream no matter how much it hurts. You cannot scream.

Luke put the top of the blade against the top of his earlobe on the outside and stood that way for a few seconds that felt like a few eternities. Then he lowered the knife.

I can't.

You must.

I can't.

Oh God, I have to.

He placed the edge of the knife against that tender unarmored flesh again and pulled down at once, before he had time to do more than pray for the edge to be sharp enough to do the job in a single stroke.

The blade *was* sharp, but his strength failed him a little at the last moment, and instead of coming off, the earlobe dangled by a shred of gristle. At first there was no pain, just the warmth of blood flowing down the side of his neck. Then the pain came. It was as if a wasp, one as big as a pint bottle, had stung him and injected its poison. Luke inhaled in a long sibilant hiss, grasped the dangling earlobe, and pulled it off like skin from a chicken drumstick. He bent over it, knowing he had gotten the damned thing but needing to see it anyway. Needing to be positive. It was there.

Luke made sure he was even with the trampoline. He put his back to it, then turned a step—a medium one, he hoped—to the right. Ahead of him was the dark bulk of the northern Maine woods, stretching for God only knew how many miles. He looked up and spotted the Big Dipper, with one corner star straight ahead. Keep following that, he told himself. That's all you have to do. It won't be straight on till morning, either, she told Avery it's only a mile or so, and then it's on to the next step. Ignore the pain in your shoulderblades, the worse pain in your calf, the worst pain of all in your Van Gogh ear. Ignore the way your arms and legs are trembling. Get going. But first . . .

He drew his fisted right hand back to his shoulder and flung the scrap of flesh in which the tracker was still embedded over the fence. He heard (or imagined he heard) the small click it made as it struck the asphalt surrounding the playground's paltry excuse for a basketball court. Let them find it there.

He began to walk, eyes up and fixed on that one single star.

21

Luke had it to guide him for less than thirty seconds. As soon as he entered the trees, it was gone. He stopped where he was, the Institute still partly visible behind him through the first interlacing branches of the woodlands.

Only a mile, he told himself, and you should find it even if you go off-course a little, because she told Avery it's big. *Fairly* big, anyway. So walk slowly. You're right-handed, which means you're right-side dominant, so try to compensate for that, but not too much, or you'll go off-course to the left. And keep count. A mile should be between two thousand and twenty-five hundred steps. Ballpark figure, of course, depending on the terrain. And be careful not to poke your eye out on a branch. You've got enough holes in you already.

Luke began walking. At least there weren't any

thickets to plow through; these were old-growth trees, which had created a lot of shade above and a thick layer of underbrush-discouraging pine duff on the ground. Every time he had to detour around one of the elderly trees (probably they were pines, but in the dark who really knew), he tried to re-orient himself and continue on a straight line which was now—he had to admit it—largely hypothetical. It was like trying to find your way across a huge room filled with barely glimpsed objects.

Something on his left made a sudden grunting sound and then ran, snapping one branch and rattling others. Luke the city boy froze in his tracks. Was that a deer? Christ, what if it was a bear? A deer would be running away, but a bear might be hungry for a mid-night snack. It might be coming at him now, attracted by the smell of blood. God knew Luke's neck and the right shoulder of his shirt were soaked with it.

Then the sound was gone, and he could only hear crickets and the occasional *hoo* of that owl. He had been at eight hundred steps when he heard the whatever-it-was. Now he began to walk again, holding his hands out in front of him like a blind man, ticking the steps off in his mind. A thousand . . . twelve hundred . . . here's a tree, a real monster, the first branches far over my head, too high up to see, go around . . . fourteen hundred . . . fifteen hun—

He stumbled over a downed trunk and went sprawling. Something, a stub of branch, dug into his left leg high up, and he grunted with pain. He lay on the duff for a moment, getting his breath back, and longing—here was the ultimate, deadly absurdity— for his room back in the Institute. A room where there was a place for everything and everything was in its place and no animals of indeterminate size went crashing around in the trees. A safe place.

"Yeah, until it's not," he whispered, and got to his feet, rubbing the new tear in his jeans and the new tear in his skin beneath. At least they don't have dogs, he thought, remembering some old black-and-white prison flick where a couple of chained-together cons had made a dash for freedom with a pack of bloodhounds baying behind them. Plus, those guys had been in a swamp. Where there were alligators.

See, Lukey? he heard Kalisha saying. It's all good. Just keep going. Straight line. Straight as you can, anyway.

At two thousand steps, Luke started looking for lights up ahead, shining through the trees. *There's always a few*, Maureen had told Avery, *but the yellow one is the brightest.* At twenty-five hundred, he began to feel anxious. At thirty-five hundred, he began to be sure he had gone off-course, and not just by a little.

It was that tree I fell over, he thought. That goddam tree. When I got up, I must have gone wrong. For all I know, I'm headed for Canada. If the Institute guys don't find me, I'll die in these woods.

But because going back wasn't an option (he couldn't have retraced his steps even if he wanted to), Luke kept walking, hands waving in front of him for branches that might try to wound him in new places. His ear throbbed.

He quit counting his steps, but he must have been around five thousand—well over two miles—when he saw a faint yellowy-orange gleam through the trees. Luke first mistook it for either a hallucination or one of the dots, soon to be joined by swarms of them.

Another dozen steps put paid to those worries. The yellow-orange light was clearer, and had been joined by two more, much dimmer. Those had to be electric lights. He thought the brighter one was an arc-sodium, the kind they had in big parking lots. Rolf's father had told them one night when he had taken Luke and Rolf to a movie at the AMC Southdale, that those kinds of lights were supposed to stop muggings and car break-ins.

Luke felt an urge to simply bolt forward and restrained it. The last thing he wanted to do was trip over another downed tree or step in a hole and break his leg. There were more lights now, but he kept his eyes firmly fixed on the first one. The Big Dipper hadn't lasted long, but here was a new guiding star, a better one. Ten minutes after first spotting it, Luke came to the edge of the trees. Across fifty yards or so of open ground, there was another chainlink fence. This one was topped with barbed wire, and there were light-posts along it at roughly thirty-foot intervals. Motion-activated, Maureen had told Avery. Tell Luke to stay well back. That was advice he hardly needed.

Beyond the fence were little houses. *Very* little. Not enough room to swing a cat in, Luke's own father might have said. They could contain three rooms at most, and probably just two. They were all the same. Avery said Maureen called this the village, but to Luke it looked like an Army barracks. The houses were arranged in blocks of four, with a patch of grass in the center of each block. There were lights shining in a few of the houses, probably the kind people left on in the bathroom so they wouldn't trip over something if they had to get up and use the toilet.

There was a single street, which ended at a larger

building. To either side of this building was a small
parking lot filled with cars and pickup trucks parked
hip to hip. Thirty or forty in all, Luke estimated. He
remembered wondering where the Institute staff kept
their vehicles. Now he knew, although how food was
supplied was still a mystery. The arc-sodium was on a
pole in front of this larger building, and it shone down
on two gas pumps. Luke thought the place almost had
to be some kind of store, the Institute's version of a
PX.

So now he understood a little more. Staff got time
off—Maureen had had a week to go back to Vermont—
but mostly they stayed right here, and when they were
off-shift, they lived in those ticky-tacky little houses.
Work schedules might be staggered so they could share
accommodations. When in need of recreation, they
hopped in their personal vehicles and drove to the nearest town, which happened to be Dennison River Bend.

The locals would certainly be curious about what
these men and women were up to out there in the
woods, they'd ask questions, and there had to be
some sort of cover story to handle them. Luke didn't
have any idea what it might be (and at this moment
couldn't care less), but it must be pretty decent to
have held up for so many years.

Go right along the fence. Look for a scarf.

Luke got moving, the fence and the village to his
left, the edge of the woods to his right. Again he had
to fight the urge to speed along, especially now that he
could see a little better. Their time with Maureen had
necessarily been short, partly because if their palaver
went on too long it might raise suspicion, and partly
because Luke was afraid too much of Avery's ostenta-
tious nose-grabbing might give the game away. As a

result, he had no idea where this scarf might be, and he was afraid of missing it.

It turned out not to be a problem. Maureen had tied it to the low-hanging branch of a tall pine tree just before the place where the security fence made a left-angle turn away from the woods. Luke took it down and knotted it around his waist, not wanting to leave such an obvious marker to those who would soon be pursuing him. That made him wonder how long it would be before Mrs. Sigsby and Stackhouse found out, and realized who had helped him escape. Not long at all, probably.

Tell them everything, Maureen, he thought. Don't make them torture you. Because if you try to hold out, they will, and you're too old and too sick for the tank.

The bright light at the building that might be a company store was quite far behind him now, and Luke had to cast around carefully before he found the old road leading back into the forest, one that might have been used by pulp-cutting woodsmen a generation ago. Its start was screened by a thick stand of blueberry bushes, and in spite of the need he felt to hurry, he stopped long enough to pick a double handful and throw them into his mouth. They were sweet and delicious. They tasted of *outside*.

Once he found the old track, it was easy to follow, even in the darkness. Plenty of underbrush was growing on its eroded crown, and a double line of weeds padded what had once been wheel-ruts. There were downed branches to step over (or trip over), but it was impossible to wander back into the forest.

He tried counting steps again, managed to keep a fairly accurate tally up to four thousand, then gave up. The track rose occasionally, but mostly it tended downward. A couple of times he came to deadfalls, and once a tangle of bushes so thick he feared the old road just stopped there, but when he pushed through, he found it again and continued. He had no sense of how much time had passed. It might have been an hour; it was probably more like two. All he knew for sure was that it was still night, and although being out here in the dark was spooky, especially for a city kid, he hoped it would stay dark for a long, long time. Except it wouldn't. At this time of year, light would start creeping back into the sky by four o'clock.

He reached the top of another rise and stopped for a moment to rest. He did this standing up. He didn't really believe he would fall asleep if he sat down, but the thought that he might scared him. The adrenaline which had brought him scratching and scrabbling under the fence, then through the woods to the village, was all gone now. The bleeding from the cuts on his back and leg and earlobe had stopped, but all those places throbbed and stung. His ear was the worst by far. He touched it tentatively, then pulled his fingers back with a hiss of pain through clenched teeth. Not before he'd felt an irregular knob of blood and scab there, however.

I mutilated myself, he thought. That earlobe is never going to come back.

"Fuckers made me do it," he whispered. "They *made* me."

Since he didn't dare sit, he bent over and grasped his knees, a position in which he had seen Maureen on many occasions. It did nothing for the fence slashes across his back, his sore ass, or his mutilated earlobe, but it eased his tired muscles a little. He straightened up, ready to go on, then paused. He could hear a faint sound from ahead. A kind of rushing, like the wind in the pines, but there wasn't even a breath of breeze where he was standing on this little rise.

Don't let it be a hallucination, he thought. Let it be real.

Another five hundred steps—these he counted—and Luke knew the sound really was running water. The track grew wider and steeper, finally steep enough that he had to walk sideways, holding onto tree branches to keep from falling on his ass. He stopped when the trees on either side disappeared. Here the woods hadn't just been cut, but stumped as well, creating a clearing that was now overgrown with bushes. Beyond and below was a wide band of black silk, running smooth enough to reflect ripples of starlight from above. He could imagine those long-ago loggers—men who might have worked in these north woods before the Second World War—using old Ford or International Harvester logging trucks to haul their cutwood this far, maybe even teams of horses. The clearing had been their turnaround point. Here they had unloaded their pulpwood and sent it skidding down to the Dennison River, where it would start its ride to the various mill towns downstate.

Luke made his way down this last slope on legs that ached and trembled. The final two hundred feet were the steepest yet, the track sunk all the way to bedrock by the passage of those long-ago logs. He sat down and let himself slide, grabbing at bushes to slow his progress a little and finally coming to a tooth-rattling stop on a rocky bank three or four feet above the water. And here, just as Maureen had promised, the prow of a splintery old rowboat peeped from beneath a green tarp drifted with pine needles. It was tethered to a ragged stump.

How had Maureen known about this place? Had she been told? That didn't seem sure enough, not when a boy's life might depend on that rickety old boat. Maybe before she'd gotten sick, she had found it on a walk by herself. Or she and a few others—maybe a couple of the cafeteria women with whom she seemed friendly—had come down here from their quasi-military village to picnic: sandwiches and Cokes or a bottle of wine. It didn't matter. The boat was here.

Luke eased himself into the water, which came up to his shins. He bent and scooped double handfuls into his mouth. The river water was cold and tasted even sweeter than the blueberries. Once his thirst was slaked, he tried to untie the rope tethering the boat to the stump, but the knots were complex, and time was passing. In the end he used the paring knife to saw through the tether, and that started his right palm bleeding again. Worse, the boat immediately began to drift away.

He lunged for it, grabbed the prow, and hauled it back. Now both of his palms were bleeding. He tried to yank off the tarp, but as soon as he let go of the boat's prow, the current began to pull it away again. He cursed himself for not getting the tarpaulin off first. There wasn't enough ground to beach the boat, and in the end he did the only thing he could: got his top half over the side and under the tarp with its somehow fishy smell of ancient canvas, then pulled on the splintery midships bench until he was all the way in. He landed in a puddle of water and on something long and angular. By now the boat was being pulled downstream by the gentle current, stern first.

I am having quite the adventure, Luke thought. Yes indeed, quite the adventure for me.

He sat up under the tarp. It billowed around him, producing an even stronger stink. He pushed and paddled at it with his bleeding hands until it flopped over the side. It floated beside the rowboat at first, then began to sink. The angular thing he'd landed on turned out to be an oar. Unlike the boat, it looked relatively new. Maureen had placed the scarf; had she also placed the oar for him? He wasn't sure she was capable of making the walk down the old logging road in her current condition, let alone down that last steep slope. If she *had* done it, she deserved an epic poem in her honor, at the very least. And all just because he'd looked some stuff up for her on the Internet, stuff she probably could have found herself if she hadn't been so sick? He hardly knew how to think about such a thing, let alone understand it. He only knew the oar was here, and he had to use it, tired or not, bleeding hands or not.

At least he knew how. He was a city boy, but Minnesota was the land of ten thousand lakes, and Luke had been out fishing with his paternal grandfather (who liked to call himself "just another old basshole from Mankato") many times. He settled himself on the center seat and first used the oar to get the fore end of the boat pointed downstream. With that accomplished, he paddled out to the center of the river, which was about eighty yards wide at this point, and shipped the oar. He took off his sneakers and started to set them on the stubby aft seat to dry. Something was printed on that seat in faded black paint, and when he leaned close, he was able to read it: S.S. *Pokey*. That made him grin. Luke leaned back on his elbows, looking up at the crazy sprawl of the stars, and tried to convince himself that this wasn't a dream—that he had really gotten out.

From somewhere behind him on the left came the double blast of an electric horn. He turned and saw a single bright headlight flickering through the trees, first coming level with his boat, then passing it. He couldn't see the engine or the train it was hauling, there were too many trees in the way, but he could hear the rumble of the trucks and the bratty squall of steel wheels on steel rails. That was what finally nailed it for him. This was not some incredibly detailed fantasy going on inside his brain as he lay sleeping in his West Wing bed. That was a real train over there, probably headed for Dennison River Bend. This was a real boat he was in, sliding south on this slow and beautiful current. Those were real stars overhead. The Minions of Sigsby would come after him, of course, but—

"I'm never going to Back Half. *Never*."

He put one hand over the side of the S.S. *Pokey*, splayed his fingers, and watched four tiny wakes speed away behind him into the dark. He had done this before, in his grandfather's little aluminum fishing skiff with its putt-putting two-stroke engine, many times, but he had never—not even as a four-year-old to whom everything was new and amazing—been so overwhelmed by the sight of those momentary grooves. It came to him, with the force of a revelation, that you had to have been imprisoned to fully understand what freedom was.

"I'll die before I let them take me back."

He understood that this was true, and that it might come to that, but he also understood that right now it had not. Luke Ellis raised his cut and dripping hands to the night, feeling free air rush past them, and began to cry.

22

He dozed off sitting on the midships bench, his chin on his chest, his hands dangling between his legs, his bare feet in the little puddle of water at the bottom of the boat, and might have still been sleeping as the *Pokey* carried him past the next stop on his improbable pilgrimage if not for the sound of another train horn, this one coming not from the riverbank but ahead and above. It was much louder, too—not a lonely honk but an imperative *WHAAA* that brought Luke around with such a jerk that he almost went sprawling backward into the stern. He raised his hands in an instinctive gesture of protection, realizing it was pathetic even as he did it. The horn quit and was supplanted by metallic squeals and vast hollow rumblings. Luke grabbed the sides of the boat where it narrowed toward the prow, and looked ahead with wild eyes, sure he was about to be run down.

It wasn't quite dawn, but the sky had begun to brighten, putting a sheen on the river, which was much wider now. A quarter of a mile downstream, a freight train was crossing a trestle, slowing down. As he watched, Luke saw boxcars marked New England Land Express, Massachusetts Red, a couple of car carriers, several tankers, one marked Canadian CleanGas and another Virginia Util-X. He passed beneath the trestle and raised a hand against the soot that came sifting down. A couple of clinkers splashed into the water on either side of his craft.

Luke grabbed the paddle and began to angle the rowboat toward the righthand shore, where he could now see a few sad-looking buildings with boarded-up windows and a crane that looked rusty and long disused. The bank was littered with paper trash, old tires, and discarded cans. Now the train he had passed beneath was over on that side, still slowing down, screeching and banging. Vic Destin, his friend Rolf's father, said there had never been a mode of transportation as dirty and noisy as transportation by rail. He said it with satisfaction rather than disgust, which surprised neither of the boys. Mr. Destin was into trains bigtime.

Luke had almost reached the end of Maureen's steps, and now it was actual steps he was looking for. Red ones. *Not real red, though*, Avery told him. *Not anymore. She says they're more like pink these days*. And when Luke spotted them just five minutes after passing beneath the trestle, they were hardly even that. Although there was some pinky-red color left on the risers, the steps themselves were mostly gray. They rose from the water's edge to the top of the embankment, maybe a hundred and fifty feet up. He paddled for them, and the keel of his little ship came aground on one just below the surface.

Luke debarked slowly, feeling as creaky as an old man. He thought of tying the S.S. *Pokey* up—enough rust had scaled off the posts to either side of the steps to tell him others had done that, probably fishermen—but the remainder of the rope tethered to the bow looked too short.

He let go of the boat, watched it start to drift away as the mild current grabbed it, then saw his footgear, with the socks tucked into them, still sitting on the stern seat. He dropped to his knees on the submerged step and managed to grab the rowboat just in time. He drew it past him hand over hand until he could grab his sneakers. Then he murmured "Thanks, *Pokey*," and let it go.

He climbed a couple of steps and sat down to put on his shoes. They had dried pretty well, but now the rest of him was soaked. It hurt his scraped back to laugh, but he laughed anyway. He climbed the stairs that used to be red, pausing every now and then to rest his legs. Maureen's scarf—in the morning light he could see that it was purple—came loose from around his waist. He thought of leaving it, then cinched it tight again. He didn't see how they could follow him this far, but the town was a logical destination, and he didn't want to leave a marker they might find, if only by chance. Besides, now the scarf felt important. It felt . . . he groped for a word that was at least close. Not lucky; talismanic. Because it was from her, and she was his savior.

By the time he got to the top of the steps, the sun was over the horizon, big and red, casting a bright glow on a tangle of railroad tracks. The freight beneath which he'd passed was now stopped in the Dennison River Bend switching yard. As the engine that had hauled it trundled slowly away, a bright yellow switch-engine pulled up to the rear of the train and would soon start it moving again, shoving it into the hump yard, where trains were broken up and reassembled.

The ins and outs of freight transport hadn't been

taught at the Broderick School, where the faculty was interested in more esoteric subjects like advanced math, climatology, and the later English poets; train lessons had been imparted by Vic Destin, balls-to-the-wall train freak and proud possessor of a huge Lionel set-up in his basement man cave. Luke and Rolf had spent a lot of hours there as his willing acolytes. Rolf liked running the model trains; the info about actual trains he could take or leave. Luke liked both. If Vic Destin had been a stamp collector, Luke would have examined his forays into philately with the same interest. It was just how he was built. He supposed that made him a bit on the creepy side (he had certainly caught Alicia Destin looking at him in a way which suggested that from time to time), but right now he blessed Mr. Destin's excited lectures.

Maureen, on the other hand, knew next to nothing about trains, only that Dennison River Bend had a depot, and she thought the trains that came through it went to all sorts of places. What those places might be, she did not know.

"She thinks if you make it that far, maybe you can hop a freight," Avery had said.

Well, he *had* made it this far. Whether or not he could actually hop a freight was another matter. He had seen it done in the movies, and with ease, but most movies were full of shit. It might be better to go to whatever passed for a downtown in this north country burg. Find the police station if there was one, call the State Police if there wasn't. Only call with what? He had no cell, and pay phones were an endangered species. If he did find one, what was he supposed to drop into the coin slot? One of his

Institute tokens? He supposed he could call 911 for free, but was that the right move? Something told him no.

He stood where he was in a day that was brightening entirely too fast for his liking, tugging nervously at the scarf around his waist. There were drawbacks to calling or going to the cops this close to the Institute; he could see them even in his current state of fear and exhaustion. The police would find out in short order that his parents were dead, murdered, and he was the most likely suspect. Another drawback was Dennison River Bend itself. Towns only existed if there was money coming in, money was their life-blood, and where did Dennison River Bend's money come from? Not from this trainyard, which would be largely automated. Not from those sad-looking buildings he'd seen. They might once have been factories, but no more. On the other hand, there was some sort of installation out there in one of the unincorporated townships ("government stuff," the locals would say, nodding wisely to each other in the barber shop or the town square), and the people who worked there had money. Men and women who came to town, and not just to patronize that Outlaw Country place on the nights when some shitkicking band or other was playing. They brought in dollars. And maybe the Institute was contributing to the town's welfare. They might have funded a community center, or a sports field, or kicked in for road maintenance. Anything that jeopardized those dollars would be looked at with skepticism and displeasure. For all Luke knew, the town officials might be getting regular payoffs to make sure the Institute didn't attract attention from the wrong people. Was that paranoid thinking? Maybe. And maybe not.

Luke was dying to blow the whistle on Mrs. Sigsby and her minions, but he thought the best, safest thing he could do right now was get as far away from the Institute as fast as he could.

The switch-engine was pushing the current bunch of freight cars up the hill trainyard people called the hump. There were two rocking chairs on the porch of the yard's tidy little office building. A man wearing jeans and bright red rubber boots sat in one of them, reading a newspaper and drinking coffee. When the engine driver hit the horn, the guy put his paper aside and trotted down the steps, pausing to wave up at a glassed-in booth on steel stilts. A guy inside waved back. That would be the hump tower operator, and the guy in the red boots would be the pin-puller.

Rolf's dad used to mourn over the moribund state of American rail transport, and now Luke saw his point. There were tracks heading in every direction, but it looked as though only four or five sets were currently operational. The others were flecked with rust, weeds growing up between the ties. There were stranded boxcars and flatcars on some of these, and Luke used them for cover, moving in on the office. He could see a clipboard hanging from a nail on one of the porch support posts. If that was today's transport schedule, he wanted to read it.

He squatted behind an abandoned boxcar close to the rear of the tower, watching from beneath as the pin-puller went to the hump track. The newly arrived freight was at the top of the hump now, and all of the operator's attention would be fixed there. If Luke was spotted, he'd probably be dismissed as just a kid who was, like Mr. Destin, a balls-to-the-wall train freak. Of course most kids didn't come out at five-thirty in the morning to look at trains no matter how balls to the wall they were. Especially kids who were soaked in river water and sporting a badly mutilated ear.

No choice. He had to see what was on that clipboard.

Mr. Red Boots stepped forward as the first car in line rolled slowly past him, and pulled the pin coupling it to the next. The box—STATE OF MAINE PRODUCTS emblazoned on the side in red, white, and blue—went rolling down the hill, pulled by gravity, its speed controlled by radar-operated retarders. The hump tower operator yanked a lever, and STATE OF MAINE PRODUCTS diverted onto Track 4.

Luke walked around the boxcar and ambled toward the station office, hands in his pockets. He didn't breathe freely until he was below the tower and out of the operator's sightline. Besides, Luke thought, if he's doing his job right, he's got eyes on the current job and nowhere else.

The next car, a tanker, was sent to Track 3. Two car carriers also went to Track 3. They bumped and clashed and rolled. Vic Destin's Lionel trains were pretty quiet, but this place was a looneybin of sound. Luke guessed that houses closer than a mile would get an earful three or four times each day. Maybe they get used to it, he thought. That was hard to believe until he thought of the kids going about their lives every day in the Institute—eating big meals, drinking nips, smoking the occasional cigarette, goofing on the playground, and running around at night, yelling their fool heads off. Luke guessed you could get used to anything. It was a horrible idea.

He reached the porch of the office, still well out of view of the tower operator, and the pin-puller's back was to him. Luke didn't think he'd turn around. "Lose focus in a job like that, and you're apt to lose a hand," Mr. Destin had told the boys once.

The computer sheet on top of the clipboard didn't contain much; the columns for Tracks 2 and 5 bore only two words: NOTHING SCHEDULED. Track 1 had a freight to New Brunswick, Canada, scheduled in at 5 PM—no help there. Track 4 was due out for Burlington and Montreal at 2:30 PM. Better, but still not good enough; if he wasn't gone by 2:30, he'd almost certainly be in big trouble. Track 3, where the pin-puller was now sending the New England Land Express box Luke had observed crossing the trestle, looked good. The cut-off for Train 4297—the time after which the station manager would not (theoretically at least) accept more freight—was 9 AM, and at 10 AM, '97 was scheduled out of Dennison River Bend for Portland/ME, Portsmouth/NH, and Sturbridge/MA. That last town had to be at least three hundred miles away, maybe a lot more.

Luke retreated to the abandoned boxcar and watched as the cars continued to roll down the hump onto various tracks, some of them for the trains that would be heading out that day, others that would simply be left on various sidings until they were needed.

The pin-puller finished his job and climbed the switch-engine's step to talk to the driver. The ops guy came out and joined them. There was laughter. It carried clearly to Luke on the still morning air, and he liked the sound. He had heard plenty of adult laughter in the C-Level break room, but it had always sounded sinister to him, like the laughter of orcs in a Tolkien story. This was coming from men who had never locked up a bunch of kids, or dunked them in an immersion tank. The laughter of men who did not carry the special Tasers known as zap-sticks.

The switch driver handed out a bag. The pin-puller took it and stepped down. As the engine started slowly down the hump, the pin-puller and the station operator each took a doughnut from the bag. Big ones dusted with sugar and probably stuffed with jelly. Luke's stomach rumbled.

The two men sat in the porch rocking chairs and munched their doughnuts. Luke, meanwhile, turned his attention to the cars waiting on Track 3. There were twelve in all, half of them boxcars. Probably not enough to make up a train going to Massachusetts, but others might be sent over from the transfer yard, where there were fifty or more just waiting around.

Meanwhile, a sixteen-wheeler pulled into the trainyard and bumped across several sets of tracks to the boxcar labeled STATE OF MAINE PRODUCTS. It was followed by a panel truck. Several men got out of the panel and began loading barrels from the traincar into the semi. Luke could hear them talking in Spanish, and was able to pick out a few words. One of the barrels tipped over and potatoes poured out. There was a lot of good-natured laughter, and a brief potato fight. Luke watched with longing.

The station operator and the pin-puller watched the potato fight from the porch rockers, then went inside. The semi left, now loaded with fresh spuds bound for McDonald's or Burger King. It was followed by the panel truck. The yard was momentarily deserted, but it wouldn't stay that way for long; there could be more loading and unloading, and the switch-engine driver might be busy adding more cars to the freight scheduled to leave at 10 AM.

Luke decided to take his chance. He started out from behind the deserted boxcar, then darted back when he saw the switch-engine driver walking up the hump, holding a phone to his ear. He stopped for a moment, and Luke was afraid he might have been seen, but the guy was apparently just finishing his call. He put his phone in the bib pocket of his overalls and passed the box Luke was hiding behind without so much as a glance. He mounted the porch steps and went into the office.

Luke didn't wait, and this time he didn't amble. He sprinted down the hump, ignoring the pain in his back and tired legs, hopping over tracks and retarder braking pads, dodging around speed sensor posts. The cars waiting for the Portland-Portsmouth-Sturbridge run included a red box with SOUTHWAY EXPRESS on the side, the words barely readable beneath all the graffiti that had been added over its years of service. It was grimy, nondescript, and strictly utilitarian, but it had one undeniable attraction: the sliding side door wasn't entirely shut. Enough of a gap, maybe, for a skinny, desperate boy to slip through.

Luke caught a rust-streaked grab-handle and pulled himself up. The gap *was* wide enough. Wider, in fact, than the one he'd dug beneath the chainlink fence at the Institute. That seemed a very long time ago, almost in another life. The side of the door scraped his already painful back and buttocks, starting new trickles of blood, but then he was inside. The car was about three-quarters full, and although it looked like a mutt on the outside, it smelled pretty great on the inside: wood, paint, furniture- and engine-oil.

The contents were a mishmash that made Luke think of his Aunt Lacey's attic, although the stuff she had stored was old, and all of this was new. To the left there were lawnmowers, weed-whackers, leaf-blowers, chainsaws, and cartons containing automotive parts and outboard motors. To the right was furniture, some in boxes but most mummified in yards of protective plastic. There was a pyramid of standing lamps on their sides, bubble-wrapped and taped together in threes. There were chairs, tables, loveseats, even sofas. Luke went to a sofa close to the partially opened door and read the invoice taped to the bubble wrap. It (and presumably the rest of the furniture) was to be delivered to Bender and Bowen Fine Furniture, in Sturbridge, Massachusetts.

Luke smiled. Train '97 might lose some cars in the Portland and Portsmouth yards, but this one was going all the way to the end of the line. His luck had not run out yet.

"Somebody up there likes me," he whispered. Then he remembered his mother and father were dead, and thought, But not that much.

He pushed some of the Bender and Bowen cartons a little way out from the far sidewall of the boxcar and was delighted to see a pile of furniture pads behind them. They smelled musty but not moldy. He crawled into the gap and pulled the boxes back as much as he could.

He was finally in a relatively safe place, he had a pile of soft pads to lie on, and he was exhausted—not just from his night run, but from the days of broken rest and escalating fear that had led up to his escape. But he did not dare sleep yet. Once he actually did doze off, but then he heard the sound of the approaching switch-engine, and the Southway Express boxcar jerked into motion. Luke got up and peered out through the partially open door. He saw the trainyard passing. Then the car jolted to a stop, almost knocking him off his feet. There was a metallic crunch that he assumed was his box being attached to another car.

Over the next hour or so there were more thumps and jolts as more cars were added to what would soon be Number 4297, headed into southern New England and away from the Institute.

Away, Luke thought. Away, away, away.

A couple of times he heard men talking, once quite close, but there was too much noise to make out what they were saying. Luke listened and chewed at fingernails that were already chewed down to the quick. What if they were talking about him? He remembered the switch-engine driver gabbing on his cell phone. What if Maureen had talked? What if he had been discovered missing? What if one of Mrs. Sigsby's minions—Stackhouse seemed the most likely—had called the trainyard and told the station operator to search all outgoing cars? If that happened, would the man start with boxcars that had slightly open side doors? Did a bear shit in the woods?

Then the voices dwindled and were lost. The bumps and shoves continued as 4297 took on weight and freight. Vehicles came and went. Sometimes there were honks. Luke jumped at every one. He wished to God he knew what time it was, but he didn't. He could only wait.

After what seemed forever, the bumps and thumps ceased. Nothing happened. Luke began to edge toward another doze and had almost made it when the biggest thump of all came, tossing him sideways. There was a pause, then the train began to move again.

Luke squirmed out of his hiding place and went to the partially open door. He looked out just in time to see the green-painted office building slide past. The operator and the pin-puller were back in their rocking chairs, each with a piece of the newspaper. 4297 thudded over a final junction point, then passed another cluster of deserted buildings. Next came a weedy ballfield, a trash dump, a couple of empty lots. The train rolled by a trailer park where kids were playing.

Minutes later, Luke found himself looking at downtown Dennison River Bend. He could see shops, streetlights, slant parking, sidewalks, a Shell station. He could see a dirty white pickup waiting for the train to pass. These things were just as amazing to him as the sight of the stars over the river had been. He was out. There were no techs, no caretakers, no token-operated machines where kids could buy booze and cigarettes. As the car swayed into a mild turn, Luke braced his hands against the boxcar's sidewalls and shuffled his feet. He was too tired to lift them, and so it was a very poor excuse for a victory dance, but that was what it was, just the same.

23

Once the town was gone, replaced by deep forest, exhaustion slammed Luke. It was like being buried under an avalanche. He crawled behind the cartons again, first lying on his back, which was his preferred sleeping position, then turning over on his stomach when the lacerations on his shoulderblades and buttocks protested. He was asleep at once. He slept through the stop at Portland and the one in Portsmouth, although the train jerked each time a few old cars were subtracted from 4297's pull-load and others were added. He was still asleep when the train stopped at Sturbridge, and only struggled back to consciousness when the door of his box was rattled open, filling it with the hot light of a July late afternoon.

Two men came in and started loading the furniture into a truck backed up to the open boxcar door—first the sofas, then the lamp trios, then the chairs. Soon they would start on the cartons, and Luke would be discovered. There were all those engines and lawn-mowers, and plenty of room to hide behind them in the far corner, but if he moved he would also be discovered.

One of the loading guys approached. He was close enough for Luke to smell his aftershave when someone called from outside. "Hey, you guys, there's a delay on the engine transfer. Shouldn't be long, but you got time for a coffee, if you want one."

"How about a beer?" asked the man who would have seen Luke on his bed of furniture pads in another three seconds.

This was greeted with laughter, and the men left. Luke backed out of his space and hobbled to the door on legs that were stiff and painful. Around the edge of the truck that was being loaded, he saw three men strolling toward the station-house. This one was painted red instead of green, and was four times the size of the one at Dennison River Bend. The sign on the front of the building said STURBRIDGE MASSACHUSETTS.

Luke thought of slipping out through the gap

between the boxcar and the truck, but this trainyard was in full swing, with lots of workmen (and a few workwomen) going here and there on foot and in vehicles. He would be seen, he would be questioned, and he knew he could not tell his story coherently in his present condition. He was vaguely aware that he was hungry, and a little more aware of his throbbing ear, but those things paled before his need for more sleep. Perhaps this boxcar would be shunted onto a sidetrack once the furniture was unloaded, and once it was dark, he could find the nearest police station. By then he might be able to talk without sounding like a lunatic. Or not *completely* like one. They might not believe him, but he was sure they would give him something to eat, and maybe some Tylenol for his throbbing ear. Telling them about his parents was his trump card. That was something they could verify. He would be returned to Minneapolis. That would be good, even if it meant going to some kind of kiddy facility. There would be locks on the doors, but no immersion tank.

Massachusetts was an excellent start, he had been fortunate to get this far, but it was still too close to the Institute. Minneapolis, on the other hand, was home. He knew people. Mr. Destin might believe him. Or Mr. Greer, at the Broderick School. Or . . .

But he couldn't think of anyone else. He was too tired. Trying to think was like trying to look through a window bleared with grease. He got on his knees and crawled to the far-right corner of the Southway Express box and peered out from between two roto-tillers, waiting for the men from the truck to come back and finish loading the furniture destined for Bender and Bowen Fine Furniture. They might still find him, he knew. They were guys, and guys liked to inspect anything with a motor in it. They might want to look at the riding mowers, or the weed-whackers. They might want to check the horsepower on the new Evinrudes—they were crated, but all the info would be on the invoices. He would wait, he would make himself small, he would hope that his luck—already stretched thin—would stretch a little further. And if they didn't find him, he would sink back into sleep.

Only there was no waiting or watching for Luke. He lay on one arm and was asleep again in minutes. He slept when the two men came back and finished their loading chores. He slept when one of them bent to check out a John Deere garden tractor not four feet from where Luke lay curled up and dead to the world. He slept when they left and one of the yard workers closed the Southway's door, this time all the way. He slept through the thud and thump of new cars being added, and stirred just slightly when a new engine replaced 4297. Then he slept again, a twelve-year-old fugitive who had been harried and hurt and terrified.

Train 4297 had a pull-limit of forty cars. Vic Destin would have identified the new loco as a GE AC6000CW, the 6000 standing for the horsepower it was capable of generating. It was one of the most powerful diesel locomotives at work in America, able to pull a train over a mile long. Running out of Sturbridge, first southeast and then dead south, this express train, 9956, was pulling seventy cars.

Luke's box was mostly empty now, and would remain that way until 9956 stopped in Richmond, Virginia, where two dozen Kohler home generators would be added to its load. Most of these were tagged for Wilmington, but two—and the entire assortment of small-engine appliances and doodads behind which Luke was now sleeping—were going to Fromie's Small Engine Sales and Service, in the little town of DuPray, South Carolina. 9956 stopped there three times a week.

Great events turn on small hinges.

HELL IS WAITING

1

As Train 4297 was leaving the Portsmouth, New Hampshire, yard, bound for Sturbridge, Mrs. Sigsby was studying the files and BDNF levels of two children who would shortly be residing at the Institute. One was male, one female. Ruby Red team would be bringing them in later that evening. The boy, a ten-year-old from Sault Ste. Marie, was just 80 on the BDNF scale. The girl, a fourteen-year-old from Chicago, was an 86. According to the file, she was autistic. That would make her difficult, both for staff and the other residents. If she had been below 80, they might have passed on her. But 86 was an outstanding score.

BDNF stood for brain-derived neurotrophic factor. Mrs. Sigsby understood very little of its chemical underpinnings, that was Dr. Hendricks's bailiwick, but she understood the basics. Like BMR, basal metabolic rate, BDNF was a scale. What it measured was the growth and survival rate of neurons throughout the body, and especially in the brain.

Those few with high BDNF readings, not even .5 per cent of the population, were the luckiest people in the world; Hendricks said they were what God had intended when He made human beings. They were rarely affected by memory loss, depression, or neuropathic pain. They rarely suffered from obesity or the extreme malnutrition that afflicted anorexics and bulimics. They socialized well with others (the incoming girl being a rare exception), were apt to stop trouble rather than start it (Nick Wilholm being another rare exception), they had low susceptibility to such neuroses as obsessive-compulsive disorder, and they had high verbal skills. They got few headaches and almost never suffered from migraines. Their cholesterol stayed low no matter what they ate. They did tend to have below average or poor sleep cycles but compensated for this by napping rather than taking sleeping aids.

While not fragile, BDNF could be damaged, sometimes catastrophically. The most common cause was what Hendricks called chronic traumatic encephalopathy, CTE for short. As far as Mrs. Sigsby could tell, that came down to plain old head-banging concussion. Average BDNF was 60 units per milliliter; football players who'd been in the game ten years or more usually measured in the mid-30s, sometimes in the 20s. BDNF declined slowly with normal ageing, much faster with those suffering from Alzheimer's. None of this mattered to Mrs. Sigsby, who was tasked only with getting results, and over her years at the Institute, results had been good.

What mattered to her, to the Institute, and to those who funded the Institute and had kept it a hard secret since 1955, was that children with high BDNF levels came with certain psychic abilities as part of the package: TK, TP, or (in rare cases) a combination of the two.

The children themselves sometimes didn't know about these abilities, because the talents were usually latent. Those who did know—usually high-functioning TPs like Avery Dixon—were sometimes able to use their talents when it seemed useful to do so, but ignored them the rest of the time.

Almost all newborns were tested for BDNF. Children such as the two whose files Mrs. Sigsby was now reading were flagged, followed, and eventually taken. Their low-level psychic abilities were refined and enhanced. According to Dr. Hendricks, those talents could also be expanded, TK added to TP and vice-versa, although such expansion did not affect the Institute's mission—its raison d'etre—in the slightest. The occasional success he'd had with the pinks he was given as guinea pigs would never be written up. She was sure Donkey Kong mourned that, even though he had to know that publication in any medical journal would land him in a maximum security prison instead of winning him a Nobel Prize.

There was a perfunctory knock at the door, and then Rosalind stuck her head in, looking apologetic. "I'm sorry to disturb you, ma'am, but it's Fred Clark, asking to see you. He seems—"

"Refresh me. Who is Fred Clark?" Mrs. Sigsby took off her reading glasses and rubbed the sides of her nose.

"One of the janitors."

"Find out what he wants and tell me later. If we've got mice chewing the wiring again, it can wait. I'm busy."

"He says it's important, and he seems extremely upset."

Mrs. Sigsby sighed, closed the folder, and put it in a drawer. "All right, send him in. But this better be good."

It wasn't. It was bad. Very.

2

Mrs. Sigsby recognized Clark, she'd seen him in the halls many times, pushing a broom or swishing a mop, but she had never seen him like this. He was dead pale, his graying hair was in a tangle, as if he had been rubbing or yanking at it, and his mouth was twitching infirmly.

"What's the problem, Clark? You look like you've seen a ghost."

"You have to come, Mrs. Sigsby. You have to see."

"See what?"

He shook his head and repeated, "You have to come."

She went with him along the walkway between the administration building and the West Wing of the residence building. She asked Clark twice more exactly what the problem was, but he would only shake his head and repeat that she had to see it for herself. Mrs. Sigsby's irritation at being interrupted began to be supplanted by a feeling of unease. One of the kids? A test gone bad, as with the Cross boy? Surely not. If there was a problem with one of them, a caretaker, a tech, or one of the doctors would have been more likely to discover it than a janitor.

Halfway down the mostly deserted West Wing corridor, a boy with a big belly pooching out his sloppily untucked shirt was peering at a piece of paper hanging from the knob of a closed door. He saw Mrs. Sigsby coming and immediately looked alarmed. Which was just the way he should look, in Mrs. Sigsby's opinion.

"Whipple, isn't it?"

"Yeah."

"What did you say to me?"

Stevie chewed his lower lip as he considered this. "Yes, Mrs. Sigsby."

"Better. Now get out of here. If you're not being tested, find something to do."

"Okay. I mean yes, Mrs. Sigsby."

Stevie headed off, casting one glance back over his shoulder. Mrs. Sigsby didn't see it. She was looking at the sheet of paper that had been pushed over the door-knob. DO NOT ENTER was written on it, probably by the pen clipped to one of Clark's shirt pockets.

"I would have locked it if I had a key," Fred said.

The janitors had keys to the various supply clos-ets on A-Level, also to the vending machines so they could resupply them, but not to the exam or residence rooms. The latter were rarely locked, anyway, except when some bad actor got up to nonsense and had to be restricted for a day as punishment. Nor did the jani-tors have elevator key cards. If they needed to go to one of the lower levels, they had to find a caretaker or a tech and ride down with them.

Clark said, "If that fat kid had gone in there, he would have gotten the shock of his young life."

Mrs. Sigsby opened the door without replying and beheld an empty room—no pictures or posters on the wall, nothing on the bed but a bare mattress. No different from any number of rooms in the residence wing these last dozen or so years, when the once strong inflow of high-BDNF children had slowed to a trickle.

It was Dr. Hendricks's theory that high BDNF was being bred out of the human genome, as were certain other human characteristics, like keen vision and hearing. Or, according to him, the ability to wiggle one's ears. Which might or might not have been a joke. With Donkey Kong, you could never be sure.

She turned to look at Fred.

"It's in the bathroom. I closed the door, just in case."

Mrs. Sigsby opened it and stood frozen for a space of seconds. She had seen a great deal during her tenure as Institute head, including the suicide of one resident and the attempted suicide of two others, but she had never seen the suicide of an employee.

The housekeeper (there was no mistaking the brown uniform) had hung herself from the shower head, which would have broken under the weight of someone heavier—the Whipple boy she'd just shooed away, for instance. The dead face glaring back at Mrs. Sigsby was black and swollen. Her tongue protruded from between her lips, almost as if she were giving them a final raspberry. Written on the tile wall in straggling letters was a final message.

"It's Maureen," Fred said in a low voice. He took a wad of handkerchief from the back pocket of his work pants and wiped his lips with it. "Maureen Alvorson. She—"

Mrs. Sigsby broke through the ice of shock and looked over her shoulder. The door to the hall was standing open. "Close that."

"She—"

"*Close that door!*"

The janitor did as he was told. Mrs. Sigsby felt in the right pocket of her suit jacket, but it was flat. Shit, she thought. Shit, shit, shit. Careless to have forgotten to bring her walkie, but who knew something like this was in store?

"Go back to my office. Tell Rosalind to give you my walkie-talkie. Bring it to me."

"You—"

"Shut up." She turned to him. Her mouth had thinned to a slit, and the way her eyes were bulging from her narrow face made Fred retreat a step. She looked crazy. "Do it, do it fast, and not a word to anyone about this."

"Okay, you bet."

He went out, closing the door behind him. Mrs. Sigsby sat down on the bare mattress and looked at the woman hanging from the shower head. And at the message she had written with the lipstick Mrs. Sigsby now observed lying in front of the toilet.

HELL IS WAITING. I'LL BE HERE TO MEET YOU.

3

Stackhouse was in the Institute's village, and when he answered her call, he sounded groggy. She assumed he had been living it up at Outlaw Country the night before, possibly in his brown suit, but didn't bother asking. She just told him to come to the West Wing at once. He'd know which room; a janitor would be standing outside the door.

Hendricks and Evans were on C-Level, conducting tests. Mrs. Sigsby told them to drop what they were doing and send their subjects back to residence. Both doctors were needed in the West Wing. Hendricks, who could be extremely irritating even at the best of times, wanted to know why. Mrs. Sigsby told him to shut up and come.

Stackhouse arrived first. The doctors were right behind him.

"Jim," Stackhouse said to Evans, after he had taken in the situation. "Lift her. Get me some slack in that rope."

Evans put his arms around the dead woman's waist—for a moment it almost looked as if they were dancing—and lifted her. Stackhouse began picking at the knot under her jaw.

"Hurry up," Evans said. "She's got a load in her drawers."

"I'm sure you've smelled worse," Stackhouse said. "Almost got it . . . wait . . . okay, here we go."

He lifted the noose over the dead woman's head (swearing under his breath when one of her arms flopped chummily down on the nape of his neck) and carried her to the mattress. The noose had left a blackish-purple brand on her neck. The four of them regarded her without speaking. At six-three, Trevor Stackhouse was tall, but Hendricks overtopped him by at least four inches. Standing between them, Mrs. Sigsby looked elfin.

Stackhouse looked at Mrs. Sigsby, eyebrows raised. She looked back without speaking.

On the table beside the bed was a brown pill bottle. Dr. Hendricks picked it up and rattled it. "Oxy. Forty milligrams. Not the highest dosage, but very high, just the same. The 'scrip is for ninety tablets, and there are only three left. I'm assuming we won't do an autopsy—"

You got that right, Stackhouse thought.

"—but if one *were* to be performed, I believe we'd find she took most of them before putting the rope around her neck."

"Which would have been enough to kill her in any case," Evans said. "This woman can't have weighed more than a hundred pounds. It's obvious that sciatica wasn't her primary problem, whatever she may have said. She couldn't have kept up with her duties for much longer no matter what, so just . . ."

"Just decided to end it," Hendricks finished.

Stackhouse was looking at the message on the wall. "Hell is waiting," he mused. "Considering what we're doing here, some might call that a reasonable assumption."

Not prone for vulgarity as a general rule, Mrs. Sigsby said, "Bullshit."

Stackhouse shrugged. His bald head gleamed beneath the light fixture as if Turtle Waxed. "Outsiders is what I meant, people who don't know the score. Doesn't matter. What we're seeing here is simple enough. A woman with a terminal disease decided to pull the plug." He pointed at the wall. "After declaring her guilt. And ours."

It made sense, but Mrs. Sigsby didn't like it. Alvorson's final communication to the world might have expressed guilt, but there was also something triumphant about it.

"She had a week off not very long ago," Fred the janitor volunteered. Mrs. Sigsby hadn't realized he was still in the room. Somebody should have dismissed him. *She* should have dismissed him. "She went back home to Vermont. That's prob'ly where she got the pills."

"Thanks," Stackhouse said. "That's very Sherlockian. Now don't you have floors to buff?"

"And clean those camera housings," Mrs. Sigsby snapped. "I asked for that to be done last week. I won't ask again."

"Yes, ma'am."

"Not a word about this, Mr. Clark."

"No, ma'am. Course not."

"Cremation?" Stackhouse asked when the janitor was gone.

"Yes. We'll have a couple of the caretakers take her to the elevator while the residents are at lunch. Which will be"—Mrs. Sigsby checked her watch—"in less than an hour."

"Is there a problem?" Stackhouse asked. "Other than keeping this from the residents, I mean? I ask because you look like there's a problem."

Mrs. Sigsby looked from the words printed on the bathroom tiles to the dead woman's black face, the tongue protruding. She turned from that final raspberry to the two doctors. "I'd like you to both step out. I need to speak to Mr. Stackhouse privately."

Hendricks and Evans exchanged a look, then left.

4

"She was your snitch. That's your problem?"

"*Our* snitch, Trevor, but yes, that's the problem. Or might be."

A year ago—no, more like sixteen months, there had still been snow on the ground—Maureen Alvorson had requested an appointment with Mrs. Sigsby and asked for any job that might provide extra income. Mrs. Sigsby, who'd had a pet project in mind for almost a year but no clear idea of how to implement it, asked if Alvorson would have a problem bringing any information she gleaned from the children. Alvorson agreed, and had even demonstrated a certain level of low cunning by suggesting the story about various supposed dead zones, where the microphones worked poorly or not at all.

Stackhouse shrugged. "What she brought us rarely rose above the level of gossip. Which boy was spending the night with which girl, who wrote TONY SUCKS on a table in the caff, that sort of thing." He paused. "Although snitching might have added to her guilt, I suppose."

"She was married," Mrs. Sigsby said, "but you'll notice she's no longer wearing her wedding ring. How much do we know about her life in Vermont?"

"I don't recall offhand, but it will be in her file, and I'm happy to look it up."

Mrs. Sigsby considered this, and realized how little she herself knew about Maureen Alvorson. Yes, she had known Alvorson was married, because she had seen the ring. Yes, she was retired military, as were many on the Institute's staff. Yes, she knew that Alvorson's home was in Vermont. But she knew little else, and how could that be, when she had hired the woman to spy on the residents? It might not matter now, not with Alvorson dead, but it made Mrs. Sigsby think of how she had left her walkie-talkie behind, assuming that the janitor had his knickers in a twist about nothing. It also made her think about the dusty camera housings, the slow computers and the small and inefficient staff in charge of them, the frequent food spoilage in the caff, the mouse-chewed wires, and the slipshod surveillance reports, especially on the night shift that ran from 11 PM to 7 AM, when the residents were asleep.

It made her think about carelessness.

"Julia? I said I'd—"

"I heard you. I'm not deaf. Who is on surveillance right now?"

Stackhouse looked at his watch. "Probably no one. It's the middle of the day. The kids will either be in their rooms or doing the usual kid things."

So you assume, she thought, and what is the mother of carelessness if not assumption? The Institute had been in operation for over sixty years, well over, and there had never been a leak. Never a reason (not on her watch, anyway) to use the special phone, the one they called the Zero Phone, for anything other than routine updates. Nothing, in short, they hadn't been able to handle in-house.

There were rumors in the Bend, of course. The most common among the citizens being that the compound out in the woods was some kind of nuclear missile base. Or that it had to do with germ or chemical warfare. Another, and this was closer to the truth, was that it was a government experimental station. Rumors were okay. Rumors were self-generated disinformation.

Everything is okay, she told herself. Everything is as it should be. The suicide of a disease-riddled housekeeper is just a bump in the road, and a minor one at that. Still, it was suggestive, of larger . . . well, not *problems*, it would be alarmist to call them that, but concerns, for sure. And some of it was her own fault. In the early days of Mrs. Sigsby's tour, the camera housings never would have been dusty, and she never would have left her office without her walkie. In those days she would have known a lot more about the woman she was paying to snitch on the residents.

She thought about entropy. The tendency to coast when things were going well.

To assume.

"Mrs. Sigsby? Julia? Do you have orders for me?"

She came back to the here and now. "Yes. I want to know everything about her, and if there's nobody in the surveillance room, I want someone there ASAP. Jerry, I think." Jerry Symonds was one of their two computer techs, and the best they had when it came to nursing the old equipment along.

"Jerry's on furlough," Stackhouse said. "Fishing in Nassau."

"Andy, then."

Stackhouse shook his head. "Fellowes is in the village. I saw him coming out of the commissary."

"Goddammit, he should be here. Zeke, then. Zeke the Greek. He's worked surveillance before, hasn't he?"

"I think so," Stackhouse said, and there it was again. Vagueness. Supposition. *Assumption*.

Dusty camera housings. Dirty baseboards. Careless talk on B-Level. The surveillance room standing empty.

Mrs. Sigsby decided on the spur of the moment that some big changes were going to be made, and before the leaves started to turn color and fall off the trees. If the Alvorson woman's suicide served no other purpose, it was a wake-up call. She didn't like speaking to the man on the other end of the Zero Phone, always felt a slight chill when she heard the faint lisp in his greeting (never *Sigsby*, always *Thigby*), but it had to be done. A written report wouldn't do. They had stringers all over the country. They had a private jet on call. The staff was well paid, and their various jobs came with all the bennies. Yet this facility more and more resembled a Dollar Store in a strip mall on the verge of abandonment. It was mad. Things had to change. Things *would* change.

She said, "Tell Zeke to run a check on the locater buttons. Let's make sure all of our charges are present and accounted for. I'm especially interested in Luke Ellis and Avery Dixon. She was talking to them a lot."

"We know what they've been talking about, and it doesn't come to much."

"Just do it."

"Happy to. In the meantime, you need to relax." He pointed to the corpse with her blackened face and impudently protruding tongue. "And get some perspective. This was a very sick woman who saw the end approaching and high-sided it."

"Run a check on the residents, Trevor. If they're all in their places—bright shiny faces optional—*then* I'll relax."

Only she wouldn't. There had been too much relaxation already.

5

Back in her office, she told Rosalind she didn't want to be disturbed unless it was Stackhouse or Zeke Ionidis, who was currently running a surveillance check on D-Level. She sat behind her desk, looking at the screen saver on her computer. It showed a white sand beach on Siesta Key, where she told people she planned to retire. She had given up telling herself that. Mrs. Sigsby fully expected to die here in the woods, possibly in her little house in the village, more likely behind this very desk. Two of her favorite writers, Thomas Hardy and

Rudyard Kipling, had died at their desks; why not her? The Institute had become her life, and she was okay with that.

Most of the staff was the same. Once they had been soldiers, or security personnel at hard-edged companies like Blackwater and Tomahawk Global, or law enforcement. Denny Williams and Michelle Robertson of the Ruby Red team had been FBI. If the Institute wasn't their lives when they were recruited and came on-station, it *became* their lives. It wasn't the pay. It wasn't the bennies or the retirement options. Part of it had to do with a manner of living that was so familiar to them it was a kind of sleep. The Institute was like a small military base; the adjacent village even had a PX where they could buy a wide range of goods at cheap prices and gas up their cars and trucks, paying ninety cents a gallon for regular and a dollar-five for hi-test. Mrs. Sigsby had spent time at Ramstein Air Base in Germany, and the town of Dennison River Bend reminded her—on a much smaller scale, granted—of Kaiserslautern, where she and her friends sometimes went to blow off steam. Ramstein had everything, even a twinplex theater and a Johnny Rockets, but sometimes you just wanted to get away. The same was true here.

But they always come back, she thought, looking at a sand beach she sometimes visited but where she would never live. They always come back and no matter how sloppy some things have become around here, they don't talk. That's one thing they are never sloppy about. Because if people found out what we're doing, the hundreds of children we have destroyed, we'd be tried and executed by the dozens. Given the needle like Timothy McVeigh.

That was the dark side of the coin. The bright side was simple: the entire staff, from the often annoying but undoubtedly competent Dr. Dan "Donkey Kong" Hendricks and Drs. Heckle and Jeckle in Back Half, right down to the lowliest janitor, understood that nothing less than the fate of the world was in their hands, as it had been in the hands of those who had come before them. Not just the survival of the human race, but the survival of the planet. They understood there was no limit to what they could and would do in pursuit of those ends. No one who fully grasped the Institute's work could regard it as monstrous.

Life here was good—good enough, anyway, especially for men and women who'd eaten sand in the Mideast and seen fellow soldiers lying in shitty villages with their legs blown off or their guts hanging out. You got the occasional furlough; you could go home and spend time with your family, assuming you had one (many Institute employees did not). Of course you couldn't talk to them about what you did, and after awhile they—the wives, the husbands, the children—would realize that it was the job that mattered, not them. Because it took you over. Your life became, in descending order, the Institute, the village, and the town of Dennison River Bend, with its three bars, one featuring live country music. And once the realization set in, the wedding ring would more often than not come off, as Alvorson's had done.

Mrs. Sigsby unlocked the bottom drawer of her desk and took out a phone that looked similar to the ones the extraction teams carried: big and blocky, like a refugee from a time when cassette tapes were giving way to CDs and portable phones were just starting to show up in electronics stores. It was sometimes called the Green Phone, because of its color, and more often the Zero Phone, because there was no screen and no numbers, just three small white circles.

I will call, she thought. Maybe they'll applaud my forward thinking and congratulate me on my initiative. Maybe they'll decide I'm jumping at shadows and it's time to think of a replacement. Either way it has to be done. Duty calls, and it should have called sooner.

"But not today," she murmured.

No, not today, not while there was Alvorson to take care of (and dispose of). Maybe not tomorrow or even this week. What she was thinking of doing was no small thing. She would want to make notes, so that when she *did* call, she could be as on-point as possible. If she really meant to use the Zero, it was imperative that she be ready to reply concisely when she heard the man at the other end say *Hello, Mithith Thigby, how can I help?*

It's not the same as procrastinating, she told herself. Not at all. And I don't necessarily want to get anyone in trouble, but—

Her intercom gave a soft tone. "I have Zeke for you, Mrs. Sigsby. Line three."

Mrs. Sigsby picked up. "What have you got for me, Ionidis?"

"Perfect attendance," he said. "Twenty-eight locater blips in Back Half. In Front Half there's two kids in the lounge, six in the playground, five in their rooms."

"Very good. Thank you."

"You're welcome, ma'am."

Mrs. Sigsby got up feeling a little better, although she couldn't have said precisely why. Of *course* the residents were all accounted for. What had she been thinking, that some of them had gone off to Disney World?

Meanwhile, on to the next chore.

6

Once all the residents were at lunch, Fred the janitor pushed a trolley borrowed from the cafeteria kitchen to the door of the room where Maureen Alvorson had ended her life. Fred and Stackhouse wrapped her in a swatch of green canvas and rolled her up the corridor, double-time. From further on came the sound of the animals at feeding time, but here all was deserted, although someone had left a teddy bear lying on the floor in front of the elevator annex. It stared at the ceiling with its glassy shoebutton eyes. Fred gave it an irritated kick.

Stackhouse looked at him reproachfully. "Bad luck, pal. That's some child's comfort-stuffy."

"I don't care," Fred said. "They're always leaving their shit around for us to pick up."

When the elevator doors opened, Fred started to pull the trolley in. Stackhouse pushed him back, and not gently. "Your services are not required beyond this point. Pick up that teddy and put it in the lounge or in the canteen, where its owner will see it when he or she comes out. And then start dusting those fucking bulbs." He pointed up at one of the overhead camera housings, rolled the trolley in, and held his card up to the reader.

Fred Clark waited until the doors were shut before giving him the finger. But orders were orders, and he'd clean the housings. Eventually.

7

Mrs. Sigsby was waiting for Stackhouse on F-Level. It was cold down here, and she was wearing a sweater over her suit jacket. She nodded to him. Stackhouse nodded back and rolled the trolley into the tunnel between Front Half and Back Half. It was the very definition of utilitarian, with its concrete floor, curved tile walls, and overhead fluorescents. A few of these were stuttering, giving the tunnel a horror movie feel, and a few others were dead out. Someone had pasted a New England Patriots bumper sticker on one wall.

More carelessness, she thought. More drift.

The door at the Back Half end of the corridor bore a sign reading AUTHORIZED PERSONNEL ONLY. Mrs. Sigsby used her card and pushed it open. Beyond was another elevator lobby. A short upward journey brought them to a lounge only slightly less utilitarian than the service tunnel they had taken to get to Back Half. Heckle—real name Dr. Everett Hallas—was waiting for them. He was wearing a big grin and constantly touching the corner of his mouth. It reminded Mrs. Sigsby of the Dixon boy's obsessive nose-pulling. Except Dixon was only a kid, and Hallas was in his fifties. Working in Back Half took a toll, the way working in an environment polluted with low-level radiation would take a toll.

"*Hello*, Mrs. Sigsby! *Hello*, Security Director Stackhouse! How wonderful to see you! We should get together more often! I'm sorry about the circumstances that have brought you here today, however!" He bent and patted the canvas bundle containing Maureen Alvorson. Then touched the corner of his mouth, as if patting at a cold sore only he could see or feel. "In the midst of life, cetra-cetra."

"We need to make this quick," Stackhouse said. Meaning, Mrs. Sigsby supposed, we have to get out of here. She quite concurred. This was where the real work was done, and Drs. Heckle and Jeckle (real name Joanne James) were heroes for doing it, but that didn't make it any easier to be here. She could already feel the atmosphere of the place. It was like being in a low-level electrical field.

"Yes, of course you do, the work never ends, wheels within wheels, big fleas with little fleas to bite em, don't I know, right this way."

From the lounge, with its ugly chairs, equally ugly sofa, and elderly flatscreen, they entered a hall with a thick blue carpet on the floor—in Back Half, the children sometimes fell down and bumped their valuable little heads. The trolley's wheels left tracks in the nap. This looked much like a corridor on the residence level of Front Half, except for the locks on the doors, which were all shut. From behind one of them, Mrs. Sigsby heard pounding and muffled cries of "Let me out!" and "At least give me a fucking aspirin!"

"Iris Stanhope," Heckle said. "She's not feeling well today, I'm afraid. On the upside, several of our other recent arrivals are holding up remarkably well. We're having a movie this evening, you know. And fireworks tomorrow." He giggled and touched the corner of his mouth, reminding Mrs. Sigsby—grotesquely—of Shirley Temple.

She brushed at her hair to make sure it was still in place. It was, of course. What she was feeling—that low buzz along her exposed skin, the sense that her eyeballs were vibrating in their sockets—wasn't electricity.

They passed the screening room with its dozen or so plush seats. Sitting in the front row were Kalisha Benson, Nick Wilholm, and George Iles. They were wearing their red and blue singlets. The Benson girl was sucking on a candy cigarette; Wilholm was smoking a real one, the air around his head wreathed with gray smoke. Iles was rubbing lightly at his temples. Benson and Iles turned to look at them as they rolled past with their canvas-wrapped burden; Wilholm just went on staring at the blank movie screen. *A lot of steam has been taken out of that hotdog,* Mrs. Sigsby thought with satisfaction.

The cafeteria was beyond the screening room, on the other side of the corridor. It was much smaller than the one in Front Half. There were always more children here, but the longer they stayed in Back Half, the less they ate. Mrs. Sigsby supposed an English major might call that irony. Three kids were currently present, two slurping up what looked like oatmeal, the other—a girl of about twelve—simply sitting with a full bowl in front of her. But when she saw them passing with the trolley, she brightened.

"Hi! What you got there? Is it a dead person? It is, isn't it? Was her name Morris? That's a funny name for a girl. Maybe it's Morin. Can I see? Are her eyes open?"

"That's Donna," Heckle said. "Ignore her. She'll be at the movie tonight, but pretty soon I expect she'll be moving on. Maybe later this week. Greener pastures, cetra-cetra. You know."

Mrs. Sigsby did know. There was Front Half, there was Back Half . . . and there was the back half of Back Half. The end of the line. She put her hand to her hair again. Still in place. Of course it was. She thought of a tricycle she'd had as a very young child, the warm squirt of urine in her pants as she rode it up and down the driveway. She thought of broken shoelaces. She thought of her first car, a—

"It was a Valium!" the girl named Donna screamed. She leaped up, knocking her chair over. The other two children looked at her dully, one with oatmeal dripping from his chin. "A Plymouth Valium, I know that! Oh God I want to go *home*! Oh God stop my *head*!"

Two caretakers in red scrubs appeared from . . . from Mrs. Sigsby didn't know where. Nor did she care. They grabbed the girl by her arms.

"That's right, take her back to her room," Heckle said. "No pills, though. We need her tonight."

Donna Gibson, who had once shared girl-secrets with Kalisha when they were both still in Front Half, began to scream and struggle. The caretakers led her away with the toes of her sneakers brushing the carpet. The broken thoughts in Mrs. Sigsby's mind first dimmed, then faded. The buzz along her skin, even in the fillings of her teeth, remained, however. Over here it was constant, like the buzz of the fluorescent lights in the corridor.

"All right?" Stackhouse asked Mrs. Sigsby.

"Yes." *Just get me out of here.*

"I feel it, too. If it's any comfort."

It wasn't. "Trevor, can you explain to me why bodies bound for the crematorium have to be rolled right through these children's living quarters?"

"There are tons of beans in Beantown," Stackhouse replied.

"What?" Mrs. Sigsby asked. "What did you say?"

Stackhouse shook his head as if to clear it. "I'm sorry. That came into my head—"

"Yes, yes," Hallas said. "There are a lot of . . . uh, shall we say *loose transmissions* in the air today."

"I know what it was," Stackhouse said. "I had to get it out, that's all. It felt like . . ."

"Choking on food," Dr. Hallas said matter-of-factly. "The answer to your question, Mrs. Sigsby is . . . *nobody knows*." He tittered and touched the corner of his mouth.

Just get me out of here, she thought again. "Where is Dr. James, Dr. Hallas?"

"In her quarters. Not feeling well today, I'm afraid. But she sends her regards. Hopes you're well, fit as a fiddle, in the pink, cetra-cetra." He smiled and did the Shirley Temple thing again—*ain't I cute?*

8

In the screening room, Kalisha plucked the cigarette from Nicky's fingers, took a final puff from the filterless stub, dropped it to the floor, stepped on it. Then she put an arm around his shoulders. "Bad?"

"I've had worse."

"The movie will make it better."

"Yeah. But there's always tomorrow. Now I know why my dad was so butt-ugly when he had a hangover. How about you, Sha?"

"Doing okay." And she was. Just a low throb over her left eye. Tonight it would be gone. Tomorrow it would be back, and not low. Tomorrow it would be pain that would make the hangovers suffered by Nicky's dad (and her own parents, from time to time) look like fun in the sun: a steady pounding thud, as if some demonic elf were imprisoned in her head, hammering at her skull in an effort to get out. Even that, she knew, wasn't as bad as it could be. Nicky's headaches were worse, Iris's worse still, and it took longer and longer for the pain to go away.

George was the lucky one; in spite of his strong TK, he had so far felt almost no pain at all. An ache in his temples, he said, and at the back of his skull. But it would get worse. It always did, at least until it was finally over. And then? Ward A. The drone. The hum. The back half of Back Half. Kalisha didn't look forward to it yet, the idea of being erased as a person still horrified her, but that would change. For Iris, it already had; most of the time she looked like a zombie on *The Walking Dead*. Helen Simms had pretty much articulated Kalisha's feelings about Ward A when she said anything was better than the Stasi Lights and a screaming headache that never stopped.

George leaned forward, looking at her across Nick with bright eyes that were still relatively pain-free. "He got out," he whispered. "Concentrate on that. And hold on."

"We will," Kalisha said. "Won't we, Nick?"

"We'll try," Nick said, and managed a smile. "Although the idea of a guy as horrible at HORSE as Lukey Ellis bringing the cavalry is pretty farfetched."

"He may be bad at HORSE but he's good at chess," George said. "Don't count him out."

One of the red caretakers appeared in the open doors of the screening room. The caretakers in Front Half wore nametags, but down here no one did. Down here the caretakers were interchangeable. There were no techs, either, only the two Back Half doctors and sometimes Dr. Hendricks: Heckle, Jeckle, and Donkey Kong. The Terrible Trio. "Free time is over. If you're not going to eat, go back to your rooms."

The old Nicky might have told this over-muscled lowbrow to go fuck himself. The new version just got to his feet, staggering and grabbing a seatback to keep his balance. It broke Kalisha's heart to see him this way. What had been taken from Nicky was in some ways worse than murder. In *many* ways.

"Come on," she said. "We'll go together. Right, George?"

"Well," George said, "I was planning to catch a matinee of *Jersey Boys* this afternoon, but since you insist."

Here we are, the three fucked-up musketeers, Kalisha thought.

Out in the hall, the drone was much stronger. Yes, she knew Luke was out, Avery had told her, and that was good. The complacent assholes didn't even know he was gone yet, which was better. But the headaches made hope seem less hopeful. Even when they let up, you were waiting for them to come back, which was its own special brand of hell. And the drone coming from Ward A made hope seem irrelevant, which was awful. She had never felt so lonely, so cornered.

But I have to hold on for as long as I can, she thought. No matter what they do to us with those lights and those goddam movies, I have to hold on. I have to hold on to my mind.

They walked slowly down the hall under the eye of the caretaker, not like children but like invalids. Or old people, whiling away their final weeks in an unpleasant hospice.

9

Led by Dr. Everett Hallas, Mrs. Sigsby and Stackhouse walked past the closed doors marked Ward A, Stackhouse rolling the trolley. There were no shouts or screams coming from behind those closed doors, but that sense of being in an electrical field was even stronger; it raced over her skin like invisible mouse feet. Stackhouse felt it, too. The hand not busy pushing Maureen Alvorson's makeshift bier was rubbing his smooth bald dome.

"To me it always feels like cobwebs," he said. Then, to Heckle, "You don't feel it?"

"I'm used to it," he said, and touched the corner of his mouth. "It's a process of assimilation." He stopped. "No, that's not the right word. *Acclimation*, I think. Or is it acclimatization? Could be either."

Mrs. Sigsby was struck by a curiosity that was almost whimsical. "Dr. Hallas, when's your birthday? Do you remember?"

"September ninth. And I know what you're thinking." He looked back over his shoulder at the doors with *Ward A* on them in red, then at Mrs. Sigsby. "I'm fine, howsomever."

"September ninth," she said. "That would make you . . . what? A Libra?"

"Aquarius," Heckle said, giving her a roguish look that seemed to say *You do not fool me so easily, my lady.* "When the moon is in the seventh house and Mercury aligns with Mars. Cetra-cetra. Duck, Mr. Stackhouse. Low bridge here."

They passed along a short, dim hallway, descended a flight of stairs with Stackhouse braking the trolley in front and Mrs Sigsby controlling it from behind, and came to another closed door. Heckle used his key card and they entered a circular room that was uncomfortably warm. There was no furniture, but on one wall was a framed sign: **REMEMBER THESE WERE HEROES.** It was under dirty smeared glass that badly needed a dose of Windex. On the far side of the room, halfway up a rough cement wall, was a steel hatch, as if for an industrial meat locker. To the left of this was a small readout screen, currently blank. To the right was a pair of buttons, one red and one green.

In here, the broken thoughts and fragments of memory that had troubled Mrs. Sigsby ceased, and the fugitive headache which had been hovering at her temples lifted a bit. That was good, but she couldn't wait to be out. She seldom visited Back Half, because her presence was unnecessary; the commander of an army rarely needed to visit the front lines as long as the war was going well. And even though she felt better, being in this bare round room was still flat-out horrible.

Hallas also seemed better, no longer Heckle but the man who had spent twenty-five years as an Army doctor and won a Bronze Star. He had straightened, and he had stopped touching his finger to the side of his mouth. His eyes were clear, his questions concise.

"Is she wearing jewelry?"

"No," Mrs. Sigsby said, thinking of Alvorson's missing wedding ring.

"I may assume she's dressed?"

"Of course." Mrs. Sigsby felt obscurely offended by the question.

"Have you checked her pockets?"

She looked at Stackhouse. He shook his head.

"Do you want to? This is your only chance, if you do."

Mrs. Sigsby considered the idea and dismissed it. The woman had left her suicide note on the bathroom wall, and her purse would be in her locker. That would need checking, just as a matter of routine, but she wasn't going to unwrap the housekeeper's body and expose that protruding impudent tongue again just to find a ChapStick, a roll of Tums, and a few wadded-up Kleenex.

"Not me. What about you, Trevor?"

Stackhouse shook his head again. He had a year-round tan, but today he looked pale beneath it. The Back Half walk-through had taken a toll on him, too. Maybe we should do it more often, she thought. Stay in touch with the process. Then she thought of Dr. Hallas proclaiming himself an Aquarian and Stackhouse saying there were tons of beans in Beantown. She decided that staying in touch with the process was a really bad idea. And by the way, did September 9th really make Hallas a Libra? That didn't seem quite right. Wasn't it Virgo?

"Let's do this," she said.

"All *righty*, then," Dr. Hallas said, and flashed an ear-to-ear smile that was all Heckle. He yanked the handle of the stainless steel door and swung it open. Beyond was blackness, a smell of cooked meat, and a sooty conveyer belt that angled down into darkness.

That sign needs to be cleaned off, Mrs. Sigsby thought. And that belt needs to be scrubbed before it gets clogged and breaks down. More carelessness.

"I hope you don't need help lifting her," Heckle said, still wearing his game-show host smile. "I'm afraid I'm feeling rather weakly today. Didn't eat my Wheaties this morning."

Stackhouse lifted the wrapped body and placed it on the belt. The bottom fold of the canvas dropped open, revealing one shoe. Mrs. Sigsby felt an urge to turn away from that scuffed sole and quelled it.

"Any final words?" Hallas asked. "Hail and farewell? Jenny we hardly knew ye?"

"Don't be an idiot," Mrs. Sigsby said.

Dr. Hallas closed the door and pushed the green button. Mrs. Sigsby heard a trundle and squeak as the dirty conveyer belt began to move. When that stopped, Hallas pushed the red button. The readout came to life, quickly jumping from 200 to 400 to 800 to 1600 and finally to 3200.

"Much hotter than your average crematory," Hallas said. "Also much faster, but it still takes awhile. You're welcome to stick around; I could give you the full tour." Still smiling the big smile.

"Not today," Mrs. Sigsby said. "Far too busy."

"That's what I thought. Another time, perhaps. We see you so seldom, and we're always open for business."

10

As Maureen Alvorson was starting her final slide, Stevie Whipple was eating mac and cheese in the Front Half cafeteria. Avery Dixon grabbed him by one meaty, freckled arm. "Come out to the playground with me."

"I ain't done eating, Avery."

"I don't care." He lowered his voice. "It's important."

Stevie took a final enormous bite, wiped his mouth

with the back of his hand, and followed Avery. The playground was deserted except for Frieda Brown, who was sitting on the asphalt surrounding the basketball hoop and drawing cartoon figures in chalk. Rather good ones. All smiling. She didn't look up as the boys passed.

When they arrived at the chainlink fence, Avery pointed at a trench in the dirt and gravel. Stevie stared at it with big eyes. "What did that? Woodchuck or sumpin?" He looked around as if he expected to see a woodchuck—possibly rabid—hiding under the trampoline or crouching beneath the picnic table.

"Wasn't a woodchuck, nope," Avery said.

"I bet you could squiggle right through there, Aves. Make an excape."

Don't think it hasn't crossed my mind, Avery thought, but I'd get lost in the woods. Even if I didn't, the boat is gone. "Never mind. You have to help me fill it in."

"Why?"

"Just because. And don't say *excape*, it sounds ignorant. *Ess*, Stevie. *Ess*cape." Which is just what his friend had done, God love and bless him. Where was he now? Avery had no idea. He'd lost touch.

"*Ess*cape," Stevie said. "Got it."

"Terrific. Now help me."

The boys got down on their knees and began to fill in the depression under the fence, scooping with their hands and raising a cloud of dust. It was hot work, and they were both soon sweating. Stevie's face was bright red.

"What are you boys doing?"

They looked around. It was Gladys, her usual big smile nowhere in sight.

"Nothing," Avery said.

"Nothing," Stevie agreed. "Just playin in the dirt. You know, the dirty ole dirt."

"Let me see. Move." And when neither of them did, she kicked Avery in the side.

"*Ow!*" he cried, and curled up. "*Ow, that hurt!*"

Stevie said, "What are you, on the rag or some—" Then he got his own kick, high up on the shoulder.

Gladys looked at the trench, only partially filled in, then at Frieda, still absorbed in her artistic endeavors. "Did you do this?"

Frieda shook her head without looking up.

Gladys pulled her walkie from the pocket of her white pants and keyed it. "Mr. Stackhouse? This is Gladys for Mr. Stackhouse."

There was a pause, then: "This is Stackhouse, go."

"I think you need to come out to the playground as soon as possible. There's something you need to see. Maybe it's nothing, but I don't like it."

11

After notifying the security chief, Gladys called Winona to take the two boys back to their rooms. They were to stay there until further notice.

"I don't know nothing about that hole," Stevie said sulkily. "I thought a woodchuck done it."

Winona told him to shut up and herded the boys back inside.

Stackhouse arrived with Mrs. Sigsby. She bent and he squatted, first looking at the dip under the chain-link, then at the fence itself.

"Nobody could crawl under there," Mrs. Sigsby

said. "Well, maybe Dixon, he's not much bigger than those Wilcox twins were, but no one else."

Stackhouse scooped away the loose mix of rocks and dirt the two boys had put back in, deepening the dip to a trench. "Are you sure of that?"

Mrs. Sigsby realized she was biting at her lip, and made herself stop. *The idea is ridiculous*, she thought. *We have cameras, we have microphones, we have the caretakers and the janitors and the housekeepers, we have security. All to take care of a bunch of kids so terrified they wouldn't say boo to a goose.*

Of course there was Wilholm, who definitely *would* say boo to a goose, and there had been a few others like him over the years. But still . . .

"Julia." Very low.

"What?"

"Get down here with me."

She started to do it, then saw the Brown girl staring at them. "Get inside," she snapped. "This second."

Frieda went in a hurry, dusting off her chalky hands, leaving her smiling cartoon people behind. As the girl entered the lounge, Mrs. Sigsby saw a small cluster of children gawking out. Where were the caretakers when you needed them? In the break room, swapping stories with one of the extraction teams? Telling dirty jo—

"Julia!"

She dropped to one knee, wincing when a sharp piece of gravel bit into her.

"There's blood on this fence. See it?"

She didn't want to, but she did. Yes, that was blood. Dried to maroon, but definitely blood.

"Now look over there."

He poked a finger through one of the chainlink diamonds, pointing at a partially uprooted bush. There was blood on that, too. As Mrs. Sigsby looked at those few spots, spots that were *outside*, her stomach dropped and for one alarming moment she thought she was going to wet her pants, as she had on that long-ago trike. She thought of the Zero Phone and saw her life as head of the Institute—because that was what it was, not her job but her life—disappearing into it. What would the lisping man on the other end say if she had to call and tell him that, in what was supposed to be the most secret and secure facility in the country—not to mention the most *vital* facility in the country—a child had escaped by *going under a fence*?

They would say she was done, of course. Done and dusted.

"The residents are all here," she said in a hoarse whisper. She grasped Stackhouse's wrist, her fingernails biting into his skin. He didn't seem to notice. He was still staring at the partially uprooted bush as if hypnotized. This was as bad for him as for her. Not worse, there *was* no worse, but just as bad. "Trevor, *they are all here*. I checked."

"I think you better check again. Don't you?"

She had her walkie this time (thoughts of locking the barn door after the livestock was stolen flashed through her mind), and she keyed it. "Zeke. This is Mrs. Sigsby for Zeke." You better be there, Ionidis. You just better.

He was. "This is Zeke, Mrs. Sigsby. I've been checking up on Alvorson, Mr. Stackhouse told me to since Jerry's off and Andy's not here, and I reached her next-door neigh—"

"Never mind that now. Look at the locater blips again for me."

"Okay." He sounded suddenly cautious. Must have heard the strain in my voice, she thought. "Hold on, everything's running slow this morning . . . couple more seconds . . ."

She felt as if she would scream. Stackhouse was still peering through the fence, as if expecting a magic fucking hobbit to appear and explain the whole thing.

"Okay," Zeke said. "Forty-one residents, still perfect attendance."

Relief cooled her face like a breeze. "All right, that's good. That's very—"

Stackhouse took the walkie from her. "Where are they currently?"

"Uh . . . still twenty-eight in Back Half, now four in the East Wing lounge . . . three in the caff . . . two in their rooms . . . three in the hall . . ."

Those three would be Dixon, Whipple, and the artist-girl, Mrs. Sigsby thought.

"Plus one in the playground," Zeke finished. "Forty-one. Like I said."

"Wait one, Zeke." Stackhouse looked at Mrs. Sigsby. "Do you see a kid in the playground?"

She didn't answer him. She didn't need to.

Stackhouse raised the walkie again. "Zeke?"

"Go, Mr. Stackhouse. Right here."

"Can you pinpoint the exact location of the kid in the playground?"

"Uh . . . let me zoom . . . there's a button for that . . ."

"Don't bother," Mrs. Sigsby said. She had spotted an object glittering in the early afternoon sun. She walked onto the basketball court, stooped at the foul line, and picked it up. She returned to her security chief and held out her hand. In her palm was most of an earlobe with the tracker button still embedded in it.

12

The Front Half residents were told to return to their rooms and stay there. If any were caught in the hall, they would be severely punished. The Institute's security force totaled just four, counting Stackhouse himself. Two of these men were in the Institute village and came quickly, using the golf-cart track Maureen had expected Luke to find, and which he had missed by less than a hundred feet. The third member of Stackhouse's team was in Dennison River Bend. Stackhouse had no intention of waiting for her to turn up. Denny Williams and Robin Lecks of the Ruby Red team were on-site, though, waiting for their next assignment, and perfectly willing to be drafted. They were joined by two widebodies—Joe Brinks and Chad Greenlee.

"The Minnesota boy," Denny said, once this makeshift search party was assembled and the tale was told. "The one we brought in last month."

"That's right," Stackhouse agreed, "the Minnesota boy."

"And you say he ripped the tracker right out of his ear?" Robin asked.

"The cut's a little smoother than that. Used a knife, I think."

"Took balls, either way," Denny said.

"I'll *have* his balls when we catch up to him," Joe said. "He doesn't fight like Wilholm did, but he's got a fuck-you look in his eyes."

"He'll be wandering around in the woods, so lost

he'll probably hug us when we find him," Chad said. He paused. "*If* we find him. Lot of trees out there."

"He was bleeding from his ear and probably all down his back from going under the fence," Stackhouse said. "Must have got it on his hands, too. We'll follow the blood as far as we can."

"It'd be good if we had a dog," Denny Williams said. "A bloodhound or a good old bluetick."

"It would be good if he'd never gotten out in the first place," Robin said. "Under the fence, huh?" She almost laughed, then saw Stackhouse's drawn face and furious eyes and reconsidered.

Rafe Pullman and John Walsh, the two security guys from the village, arrived just then.

Stackhouse said, "We are not going to kill him, understand that, but we *are* going to zap the living shit out of the little son of a bitch when we find him."

"*If* we find him," Chad the caretaker repeated.

"We'll find him," Stackhouse said. Because if we don't, he thought, I'm toast. This whole place might be toast.

"I'm going back to my office," Mrs. Sigsby said.

Stackhouse caught her by the elbow. "And do what?"

"Think."

"That's good. Think all you want, but no calls. Are we agreed on that?"

Mrs. Sigsby looked at him with contempt, but the way she was biting her lips suggested she might also be afraid. If so, that made two of them. "Of course."

But when she got to her office—the blessed air-conditioned silence of her office—she found thinking was hard. Her eyes kept straying to the locked drawer of her desk. As if it wasn't a phone inside, but a hand grenade.

13

Three o'clock in the afternoon.

No news from the men hunting for Luke Ellis in the woods. Plenty of communications, yes, but no news. Every member of the Institute staff had been notified of the escape; it was all hands on deck. Some had joined the searchers. Others were combing the Institute village, searching all empty quarters, looking for the boy or at least some sign that he'd been there. All personal vehicles were accounted for. The golf carts the employees sometimes used to get around were all where they belonged. Their stringers in Dennison River Bend—including two members of the town's small police force—had been alerted and given Ellis's description, but there had been no sightings.

With Alvorson there *was* news.

Ionidis had shown initiative and guile of which Jerry Symonds and Andy Fellowes, their IT techs, would have been incapable. First using Google Earth and then a phone locater app, Zeke had gotten in touch with Alvorson's next-door neighbor in the little Vermont town where Alvorson still maintained a residence. He represented himself to this neighbor as an IRS agent, and she bought it without a single question. Showing no signs of the reticence Yankees were supposedly famous for, she told him that Maureen had asked her to witness several documents the last time Mo had been home. A woman lawyer had been present. The documents were addressed to several collection agencies. The lawyer called the documents C-and-D orders, which the neighbor rightly took to mean cease and desist.

"Those letters were all about her husband's credit cards," the neighbor lady told Zeke. "Mo didn't explain, but she didn't need to. I wasn't born yesterday. Handling that deadbeat's bills is what she was doing. If the IRS can sue her for that, you better move fast. She looked sick as hell."

Mrs. Sigsby thought the Vermont neighbor had it right. The question was why Alvorson would do it that way; it was carrying coals to Newcastle. All Institute employees knew that if they got into any kind of financial jam (gambling was the most common), they could count on loans that were next door to interest-free. That part of the benefits package was explained at every new employee's intake orientation. It really wasn't a benefit at all, but a protection. People who were in debt could be tempted to sell secrets.

The easy explanation for such behavior was pride, maybe combined with shame at having been taken advantage of by her runaway husband, but Mrs. Sigsby didn't like it. The woman had been nearing the end of her life and must have known that for some time. She had decided to clean her hands, and taking money from the organization that had dirtied them was not the way to start. That felt right—or close to right, anyway. It fit with Alvorson's reference to hell.

That bitch helped him escape, Mrs. Sigsby thought. *Of course she did, it was her idea of atonement. But I can't question her about it, she made sure of that. Of course she did—she knows our methods. So what do I do? What* will *I do if that too-smart-for-his-own-good boy isn't back here before dark?*

She knew the answer, and was sure Trevor did, too. She would have to take the Zero Phone out of its locked drawer and hit all three of the white buttons. The lisping man would answer. When she told him that a resident had escaped for the first time in the Institute's history—had dug his way out in the middle of the night under the fence—what would that person say? Gosh, I'm thorry? Thath's too bad? Don't worry about it?

Like hell.

Think, she told herself. Think, think, *think*. Who might the troublesome housekeeper have told? For that matter, who might *Ellis* have t—

"Fuck. *Fuck!*"

It was right in front of her, and had been ever since discovering the hole under the fence. She sat up straight in her chair, eyes wide, the Zero Phone out of her mind for the first time since Stackhouse had called in to report the blood-trail had disappeared just fifty yards into the woods.

She powered up her computer and found the file she wanted. She clicked, and a video began to play. Alvorson, Ellis, and Dixon, standing by the snack machines.

We can talk here. There's a mic, but it hasn't worked for years.

Luke Ellis did most of the talking. He voiced concern about those twins and the Cross boy. Alvorson soothed him. Dixon stood by, saying little, just scratching his arms and yanking at his nose.

Jesus Christ, Stackhouse had said. *If you have to pick it, go on and pick it.* Only now, looking at this video with new eyes, Mrs. Sigsby saw what had really been going on.

She closed her laptop and thumbed her intercom. "Rosalind, I want to see the Dixon boy. Have Tony and Winona bring him. Right away."

14

Avery Dixon, dressed in a Batman tee-shirt and dirty shorts that displayed his scabby knees, stood in front of Mrs. Sigsby's desk, looking at her with frightened eyes. Small to begin with and now flanked by Winona and Tony, he didn't look ten; he looked barely old enough for first grade.

Mrs. Sigsby offered him a thin smile. "I should have gotten to you much sooner, Mr. Dixon. I must be slipping."

"Yes, ma'am," Avery whispered.

"So you agree? You think I'm slipping?"

"No, ma'am!" Avery's tongue flicked out and wet his lips. No nose-pulling, though, not today.

Mrs. Sigsby leaned forward, hands clasped. "If I have been, the slippage is over now. Changes will be made. But first it's important . . . *imperative* . . . that we bring Luke back home."

"Yes, ma'am."

She nodded. "We agree, and that's good. A good start. So where did he go?"

"I don't know, ma'am."

"I think you do. You and Steven Whipple were filling in the hole he escaped through. Which was stupid. You should have left it alone."

"We thought a woodchuck made it, ma'am."

"Nonsense. You know exactly who made it. Your friend Luke. Now." She spread her hands on her desk and smiled at him. "He's a smart boy and smart boys don't just plunge off into the woods. Going under the fence might have been his idea, but he needed Alvorson to give him the lay of the land on the other side of it. She gave you the directions piece by piece, every time you yanked on your nose. Beamed it right into your talented little head, didn't she? Later on, you gave it to Ellis. There's no point in denying it, Mr. Dixon, I've seen the video of your conversation. It is—if you don't mind a silly old lady making a joke—as plain as the nose on your face. I should have realized it sooner."

And Trevor, she thought. He saw it, too, and also should have seen what was going on. If there's a comprehensive debriefing when this is over, how blind we will look.

"Now tell me where he went."

"I really don't know."

"You're shifting your eyes around, Mr. Dixon. That's what liars do. Look straight at me. Otherwise, Tony is going to twist your arm behind your back, and that will hurt."

She nodded at Tony. He grabbed one of Avery's thin wrists.

Avery looked straight at her. It was hard, because her face was thin and scary, a mean teacher's face that said *tell me everything*, but he did it. Tears began to well up and roll down his cheeks. He had always been a crier; his two older sisters had called him Little Crybaby Cry, and in the schoolyard at recess he had been anybody's punching bag. The playground here was better. He missed his mother and father, missed them *bad*, but at least he had friends. Harry had pushed him down, but then had been a friend. At least until he died. Until they killed him with one of their stupid tests. Sha and Helen were gone, but the new girl, Frieda, was nice to him, and had let him win at HORSE. Only once, but still. And Luke. He was the best of all. The best friend Avery had ever had.

"Where did Alvorson tell him to go, Mr. Dixon? What was the plan?"

"I don't know."

Mrs. Sigsby nodded to Tony, who twisted Avery's arm behind his back and hoisted his wrist almost to his shoulderblade. The pain was incredible. Avery screamed.

"Where did he go? What was the plan?"

"I don't know!"

"Let him go, Tony."

Tony did so, and Avery collapsed to his knees, sobbing. "That really hurt, don't hurt me anymore, please don't." He thought of adding *it's not fair*, but what did these people care about what was fair? Nothing, that was what.

"I don't want to," Mrs. Sigsby said. This was a thin truth, at best. The thicker one was that years spent in this office had inured her to the pain of children. And while the sign in the crematorium was right—they were heroes, no matter how reluctant their heroism might be—some of them could try one's patience. Sometimes until one's patience snapped.

"I don't know where he went, honest."

"When people have to say they're being honest, that means they're not. I've been around the block a few times, and I know that. So tell me: Where did he go, and what was the plan?"

"I don't know!"

"Tony, lift up his shirt. Winona, your Taser. Medium power."

"No!" Avery screamed, trying to pull away. "No zap-stick! Please, no zap-stick!"

Tony caught him around the middle and lifted his shirt. Winona positioned her zap-stick just above

Avery's belly button and triggered it. Avery shrieked. His legs jerked and piss watered the carpet.

"Where did he go, Mr. Dixon?" The boy's face was blotchy and snotty, there were dark circles beneath his eyes, he had wet his pants, and still the little runt was holding out. Mrs. Sigsby could hardly believe it. "Where did he go and what was the plan?"

"I don't know!"

"Winona? Again. Medium power."

"Ma'am, are you s—"

"A little higher this time, if you please. Just below the solar plexus."

Avery's arms were greased with sweat and he wriggled out of Tony's grip, almost making a rotten situation even worse—he'd have gone flying around her office like a bird trapped in a garage, knocking things over and bouncing off the walls—but Winona tripped him and pulled him to his feet by his arms. So it was Tony who used the Taser. Avery screamed and went limp.

"Is he out?" Mrs. Sigsby asked. "If he is, get Dr. Evans in here to give him a shot. We need answers fast."

Tony grabbed one of Avery's cheeks (plump when he'd come here; much thinner now) and twisted it. Avery's eyes flew open. "He's not out."

Mrs. Sigsby said, "Mr. Dixon, this pain is stupid and unnecessary. Tell me what I want to know and it will stop. Where did he go? What was the plan?"

"I don't know," Avery whispered. "I really really really don't kn—"

"Winona? Please remove Mr. Avery's pants and apply your Taser to his testes. Full power."

Although Winona was as apt to slap a sassbox resident as look at him, she was clearly unhappy with this command. Nevertheless, she reached for the waistband of his pants. That was when Avery broke.

"Okay! Okay! I'll tell! Just don't hurt me anymore!"

"That is a relief for both of us."

"Maureen told him to go through the woods. She said he might find a track for golf carts but to keep going straight even if he didn't. She said he'd see lights, especially a bright yellow one. She said when he got to the houses, he should follow the fence until he saw a scarf tied to a bush or a tree, I don't remember which. She said there was a path behind it . . . or a road . . . I don't remember that, either. But she said it would take him to the river. She said there was a boat."

He stopped. Mrs. Sigsby gave him a nod and a benign smile, but inside, her heart was beating triple-time. This was both good news and bad. Stackhouse's search party could stop floundering around in the woods, but a boat? Ellis had gotten to the *river*? And he was hours ahead of them.

"Then what, Mr. Dixon? Where did she tell him to get off the river? The Bend, am I right? Dennison River Bend?"

Avery shook his head and made himself look directly at her, all wide eyes and terrified honesty. "No, she said that was too close, she said to keep on the river as far as Presque Isle."

"Very good, Mr. Dixon, you can go back to your room. But if I should find out that you've lied . . ."

"I'll be in trouble," Avery said, wiping at the tears on his cheeks with trembling hands.

At that, Mrs. Sigsby actually laughed. "You read my mind," she said.

15

Five o'clock in the afternoon.

Ellis gone at least eighteen hours, maybe longer. The playground cams didn't record, so it was impossible to tell for sure. Mrs. Sigsby and Stackhouse were in Mrs. Sigsby's office, monitoring developments and listening for reports from their stringers. They had these all over the country. For the most part, the Institute's stringers did no more than groundwork: keeping an eye on children with high BDNF scores and compiling information on their friends, family, neighborhoods, school situations. And their homes, of course. Everything about their homes, especially alarm systems. All that background was useful to the extraction teams when the time came. They also kept an eye out for special children not already on the Institute's radar. These did show up from time to time. BDNF testing, along with the heel-stick PKU and the Apgar score, was routine for infants born in American hospitals, but of course not all babies were born in hospitals, and plenty of parents, such as the ever more vocal anti-vaxxer contingent, forewent the tests.

These stringers had no idea to whom they were reporting, or to what purpose; many assumed (incorrectly) that it was some kind of US government Big Brother thing. Most simply banked the extra income of five hundred dollars a month, made their reports when reports had to be made, and asked no questions. Of course every now and then one *would* ask questions, and that one would discover that as well as killing cats, curiosity killed their monthly dividend.

The thickest concentration of stringers, almost fifty,

was in the area surrounding the Institute, and tracking talented children was not their major concern. The chief job of these stringers was to listen for people asking the wrong questions. They were tripwires, an early warning system.

Stackhouse was careful to alert half a dozen in Dennison River Bend, just in case the Dixon boy was mistaken or lying ("He wasn't lying, I would have known," Mrs. Sigsby insisted), but most he sent to the Presque Isle area. One of these was tasked with contacting the PI police and telling them that he was quite sure he'd seen a boy who had been in a news story on CNN. This boy, according to the news, was wanted for questioning in the murders of his parents. His name was Luke Ellis. The stringer told the police he wasn't positive it was that kid, but it sure did look like him, and he'd asked for money in a threatening, disjointed way. Both Mrs. Sigsby and Stackhouse knew that having the police pick up their wandering boy wasn't the ideal solution to their problems, but police could be handled. Besides, anything Ellis told them would be dismissed as the ravings of an unbalanced child.

Cell phones didn't work in the Institute or in the village—indeed, not for a two-mile radius—so the searchers used walkies. And there *were* landlines. Now the one on Mrs. Sigsby's desk rang. Stackhouse grabbed it. "What? Who am I talking to?"

It was Dr. Felicia Richardson, who had spelled Zeke in the comm room. She had been eager to do it. Her ass was also on the line, a fact she fully grasped. "I've got one of our stringers on hold. Guy named Jean Levesque. He says he found the boat Ellis used. Want me to transfer him to you?"

"Immediately!"

Mrs. Sigsby was standing in front of Stackhouse now, hands raised, lips forming the word *What?*

Stackhouse ignored her. There was a click, and Levesque came on the line. He had a St. John Valley accent thick enough to cut pulpwood. Stackhouse had never seen him, but pictured a tanned old guy under a hat with a bunch of fishing lures stuck in the brim.

"Found dat boat, me."

"So I'm told. Where?"

"She come aground on a bank about five miles up-river from Presque Isle. Ship quite a bit of water she did, but the handle of the oar—just one oar—was prop on the seat. Left it right where it was. Didn't call nobody. Dere's blood on the oar. Tell you what, dere's a l'il bit of a rapids a little further up. If dat boy you lookin for wasn't used to boats, specially a l'il one like that—"

"It might have spilled him out," Stackhouse finished. "Stay where you are, I'm going to send a couple of guys. And thank you."

"What you pay me for," Levesque said. "Don't suppose you can tell me what he do."

Stackhouse killed the call, which answered *that* particular foolish question, and filled in Mrs. Sigsby. "With any luck, the little bastard drowned and someone will find his body tonight or tomorrow, but we can't count on being that lucky. I want to get Rafe and John—all I've got for security, and *that's* going to change when this is over—to downtown Presque Isle, ASAP. If Ellis is on foot, that's where he'll go first. If he hitches a ride, either the State Police or some townie cop will pick him up and hold him. He's the crazy kid who killed his parents, after all, then ran all the way to Maine."

"Are you as hopeful as you sound?" She was honestly curious.

"No."

16

The residents were allowed out of their rooms for dinner. It was, by and large, an outwardly silent meal. There were several caretakers and techs present, circling like sharks. They were clearly on edge, more than ready to strike or zap anyone who gave them lip. Yet in that quiet, running secretly behind it, was a nervous elation so strong that it made Frieda Brown feel slightly drunk. There had been an escape. All of the kids were glad and none of them wanted to show it. Was *she* glad? Frieda wasn't so sure. Part of her was, but . . .

Avery was sitting beside her, burying his two hot-dogs in baked beans, then digging them up. Interring them and exhuming them. Frieda wasn't as bright as Luke Ellis, but she was plenty smart, and knew what *interring* and *exhuming* meant. What she didn't know was what would happen if Luke tattled about what was going on here to someone who believed him. Specifically, what would happen to *them*. Would they be freed? Sent home to their parents? She was sure it was what these kids wanted to believe—hence that secret current—but Frieda had her doubts. She was only fourteen, but she was already a hardened cynic. Her cartoon people smiled; she rarely did. Also, she knew something the rest of them didn't. Avery had been taken to Mrs. Sigsby's office, and there he had undoubtedly spilled his guts.

Which meant Luke wasn't going to get away.

"Are you going to eat that shizzle, or just play with it?"

Avery pushed the plate away and stood up. Ever since coming back from Mrs. Sigsby's office, he had looked like a boy who had seen a ghost.

"There's apple pie à la mode and chocolate pudding for dessert on the menu," Frieda said. "And it's not like home—mine, anyway—where you have to eat everything on your plate to get it."

"Not hungry," Avery said, and left the cafeteria.

But two hours later, after the kids had been sent back to their rooms (the lounge and canteen had both been declared off-limits this evening, and the door to the playground was locked), he padded down to Frieda's room in his jammies, said he was hungry, and asked if she had any tokens.

"Are you kidding?" Frieda asked. "I just barely got here." She actually had three, but she wasn't giving them to Avery. She liked him, but not *that* much.

"Oh. Okay."

"Go to bed. You won't be hungry while you're asleep, and when you wake up it'll be breakfast."

"Can I sleep with you, Frieda? Since Luke's gone?"

"You should be in your room. You could get us in trouble."

"I don't want to sleep alone. They hurt me. They gave me lectric shocks. What if they come back and hurt me some more? They might, if they find out—"

"What?"

"Nothing."

She considered. She considered many things, actually. An ace considerer was Frieda Brown of Springfield, Missouri. "Well . . . okay. Get into bed. I'm going to stay up awhile longer. There's a show on TV about wild animals I want to see. Did you know some wild animals eat their babies?"

"Do they?" Avery looked stricken. "That's awful sad."

She patted his shoulder. "Mostly they don't."

"Oh. Oh, good."

"Yes. Now get into bed, and don't talk. I hate people talking when I'm trying to watch a show."

Avery got into bed. Frieda watched the wild animal show. An alligator fought with a lion. Or maybe it was a crocodile. Either way, it was interesting. And Avery was interesting. Because Avery had a secret. If she had been a TP as strong as he was, she would have known it already. As it was, she only knew it was there.

When she was sure he was asleep (he snored—polite little-boy snores), she turned out the lights, got into bed with him, and shook him. "Avery."

He grunted and tried to turn away from her. She wouldn't let him.

"Avery, where did Luke go?"

"Prekile," he muttered.

She had no idea what *Prekile* was, and didn't care, because it wasn't the truth.

"Come on, where did he go? I won't tell."

"Up the red steps," Avery said. He was still mostly asleep. Probably thought he was dreaming this.

"What red steps?" She whispered it in his ear.

He didn't answer, and when he tried to turn away from her this time, Frieda let him. Because she had what she needed. Unlike Avery (and Kalisha, at least on good days), she could not exactly read thoughts. What she had were intuitions that were probably based on thoughts, and sometimes, if a person were unusually open (like a little boy who was mostly asleep), she got brief, brilliant pictures.

She lay on her back, looking up at the ceiling of her room, thinking.

17

Ten o'clock. The Institute was quiet.

Sophie Turner, one of the night caretakers, was sitting at the picnic table in the playground, smoking an illicit cigarette and tapping her ashes into the cap of a Vitaminwater bottle. Dr. Evans was beside her, with a hand on her thigh. He leaned over and kissed her neck.

"Don't do that, Jimmy," she said. "Not tonight, with the whole place on red alert. You don't know who's watching."

"You're an Institute employee smoking a cigarette while the whole place is on red alert," he said. "If you're going to be a bad girl, why not be a *bad* girl?"

He slid his hand higher, and she was debating whether or not to leave it there, when she looked around and saw a little girl—one of the new ones—standing at the lounge doors. Her palms were on the glass, and she was looking out at them.

"God*dammit*!" Sophie said. She removed Evans's hand and squashed her cigarette out. She strode to the door and unlocked it and jerked it open and grabbed Peeping Thomasina by the neck. "What are you doing up? No walking around tonight, didn't you get the message? The lounge and canteen are off-limits! So if you don't want your ass slapped good and hard, get back to your—"

"I want to talk to Mrs. Sigsby," Frieda said. "Right away."

"Are you out of your mind? For the last time, get back—"

Dr. Evans pushed past Sophie, and without apology. There would be no more touchie-feelie for him tonight, Sophie decided.

"Frieda? You're Frieda, right?"

"Yes."

"Why don't you tell me what's on your mind?"

"I can only talk to her. Because she's the boss."

"That's right, and the boss has had a busy day. Why don't you tell me, and I'll decide if it's important enough to tell her."

"Oh, please," Sophie said. "Can't you see when one of these brats is scamming you?"

"I know where Luke went," Frieda said. "I won't tell you, but I'll tell her."

"She's lying," Sophie said.

Frieda never looked at her. She kept her eyes on Dr. Evans. "Not."

Evans's interior debate was short. Luke Ellis would soon have been gone for a full twenty-four hours, he could be anywhere and telling anything to anyone— a cop, or please God no, a reporter. It wasn't Evans's job to pass judgement on the girl's claim, farfetched as it was. That was Mrs. Sigsby's job. His job was not to make a mistake that ended him up shit creek without a paddle.

"You better be telling the truth, Frieda, or you're going to be in a world of hurt. You know that, don't you?"

She only looked at him.

18

Ten-twenty.

The Southway Express box, in which Luke slept behind the rototillers, lawn tractors, and boxed outboard motors, was now leaving New York State for Pennsylvania and entering an enhanced speed corridor along which it would travel for the next three hours. Its speed rose to 79 miles an hour, and woe to anyone stalled on a crossing or asleep on the tracks.

In Mrs. Sigsby's office, Frieda Brown was standing in front of the desk. She was wearing pink footie pajamas nicer than any she had at home. Her hair was in daytime pigtails and her hands were clasped behind her back.

Stackhouse was in the small private quarters adjacent to the office, cat-napping on the couch. Mrs. Sigsby saw no reason to wake him. At least not yet. She examined the girl and saw nothing remarkable. She was as brown as her name: brown eyes, mouse-brown hair, skin tanned a summer café au lait. According to her file, her BDNF was likewise unremarkable, at least by Institute standards; useful but hardly amazing. Yet there was something in those brown eyes, *something*. It could have been the look of a bridge or whist player who has a hand filled with high trumps.

"Dr. Evans says you think you know where our missing child is," Mrs. Sigsby said. "Perhaps you'd like to tell me where this brainwave came from."

"Avery," Frieda said. "He came down to my room. He's sleeping there."

Mrs. Sigsby smiled. "I'm afraid you're a little late,

dear. Mr. Dixon has already told us everything he knows."

"He lied to you." Still with her hands clasped behind her back, and still maintaining a surface calm, but Mrs. Sigsby had dealt with many, many children, and knew this girl was scared to be here. She understood the risk. Yet the certainty in those brown eyes remained. It was fascinating.

Stackhouse came into the room, tucking in his shirt. "Who's this?"

"Frieda Brown. A little girl who's confabulating. I bet you don't know what that means, dear."

"Yes I do," Frieda said. "It means lying, and I'm not."

"Neither was Avery Dixon. I told Mr. Stackhouse, and now I tell you: I know when a child is lying."

"Oh, he probably told the truth about most of it. That's why you believed him. But he didn't tell the truth about Prekile."

A frown creased her brow. "What's—"

"Presque Isle?" Stackhouse came to her and took her by the arm. "Is that what you're saying?"

"It's what *Avery* said. But that was a lie."

"How did you—" Mrs. Sigsby began, but Stackhouse held up a hand to stop her.

"If he lied about Presque Isle, what's the truth?"

She gave him a cunning smile. "What do I get if I tell?"

"What you *won't* get is electricity," Mrs. Sigsby said. "Within an inch of your life."

"If you zap me, I'll tell you something, but it might not be the truth. Like Avery didn't tell you the truth when you zapped *him*."

Mrs. Sigsby slammed a hand down on her desk.

"Don't try that with me, missy! If you've got something to say—"

Stackhouse held his hand up again. He knelt in front of Frieda. Tall as he was, they still weren't eye to eye, but close. "What do you want, Frieda? To go home? I'm telling you straight out, that can't happen."

Frieda almost laughed. Want to go home? To her el dopo mother, with her succession of el dopo boyfriends? The last one had wanted her to show him her breasts, so he could see "how fast she was developing."

"I don't want that."

"Okay then, what?"

"I want to stay here."

"That's a rather unusual request."

"But I don't want the needle sticks, and I don't want any more tests, and I don't want to go to Back Half. Ever. I want to stay here and grow up to be a caretaker like Gladys or Winona. Or a tech like Tony and Evan. Or I could even learn to cook and be a chef like Chef Doug."

Stackhouse looked over the girl's shoulder to see if Mrs. Sigsby was as amazed by this as he was. She appeared to be.

"Let's say that . . . um . . . permanent residency could be arranged," he said. "Let's say it *will* be arranged, if your information is good and we catch him."

"Catching him can't be part of the deal, because it's not fair. Catching him is *your* job. Just if my information is good. And it is."

He looked over Frieda's shoulder again at Mrs. Sigsby. Who nodded slightly.

"Okay," he said. "It's a deal. Now spill it."

She gave him a sly smile, and he thought about

slapping it off her face. Only for a moment, but it was a serious thought. "And I want fifty tokens."

"No."

"Forty, then."

"Twenty," Mrs. Sigsby said from behind her. "And only if your information is good."

Frieda considered it. "All right. Only how do I know if you'll keep your promises?"

"You'll have to trust us," Mrs. Sigsby said.

Frieda sighed. "I guess so."

Stackhouse: "No more dickering. If you have something to say, then say it."

"He got off the river before Prekile. He got off at some red steps." She hesitated, then gave up the rest. The important part. "There was a train station at the top of the steps. That's where he went. The train station."

19

After Frieda was sent back to her room with her tokens (and with a threat that all promises would be off if she spoke a single word about what had transpired in Mrs. Sigsby's office to anyone), Stackhouse called down to the computer room. Andy Fellowes had come in from the village and spelled Felicia Richardson. Stackhouse told Fellowes what he wanted, and asked if he could get it without alerting anyone. Fellowes said he could, but would need a few minutes.

"Make it a very few," Stackhouse said. He hung up and used his box phone to call Rafe Pullman and John Walsh, his two security men who were standing by.

"Shouldn't you get one of our pet cops to go down

there to the trainyard instead?" Mrs. Sigsby asked
when he finished the call. Two members of the Dennison River Bend Police were stringers for the Institute,
which amounted to twenty per cent of the entire force.
"Wouldn't that be quicker?"

"Quicker but maybe not safer. I don't want knowledge of this shit-show to go any further than it already
has unless and until it becomes absolutely necessary."

"But if he got on a train, he could be *anywhere*!"

"We don't know that he was even there. The girl
could have been bullshitting."

"I don't think she was."

"You didn't think *Dixon* was."

It was true—and embarrassing—but she stayed on
message. The situation was far too serious to do anything else. "Point taken, Trevor. But if he'd stayed in
a town that small, he'd have been spotted hours ago!"

"Maybe not. He's one smart kid. He might have
gone to ground somewhere."

"But a train is the most likely, and you know it."

The phone rang again. They both went for it. Stackhouse won.

"Yes, Andy. You did? Good, give it to me." He
grabbed a notepad and jotted on it rapidly. She leaned
over his shoulder to read.

4297 at 10 AM.

16 at 2:30 PM.

77 at 5 PM.

He circled *4297 at 10 AM*, asked for its destination, then jotted *Port, Ports, Stur.* "What time was that
train due into Sturbridge?"

He jotted *4–5 PM* on the pad. Mrs. Sigsby looked
at it with dismay. She knew what Trevor was thinking:
the boy would have wanted to get as far away as pos-

sible before leaving the train—assuming he had been on it. That would be Sturbridge, and even if the train had pulled in late, it would have arrived at least five hours ago.

"Thanks, Andy," Stackhouse said. "Sturbridge is in Western Mass, right?"

He listened, nodding.

"Okay, so it's on the turnpike, but it's still got to be a pretty small port of call. Maybe it's a switching point. Can you find out if that train, or any part of it, goes on from there? Maybe with a different engine, or something?"

He listened.

"No, just a hunch. If he stowed away on that train, Sturbridge might not be far enough for him to feel comfortable. He might want to keep running. It's what I'd do in his place. Check it out and get back to me ASAP."

He hung up. "Andy got the info off the station website," he said. "No problem. Isn't that amazing? Everything's on the Internet these days."

"Not us," she said.

"Not yet," he countered.

"What now?"

"We wait for Rafe and John."

They did so. The witching hour came and went. At just past twelve-thirty, the phone on her desk rang. Mrs. Sigsby beat him to it this time, barked her name, then listened, nodding along.

"All right. All understood. Now go on up to the train station . . . depot . . . yard . . . whatever they call it . . . and see if anyone is still . . . oh. All right. Thank you."

She hung up and turned to Stackhouse.

"That was your security force." This was delivered with some sarcasm, since Stackhouse's security force tonight consisted of just two men in their fifties and neither in wonderful physical shape. "The Brown girl had it right. They found the stairs, they found shoe prints, they even found a couple of bloody finger-marks, about halfway up the stairs. Rafe theorizes that Ellis either stopped there to rest, or maybe to re-tie his shoes. They're using flashlights, but John says they could probably find more signs once it's daylight." She paused. "And they checked the station. No one there, not even a night watchman."

Although the room was air conditioned to a pleasant seventy-two degrees, Stackhouse armed sweat from his forehead. "This is bad, Julia, but we still might be able to contain it without using that." He pointed to the bottom drawer of her desk, where the Zero Phone was waiting. "Of course if he went to the cops in Stur-bridge, our situation becomes a lot shakier. And he's had five hours to do it."

"Even if he did get off there he might not've," she said.

"Why wouldn't he? He doesn't know he's on the hook for killing his parents. How could he, when he doesn't know they're dead?"

"Even if he doesn't know, he suspects. He's very bright, Trevor, it won't do for you to forget that. If I were him, you know the first thing I'd do if I did get off a train in Sturbridge, Massachusetts, at . . ." She looked at the pad. ". . . at four or five in the afternoon? I'd beat feet to the library and get on the Internet. Get current with events back home."

This time they both looked at the locked drawer.

Stackhouse said, "Okay, we need to take this wider.

I don't like it, but there's really no choice. Let's find out who we've got in the vicinity of Sturbridge. See if he's shown up there."

Mrs. Sigsby sat down at her desk to put that in motion, but the phone rang even as she reached for it. She listened briefly, then handed it to Stackhouse.

It was Andy Fellowes. He had been busy. There *was* a night-crew at Sturbridge, it seemed, and when Fellowes represented himself as an inventory manager for Downeast Freight, checking on a shipment of live lobsters that might have gone astray, the graveyard shift stationmaster was happy to help out. No, no live lobsters offloaded at Sturbridge. And yes, most of 4297 went on from there, only with a much more powerful engine pulling it. It became Train 9956, running south to Richmond, Wilmington, DuPray, Brunswick, Tampa, and finally Miami.

Stackhouse jotted all this down, then asked about the two towns he didn't know.

"DuPray's in South Carolina," Fellowes told him. "Just a whistlestop—you know, six sticks and nine hicks—but it's a connecting point for trains coming in from the west. They have a bunch of warehouses there. Probably why the town even exists. Brunswick's in Georgia. It's quite a bit bigger. I imagine they load in a fair amount of produce and seafood there."

Stackhouse hung up and looked at Mrs. Sigsby. "Let's assume—"

"Assume," Mrs. Sigsby said. "A word that makes an ass out of you and—"

"Stow it."

No one else could have spoken to Mrs. Sigsby in such an abrupt way (not to mention so rudely), but no one else was allowed to call her by her first name, either. Stackhouse began to pace, his bald head gleaming under the lights. Sometimes she wondered if he really *did* wax it.

"What do we have in this facility?" he asked. "I'll tell you. Forty or so employees in Front Half and another two dozen in Back Half, not counting Heckle and Jeckle. Because we keep our wagons in a tight circle. We have to, but that doesn't help us tonight. There's a phone in that drawer that would get us all kinds of high-powered help, but if we use it, our lives will change, and not for the better."

"If we have to use that phone, we might not *have* lives," Mrs. Sigsby said.

He ignored this. "We have stringers nationwide, a good information network that includes low-level cops and medical people, hotel employees, news reporters on small-town weeklies, and retirees who have lots of time to spend scanning Internet sites. We also have two extraction teams at our disposal and a Challenger aircraft that can get them to practically anywhere fast. And we have our brains, Julia, our brains. He's a chess player, the caretakers used to see him out there playing with Wilholm all the time, but this is real-world chess, and that's a game he's never played before. So let's assume."

"All right."

"We'll get a stringer to check with the police in Sturbridge. Same story we floated in Presque Isle—our guy says he thinks he saw a kid who might have been Ellis. We better do the same check in Portland and Portsmouth, although I don't believe for a minute he would have gotten off so soon. Sturbridge is much more likely, but I think our guy will draw a blank there, too."

"Are you sure that's not just wishful thinking?"

"Oh, I'm wishing my ass off. But if he's thinking as well as running, it makes sense."

"When Train 4297 became Train 9956, he stayed on. That's your assumption."

"Yes. 9956 stops in Richmond at approximately 2 AM. We need someone, preferably several someones, watching that train. Same with Wilmington, where it stops between 5 AM and 6. But you know what? I don't think he'll get off at either place."

"You think he's going to ride it to the end of the line." Trevor, she thought, you keep climbing higher and higher on the assumption tree, and each branch is thinner than the last.

But what else was there, now that the kid was gone? If she had to use the Zero Phone, she would be told they should have been prepared for something like this. It was easy to say, but how could *anyone* have foreseen a twelve-year-old child desperate enough to saw off his own earlobe to get rid of the tracker? Or a housekeeper willing to aid and abet him? Next she would be told the Institute staff had gotten lazy and complacent . . . and what would she say to that?

"—the line."

She came back to the here and now, and asked him to repeat.

"I said he won't necessarily ride it to the end of the line. A kid as smart as this one will *know* we'd put people there, if we figured out the train part. I don't think he'll want to get off in any metro area, either. Especially not in Richmond, a strange city in the middle of the night. Wilmington's possible—it's smaller, and it'll be daylight when 9956 gets there—but I'm leaning toward one of the whistlestops. I think either

DuPray, South Carolina, or Brunswick, Georgia. Assuming he's on that train at all."

"He might not even know where it was going once it left Sturbridge. In which case he *might* ride it all the way."

"If he's in with a bunch of tagged freight, he knows."

Mrs. Sigsby realized it had been years since she had been this afraid. Maybe she had never been this afraid. Were they assuming or just guessing? And if the latter, was it likely they could make this many good ones in a row? But it was all they had, so she nodded. "If he gets off at one of the smaller stops, we could send an extraction team to take him back. God, Trevor, that would be ideal."

"*Two* teams. Opal and Ruby Red. Ruby's the same team that brought him in. That would have a nice roundness, don't you think?"

Mrs. Sigsby sighed. "I wish we could be positive he got on that train."

"I'm not positive, but I'm pretty sure, and that'll have to do." Stackhouse gave her a smile. "Get on the phone. Wake some people up. Start with Richmond. Nationwide we must pay these guys and gals what, a million a year? Let's make some of them earn their money."

Thirty minutes later, Mrs. Sigsby set the phone back into its cradle. "If he's in Sturbridge, he must be hiding in a culvert or an abandoned house or something—the police don't have him, there'd be something about it on their scanners if they did. We'll have people in both Richmond and Wilmington with eyes on that train when it's there, and they've got a good cover story."

"I heard. Nicely done, Julia."

She lifted a weary hand to acknowledge this. "Sighting earns a substantial bonus, and there will be an even more substantial bonus—more like a windfall—if our people should see a chance to grab the boy and take him to a safe house for pickup. Not likely in Richmond, both of our people there are just John Q. Citizens, but one of the guys in Wilmington is a cop. Pray that it happens there."

"What about DuPray and Brunswick?"

"We'll have two people watching in Brunswick, the pastor of a nearby Methodist church and his wife. Only one in DuPray, but the guy actually lives there. He owns the town's only motel."

20

Luke was in the immersion tank again. Zeke was holding him down, and the Stasi Lights were swirling in front of him. They were also inside his head, which was ten times worse. He was going to drown looking at them.

At first he thought the screaming he heard when he flailed his way back to consciousness was coming from him, and wondered how he could possibly make such an ungodly racket underwater. Then he remembered that he was in a boxcar, the boxcar was part of a moving train, and it was slowing down fast. The screeching was steel wheels on steel rails.

The colored dots remained for a moment or two, then faded. The boxcar was pitch black. He tried to stretch his cramped muscles and discovered he was hemmed in. Three or four of the outboard motor cartons had fallen over. He wanted to believe he'd done that thrashing around in his nightmare, but he thought he might have done it with his mind, while in the grip of those damned lights. Once upon a time the limit of his mind-power was pushing pizza pans off restaurant tables or fluttering the pages of a book, but times had changed. *He* had changed. Just how much he didn't know, and didn't want to.

The train slowed more and began rumbling over switching points. Luke was aware that he was in a fair amount of distress. His body wasn't on red alert, not yet, but it had definitely reached Code Yellow. He was hungry, and that was bad, but his thirst made his empty belly seem minor in comparison. He remembered sliding down the riverbank to where the S.S. *Pokey* had been tethered, and how he had splashed the cold water over his face and scooped it into his mouth. He would give anything for a drink of that river water now. He ran his tongue over his lips, but it wasn't much help; his tongue was also pretty dry.

The train came to a stop, and Luke stacked the boxes again, working by feel. They were heavy, but he managed. He had no idea where he was, because in Sturbridge the door of the Southway Express box had been shut all the way. He went back to his hidey-hole behind the boxes and small engine equipment and waited, feeling miserable.

He was dozing again in spite of his hunger, thirst, full bladder, and throbbing ear, when the door of the boxcar rattled open, letting in a flood of moonlight. At least it seemed like a flood to Luke after the pure dark he'd found himself in when he woke. A truck was backing up to the door, and a guy was hollering.

"Come on . . . little more . . . easy . . . little more . . . . *ho*!"

The truck's engine switched off. There was the sound of its cargo door rattling up, and then a man jumped into the boxcar. Luke could smell coffee, and his belly rumbled, surely loud enough for the man to hear. But no—when he peeked out between a lawn tractor and a riding lawnmower, he saw the guy, dressed in work fatigues, was wearing earbuds.

Another man joined him and set down a square battery light which was—thankfully—aimed at the door and not in Luke's direction. They laid down a steel ramp and began to dolly crates from the truck to the boxcar. Each was stamped KOHLER, THIS SIDE UP, and USE CAUTION. So wherever this was, it wasn't the end of the line.

The men paused after loading ten or twelve of the crates and ate doughnuts from a paper sack. It took everything Luke had—thoughts of Zeke holding him down in the tank, thoughts of the Wilcox twins, thoughts of Kalisha and Nicky and God knew how many others depending on him—to keep from breaking cover and begging those men for a bite, just one bite. He might have done it anyway, had one of them not said something that froze him in place.

"Hey, you didn't see a kid running around, did you?"

"What?" Through a mouthful of doughnut.

"A kid, a kid. When you went up to take the engineer that Thermos."

"What would a kid be doing out here? It's two-thirty in the morning."

"Aw, some guy asked me when I went to get the doughnuts. Said his brother-in-law called him from up in Massachusetts, woke him out of a sound sleep and asked him to check the train station. The Massachusetts guy's kid ran away. Said he was always talking about hopping a freight out to California."

"That's on the other side of the country."

"*I* know that. *You* know that. Would a kid know that?"

"If he's any good in school, he'd know Richmond is a fuck of a long way from Los Angeles."

"Yeah, but it's also a junction point. The guy said he might be on this train, then get off and try to hop one going west."

"Well, I didn't see any kid."

"The guy said his brother-in-law would pay a reward."

"It could be a million dollars, Billy, and I still couldn't see any kid unless a kid was there to see."

If my belly rumbles again, I'm finished, Luke thought. Deep-fried. Nuked.

From outside, someone shouted: "Billy! Duane! Twenty minutes, boys, finish up!"

Billy and Duane loaded a few more Kohler crates into the boxcar, then rolled their ramp back into the truck and drove away. Luke had time to catch a glimpse of a city skyline—what city he didn't know—and then a man in overalls and a railroad cap came along and ran the Southway door shut . . . but this time not all the way. Luke guessed there was a sticky place in the track. Another five minutes passed before the train jerked into motion again, slowly at first, clicking over points and crossings, then picking up speed.

Some guy calling himself some other guy's brother-in-law.

Said he was always talking about hopping a freight.

They knew he was gone, and even if they found the

Pokey downstream from Dennison River Bend, they hadn't been fooled. They must have made Maureen talk. Or Avery. The thought of them torturing the information out of the Avester was too horrible to contemplate, and Luke pushed it away. If they had people watching for him to get off here, they'd have people waiting at the next stop, too, and by then it might be daylight. They might not want to cause trouble, might just observe and report, but it was possible they'd try to take him prisoner. Depending on how many people were around, of course. And how desperate they were. That, too.

I might have outsmarted myself by taking the train, Luke thought, but what else could I do? They weren't supposed to find out so *fast*.

In the meantime, there was one discomfort of which he could rid himself. Holding to the seat of a riding lawnmower to keep his balance, he unscrewed the fuel cap of a John Deere rototiller, opened his fly, and pissed what felt like two gallons into the empty gas tank. Not a nice thing to do, an extremely mean trick on whoever ended up with the rototiller, but these were extraordinary circumstances. He put the gas cap back on and screwed it tight. Then he sat down on the seat of the riding lawnmower, put his hands over his empty belly, and closed his eyes.

Think about your ear, he told himself. Think about the scratches on your back, too. Think about how bad those things hurt and you'll forget all about being hungry and thirsty.

It worked until it didn't. What crept in were images of kids leaving their rooms and going down to the caff for breakfast a few hours from now. Luke was helpless to dispel images of pitchers filled with orange juice, and the bubbler filled with red Hawaiian Punch. He wished he was there right now. He'd drink a glass of each, then load up his plate with scrambled eggs and bacon from the steam table.

You don't wish you were there. Wishing that would be crazy.

Nevertheless, part of him did.

He opened his eyes to get rid of the images. The one of the orange juice pitchers was stubborn, it didn't want to go . . . and then he saw something in the empty space between the new crates and the small engine gizmos. At first he thought it was a trick of the moonlight coming through the partly opened boxcar door, or an outright hallucination, but when he blinked his eyes twice and it was still there, he got off the seat of the mower and crawled to it. To his right, moon-washed fields flashed past the boxcar door. Leaving Dennison River Bend, Luke had drunk in all that he saw with wonder and fascination, but he had no eyes for the outside world now. He could only look at what was on the floor of the boxcar: doughnut crumbs.

And one piece that was bigger than a crumb.

He picked that one up first. To get the smaller ones, he wet a thumb and picked them up that way. Afraid of losing the smallest into the cracks in the boxcar floor, he bent over, stuck out his tongue, and licked them up.

21

It was Mrs. Sigsby's turn to catch some sleep on the couch in the inner room, and Stackhouse had closed the door so neither phone—the landline or his box phone—would disturb her. Fellowes called from the computer room at ten to three.

"9956 has left Richmond," he said. "No sign of the boy."

Stackhouse sighed and rubbed at his chin, feeling the rasp of stubble there. "Okay."

"Shame we can't just have that train pulled over on a siding and searched. Settle the question of whether or not he's on there once and for all."

"It's a shame everyone in the world isn't in a big circle, singing 'Give Peace a Chance.' What time does it get to Wilmington?"

"Should be there by six. Earlier, if they make up some time."

"How many guys have we got there?"

"Two now, another on his way from Goldsboro."

"They know better than to get intense, right? Intense people rouse suspicions."

"I think they'll be fine. It's a good story. Runaway boy, concerned folks."

"You better hope they're fine. Tell me how it goes."

Dr. Hendricks came into the office without bothering to knock. There were circles under his eyes, his clothes were wrinkled, and his hair was standing up in a steel-gray ruff. "Any word?"

"Not yet."

"Where's Mrs. Sigsby?"

"Getting some badly needed rest." Stackhouse leaned back in her chair and stretched. "The Dixon boy hasn't had the tank, has he?"

"Of course not." Donkey Kong looked vaguely offended at the very idea. "He's not a pink. Farthest thing from one. To risk damaging a BDNF as high as his would be insane. Or to risk extending his abilities. Which would be unlikely but not impossible. Sigsby would have my head."

"She won't and he goes in it today," Stackhouse said. "Dunk that little motherfucker until he thinks he's dead, then dunk him some more."

"Are you serious? He's valuable property! One of the highest TP-positives we've had in years!"

"I don't care if he can walk on water and shoot electricity out of his asshole when he farts. He helped Ellis get away. Have the Greek do it as soon as he comes back on duty. He loves putting them in the tank. Tell Zeke not to kill him, I do understand his value, but I want him to have an experience he'll remember for as long as he *can* remember. Then take him to Back Half."

"But Mrs. Sigsby—"

"Mrs. Sigsby agrees completely."

Both men swung around. She was standing in the door between the office and her private quarters. Stackhouse's first thought was that she looked as if she had seen a ghost, but that wasn't quite right. She looked as if she *were* a ghost.

"Do it just the way he told you, Dan. If it damages his BDNF, so be it. He needs to pay."

22

The train jerked into motion again, and Luke thought of some other song his grandma used to sing. Was it the one about the Midnight Special? He couldn't remember. The doughnut crumbs had done nothing but sharpen his hunger and increase his thirst. His mouth was a desert, his tongue a sand dune within. He dozed, but couldn't sleep. Time passed, he had no idea how much, but eventually pre-dawn light began to filter into the car.

Luke crawled over the swaying floor to the partially open door of the boxcar and peered out. There were trees, mostly straggly, second-growth pines, small towns, fields, then more trees. The train charged across a trestle, and he looked down at the river below with longing eyes. This time it wasn't a song that came to mind but Coleridge. Water, water everywhere, Luke thought, the boxcar boards did shrink. Water, water, everywhere and not a drop to drink.

Probably polluted anyway, he told himself, and knew he would drink from it even if it was. Until his belly was bulging. Puking it up would be a pleasure because then he could drink more.

Just before the sun came up, red and hot, he began to smell salt in the air. Instead of farms, the buildings sliding past were now mostly warehouses and old brick factories with their windows boarded up. Cranes reared against the brightening sky. Planes were taking off not far away. For awhile the train ran beside a four-lane road. Luke saw people in cars with nothing to worry about but a day's work. Now he could smell mudflats, dead fish, or both.

I would eat a dead fish if it wasn't all maggoty, he thought. Maybe even if it was. According to *National Geographic*, maggots are a good source of organic protein.

The train began slowing, and Luke retreated to his hiding place. There were more thumps and bumps as his car went over points and crossings. At last it came to a stop.

It was an early hour, but this was a busy place, even so. Luke heard trucks. He heard men laughing and talking. A boombox or truck radio was playing Kanye, bass like a heartbeat first swelling, then fading. An engine went by on some other track, leaving behind a stink of diesel. There were several tremendous jerks as cars were coupled or uncoupled from Luke's train. Men shouted in Spanish, and Luke picked out some of the profanities: *puta mierda, hijo de puta, chupapollas*.

More time went by. It felt like an hour, but might only have been fifteen minutes. At last another truck backed up to the Southway Express box. A guy in overalls rolled the door all the way open. Luke peered out from between a rototiller and a lawn tractor. The guy jumped into the boxcar, and another steel ramp was laid between the truck and the box. This time there were four men in the crew, two black, two white, all big and tatted out. They were laughing and talk-ing in deep southern accents, which made them sound to Luke like the country singers on BUZ'N 102 back home in Minneapolis.

One of the white guys said he'd gone dancing last night with the wife of one of the black guys. The black guy pretended to hit him, and the white guy pretended to stagger backward, sitting down on the pile of outboard motor cartons Luke had recently re-stacked.

"Come on, come on," said the other white guy. "I want my breffus."

So do I, Luke thought. Oh man, so do I.

When they began loading the Kohler crates into the truck, Luke thought it was like a movie of the last stop, only run in reverse. That made him think of the movies Avery said the kids had to watch in Back Half, and that made the dots start to come back again—big juicy ones. The boxcar door jerked on its track, as if it meant to shut itself.

"Whoa!" the second black guy said. "Who's out there?" He looked. "Huh. Nobody."

"Boogeyman," said the black guy who had pretended to smack the white guy. "Come on, come on, let's get it done. Stationmaster say this bitch is runnin late."

Still not the end of the line, Luke thought. I won't be in here until I starve to death, there's that, but only because I'll die of thirst first. He knew from his reading that a person could go for at least three days without water before lapsing into the unconsciousness that preceded death, but it didn't seem that way to him now.

The four-man crew loaded all but two of the big crates into their truck. Luke waited for them to start on the small engine stuff, which was when they would discover him, but instead of doing that, they ran their ramp back into the truck and yanked its pull-down door shut.

"You guys go on," one of the white guys said. He was the one who'd joked about going dancing with the black guy's wife. "I gotta visit the caboose shithouse. See a man about a dog."

"Come on, Mattie, squeeze it a little."

"Can't," the white guy said. "This one's so big I'm gonna have to climb down off'n it."

The truck started up and drove away. There were a few moments of quiet, and then the white guy, Mattie, climbed back into the boxcar, biceps flexing in his sleeveless tee. Luke's once-upon-a-time best friend Rolf Destin would have said *the guns are fully loaded*.

"Okay, outlaw. I seen you when I sat down on those boxes. You can come out now."

23

For a moment Luke stayed where he was, thinking that if he remained perfectly still and perfectly silent, the man would decide he'd been mistaken and go away. But that was childish thinking, and he was no longer a child. Not even close. So he crept out and tried to stand, but his legs were stiff and his head was light. He would have fallen over if the white guy hadn't grabbed him.

"Holy shit, kid, who tore your ear off?"

Luke tried to speak. At first nothing came out but a croak. He cleared his throat and tried again. "I had some trouble. Sir, do you have anything to eat? Or drink? I'm awfully hungry and thirsty."

Still not taking his eyes from Luke's mutilated ear, the white guy—Mattie—reached into his pocket and brought out half a roll of Life Savers. Luke grabbed it, tore away the paper, and tossed four into his mouth. He would have said all his saliva was gone, re-absorbed by his thirsty body, but more squirted, as if from invisible jets, and the sugar hit his head like a bomb. The dots flared briefly into existence, racing across the white guy's face. Mattie looked around, as if he had sensed someone coming up behind him, then redirected his attention to Luke.

"When's the last time you ate?"

"Don't know," Luke said. "Can't exactly remember."

"How long you been on the train?"

"About a day." That had to be right, but it seemed much longer.

"All the way from Yankeeland, right?"

"Yes." Maine was about as Yankeeland as you could get, Luke thought.

Mattie pointed at Luke's ear. "Who done that? Was it your dad? Stepdad?"

Luke stared at him, alarmed. "Who . . . how did you get that idea?" But even in his current state, the answer was obvious. "Someone's looking for me. It was the same at the last place the train stopped. How many are there? What did they say? That I ran away from home?"

"That's it. Your uncle. He brought a couple of friends, and one's a cop from Wrightsville Beach. They didn't say why, but yeah, they said you ran away from up in Massachusetts. And if someone done that, I get it."

That one of the waiting men was a cop scared Luke badly. "I got on in Maine, not Massachusetts, and my dad is dead. My mom, too. Everything they say is a lie."

The white guy considered this. "So who done that to your ear, outlaw? Some foster home asshole?"

That was not so far from the truth, Luke thought. Yes, he had been in a kind of foster home, and yes, it had been run by assholes. "It's complicated. Just . . . sir . . . if those men see me, they'll take me away. Maybe they couldn't do that if they didn't have a cop with them, but they do. They'll take me back to where this happened." He pointed to his ear. "Please don't tell. Please just let me stay on the train."

Mattie scratched his head. "I don't know about that. You're a kid, and you're a mess."

"I'll look a whole lot worse if those men take me."

Believe that, he thought with all his force. *Believe that, believe that.*

"Well, I don't know," Mattie repeated. "Although I didn't much care for the look of those three, tell you the God's honest. They seemed kinda nervy, even the cop. Also, you're lookin at a guy who run from home three times before I finally made it. First time I was about your age."

Luke said nothing. Mattie was headed in the right direction, at least.

"Where you going? Do you even know?"

"Someplace where I can get some food and some water and *think*," Luke said. "I need to think, because nobody's going to want to believe the story I've got to tell. Especially not coming from a kid."

"*Mattie!*" someone shouted. "*Come on, man! Unless you want a free trip to South Carolina!*"

"Kid, were you kidnapped?"

"*Yes*," Luke said, and began to cry. "And those men . . . the one who says he's my uncle, and the cop . . ."

"*MATTIE! Wipe your ass and come ON!*"

"I'm telling the truth," Luke said simply. "If you want to help me, let me go."

"Well, shit." Mattie spat over the side of the boxcar. "Seems wrong, but that ear of yours . . . those men, you're sure they're bad guys?"

"The worst," Luke said. He was actually ahead of the worst ones, but whether or not he was able to stay there depended on what this man decided to do.

"Do you even know where you are now?"

Luke shook his head.

"This is Wilmington. Train's gonna stop in Georgia, then at Tampa, and finish up its run in Miami. If people are looking for you, APB or AMBER Alert or whatever they call it, they'll be looking in all those places. But the *next* place it stops is just a shit-splat on the map. You might—"

"Mattie, where the fuck are you?" Much closer now. "Stop fuckin around. We gotta sign out."

Mattie gave Luke another dubious look.

"Please," Luke said. "They put me in a tank. Almost drowned me. I know that's hard to believe, but it's true."

Footsteps crunched on gravel, approaching. Mattie jumped down and trundled the boxcar door three-quarters of the way closed. Luke crawled back into his nest behind the small engine gear.

"Thought you said you were gonna take a shit. What were you doing in there?"

Luke waited for Mattie to say *There's a kid stowed away in that box, gave me some crazy story about being kidnapped up in Maine and stuck in a water-tank so he don't have to go with his uncle.*

"I did my bi'ness then wanted a look at those Kubota walk-behinds," Mattie said. "My Lawn-Boy's just about to drop dead."

"Well, come on, train can't wait. Hey, you didn't see any kid running around, did you? Like maybe he hopped onboard up north and decided Wimmington would be a nice place to visit?"

There was a pause. Then Mattie said, "No."

Luke had been sitting forward. At that single word, he put his head back against the boxcar wall and closed his eyes.

Ten minutes or so later, Train 9956 gave a hard jerk

that ran through the cars—there were now an even one hundred—like a shudder. The trainyard began to roll past, slowly at first, then picking up speed. The shadow of a signal tower ran across the floor of the boxcar, and then another shadow appeared. A man-shadow. A grease-spotted paper bag flew into the car and landed on the floor.

He didn't see Mattie, only heard him: "Good luck, outlaw." Then the shadow was gone.

Luke crawled out of his hiding place so fast he cracked the good-ear side of his head on the housing of a riding lawnmower. He didn't even notice. Heaven was in that bag. He could smell it.

Heaven turned out to be a cheese-and-sausage biscuit, a Hostess Fruit Pie, and a bottle of Carolina Sweetheart Spring Water. Luke had to use all his will-power to keep from drinking the whole sixteen-ounce bottle of water at a single go. He left a quarter of it, set it down, then snatched it up again and screwed on the cap. He thought if the train took a sudden yaw and it spilled, he would go insane. He gobbled the sausage biscuit in five snatching bites and chased it with an-other big swallow of water. He licked the grease from his palm, then took the water and the Hostess pie and crept back into his nest. For the first time since rid-ing down the river in the S.S. *Pokey* and looking up at the stars, he felt that his life might be worth living. And although he did not exactly believe in God, hav-ing found the evidence against just slightly stronger than the evidence for, he prayed anyway, but not for himself. He prayed for the highly hypothetical higher power to bless the man who had called him outlaw and thrown that brown bag into the boxcar.

24

With his belly full, he felt like dozing again, but forced himself to stay awake.

Train's gonna stop in Georgia, then at Tampa, and finish up its run in Miami, Mattie had said. *If people are looking for you, they'll be looking in all those places. But the next place it stops is just a shit-splat on the map.*

There might be people watching for him even in a little town, but Luke had no intention of going on to Tampa and Miami. Getting lost in a large population had its attractions, but there were too many cops in big cities, and by now all of them probably had a photo of the boy suspected of killing his parents. Besides, logic told him he could only run so long. That Mattie hadn't turned him in had been a fantastic stroke of good fortune; to count on another would be idiotic.

Luke thought he might have one high card in his hand. The paring knife Maureen had left under his mattress had disappeared somewhere along the way, but he still had the flash drive. He had no idea what was on it, for all he knew nothing but a rambling, guilt-ridden confession that would sound like gibberish, stuff about the baby she'd given away, maybe. On the other hand, it might be proof. Documents.

At last the train began to slow again. Luke went to the door, held it to keep his balance, and leaned out. He saw a lot of trees, a two-lane blacktop road, then the backs of houses and buildings. The train passed a signal: yellow. This might be the approach to the shit-splat Mattie had told him about; it might just be a slowdown while his train waited for another to clear the tracks somewhere up ahead. That might actually be better for him, because if there was a concerned uncle waiting for him at the next stop, he'd be at the depot. Up ahead he could see warehouses with glittering metal roofs. Beyond the warehouses was the two-lane road, and beyond the road were more trees.

Your mission, he told himself, is to get off this train and into those trees as fast as you can. And remember to hit the ground running so you don't face-plant in the cinders.

He began to sway back and forth, still holding the door, lips pressed together in a thin stress-line of concentration. It *was* the stop Mattie had told him about, because now he could see a station-house up ahead. On the roof, DUPRAY SOUTHERN & WESTERN had been painted on faded green shingles.

Got to get off now, Luke thought. Absolutely do not want to meet any uncles.

"One . . ."

He swayed forward.

"Two . . ."

He swayed back.

"Three!"

Luke jumped. He started running in midair, but hit the cinders beside the track with his body going at train speed, which was still a bit faster than his legs could carry him. His upper body tilted forward, and with his arms extended behind him in an effort to maintain his balance, he looked like a speed-skater approaching the finish line.

Just as he began to think he might catch up with

himself before he went sprawling, someone shouted *"Hey, look out!"*

He snapped his head up and saw a man on a forklift halfway between the warehouses and the depot. Another man was rising from a rocker in the shade of the station's roof, the magazine he'd been reading still in his hand. This one shouted *"Ware that post!"*

Luke saw the second signal-post, this one flashing red, too late to slow down. He instinctively turned his head and tried to raise his arm, but hit the steel post at full running speed before he could get it all the way up. The right side of his face collided with the post, his bad ear taking the brunt of the blow. He rebounded, hit the cinders, and rolled away from the tracks. He didn't lose consciousness, but he lost the *immediacy* of consciousness as the sky swung away, swung back, then swung away again. He felt warmth cascading down his cheek and knew his ear had opened up again—his poor abused ear. An interior voice was screaming at him to get up, to beat feet into the woods, but hearing and heeding were two different things. When he tried scrambling to his feet, it didn't work.

My scrambler's broke, he thought. Shit. What a fuckup.

Then the man from the forklift was standing over him. From where Luke lay, he looked about sixteen feet tall. The lenses of his glasses caught the sun, making it impossible to see his eyes. "Jesus, kid, what in the hell did you think you were doing?"

"Trying to get away." Luke wasn't sure he was actually speaking, but thought he probably was. "I can't let them get me, please don't let them get me."

The man bent down. "Stop trying to talk, I can't understand you anyway. You took a hell of a whack on that post, and you're bleeding like a stuck pig. Move your legs for me."

Luke did.

"Now move your arms."

Luke held them up.

Rocking Chair Man joined Forklift Man. Luke tried to use his newly acquired TP to read one or both of them, find out what they knew. He got nothing; when it came to thought-reading, the tide was currently out. For all he knew, the whack he'd taken had knocked the TP clean out of his head.

"He all right, Tim?"

"I think so. I hope so. First aid protocol says not to move a head injury, but I'm going to take a chance."

"Which of you is supposed to be my uncle?" Luke asked. "Or is it both of you?"

Rocking Chair Man frowned. "Can you understand what he's saying?"

"No. I'm going to put him in Mr. Jackson's back room."

"I'll take his legs."

Luke was coming back now. His ear was actually helping in that regard. It felt as if it wanted to drill right into his head. And maybe hide there.

"No, I got him," Forklift Man said. "He's not heavy. I want you to call Doc Roper, and ask him to make a house call."

"More of a *ware*house call," Rocking Chair Man said, and laughed, exposing the yellowed pegs of his teeth.

"Whatever. Go and do it. Use the station phone."

"Yessir." Rocking Chair Man gave Forklift Man a half-assed salute, and set off. Forklift Man picked Luke up.

"Put me down," Luke said. "I can walk."

"You think so? Let's see you do it."

Luke swayed on his feet for a moment, then steadied.

"What's your name, son?"

Luke considered, not sure he wanted to give it when he didn't know if this man was an uncle. He looked okay . . . but then, so did Zeke back at the Institute, when he was in one of his rare good moods.

"What's yours?" he countered.

"Tim Jamieson. Come on, let's at least get you out of the sun."

25

Norbert Hollister, owner of a decrepit motel which only kept operating thanks to his monthly stipend as an Institute stringer, used the station-house phone to call Doc Roper, but first he used his cell to call a number he had gotten in the early hours of the morning. Then, he had been pissed off at being awakened. Now, however, he was delighted.

"That kid," he said. "He's here."

"Just a second," Andy Fellowes said. "I'm transferring you."

There was a brief silence and then another voice said, "Are you Hollister? In DuPray, South Carolina?"

"Yeah. That kid you're looking for just jumped off a freight. Ear's all tore up. Is there still a reward for him?"

"Yes. And it will be bigger if you make sure he stays in town."

Norbert laughed. "Oh, I think he'll be stayin. He banged into a signal-post and it conked him silly."

"Don't lose track of him," Stackhouse said. "I want a call every hour. Understood?"

"Like an update."

"Yes, like that. We'll take care of the rest."

HELL IS HERE

1

Tim led the bloodied-up kid, obviously still dazed but walking on his own, through Craig Jackson's office. The owner of DuPray Storage & Warehousing lived in the nearby town of Dunning, but had been divorced for five years, and the spacious, air-conditioned room behind the office served him as auxiliary living quarters. Jackson wasn't there now, which was no surprise to Tim; on days when '56 stopped rather than barreling straight on through, Craig had a tendency to make himself scarce.

Past the little kitchenette with its microwave, hotplate, and tiny sink was a living area that consisted of an easy chair planted in front of an HD television set. Beyond that, old centerfolds from *Playboy* and *Penthouse* looked down on a neatly made camp bed. Tim's idea was to get the kid to lie down on it until Doc Roper came, but the boy shook his head.

"Chair."

"You sure?"

"Yes."

The kid sat. The cushion made a tired woofing sound. Tim took a knee before him. "Now how about a name?"

The kid looked at him doubtfully. He had stopped bleeding, but his cheek was covered with gore, and his right ear was a tattered horror. "Were you waiting for me?"

"For the train. I work here mornings. Longer, when the 9956 is scheduled. Now what's your name?"

"Who was the other guy?"

"No more questions until I get a name."

The kid thought it over, then licked his lips and said, "I'm Nick. Nick Wilholm."

"Okay, Nick." Tim made a peace sign. "How many fingers do you see?"

"Two."

"Now?"

"Three. The other guy, did he say he was my uncle?"

Tim frowned. "That was Norbert Hollister. He owns the local motel. If he's anyone's uncle, I don't know about it." Tim held up a single finger. "Follow it. Let me see your eyes move."

Nicky's eyes followed his finger left and right, then up and down.

"I guess you're not scrambled too badly," Tim said. "We can hope, anyway. Who are you running away from, Nick?"

The kid looked alarmed and tried to get out of the chair. "Who told you that?"

Tim pushed him gently back. "No one. It's just that whenever I see a kid in dirty torn-up clothes and a torn-up ear jump from a train, I make this wild assumption that he's a runaway. Now who—"

"What's all the shouting about? I heard . . . oh dear-to-Jesus, what happened to that boy?"

Tim turned and saw Orphan Annie Ledoux. She must have been in her tent behind the depot. She often went there to snooze in the middle of the day. Although the thermometer outside the station had registered eighty-five degrees at ten that morning, Annie was dressed in what Tim thought of as her Full Mexican outfit: serape, sombrero, junk bracelets, and rescued cowboy boots sprung along the seams.

"This is Nick Wilholm," Tim said. "He's visiting our fair village from God knows where. Jumped off the '56 and ran full-tilt-boogie into a signal-post. Nick, this is Annie Ledoux."

"Very pleased to meet you," Luke said.

"Thank you, son, same goes back. Was it the signal-post that ripped off half his ear, Tim?"

"I don't believe so," Tim said. "I was hoping to get that story."

"Were *you* waiting for the train to come in?" the boy asked her. He seemed fixated on that. Maybe because he'd had his bell rung pretty hard, maybe for some other reason.

"I'm waiting for nothing but the return of Our Lord Jesus Christ," Annie said. She glanced around. "Mr. Jackson has naughty pictures on his wall. I can't say I'm surprised." *Can't* came out *cain't*.

Just then an olive-skinned man wearing biballs over a white shirt and dark tie came into the room. A railroader's pillowtick cap was perched on his head. "Hello, Hector," Tim said.

"Hello to you," Hector said. He glanced at the bloody boy sitting in Craig Jackson's easy chair, not showing much interest, then returned his attention to Tim. "My secondman tells me I have a couple of generators for you, a bunch of lawn tractors and such, about a ton of canned goods, and another ton of fresh produce. I am running late, Timmy my boy, and if you don't unload me, you can send the fleet of trucks this town doesn't have to pick up your goods in Brunswick."

Tim stood up. "Annie, can you keep this young man company until the doctor gets here? I have to go run a forklift for awhile."

"I can handle that. If he pitches a fit I'll put something in his mouth."

"I'm not going to pitch a fit," the boy said.

"That's what they all say," Annie retorted, rather obscurely.

"Son," Hector said, "did you stow away on my train?"

"Yes, sir. I'm sorry."

"Well, since you're off it now that's nothing to me. The cops'll deal with you, I guess. Tim, I see you got a situation here, but goods won't wait, so help a man out. Where's your goddam crew? I only seen one guy, and he's in the office on the phone."

"That's Hollister from the local motel, and I can't see him unloading anything. Except maybe for his bowels, first thing in the morning."

"Nasty," Orphan Annie said, although she might have been referring to the gatefolds, which she was still studying.

"The Beeman boys are supposed to be here, but those two no-accounts seem to be running late. Like you."

"Ah, Christ." Hector took off his cap and ran a hand through his thick black hair. "I hate these milk-runs. Unloading went slow in Wilmington, too. A goddam Lexus got stuck on one of the carriers. Well, let's see what we can do."

Tim followed Hector to the door, then turned back. "Your name isn't Nick, is it?"

The boy considered, then said, "It will do for now."

"Don't let him move," Tim said to Annie. "If he tries, give me a holler." And to the bloody boy, who looked very small and badly used: "We're going to discuss this when I get back. That work for you?"

The kid thought it over, then gave a tired nod. "I guess it has to."

2

When the men were gone, Orphan Annie found a couple of clean rags in a basket under the sink. After wetting them with cold water, she wrung one out tight and the other loose. She handed him the tight one. "Put that on your ear."

Luke did so. It stung. She used the other to clean the blood from his face, working with a gentleness that made him think of his mother. Annie stopped what she was doing and asked him—with equal gentleness— why he was crying.

"I miss my mom."

"Why, now, I bet she misses you, too."

"Not unless consciousness somehow continues after death. I'd like to believe it, but empirical evidence suggests that's not the case."

"Continues? Oh, it surely *does*." Annie went to the sink and began rinsing blood from the rag she'd been using. "Some say that souls gone on take no interest in the earthly sphere, nummore than we care about the goings-ons of ants in anthills, but I ain't one of those some. I believe they pay attention. I'm sorry she's passed, son."

"Do you think their love continues?" The idea was silly, he knew that, but it was *good* silly.

"Sure. Love don't die with the earthly body, son. It's a purely ridiculous notion. How long since she went on?"

"Maybe a month, maybe six weeks. I've pretty much lost track of time. They were murdered, and I was kidnapped. I know that's hard to believe—"

Annie went to work on the rest of the blood. "Not hard if you're in the know." She tapped her temple below the brim of her sombrero. "Did they come in black cars?"

"I don't know," Luke said, "but I wouldn't be surprised."

"And were they doing experiments on you?"

Luke's mouth dropped open. "How did you know that?"

"George Allman," she said. "He's on WMDK from midnight until four in the morning. His show is about walk-ins, and UFOs, and psychic powers."

"Psychic powers? Really?"

"Yes, and the conspiracy. Do you know about the conspiracy, son?"

"Sort of," Luke said.

"George Allman's show is called *The Outsiders*. People call in, but mostly it's just him talking. He doesn't say it's aliens, or the government, or the government *working* with aliens, he's careful because he doesn't want to disappear or get shot like Jack and Bobby, but he talks about the black cars all the time, and the experiments. Things that would turn your hair white. Did you know that Son of Sam was a walk-in?

No? Well, he was. Then the devil that was inside him walked back out, leaving only a shell. Raise your head, son, that blood's all down your neck, and if it dries before I can get it, I'll have to scrub."

3

The Beeman boys, a pair of great hulking teenagers from the trailer park south of town, showed up at quarter past noon, well into what was usually Tim's lunch hour. By then most of the stuff for Fromie's Small Engine Sales and Service was on the cracked concrete of the station tarmac. If it had been up to Tim, he would have fired the Beemans on the spot, but they were related to Mr. Jackson in some complicated southern way, so that wasn't an option. Besides, he needed them.

Del Beeman got the big truck with the stake sides backed up to the door of the Carolina Produce boxcar by twelve-thirty, and they began loading in crates of lettuce, tomatoes, cucumbers, and summer squash. Hector and his secondman, interested not in fresh veggies but only in getting the hell out of South Carolina, pitched in. Norb Hollister stood in the shade of the depot overhang, doing some heavy looking-on but nothing else. Tim found the man's continued presence a trifle peculiar—he'd shown no interest in the arrivals and departures of the trains before—but was too busy to consider it.

An old Ford station wagon pulled into the station's small parking lot at ten to one, just as Tim was forklifting the last crates of produce into the back of the truck that would deliver them to the DuPray Grocery . . . assuming that Phil Beeman got it there all right. It was less than a mile, but this morning Phil's speech was slow and his eyes were as red as those of a small animal trying to stay ahead of a brushfire. It didn't take Sherlock Holmes to deduce he'd been indulging in a bit of wacky tobacky. He and his brother both.

Doc Roper got out of his station wagon. Tim tipped him a wave and pointed to the warehouse where Mr. Jackson kept his office/apartment. Roper waved back and headed in that direction. He was old-school, almost a caricature; the kind of doctor who still survives in a thousand poor-ass rural areas where the nearest hospital is forty or fifty miles away, Obamacare is looked upon as a libtard blasphemy, and a trip to Walmart is considered an occasion. He was overweight and over sixty, a hardshell Baptist who carried a Bible as well as a stethoscope in a black bag which had been handed down, father to son, for three generations.

"What's with that kid?" the train's secondman asked, using a bandanna to mop his forehead.

"I don't know," Tim said, "but I intend to find out. Go on, you guys, rev it up and go. Unless you want to leave me one of those Lexuses, Hector. Happy to roll it off myself if you do."

"Chupa mi polla," Hector said. Then he shook Tim's hand and headed back to his engine, hoping to make up time between DuPray and Brunswick.

4

Stackhouse intended to make the trip on the Challenger with the two extraction teams, but Mrs. Sigsby overruled him. She could do that because she was the boss. Nevertheless, Stackhouse's expression of dismay at this idea bordered on insulting.

"Wipe that look off your face," she said. "Whose head do you think will roll if this goes pear-shaped?"

"Both of our heads, and it won't stop with us."

"Yes, but whose will come off first and roll the farthest?"

"Julia, this is a field operation, and you've never been in the field before."

"I'll have both Ruby and Opal teams with me, four good men and three tough women. We'll also have Tony Fizzale, who's ex-Marines, Dr. Evans, and Winona Briggs. She's ex-Army, and has some triage skills. Denny Williams will be in charge once the operation begins, but I intend to be there, and I intend to write my report from a ground-level perspective." She paused. "If there needs to be a report, that is, and I'm starting to believe there will be no way to avoid it." She glanced at her watch. Twelve-thirty. "No more discussion. We need to get this on wheels. You run the place, and if all goes well, I'll be back here by two tomorrow morning."

He walked with her out the door and down to the gated dirt road that eventually led to two-lane blacktop three miles east. The day was hot. Crickets sang in the thick woods through which the fucking kid had somehow found his way. A Ford Windstar soccer-mom van was idling in front of the gate, with Robin Lecks behind the wheel. Michelle Robertson was sitting beside her. Both women wore jeans and black tee-shirts.

"From here to Presque Isle," Mrs. Sigsby said. "Ninety minutes. From Presque Isle to Erie, Pennsylvania, another seventy minutes. We pick up Opal Team there. From Erie to Alcolu, South Carolina, two hours, give or take. If all goes well, we'll be in DuPray by seven this evening."

"Stay in touch, and remember that Williams is in charge once you go hot. Not you."

"I will."

"Julia, I really think this is a mistake. It ought to be me."

She faced him. "Say it again, and I'll haul off on you." She walked to the van. Denny Williams unrolled the side door for her. Mrs. Sigsby started to get in, then turned to Stackhouse. "And make sure Avery Dixon is well dunked and in Back Half by the time I return."

"Donkey Kong doesn't like the idea."

She gave him a terrifying smile. "Do I look like I care?"

5

Tim watched the train pull out, then returned to the shade of the depot's overhang. His shirt was soaked with sweat. He was surprised to see Norbert Hollister still standing there. As usual, he was wearing his paisley vest and dirty khakis, today cinched with a braided belt just below his breastbone. Tim wondered (and not for the first time) how he could wear pants that high and not squash the hell out of his balls.

"What are you still doing here, Norbert?"

Hollister shrugged and smiled, revealing teeth Tim could have done without viewing before lunch. "Just passing the time. Afternoons ain't exactly busy back at the old ranchero."

As if mornings or evenings were, Tim thought. "Well, why don't you put an egg in your shoe and beat it?"

Norbert pulled a pouch of Red Man from his back pocket and stuffed some in his mouth. It went a long way, Tim thought, to explaining the color of his teeth. "Who died and made you Pope?"

"I guess that sounded like a request," Tim said. "It wasn't. Go."

"Fine, fine, I can take a hint. You have a good day, Mr. Night Knocker."

Norbert ambled off. Tim looked after him, frowning. He sometimes saw Hollister in Bev's Eatery, or down at Zoney's, buying boiled peanuts or a hard-boiled egg out of the jar on the counter, but otherwise he rarely left his motel office, where he watched sports and porn on his satellite TV. Which, unlike the ones in the rooms, worked.

Orphan Annie was waiting for Tim in Mr. Jackson's outer office, sitting behind the desk and thumbing through the papers in Jackson's IN/OUT basket.

"That's not your business, Annie," Tim said mildly. "And if you mess that stuff up, I'll be the one in trouble."

"Nothing in'dresting, anyway," she said. "Just invoices and schedules and such. Although he *does* have a meal punch-card for that topless café down Hardeeville. Two more punches and he gets a free buffet lunch. Although eating lunch while looking at some woman's snatchola . . . *brrr*."

Tim had never thought of it that way, and now that he had, wished he hadn't. "The doc's in with the kid?"

"Yeah. I stopped the bleeding, but he'll have to wear his hair long from now on because that ear is never gonna look the same. Now listen to me. That boy's parents were murdered and he was kidnapped."

"Part of the conspiracy?" He and Annie had had many conversations about the conspiracy on his night-knocker rounds.

"That's right. They came for him in the black cars, count on it, and if they trace him to here, they'll *come* for him here."

"Noted," he said, "and I'll be sure to discuss it with Sheriff John. Thanks for cleaning him up and watching him, but now I think you better head out."

She got up and shook out her serape. "That's right, you tell Sheriff John. You-all need to be on your guard. They're apt to come locked and loaded. There's a town in Maine, Jerusalem's Lot, and you could ask the people who lived there about the men in the black cars. If you could find any people, that is. They all disappeared forty or more years ago. George Allman talks about that town all the time."

"Got it."

She went to the door, serape swishing, then turned. "You don't believe me, and I ain't a bit surprised. Why would I be? I been the town weirdo for years before you came, and if the Lord doesn't take me, I'll be the town weirdo years after you're gone."

"Annie, I never—"

"Hush." She stared at him fiercely from beneath her sombrero. "It's all right. But pay attention, now. I'm telling you . . . but *he* told *me*. That boy. So that's two of us, all right? And you remember what I said. *They come in black cars*."

6

Doc Roper was putting the few tools of examination he'd used back into his bag. The boy was still sitting in Mr. Jackson's easy chair. His face had been cleaned of blood and his ear was bandaged. He was raising a good bruise down the right side of his face from his argument with the signal-post, but his eyes were clear and alert. The doc had found a bottle of ginger ale in the little fridge, and the boy was making short work of it.

"Sit there easy, young man," Roper said. He snapped his bag shut and walked over to Tim, who was standing just inside the door to the outer office.

"Is he okay?" Tim asked, keeping his voice low.

"He's dehydrated, and he's hungry, hasn't had much to eat in quite awhile, but otherwise he seems fine to me. Kids his age bounce back from worse. He says he's twelve, he says his name is Nick Wilholm, and he says he got on that train where it started, way up in northern Maine. I ask him what he was doing there, he says he can't tell me. I ask him for his address, he says he can't remember. Plausible, a hard knock on the head can cause temporary disorientation and scramble memory, but I've been around the block a few times, and I can tell the difference between amnesia and reticence, especially in a kid. He's hiding something. Maybe a lot."

"Okay."

"My advice? Promise to feed him a big old meal at the café, and you'll get the whole story."

"Thanks, Doc. Send me the bill."

Roper waved this away. "You buy *me* a big old meal someplace classier than Bev's, and we'll call it square." In the doc's thick Dixie accent, *square* came out *squarr*. "And when you get his story, I want to hear it."

When he was gone, Tim closed the door so it was just him and the boy, and took his cell phone from his pocket. He called Bill Wicklow, the deputy who was scheduled to take over the night knocker's job after Christmas. The boy watched him closely, finishing the last of his cold drink.

"Bill? This is Tim. Yeah, fine. Just wondering if you'd like a little dry run on the night-knocking job tonight. This is usually my time to sleep, but something's come up down at the trainyard." He listened. "Excellent. I owe you one. I'll leave the time clock at the cop-shop. Don't forget you have to wind it up. And thanks."

He ended the call and studied the boy. The bruises on his face would bloom, then fade in a week or two. The look in his eyes might take longer. "You feeling better? Headache going away?"

"Yes, sir."

"Never mind the sir, you can call me Tim. Now what do I call you? What's your real name?"

After a brief hesitation, Luke told him.

7

The poorly lit tunnel between Front Half and Back Half was chilly, and Avery began to shiver immediately. He still had on the clothes he'd been wearing when Zeke and Carlos had hauled his small unconscious body out of the immersion tank, and he was soaked. His teeth began to chatter. Still, he held onto what he had learned. It was important. Everything was important now.

"Stop with the teeth," Gladys said. "That's a disgusting sound." She was pushing him in a wheelchair, her smile nowhere in evidence. Word of what this little shit had done was everywhere now, and like all the other Institute employees, she was terrified and would remain so until Luke Ellis was hauled back and they could all breathe a sigh of relief.

"I c-c-c-can't h-h-help ih-it," Avery said. "I'm so c-c-cold."

"Do you think I give a shit?" Gladys's raised voice echoed back from the tile walls. "Do you have any idea of what you did? Do you have any *idea*?"

Avery did. In fact, he had many ideas, some of them Gladys's (her fear was like a rat running on a wheel in the middle of her head), some of them entirely his own.

Once they were through the door marked AUTHORIZED PERSONNEL ONLY, it was a little warmer, and in the tatty lounge where Dr. James was waiting for them (her white lab coat misbuttoned, her hair in disarray, a big goofy smile on her face), it was warmer still.

Avery's shivering slowed, then ceased, but the colored Stasi Lights came back. That was all right, because he could make them go away any time he wanted. Zeke had nearly killed him in that tank, in fact before Avery passed out he thought he *was* dead, but the tank had also done something to him. He understood that it did stuff to some of the other kids who went into it, but he thought this was something more. TK as well as TP was the least of it. Gladys was terrified of what might happen because of Luke, but Avery had an idea that he, Avery, could terrify her of *him*, if he wanted.

But this wasn't the time.

"Hello, young man!" Dr. James cried. She sounded like a politician on a TV ad, and her thoughts were flying around like scraps of paper caught in a strong wind.

Something is really, really wrong with her, Avery thought. It's like radiation poisoning, only in her brain instead of her bones.

"Hello," Avery said.

Dr. Jeckle threw back her head and laughed as if *Hello* were the punchline of the funniest joke she'd ever heard. "We weren't expecting you so soon, but welcome, welcome! Some of your friends are here!"

I know, Avery thought, and I can't wait to see them. And I think they'll be glad to see me.

"First, though, we need to get you out of those wet clothes." She gave Gladys a reproachful look, but Gladys was busy scratching at her arms, trying to get rid of the buzz running over her skin (or just under it). Good luck with that, Avery thought. "I'll have Henry take you to your room. We have nice caretakers here. Can you walk on your own?"

"Yes."

Dr. Jeckle did some more laughing, head back and throat working. Avery got out of the wheelchair, and gave Gladys a long, measuring look. She stopped scratching and now *she* was the one who shivered. Not because she was wet, and not because she was cold. It was because of him. She felt him, and she didn't like it.

But Avery did. It was sort of beautiful.

8

Because there was no other chair in Mr. Jackson's living room, Tim brought one in from the outer office. He considered putting it in front of the boy, then decided that would be too much like the set-up in a police interrogation room. He slid it beside the La-Z-Boy instead, sitting next to the boy the way you'd sit with a friend, maybe to watch a favorite TV show. Only Mr. Jackson's flatscreen was blank.

"Now, Luke," he said. "According to Annie, you were kidnapped, but Annie isn't always . . . completely on the beam, let's say."

"She's on the beam about that," Luke said.

"Okay, then. Kidnapped from where?"

"Minneapolis. They knocked me out. And they killed my parents." He swiped a hand across his eyes.

"These kidnappers took you from Minneapolis to Maine. How did they do that?"

"I don't know. I was unconscious. Probably in a plane. I really am from Minneapolis. You can check that out, all you have to do is call my school. It's called the Broderick School for Exceptional Children."

"Which would make you a bright boy, I'm assuming."

"Oh, sure," Luke said, with no pride in his voice. "I'm a bright boy. And right now I'm a very hungry boy. I haven't had anything for a couple of days but a sausage biscuit and a fruit pie. I think a couple of days. I've kind of lost track of time. A man named Mattie gave them to me."

"Nothing else?"

"A piece of doughnut," Luke said. "It wasn't very big."

"Jesus, let's get you something to eat."

"Yes," Luke said, then added, "Please."

Tim took his cell phone from his pocket. "Wendy? This is Tim. I wonder if you could do me a favor."

9

Avery's room in Back Half was stark. The bed was your basic cot. There were no Nickelodeon posters on the walls, and no G.I. Joes on the bureau to play with. That was okay with Avery. He was only ten, but now he had to be a grownup, and grownups didn't play with toy soldiers.

Only I can't do it alone, he thought.

He remembered Christmas, the year before. It hurt to think about that, but he thought about it, anyway. He had gotten the Lego castle he'd asked for, but when the pieces were spread out before him, he didn't know how to get from that scatter to the beautiful castle on the box, with its turrets and gates and the drawbridge that went up and down. He'd started to cry. Then his father (dead now, he was sure of it) knelt down beside him and said, *We'll follow the instructions and do it together. One step at a time.* And they had. The castle had stayed on his bureau in his room with his G.I. Joes guarding it, and that castle was one thing they hadn't been able to duplicate when he woke up in Front Half.

Now he lay on the cot in this barren room, dressed in dry clothes, thinking of how fine the castle had looked when it was done. And feeling the hum. It was constant here in Back Half. Loud in the rooms, louder in the halls, loudest of all down past the cafeteria, where a double-locked door beyond the caretakers' break room led to the back half of Back Half. The caretakers often called that part Gorky Park, because the kids who lived there (if you could call it living) were gorks. Hummers. But they were useful, Avery supposed. The way the wrapper your Hershey bar came in was useful, until you licked it clean. Then you could throw it away.

The doors here had locks. Avery concentrated, trying to turn his. Not that there was anywhere to go except for the hallway with its blue carpet, but it was an interesting experiment. He could feel the lock *trying* to turn, but he couldn't quite manage it. He wondered if George Iles would be able to, because George had been a strong TK-pos to begin with. Avery guessed he could, with a little help. He thought again about what his father had said: *We'll do it together. One step at a time.*

At five o'clock, the door opened and a red-clad caretaker poked his unsmiling face in. They didn't wear nametags here, but Avery didn't need a nametag. This was Jacob, known to his colleagues as Jake the Snake. He was ex-Navy. You tried to be a SEAL, Avery thought, but you couldn't make it. They kicked you out. I think maybe you liked hurting people too much.

"Dinner," Jake the Snake said. "If you want it, come on. If you don't, I'll lock you in until movie time."

"I want it."

"All right. You like movies, kiddo?"

"Yes," Avery said, and thought, But I won't like these. These movies kill people.

"You'll like these," Jake said. "There's always a cartoon to start with. Caff's right down there on your left.

And quit lollygagging." Jake gave him a hefty swat on the ass to get him going.

In the cafeteria—a dreary room painted the same dark green as the residence corridor in Front Half—about a dozen kids sat eating what smelled to Avery like Dinty Moore Beef Stew. His mom served it at least twice a week back home, because his little sister liked it. She was probably dead, too. Most of the kids looked like zombies, and there was a lot of slobbering. He saw one kid, a girl, who was smoking a cigarette as she ate. As Avery watched, she tapped ash into her bowl, looked around vacantly, and began eating from it again.

He had felt Kalisha even down in the tunnel and now he saw her, sitting at a table near the back. He had to restrain an urge to run to her and throw his arms around her neck. That would attract attention, and Avery didn't want to do that. Just the opposite. Helen Simms was sitting next to Sha, hands lying limply on either side of her bowl. Her eyes were fixed on the ceiling. Her hair, so razzily colored when she showed up in Front Half, was now dull and dank, hanging around her face—her much *thinner* face—in clumps. Kalisha was feeding her, or trying to.

"Come on, Hel, come on, Hell on Wheels, here we go." Sha got a spoonful of the stew into Helen's mouth. When a brown lump of mystery meat tried to come out over Helen's lower lip, Sha used the spoon to push it back in. This time Helen swallowed, and Sha smiled. "*That's* right, good."

Sha, Avery thought. *Hey, Kalisha.*

She looked around, startled, saw him, and broke into a broad smile.

Avester!

A drool of brown gravy ran down Helen's chin. Nicky, sitting on her other side, used a paper napkin to wipe it off. Then he also saw Avery, grinned, and gave him a thumbs-up. George, sitting directly across from Nicky, turned around.

"Hey, check it out, it's the Avester," George said. "Sha thought you might be coming. Welcome to our happy home, little hero."

"If you're gonna eat, get a bowl," said a hard-faced older woman. Her name was Corinne, Avery knew, and she liked slapping. Slapping made her feel good. "I gotta shut down early, on account of it's movie night."

Avery got a bowl and ladled up some of the stew. Yes, it was Dinty Moore. He put a piece of spongy white bread on top of it, then took his meal over to his friends and sat down. Sha smiled at him. Her headache was bad today, but she smiled anyway, and that made him feel like laughing and crying at the same time.

"Eat up, buddy," Nicky said, but he wasn't taking his own advice; his bowl was still mostly full. His eyes were bloodshot, and he was rubbing at his left temple. "I know it looks like diarrhea, but you don't want to go to the movies on an empty stomach."

Have they caught Luke? Sha sent.

No. They're all scared shitless.

Good. Good!

Will we get hurty shots before the movie?

I don't think so tonight, this is still a new one, we've only seen it once.

George was looking at them with wise eyes. He had heard. Once upon a Front Half time George Iles had only been a TK, but now he was something more. They all were. Back Half increased whatever you had, but thanks to the immersion tank, none of them were like Avery. He knew stuff. The tests in Front Half, for example. A lot of them were side projects of Dr. Hendricks, but the injections were matters of practicality. Some of them were limiters, and Avery hadn't had those. He had gone straight to the immersion tank, where he had been taken to death's door or maybe right through it, and as a result he could make the Stasi Lights almost any time he wanted to. He didn't need the movies, and he didn't need to be part of the group-think. Creating that group-think was Back Half's main job.

But he was still only ten. Which was a problem.

As he began to eat, he probed for Helen, and was delighted to discover she was still in there. He liked Helen. She wasn't like that bitch Frieda. He didn't need to read Frieda's mind to know she had tricked him into telling her stuff, then snitched on him; who else *could* it have been?

Helen?

No. Don't talk to me, Avery. I have to . . .

The rest was gone, but Avery thought he understood. She had to hide. There was a sponge filled with pain inside her head, and she was hiding from it as best she could. Hiding from pain was a sensible response, as far as it went. The problem was how the sponge kept swelling. It would keep on until there was nowhere to hide, and then it would squash her against the back of her own skull like a fly on a wall. Then she'd be done. As Helen, at least.

Avery reached into her mind. It was easier than trying to turn the lock on the door of his room, because he'd been a powerful TP to begin with, and TK was new to him. He was clumsy and had to be careful.

He couldn't fix her, but he thought he could *ease* her. Shield her a bit. That would be good for her, and it would be good for them . . . because they were going to need all the help they could get.

He found the headache-sponge deep inside Helen's head. He told it to stop spreading. He told it to go away. It didn't want to. He pushed it. The colored lights started to appear in front of him, swirling slowly, like cream into coffee. He pushed harder. The sponge was pliable but firm.

Kalisha. Help me.

With what? What are you doing?

He told her. She came in, tentatively at first. They pushed together. The headache-sponge gave a little.

George, Avery sent. *Nicky. Help us.*

Nicky was able to, a little. George looked puzzled at first, then joined in, but after a moment he backed out again. "I can't," he whispered. "It's dark."

Never mind the dark! That was Sha. *I think we can help!*

George came back. He was reluctant, and he wasn't much help, but at least he was with them.

It's only a sponge, Avery told them. He could no longer see his bowl of stew. It had been replaced by the heartbeat swirl of the Stasi Lights. *It can't hurt you. Push it! All together!*

They tried, and something happened. Helen looked down from the ceiling. She looked at Avery instead.

"Look who's here," she said in a rusty voice. "My headache's a little better. Thank God." She began to eat on her own.

"Holy shit," George said. "That was us."

Nick was grinning and holding up a hand. "Five, Avery."

Avery slapped him five, but any good feeling left with the dots. Helen's headache would come back, and it would worsen each time she watched the movies. Helen's would, Sha's would, Nicky's would. His would, too. Eventually all of them would join the hum emanating from Gorky Park.

But maybe . . . if they were all together, in their own group-think . . . and if there was a way to make a shield . . .

Sha.

She looked at him. She listened. Nicky and George also listened, at least as well as they could. It was like they were partially deaf. But Sha heard. She ate a bite of stew, then put her spoon down and shook her head.

We can't escape, Avery. If that's what you're thinking, forget it.

I know we can't. But we have to do something. We have to help Luke, and we have to help ourselves. I see the pieces, but I don't know how to put them together. I don't . . .

"You don't know how to build the castle," Nicky said in a low, musing voice. Helen had stopped eating again, and had resumed her inspection of the ceiling. The headache-sponge was growing again already, swelling as it gorged on her mind. Nicky helped her to another bite.

"Cigarettes!" one of the caretakers was shouting. He held up a box. Smokes were free back here, it seemed. Encouraged, even. "Who wants a cigarette before the show?"

We can't escape, Avery sent, *so help me build a castle. A wall. A shield. Our castle. Our wall. Our shield.*

He looked from Sha to Nicky to George and back to Sha again, pleading for her to understand. Her eyes brightened.

She gets it, Avery thought. Thank God, she gets it.

She started to speak, but closed her mouth again as the caretaker—his name was Clint—passed them by, bawling, "Cigarettes! Who wants one before the show?"

When he was gone, she said, "If we can't escape, we have to take the place over."

10

Deputy Wendy Gullickson's original frosty attitude toward Tim had warmed considerably since their first date at the Mexican restaurant in Hardeeville. They were now an acknowledged couple, and when she came into Mr. Jackson's back room apartment with a large paper bag, she kissed him first on the cheek and then quickly on the mouth.

"This is Deputy Gullickson," Tim said, "but you can call her Wendy, if that's okay with her."

"It is," Wendy said. "What's your name?"

Luke looked to Tim, who gave him a slight nod.

"Luke Ellis."

"Pleased to meet you, Luke. That's quite a bruise you've got there."

"Yes, ma'am. Ran into something."

"Yes, *Wendy*. And the bandage over your ear? Did you cut yourself, as well?"

That made him smile a little, because it was the stone truth. "Something like that."

"Tim said you might be hungry, so I grabbed some take-out from the restaurant on Main Street. I've got Co'-Cola, chicken, burgers, and fries. What do you want?"

"All of it," Luke said, which made Wendy and Tim laugh.

They watched him eat two drumsticks, then a hamburger and most of the fries, finally a good-sized go-cup of rice pudding. Tim, who had missed his lunch, ate the rest of the chicken and drank a Coke.

"All right now?" Tim asked when the food was gone.

Instead of speaking, Luke burst into tears.

Wendy hugged him and stroked his hair, working some of the tangles out with her fingers. When Luke's sobs finally eased, Tim squatted beside him.

"Sorry," Luke said. "Sorry, sorry, sorry."

"That's okay. You're allowed."

"It's because I feel alive again. I don't know why that would make me cry, but it did."

"I think it's called relief," Wendy said.

"Luke claims his parents were murdered and he was kidnapped," Luke said. Wendy's eyes widened.

"It's not a claim!" Luke said, sitting forward in Mr. Jackson's easy chair. "It's the truth!"

"Bad word choice, maybe. Let's have your story, Luke."

Luke considered this, then said, "Will you do something for me first?"

"If I can," Tim said.

"Look outside. See if that other guy is still there."

"Norbert Hollister?" Tim smiled. "I told him to scram. By now he's probably down at the Go-Mart, buying lottery tickets. He's convinced he's going to be South Carolina's next millionaire."

"Just check."

Tim looked at Wendy, who shrugged and said, "I'll do it."

She came back a minute later, frowning. "As a matter of fact, he's sitting in a rocking chair over at the depot. Reading a magazine."

"I think he's an uncle," Luke said in a low voice. "I had uncles in Richmond and Wilmington. Maybe in Sturbridge, too. I never knew I had so many uncles." He laughed. It was a metallic sound.

Tim got up and went to the door just in time to see Norbert Hollister rise and amble away in the direction of his going-to-seed motel. He didn't look back. Tim returned to Luke and Wendy.

"He's gone, son."

"Maybe to call them," Luke said. He poked at his empty Coke can. "I won't let them take me back. I thought I was going to die there."

"Where?" Tim asked.

"The Institute."

"Start at the beginning and tell us everything," Wendy said.

Luke did.

11

When he was finished—it took almost half an hour, and Luke consumed a second Coke during the telling— there was a moment of silence. Then Tim said, very quietly, "It's not possible. Just to begin with, that many abductions would raise red flags."

Wendy shook her head at that. "You were a cop. You should know better. There was a study a few years back that said over half a million kids go missing each year in the United States. Pretty staggering figure, wouldn't you say?"

"I know the numbers are high, there were almost five hundred missing kids reported in Sarasota County the last year I was on the cops there, but the majority—the *great* majority—are kids who come back on their own." Tim was thinking of Robert and Roland Bilson, the twins he'd spotted on their way to the Dunning Agricultural Fair in the wee hours of the morning.

"That still leaves thousands," she said. "*Tens* of thousands."

"Agreed, but how many of those disappear leaving murdered parents behind?"

"No idea. I doubt if anyone's done a study." She turned her attention back to Luke, who had been following their conversation with his eyes, as if watching a tennis match. His hand was in his pocket, touching the thumb drive as if it were a lucky rabbit's foot.

"Sometimes," he said, "they probably make it look like accidents."

Tim had a sudden vision of this boy living with Orphan Annie in her tent, the two of them listening to that late-night kook of hers on the radio. Talking about the conspiracy. Talking about *they*.

"You say you cut your earlobe off because there was a tracking device in it," Wendy said. "Is that really the truth, Luke?"

"Yes."

Wendy didn't seem to know where to take it from there. The expression she looked at Tim said *Over to you*.

Tim picked up Luke's empty Coke can and dropped it into the take-out bag, which now contained nothing but wrappers and chicken bones. "You're talking about a secret installation running a secret program on domestic soil, one that stretches back God knows how many years. Once upon a time that might have been possible, I suppose—theoretically—but not in the age of the computer. The government's biggest secrets get dumped onto the Internet by this rogue outfit called—"

"WikiLeaks, I know about WikiLeaks." Luke sounded impatient. "I know how hard it is to keep secrets, and I know how crazy this sounds. On the other hand, the Germans had concentration camps during World War II where they managed to kill seven million Jews. Also gypsies and gays."

"But the people around those camps knew what was going on," Wendy said. She tried to take his hand.

Luke took it back. "And I'd bet a million bucks the people in Dennison River Bend, that's the closest town, know *something's* going on. Something bad. Not what, because they don't *want* to know. Why would they? It keeps them going, and besides, who'd believe it, anyway? You've still got people today who don't believe the Germans killed all those Jews, as far as that goes. It's called denial."

Yes, Tim thought, the boy is bright. His cover story for whatever really happened to him is loony, but he does have a ton of brains.

"I want to be sure I have this straight," Wendy said. She was speaking gently. They both were. Luke got it. You didn't have to be a child fucking prodigy to know this was how people talked to someone who was mentally unbalanced. He was disappointed but not surprised. What else could he have expected? "They somehow find kids who are telepaths and what you call teleki-something—"

"Telekinetics. TK. Usually the talents are small—

even TK-pos kids don't have much. But the Institute doctors make them stronger. Shots for dots, that's what they say, what we all say, only the dots are really the Stasi Lights I told you about. The shots that bring on the lights are supposed to boost what we have. I think some of the others might be to make us last longer. Or . . ." Here was something he just thought of. "Or to keep us from getting too much. Which could make us dangerous to them."

"Like vaccinations?" Tim asked.

"I guess you could say that, yeah."

"Before you were taken, you could move objects with your mind," Tim said in his gentle I'm-talking-to-a-lunatic voice.

"*Small* objects."

"And since this near-death experience in the immersion tank, you can also read thoughts."

"Even before. The tank . . . boosted it higher. But I'm still not . . ." He massaged the back of his neck. This was hard to explain, and their voices, so low and so calm, were getting on his nerves, which were already raw. Soon he would be as nuts as they thought he was. Still, he had to try. "But I'm still not very strong. None of us are, except maybe for Avery. He's awesome."

Tim said, "Let me make sure I have this straight. They kidnap kids who have weak psychic powers, feed them mental steroids, then get them to kill people. Like that politician who was planning to run for president. Mark Berkowitz."

"Yes."

"Why not Bin Laden?" Wendy asked. "I would have thought he'd be a natural target for this . . . this mental assassination."

"I don't know," Luke said. He sounded exhausted. The bruise on his cheek seemed to be growing more colorful by the minute. "I don't have a clue how they pick their targets. I talked about it one time with my friend Kalisha. She didn't have any idea, either."

"Why wouldn't this mystery organization just use hit men? Wouldn't that be simpler?"

"It looks simple in the movies," Luke said. "In real life I think they mostly fail, or get caught. Like the guys who killed Bin Laden almost got caught."

"Let's have a demonstration," Tim said. "I'm thinking of a number. Tell me what it is."

Luke tried. He concentrated and waited for the colored dots to appear, but they didn't come. "I can't get it."

"Move something, then. Isn't that your basic talent, the one they grabbed you for?"

Wendy shook her head. Tim was no telepath, but he knew what she was thinking: *Stop badgering him, he's disturbed and disoriented and on the run.* But Tim thought if he could break through the kid's cockamamie story, maybe they could get to something real and figure out where to go from there.

"How about the take-out bag? No food in it now, it's light, you should be able to move it."

Luke looked at it, his brow furrowing more deeply. For a moment Tim thought he felt something— a whisper along his skin, like a faint draft—but then it was gone, and the bag didn't move. Of course it didn't.

"Okay," Wendy said, "I think that enough for n—"

"I know you two are boyfriend and girlfriend," Luke said. "I know that much."

Tim smiled. "Not too impressive, kiddo. You saw her kiss me when she came in."

Luke turned his attention to Wendy. "You're going on a trip. To see your sister, is it?"

Her eyes went wide. "How—"

"Don't fall for it," Tim said . . . but gently. "It's an old medium's trick—the educated guess. Although I'll admit the kid does it well."

"What education have I had about Wendy's sister?" Luke asked, although without much hope. He had played his cards one by one, and now there was only one left. And he was so tired. What sleep he'd gotten on the train had been thin and haunted by bad dreams. Mostly of the immersion tank.

"Will you excuse us for a minute?" Tim asked. Without waiting for a reply, he took Wendy over to the door to the outer office. He spoke to her briefly. She nodded and left the room, taking her phone from her pocket as she went. Tim came back. "I think we better take you to the station."

At first Luke thought he was talking about the train station. Putting him on another freight, so he and his girlfriend didn't have to deal with the runaway kid and his crazy story. Then he realized that wasn't the kind of station Tim meant.

Oh, so what? Luke thought. I always knew I'd end up in a police station somewhere. And maybe a small one is better than a big one, where they'd have a hundred different people—perps—to deal with.

Only they thought he was just being paranoid about that guy Hollister, and that wasn't good. For now he'd have to hope they were right, and Hollister was nobody special. They probably *were* right. After all, the Institute couldn't have guys everywhere, could they?

"Okay, but first I need to tell you something and show you something."

"Go for it," Tim said. He leaned forward, looking intently into Luke's face. Maybe he was just humoring the crazy kid, but at least he was listening, and Luke supposed that was the best he could expect for now.

"If they know I'm here, they'll come for me. Probably with guns. Because they're scared to death someone might believe me."

"Duly noted," Tim said, "but we've got a pretty good little police force here, Luke. I think you'll be safe."

You have no idea what you might be up against, Luke thought, but he couldn't try to convince this guy anymore just now. He was just too worn out. Wendy came back and gave Tim a nod. Luke was too beat to care about that, either.

"The woman who helped me escape from the Institute gave me two things. One was the knife I used to cut off the part of my ear that had the tracker in it. The other was this." From his pocket he drew out the flash drive. "I don't know what's on it, but I think you should look at it before you do anything else."

He handed it to Tim.

12

The residents of Back Half—the front half of Back Half, that was; the eighteen currently in Gorky Park remained behind their locked door, humming away— were given twenty minutes of free time before the movie started. Jimmy Cullum zombie-walked his aching head to his room; Hal, Donna, and Len sat in the cafeteria, the two boys staring at their half-eaten desserts (chocolate pudding tonight), Donna regarding a smoldering cigarette she seemed to have forgotten how to smoke.

Kalisha, Nick, George, Avery, and Helen went down to the lounge with its ugly thrift-store furniture and the old flatscreen, which showed only prehistoric sitcoms like *Bewitched* and *Happy Days*. Katie Givens was there. She didn't look around at them, only at the currently blank TV. To Kalisha's surprise, they were joined by Iris, who looked better than she had in days. Brighter.

Kalisha was thinking hard, and she could think, because she *felt* better than she had in days. What they had done to Helen's headache—Avery, mostly, but they had all pitched in—had helped her own. The same was true of Nicky and George. She could see it.

Take the place over.

A bold and delicious idea, but questions immediately arose. The most obvious was how they were supposed to do it, when there were at least twelve caretakers on duty—there were always more on movie days. The second was why they had never thought of this before.

I did, Nicky told her . . . and was his mental voice stronger? She thought it was, and she thought Avery might have also played a part in that. Because *he* was stronger now. *I thought about it when they first brought me here.*

That was as much as Nicky could manage to tell her mind to mind, so he put his mouth to her ear and whispered the rest. "I was the one who always fought, remember?"

It was true. Nicky with his black eyes. Nicky with his bruised mouth.

"We're not strong enough," he murmured. "Even in here, even after the lights, we only have little powers."

Avery, meanwhile, was looking at Kalisha with desperate hope. He was thinking into her head, but hardly needed to. His eyes said it all. *Here are the pieces, Sha. I'm pretty sure all of them are here. Help me put them together. Help me build a castle where we can be safe, at least for awhile.*

Sha thought of the old, faded Hillary Clinton sticker on the back bumper of her mom's Subaru. It said STRONGER TOGETHER, and of course that was how it worked here in Back Half. That was why they watched the movies together. That was why they could reach across thousands of miles, sometimes even halfway around the world, to the people who were *in* the movies. If the five of them (make it six, if they could work on Iris's headache the way they had worked on Helen's) were able to create that united mental force, a kind of Vulcan mind meld, shouldn't that be enough to mutiny and take Back Half over?

"It's a great idea, but I don't think so," George said. He took her hand and gave it a brief squeeze. "We might be able to screw with their heads a little, maybe scare the hell out of them, but they've got those zap-sticks, and as soon as they jolted one or two of us, it would be game over."

Kalisha didn't want to admit it, but told him he was probably right.

Avery: *One step at a time.*

Iris said, "I can't hear what you guys are thinking. I know you're thinking something, but my head still hurts bad."

Avery: *Let's see what we can do for her. All of us together.*

Kalisha looked at Nick, who nodded. At George, who shrugged and also nodded.

Avery led them into Iris Stanhope's head like an explorer leading his party into a cave. The sponge in her mind was very big. Avery saw it as blood-colored, so they all saw it that way. They ranged themselves around it and began to push. It gave a little . . . and a little more . . . but then it stopped, resisting their efforts. George backed out first, then Helen (who hadn't had all that much to contribute, anyway), then Nick and Kalisha. Avery came last, dealing the headache-sponge a petulant mental kick before withdrawing.

"Any better, Iris?" Kalisha asked, without much hope.

"What's better?" It was Katie Givens. She had drifted to join them.

"My headache," Iris said. "And it is. A little, anyway." She smiled at Katie, and for a moment the girl who had won the Abilene Spelling Bee was in the room.

Katie turned her attention back to the TV. "Where's Richie Cunningham and the Fonz?" she asked, and began rubbing at her temples. "I wish mine was better, my headache hurts like *poop*."

You see the problem, George thought to the others.

Kalisha did. They were stronger together, yes, but still not strong enough. No more than Hillary Clinton had been when she ran for president a few years back. Because the guy running against her, and his supporters, had had the political equivalent of the caretakers' zap-sticks.

"It helped me, though," Helen said. "My own headache is almost gone. It's like a miracle."

"Don't worry," Nicky said. Hearing him sound so defeated scared Kalisha. "It'll be back."

Corinne, the caretaker who liked to slap, came into the room. She had one hand on her holstered zap-stick, as if she had felt something. Probably did, Kalisha thought, but she doesn't know what it was.

"Movie time," she said. "Come on, kiddies, move your asses."

13

Two caretakers, Jake and Phil (known respectively as the Snake and the Pill), were standing outside the screening room's open doors, each holding a basket. As the kids filed in, those with cigarettes and matches (lighters weren't allowed in Back Half) deposited them in the baskets. They could have them back when the show was over . . . if they remembered to take them, that was. Hal, Donna, and Len sat in the back row, staring vacantly at the blank screen. Katie Givens sat in a middle row next to Jimmy Cullum, who was lackadaisically picking his nose.

Kalisha, Nick, George, Helen, Iris, and Avery sat down front.

"Welcome to another fun-filled evening," Nicky said in a loud announcer's voice. "This year's feature, an Academy Award winner in the category of Shittiest Documentary—"

Phil the Pill slapped him across the back of the head. "Shut up, asshole, and enjoy the show."

He retreated. The lights went down, and Dr. Hendricks appeared on the screen. Just seeing the unlit sparkler in his hand made Kalisha's mouth dry up.

There was something she was missing. Some vital piece of Avery's castle. But it wasn't lost; she just wasn't seeing it.

Stronger together, but not strong enough. Even if those poor almost-gorks like Jimmy and Hal and Donna were with us, we wouldn't be. But we could *be. On nights when the sparkler is lit, we* are. *When the sparkler is lit, we're destroyers, so what am I missing?*

"Welcome, boys and girls," Dr. Hendricks was saying, "and thank you for helping us! Let's begin with a few laughs, shall we? And I'll see you later." He wagged the unlit sparkler and actually winked. It made Kalisha feel like vomiting.

If we can reach all the way to the other side of the world, then why can't we—

For a moment she almost had it, but then Katie gave a loud cry, not of pain or sorrow but of joy. *"Road Runner! He's the best!"* She began to sing in a half-screaming falsetto that drilled into Kalisha's brain. *"Road Runner, Road Runner, the coyote's after YOU! Road Runner, Road Runner, if he catches you you're THROUGH!"*

"Shut it, Kates," George said, not unkindly, and as Road Runner went *meep-meep*ing down a deserted desert highway, and as Wile E. Coyote looked at him and saw a Thanksgiving dinner, Kalisha felt whatever had almost been in her grasp float away.

When the cartoon was over and Wile E. Coyote had once more been vanquished, a guy in a suit came on the screen. He had a microphone in his hand. Kalisha thought he was a businessman, and maybe he was, sort of, but that wasn't his main claim to fame. He was really a preacherman, because when the camera drew back you could see a big old cross behind him outlined in red neon, and when the camera panned away you could see an arena, or maybe it was a sports stadium, filled with thousands of people. They rose to their feet, some waving their hands back and forth in the air, some waving Bibles.

At first he did a regular sermon, citing chapters and verses from the Bible, but then he got off onto how the country was falling apart because of OPE-e-oids and for-ni-CAY-tion. Then it was politics, and judges, and how America was a shining city on a hill that the godless wanted to smirch with mud. He was starting about how sorcery had bewitched the people of Samaria (what that had to do with America was unclear to Kalisha), but then the colored dots came, flashing on and off. The hum rose and fell. Kalisha could even feel it in her nose, vibrating the tiny hairs in there.

When the dots cleared, they saw the preacherman getting on an airplane with a woman who was probably Mrs. Preacherman. The dots came back. The hum rose and fell. Kalisha heard Avery in her head, something that sounded like *they see it.*

Who sees it?

Avery didn't answer, probably because he was getting into the movie. That was what the Stasi Lights did; they got you into it bigtime. Preacherman was hitting it again, hitting it hard, this time from the back of a flatbed truck, using a bullhorn. Signs said HOUSTON LOVES YOU and GOD GAVE NOAH THE RAIN-BOW SIGN and JOHN 3:16. Then the dots. And the hum. Several of the empty movie theater seats began to flap up and down by themselves, like unmoored shutters in a strong wind. The screening room doors flew open. Jake the Snake and Phil the Pill slammed them shut again, putting their shoulders into it.

Now the preacherman was in some kind of homeless shelter, wearing a cook's apron and stirring a huge vat of spaghetti sauce. His wife was by his side, both of them grinning, and this time it was Nick in her head: *Smile for the camera!* Kalisha was vaguely aware that her hair was standing up, like in some kind of electrical experiment.

Dots. Hum.

Next, the preacherman was on a TV news show with some other people. One of the other people accused the preacherman of being . . . something . . . big words, college words she was sure Lukey would have understood . . . and the preachman was laughing like it was the biggest joke in the world. He had a great laugh. It made you want to laugh along. If you weren't going crazy, that was.

Dots. Hum.

Each time the Stasi Lights came back, they seemed brighter, and each time they seemed to delve deeper into Kalisha's head. In her current state, all the clips that made up the movie were fascinating. They had *levers*. When the time came—probably tomorrow night, maybe the next—the kids in Back Half would pull them.

"I hate this," Helen said in a small, dismayed voice. "When will it be over?"

Preacherman was standing in front of a fancy mansion where a party seemed to be going on. Preacherman was in a motorcade. Preacherman was at an outdoor barbecue and there was red, white, and blue bunting on the buildings behind him. People were eating corndogs and big slices of pizza. He was preaching about perverting the natural order of things which God had ordained, but then his voice cut out and was replaced by that of Dr. Hendricks.

"This is Paul Westin, kids. His home is in Deerfield, Indiana. Paul Westin. Deerfield, Indiana. Paul Westin, Deerfield, Indiana. Say it with me, boys and girls."

Partly because they had no choice, partly because it would bring a merciful end to the colored dots and the rising and falling of the hum, mostly because now *they were really into it*, the ten children in the screening room began to chant. Kalisha joined in. She didn't know about the others, but for her, this was the absolute worst part of movie nights. She hated that it felt good. She hated that feeling of *levers* just waiting to be yanked. Begging for it! She felt like a ventriloquist's dummy on that fucking doctor's knee.

"Paul Westin, Deerfield, Indiana! Paul Westin, Deerfield, Indiana! PAUL WESTIN, DEERFIELD, INDIANA!"

Then Dr. Hendricks came back on the screen, smiling and holding the unlit sparkler. "That's right. Paul Westin, Deerfield, Indiana. Thank you, kids, and have a good night. See you tomorrow!"

The Stasi Lights came back one final time, blinking and swirling and spiraling. Kalisha gritted her teeth and waited for them to be gone, feeling like a tiny space capsule hurtling into a storm of giant asteroids. The hum was louder than ever, but when the dots disappeared the hum cut off instantly, as if a plug had been pulled on an amplifier.

They see it, Avery had said. Was that the missing piece? If so, who was *they*?

The screening room lights came up. The doors opened, Jake the Snake on one and Phil the Pill on the other. Most of the kids walked out, but Donna, Len, Hal, and Jimmy sat where they were. Might sit there lolling in the comfortable seats until the caretakers came to shoo them back to their rooms, and one or two or maybe even all four might be in Gorky Park after the show tomorrow. The big show. Where they did whatever was supposed to be done to the preacherman.

They were allowed another half hour in the lounge before being locked in their rooms for the night. Kalisha went there. George, Nicky, and Avery followed. After a few minutes, Helen shuffled in and sat on the floor with an unlit cigarette in her hand and her once bright hair hanging in her face. Iris and Katie came last.

"Headache's better," Katie announced.

Yes, Kalisha thought, the headaches get better after the movies . . . but only for a little while. A shorter little while each time.

"Another fun night at the movies," George muttered.

"All right, children, what have we learned?" Nicky asked. "That somebody somewhere don't much care for the Reverend Paul Westin, of Deerfield, Indiana."

Kalisha zipped a thumb across her lips and looked at the ceiling. *Bugs*, she thought at Nicky. *Be careful.*

Nick put a finger-gun to his head and pretended to shoot himself. It made the others smile. It would be different tomorrow, Kalisha knew. No smiles then. After tomorrow's show, Dr. Hendricks would appear with his sparkler lit, and the hum would rise to a white-noise roar. Levers would be pulled. There would be a period of unknown length, both sublime and horrible, when their headaches would be banished completely. Instead of a clear fifteen or twenty minutes afterward, there might be six or eight hours of blessed relief. And somewhere, Paul Westin of Deerfield,

Indiana, would do something that would change his life or end it. For the kids in Back Half, life would go on . . . if you could call it living. The headaches would come back, and worse. Worse each time. Until instead of just feeling the hum, they would become part of it. Just another one of the—

The gorks!

That was Avery. No one else could project with such clean strength. It was as if he were living inside her head. *That's how it works, Sha! Because they—*

"They see it," Kalisha whispered, and there it was, bingo, the missing piece. She put the heels of her hands against her forehead, not because the headache was back, but because it was so beautifully obvious. She grasped Avery's small, bony shoulder.

The gorks see what we see. Why else would they keep them?

Nicky put his arm around Kalisha and whispered in her ear. The touch of his lips made her shiver. "What are you talking about? Their minds are gone. Like ours will be, before long."

Avery: *That's what makes them stronger. Everything else is gone. Stripped away. They're the battery. All we are is . . .*

"The switch," Kalisha whispered. "The ignition switch."

Avery nodded. "We need to use them."

When? Helen Simms's mental voice was that of a small, frightened child. *It has to be soon, because I can't take much more of this.*

"None of us can," George said. "Besides, right now that bitch—"

Kalisha gave her head a warning shake, and George continued mentally. He wasn't very good at it, at least not yet, but Kalisha got the gist. They all did. Right now that bitch Mrs. Sigsby would be concentrating on Luke. Stackhouse, too. Everyone in the Institute would be, because they all knew he'd escaped. This was their chance, while everyone was scared and distracted. They would never get another one so good.

Nicky began to smile. *No time like the present.*

"How?" Iris asked. "How can we do it?"

Avery: *I think I know, but we need Hal and Donna and Len.*

"Are you sure?" Kalisha asked, then added, *They're almost gone.*

"I'll get them," Nicky said. He got up. He was smiling. *The Avester's right. Every little bit helps.*

His mental voice was stronger, Kalisha realized. Was that on the sending or receiving end?

Both, Avery said. He was smiling, too. *Because now we're doing it for ourselves.*

Yes, Kalisha thought. Because they were doing it for themselves. They didn't have to be a bunch of dazed dummies sitting on the ventriloquist's knee. It was so simple, but it was a revelation: what you did for yourself was what gave you the power.

14

Around the time Avery—dripping wet and shivering— was being pushed through the access tunnel between Front Half and Back Half, the Institute's Challenger aircraft (940NF on the tail and MAINE PAPER IN- DUSTRIES on the fuselage) was lifting off from Erie, Pennsylvania, now with its full assault team on board. As the plane reached cruising altitude and set out for the small town of Alcolu, Tim Jamieson and Wendy

Gullickson were escorting Luke Ellis into the Fairlee County Sheriff's Department.

Many wheels moving in the same machine.

"This is Luke Ellis," Tim said. "Luke, meet Deputies Faraday and Wicklow."

"Pleased to meet you," Luke said, without much enthusiasm.

Bill Wicklow was studying Luke's bruised face and bandaged ear. "How's the other guy look?"

"It's a long story," Wendy said before Luke could reply. "Where's Sheriff John?"

"In Dunning," Bill said. "His mother's in the old folks' home there. She's got the . . . you know." He tapped one temple. "Said he'd be back around five, unless she was having a good day. Then he might stay and eat dinner with her." He looked at Luke, a beat-up boy in dirty clothes who might as well have been wearing a sign reading RUNAWAY. "Is this an emergency?"

"A good question," Tim said. "Tag, did you get that info Wendy requested?"

"I did," the one named Faraday said. "If you want to step into Sheriff John's office, I can give it to you."

"That won't be necessary," Tim said. "I don't think you're going to tell me anything Luke doesn't already know."

"You sure?"

Tim glanced at Wendy, who nodded, then at Luke, who shrugged. "Yes."

"Okay. This boy's parents, Herbert and Eileen Ellis, were murdered in their home about seven weeks ago. Shot to death in their bedroom."

Luke felt as if he were having an out-of-body experience. The dots didn't come back, but this was the way he felt when they did. He took two steps to the swivel chair in front of the dispatch desk and collapsed onto it. It rolled backward and would have tipped him over if it hadn't banged into the wall first.

"Okay, Luke?" Wendy asked.

"No. Yes. As much as I can be. The assholes in the Institute—Dr. Hendricks and Mrs. Sigsby and the caretakers—told me they were okay, just fine, but I knew they were dead even before I saw it on my computer. I knew it, but it's still . . . awful."

"You had a *computer* in that place?" Wendy asked.

"Yes. To play games with, mostly, or look at You-Tube music videos. Non-substantive stuff like that. News sites were supposed to be blocked, but I knew a work-around. They should have been monitoring my searches and caught me, but they were just . . . just lazy. Complacent. I wouldn't have gotten out, other-wise."

"What the hell's he talking about?" Deputy Wick-low asked.

Tim shook his head. He was still focused on Tag. "You didn't get this from the Minneapolis police, right?"

"No, but not because you told me not to. Sheriff John will decide who to contact and when. That's the way it works here. Meanwhile, though, Google had plenty." He gave Luke a *you might be poison* stare. "He's listed in the database of the National Center for Miss-ing and Exploited Children, and there are also beau-coup stories about him in the Minneapolis *Star Tribune* and the St. Paul *Pioneer Press.* According to the papers, he's supposed to be brilliant. A child prodigy."

"Sounds that way to me," Bill said. "Uses a lot of big words."

I'm right here, Luke thought. Talk about me like I'm here.

"The police aren't calling him a person of interest," Tag said, "at least not in the newspaper stories, but they sure do want to question him."

Luke spoke up. "You bet they do. And the first question they ask will probably be 'Where'd you get the gun, kid?'"

"*Did* you kill them?" Bill asked the question casually, as if just passing the time. "Tell the truth now, son. It'll do you a world of good."

"No. I love my parents. The people who killed them were thieves, and I was what they came to steal. They didn't want me because I scored fifteen-eighty on the SATs, or because I can do complex equations in my head, or because I know that Hart Crane committed suicide by jumping off a boat in the Gulf of Mexico. They killed my mom and dad and kidnapped me because sometimes I could blow out a candle just by looking at it, or flip a pizza pan off the table at Rocket Pizza. An *empty* pizza pan. A full one would have stayed right where it was." He glanced at Tim and Wendy and laughed. "I couldn't even get a job in a lousy roadside carnival."

"I don't see anything funny about any of this," Tag said, frowning.

"Neither do I," Luke said, "but sometimes I laugh, anyway. I laughed a lot with my friends Kalisha and Nick in spite of everything we were going through. Besides, it's been a long summer." He didn't laugh this time, but he smiled. "You have no idea."

"I'm thinking you could use some rest," Tim said. "Tag, have you got anybody in the cells?"

"Nope."

"Okay, why don't we—"

Luke took a step backward, alarm on his face. "No way. No *way.*"

Tim held up his hands. "Nobody's going to lock you up. We'd leave the door wide open."

"No. Please don't do that. Please don't make me go in a cell." Alarm had become terror, and for the first time Tim began to believe at least one part of the boy's story. The psychic stuff was bullshit, but he had seen before what he was seeing now, while on the cops—the look and behavior of a child who has been abused.

"Okay, how about the couch in the waiting area?" Wendy pointed. "It's lumpy, but not too bad. I've stretched out on it a few times."

If she had, Tim had never seen her do it, but the kid was clearly relieved. "Okay, I'll do that. Mr. Jamieson— Tim—you still have the flash drive, right?"

Tim took it out of his breast pocket and held it up. "Right here."

"Good." He trudged to the couch. "I wish you'd check on that Mr. Hollister. I really think he might be an uncle."

Tag and Bill gave Tim identical looks of puzzlement. Tim shook his head.

"Guys who watch for me," Luke said. "They pretend to be my uncle. Or maybe a cousin or just a friend of the family." He caught Tag and Bill rolling their eyes at each other, and smiled again. It was both tired and sweet. "Yeah, I know how it sounds."

"Wendy, why don't you take these officers into Sheriff John's office and bring them up to speed on what Luke told us? I'll stay here."

"That's right, you will," Tag said. "Because until Sheriff John gives you a badge, you're just the town night knocker."

"Duly noted," Tim said.

"What's on the drive?" Bill asked.

"I don't know. When the sheriff gets here, we'll all look at it together."

Wendy escorted the two deputies into Sheriff Ashworth's office and closed the door. Tim heard the murmur of voices. This was his usual time to sleep, but he felt more fully awake than he had in a long time. Since leaving the Sarasota PD, maybe. He wanted to know who the boy beneath the nutty story really was, and where he had been, and what had happened to him.

He got a cup of coffee from the Bunn in the corner. It was strong but not undrinkable, as it would be by ten o'clock, when he usually stopped in on his night-knocking rounds. He took it back to the dispatch chair. The boy had either gone to sleep or was doing a hell of a good job faking it. On a whim, he grabbed the looseleaf binder that listed all of DuPray's businesses, and called the DuPray Motel. The phone went unanswered. Hollister hadn't gone back to his rat trap of a motel after all, it seemed. Which meant nothing, of course.

Tim hung up, took the flash drive out of his pocket, and looked at it. It also meant nothing, more than likely, but as Tag Faraday had been at pains to point out, that was Sheriff Ashworth's call. They could wait.

In the meantime, let the boy get his sleep. If he really had come all the way from Maine in a boxcar, he could use it.

15

The Challenger carrying its eleven passengers—Mrs. Sigsby, Tony Fizzale, Winona Briggs, Dr. Evans, and the combined Ruby Red and Opal teams—touched down in Alcolu at quarter past five. For purposes of reporting back to Stackhouse at the Institute, this short dozen was now called Gold team. Mrs. Sigsby was first off the plane. Denny Williams from Ruby Red and Louis Grant from Opal remained onboard, taking care of Gold team's rather specialized baggage. Mrs. Sigsby stood on the tarmac in spite of the staggering heat and used her cell to call her office landline. Rosalind answered and handed her off to Stackhouse.

"Have you—" she began, then paused to let the pilot and co-pilot pass, which they did without speaking. One was ex–Air Force, one ex-ANG, and both were like the Nazi guards in that old sitcom *Hogan's Heroes*: they saw nothing, they heard nothing. Their job was strictly pickup and delivery.

Once they were gone, she asked Stackhouse if he had heard anything from their man in DuPray.

"Indeed I have. Ellis sustained a booboo when he jumped off the train. Did a header into a signal-post. Instant death from a subdural hematoma would have solved most of our problems, but this Hollister says it didn't even knock him out. A guy running a forklift saw Ellis, took him inside a warehouse near the station, called the local sawbones. He came. A little later a female deputy showed up. Deputy and forklift guy took our boy to the sheriff's office. The ear that had the tracker in it was bandaged."

Denny and Louis Grant emerged from the plane,

each on one end of a long steel chest. They muscled it down the air-stairs and carried it inside.

Mrs. Sigsby sighed. "Well, we might have expected it. We did, in fact. This is a small town we're talking about, right? With small-town law enforcement?"

"Middle of nowhere," Stackhouse agreed. "Which is good news. And there might be more. Our guy says the sheriff drives a big old silver Titan pickup, and it wasn't parked in front of the station or in the lot for town employees out back. So Hollister took a walk down to the local convenience store. He says the ragheads who work there—his term, not mine—know everything about everyone. The one on duty told him the sheriff stopped in for a pack of Swisher Sweets and said he was going to visit his mother, who's in a retirement home or hospice or something in the next town over. But the next town over is like thirty miles away."

"And this is good news for us how?" Mrs. Sigsby fanned the top of her blouse against her neck.

"Can't be completely sure cops in a one-stoplight town like DuPray will follow protocol, but if they do, they'll just hold the kid until the big dog gets back. Let him decide what to do next. How long will it take you to get there?"

"Two hours. We could do it in less, but we're carrying a lot of mother's helpers, and it would be unwise to exceed the speed limit."

"Indeed it would," Stackhouse said. "Listen, Julia. The DuPray yokels could contact the Minneapolis cops at any time. May have contacted them already. It makes no difference either way. You understand that, right?"

"Of course."

"We'll worry about any messes that need to be

cleaned up later. For now, just deal with our wandering boy."

Killing was what Stackhouse meant, and killing was what it would probably take. Ellis, and anyone who tried to get in their way. That sort of mess would mean calling the Zero Phone, but if she could assure the gentle, lisping voice on the other end that the crucial problem had been solved, she thought she might escape with her life. Possibly even her job, but she would settle for her life, if it came to that.

"I know what needs to be done, Trevor. Let me get to it."

She ended the call and went inside. The air conditioning in the little waiting room hit her sweaty skin like a slap. Denny Williams was standing by.

"Are we set?" she asked.

"Yes, ma'am. Ready to rock and roll. I'll take over when you give me the word."

Mrs. Sigsby had been busy with her iPad on the flight from Erie. "We'll be making a brief stop at Exit 181. That's where I'll turn command of the operation over to you. Are you good with that?"

"Excellent with it."

They found the others standing outside. There were no black SUVs with tinted windows, only three more mom vans in unobtrusive colors: blue, green, and gray. Orphan Annie would have been disappointed.

16

Exit 181 dumped the Gold team caravan off the turnpike and into your basic Nowheresville. There was a gas station and a Waffle House, and that was the whole deal. The nearest town, Latta, was twelve miles away. Five minutes past the Waffle House, Mrs. Sigsby, riding up front in the lead van, directed Denny to pull in behind a restaurant that looked as if it had gone broke around the time Obama became president. Even the sign reading OWNER WILL BUILD TO SUIT looked desolate.

The steel case Denny and Louis had carried off the Challenger was opened, and Gold team gunned up. The seven members of Ruby Red and Opal took Glock 37s, the weapon they carried on their extraction missions. Tony Fizzale was issued another, and Denny was glad to see him immediately rack the slide and make sure the chamber was empty.

"A holster would be nice," Tony said. "I don't really want to stuff it down my belt in back, like some MS-13 gangbanger."

"For now, just stow it under the seat," Denny said.

Mrs. Sigsby and Winona Briggs were issued Sig Sauer P238s, petite enough to fit in their purses. When Denny offered one to Evans, the doctor held up his hands and took a step back. Tom Jones of Opal bent to the portable armory and brought out one of two HK37 assault rifles. "How about this, Doc? Thirty-round clip, blow a cow through the side of a barn. Got some flash-bangs, too."

Evans shook his head. "I'm here under protest. If you mean to kill the boy, I'm not sure why I'm here at all."

"Fuck your protest," said Alice Green, also of Opal. This was greeted by the kind of laughter—brittle, eager, a little crazy—that only came before an op where there was apt to be shooting.

"That's enough," Mrs. Sigsby said. "Doctor Evans,

it's possible that we can take the boy alive. Denny, you have a map of DuPray on your pad?"

"Yes, ma'am."

"Then this operation is now yours."

"Very good. Gather round, people. You too, Doc, don't be shy."

They gathered around Denny Williams in the simmering late-day heat. Mrs. Sigsby checked her watch. Quarter past six. An hour from their destination, maybe a bit more. Slightly behind schedule, but acceptable, given the speed with which this had been put together.

"Here's downtown DuPray, what there is of it," Denny Williams said. "Just one main street. Halfway down it is the County Sheriff's Department, right between the Town Office and the DuPray Mercantile Store."

"What's a mercantile store?" This was Josh Gottfried, of Opal.

"Like a department store," Robin Lecks said.

"More like an old-time five-and-dime." That was Tony Fizzale. "I spent about ten years in Alabama, most of it on MP duty, and I can tell you that these small southern towns, it's like you went back fifty years in a time machine. Except for the Walmart. Most of em have one of those."

"Stow the chatter," Mrs. Sigsby said, and nodded for Denny to go on.

"Not much to it," Denny said. "We park here, behind the town movieshow, which is closed down. We get confirmation from Mrs. Sigsby's source that the target is still in the police station. Michelle and I will play a married couple, on a vacation taking us through little-visited towns in the American south—"

"Crazy, in other words," Tony said, which produced more of that brittle laughter.

"We will idle our way up the street, checking the surroundings—"

"Holding hands like the lovebirds we are," Michelle Robertson said, taking Denny's and giving him a coy but worshipful smile.

"What about having your local man check things out?" Louis Grant asked. "Wouldn't that be safer?"

"Don't know him, therefore don't trust his intel," Denny said. "Also, he's a civilian."

He looked to Mrs. Sigsby, who nodded for him to go on.

"Maybe we'll go into the station and ask directions. Maybe not. We'll play that part by ear. What we want is an idea of how many officers are present, and where they are. Then . . ." He shrugged. "We hit em. If there's a firefight, which I don't expect, we terminate the boy there. If not, we extract him. Less mess to clean up if it looks like an abduction."

Mrs. Sigsby left Denny to fill them in on where the Challenger would be waiting, and called Stackhouse for an update.

"Just hung up with our pal Hollister," he said. "The sheriff pulled up in front of the station five or so minutes ago. By now he'll be getting introduced to our wayward boy. Time to get a move on."

"Yes." She felt a not entirely unpleasurable tightening in her stomach and groin. "I'll call you when it's over."

"Do the deed, Julia. Bail us out of this fucking mess."

She ended the call.

17

Sheriff John Ashworth got back to DuPray around six-twenty. Fourteen hundred miles north, dazed children were dumping cigarettes and matches into baskets and filing into a screening room where the star of that evening's film would be a megachurch minister from Indiana with many powerful political friends.

The sheriff stopped just inside the door and surveyed the big main room of the station with his hands on his well-padded hips, noting that his entire staff was there with the exception of Ronnie Gibson, who was vacationing at her mother's time-share in St. Petersburg. Tim Jamieson was there as well.

"Wellnow, howdy-do," he said. "This can't be a surprise party, because it's not my birthday. And who might that be?" He pointed to the boy on the small waiting room couch. Luke was curled into as much of a fetal position as it would allow. Ashworth turned to Tag Faraday, the deputy in charge. "Also, just by the way, who beat him up?"

Instead of answering, Tag turned to Tim and swept out a hand in an *after you* gesture.

"His name is Luke Ellis, and nobody here beat him up," Tim said. "He jumped off a freight and ran into a signal-post. That's where the bruises came from. As for the bandage, he says he was kidnapped and the kidnappers put a tracking device in his ear. He claims he cut off his earlobe to get rid of it."

"With a paring knife," Wendy added.

"His parents are dead," Tag said. "Murdered. That much of his story is true. I checked it out. Way to hell and gone in Minnesota."

"But he says the place he escaped from was in Maine," Bill Wicklow said.

Ashworth was silent for a moment, hands still on his hips, looking from his deputies and his night knocker to the boy asleep on the couch. The conversation showed no sign of bringing Luke around; he was dead to the world. At last Sheriff John looked back at his assembled law enforcement crew. "I'm starting to wish I'd stayed to have dinner with my ma."

"Aw, was she poorly?" Bill asked.

Sheriff John ignored this. "Assuming y'all haven't been smoking dope, could I get a coherent story here?"

"Sit down," Tim said. "I'll bring you up to speed, and then I think we might want to watch this." He put the flash drive down on the dispatch desk. "After that, you can decide what comes next."

"Also might want to call the police in Minneapolis, or the State Police in Charleston," Deputy Burkett said. "Maybe both." He tilted his head toward Luke. "Let them figure out what to do with him."

Ashworth sat. "On second thought, I'm glad I came back early. This is kind of interesting, wouldn't you say?"

"Very," Wendy said.

"Well, that's all right. Not much interesting around here as a general rule, we can use the change. Do the Minneapolis cops think he killed his folks?"

"That's the way the newspaper stories sound," Tag said. "Although they're careful, him being a minor and all."

"He's awesomely bright," Wendy said, "but otherwise he seems like a nice enough kid."

"Uh-huh, uh-huh, how nice or nasty he is will end up being someone else's concern, but for now my curiosity's up. Bill, stop fiddling with that time clock before you bust it, and bring me a Co'-Cola from my office."

18

While Tim was telling Sheriff Ashworth the story Luke had told him and Wendy, and while Gold team was approaching the I-95 Hardeeville exit, where they would double back to the little town of Du-Pray, Nick Wilholm was herding the kids who had remained in the screening room into the little Back Half lounge.

Sometimes kids lasted a surprisingly long time; George Iles was a case in point. Sometimes, however, they seemed to unravel all at once. That appeared to be happening to Iris Stanhope. What Back Half kids called the bounce—a brief post-movie respite from the headaches—hadn't happened for her this time. Her eyes were blank, and her mouth hung open. She stood against the wall of the lounge with her head down and her hair in her eyes. Helen went to her and put an arm around her, but Iris didn't seem to notice.

"What are we doing here?" Donna asked. "I want to go back to my room. I want to go to sleep. I *hate* movie nights." She sounded querulous and on the verge of tears, but at least she was still present and accounted for. The same seemed true of Jimmy and Hal. They looked dazed, but not exactly hammered, the way Iris did.

Not going to be any more movies, Avery said. *Not ever.*

His voice was louder in Kalisha's head than it had

ever been, and for her that just about proved it—they really were stronger together.

"A bold prediction," Nicky said. "Especially coming from a little shit like you, Avester."

Hal and Jimmy smiled at that, and Katie even giggled. Only Iris still seemed completely lost, now scratching unselfconsciously at her crotch. Len had been distracted by the television, although nothing was on. Kalisha thought maybe he was studying his own reflection.

We don't have much time, Avery said. *One of them will come soon to take us back to our rooms.*

"Probably Corinne," Kalisha said.

"Yeah," Helen said. "The Wicked Bitch of the East."

"What do we do?" George asked.

For a moment Avery seemed at a loss, and Kalisha was afraid. Then the little boy who had thought earlier in the day that his life was going to end in the immersion tank held out his hands. "Grab on," he said. *Make a circle.*

All of them except Iris shuffled forward. Helen Simms took Iris's shoulders and steered her into the rough circle the others had formed. Len looked longingly back over his shoulder at the TV, then sighed and put out his hands. "Fuck it. Whatever."

"That's right, fuck it," Kalisha said. "Nothing to lose." She took Len's right hand in her left, and Nicky's left hand in her right. Iris was the last one to join up, and the instant she was linked to Jimmy Cullum on one side and Helen on the other, her head came up.

"Where am I? What are we doing? Is the movie over?"

"Hush," Kalisha said.

"My head feels better!"

"Good. Hush, now."

And the others joined in: *Hush . . . hush . . . Iris, hush*.

Each *hush* was louder. Something was changing. Something was *charging*.

Levers, Kalisha thought. *There are levers, Avery.*

He nodded at her from the other side of their circle.

It wasn't power, at least not yet, and she knew it would be a fatal mistake to believe it was, but the *potential* for power was present. Kalisha thought, This is like breathing air just before the summer's biggest thunderstorm lets rip.

"Guys?" Len said in a timid voice. "My head's clear. I can't remember the last time it was clear like this." He looked at Kalisha with something like panic. "Don't let go of me, Sha!"

You're okay, she thought at him. *You're safe.*

But he wasn't. None of them were.

Kalisha knew what came next, what *had* to come next, and she dreaded it. Of course, she also wanted it. Only it was more than wanting. It was lusting. They were children with high explosives, and that might be wrong, but it felt so right.

Avery spoke in a low, clear voice. "Think. Think with me, guys."

He began, the thought and the image that went with it strong and clear. Nicky joined him. Katie, George, and Helen chimed in. So did Kalisha. Then the rest of them. They chanted at the end of the movies, and they chanted now.

Think of the sparkler. Think of the sparkler. Think of the sparkler.

The dots came, brighter than they had ever been. The hum came, louder than it had ever been. The sparkler came, spitting brilliance.

And suddenly they weren't just eleven. Suddenly they were twenty-eight.

Ignition, Kalisha thought. She was terrified; she was exultant; she was holy.

OH MY GOD

19

When Tim finished telling Luke's story, Sheriff Ashworth sat silent for several seconds in the dispatch chair, his fingers laced together on his considerable belly. Then he picked up the flash drive, studied it as if he had never seen such a thing before, and set it down. "He told you he doesn't know what's on it, is that right? Just got it from the housekeeper, along with a knife he used to do surgery on his earlobe."

"That's what he said," Tim agreed.

"Went under a fence, went through the woods, took a boat downriver just like Huck and Jim, then rode a boxcar most of the way down the East Coast."

"According to him, yes," Wendy said.

"Well, that's quite a tale. I especially like the part about the telepathy and mind over matter. Like the stories the old grannies tell at their quilting bees and canning parties about rains of blood and stumpwater cures. Wendy, wake the boy up. Do it easy, I can see he's been through a lot no matter what his real story is, but when we look at this, I want him looking with us."

Wendy crossed the room and shook Luke's shoulder. Gently at first, then a little harder. He muttered, moaned, and tried to pull away from her. She took his arm. "Come on, now, Luke, open your eyes and—"

He surged up so suddenly that Wendy stumbled backward. His eyes were open but unseeing, his hair sticking up in front and all around his head like quills. *"They're doing something! I saw the sparkler!"*

"What's he talking about?" George Burkett asked.

"Luke!" Tim said. "You're okay, you were having a dre—"

"Kill them!" Luke shouted, and in the station's small holding annex, the doors of all four cells clashed shut. *"Obliterate those motherfuckers!"*

Papers flew up from the dispatch desk like a flock of startled birds. Tim felt a gust of wind buffet past him, real enough to ruffle his hair. Wendy gave a little cry, not quite a scream. Sheriff John was on his feet.

Tim gave the boy a single hard shake. "Wake up, Luke, *wake up*!"

The papers fluttering around the room fell to the floor. The assembled cops, Sheriff John included, were staring at Luke with their mouths open.

Luke was pawing at the air. "Go away," he muttered. "Go away."

"Okay," Tim said, and let go of Luke's shoulder.

"Not you, the dots. The Stasi Li . . ." He blew out a breath and ran a hand through his dirty hair. "Okay. They're gone."

"You did that?" Wendy asked. She gestured at the fallen paperwork. "You really did that?"

"Something sure did it," Bill Wicklow said. He was looking at the night knocker's time clock. "The hands on this thing were going around . . . *whizzing* around . . . but now they've stopped."

"They're doing something," Luke said. "My friends

are doing something. I felt it, even way down here. How could that happen? Jesus, my *head*."

Ashworth approached Luke and held out a hand. Tim noticed he kept the other on the butt of his holstered gun. "I'm Sheriff Ashworth, son. Want to give me a shake?"

Luke shook his hand.

"Good. Good start. Now I want the truth. Did you do that just now?"

"I don't know if it was me or them," Luke said. "I don't know how it *could* be them, they're so far away, but I don't know how it could be me, either. I never did anything like that in my life."

"You specialize in pizza pans," Wendy said. "Empty ones."

Luke smiled faintly. "Yeah. You didn't see the lights? Any of you? A bunch of colored dots?"

"I didn't see anything but flying papers," Sheriff John said. "And heard those cell doors slam shut. Frank, George, pick that stuff up, would you? Wendy, get this boy an aspirin. Then we're going to see what's on that little computer widget."

Luke said, "This afternoon all your mother could talk about was her barrettes. She said someone stole her barrettes."

Sheriff John's mouth fell open. "How do you know that?"

Luke shook his head. "I don't know. I mean, I'm not even trying. Christ, I wish I knew what they were doing. And I wish I was with them."

Tag said, "I'm thinking there might be something to this kid's story, after all."

"I want to look at that flash drive, and I want to look at it right now," Sheriff Ashworth said.

20

What they saw first was an empty chair, an old-fashioned wingback placed in front of a wall with a framed Currier & Ives sailing ship on it. Then a woman's face poked into the frame, staring at the lens.

"That's her," Luke said. "That's Maureen, the lady who helped me get out."

"Is this on?" Maureen said. "The little light's on, so I guess it is. I hope so, because I don't think I have the strength to do this twice." Her face left the screen of the laptop computer the officers were watching. Tim found that something of a relief. The extreme closeup was like looking at a woman trapped inside a fishbowl.

Her voice faded a bit, but was still audible. "But if I have to, I will." She sat down in the chair and adjusted the hem of her floral skirt over her knees. She wore a red blouse above it. Luke, who had never seen her out of her uniform, thought it was a pretty combination, but bright colors couldn't conceal how thin her face was, or how haggard.

"Max the audio," Frank Potter said. "She should have been wearing a lav mike."

Meanwhile, she was talking. Tag reversed the video, turned up the sound, and hit play again. Maureen once more returned to the wingback chair and once more adjusted the hem of her skirt. Then she looked directly into the camera's lens.

"Luke?"

He was so startled by his name out of her mouth that he almost answered, but she went on before he could, and what she said next put a dagger of ice into his heart. Although he had known, hadn't he? Just as he hadn't needed the *Star Tribune* to give him the news about his parents.

"If you're looking at this, then you're out and I'm dead."

The deputy named Potter said something to the one named Faraday, but Luke paid no attention. He was completely focused on the woman who'd been his only grownup friend in the Institute.

"I'm not going to tell you my life story," the dead woman in the wingback chair said. "There's no time for that, and I'm glad, because I'm ashamed of a lot of it. Not of my boy, though. I'm proud of the way he turned out. He's going to college. He'll never know I'm the one who gave him the money, but that's all right. That's good, the way it should be, because I gave him up. And Luke, without you to help me, I might have lost that money and that chance to do right by him. I only hope I did right by you."

She paused, seeming to gather herself.

"I will tell one part of my story, because it's important. I was in Iraq during the second Gulf war, and I was in Afghanistan, and I was involved in what was called enhanced interrogation."

To Luke, her calm fluency—no uhs, no you-knows, no kinda or sorta—was a revelation. It made him feel embarrassment as well as grief. She sounded so much more intelligent than she had during their whispered conversations near the ice machine. Because she had been playing dumb? Maybe, but maybe—*probably*—he had seen a woman in a brown housekeeper's uniform and just assumed she didn't have a lot going on upstairs.

Not like me, in other words, Luke thought, and realized embarrassment didn't accurately describe what he was feeling. The right word for that was shame.

"I saw waterboarding, and I saw men—women, too, a couple—standing in basins of water with electrodes on their fingers or up their rectums. I saw toenails pulled out with pliers. I saw a man shot in the kneecap when he spit in an interrogator's face. I was shocked at first, but after awhile I wasn't. Sometimes, when it was men who'd planted IEDs on our boys or sent suicide bombers into crowded markets, I was glad. Mostly I got . . . I know the word . . ."

"Desensitized," Tim said.

"Desensitized," Maureen said.

"Christ, like she heard you," Deputy Burkett said.

"Hush," Wendy said, and something about that word made Luke shiver. It was as if someone else had said it just before her. He turned his attention back to the video.

"—never took part after the first two or three, because they gave me another job. When they wouldn't talk, I was the kindly noncom who came in and gave them a drink or snuck them something to eat out of my pocket, a Quest Bar or a couple of Oreos. I told them the interrogators had all gone off on a break or to eat a meal, and the microphones were turned off. I said I felt sorry for them and wanted to help them. I said that if they didn't talk, they would be killed, even though it was against the rules. I never said against the Geneva Convention, because most of them didn't know what that was. I said if they didn't talk, their *families* would be killed, and I *really* didn't want that. Usually it didn't work—they suspected—but sometimes when the interrogators came back, the prisoners told them what they wanted to hear, either because they believed me or wanted to. Sometimes they said things to me, because they were confused . . . disoriented . . . and because they trusted me. God help me, I had a very trustworthy face."

I know why she's telling me this, Luke thought.

"How I wound up at the Institute . . . that story's too long for a tired, sick woman to go into. Someone came to see me, leave it at that. Not Mrs. Sigsby, Luke, and not Mr. Stackhouse. Not a government man, either. He was old. He said he was a recruiter. He asked me if I wanted a job when my tour was over. Easy work, he said, but only for a person who could keep her lip buttoned. I'd been thinking about re-upping, but this sounded better. Because the man said I'd be helping my country a lot more than I ever could in sandland. So I took the job, and when they put me in housekeeping, I was okay with that. I knew what they were doing, but at first I was okay with that, too, because I knew why. Good for me, because the Institute is like what they say about the mafia— once you're in, you can't get out. When I came up short on money to pay my husband's bills, and when I started to be afraid the vultures would take the money I'd saved for my boy, I asked for the job I'd been doing downrange, and Mrs. Sigsby and Mr. Stackhouse let me try."

"Tattling," Luke murmured.

"It was easy, like slipping on an old pair of shoes. I was there for twelve years, but only snitched the last sixteen months or so, and by the end I was starting to feel bad about what I was doing, and I'm not just talking about the snitching part. I got desensitized in what we called the black houses, and I stayed desensitized in the Institute, but eventually that started to wear off, the way a wax shine will wear off a car if you don't put on a fresh coat every now and then. They're just kids, you know, and kids want to trust a grownup who's kind and sympathetic. It wasn't as if they had ever blown anybody up. *They* were the ones who got blown up, them and their families. But maybe I would have kept on with it, anyway. If I'm going to be honest—and it's too late to be anything else—I guess I probably would have. But then I got sick, and I met you, Luke. You helped me, but that's not why I helped you. Not the only reason, anyway, and not the main reason. I saw how smart you were, way beyond any of the other kids, way beyond the people who stole you away. I knew they didn't care about your fine mind, or your little sense of humor, or how you were willing to help an old sick bag like me, even though you knew it might get you in trouble. To them you were just another cog in the machine, to be used until it wore out. In the end you would have gone the way of all the others. Hundreds of them. Maybe thousands, going all the way back to the beginning."

"Is she crazy?" George Burkett asked.

"Shut up!" Ashworth said. He was leaning forward over his belly, eyes fixed on the screen.

Maureen had stopped to take a drink of water and then to rub her eyes, which were sunk deep in their hollows of flesh. Sick eyes. Sad eyes. Dying eyes, Luke thought, staring eternity right in the face.

"It was still a hard decision, and not just because of what they might do to me or to you, Luke. It was hard because if you *do* get away, if they don't catch you in the woods or in Dennison River Bend, and if you can find someone to believe you . . . if you get past all those *ifs*, you might be able to drag what's been going on here for fifty or sixty years out into the open. Bring it all down on their heads."

Like Samson in the temple, Luke thought.

She leaned forward, looking directly into the lens. Directly at him.

"And that might mean the end of the world."

21

The westering sun turned the railroad tracks running close to State Route 92 into pinkish-red lines of fire, and seemed to spotlight the sign just ahead:

> WELCOME TO DuPRAY, S.C.
> FAIRLEE COUNTY SEAT
> POPULATION 1,369
> *A NICE PLACE TO VISIT &*
> *A NICER PLACE TO LIVE!*

Denny Williams pulled the lead van onto the dirt shoulder. The others followed. He spoke to those in his own van—Mrs. Sigsby, Dr. Evans, Michelle Robertson—then went to the other two. "Radios off, earpieces out. We don't know what frequencies the locals or the Staties might be listening to. Cell phones off. This is now a sealed operation and will remain so until we are back at the airfield."

He returned to the lead van, got back behind the wheel, and turned to Mrs. Sigsby. "All good, ma'am?"

"All good."

"I am here under protest," Dr. Evans said again.

"Shut up," Mrs. Sigsby said. "Denny? Let's go."

They rolled into Fairlee County. There were barns

and fields and stands of pine on one side of the road; railroad tracks and more trees on the other. The town itself was now just two miles away.

22

Corinne Rawson was standing in front of the screening room, shooting the shit with Jake "the Snake" Howland and Phil "the Pill" Chaffitz. Abused as a child by both her father and two of her four older brothers, Corinne had never had a problem with her work in Back Half. She knew the kiddos called her Corinne the Slapper, and that was okay. She had been slapped plenty in the Reno trailer park where she had grown up, and the way she looked at it, what goes around comes around. Plus, it was for a good cause. What you called your basic win-win situation.

Of course there were drawbacks to working in Back Half. For one thing, your head got jammed up with too much information. She knew that Phil wanted to fuck her and Jake didn't because Jake only liked women with double-wide racks in front and extra junk in the trunk. And she knew that *they* knew she didn't want anything to do with either of them, at least not in that way; since the age of seventeen, she had batted strictly for the other side.

Telepathy always sounded great in stories and movies, but it was annoying as fuck in real life. It came with the hum, which was a drawback. And it was cumulative, which was a *major* drawback. The housekeepers and janitors swapped back and forth between Front Half and Back Half, which helped, but the red caretakers worked here and nowhere else. There were two teams, Alpha and Beta. Each worked four months on, then had four months off. Corinne was almost at the end of her current four-month swing. She would spend a week or two decompressing in the adjacent staff village, recovering her essential self, and then would go to her little house in New Jersey, where she lived with Andrea, who believed her partner worked in a top-secret military project. Top-secret it was; military it was not.

The low-level telepathy would fade during her time in the village, and by the time she got back to Andrea, it would be gone. Then, a few days into her next swing, it would start to creep back. If she had been able to feel sympathy (a sensibility that had been mostly beaten out of her by the age of thirteen), she would have felt it for Dr. Hallas and Dr. James. They were here almost all of the time, which meant they were almost constantly exposed to the hum, and you could see what it was doing to them. She knew that Dr. Hendricks, the Institute's chief medical officer, gave the Back Half docs injections that were supposed to limit the constant erosion, but there was a big difference between limiting a thing and halting it.

Horace Keller, a red caretaker with whom she was friendly, called Heckle and Jeckle high-functioning crazies. He said that eventually one or both of them would freak out, and then the topsiders would have to find fresh medical talent. That was nothing to Corinne. Her job was to make sure the kids ate when they were supposed to eat, went into their rooms when they were supposed to go to their rooms (what they did in there was also no concern of hers), attended the movies on movie nights, and didn't get out of line. When they did, she slapped them down.

"The gorks are restless tonight," Jake the Snake said. "You can hear them in there. Tasers at the ready when we do the eight o'clock feeding, right?"

"They're always worse at night," Phil said. "I don't . . . hey, what the *fuck*?"

Corinne felt it, too. They were used to the hum, the way you got used to the sound of a noisy fridge or a rattling air conditioner. Now, suddenly, it ramped up to the level they had to endure on movie nights that were also sparkler nights. Only on movie nights it mostly came from behind the closed and locked doors of Ward A, also known as Gorky Park. She could feel it coming from there now, but it was also coming from another direction, like the push of a strong wind. From the lounge, where those kids had gone to spend their free time when the show was over. First one bunch went down there, those who were still high-functioning, then a couple Corinne thought of as pre-gorks.

"What the fuck are they doing?" Phil shouted. He put his hands to the sides of his head.

Corinne ran for the lounge, pulling her zap-stick. Jake was behind her. Phil—perhaps more sensitized to the hum, maybe just scared—stayed where he was, palms pressed to his temples as if to keep his brains from exploding.

What Corinne saw when she got to the door was almost a dozen children. Even Iris Stanhope, who would certainly go to Gorky Park after tomorrow's movie, was there. They were standing in a circle, hands joined, and now the hum was strong enough to make Corinne's eyes water. She thought she could even feel her fillings vibrating.

Get the new one, she thought. The shrimp. I think

he's the one driving this. Zap him and it might break the circuit.

But even as she thought it, her fingers opened and her zap-stick dropped to the carpet. Behind her, almost lost in the hum, she heard Jake shouting for the kids to stop whatever they were doing and go to their rooms. The black girl was looking at Corinne, and there was an insolent smile on her lips.

I'll slap that look right off you, missy, Corinne thought, and when she raised her hand, the black girl nodded.

That's right, slap.

Another voice joined Kalisha's: *Slap!*

Then all the others: *Slap! Slap! Slap!*

Corinne Rawson began to slap herself, first with her right hand, then with her left, back and forth, harder and harder, aware that her cheeks were first hot and then burning, but that awareness was faint and far away, because now the hum wasn't a hum at all but a huge *BWAAAAAA* of internal feedback.

She was knocked to her knees as Jake rushed past her. "Stop whatever you're doing, you fucking little—"

His hand swept up and there was a crackle of electricity as he zapped himself between the eyes. He jerked backward, legs first splaying out and then coming together in a funky dance floor move, eyes bulging. His mouth dropped open and he plugged the barrel of his zap-stick into it. The crackle of electricity was muffled, but the results were visible. His throat swelled like a bladder. Momentary blue light shone from his nostrils. Then he fell forward on his face, cramming the zap-stick's slim barrel into his mouth all the way to the butt, his finger still convulsing on the trigger.

Kalisha led them into the resident corridor with their hands linked, like first-graders on a school outing. Phil the Pill saw them and cringed back, holding his zap-stick in one hand and gripping one of the screening room doors in the other. Farther down the corridor, between the cafeteria on one side and Ward A on the other, stood Dr. Everett Hallas, with his mouth hanging open.

Now fists began to hammer on Gorky Park's locked double doors. Phil dropped his zap-stick and raised the hand that had been holding it, showing the oncoming children that it was empty.

"I won't be a problem," he said. "Whatever you mean to do, I won't be a prob—"

The screening room doors slammed shut, cutting off his voice and also three of his fingers.

Dr. Hallas turned and fled.

Two other red caretakers emerged from the staff lounge beyond the stairway to the crematorium. They ran toward Kalisha and her makeshift cadre, both with drawn zap-sticks. They stopped outside the locked doors of Ward A, zapped each other, and dropped to their knees. There they continued to exchange bolts of electricity until both of them collapsed, insensible. More caretakers appeared, either saw or felt what was happening, and retreated, some few down the stairs to the crematorium (a dead end in more ways than one), others back to the staff lounge or the doctors' lounge beyond it.

Come on, Sha. Avery was looking down the hall, past Phil—howling over the spouting stumps of his fingers—and the two dazed caretakers.

Aren't we getting out?

Yes. But we're letting them *out, first.*

The line of children began to walk down the hall to Ward A, into the heart of the hum.

23

"I don't know how they pick their targets," Maureen was saying. "I've often wondered about that, but it must work, because no one has dropped an atomic bomb or started a world-wide war in over seventy-five years. Think about what a fantastic accomplishment that is. I know some people say God is watching out for us, and some say it's diplomacy, or what they call MAD, mutual assured destruction, but I don't believe any of that. It's the Institute."

She paused for another drink of water, then resumed.

"They know which kids to take because of a test most children have at birth. I'm not supposed to know what that test is, I'm just a lowly housekeeper, but I listen as well as snitch. And I snoop. It's called BDNF, which stands for brain-derived neurotrophic factor. Kids with a high BDNF are targeted, followed, and eventually taken and brought to the Institute. Sometimes they're as old as sixteen, but most are younger. They grab those with really high BDNF scores as soon as possible. We've had kids here as young as eight."

That explains Avery, Luke thought. And the Wilcox twins.

"They're prepared in Front Half. Part of the prep is done with injections, part of it with exposure to something Dr. Hendricks calls the Stasi Lights. Some of the kids who come in here have telepathic ability— thought-readers. Some are telekinetics—mind over matter. After the injections and exposure to the Stasi Lights, some of the kids stay the same, but most get at least a little stronger in whatever ability they were taken for. And there are a few, what Hendricks calls pinks, who get extra tests and shots and sometimes develop *both* abilities. I heard Dr. Hendricks say once that there might be even more abilities, and discovering them could change everything for the better."

"TP as well as TK," Luke murmured. "It happened to me, but I hid it. At least I tried to."

"When they're ready to . . . to be put to work, they're moved from Front Half into Back Half. They see movies that show the same person over and over. At home, at work, at play, at family get-togethers. Then they get a trigger image that brings back the Stasi Lights and also binds them together. You see . . . the way it works . . . when they're alone, their powers are small even after the enhancements, but when they're together, their strength increases in a way . . . there's a math word for it . . ."

"Exponentially," Luke said.

"I don't know the word. I'm tired. The important thing is these children are used to eliminate certain people. Sometimes it looks like an accident. Sometimes it looks like suicide. Sometimes like murder. But it's always the kids. That politician, Mark Berkowitz? That was the kids. Jangi Gafoor, that man who supposedly blew himself up by accident in his bomb-making factory in Kunduz Province two years ago? That was the kids. There have been plenty of others, just in my time at the Institute. You'd say there was no rhyme or reason to any of it—six years ago it was an Argentinian poet who swallowed lye—and there's none that I can see, but there must be, because the world is still here. I once heard Mrs. Sigsby, she's the big boss, say that we were like people constantly bailing out a boat that would otherwise sink, and I believe her."

Maureen once more scrubbed at her eyes, then leaned forward, looking intently into the camera.

"They need a constant supply of children with high BDNF scores, because Back Half uses them up. They have headaches that get worse and worse, and each time they experience the Stasi Lights, or see Dr. Hendricks with his sparkler, they lose more of their essential selves. By the end, when they get sent to Gorky Park—that's what the staff calls Ward A—they're like children suffering from dementia or advanced Alzheimer's disease. It gets worse and worse until they die. It's usually pneumonia, because they keep Gorky Park cold on purpose. Sometimes it's like . . ." She shrugged. "Oh God, like they just forget how to take the next breath. As for getting rid of the bodies, the Institute has a state-of-the-art crematorium."

"No," Sheriff Ashworth said softly. "Ah, *no*."

"The staff in Back Half works in what they call long swings. That's a few months on and a few months off. It has to be that way, because the atmosphere is toxic. But because none of the staff has high BDNF scores, the process works slower on them. Some it hardly seems to affect at all."

She paused for a sip of water.

"There are two docs who work there almost all of the time, and they're both losing their minds. I know, because I've been there. Housekeepers and janitors have shorter swings between Front Half and Back Half. Same with the cafeteria staff. I know this is a lot to take in, and there's more, but that's all I can manage now. I have to go, but I have something to show you, Luke. You and whoever might be watching this with you. It's hard to look at, but I hope you can, because I risked my life to get it."

She drew in a trembling breath and tried to smile. Luke began to cry, soundlessly at first.

"Luke, helping you escape was the hardest decision of my life, even with death staring me in the face and hell, I have no doubt, on the other side of death. It was hard because now the boat may sink, and that will be my fault. I had to choose between your life and maybe the lives of the billions of people on earth who depend on the Institute's work without even knowing it. I chose you over all of them, and may God forgive me."

The screen went blue. Tag reached for the laptop's keyboard, but Tim grabbed his hand. "Wait."

There was a line of static, a stutter of sound, and then a new video began. The camera was moving down a corridor with a thick blue carpet on the floor. There was an intermittent rasping noise, and every now and then the picture was interrupted by darkness that came and went like a shutter.

She's shooting video, Luke thought. Shooting it through a hole or a rip she made in the pocket of her uniform. That rasping noise is cloth rubbing over the mic.

He doubted if cell phones even worked for making calls in the deep woods of northern Maine, but guessed they were absolutely *verboten* in the Institute just the same, because the *cameras* would still work. If Maureen had been caught, she wouldn't have just had her salary docked or lost her job. She really had risked her life. It made the tears come faster. He felt Officer Gullickson—Wendy—put an arm around him. He leaned gratefully against her side, but he kept his eyes on the laptop screen. Here, finally, was Back Half. Here was what he had escaped. Here was where Avery undoubtedly was now, assuming he was still alive.

The camera passed open double doors on the right. Maureen turned briefly, giving the watchers a view of a screening room with maybe two dozen plush seats. A couple of kids were sitting in there.

"Is that girl *smoking?*" Wendy asked.

"Yes," Luke said. "I guess they let them have cigarettes in Back Half, too. The girl is one of my friends. Her name is Iris Stanhope. They took her away before I got out. I wonder if she's still alive? And if she can still think, if she is?"

The camera swiveled back to the corridor. A couple of other kids passed, looking up at Maureen with no appreciable interest before leaving the frame. A caretaker in a red smock appeared. His voice was muffled by the pocket in which Maureen's phone was hidden, but the words were understandable: he was asking her if she was glad to be back. Maureen asked him if she looked crazy, and he laughed. He said something about coffee, but the cloth of the pocket was rustling loudly, and Luke couldn't pick it up.

"Is that a pistol he's wearing?" Sheriff John asked.

"It's a zap-stick," Luke said. "You know, a Taser. There's a dial on them that ramps up the voltage."

Frank Potter: "You're shitting me!"

The camera passed another set of open double doors, this time on the left, went two or three dozen steps further, and then stopped at a door that was closed. Printed on it in red was WARD A. In a low voice, Maureen said, "This is Gorky Park."

Her hand, clad in a blue latex glove, came into

the frame. She was holding a key card. Except for the color, bright orange, it looked to Luke like the one he had stolen, but he had an idea that people who worked in Back Half weren't so careless with these. Maureen pressed it to the electronic square above the doorknob, there was a buzz, and then she opened the door.

Hell was beyond it.

24

Orphan Annie was a baseball fan, and she usually spent warm summer evenings in her tent, listening to the Fireflies, a minor league team out of Columbia. She was happy when one of their players got sent up to the Rumble Ponies, the Double-A franchise in Binghamton, but she was always sorry to lose them. When the game was over, she might sleep a little, then wake and tune to George Allman's show, and see what was going on in what George called the Wonderful World of Weird.

Tonight, however, she was curious about the boy who had jumped from the train. She decided to drift on over to the sheriff's station and see if she could find anything out. They probably wouldn't let her in the front, but sometimes Frankie Potter or Billy Wicklow came out into the alley, where she kept her air mattress and spare supplies, to have a smoke. They might tell her what the kid's story was if she asked nice. After all, she had cleaned him up and comforted him some, and that gave her a rooting interest.

A path from her tent near the warehouses ran through the woods on the west side of town. When she went to the alley to spend the night on her air mattress (or inside, if it was chilly—they let her do that now, thanks to helping Tim with his go-slow banner), she followed the path as far as the backside of the Gem, the town's movie theater, where she had seen many interesting movies as a younger (and slightly saner) woman. Ole Gemmie had been closed for the last fifteen years, and the parking lot behind it was a wilderness of weeds and goldenrod. She usually cut through this and went up the old theater's crumbling brick flank to the sidewalk. The sheriff's station and the DuPray Mercantile were on the other side of Main Street, with her alley (so she thought of it) running between them.

This evening, just as she was about to leave the path for the parking lot, she saw a vehicle turn down Pine Street. It was followed by another . . . and another. Three vans, going just about nose to tail. And although twilight was advancing, they didn't even have their parking lights on. Annie stood in the trees, watching, as they entered the lot she had been about to cross. They turned as if in formation, and stopped in a row, with their noses pointed back toward Pine Street. Almost like they might need to make a quick getaway, she thought.

The doors opened. Some men and women got out. One of the men was wearing a sportcoat and nice-looking trousers with a crease in them. One of the women, older than the others, was wearing a dark red pant suit. Another was wearing a dress with flowers on it. That one had a purse. The other four women didn't. Most of them were wearing jeans and dark shirts.

Except for the sportcoat man, who just stood back and watched, they moved quickly and purposefully, like folks on a mission. To Annie they looked sort of military, and this impression was confirmed in short

order. Two of the men and one of the younger women
opened the back doors of the vans. The men took a
long steel box from one of them. From the back of another van came holster-belts, which the woman handed
around to everyone except for the sportcoat man, another man with short blond hair, and the woman in
the flower-dress. The steel box was opened, and from
this came a couple of long guns that were not hunting rifles. They were what Annie Ledoux thought of as
school shooter guns.

The woman in the flower-dress put a small handgun
in her purse. The man beside her stuck a bigger one
in his belt at the small of his back, then dropped the
tail of his shirt over it. The others holstered up. They
looked like a raiding party. Hell, they *were* a raiding
party. Annie didn't see how they could be anything
else.

A normally wired person—one who didn't get her
nightly news from George Allman, for instance—
might have merely stared in dismayed confusion,
wondering what on earth a bunch of armed men and
women might be doing in a sleepy South Carolina
town where there was only a single bank, and that
one locked up for the night. A normally wired person
might have whipped out her cell phone and called 911.
Annie, however, was not a normally wired person, and
she knew exactly what these armed men and women,
at least ten of them and maybe more, were up to. They
hadn't come in the black SUVs she would have expected, but they were here for the boy. Of course they
were.

Calling 911 to alert the folks in the sheriff's station
wasn't an option in any case, because she wouldn't
have carried a cell phone even if she'd been able to

afford one. Cell phones shot radiation into your head, any fool knew that, and besides, *they* could track you that way. So Annie continued along the path, running now, until she reached the back of the DuPray Barber Shop two buildings down. A rickety flight of stairs led to the apartment above. Annie climbed them as fast as she could, holding up her serape and the long skirt beneath so she wouldn't trip and take a tumble. At the top, she hammered on the door until she saw Corbett Denton through the ragged curtain, shuffling toward her with his big belly leading the way. He pushed the curtain aside and peered out, his bald head gleaming beneath the light of the kitchen's fly-specked overhead globe.

"Annie? What do you want? I'm not giving you anything to eat, if that's—"

"There's men," she said, panting to catch her breath. She could have added there were also women, but just saying *men* sounded more fearsome, at least to her. "They're parked behind the Gem!"

"Go away, Annie. I don't have time for your foolish—"

"There's a boy! I think those men mean to go to the station and take him away! I think there's going to be shooting!"

"What the hell are you—"

"Please, Drummer, *please*! They had machine guns, I think, and that boy, he's a nice boy!"

He opened the door. "Let me smell your breath."

She seized him by the front of his pajama shirt. "I haven't had a drink in ten years! Please, Drummer, they came for the boy!"

He sniffed, frowning now. "No booze. Are you hallucinating?"

"No!"

"You said machine guns. Do you mean automatic rifles, like AR-15s?" Drummer Denton was beginning to look interested.

"Yes! No! I don't know! But you have guns, I know you do! You should bring them!"

"You're out of your mind," he said, and that was when Annie began to cry. Drummer had known her most of his life, had even gone stepping with her a time or two when they were much younger, and he had never seen her cry. She really believed something was going on, and Drummer decided what the hell. He had only been doing what he did every night, which was thinking about the basic stupidity of life.

"All right, let's go look."

"And your guns? You'll bring your guns?"

"Hell no. I said we're going to look."

"Drummer, please!"

"*Look*," he said. "That's all I'm willing to do. Take it or leave it."

With no other choice, Orphan Annie took it.

25

"Oh my dear God, what am I looking at?"

Wendy's words were muffled, because she had a hand over her mouth. No one answered. They were staring at the screen, Luke as frozen with wonder and horror as the rest.

The back half of Back Half—Ward A, Gorky Park—was a long, high room that looked to Luke like the sort of abandoned factory where shoot-outs always happened at the end of the action movies he and Rolf had liked to watch a thousand years ago, back when he had been a real kid. It was lit by fluorescent bars behind wire mesh that cast shadows and gave the ward an eerie undersea look. There were long, narrow windows covered by heavier mesh. There were no beds, only bare mattresses. Some of these had been pushed into the aisles, a couple were overturned, and one leaned drunkenly against a bare cinderblock wall. It was splotched with yellow gunk that might have been vomit.

A long gutter filled with running water ran alongside one cinderblock wall, where a stenciled motto read YOU ARE SAVIORS! A girl, naked except for a pair of dirty socks, squatted over this gutter with her back against the wall and her hands on her knees. She was defecating. There was that rasping sound as cloth rubbed across the phone in Maureen's pocket, where it was perhaps taped in place, and the image was momentarily blotted out as the slit the camera was peering through closed. When it opened again, the girl was walking away in a kind of drunken amble, and her shit was being carried down the gutter.

A woman in a brown housekeeper's uniform was using a Rinsenvac to clean up what might have been more puke, more shit, spilled food, God knew what. She saw Maureen, waved, and said something none of them could pick up, not just because of the Rinsenvac but because Gorky Park was a looneybin of mingled voices and cries. A girl was doing cartwheels down one of the ragged aisles. A boy in dirty underpants with pimples on his face and smeary glasses sliding down his nose walked past. He was yelling "ya-*ya*-ya-*ya*-ya-*ya*" and hitting the top of his head on every emphasized syllable. Luke remembered Kalisha mentioning a boy with zits and glasses. On his first day at the Institute, that had been. *Seems like Petey's been gone forever, but it was only last week*, she had said, and here that boy was. Or what was left of him.

"Littlejohn," Luke murmured. "I think that's his name. Pete Littlejohn."

No one heard him. They were staring at the screen as if hypnotized.

Across from the gutter used for eliminatory purposes was a long trough on steel legs. Two girls and a boy were standing there. The girls were using their hands to scoop some brown gunk into their mouths. Tim, staring at this with disbelief and sickened wonder, thought it looked like Maypo, the cereal of his childhood. The boy was bent over with his face in the stuff, his hands held out at his sides, snapping his fingers. A few other kids just lay on their mattresses, staring up at the ceiling, their faces tattooed with the shadows of the mesh.

As Maureen walked toward the Rinsenvac woman, presumably to take over her job, the picture cut out and the blue screen came back. They waited to see if Maureen would appear again in her wingback chair, perhaps to offer some further explanation, but there was nothing else.

"My God, what *was* that?" Frank Potter asked.

"The back half of Back Half," Luke said. He was whiter than ever.

"What kind of people would put *children* in a—"

"Monsters," Luke said. He got up, then put a hand to his head and staggered.

Tim grabbed him. "Are you going to faint?"

"No. I don't know. I need to get outside. I need to breathe some fresh air. It's like the walls are closing in."

Tim looked at Sheriff John, who nodded. "Take him out in the alley. See if you can get him right."

"I'll come with you," Wendy said. "You'll need me to open the door, anyway."

The door at the far end of the holding area had big white capital letters printed across it: EMERGENCY EXIT ALARM WILL SOUND. Wendy used a key from her ring to turn off the alarm. Tim hit the push-bar with the heel of his hand and used the other to lead Luke, not staggering now but still horribly pale, out into the alley. Tim knew what PTSD was, but had never seen it except on TV. He was seeing it now, in this boy who wouldn't be old enough to shave for another three years.

"Don't step on any of Annie's stuff," Wendy said. "Especially not her air mattress. She wouldn't thank you for that."

Luke didn't ask what an air mattress, two backpacks, a three-wheeled grocery cart, and a rolled-up sleeping bag were doing in the alley. He walked slowly toward Main Street, taking deep breaths, pausing once to bend over and grip his knees.

"Any better?" Tim asked.

"My friends are going to let them out," Luke said, still bent over.

"Let who out?" Wendy asked. "Those . . ." She didn't know how to finish. It didn't matter, because Luke didn't seem to hear her.

"I can't see them, but I know. I don't understand how I can, but I do. I think it's the Avester. Avery, I mean. Kalisha is with him. And Nicky. George. God, they're so strong! So strong together!"

Luke straightened up and began walking again. As he stopped at the mouth of the alley, Main Street's six streetlights came on. He looked at Tim and Wendy, amazed. "Did I do that?"

"No, honey," Wendy said, laughing a little. "It's just their regular time. Let's go back inside, now. You need to drink one of Sheriff John's Cokes."

She touched his shoulder. Luke shook her off. "Wait."

A hand-holding couple was crossing the deserted street. The man had short blond hair. The woman was wearing a dress with flowers on it.

26

The power the kids generated dropped when Nicky let go of Kalisha's and George's hands, but only a little. Because the others were gathered behind the Ward A door now, and they were providing most of the power.

It's like a seesaw, Nick thought. As the ability to think goes down, TP and TK goes up. And the ones behind that door have almost no minds left.

That's right, Avery said. *That's how it works. They're the battery.*

Nicky's head was clear—absolutely no pain. Looking at the others, he guessed they were the same. Whether the headaches would come back—or when—was impossible to say. For now he was only grateful.

No more need for the sparkler; they were past that now. They were riding the hum.

Nicky bent over the caretakers who had Tased themselves into unconsciousness and started going through their pockets. He found what he was looking for and handed it to Kalisha, who handed it to Avery. "You do it," she said.

Avery Dixon—who should have been home eating supper with his parents after another hard day of being the smallest boy in his fifth-grade class—took the orange key card and pressed it to the sensor panel. The lock thumped, and the door opened. The residents of Gorky Park were clustered on the other side like sheep huddled together in a storm. They were dirty, mostly undressed, dazed. Several of them were drooling. Petey Littlejohn was going "ya-*ya*-ya-*ya*-ya-*ya*" as he thumped his head.

They are never coming back, Avery thought. Their gears are too stripped to recover. Maybe Iris, too.

George: *But the rest of us might have a chance.*

Yes.

Kalisha, knowing it was cold, also knowing it was necessary: *In the meantime, we can use them.*

"What now?" Katie asked. "What now what *now*?"

For a moment none of them answered, because none of them knew. Then Avery spoke up.

Front Half. Let's get the rest of the kids and get out of here.

Helen: *And go where?*

An alarm began to blare, *whoop-whoop-whoop*ing in rising and falling cycles. None of them paid any attention.

"We'll worry about where later," Nicky said. He joined hands with Kalisha and George again. "First, let's get some payback. Let's do some damage. Anyone got a problem with that?"

No one did. Hands once more linked, the eleven who had begun the revolt started back down the hall toward the Back Half lounge, and the elevator lobby beyond. The residents of Ward A followed in a kind of zombie shuffle, perhaps drawn by the magnetism of children who could still think. The hum had dropped to a drone, but it was there.

Avery Dixon reached out, searching for Luke, hoping to find him in a place too far away to be of any help to them. Because that would mean at least one of the Institute's child slaves was safe. There was a good chance the rest of them were going to die, because the staff of this hellhole would do anything to keep them from escaping.

Anything.

27

Trevor Stackhouse was in his office down the hall from Mrs. Sigsby's, pacing up and down because he was too wired to sit, and would remain that way until he heard from Julia. Her news might be good or bad, but any news would be better than this waiting.

A telephone rang, but it was neither the traditional jingle of the landline or the *brrt-brrt* of his box phone; it was the imperative double-honk of the red security phone. The last time it had rung was when the shitshow with those twins and the Cross boy had gone down in the cafeteria. Stackhouse picked it up, and before he could say a word, Dr. Hallas was gibbering in his ear.

"They're out, the ones who watch the movies for sure and I think the gorks are out, too, they've hurt at least three of the caretakers, no, four, Corinne says she thinks Jake Howland is dead, electrocu—"

"SHUT UP!" Stackhouse yelled into the phone. And then, when he was sure (no, not sure, just hopeful) that he had Heckle's attention, he said: "Put your thoughts in order and tell me what happened."

Hallas, shocked back to an approximation of his once-upon-a-time rationality, told Stackhouse what he had seen. As he was nearing the end of his story, the Institute's general alarm began to go off.

"Christ, did you turn that on, Everett?"

"No, no, not me, it must have been Joanne. Dr. James. She was in the crematory. She goes there to meditate."

Stackhouse was almost sidetracked by the bizarre image this raised in his mind, Dr. Jeckle sitting crosslegged in front of the oven door, perhaps praying for serenity, and then he forced his mind back to the situation at hand: the Back Half children had raised some kind of half-assed mutiny. How could it have happened? It had never happened before. And why *now*?

Heckle was still talking, but Stackhouse had heard all he needed. "Listen to me, Everett. Get every orange card you can find and burn them, okay? *Burn them.*"

"How . . . how am I supposed to . . ."

"You've got a goddam furnace on E-Level!" Stackhouse roared. "Use the fucking thing for something besides kids!"

He hung up and used the landline to call Fellowes in the computer room. Andy wanted to know what the alarm was about. He sounded scared.

"We have a problem in Back Half, but I'm handling it. Feed the cameras from over there to my computer. Don't ask questions, just do it."

He turned on his desktop—had the elderly thing ever booted up so slowly?—and clicked on SECURITY CAMERAS. He saw the Front Half cafeteria, mostly empty . . . a few kids in the playground . . .

"Andy!" he shouted. "Not Front Half, *Back* Half! Stop fucking arou—"

The picture flipped, and he saw Heckle through a film of lens dust, cowering in his office just as Jeckle came in, presumably from her interrupted meditation session. She was looking back over her shoulder.

"Okay, that's better. I'll take it from here."

He flipped the image and saw the caretakers' lounge. A bunch of them were cowering in there with the door to the corridor closed and presumably locked. No help there.

Flip, and here was the blue-carpeted main corridor, with at least three caretakers down. No, make it four. Phil Chaffitz was sitting on the floor outside the screening room, cradling his hand against his smock top, which was drenched with blood.

Flip, and here was the cafeteria, empty.

Flip, and here was the lounge. Corinne Rawson was kneeling next to Jake Howland, blabbing to someone on her walkie-talkie. Jake did indeed look dead.

Flip, and here was the elevator lobby, the door to the elevator just beginning to slide shut. The car was the size of those used to transport patients in hospitals, and it was crammed with residents. Most undressed. The gorks from Ward A, then. If he could stop them there . . . trap them there . . .

Flip, and through that irritating film of dust and smear, Stackhouse saw more kids on E-Level, close to a dozen, milling around in front of the elevator doors and waiting for them to open and disgorge the rest of the kiddie mutineers. Waiting outside the access tunnel leading to Front Half. Not good.

Stackhouse picked up the landline and heard nothing but silence. Fellowes had hung up on his end. Cursing the wasted time, Stackhouse dialed him back.

"Can you kill the power to the Back Half elevator? Stop it in the shaft?"

"I don't know," Fellowes said. "Maybe. It might be in the Emergency Procedures booklet. Just let me ch—"

But it was already too late. The elevator doors slid open on E-Level and the escapees from Gorky Park wandered out, staring around at the tiled elevator lobby as if there was something to see there. That was bad, but Stackhouse saw something worse. Heckle and Jeckle could collect dozens of Back Half key cards and burn them, but it would make no difference. Because one of the kids—it was the pipsqueak who'd collaborated with the housekeeper on Ellis's escape—had an orange key card in his hand. It would open the door to the tunnel, and it would also open the door that gave on F-Level in Front Half. If they got to Front Half, anything might happen.

For a moment, one that seemed endless, Stackhouse froze. Fellowes was squawking in his ear, but the sound was far away. Because yes, the little shit was using the orange card and leading his merry band into the tunnel. A two-hundred-yard walk would take them to Front Half. The door closed behind the last of them, leaving the lower elevator lobby empty. Stackhouse flipped to a new camera and got them walking along the tiled tunnel.

Dr. Hendricks came bursting in, good old Donkey Kong with his shirttail flapping and his fly half-zipped and his eyes all red-rimmed and buggy. "What's happening? What's—"

And, just to add to the lunacy, his box phone began its *brrt-brrt-brrt*. Stackhouse held his hand up to silence Hendricks. The box phone continued its demands.

"Andy. They're in the tunnel. They're coming, and they have a key card. We need to stop them. Do you have any ideas at all?"

He expected nothing but more panic, but Fellowes surprised him. "I guess I could kill the locks."

"What?"

"I can't deactivate the cards, but I can freeze the locks. The entry codes are computer generated, and so—"

"Are you saying you can bottle them up?"

"Well, yes."

"Do it! Do it right now!"

"What is it?" Hendricks asked. "Jesus, I was just getting ready to leave and the alarm—"

"Shut up," Stackhouse said. "But stay here. I may need you."

The box phone continued braying. Still watching the tunnel and the marching morons, he picked it up. Now he was holding a phone to each ear, like a character in some old slapstick comedy. "What? *What?*"

"We are here, and the boy is here," Mrs. Sigsby said. The connection was good; she might have been in the next room. "I expect to have him back in our custody shortly." She paused. "Or dead."

"Good for you, Julia, but we have a situation here. There's been a—"

"Whatever it is, handle it. This is happening *now*. I'll call you when we're on our way out of town."

She was gone. Stackhouse didn't care, because if Fellowes didn't work computer magic, Julia might have nothing to come back *to*.

"Andy! Are you still there?"

"I'm here."

"Did you do it?"

Stackhouse felt a dreadful certainty that Fellowes would say that their old computer system had picked this critical moment to seize up.

"Yes. Well, pretty sure. I'm looking at a message on my screen that says ORANGE KEY CARDS IN-VALID INSERT NEW AUTHORIZATION CODE."

A pretty-sure from Andy Fellowes did jackshit to ease Stackhouse's mind. He sat forward in his chair, hands locked together, watching the screen of his computer. Hendricks joined him, peering over his shoulder.

"My God, what are they doing out?"

"Coming for us would be my guess," Stackhouse said. "We're about to find out if they can."

The parade of potential escapees left the view of one camera. Stackhouse punched the key that swapped the images, briefly got Corinne Rawson holding Jake's head in her lap, then got the one he wanted. It showed the door to F-Level on the Front Half end of the access tunnel. The kids reached it.

"Crunch time," Stackhouse said. He was clenching his fists hard enough to leave marks in his palms.

Dixon raised the orange card and laid it on the reader pad. He tried the knob and when nothing happened, Trevor Stackhouse finally relaxed. Beside him, Hendricks gusted out a breath that smelled strongly of bourbon. Drinking on duty was as *verboten* as carrying a cell phone, but Stackhouse wasn't going to worry about that now.

Flies in a jar, he thought. That's all you are now, boys and girls. As to what happens to you next . . .

That, thankfully, wasn't his problem. What happened to them after the loose end in South Carolina had been snipped off was up to Mrs. Sigsby.

"That's why they pay you the big bucks, Julia," he said, and settled back in his chair to watch a bunch of the kids—now led by Wilholm—go back and try the door they had come through. With no result. The Wilholm brat threw back his head. His mouth opened. Stackhouse wished for audio, so he could hear that scream of frustration.

"We have contained the problem," he said to Hendricks.

"Um," Hendricks said.

Stackhouse turned to look at him. "What does that mean?"

"Maybe not quite."

28

Tim put a hand on Luke's shoulder. "If you feel up to it now, we really need to go back inside and sort this out. We'll get you that Coke, and—"

"Wait." Luke was staring at the hand-holding couple crossing the street. They hadn't noticed the trio standing at the mouth of Orphan Annie's alley; their attention was focused on the cop-shop.

"Got off the interstate and got lost," Wendy said. "Bet you anything. We get half a dozen a month. Want to go back in now?"

Luke paid no attention. He could still sense the others, the kids, and they sounded dismayed now, but they were far back in his mind, like voices coming through a ventilator from another room. That woman . . . the one in the flowery dress . . .

Something falls over and wakes me up. It must be the trophy from when we won the Northwest Debate Tourney, because that's the biggest and it makes a hell of a clatter. Someone is bending over me. I say *mom* because even though I know it isn't her, she's a woman and *mom* is the first word to come into my still-mostly-asleep mind. And she says—

"Sure," Luke said. "Whatever you want."

"Great!" Wendy said. "We'll just—"

"No, that's what *she* said." He pointed. The couple had reached the sidewalk in front of the sheriff's station. They were no longer holding hands. Luke turned to Tim, his eyes wide and panicky. "She's one of the ones who took me! I saw her again, in the Institute! In the break room! They're here! I told you they'd come and *they're here*!"

Luke whirled and ran for the door, which was unlocked on this side, so Annie could get in late at night, should she so desire.

"What—" Wendy began, but Tim didn't let her finish. He ran after the boy from the train, and the thought in his mind was that just maybe the kid had been right about Norbert Hollister after all.

29

"Well?" Orphan Annie's whisper was almost too fierce to be called one. "Do you believe me now, Mr. Corbett Denton?"

Drummer didn't reply at first, because he was trying to process what he was looking at: three vans parked side by side, and beyond them, a cluster of men and women. Looked like nine of them, enough to field a damn baseball team. And Annie was right, they were armed. It was twilight now, but the light lingered long in late summer, and besides, the streetlights had come on. Drummer could see holstered sidearms and two long guns that looked to him like HKs. People-killing machines. The baseball team was clustered near the front of the old movie theater, but mostly shielded from the sidewalk by its brick flank. They were obviously waiting for something.

"They got scouts!" Annie hissed. "See them crossing the street? They'll be checking the sheriff's to see how many are in there! Will you get your goddam guns now, or do I have to go get em myself?"

Drummer turned, and for the first time in twenty years, maybe even thirty, broke into a full-out run. He mounted the steps to the apartment over his barber shop and stopped on the landing long enough to tear in three or four huge breaths. Also long enough to wonder if his heart would be able to stand the strain or if it would simply explode.

His .30–06, which he planned to shoot himself with one of these fine South Carolina nights (might have done it already, if not for an occasional interesting conversation with the town's new night knocker) was in the closet, and it was loaded. So were the .45 automatic pistol and .38 revolver on the high shelf.

He took all three weapons and ran back down the stairs, panting and sweating and probably stinking like a hog in a steambath, but feeling fully alive for the first time in years. He listened for the sound of shooting, but so far there was nothing.

Maybe they're cops, he thought, but that seemed unlikely. Cops would have walked right in, showed their IDs, and announced their business. Also, they would have come in black SUVs, Suburbans or Escalades.

At least that was the way they did it on TV.

30

Nick Wilholm led the ragtag troop of lost boys and girls back down the slightly slanted tunnel to the locked door on the Front Half side. Some of the Ward A inmates followed; some just milled around. Pete Littlejohn began to hit the top of his head again, yelling, "Ya-*ya*-ya-*ya*-ya-*ya*." There was an echo in the tunnel that made his rhythmic chant not just annoying but maddening.

"Join hands," Nicky said. "All of us." He lifted his chin to indicate the milling gorks, and added, *I think it will bring them.*

Like bugs to a bug light, Kalisha thought. It wasn't very nice, but the truth so seldom was.

They came. As each one joined the circle, the hum became louder. The sides of the tunnel forced their circle into more of a capsule shape, but that was okay. The power was here.

Kalisha understood what Nicky was thinking, not just because she was picking it up but because it was the only play they had left.

Stronger together, she thought, and then, out loud to Avery: "Bust that lock, Avester."

The hum rose to that feedback scream, and if any one of them had still had a headache, it would have fled in terror. Once again Kalisha had that sense of sublime power. It came on sparkler nights, but then it was dirty. This was clean, because it was *them*. The

Ward A children were silent, but smiling. They felt it, too. And liked it. Kalisha supposed it was the closest to thinking they might ever get.

There was a faint creaking noise from the door, and they could see it settle back in its frame, but that was all. Avery had been standing on his tiptoes, his small face clenched in concentration. Now he slumped and let out his breath.

George: *No?*

Avery: *No. If it was just locked, I think we could, but it's like the lock isn't even there.*

"Dead," Iris said. "Dead, dead, can't be fed, that's what I said, the lock is dead."

"Froze them somehow," Nicky said. *And we can't bust through, can we?*

Avery: *No, solid steel.*

"Where's Superman when you need him?" George said. He scrubbed his hands up his cheeks, producing a humorless smile.

Helen sat down, put her hands to her face, and began to cry. "What good are we?" She said it again, this time as a mental echo: *What good are we?*

Nicky turned to Kalisha. *Any ideas?*

No.

He turned to Avery. *What about you?*

Avery shook his head.

31

"What do you mean, not quite?" Stackhouse asked.

Instead of answering, Donkey Kong hurried across the room to Stackhouse's intercom. The top of the casing was thick with dust. Stackhouse had never used it a single time—it wasn't as if he had to announce up-coming dances or trivia nights. Dr. Hendricks bent to inspect the rudimentary controls and flicked a switch, lighting a green go-lamp.

"What do you mean—"

It was Hendricks's turn to say shut up, and instead of being angry, Stackhouse felt a certain admiration. Whatever the good doctor was up to, he thought it was important.

Hendricks took the microphone, then paused. "Is there a way to make sure those escaped children don't hear what I'm going to say? No sense giving them ideas."

"There are no speakers in the access tunnel," Stackhouse said, hoping he was correct about that. "As for Back Half, I believe they have their own separate intercom system. What are you up to?"

Hendricks looked at him as if he were an idiot. "Just because their bodies are locked up, that doesn't mean their minds are."

Oh shit, Stackhouse thought. I forgot what they're here for.

"Now how does this . . . never mind, I see." Hendricks depressed the button on the side of the mic, cleared his throat, and began to speak. "Attention, please. All staff, attention. This is Dr. Hendricks." He ran a hand through his thinning hair, making what had been crazy to begin with crazier still. "Children have escaped from Back Half, but there is no cause for alarm. I repeat, no cause for alarm. They are penned up in the access tunnel between Front Half and Back Half. They may attempt to influence you, however, the way they . . ." He paused, licking his lips. "The way they influence certain people when they do their jobs. They may attempt to make you harm yourselves. Or . . . well . . . to turn you against one another."

Oh, Jesus, Stackhouse thought, *there's* a cheerful idea.

"Listen carefully," Hendricks said. "They are only able to succeed in such mental infiltration if the targets are unsuspecting. If you feel something . . . if you sense thoughts that are not your own . . . remain calm and resist them. Expel them. You will be able to do this quite easily. It may help to speak aloud. To say *I am not listening to you*."

He started to put the mic down, but Stackhouse took it. "This is Stackhouse. Front Half personnel, all children must go back to their rooms immediately. If any resist, zap them."

He flicked off the intercom and turned to Hendricks. "Maybe the little fucks in the tunnel won't think of it. They're only children, after all."

"Oh, they'll think of it," Hendricks said. "After all, they've had practice."

32

Tim overtook Luke as the boy opened the door to the holding area. "Stay here, Luke. Wendy, you're with me."

"You don't really think—"

"I don't know what I think. Don't draw your gun, but make sure the strap is off."

As Tim and Wendy hurried up the short aisle between the four empty cells, they heard a man's voice. He sounded pleasant enough. Good humored, even. "My wife and I were told there are some interesting old buildings in Beaufort, and we thought we'd take a shortcut, but our GPS kinda screwed the pooch."

"I made him stop to ask for directions," the woman said, and as Tim entered the office, he saw her looking up at her husband—if that was what the blond man really was—with amused exasperation. "He didn't want to. Men always think they know where they're going, don't they?"

"I tell you what, we're a little busy just now," Sheriff John said, "and I don't have time—"

"It's *her*!" Luke shouted from behind Tim and Wendy, making them both jump. The other officers looked around. Luke shoved past Wendy hard enough to make her stagger against the wall. "She's the one who sprayed me in the face and knocked me out! *You bitch, you killed my parents!*"

He tried to run at her. Tim caught him by the neck of his shirt and yanked him back. The blond man and the flower-dress woman looked surprised and puzzled. Completely normal, in other words. Except Tim thought he'd seen another expression on the woman's face, just for an instant: a look of narrow recognition.

"I think there's some kind of mistake," she was saying. She tried on a bewildered smile. "Who is this boy? Is he crazy?"

Although he was only the town night knocker and would be for the next five months, Tim reverted to cop mode without thinking, as he had on the night those kids had stuck up the Zoney's and shot Absimil Dobira. "I'd like to see your IDs, folks."

"Really, there's no need of that, is there?" the woman said. "I don't know who that boy thinks we are, but we're lost, and when I was a little girl, my mom used to tell me that if you get lost, ask a policeman."

Sheriff John stood up. "Uh-huh, uh-huh, that may be true, and if it is, you won't mind showing us your drivers' licenses, will you?"

"Not at all," the man said. "Just let me get my wallet." The woman was already reaching into her purse, looking exasperated.

"Look out!" Luke shouted. *"They have guns!"*

Tag Faraday and George Burkett looked astounded, Frank Potter and Bill Wicklow perplexed.

"Whoa a second!" Sheriff John said. "Hands where I can see them!"

Neither of them paused. Michelle Robertson's hand came out of her purse holding not her driver's license but the Sig Sauer Nightmare Micro she had been issued. Denny Williams had reached behind him for the Glock in his belt rather than his wallet. Both the sheriff and Deputy Faraday were reaching for their service weapons, but they were slow, slow.

Tim was not. He pulled Wendy's gun from her holster and pointed it with both hands. *"Drop the weapons, drop them!"*

They did not. Robertson aimed at Luke, and Tim shot her a single time, driving her backward against one of the station's big double doors hard enough to crack the frosted glass.

Williams dropped to one knee and aimed at Tim, who had just time to think, This guy's a pro and I'm dead. But the man's gun jerked upward, as if pulled by an invisible cord, and the bullet meant for Tim went into the ceiling. Sheriff John Ashworth punted the blond man in the side of the head, sending him sprawling. Billy Wicklow stomped on his wrist.

"Give it up, motherfucker, just give it—"

That was when Mrs. Sigsby, realizing things had gone wrong, told Louis Grant and Tom Jones to open up with the big guns. Williams and Robertson weren't important.

The boy was.

33

The two HK37s filled DuPray's formerly peaceful twilight with thunder. Grant and Jones raked the brick front of the sheriff's station, raising puffs of pinkish-red dust, blowing the windows and the glass door panels inward. They were on the sidewalk; the rest of Gold team was standing spread out behind them in the street. The only exception was Dr. Evans, standing off to one side, his hands over his ears.

"*Yeah!*" Winona Briggs shouted. She was dancing from foot to foot, as if she needed to go to the bathroom. *"Kill their asses!"*

"Go!" Mrs. Sigsby shouted. "All of you go now! Take the boy or kill him! Take him or—"

Then, from behind them: "You're not going anywhere, ma'am. I swear by the Savior a bunch of you goan be dead if you try. You two fellas up front, put down those grease guns this minute."

Louis Grant and Tom Jones turned, but did not put down the HKs.

"Do it fast," Annie said, "or you're dead. This isn't playin, boys. You're in the south now."

They looked at each other, then put the autos carefully down on the pavement.

Mrs. Sigsby saw two unlikely ambushers standing

beneath the Gem's sagging marquee: a fat bald man in a pajama top and a wild-haired woman in what looked like a Mexican serape. The man had a rifle. The woman in the serape had an automatic in one hand and a revolver in the other.

"Now the rest of you folks do the same," Drummer Denton said. "You're covered."

Mrs. Sigsby looked at the two yokels standing in front of the abandoned theater, and her thought was both simple and weary: Would this never end?

A gunshot from inside the sheriff's station, a brief pause, then another. When the yokels glanced that way, Grant and Jones bent to pick up their weapons.

"Don't you do it!" the woman in the serape shouted.

Robin Lecks, who not so long ago had shot Luke's father through a pillow, took that small window of opportunity to draw her Sig Micro. The other members of Gold team dropped, to give Grant and Jones a clear field of fire. This was how they had been taught to react. Mrs. Sigsby stood where she was, as if her anger at this unexpected problem would protect her.

34

As the confrontation in South Carolina began, Kalisha and her friends were sitting in slumped postures of disconsolation near the access door to Front Half. The door they couldn't open because Iris was right: the lock was dead.

Nicky: *Maybe we can still do something. Get the staff in Front Half the way we got the red caretakers.*

Avery was shaking his head. He looked less like a little boy and more like a weary old man. *I tried.*

Reached out to Gladys, because I hate her. Her and her fake smile. She said she wasn't listening and pushed me away.

Kalisha looked at the Ward A kids, who were once more wandering off, as if there were anywhere to go. A girl was doing cartwheels; a boy wearing filthy board shorts and a torn tee-shirt was knocking his head lightly against the wall; Pete Littlejohn was still getting his ya-ya's out. But they would come if called, and there was plenty of power there. She took Avery's hand. "All of us together—"

"No," Avery said. *We might be able to make them feel a little weird, dizzy and sick to their stomachs . . .* ". . . but that's all."

Kalisha: *But why?* Why? *If we could kill that bomb-making guy way over in Afghanistan—*

Avery: *Because the bomb-making guy didn't know. The preacher, that Westin guy,* he *doesn't know. When they know . . .*

George: *They can keep us out.*

Avery nodded.

"Then what can we do?" Helen asked. *"Anything?"*

Avery shook his head. *I don't know.*

"There's one thing," Kalisha said. "We're stuck here, but we know someone who isn't. But we'll need everybody." She tilted her head toward the wandering exiles from Ward A. "Let's call them."

"I don't know, Sha," Avery said. "I'm pretty tired."

"Just this one more thing," she coaxed.

Avery sighed and held out his hands. Kalisha, Nicky, George, Helen, and Katie linked up. After a moment, Iris did, too. Once again, the others drifted to them. They made the capsule shape, and the hum rose. In Front Half, caretakers and techs and janitors felt it and feared it, but it wasn't directed at them. Fourteen hundred miles away, Tim had just put a bullet between Michelle Robertson's breasts; Grant and Jones were just raising their automatic rifles to rake the front of the sheriff's station; Billy Wicklow was standing on Denny Williams's hand with Sheriff John beside him.

The children of the Institute called out to Luke.

35

Luke didn't think about reaching out with his mind to knock the blond man's gun up; he just did it. The Stasi Lights came back, momentarily blotting out everything. When they began to fade, he saw one of the cops standing on the blond man's wrist, trying to make him let go of the gun in his hand. The blond man's lips were stretched in a snarl of pain, and blood was pouring down the side of his face, but he was holding on. The sheriff brought his foot back, apparently meaning to kick the blond man in the head again.

Luke saw this much, but then the Stasi Lights returned, brighter than ever, and the voices of his friends hit him like a hammer blow in the middle of his head. He stumbled backward through the doorway to the holding area, raising his hands as if to ward off a punch, and tripped over his own feet. He landed on his butt just as Grant and Jones opened up with their automatic rifles.

He saw Tim tackle Wendy and bring her to the floor, shielding her body with his own. He saw bullets tear into the sheriff and the deputy standing on the blond man's hand. They both went down. Glass flew. Somebody was screaming. Luke thought it was Wendy. Outside, Luke heard the woman who sounded weirdly like Mrs. Sigsby shout something that sounded like *all of you now*.

For Luke, dazed from a double dose of the Stasi Lights and the combined voices of his friends, the world seemed to slow down. He saw one of the other deputies—wounded, there was blood running down his arm—pivot toward the broken main doors, probably to see who had been shooting. He seemed to be moving very slowly. The blond man was getting to his knees, and he also seemed to be moving slowly. It was like watching an underwater ballet. He shot the deputy in the back, then began turning toward Luke. Faster now, the world speeding up again. Before the blond man could fire, the redheaded deputy bent down, almost bowing, and shot him in the temple. The blond man flew sideways and landed on top of the woman who had claimed to be his wife.

A woman outside—not the one who sounded like Mrs. Sigsby, another one with a southern accent—shouted, "Don't you do it!"

More gunfire followed, and then the first woman yelled, *"The boy! We have to get the boy!"*

It *is* her, Luke thought. I don't know how it can be, but it is. That's Mrs. Sigsby out there.

36

Robin Lecks was a good shot, but the twilight was deepening and the distance was long for a handgun as small as the Micro. Her bullet got Drummer Denton high in the shoulder instead of hitting him center mass. It drove him back against the boarded-up box office, and her next two shots went wild. Orphan Annie stood her ground. She had been raised that way in the Georgia canebrakes by a father who told her, "You don't back down, girl, not for nothin." Jean Ledoux had been a crack shot whether drunk or sober, and he had taught her well. Now she opened fire with both of Drummer's handguns, compensating for the .45 auto's heavier recoil without even thinking about it. She took down one of the automatic riflemen (it was Tony Fizzale, who would never wield a zap-stick again), never minding the three or four bullets that whizzed past her, one of them giving a flirty little flick to the hem of her serape.

Drummer came back and aimed at the woman who had shot him. Robin was down on one knee in the middle of the street, cursing her Sig, which had jammed. Drummer socked the .30–06 into the hollow of the shoulder that wasn't bleeding and put her down the rest of the way.

"Stop shooting!" Mrs. Sigsby was screaming. *"We have to get the boy! We have to make sure of the boy! Tom Jones! Alice Green! Louis Grant! Wait for me! Josh Gottfried! Winona Briggs! Hold steady!"*

Drummer and Annie looked at each other. "Do *we* keep shooting or not?" Annie asked.

"Fuck if I know," Drummer said.

Tom Jones and Alice Green were flanking the battered doors of the sheriff's station. Josh Gottfried and Winona Briggs walked backward, likewise flanking Mrs. Sigsby and keeping their guns on the unexpected shooters who had blindsided them. Dr. James Evans, who had not been assigned a position, assigned his own. He walked past Mrs. Sigsby and approached Drummer and Orphan Annie with his hands raised and a placating smile on his face.

"Get back here, you fool!" Mrs. Sigsby snapped.

He ignored her. "I'm not a part of this," he said, speaking to the fat man in the pajama top, who looked to be the saner of the two ambushers. "I never wanted to be a part of this, so I think I'll just—"

"Oh, sit down," Annie said, and shot him in the foot. She was considerate enough to do it with the .38, which would cause less damage. In theory, at least.

That left the woman in the red pant suit, the one in charge. If the shooting started again, she would probably be cut to pieces in the crossfire, but she showed no fear, only a kind of pissed-off concentration.

"I'm going into the station now," she said to Drummer and Orphan Annie. "There doesn't need to be any more of this nonsense. Stand pat and you'll be fine. Start shooting and Josh and Winona will take you out. Understood?"

She didn't wait for an answer, simply turned away and walked toward the remains of her force, low heels clacking on the pavement.

"Drummer?" Annie said. "What do we do?"

"Maybe we don't have to do anything," he said. "Look to your left. Don't move your head, just cut your eyes."

She did, and saw one of the Dobira brothers hustling up the sidewalk. He had a pistol. Later he would tell the State Police that although he and his brother were peaceful men, they had thought it wise to keep a gun in the store since the holdup.

"Now to the right. Don't move your head."

She cut her eyes that way and saw the widow Goolsby and Mr. Bilson, father of the Bilson twins. Addie Goolsby was in her robe and slippers. Richard Bilson was wearing madras shorts and a red Crimson

Tide tee-shirt. Both had hunting rifles. The cluster in front of the sheriff's station didn't see them; their attention was on whatever business they'd come here to transact.

You're in the south now, Annie had told these gunned-up interlopers. She had an idea they were about to find out just how true that was.

"Tom and Alice," Mrs. Sigsby said. "Go in. Make sure you get the boy."

They went.

37

Tim pulled Wendy to her feet. She looked dazed, not entirely sure where she was. There was a shredded piece of paper caught in her hair. The shooting outside had stopped, at least for the moment. It had been replaced by talking, but Tim's ears were ringing, and he couldn't make out the words. And it didn't matter. If they were making peace out there, good. It would be prudent, however, to expect more war.

"Wendy, okay?"

"They . . . Tim, they killed Sheriff John! How many others?"

He shook her. *"Are you okay?"*

She nodded. "Y-Yes. I think s—"

"Take Luke out the back."

She reached for him. Luke evaded her and ran for the sheriff's desk. Tag Faraday tried to grab his arm, but Luke evaded him, too. A bullet had clipped the laptop, knocking it askew, but the home screen, although cracked, was still up, and the flash drive's little orange ready light was blinking steadily. His ears were also ringing, but he was close to the door now, and heard Mrs. Sigsby say *Make sure you get the boy*.

Oh you bitch, he thought. You relentless bitch.

Luke grabbed the laptop and dropped to his knees, cradling it to his chest as Alice Green and Tom Jones came through the shattered double doors. Tag raised his sidearm but took a burst from the HK before he could fire, the back of his uniform shirt shredding. The Glock flew from his hand and spun across the floor. The only other deputy still standing, Frank Potter, never moved to defend himself. There was a stunned, unbelieving expression on his face. Alice Green shot him once in the head, then ducked as more gunfire erupted in the street behind them. There were yells and a scream of pain.

The gunfire and the scream momentarily distracted the man with the HK. Jones wheeled in that direction, and Tim double-tapped him, one in the back of the neck and the other in the head. Alice Green straightened and came on, stepping over Jones, her face set, and now Tim saw another woman crowding in behind her. An older woman wearing a red pant suit, also holding a gun. Dear Christ, he thought, how many are there? Did they send an army for one little boy?

"He's behind the desk, Alice," the older woman said. Considering the carnage, she sounded eerily calm. "I can see a bandage on his ear sticking up. Pull him out and shoot him."

The woman named Alice came around the desk. Tim didn't bother telling her to stop—they were way past that—only pulled the trigger of Wendy's Glock. It clicked dry, although there should have been at least one more round in the clip, and probably two. Even in this do-or-die moment, he understood the reason:

Wendy hadn't fully reloaded after the last time she took target practice with it on the gun-range over in Dunning. Such things were not high on her list of priorities. He even had time to think—as he had during his early days in DuPray—that Wendy had never been cut out to be a cop.

Should have stuck to dispatch, he thought, but too late now. I think we're all going to die.

Luke rose up from behind the dispatch desk, the laptop held in both hands. He swung it and hit Alice Green full in the face. The cracked screen shattered. Green staggered back into the woman in the pant suit, her nose and mouth bleeding, then raised her gun again.

"Drop it, drop it, drop it!" Wendy screamed. She had scooped up Tag Faraday's Glock. Green took no notice. She was aiming at Luke, who was pulling Maureen Alvorson's flash drive from the laptop's port instead of ducking for cover. Wendy fired three times, eyes slitted, uttering a shrill cry with each trigger-pull. The first bullet took Alice Green just above the bridge of her nose. The second went through one of the empty holes in the door where a frosted glass panel had been only a hundred and fifty seconds before.

The third struck Julia Sigsby in the leg. Her gun flew from her hand and she folded to the floor, a look of unbelief on her face. "You shot me. Why did you shoot me?"

"Are you stupid? Why do you think?" Wendy said. She walked to the woman sitting against the wall, her shoes crunching on broken glass. The air stank of gunpowder, and the office—once neat, now a shambles—was filled with drifting blue smoke. "You were telling them to shoot the kid."

Mrs. Sigsby gave her the sort of smile reserved for those who must suffer fools. "You don't understand. How could you? He belongs to me. He's *property*."

"Not anymore," Tim said.

Luke knelt beside Mrs. Sigsby. There were spatters of blood on his cheeks and a shard of glass in one eyebrow. "Who did you leave in charge at the Institute? Stackhouse? Is he the one?"

She only looked at him.

"Is it Stackhouse?"

Nothing.

Drummer Denton stepped in and looked around. His pajama shirt was soaked with blood down one side, but he looked remarkably alert in spite of that. Gutaale Dobira was peering over his shoulder, eyes wide.

"Holy shit," Drummer said. "It's a massacree."

"I had to shoot a man," Gutaale said. "Mrs. Goolsby, she was shooting a woman who was trying to shoot her. It was a clear case of self-defense."

"How many outside?" Tim asked them. "Are they all down, or are some still active?"

Annie pushed Gutaale Dobira aside and stood next to Drummer. In her serape, with a smoking gun in each hand, she looked like a character from a spaghetti western. Tim wasn't surprised. He was beyond surprise. "I believe everyone who got out of those vans is accounted for," she said. "A couple wounded, one with a bullet in his foot, one hurt bad. That was the one Dobira shot. The rest of the sons of bitches look like they are dead in here." She surveyed the room. "And Christ, who's left in the Sheriff's Department?"

Wendy, Tim thought but did not say. I guess she's the acting sheriff now. Or maybe Ronnie Gibson will be when she comes back from vacation. Probably Ronnie. Wendy won't want the job.

Addie Goolsby and Richard Bilson were now standing with Gutaale, behind Annie and Drummer. Bilson surveyed the main room with dismay—bullet-riddled walls, broken glass, pools of blood on the floor, sprawled bodies—and put a hand to his mouth.

Addie was made of sterner stuff. "Doc's on his way. Half the town's out there in the street, most of em armed. What happened here? And who's that?" She pointed at the skinny boy with the bandage on his ear.

Luke took no notice. He was fixated on the woman in the pant suit. "Stackhouse, sure. Has to be. I need to get in touch with him. How do I do that?"

Mrs. Sigsby only stared at him. Tim knelt beside Luke. What he saw in the pant suit woman's eyes was pain, disbelief, and hate. He couldn't be sure which of those predominated, but if forced to guess, he would have said hate. It was always the strongest, at least in the short term.

"Luke—"

Luke paid no attention. All of his attention was focused on the wounded woman. "I need to get in touch with him, Mrs. Sigsby. He's holding my friends prisoner."

"They're not prisoners, they're *property*!"

Wendy joined them. "I'm thinking you must have been absent on the day your class learned about Lincoln freeing the slaves, ma'am."

"Come in here, shooting up our town," Annie said. "Guess you found out, didn't you?"

"Hush, Annie," Wendy said.

"I need to get in touch with him, Mrs. Sigsby. I need to make a deal. Tell me how to do it."

When she didn't reply, Luke jammed his thumb into the bullet hole in her red pants. Mrs. Sigsby shrieked. *"Don't, oh don't, that HURTS!"*

"Zap-sticks hurt!" Luke shouted at her. Glass shards rattled across the floor, forming small creeks. Annie stared, eyes wide with fascination. "Injections hurt! Being half-drowned hurts! And having your mind ripped open?" He jammed his thumb against the bullet wound again. The door to the holding area slammed shut, making them all jump. "Having your mind *destroyed*? That hurts most of all!"

"Make him stop!" Mrs. Sigsby screamed. *"Make him stop hurting me!"*

Wendy bent to pull Luke away. Tim shook his head and took her arm. "No."

"It's the conspiracy," Annie whispered to Drummer. Her eyes were huge. "That woman works for the conspiracy. They all do! I knew it all along, I *said* it, and nobody believed me!"

The ringing in Tim's ears was starting to fade. He heard no sirens, which didn't surprise him. He guessed the Staties might not even know there had been a shoot-out in DuPray, at least not yet. And anyone calling 911 would have reached not the South Carolina Highway Patrol but the Fairlee County sheriff—this shambles, in other words. He glanced at his watch and saw with disbelief that the world had been rightside up only five minutes ago. Six, at most.

"Mrs. Sigsby, is it?" he asked, kneeling beside Luke.

She said nothing.

"You are in a great deal of trouble, Mrs. Sigsby. I advise you to tell Luke here what he wants to know."

"I need medical attention."

Tim shook his head. "What you need is to do some talking. Then we'll see about medical attention."

"Luke was telling the truth," Wendy said to no one in particular. "About everything."

"Didn't I just say that?" Annie almost crowed.

Doc Roper pushed his way into the office. "Holy Jesus on Resurrection Morn," he said. "Who's still alive? How badly is that woman hurt? Was it some kind of terrorist thing?"

"They're torturing me," Mrs. Sigsby said. "If you are a doctor, as that black bag you're carrying would seem to suggest, you have an obligation to make them stop."

Tim said, "The boy you treated was running away from this woman and the raiding party she brought with her, Doc. I don't know how many are dead out there, but we lost five, including the sheriff, and it was on this woman's orders."

"We'll deal with that later," Roper said. "Right now I need to take care of her. She's bleeding. And somebody needs to call a goddam ambulance."

Mrs. Sigsby looked at Luke, bared her teeth in a smile that said *I win*, then looked back at Roper. "Thank you, Doctor. Thank you."

"There's a biddy with sand in her craw," Annie said, and not without admiration. "Fella I shot in the foot, maybe not so much. I'd go see him, were I you. I think he'd sell his own grammaw into white slavery for a shot of morphine."

Mrs. Sigsby's eyes widened in alarm. "Leave him alone. I forbid you to talk to him."

Tim got to his feet. "Forbid and be damned. I don't know who you work for, lady, but I believe your days of kidnapping children are over. Luke, Wendy, come with me."

38

House lights had come on all over town, and DuPray's main street was full of milling people. The bodies of the dead were being covered by whatever came to hand. Someone had taken Orphan Annie's sleeping bag out of the alley and draped it over Robin Lecks.

Dr. Evans had been completely forgotten. He could conceivably have limped his way to one of the parked mom vans and gotten away, but had made no effort to do so. Tim, Wendy, and Luke found him sitting on the curb in front of the Gem. His cheeks gleamed with tears. He had managed to work his shoe off, and was now staring at a bloody sock covering what looked like a badly deformed foot. How much of that was bone damage and how much swelling that would eventually go down, Tim neither knew nor cared.

"What is your name, sir?" Tim asked.

"Never mind my name. I want a lawyer. And I want a doctor. A woman shot me. I want her arrested."

"His name is James Evans," Luke said. "And *he's* a doctor. Just like Josef Mengele was."

Evans seemed to notice Luke for the first time. He pointed at the boy with a trembling finger. "This is all your fault."

Luke lunged at Evans, but this time Tim held him back and pushed him gently but firmly to Wendy, who took him by the shoulders.

Tim squatted on his hunkers so he could look the pallid, frightened man dead in the eye. "Listen to me, Dr. Evans. Listen closely. You and your friends came high-riding into town to get this boy and killed five people. All police officers. Now, you might not know it, but South Carolina has the death penalty, and if you think they won't use it, and double-quick, for killing a county sheriff and four deputies—"

"I had nothing to do with it!" Evans squawked. "I was here under protest! I—"

"Shut up!" Wendy said. She still had the late Tag Faraday's Glock, and now she pointed it at the foot that was still shod. "Those officers were also my friends. If you think I'm going to read you your rights or something, you're out your goddam mind. What I'm going to do if you don't tell Luke what he wants is put a bullet in your other—"

"All right! All right! Yes!" Evans reached down and put protective hands over his good foot, which almost made Tim feel sorry for him. Almost. "What is it? What do you want to know?"

"I need to talk to Stackhouse," Luke said. "How do I do that?"

"Her phone," Evans said. "She has a special phone. She called him before they attempted . . . you know . . . the extraction. I saw her put it in her coat pocket."

"I'll get it," Wendy said, and turned back toward the sheriff's station.

"Don't just bring the phone," Luke said. "Bring *her*."

"Luke . . . she's been shot."

"We might need her," Luke said. His eyes were stony. "Why?"

Because it was chess now, and in chess you never lived in the move you were about to make, or even the next one. Three moves ahead, that was the rule. And three alternates to each of those, depending on what your opponent did.

She looked at Tim, who nodded. "Bring her. Cuff her if you need to. You're the law, after all."

"Jesus, what a thought," she said, and left.

Now, at last, Tim heard a siren. Maybe even two of them. Still faint, though.

Luke grabbed his wrist. Tim thought the boy looked totally focused, totally aware, and also tired to death. "I can't get caught in this. They have my friends. They're trapped and there's nobody to help them but me."

"Trapped in this Institute."

"Yes. You believe me now, don't you."

"It'd be hard not to after what was on the flash drive, and all this. What about that drive? Do you still have it?"

Luke patted his pocket.

"Mrs. Sigsby and the people she works with mean to do something to these friends of yours so they end up like the kids in that ward?"

"They were already doing it, but then they got out. Mostly because of Avery, and Avery was there because he helped me get out. I guess you'd call that irony. But I'm pretty sure they're trapped again. I'm afraid Stackhouse will kill them if I can't make a deal."

Wendy was coming back. She had a boxy device that Tim supposed was a phone. There were three bleeding scratches across the back of the hand that held it.

"She didn't want to give it up. And she's surprisingly strong, even after taking a bullet." She handed Tim the gadget and looked back over her shoulder. Orphan Annie and Drummer Denton were supporting Mrs. Sigsby across the street. Although she was pale and in pain, she was resisting them as much as she could. At least three dozen DuPray townsfolk trailed behind them, with Doc Roper leading the pack.

"Here she is, Timmy," Orphan Annie said. She was panting for breath, and there were red marks on her cheek and temple where Mrs. Sigsby had slapped at her, but Annie looked not the slightest bit discomposed. "What do you want us to do with her? I s'pose stringing her up is pretty much out of the question, but ain't it an attractive idea."

Doc Roper set down his black bag, grabbed Annie by the serape, and pulled her aside so he could face Tim. "What in God's name are you thinking of? You can't transport this woman anywhere! You're apt to kill her!"

"I don't think she's exactly at death's door, Doc," Drummer said. "Hit me a lick like to break my nose." Then he laughed. Tim didn't believe he had ever heard the man laugh before.

Wendy ignored both Drummer and the doctor. "If we're going to go somewhere, Tim, we better do it before the State Police get here."

"Please." Luke looked first to Tim, then to Doc Roper. "My friends will die if we don't do something, I know they will. And there are others with them, the ones they call the gorks."

"I want to go to the hospital," Mrs. Sigsby said. "I've lost a lot of blood. And I want to see a lawyer."

"Shut your cakehole or I'll shut it for you," Annie said. She looked at Tim. "She ain't hurt as bad as she's trying to make out. Bleeding's already stopped."

Tim didn't answer immediately. He was thinking of the day, not so long ago, when he had swung into Sarasota's Westfield Mall to buy a pair of shoes, nothing more than that, and a woman had run up to him because he was in uniform. A boy was waving a gun around up by the movie theater, she said, so Tim had gone to see, and had been faced with a decision that had changed his life. A decision that had, in fact, brought him here. Now he had another decision to make.

"Bandage her up, Doc. I think Wendy and Luke and I are going to take these two for a little ride and see if we can straighten this thing out."

"Give her something for pain, too," Wendy said.

Tim shook his head. "Give it to me. I'll decide when she gets it."

Doc Roper was looking at Tim—and Wendy, her too—as if he had never seen them in his life. "This is *wrong*."

"No, Doc." It was Annie, and she spoke with surprising gentleness. She took Roper by the shoulder and pointed him past the covered bodies in the street and at the sheriff's station, with its smashed windows and doors. "*That's* wrong."

The doctor stood where he was for a moment, looking at the bodies and the shot-up station. Then he came to a decision. "Let's see what the damage is. If she's still bleeding heavily, or if her femur's shattered, I won't let you take her."

You will, though, Tim thought. Because there's no way you can stop us.

Roper knelt, opened his bag, and took out a pair of surgical scissors.

"No," Mrs. Sigsby said, pulling back from Drummer. He grabbed her again immediately, but Tim was interested to see that before he did, she was able to put her weight on her wounded leg. Roper saw it, too. He was getting on, but he still didn't miss much. "You're not going to do field surgery on me in this street!"

"The only thing I'm going to do surgery on is the

leg of your pants," Roper said. "Unless you keep struggling that is. Do that, and I can't guarantee what will happen."

"No! I forbid you to—"

Annie seized her by the neck. "Woman, I don't want to hear no more of what you forbid. Hold still, or your leg's the last thing you'll be worrying about."

"Get your hands off me!"

"Only if you'll be still. Otherwise I'm apt to wring your scrawny neck."

"Better do it," Addie Goolsby advised. "She can be crazy when she gets one of her spells."

Mrs. Sigsby stopped struggling, perhaps as much from exhaustion as the threat of strangulation. Roper scissored neatly around her slacks two inches above the wound. The pantleg collapsed around her ankle, exposing white skin, a tracery of varicose veins, and something that looked more like a knife-slash than a bullet hole.

"Well, sugar," Roper said, sounding relieved. "This isn't bad. Worse than a graze, but not much. You got lucky, ma'am. It's already clotting."

"I am badly hurt!" Mrs. Sigsby cried.

"You will be, if you don't shut up," Drummer said.

The doctor swabbed the wound with disinfectant, wrapped a bandage around it, and secured it with butterfly clips. By the time he finished, it seemed that all of DuPray—those who lived in town, at least—were spectating. Tim, meanwhile, looked at the woman's phone. A button on the side lit up the screen and a message reading POWER LEVEL 75%.

He powered it down again and handed it to Luke. "You keep this for now."

As Luke put it into the pocket containing the flash

drive, a hand tugged his pants. It was Evans. "You need to be careful, young Luke. If you don't want to have to hold yourself responsible, that is."

"Responsible for what?" Wendy asked.

"For the end of the world, miss. For the end of the world."

"Shut up, you fool," Mrs. Sigsby said.

Tim considered her for a moment. Then he turned to the doc. "I don't know exactly what we're dealing with here, but I know it's something extraordinary. We need some time with these two. When the state cops show up, tell them we'll be back in an hour. Two, at most. Then we'll try to get on with something at least approximating normal police procedure."

This was a promise he doubted he would be able to keep. He thought his time in DuPray, South Carolina, was almost certainly over, and he was sorry for that.

He thought he could have lived here. Perhaps with Wendy.

39

Gladys Hickson stood in front of Stackhouse at parade rest, her feet apart and her hands behind her back. The fake smile that every child in the Institute came to know (and hate) was nowhere in evidence.

"You understand the current situation, Gladys?"

"Yes, sir. The Back Half residents are in the access tunnel."

"Correct. They can't get out, but as of now, we can't get in. I understand that they have tried to . . . shall we say *fiddle* with some of the staff, using their psychic abilities?"

"Yes, sir. It doesn't work."

"But it's uncomfortable."

"Yes, sir, a bit. There's a kind of . . . *humming*. It's distracting. It's not here in admin, at least not yet, but everybody in Front Half feels it."

Which made sense, Stackhouse thought. Front Half was closer to the tunnel. Right on top of it, you could say.

"It seems to be getting stronger, sir."

Maybe that was just her imagination. Stackhouse could hope so, and he could hope Donkey Kong was right when he insisted that Dixon and his friends couldn't influence prepared minds, not even if the gorks were adding their undeniable force to the equation, but as his grandfather used to say, hope don't win horse races.

Perhaps made uneasy by his silence, she went on. "But we know what they're up to, sir, and it's no problem. We got em by the short and curlies."

"That's well put, Gladys. Now as to why I asked you here. I understand that you attended the University of Massachusetts in the days of your youth."

"That's correct, sir, but only for three semesters. It wasn't for me, so I left and joined the Marines."

Stackhouse nodded. No need to embarrass her by pointing out what was in her file: after doing well in her first year, Gladys had run into fairly serious trouble during her second. In a student hangout near the campus, she had knocked a rival for her boyfriend's affections unconscious with a beer stein and been asked to leave not just the joint but the college. The incident had not been her first outburst of bad temper. No wonder she'd picked the Marines.

"I understand you were a chem major."

"No, sir, not exactly. I hadn't declared a major before I . . . before I decided to leave."

"But that was your intention."

"Um, yes, sir, at that time."

"Gladys, suppose we needed—to use an unjustly vilified phrase—a final solution concerning those residents in the access tunnel. Not saying it will happen, not saying that at all, but supposing it did."

"Are you asking if they could be poisoned somehow, sir?"

"Let's say I am."

Now Gladys did smile, and this one was perfectly genuine. Perhaps even relieved. If the residents were gone, that annoying hum would cease. "Easiest thing in the world, sir, assuming the access tunnel is hooked up to the HVAC system, and I'm sure it is."

"HVAC?"

"Heating, ventilation, and air conditioning, sir. What you'd want is bleach and toilet bowl cleaner. Housekeeping will have plenty of both. Mix em up and you get chlorine gas. Put a few buckets of the stuff under the HVAC intake duct that feeds the tunnel, cover it with a tarp to get a good suck going on, and there you are." She paused, thinking. "Of course, you might want to clear out the staff in Back Half before you did it. There might be only one intake for that part of the compound. Not sure. I could look at the heating plans, if you—"

"That won't be necessary," Stackhouse said. "But perhaps you and Fred Clark from janitorial could get the . . . uh . . . proper ingredients ready. Just as a contingency, you understand."

"Yes, sir, absolutely." Gladys looked raring to go. "Can I ask where Mrs. Sigsby is? Her office is empty, and Rosalind said to ask you, if I wanted to know."

"Mrs. Sigsby's business is none of yours, Gladys." And since she seemed to be determined to remain in military mode, he added: "Dismissed."

She left to find Fred the janitor and start gathering the ingredients that would put an end to both the children and the hum that had settled over Front Half.

Stackhouse sat back in his chair, wondering if such a radical action would become necessary. He thought it might. And was it really so radical, considering what they had been doing here for the last seven decades or so? Death was inevitable in their business, after all, and sometimes a bad situation required a fresh start.

That fresh start depended on Mrs. Sigsby. Her expedition to South Carolina had been rather harebrained, but such plans were often the ones that worked. He remembered something Mike Tyson had said: once the punching starts, strategy goes out the window. His own exit strategy was ready in any case. Had been for years. Money put aside, false passports (three of them) put aside, travel plans in place, destination waiting. Yet he would hold here as long as he could, partly out of loyalty to Julia, mostly because he believed in the work they were doing. Keeping the world safe for democracy was secondary. Keeping it safe full stop was primary.

No reason to go yet, he told himself. The apple cart is tipping, but it hasn't turned over. Best to hang. See who's still standing once the punching is over.

He waited for the box phone to give out its strident *brrt-brrt*. When Julia filled him in on the outcome down there, he would decide what to do next. If the phone didn't ring at all, that would also be an answer.

40

There was a sad little abandoned beauty shop at the junction of US 17 and SR 92. Tim pulled in and walked around to the van's passenger side, where Mrs. Sigsby was sitting. He opened her door, then pulled the slider back. Luke and Wendy were on either side of Dr. Evans, who was staring morosely down at his misshapen foot. Wendy was holding Tag Faraday's Glock. Luke had Mrs. Sigsby's box phone.

"Luke, with me. Wendy, sit where you are, please."

Luke got out. Tim asked for the phone. Luke handed it over. Tim powered it up, then leaned in the passenger door. "How does this baby work?"

She said nothing, simply looked straight ahead at the boarded-up building with its faded sign reading *Hairport 2000*. Crickets chirruped, and from the direction of DuPray they could hear the sirens. Closer now, but still not in town, Tim judged. They would be soon.

He sighed. "Don't make this hard, ma'am. Luke says there's a chance we can make a deal, and he's smart."

"Too smart for his own good," she said, then pressed her lips together. Still looking through the windshield, arms crossed over her scant bosom.

"Given the position you're in, I'd have to say he's too smart for yours, as well. When I say don't make this hard, I mean don't make me hurt you. For someone who's been hurting children—"

"Hurting them and killing them," Luke put in. "Killing other people, as well."

"For someone who's been doing that, you seem remarkably averse to pain yourself. So stop the silent treatment and tell me how this works."

"It's voice activated," Luke said. "Isn't it?"

She looked at him, surprised. "You're TK, not TP. And not that strong in TK, at that."

"Things have changed," Luke said. "Thanks to the Stasi Lights. Activate the phone, Mrs. Sigsby."

"Make a deal?" she said, and barked a laugh. "What deal could possibly do me any good? I'm dead no matter what. I failed."

Tim leaned in the sliding door. "Wendy, hand me the gun."

She did so without argument.

Tim put the muzzle of Deputy Faraday's service automatic to the pantleg that was still there, just below the knee. "This is a Glock, ma'am. If I pull the trigger, you will never walk again."

"The shock and blood loss will kill her!" Dr. Evans squawked.

"Five dead back there, and she's responsible," Tim said. "Do you think I really care? I've had it with you, Mrs. Sigsby. This is your last chance. You might lose consciousness at once, but I'm betting your lights will stay on for awhile. Before they go out, the pain you feel will make that bullet-groove in your other leg feel like a kiss goodnight."

She said nothing.

Wendy said, "Don't do it, Tim. You can't, not in cold blood."

"I can." Tim wasn't sure this was the truth. What he did know for sure was that he didn't want to find out. "Help me, Mrs. Sigsby. Help yourself."

Nothing. And time was short. Annie wouldn't tell the State Police which way they went; neither would Drummer or Addie Goolsby. Doc Roper might. Norbert Hollister, who had kept prudently out of sight during the Main Street shoot-out, was an even more likely candidate.

"Okay. You're a murderous bitch, but I'm still sorry I have to do this. No three-count."

Luke put his hands over his ears to stifle the sound of the gunshot, and that was what convinced her. "Don't." She held out her hand. "Give me the phone."

"I think not."

"Then hold it up to my mouth."

Tim did so. Mrs. Sigsby muttered something, and the phone spoke. "Activation rejected. You have two more tries."

"You can do better," Tim said.

Mrs. Sigsby cleared her throat and this time spoke in a tone that was almost normal. "Sigsby One. Kansas City Chiefs."

The screen that appeared looked exactly like the one on Tim's iPhone. He pushed the phone icon, then RE-CENTS. There, at the very top of the list, was STACK-HOUSE.

He handed the phone to Luke. "You call. I want him to hear your voice. Then give it to me."

"Because you're the adult and he'll listen to you."

"I hope you're right."

41

Almost an hour after Julia's last contact—much too long—Stackhouse's box phone lit up and began to buzz. He grabbed it. "Have you got him, Julia?"

The voice that replied was so astounding that Stackhouse almost dropped the phone. "No," Luke Ellis said, "you've got it backward." Stackhouse could hear undeniable satisfaction in the little shit's voice. "We've got *her*."

"What . . . what . . ." At first he could think of nothing else to say. He didn't like that *we*. What steadied him was the thought of the three passports locked in his office safe, and the carefully thought-out exit strategy that went with them.

"Not following that?" Luke asked. "Maybe you need a dunk in the immersion tank. It does wonders for your mental abilities. I'm living proof. I bet Avery is, too."

Stackhouse felt a strong urge to end the call right there, to simply gather up his passports and get out of here, quickly and quietly. What stopped him was the fact that the kid was calling at all. That meant he had something to say. Maybe something to offer.

"Luke, where is Mrs. Sigsby?"

"Right here," Luke said. "She unlocked her phone for us. Wasn't that great of her?"

Us. Another bad pronoun. A *dangerous* pronoun.

"There's been a misunderstanding," Stackhouse said. "If there's any chance we can put this right, it's important that we do so. The stakes are higher than you know."

"Maybe we can," Luke said. "That would be good."

"Terrific! If you could just put Mrs. Sigsby on for a minute or two, so I know she's all right—"

"Why don't you talk to my friend instead? His name is Tim."

Stackhouse waited, sweat trickling down his cheeks. He was looking at his computer monitor. The kids in the tunnel who had started the revolt—Dixon and his friends—looked like they were asleep. The gorks weren't. They were walking around aimlessly, gabbling away and sometimes running into each other like bumper cars in an amusement park. One had a crayon or something, and was writing on the wall. Stackhouse was surprised. He wouldn't have thought any of them still capable of writing. Maybe it was just scribbling. The goddam camera wasn't good enough to make it out. Fucking substandard equipment.

"Mr. Stackhouse?"

"Yes. Who am I speaking to?"

"Tim. That's all you need right now."

"I want to speak to Mrs. Sigsby."

"Say something, but make it quick," said the man calling himself Tim.

"I'm here, Trevor," Julia said. "And I'm sorry. It just didn't work out."

"How—"

"Never mind how, Mr. Stackhouse," said the man calling himself Tim, "and never mind the queen bitch here. We need to make a deal, and we need to do it fast. Can you shut up and listen?"

"Yes." Stackhouse drew a notepad in front of him. Drops of sweat fell on it. He mopped his forehead with his sleeve, turned to a fresh page, and picked up a pen. "Go ahead."

"Luke brought a flash drive out of this Institute place where you were holding him. A woman named Maureen Alvorson made it. She tells a fantastic story, one that would be hard to believe, except she also took video of what you call either Ward A or Gorky Park. With me so far?"

"Yes."

"Luke says that you are holding a number of his friends hostage along with a number of children from Ward A."

Until this moment, Stackhouse hadn't thought of them as hostages, but he supposed that from Ellis's point of view . . .

"Let's say that's the case, Tim."

"Yes, let's say that. Now here comes the important part. As of now, only two people know Luke's story and what's on that flash drive. I'm one. My friend Wendy is the other, and she's with me and Luke. There were others who saw it, all cops, but thanks to the queen bitch here and the force she brought with her, they're all dead. Most of hers are dead, too."

"That's impossible!" Stackhouse shouted. The idea that a bunch of small-town cops could have taken out Opal and Ruby Red combined was ludicrous.

"Boss lady was a little too eager, my friend, and they were blindsided in the bargain. But let's stay on point, shall we? I have the flash drive. I also have your Mrs. Sigsby, and a Dr. James Evans. Both of them are wounded, but if they get out of this, they'll mend. You have the children. Can we trade?"

Stackhouse was dumbfounded.

"Stackhouse? I need an answer."

"It would depend on whether or not we can keep this facility secret," Stackhouse said. "Without that assurance, no deal makes any sense."

A pause, then Tim was back. "Luke says we might be able to work that out. For now, where am I going, Stackhouse? How did your pirate crew get here from Maine so fast?"

Stackhouse told him where the Challenger was waiting outside of Alcolu—he really had no choice. "Mrs. Sigsby can give you exact directions once you reach the town of Beaufort. Now I need to talk to Ellis again."

"Is that really necessary?"

"As a matter of fact, it's vital."

There was a brief pause, then the boy was on the secure line. "What do you want?"

"I assume you have been in touch with your friends," Stackhouse said. "Perhaps one friend in particular, Mr. Dixon. No need to confirm or deny, I understand that time is short. In case you don't know exactly where they are—"

"They're in the tunnel between Back Half and Front Half."

That was unsettling. Nevertheless, Stackhouse pressed on.

"That's right. If we can reach an agreement, they may get out and see the sun again. If we can't, I will fill that tunnel with chlorine gas, and they will die slowly and unpleasantly. I won't see it happen; I'll be gone two minutes after I give the order. I'm telling you this because I feel quite certain that your new friend Tim would like to leave you out of whatever deal we make. That cannot happen. Do you understand?"

There was a pause, then Luke said: "Yes. I understand. I'll come with him."

"Good. At least for now. Are we done?"

"Not quite. Will Mrs. Sigsby's phone work from the airplane?"

Faintly, Stackhouse heard Mrs. Sigsby say that it would.

"Stay close to your phone, Mr. Stackhouse," Luke said. "We'll need to talk again. And you need to stop thinking about running. If you do, I'll know. We have a policewoman with us, and if I tell her to contact Homeland Security, she will. Your picture will be at every airport in the country, and all the fake ID in the world won't do you any good. You'll be like a rabbit in an open field. Do you understand me?"

For the second time, Stackhouse was too dumbfounded to speak.

"Do you?"

"Yes," he said.

"Good. We'll be in touch to fine-tune the details."

With that, the boy was gone. Stackhouse set the phone down carefully on his desk. He noted that his hand was trembling slightly. Part of that was fright, but it was mostly fury. *We'll be in touch*, the boy had said, as though he were some hotshot Silicon Valley CEO and Stackhouse a paper-pushing underling who had to do his bidding.

We'll see about that, he thought. We'll just see.

42

Luke handed the box phone to Tim as if glad to be rid of it.

"How do you know he has fake ID?" Wendy asked. "Did you read it in his mind?"

"No," Luke said. "But I bet he has plenty—passports, driver's licenses, birth certificates. I bet a lot of them do. Maybe not the caretakers and techs and cafeteria staff, but the ones on top. They're like Eichmann or Walter Rauff, the guy who came up with the idea of building mobile gas chambers." Luke looked at Mrs. Sigsby. "Rauff would have fit right in with your people, wouldn't he?"

"Trevor may have false documents," Mrs. Sigsby said. "I do not."

And although Luke couldn't get into her mind—

she had closed it off to him—he thought she was telling the truth. There was a word for people like her, and the word was *zealot*. Eichmann, Mengele, and Rauff had run, like the opportunistic cowards they were; their zealot fuehrer had stayed and committed suicide. Luke felt quite sure that if given the opportunity, this woman would do the same. As long as it was relatively painless.

He climbed back into the van, being careful to avoid Evans's wounded foot. "Mr. Stackhouse thinks I'm coming to him, but that's not right."

"No?" Tim asked.

"No. I'm coming *for* him."

The Stasi Lights flared in front of Luke's eyes in the growing gloom, and the van's sliding door rolled shut on its own.

THE BIG PHONE

1

As far as Beaufort, the interior of the van was mostly silent. Dr. Evans did try to start a conversation once, again wanting them to know that he was an innocent party in all this. Tim told him he had a choice: either shut up and get a couple of the oxycodone tablets Dr. Roper had provided, or keep talking and endure the pain in his wounded foot. Evans opted for silence and the pills. There were a few more in the little brown bottle. Tim offered one to Mrs. Sigsby, who dry-swallowed it without bothering to say thank you.

Tim wanted quiet for Luke, who was now the brains of the operation. He knew most people would think him nuts for allowing a twelve-year-old to create a strategy intended to save the kids in that tunnel without getting killed themselves, but he noticed that Wendy was also keeping quiet. She and Tim knew what Luke had done to get here, they had seen him in operation since, and they understood.

What, exactly, was that understanding? Why, that aside from having a yard of guts, the kid also happened to be a genuine bottled-in-bond genius. These Institute thugs had taken him to obtain a talent that was (at least before its enhancement) little more than a parlor trick. They considered his brilliance a mere adjunct to what they were really after, making them like poachers willing to slaughter a twelve-thousand-pound elephant to get ninety pounds of ivory.

Tim doubted if Evans could appreciate the irony, but he guessed Sigsby could . . . if she ever allowed the idea mental house-room, that was: a clandestine operation that had lasted for decades brought down by the very thing they had considered dispensable—this child's formidable intellect.

2

Around nine o'clock, just after passing the Beaufort city limits, Luke told Tim to find a motel. "Don't stop in front, though. Go around to the back."

There was an Econo Lodge on Boundary Street, its rear parking lot shaded by magnolias. Tim parked by the fence and killed the engine.

"This is where you leave us, Officer Wendy," Luke said.

"Tim?" Wendy asked. "What's he talking about?"

"About you booking a room, and he's right," Tim said. "You stay, we go."

"Come back here after you get your key," Luke said. "And bring back some paper. Have you got a pen?"

"Of course, and I have my notebook." She tapped the front pocket of her uniform pants. "But—"

"I'll explain as much as I can when you get back, but what it comes down to is you're our insurance policy."

Mrs. Sigsby addressed Tim for the first time since

the abandoned beauty parlor. "What this boy has been through has made him crazy, and you'd be crazy to listen to what he says. The best thing the three of you could do is leave Dr. Evans and me here, and run."

"Which would mean leaving my friends to die," Luke said.

Mrs. Sigsby smiled. "Really, Luke, think. What have they ever done for you?"

"You wouldn't understand," Luke said. "Not in a million years."

"Go on, Wendy," Tim said. He took her hand and squeezed it. "Get a room, then come back."

She gave him a doubtful look but handed him the Glock, got out of the van, and headed for the office.

Dr. Evans said, "I want to emphasize that I was here under—"

"Protest, yes," Tim said. "We got that. Now shut up."

"Can we get out?" Luke asked. "I want to talk to you without . . ." He nodded at Mrs. Sigsby.

"Sure, we can do that." Tim opened both the passenger door and the slider, then stood against the fence dividing the motel from the closed car dealership next door. Luke joined him. From where Tim stood, he could see both of their unwilling passengers, and could stop them if either decided to try making a run. He didn't think that was very likely, considering one had been shot in the leg and the other in the foot.

"What's up?" Tim asked.

"Do you play chess?"

"I know the game, but I was never very good at it."

"I am," Luke said. He was speaking low. "And now I'm playing with him. Stackhouse. Do you get that?"

"I think I do."

"Trying to think three moves ahead, plus counters to *his* future moves."

Tim nodded.

"In chess, time isn't a factor unless you're playing speed-chess, and this game is. We have to get from here to the airfield where the plane is waiting. Then to someplace near Presque Isle, where the plane is based. From there to the Institute. I can't see us making it until at least two tomorrow morning. Does that sound right to you?"

Tim ran it in his mind, and nodded. "Might be a little later, but say two."

"That gives my friends five hours to do something on their own behalf, but it also gives Stackhouse five hours to re-think his position and change his mind. To gas those kids and just take off running. I told him his picture would be in every airport, and he'll buy that, I think, because there must be pictures of him somewhere online. A lot of the Institute people are ex-military. Probably he is, too."

"There might even be a photo of him on the queen bitch's phone," Tim said.

Luke nodded, although he doubted if Mrs. Sigsby had been the type to take snapshots. "But he might decide to slip across the Canadian border on foot. I'm sure he has at least one alternate escape route all picked out—an abandoned woods road or a creek. That's one of those possible future moves I have to keep in mind. Only . . ."

"Only what?"

Luke rubbed the heel of his hand up one cheek, a strangely adult gesture of weariness and indecision. "I need your input. What I'm thinking makes sense to me, but I'm still only a kid. I can't be sure. You're a grownup, and you're one of the good guys."

Tim was touched by that. He glanced toward the front of the building, but there was no sign of Wendy yet. "Tell me what you're thinking."

"That I fucked him up. Fucked up his whole world. I think he might stay just to kill me. Using my friends as bait to make sure I'll come. Does that make sense to you? Tell me the truth."

"It does," Tim said. "No way to be sure, but revenge is a powerful motivator, and this Stackhouse wouldn't be the first to ignore his own best interests in an effort to get it. And I can think of another reason he might decide to wait in place."

"What?" Luke was studying him anxiously. From around the building, Wendy Gullickson came with a key card in one hand.

Tim tipped his head toward the van's open passenger door, then brought his head close to Luke's. "Sigsby's the boss lady, right? Stackhouse is just her ramrod?"

"Yes."

"Well," Tim said, smiling a little, "who's *her* boss? Have you thought of that?"

Luke's eyes widened and his mouth dropped open a little. He got it. And smiled.

3

Nine-fifteen.

The Institute was quiet. The kids currently in Front Half were asleep, aided by sedatives Joe and Hadad had handed out. In the access tunnel, the five who had started the mutiny were also sleeping, but probably not deeply; Stackhouse hoped their headaches would be fucking them up most awesomely. The only kids still awake were the gorks, rambling around almost as if they had somewhere to go. Sometimes they made circles, like they were playing ring around the rosie.

Stackhouse had returned to Mrs. Sigsby's office and opened the locked bottom drawer of her desk with the duplicate key she had given him. Now he held the special box phone in his hand, the one they called the Green Phone, or sometimes the Zero Phone. He was thinking of something Julia had once said concerning that phone with its three buttons. This had been in the village one day last year, back when Heckle and Jeckle still had most of their brain cells working. The Back Half kids had just offed a Saudi bagman who was funneling money to terrorist cells in Europe, and it had totally looked like an accident. Life was good. Julia invited him to dinner to celebrate. They had split a bottle of wine before, and a second bottle during and after. It had loosened her tongue.

"I hate making update calls on the Zero Phone. That man with the lisping voice. I always imagine him as an albino. I don't know why. Maybe something I saw in a comic book when I was a girl. An albino villain with X-ray eyes."

Stackhouse had nodded his understanding. "Where is he? *Who* is he?"

"Don't know and don't want to know. I make the call, I give my report, then I take a shower. There would only be one thing worse than *calling* on the Zero Phone. That would be *getting* a call."

Stackhouse looked at the Zero Phone now with something like superstitious dread, as if just thinking of that conversation would make it ring in his—

"No," he said. To the empty room. To the silent phone. Silent for now, at least. "Nothing superstitious about it. You *will* ring. Simple logic."

Sure. Because the people on the other end of the Zero Phone—the lisping man and the greater organization of which he was a part—would find out about the spectacular balls-up in that little South Carolina town. Of course they would. It was going to be front-page news across the country and maybe the whole world. They might know already. If they knew about Hollister, the stringer who actually lived in DuPray, they might have been in touch with him for all the gory details.

Yet the Zero Phone hadn't rung. Did that mean they didn't know, or did it mean they were giving him time to put things right?

Stackhouse had told the man named Tim that any deal they made would depend on whether or not the Institute could be kept a secret. Stackhouse wasn't fool enough to believe its work could continue, at least not here in the Maine woods, but if he could somehow manage the situation without worldwide headlines about psychic children who had been abused and murdered . . . or *why* those things had taken place . . . that would be something. He might even be rewarded if he could manage a cover-up that was watertight, although just keeping his life would be reward enough.

Only three people knew, according to this Tim.

The others who had seen what was on the flash drive were dead. Some of the ill-starred Gold team might be alive, but they hadn't seen it, and they would maintain silence about everything else.

Get Luke Ellis and his collaborators here, he thought. That's step one. They might arrive as soon as 2 AM. Even one-thirty would give me enough time to plan an ambush. All I've got on hand are techs and widebodies, but some of them—Zeke the Greek, to name just one—are hard guys. Get the flash drive and get *them*. Then, when the man with the lisp calls—and he will—to ask if I am handling the situation, I can say . . .

"I can say it's already handled," Stackhouse said.

He put the Zero Phone on Mrs. Sigsby's desk and sent it a mental message: Don't ring. Don't you dare ring until three o'clock tomorrow morning. Four or five would be even better.

"Give me enough ti—"

The phone rang, and Stackhouse gave a startled yell. Then he laughed, although his heart was still beating way too fast. Not the Zero Phone but his own box phone. Which meant the call was coming from South Carolina.

"Hello? Is it Tim or Luke?"

"It's Luke. Listen to me, and I'll tell you how this is going to work."

4

Kalisha was lost in a very large house, and she had no idea how to get out, because she didn't know how she'd gotten in. She was in a hall that looked like

the residence corridor in Front Half, where she had
lived for awhile before being taken away to have her
brains plundered. Only this hall was furnished with
bureaus and mirrors and coat racks and something
that looked like an elephant foot filled with umbrel-
las. There was an endtable with a phone on it, one
that looked just like the phone in their kitchen back
home, and it was ringing. She picked it up, and since
she couldn't say what she had been taught to say
since the age of four ("Benson residence"), she just
said hello.

"Hola? Me escuchas?" It was a girl's voice, faint and
broken up by static, just barely audible.

Kalisha knew *hola* because she'd had a year of
Spanish in middle school, but her scant vocabulary
didn't include *escuchas*. Nevertheless, she knew what
the girl was saying, and realized this was a dream.

"Yes, uh-huh, I can hear you. Where are you? *Who*
are you?"

But the girl was gone.

Kalisha put the phone down and kept walking
along the hall. She peered into what looked like a
drawing room in an old-time movie, then into a ball-
room. It had a floor made of black-and-white squares
that made her think of Luke and Nick, playing chess
out in the playground.

Another phone began to ring. She hurried faster
and entered a nice modern kitchen. The fridge was
plastered with pictures and magnets and a bumper
sticker that said BERKOWITZ FOR PRESIDENT!
She didn't know Berkowitz from a hole in the wall,
yet she knew it was his kitchen. The phone was on
the wall. It was bigger than the one on the endtable,
certainly bigger than the one in the Benson kitchen,

almost like a joke phone. But it was ringing, so she picked it up.

"Hello? *Hola?* My name is—*me llamo*—Kalisha."

But it wasn't the Spanish girl. It was a boy. *"Bonjour, vous m'entendez?"* French. *Bonjour* was French. Different language, same question, and this time the connection was better. Not much, but a little.

"Yes, wee-wee, I hear you! Where are—"

But the boy was gone, and another phone was ringing. She dashed through a pantry and into a room with straw walls and a packed dirt floor mostly covered by a colorful woven mat. It had been the final stop for a fugitive African warlord named Badu Bokassa, who had been stabbed in the throat by one of his mistresses. Except he'd really been killed by a bunch of kids thousands of miles away. Dr. Hendricks had waved his magic wand—which just happened to be a cheap Fourth of July sparkler—and down Mr. Bokassa went. The phone on the mat was bigger still, almost the size of a table lamp. The receiver was heavy in her hand when she picked it up.

Another girl, and this time clear as a bell. As the phones got bigger, the voices got clearer, it seemed. *"Zdravo, cujes li me?"*

"Yes, I hear you fine, what is this place?"

The voice was gone, and another phone was ringing. It was in a bedroom with a chandelier, and this phone was the size of a footstool. She had to pick up the receiver with both hands.

"Hallo, hoor je me?"

"Yes! Sure! Absolutely! Talk to me!"

He didn't. No dial tone. Just gone.

The next phone was in a sunroom with a great glass roof, and it was as big as the table it sat on. The ringing hurt her ears. It was like listening to a phone channeled through an amplifier at a rock-and-roll gig. Kalisha ran at it, hands outstretched, palms tilted upward, and knocked the receiver off the phone's base, not because she expected enlightenment but to shut it up before it burst her eardrums.

"Ciao!" boomed a boy's voice. *"Mi senti? MI SENTI?"*

And that woke her up.

5

She was with her buds—Avery, Nicky, George, and Helen. The others were still sleeping, but not easily. George and Helen were moaning. Nicky was muttering something and holding out his hands, making her think of how she'd run at the big phone to make it stop. Avery was twisting around and gasping something that she had already heard: *Hoor je me? Hoor je me?*

They were dreaming what she had been dreaming, and considering what they were now—what the Institute had made them—the idea made perfect sense. They were generating some kind of group power, telepathy as well as telekinesis, so why wouldn't they share the same dream? The only question was which one of them had started it. She was guessing Avery, because he was the strongest.

Hive of bees, she thought. That's what we are now. Hive of psychic bees.

Kalisha got to her feet and looked around. Still trapped in the access tunnel, that hadn't changed, but she thought the level of that group power had. Maybe it was why the Ward A kids hadn't gone to sleep, although it had to be fairly late; Kalisha's time-sense had always been good, and she thought it was at least nine-thirty, maybe a bit later.

The hum was louder than ever, and had picked up a kind of cycling beat: *mmm-MMM-mmm-MMM*. She saw with interest (but no real surprise) that the overhead fluorescents were cycling with the hum, going bright, fading a little, then going bright again.

TK you can actually see, she thought. *For all the good it does us.*

Pete Littlejohn, the boy who had been beating on his head and going ya-*ya*-ya-*ya*, came loping toward her. In Front Half, Pete had been kind of cute and kind of annoying, like a little brother that tags after you everywhere and tries to listen in while you and your girlfriends are telling secrets. Now he was hard to look at with his wet, drooping mouth and empty eyes.

"Me escuchas?" he said. *"Hörst du mich?"*

"You dreamed it, too," Kalisha said.

Pete paid no attention, just turned back toward his wandering mates, now saying something that sounded like *styzez minny*. God only knew what the language was, but Kalisha was sure it meant the same as all the others.

"I hear you," Kalisha told no one. "But what do you want?"

About halfway down the tunnel toward the locked door into Back Half, something had been written on the wall in crayon. Kalisha walked down to look at it, dodging past several wandering Ward A kids to get there. Written in big purple letters was CALL THE BIG FONE. ANSER THE BIG FONE. So the gorks *were* dreaming it, too, only while awake. With their brains mostly wiped, maybe they were dreaming all the time. What a horrible idea, to dream and dream and dream and never be able to find the real world.

"You too, huh?"

It was Nick, eyes puffy with sleep, hair standing up in stalks and spears. It was sort of endearing. She raised her eyebrows.

"The dream. Big house, increasingly big phones? Sort of like in *The 500 Hats of Bartholomew Cubbins*?"

"Bartholomew who?"

"A Dr. Seuss book. Bartholomew kept trying to take off his hat for the king, and every time he took one off, there was a bigger and fancier one underneath."

"Never read it, but the dream, yeah. I think it came from Avery." She pointed to the boy, who was still sleeping the sleep of the totally exhausted. "Or started with him, at least."

"I don't know if he started it, or if he's receiving it and amplifying it and passing it on. Not sure it matters." Nick studied the message on the wall, then looked around. "The gorks are restless tonight."

Kalisha frowned at him. "Don't call them that. It's a slave word. Like calling me a nigger."

"Okay," Nick said, "the mentally challenged are restless tonight. That better?"

"Yes." She allowed him a smile.

"How's your head, Sha?"

"Better. Fine, in fact. Yours?"

"The same."

"Mine, too," George said, joining them. "Thanks for asking. You guys have the dream? Bigger phones and *Hello, do you hear me*?"

"Yeah," Nick said.

"That last phone, the one just before I woke up, was

bigger than me. And the hum's stronger." Then, in the same casual tone: "How long do you think before they decide to gas us? I'm surprised they haven't done it already."

6

Nine forty-five, in the parking lot of the Econo Lodge in Beaufort, South Carolina.

"I'm listening," Stackhouse said. "If you let me help you, maybe we can work this out together. Let's discuss it."

"Let's not," Luke said. "All you have to do is listen. And make notes, because I don't want to have to repeat myself."

"Is your friend Tim still with y—"

"Do you want the flash drive or not? If you don't, keep talking. If you do, *shut the fuck up.*"

Tim put a hand on Luke's shoulder. In the front seat of the van, Mrs. Sigsby was shaking her head sadly. Luke didn't have to read her mind to know what she was thinking: a boy trying to do a man's work.

Stackhouse sighed. "Go ahead. Pen and paper at the ready."

"First. Officer Wendy doesn't have the flash drive, that comes with us, but she knows the names of my friends—Kalisha, Avery, Nicky, Helen, a couple more—and where they came from. If their parents are dead, like mine, that will be enough to support an investigation, even without the flash drive. She'll never have to say a word about psychic kids or the rest of your murderous bullshit. They'll find the Institute. Even if you got away, Stackhouse, your bosses would hunt you down. We're your best chance of living through this. Got it?"

"Spare me the sell-job. What's this Officer Wendy's last name?"

Tim, who was leaning close enough to hear both sides of the conversation, shook his head. This was advice Luke didn't need.

"Never mind. Second. Call the plane your posse came down in. Tell the pilots they are to lock themselves in the cockpit as soon as they see us coming."

Tim whispered two words. Luke nodded.

"But before they do that, tell them to lower the air-stairs."

"How will they know it's you?"

"Because we'll be in one of the vans your hired killers came in." Luke was pleased to give Stackhouse this information, hoping it rammed home the point: Mrs. Sigsby had swung and missed.

"We don't see the pilot and co-pilot and they don't see us. We land where the plane took off, and they stay inside the cockpit. With me so far?"

"Yes."

"Third. I want a van waiting for us, a nine-seater, just like the one we drove out of DuPray."

"We don't—"

"Bullshit you don't, you've got a motor pool in that little barracks town of yours. I saw it. Now are you going to work with me on this, or should I just give up on you?"

Luke was sweating heavily, and not just because the night was humid. He was very glad for Tim's hand on his shoulder, and Wendy's concerned eyes. It was good not to be alone in this anymore. He really hadn't realized how heavy that burden was until now.

Stackhouse gave the sigh of a man being unfairly burdened. "Go on."

"Fourth. You're going to procure a bus."

"A *bus*? Are you *serious*?"

Luke decided to ignore this interruption, feeling that it was warranted. Certainly Tim and Wendy looked amazed.

"I'm sure you have friends everywhere, and that includes at least some of the police in Dennison River Bend. Maybe all of them. It's summer, so the kids are on vacation, and the buses will be in the town's municipal lot, along with the plows and dump trucks and all the other stuff. Have one of your cop friends unlock the building where they keep the keys. Have him put the key in the ignition of a bus that seats at least forty. One of your techs or caretakers can drive it to the Institute. Leave it by the flagpole in front of the admin building with the keys in it. Do you understand all that?"

"Yes." Businesslike. No protests or interruptions now, and Luke didn't need Tim's adult grasp of psychology and motivation to understand why. This, Stackhouse must be thinking, was a child's harebrained plan, only half a step removed from wishful thinking. He could see the same thing on Tim's face, and on Wendy's. Mrs. Sigsby was in earshot, and she looked like she was having trouble keeping a straight face.

"It's a simple exchange. You get the flash drive, I get the kids. The ones from Back Half, and the ones in Front Half, too. You have them all ready for their field trip by 2 AM tomorrow morning. Officer Wendy keeps her mouth shut. That's the deal. Oh, you also get your piece-of-shit boss and your piece-of-shit doctor."

"Can I ask a question, Luke? Is that permissible?"

"Go ahead."

"Once you have somewhere between thirty-five and forty children crammed into a big yellow school bus with DENNISON RIVER BEND on the side, where do you plan to take them? Always remembering that the majority have no minds left?"

"Disneyland," Luke said.

Tim put a hand to his brow, as if he had developed a sudden headache.

"We'll be staying in touch with Officer Wendy. Before we take off. After we land. When we get to the Institute. When we leave the Institute. If she doesn't get a call, she'll start making calls of her own, starting with the Maine State Police, then moving on to the FBI and Homeland Security. Got it?"

"Yes."

"Good. Last thing. When we get there, I want *you* there. Arms outstretched. One hand on the hood of the bus, one hand on the flagpole. As soon as the kids are on the bus and my friend Tim is behind the wheel, I hand you Maureen's flash drive and get aboard myself. Clear on that?"

"Yes."

Crisp. Trying not to sound like a man who's won the big jackpot.

He understands that Wendy might be a problem, Luke thought, because she knows the names of a bunch of missing kids, but that's a problem he thinks he can solve. The flash drive's a bigger deal, harder to dismiss as fake news. I'm offering it to him pretty much on a silver platter. How can he refuse? Answer: he can't.

"Luke—" Tim began.

Luke shook his head: not now, not while I'm thinking.

He knows his situation is still bad, but now he sees a ray of light. Thank God Tim reminded me of what I should have thought of myself: it doesn't end with Sigsby and Stackhouse. They have to have their own bosses, people they answer to. When the shit hits the fan, Stackhouse can tell them it could have been much worse; in fact they should be thanking him for saving the day.

"Will you be calling me before you take off?" Stackhouse asked.

"No. I trust you to make all the arrangements." Although trust wasn't the first word that came to mind when Luke thought of Stackhouse. "The next time we talk will be face-to-face, at the Institute. Van at the airport. Bus waiting by the flagpole. Fuck up at any point and Officer Wendy starts making her calls and telling her tale. Goodbye."

He ended the call and sagged.

7

Tim handed Wendy the Glock and gestured at their two prisoners. She nodded. Once she was standing guard, Tim drew the boy aside. They stood by the fence, in a blot of shadow cast by one of the magnolias.

"Luke, it will never work. If we go there, the van may be waiting at the airport, but if this Institute is what you say it is, the two of us will be ambushed and killed when we get there. Your friends and the other kids, as well. That leaves Wendy, and she'll do her best, but it will be days before anyone shows up there—I know how law enforcement works when something comes up outside of normal protocol. If they find the place, it will be empty except for the bodies. They may be gone, too. You say they have a disposal system for the . . ." Tim didn't know exactly how to put it. "For the used kids."

"I know all that," Luke said. "It's not about us, it's about *them*. The kids. All I'm buying is time. Something's happening there. And not just there."

"I don't understand."

"I'm stronger now," Luke said, "and we're over a thousand miles from the Institute. I'm a part of the Institute kids, but it's not just them anymore. If it was, I never could have pushed up that guy's gun with my mind. Empty pizza pans were the best I could do, remember?"

"Luke, I just don't—"

Luke concentrated. For a moment he had an image of the telephone in their front hall ringing, and knew if it was answered, someone would ask, "Do you hear me?" Then that image was replaced by the colored dots and a faint humming sound. The dots were dim rather than bright, which was good. He wanted to show Tim, but not hurt him . . . and hurting him would be so easy.

Tim stumbled forward into the chainlink fence, as if pushed by invisible hands, and got his forearms up just in time to keep from dashing his face.

"Tim?" Wendy called.

"I'm okay," Tim said. "Keep your eyes on them, Wendy." He looked at Luke. "You did that?"

"It didn't come *from* me, it came *through* me," Luke said. Because they had time now (a little at least), and because he was curious, he asked, "What was it like?"

"A strong gust of wind."

"Sure it was strong," Luke said. "Because we're stronger together. That's what Avery says."

"He's the little kid."

"Yes. He was the strongest one they've had in a long time. Maybe years. I don't know exactly what happened, but I'm thinking they must have put him in the immersion tank—given that near-death experience that enhances the Stasi Lights, only with none of the limiting injections."

"I'm not following you."

Luke didn't seem to hear him. "It was punishment, I bet, for helping me get away." He tilted his head toward the van. "Mrs. Sigsby might know. It might even have been her idea. Anyway, it backfired. It must have, because they mutinied. The Ward A kids have got the real power. Avery unlocked it."

"But not enough power to get them out of where they're trapped."

"Not *yet*," Luke said. "But I think they will."

"Why? How?"

"You got me thinking when you said Mrs. Sigsby and Stackhouse must have their own bosses. I should have figured that out for myself, but I never looked that far. Probably because parents and teachers are the only bosses kids have. If there are more bosses, why wouldn't there be more Institutes?"

A car came into the lot, passed them, and disappeared in a wink of red taillights. When it was gone, Luke continued.

"Maybe the one in Maine is the only one in America, or maybe there's one on the West Coast. You know, like bookends. But there might be one in the

UK . . . and in Russia . . . India . . . China . . . Germany . . . Korea. It stands to reason, when you think of it."

"A mind race instead of an arms race," Tim said. "That's what you're saying?"

"I don't think it's a race. I think all the Institutes are working together. I don't know that for sure, but it feels right. A common goal. A good one, sort of— killing a few kids to keep the whole human race from killing itself. A trade-off. God knows how long it's been going on, but there's never been a mutiny until now. Avery and my other friends started it, but it could spread. It might be spreading already."

Tim Jamieson was no historian or social scientist, but he kept up with current events, and he thought Luke could be right. Mutiny—or revolution, to use a less pejorative term—was like a virus, especially in the Information Age. It *could* spread.

"The power each of us has—the reason they kidnapped us and brought us to the Institute in the first place—is just little. The power of all of us together is stronger. Especially the Ward A kids. With their minds gone, the power is all that's left. But if there are more Institutes, if they know what's happening at ours, and if they were all to band together . . ."

Luke shook his head. He was thinking again of the phone in their front hall, only grown to enormous size.

"If that happened, it would be big, and I mean really big. That's why we need time. If Stackhouse thinks I'm an idiot so eager to save my friends I'd make an idiotic deal, that's good."

Tim could still feel that phantom gust of wind that

had shoved him into the fence. "We're not exactly going there to save them, are we?"

Luke regarded him soberly. With his dirty bruised face and bandaged ear, he looked like the most harmless of children. Then he smiled, and for a moment didn't look harmless at all.

"No. We're going to pick up the pieces."

8

Kalisha Benson, Avery Dixon, George Iles, Nicholas Wilholm, Helen Simms.

Five kids sitting at the end of the access tunnel, next to the locked door giving (not that it *would* give) on Front Half's F-Level. Katie Givens and Hal Leonard had been with them for awhile, but now they had joined the Ward A kids, walking with them when they walked, joining hands when they decided to make one of those rings. So had Len, and Kalisha's hopes for Iris were fading, although so far Iris was just looking on as the Ward A kids circled, broke apart, then circled again. Helen had come back, was fully with them. Iris might be too far gone. The same with Jimmy Cullum and Donna Gibson, whom Kalisha had known in Front Half—thanks to her chicken pox, she had been around much longer than the usual residents there. The Ward A kids made her sad, but Iris was worse. The possibility that she might be fucked up beyond repair . . . that idea was . . .

"Horrible," Nicky said.

She looked at him half-scoldingly. "Are you in my head?"

"Yeah, but not looking through your mental underwear drawer," Nicky said, and Kalisha snorted.

"We're all in each other's heads now," George said. He cocked a thumb at Helen. "Do you really think I wanted to know she laughed so hard at some friend's pajama party that she peed herself? That's an authentic case of TMI."

"Better than finding out you worry about psoriasis on your—" Helen began, but Kalisha told her to hush.

"What time is it, do you think?" George asked.

Kalisha consulted her bare wrist. "Skin o'clock."

"Feels like eleven to me," Nicky said.

"You know something funny?" Helen said. "I always hated the hum. I knew it was stripping my brains."

"We all knew," George said.

"Now I sort of like it."

"Because it's power," Nicky said. "*Their* power, until we took it back."

"A carrier wave," George said. "And now it's constant. Just waiting for a broadcast."

Hello, do you hear me? Kalisha thought, and the shiver that shook her was not entirely unpleasant.

Several of the Ward As linked hands. Iris and Len joined them. The hum cycled up. So did the pulse in the overhead fluorescents. Then they let go and the hum dropped back to its previous low level.

"He's in the air," Kalisha said. None of them needed to ask who she meant.

"I'd love to fly again," Helen said wistfully. "I would *love* that."

"Will they wait for him, Sha?" Nicky asked. "Or just turn on the gas? What's your thinking?"

"Who made me Professor Xavier?" She threw an elbow into Avery's side . . . but gently. "Wake up, Avester. Smell the coffee."

"I'm awake," Avery said. Not quite truthfully; he had still been drowsing, enjoying the hum. Thinking of telephones that got bigger, the way Bartholomew Cubbins's hats had grown bigger and fancier. "They'll wait. They have to, because if anything happens to us, Luke would know. And *we'll* wait until he gets here."

"And when he does?" Kalisha asked.

"We use the phone," Avery said. "The big phone. All of us together."

"How big is it?" George sounded uneasy. "Because the last one I saw was very fuckin large. Almost as big as me."

Avery only shook his head. His eyelids drooped. At bottom he was still a little kid, and up long past his bedtime.

The Ward A kids—it was hard not to think of them as the gorks, even for Kalisha—were still holding hands. The overheads brightened; one of the tubes actually shorted out. The hum deepened and strengthened. They felt it in Front Half, Kalisha was sure of that—Joe and Hadad, Chad and Dave, Priscilla and that mean one, Zeke. The rest of them, too. Were they frightened by it? Maybe a little, but—

But they believe we're trapped, she thought. They believe they're still safe. They believe the revolt has been contained. Let them go on believing that.

Somewhere there was a big phone—the *biggest* phone, one with extensions in many rooms. If they called on that phone (*when* they called on it, because there was no other choice), the power in this tunnel where they were trapped would go beyond any bomb ever exploded on the earth or below it. That hum, now just a carrier wave, might grow to a vibration that could topple buildings, maybe destroy whole cities. She didn't know that for sure, but thought it might be true. How many kids, their heads now empty of everything but the powers for which they had been taken, were waiting for a call on the big phone? A hundred? Five hundred? Maybe even more, if there were Institutes all over the world.

"Nicky?"

"What?" He had also been drowsing, and he sounded irritated.

"Maybe we can turn it on," she said, and there was no need to be specific about what *it* was. "But if we do . . . can we turn it off again?"

He considered this, then smiled. "I don't know. But after what they did to us . . . frankly, my dear, I don't give a damn."

9

Quarter past eleven.

Stackhouse was back in Mrs. Sigsby's office, with the Zero Phone—still silent—on the desk. Forty-five minutes from now, the last day of the Institute's normal operation would be over. Tomorrow this place would be abandoned, no matter how the business with Luke Ellis turned out. Containment of the program as a whole was possible in spite of the Wendy person Luke and his friend Tim were leaving down south, but this facility was blown. The important things tonight were obtaining the flash drive and making sure Luke Ellis was dead.

Rescuing Mrs. Sigsby would be nice, but it was strictly optional.

In point of fact, the Institute was being abandoned already. From where he sat, he had an angle on the road that led away from the Institute, first to Dennison River Bend, then to the rest of the lower forty-eight . . . not to mention Canada and Mexico, for those with passports. Stackhouse had called in Zeke, Chad, Chef Doug (twenty years with Halliburton), and Dr. Felicia Richardson, who had come to them from the Hawk Security Group. They were people he trusted.

As for the others . . . he had seen their departing headlights flickering through the trees. He guessed only a dozen so far, but there would be more. Soon Front Half would be deserted except for the children currently in residence there. Maybe it was already. But Zeke, Chad, Doug, and Dr. Richardson would stick; they were loyalists. And Gladys Hickson. She would stick as well, maybe after all the others were gone. Gladys wasn't just a scrapper; Stackhouse was becoming more and more certain that she was an out-and-out psycho.

I'm psycho myself for staying, Stackhouse thought. But the brat's right—they'd hunt me down. And he's walking right into it. Unless . . .

"Unless he's playing me," Stackhouse murmured.

Rosalind, Mrs. Sigsby's assistant, stuck her head in. Her usually perfect makeup had eroded over the course of the last difficult twelve hours, and her usually perfect graying hair was sticking up on the sides.

"Mr. Stackhouse?"

"Yes, Rosalind."

Rosalind looked troubled. "I believe Dr. Hendricks may have left. I believe I saw his car about ten minutes ago."

"I'm not surprised. You should go yourself, Rosalind. Head home." He smiled. It felt strange to be smiling on a night like this, but it was a good strange. "I just realized that I've known you since I came here— many moons—and I don't know where home is for you."

"Missoula," Rosalind said. She looked surprised herself. "That's in Montana. At least I suppose it's still home. I own a house in Mizzou, but I haven't been there in I guess five years. I just pay the taxes when they come due. When I have time off, I stay in the village. For vacation, I go down to Boston. I like the Red Sox and the Bruins, and the art cinema in Cambridge. But I'm always ready to come back."

Stackhouse realized it was the most Rosalind had said to him in those many moons, which stretched back over fifteen years. She had been here, Mrs. Sigsby's faithful dogsbody, when Stackhouse had retired from his service as an investigator for the US Army (JAG), and here she still was, and looking about the same. She could have been sixty-five, or a well-preserved seventy.

"Sir, do you hear that humming noise?"

"I do."

"Is it a transformer or something? I never heard it before."

"A transformer. Yes, I suppose you could call it that."

"It's very annoying." She rubbed at her ears, further disarranging her hair. "I suppose the children are doing it. Is Julia—Mrs. Sigsby—coming back? She is, isn't she?"

Stackhouse realized (with amusement rather than irritation) that Rosalind, always so proper and so unobtrusive, had been keeping her ears peeled, hum or no hum.

"I expect so, yes."

"Then I'd like to stay. I can shoot, you know. I go to the range in the Bend once a month, sometimes twice. I have the shooting club equivalent of a DM badge, and I won the small handgun competition last year."

Julia's quiet assistant not only took excellent shorthand, she had a Distinguished Marksman badge . . . or, as she said, the equivalent of. Wonders never ceased.

"What do you shoot, Rosalind?"

"Smith & Wesson M&P .45."

"Recoil doesn't bother you?"

"With the help of a wrist support, I manage the recoil very well. Sir, if it's your intention to free Mrs. Sigsby from the kidnappers holding her, I would much desire to be a part of that operation."

"All right," Stackhouse said, "you're in. I can use all the help I can get." But he would have to be careful how he used her, because saving Julia might not be possible. She had become expendable now. The important thing was the flash drive. And that fucking too-smart-for-his-own-good boy.

"Thank you, sir. I won't let you down."

"I'm sure you won't, Rosalind. I'll tell you how I expect this will play out, but first I have a question."

"Yes?"

"I know a gentleman is never supposed to ask, and a lady is never supposed to tell, but how old are you?"

"Seventy-eight, sir." She answered promptly enough, and while maintaining eye contact, but this was a lie. Rosalind Dawson was actually eighty-one.

10

Quarter of twelve.

The Challenger aircraft with 940NF on the tail and MAINE PAPER INDUSTRIES on the side droned north toward Maine at 39,000 feet. With a helping push from the jet stream, its speed was fluctuating gently between 520 and 550 miles an hour.

Their arrival at Alcolu and subsequent takeoff had gone without incident, mostly because Mrs. Sigsby had a VIP entry pass from the Regal Air FBO, and she had been more than willing to use it to open the gate. She smelled a chance—still slim, but there—of getting out of this alive. The Challenger stood in solitary splendor with its air-stairs down. Tim had raised the stairs himself, secured the door, and then hammered on the closed cockpit door with the butt of the dead deputy's Glock.

"I think we're all tight back here. If you've got a green board, let's roll."

There was no answer from the other side of the door, but the engines began to cycle up. Two minutes later they went airborne. Now they were somewhere over West Virginia, according to the monitor on the bulkhead, and DuPray was in the rearview. Tim hadn't expected to leave so suddenly, and certainly not under such cataclysmic circumstances.

Evans was dozing, and Luke was dead to the world. Only Mrs. Sigsby was still awake, sitting upright, her gaze fixed on Tim's face. There was something reptilian about those wide expressionless eyes. The last of Doc Roper's pain pills might have put her out, but she had refused in spite of what must have been fairly bad pain. She had been spared a serious gunshot wound, but even a groove hurt plenty.

"You have law enforcement experience, I believe," she said. "It's in the way you carry yourself, and in the way you reacted—quickly and well."

Tim said nothing, only looked at her. He had put the Glock beside him on the seat. Firing a gun at 39,000 feet would be a very bad idea, and really, why would he, even if they'd been at a much lower altitude? He was taking this bitch exactly where she wanted to go.

"I don't understand why you're going along with this plan." She nodded at Luke, who—with his dirty face and bandaged ear—looked much younger than twelve. "We both know he wants to save his friends, and I think we both know the plan is silly. Idiotic, really. Yet you agreed. Why was that, Tim?"

Tim said nothing.

"Why you'd get involved in the first place is a mystery to me. Help me understand."

He had no intention of doing that. One of the first things his mentor officer had taught him during the four months of his rookie probationary tour was you question perps. You never allow perps to question you.

Even if he had been disposed to talk, he didn't know what he could say that would sound even marginally sane. Could he tell her that his presence on this state-of-the-art airplane, the sort of craft only rich men and women usually saw the inside of, was an accident? That once upon a time a man bound for New York City had suddenly stood up on a much more ordinary plane, agreeing to give up his seat for a cash payment and a hotel voucher? That everything—the hitchhike north, the traffic tie-up on I-95, the walk to DuPray, the night knocker job—had followed from that single impulsive act? Or could he say that it was fate? That he had been moved to DuPray by the hand of some cosmic chess player, to save the sleeping boy from the people who had kidnapped him and wanted to use his extraordinary mind until it was used up? And if that were the case, what did it make Sheriff John, Tag Faraday, George Burkett, Frank Potter, and Bill Wicklow? Just pawns to be sacrificed in the great game? And what piece was he? It would be nice to believe himself a knight, but more likely, he was just another pawn.

"Sure you don't want that pill?" he asked.

"You don't intend to answer my question, do you?"

"No, ma'am, I do not." Tim turned his head and looked out at the leagues of darkness and the few lights down there, like fireflies at the bottom of a well.

11

Midnight.

The box phone gave its hoarse cry. Stackhouse answered. The voice on the other end belonged to one of the off-duty caretakers, a man named Ron Church. The requested van was in place at the airport, Church said. Denise Allgood, an off-duty tech (although they were all supposedly on duty now), had driven behind

Church in an Institute sedan. The idea was that, after leaving the vehicle on the tarmac, Ron would ride back here with Denise. But those two had a thing going on, which Stackhouse knew about. It was his business to know things, after all. He felt sure that with the boy's ride in place, Ron and Denise would be heading for anywhere that *wasn't* here. That was okay. Although the multiple desertions were sad, maybe they were for the best. It was time to draw a line under this operation. Enough of his people would stay for the final act, which was all that mattered.

Luke and his friend Tim were going down, there was no question in his mind about that. Either it would be good enough for the lisping man on the other end of the Zero Phone or it wouldn't. That was out of Stackhouse's hands, and it was a relief. He supposed he had carried this streak of fatalism like a dormant virus since his days in Iraq and Afghanistan, and just hadn't recognized it for what it was until now. He would do what he could, which was all any man or woman could do. The dogs barked and the caravan moved on.

There was a tap at the door and Rosalind looked in. She had done something with her hair, which was an improvement. He was less sure about the shoulder holster she was now wearing. It was a bit surreal, like a dog wearing a party hat.

"Gladys is here, Mr. Stackhouse."

"Send her in."

Gladys entered. There was an air mask dangling below her chin. Her eyes were red. Stackhouse doubted if she had been crying, so the irritation was probably from whatever bad medicine she'd been mixing up. "It's ready. All I need to do is add the toilet bowl cleaner. You say the word, Mr. Stackhouse, and we'll gas them." She gave her head a quick, hard shake. "That hum is driving me crazy."

From the look of you, you don't have far to go, Stackhouse thought, but she was right about the hum. The thing was, you couldn't get used to it. Just when you thought you might, it would rise in volume—not in your ears, exactly, but inside your head. Then, all at once, it would drop back to its former and slightly more bearable level.

"I was talking to Felicia," Gladys said. "Dr. Richardson, I mean. She's been watching them on her monitor. She says the hum gets stronger when they link up and drops when they let go of each other."

Stackhouse had already figured that out for himself. You didn't have to be a rocket scientist, as the saying went.

"Will it be soon, sir?"

He looked at his watch. "I think about three hours, give or take. The HVAC units are on the roof, correct?"

"Yes."

"I may be able to call you when it's time, Gladys, but I may not. Things will probably happen fast. If you hear shooting from the front of the admin building, start the chlorine gas whether you hear from me or not. Then come. Don't go back inside, just run along the roof to the East Wing of Front Half. Understand?"

"Yes, sir!" She gave him a brilliant smile. It was the one all the kids hated.

12

Twelve-thirty.

Kalisha was watching the Ward A kids and thinking about the Ohio State Marching Band. Her dad loved Buckeyes football, and she had always watched with him—for the closeness—but the only part she really cared about was halftime show, when the band (*"The Priiide of the Buckeyes!"* the announcer always proclaimed) would take the field, simultaneously playing their instruments and making shapes that were only discernible from above—everything from the S on Superman's chest to a fantastic *Jurassic Park* dinosaur that walked around nodding its saurian head.

The Ward A kids had no musical instruments, and all they made when they joined hands was the same circle—irregular, because the access tunnel was narrow—but they had the same . . . there was a word for it . . .

"Synchronicity," Nicky said.

She looked around, startled. He smiled at her, brushing his hair back to give her a better look at eyes that were, let's face it, sort of fascinating.

"That's a big word even for a white boy."

"I got it from Luke."

"You hear him? You're in touch with him?"

"Sort of. Off and on. It's hard to tell what's my thinking and what's his. It helped that I was asleep. Awake, my thoughts get in the way."

"Like interference?"

He shrugged. "I guess. But if you open your mind, I'm pretty sure you can hear him, too. He comes through even clearer when they make one of their circles." He nodded to the Ward A kids, who had resumed their aimless wandering. Jimmy and Donna were walking together, swinging their linked hands. "Want to try?"

Kalisha tried to stop thinking. It was surprisingly hard at first, but when she listened to the hum, it got easier. The hum was sort of like mouthwash, only for the brain.

"What's funny, K?"

"Nothing."

"Oh, I get it," Nicky said. "Mindwash instead of mouthwash. I like that."

"I'm getting something, but not much. He might be sleeping."

"Probably is. But he'll wake up soon, I think. Because we're awake."

"Synchronicity," she said. "That's some badass word. And it sounds just like him. You know the tokens they used to give us for the machines? Luke called them *emoluments*. That's another badass word."

"Luke's special because he's so smart." Nicky looked at Avery, who was leaning against Helen, both of them dead asleep. "And the Avester's special just because . . . well . . ."

"Just because he's Avery."

"Yeah." Nicky grinned. "And those idiots went and souped him up without putting a governor on his engine." His smile was, let's face it, as fascinating as his eyes. "It's the two of them together that put us where we are, you know. Luke's chocolate, Avery's peanut butter. Either of them alone, nothing would have changed. Together they're the Reese's Peanut Butter Cup that's going to rip this joint."

She laughed. It was a stupid way to put it, but also pretty accurate. At least she hoped so. "We're still stuck, though. Like rats in a plugged pipe."

His blue eyes on her brown ones. "We won't be for much longer, you know that."

She said, "We're going to die, aren't we? If they don't gas us, then . . ." She tilted her head toward the Ward A kids, who were circling again. The hum strengthened. The overhead lights brightened. "It'll happen when they cut loose. And the others, wherever they are."

The phone, she thought at him. *The big phone.*

"Probably," Nicky said. "Luke says we're going to bring them down like Samson brought the temple down on the Philistines. I don't know the story—nobody in my family bothered with the Bible—but I get the idea."

Kalisha *did* know the story, and shivered. She looked again at Avery, and thought of something else from the Bible: *a little child shall lead them.*

"Can I tell you something?" Kalisha said. "You'll probably laugh, but I don't care."

"Go for it."

"I'd like you to kiss me."

"Not exactly a tough assignment," Nicky said. He smiled.

She leaned toward him. He leaned to meet her. They kissed in the hum.

This is nice, Kalisha thought. I thought it would be, and it is.

Nicky's thought came at once, riding the hum: *Let's go for two. See if it's twice as nice.*

13

One-fifty.

The Challenger touched down on the runway of a private airstrip owned by a shell company called Maine

Paper Industries. It taxied to a small darkened building. As it approached, a trio of motion-activated lights on the roof triggered, illuminating a boxy ground power unit and a hydraulic container-loader. The waiting vehicle wasn't a mom van but a nine-passenger Chevrolet Suburban. It was black with tinted windows. Orphan Annie would have loved it.

The Challenger pulled up close to the Suburban and its engines died. For a moment Tim wasn't entirely sure that they had, because he could hear a faint hum.

"That's not the plane," Luke said. "It's the kids. It'll get stronger when we're closer."

Tim went to the front of the cabin, threw the big red lever that opened the door, and unfolded the stairs. They came down on the tarmac less than four feet from the Suburban's driver's side.

"Okay," he said, returning to the others. "Here we are. But before we go, Mrs. Sigsby, I have something for you."

On the table in the Challenger's conversation area he had found a goodly supply of glossy brochures advertising the various wonders of the totally bogus Maine Paper Industries, and half a dozen Maine Paper Industries gimme caps. He handed one to her and took another for himself.

"Put this on. Jam it down. Your hair's short, shouldn't be a problem getting it all underneath."

Mrs. Sigsby looked at the cap with distaste. "Why?"

"You're going first. If there are people waiting to ambush us, I'd like you to draw their fire."

"Why would they put people *here* when we're going *there*?"

"I admit it seems unlikely, so you won't mind

going first." Tim put on his own gimme cap, only backward, with the adjustable band cutting across his forehead. Luke thought he was too old to wear a hat that way—it was a kid thing—but kept his mouth shut. He thought maybe it was Tim's way of psyching himself up. "Evans, you're right behind her."

"No," Evans said. "I'm not leaving this plane. I'm not sure I could if I wanted to. My foot is too painful. I can't put any weight on it."

Tim considered, then looked at Luke. "What do you think?"

"He's telling the truth," Luke said. "He'd have to hop down the stairs, and they're steep. He might fall."

"I shouldn't have been here in the first place," Dr. Evans said. A fat tear squeezed from one of his eyes. "I'm a medical man!"

"You're a medical monster," Luke said. "You watched kids almost drown—they thought they *were* drowning—and you took notes. There were kids who died because they had a fatal reaction to the shots you and Hendricks gave them. And those who lived really aren't living at all, are they? Tell you what, I'd like to step on your foot. Grind my heel right into it."

"No!" Evans squealed. He shrank back in his seat and dragged his swollen foot behind the good one.

"Luke," Tim said.

"Don't worry," Luke said. "I want to but I won't. Doing that would make me like him." He looked at Mrs. Sigsby. *"You* don't get any choice. Get up and go down those stairs."

Mrs. Sigsby tugged on the Paper Industries cap and rose from her seat with such dignity as she could manage. Luke started to fall in behind her, but Tim held him back. "You're behind me. Because you're the important one."

Luke didn't argue.

Mrs. Sigsby stood at the stop of the air-stairs and raised her hands over her head. *"It's Mrs. Sigsby! If anyone is out there, hold your fire!"*

Luke caught Tim's thought clearly: *Not as sure as she claimed*.

There was no response; no outside sound but the crickets, no inside sound except the faint hum. Mrs. Sigsby made her way slowly down the stairs, holding onto the railing and favoring her bad leg.

Tim knocked on the cockpit door with the butt of the Glock. "Thank you, gentlemen. It was a good flight. You have one passenger still onboard. Take him wherever you want."

"Take him to hell," Luke said. "Single fare, no return."

Tim started down the steps, bracing for a possible gunshot—he hadn't anticipated her calling out and identifying herself. He should have, of course. In the event, no gunshot came.

"Front passenger seat," Tim said to Mrs. Sigsby. "Luke, you get in behind her. I'll have the gun, but you're my backup. If she tries to make a move on me, use some of your mental juju. Got it?"

"Yes," Luke said, and got in back.

Mrs. Sigsby sat down and fastened her seatbelt. When she reached to close the door, Tim shook his head. "Not yet." He stood with one hand on the open door and called Wendy, safe in her room at the Beaufort Econo Lodge.

"The Eagle has landed."

"Are you all right?" The connection was good; she

could have been standing next to him. He wished she was, then remembered where they were going.

"Fine so far. Stand by. I'll call you when it's over."

If I can, he thought.

Tim walked around to the driver's side and got in. The key was in the cup holder. He nodded to Mrs. Sigsby. "*Now* you can close the door."

She did, looked at him disdainfully, and said what Luke had been thinking. "You look remarkably stupid with your hat on that way, Mr. Jamieson."

"What can I say, I'm an Eminem fan. Now shut up."

14

In the darkened Maine Paper Industries arrival building, a man knelt by the windows, watching as the Suburban's lights came on and it started rolling toward the gate, which stood open. Irwin Mollison, an unemployed millworker, was one of the Institute's many Dennison River Bend stringers. Stackhouse could have ordered Ron Church to stay, but knew from experience that issuing an order to a man who might choose to disobey it was a bad idea. Better to use a stooge who only wanted to make a few extra dollars.

Mollison called a number pre-programmed into his cell. "They're on their way," he said. "A man, a woman, and a boy. The woman's wearing a cap over her hair, couldn't make out her face, but she stood in the doorway of the plane and yelled out her name. Mrs. Sigsby. Man's also wearing a cap, but turned around backward. The boy's the one you're looking for. Got a bandage on his ear and a hell of a bruise on the side of his face."

"Good," Stackhouse said. He had already gotten a call from the Challenger's co-pilot, who told him Dr. Evans had stayed on the plane. Which was fine.

So far, everything was fine . . . or as fine as it could be, under the circumstances. The bus was parked by the flagpole, as requested. He would place Doug the chef and Chad the caretaker in the trees beyond the admin building, where the Institute's driveway began. Zeke Ionidis and Felicia Richardson would take up their stations on the admin building's roof, behind a parapet that would hide them until the shooting began. Gladys would start the poison sucking into the HVAC system, then join Zeke and Felicia. Those two positions would enable a classic crossfire when the Suburban pulled in—that, at least, was the theory. Standing beside the flagpole with his hand on the hood of the bus, Stackhouse would be at least thirty yards from the crisscrossing bullets. There would be some risk of taking a spare round, he knew that, but it was an acceptable one.

Rosalind he would send to stand guard outside the door to the access tunnel on F-Level of Front Half. He wanted to make sure she didn't have a chance to realize her long-time and beloved boss was also in the crossfire, but there was more to it than that. He understood that the constant hum was power. Maybe it wasn't enough to breach the door yet, but maybe it was. Maybe they were just waiting for the Ellis boy to arrive, so they could attack from the rear and cause the sort of chaos they had already brought about in Back Half. The gorks didn't have brains enough to think of something like that, but there were the others. If that was the case, Rosalind would be there with her S&W .45, and the first ones through that door would wish they had stayed behind it. Stackhouse could only hope the twice-damned Wilholm boy would be leading the charge.

Am I ready for this? he asked himself, and the answer seemed to be yes. As ready as he could be. And it might still be all right. On the outside, after all, it was Ellis they were dealing with. Only a kid and some misguided hero he'd picked up along the way. In just ninety minutes, this shit-show would be over.

15

Three o'clock. The hum was louder now.

"Stop," Luke said. "Turn there." He was pointing to a dirt track screened by huge old pines, its mouth barely visible.

"Is this the way you came when you escaped?" Tim asked.

"God, no. They would have caught me."

"Then how do you—"

"*She* knows," Luke said. "And because she does, I do."

Tim turned to Mrs. Sigsby. "Is there a gate?"

"Ask *him*." She nearly spat the words.

"No gate," Luke said. "Just a big sign that says Maine Paper Industries Experimental Station and no trespassing."

Tim had to smile at the expression of pure frustration on Mrs. Sigsby's face. "Kid should be a cop, don't you think, Mrs. Sigsby? No alibi would get past him."

"Don't do this," she said. "You're going to get all three of us killed. Stackhouse will stop at nothing."

She looked over her shoulder at Luke. "You're the mind-reader, you know I'm telling the truth, so tell *him*."

Luke said nothing.

"How far to this Institute of yours?" Tim asked.

"Ten miles," Mrs. Sigsby said. "Maybe a bit more." She had apparently decided that stonewalling was useless.

Tim turned onto the road. Once he was past the big trees (their branches brushed at the roof and sides of the car), he found it smooth and well maintained. Overhead, a three-quarter moon cleared the slot through the trees, turning the dirt to the color of bone. Tim doused the Suburban's headlights and drove on.

16

Three-twenty.

Avery Dixon seized Kalisha's wrist with a cold hand. She had been dozing on Nicky's shoulder. Now she raised her head. "Avester?"

Wake them up. Helen and George and Nicky. Wake them up.

"What—"

If you want to live, wake them up. It's going to happen pretty soon.

Nick Wilholm already was awake. "*Can* we live?" he asked. "Do you think that's possible?"

"I hear you in there!" Rosalind's voice, coming from the other side of the door, was only slightly muffled. "What are you talking about? And why are you humming?"

Kalisha shook George and Helen awake. Kalisha could see the colored dots again. They were faint, but they were there. They went whooshing up and down the tunnel like kids on a slide, and that sort of made sense, because in a way they *were* kids, weren't they? Or the remains of them. They were thoughts made visible, looping and dancing and pirouetting through the wandering Ward A kids. And did those kids look slightly more lively? A little more there? Kalisha thought so, but maybe that was only her imagination. So much wishful thinking. You got used to wishful thinking in the Institute. You lived on it.

"I have a gun, you know!"

"So do I, lady," George said. He grabbed his crotch, then turned to Avery. *What's up, Boss Baby?*

Avery looked at them, one after another, and Kalisha saw he was crying. That made her stomach feel heavy, as if she had eaten something bad and was going to be sick.

When it happens, you have to go fast.

Helen: *When* what *happens, Avery?*

When I talk on the big phone.

Nicky: *Talk to who?*

The other kids. The far-away kids.

Kalisha nodded to the door. *That woman has a gun.*

Avery: *That's the last thing you have to worry about. Just go. All of you.*

"We," Nicky said. "*We*, Avery. We all go."

But Avery was shaking his head. Kalisha tried to get inside that head, tried to find out what was going on in there, what he knew, but all she got were three words, repeated over and over.

You're my friends. You're my friends. You're my friends.

17

Luke said, "They're his friends, but he can't go with them."

"Who can't go with who?" Tim asked. "What are you talking about?"

"About Avery. He has to stay. He's the one who has to call on the big phone."

"I don't know what you're talking about, Luke."

"I want them, but I want him, too!" Luke cried. "I want *all* of them! It's not fair!"

"He's crazy," Mrs. Sigsby said. "Surely you realize that n—"

"Shut up," Tim said. "I'm telling you for the last time."

She looked at him, read his face, did as he said.

Tim took the Suburban slowly over a rise and came to a stop. The road widened ahead. He could see lights through the trees, and the dark bulk of a building.

"I think we're here," he said. "Luke, I don't know what's going on with your friends, but that's out of our hands right now. I need you to get hold of yourself. Can you do that?"

"Yes." His voice was hoarse. He cleared his throat and tried again. "Yes. Okay."

Tim got out, walked around to the passenger door, and opened it.

"What now?" Mrs. Sigsby asked. She sounded querulous and impatient, but even in the scant light, Tim could see she was afraid. And she was right to be.

"Get out. You're driving the car the rest of the way. I'll be in back with Luke, and if you try anything clever, like driving into a tree before we get to those lights, I'll put a bullet through the seat and into your spine."

"No. *No!*"

"Yes. If Luke is right about what you've been doing to those children, you've run up quite a bill. This is where it comes due. Get out, get behind the wheel, and drive. Slowly. Ten miles an hour." He paused. "And turn your cap around backward."

18

Andy Fellowes called from the computer/surveillance center. His voice was high and excited. "They're here, Mr. Stackhouse! They're stopped about a hundred yards from where the road turns into the driveway! Their lights are off, but there's enough from the moon and the front of the building to see by. If you want me to put it up on your monitor so you can confirm, I—"

"That won't be necessary." Stackhouse tossed his box phone on the desk, gave the Zero Phone a final look—it had stayed silent, thank God for that—and headed for the door. His walkie was in his pocket, turned up to high gain and connected to the button in his ear. All of his people were on the same channel.

"Zeke?"

"I'm here, boss. With the lady doc."

"Doug? Chad?"

"In place." That was Doug, the chef. Who, in better days, had sometimes sat with the kids at dinner and showed them magic tricks that made the little ones laugh. "We also see their vehicle. Black nine-seater. Suburban or Tahoe, right?"

"Right. Gladys?"

"On the roof, Mr. Stackhouse. Stuff's all ready. Only have to combine the ingredients."

"Start it if there's shooting." But it was no longer a question of if, only of when, and when was now only three or four minutes away. Maybe less.

"Roger that."

"Rosalind?"

"In position. The hum is very loud down here. I think they are *conspiring*."

Stackhouse was sure they were, but wouldn't be for long. They would be too busy choking. "Hold steady, Rosalind. You'll be back at Fenway watching the Sox before you know it."

"Will you come with me, sir?"

"Only if I can cheer for the Yankees."

He went outside. The night air was pleasantly cool after a hot day. He felt a surge of affection for his team. The ones who had stuck with him. They would be rewarded no matter what, if he had anything to say about it. This was hard duty, and they had stayed behind to do it. The man behind the wheel of the Suburban was misguided, all right. What he didn't understand, *couldn't* understand, was that the lives of everyone he had ever loved depended on what they had done here, but that was over now. All the misguided hero could do was die.

Stackhouse approached the schoolbus parked by the flagpole and spoke to his troops for the last time. "Shooters, I want you to concentrate on the driver, all right? The one wearing his hat backward. Then rake the whole damn thing, front to back. Aim high, for the windows, knock out that dark glass, get head shots. Acknowledge."

They did.

"Start firing when I raise my hand. Repeat, when I raise my hand."

Stackhouse stood in front of the bus. He put his right hand on its chilly, dew-jeweled surface. With his left he grasped the flagpole. Then he waited.

19

"Drive," Tim said. He was on the floor behind the driver's seat. Luke was beneath him.

"Please don't make me do this," Mrs. Sigsby said. "If you'd just let me tell you why this place is so important—"

"Drive."

She drove. The lights drew closer. Now she could see the bus, and the flagpole, and Trevor standing between them.

20

It's time, Avery said.

He had expected to be afraid, he had been afraid ever since waking up in a room that looked like his room but wasn't, and then Harry Cross had knocked him down and he had been more afraid than ever. But he wasn't afraid now. He was exhilarated. There was a song his mom played on the stereo all the time when she was cleaning, and now a line of it recurred to him: *I shall be released*.

He walked to the Ward A kids, who were already circling. Kalisha, Nicky, George, and Helen followed.

Avery held out his hands. Kalisha took one and Iris—poor Iris, who might have been saved if this had happened even a day earlier—took the other.

The woman standing guard outside the door shouted something, a question, but it was lost in the rising hum. The dots came, not dim now but bright and getting brighter. The Stasi Lights filled the center of the circle, spinning and rising like the stripe on a barber pole, coming from some deep seat of power, going back there, then returning, refreshed and stronger than ever.

CLOSE YOUR EYES.

No longer a thought but a *THOUGHT*, riding the hum.

Avery watched to make sure they were doing it, then closed his. He expected to see his own room at home, or maybe their backyard with the swing set and the aboveground pool his dad inflated every Memorial Day, but he didn't. What he saw behind his closed eyes—what all of them saw—was the Institute playground. And maybe that shouldn't have been a surprise. It was true that he had been knocked down there and made to cry, which was a bad beginning to these last weeks of his life, but then he had made friends, good ones. He hadn't had friends back home. In his school back home they thought he was a weirdo, they even made fun of his name, running up to him and yelling *"Hey Avery, do me a favory"* in his face. There had been none of that here, because here they'd all been in it together. Here his friends had taken care of him, treated him like a normal person, and now he would take care of them. Kalisha, Nicky, George, and Helen: he would take care of them.

Luke most of all. If he could.

With his eyes closed, he saw the big phone.

It was sitting next to the trampoline, in front of the shallow ditch Luke had squirmed through to get under the fence, an old-fashioned telephone at least fifteen feet high and as black as death. Avery and his friends and the kids from Ward A stood around it in their circle. The Stasi Lights swirled, brighter than ever, now over the phone's dial, now skating giddily over its gigantic Bakelite handset.

Kalisha, GO. Playground!

There was no protest. Her hand left Avery's, but before the break in the circle could interrupt the power and destroy the vision, George grasped Avery's hand. The hum was everywhere now, surely they must hear it in all those faraway places where there were other children like them, standing in circles like this. Those children heard, just as the targets they'd been brought to their various Institutes to kill had heard. And like those targets, the children would obey. The difference was they would obey knowingly, and gladly. The revolt was not just here; the revolt was global.

George, GO. Playground!

George's hand dropped out and Nicky's took its place. Nicky who had stood up for him when Harry knocked him over. Nicky who called him the Avester, like it was a special name only friends could use. Avery gave his hand a squeeze and felt Nicky squeeze back. Nicky who was always bruised. Nicky who wouldn't knuckle under or take their shitty tokens.

Nicky, GO. Playground!

He was gone. Now it was Helen gripping his hand, Helen with her fading punk hair, Helen who had taught him to do forward rolls on the trampoline and spotted him "so you won't fall off and split your stupid head."

Helen, GO. Playground!

She went, the last of his friends from down here, but Katie took the hand Helen had been holding, and it was time.

Outside, faint gunfire.

Please don't let it be too late!

It was his last conscious thought as an individual, as Avery. Then he joined the hum, and the lights.

It was time to make a long-distance call.

21

Through a few remaining trees, Stackhouse saw the Suburban roll forward. The gleam of lights from the admin building slid on its chrome. It was moving very slowly, but it was coming. It occurred to him (too late to do anything about it, but wasn't that always the way) that the boy might no longer have the flash drive, that he might have left it with the one he called Officer Wendy after all. Or hidden it somewhere between the airport and here, with a last-gasp call from the misguided hero to tell Officer Wendy where it was if things went wrong.

But what could I have done about it? he thought. Nothing. There is only this.

The Suburban appeared at the head of the driveway. Stackhouse remained standing between the bus and the flagpole, arms outstretched like Christ on the cross. The hum had reached a near deafening level, and he wondered if Rosalind was still holding her position or if she had been forced to flee. He thought of Gladys and hoped she was ready to start the mix.

He squinted at the shape behind the Suburban's wheel. It was impossible to make out much, and he knew Doug and Chad wouldn't be able to see jack-shit through the darkened rear windows until they were blown out, but the windshield was clear glass, and when the Suburban closed the distance to twenty yards—a little closer than he had hoped for—he saw the expansion band of the turned-around cap cutting across the driver's forehead, and let go of the flagpole. The driver's head began to shake frantically. One hand left the wheel, pressing a starfish shape against the windshield in a stop gesture, and he realized he'd been deked. The trick was as simple as a kid escaping by crawling under a fence, and just as effective.

It wasn't the misguided hero behind the wheel. It was Mrs. Sigsby.

The Suburban stopped again, then began to back up. "I'm sorry, Julia, no help for it," he said, and raised his hand.

The shooting from admin and the trees began. At the rear of Front Half, Gladys Hickson removed the covers from two large buckets of bleach positioned under the HVAC unit which provided heating and cooling to Back Half and the access tunnel. She held her breath, dumped the bottles of toilet bowl cleaner into the buckets of bleach, gave each a quick stir with a mop handle, covered the buckets and the unit with a tarp, then sprinted for Front Half's East Wing with her eyes burning. As she ran across the roof, she realized it was moving under her feet.

22

"No, Trevor, no!" Mrs. Sigsby screamed. She was shak-ing her head back and forth. From his position behind

her, Tim saw her raise one hand and press it against the windshield. She used her other hand to put the Suburban in reverse.

It had just started to move when the shooting began, some of it coming from the right, in the woods, some from ahead and—Tim was pretty sure—from above. Holes appeared in the Suburban's windshield. The glass turned milky and sagged inward. Mrs. Sigsby became a puppet, jerking and bouncing and making stifled cries as bullets hit her.

"Stay down, Luke!" Tim shouted when the boy began to squirm beneath him. *"Stay down!"*

Bullets punched through the Suburban's rear windows. Shards of glass fell on Tim's back. Blood was running down the rear of the driver's seat. Even with the steady hum that seemed to be coming from everywhere, Tim could hear the slugs passing just above him, each one making a low *zzzz* sound.

There was the *sping-spang* of bullets punching through metal. The Suburban's hood popped up. Tim found himself thinking of the final scene in some old gangster movie, Bonnie Parker and Clyde Barrow doing a death-dance as bullets ripped into their car and into them. Whatever Luke's plan had been, it had gone disastrously wrong. Mrs. Sigsby was dead; he could see her blood spattered on the remains of the windshield. They would be next.

Then, screams from ahead and shouts from the right. Two more bullets came through the right side of the Suburban, one of them actually twitching the collar of Tim's shirt. They were the last two. Now what he heard was a vast, grinding roar.

"Let me up!" Luke gasped. "I can't breathe!"

Tim got off the boy and peered between the front

seats. He was aware that his head might be blown off at any second, but he had to see. Luke got up beside him. Tim started to tell the boy to get back down, but the words died in his throat.

This can't be real, he thought. It can't be.

But it was.

23

Avery and the others stood in a circle around the big phone. It was hard to see because of the Stasi Lights, so bright and so beautiful.

The sparkler, Avery thought. *Now we make the sparkler.*

It coalesced from the lights, ten feet high and spitting brilliance in every direction. The sparkler wavered back and forth at first, then the group mind took firmer control. It swung against the phone's gigantic receiver and knocked it from its gigantic base. The dumbbell-shape landed askew against the jungle gym. Voices in different languages spilled from the mouthpiece, all asking the same questions: *Hello, do you hear me? Hello, are you there?*

YES, the children of the Institute answered, and in one voice. *YES, WE HEAR YOU! DO IT NOW!*

A circle of children in Spain's Sierra Nevada National Park heard. A circle of Bosnian children imprisoned in the Dinaric Alps heard. On Pampus, an island guarding the entrance to Amsterdam's harbor, a circle of Dutch children heard. A circle of German children heard in the mountainous forests of Bavaria.

In Pietrapertosa, Italy.

In Namwon, South Korea.

Ten kilometers outside the Siberian ghost town of Chersky.

They heard, they answered, they became one.

24

Kalisha and the others reached the locked door between them and Front Half. They could hear the gunfire clearly now, because the hum had abruptly stopped, as if somewhere a plug had been pulled.

Oh, it's still there, Kalisha thought. It's just not for us anymore.

A groaning began in the walls, an almost human sound, and then the steel door between the access tunnel and Front Half's F-Level blew outward, smashing Rosalind Dawson before it and killing her instantly. The door landed beyond the elevator, twisted out of shape where its heavy hinges had been. Above, the wire mesh guarding the overhead fluorescent tubes was rippling, casting crazy underwater shadows.

The groaning grew louder, coming from everywhere. It was as if the building were trying to tear itself apart. In the Suburban, Tim had thought of *Bonnie and Clyde*; Kalisha thought of the Poe story about the House of Usher.

Come on, she thought at the others. *Fast!*

They ran past the torn door with the torn woman lying beneath it in a spreading pool of blood.

George: *What about the elevator? It's back there!*

Nicky: *Are you crazy? I don't know what's happening, but I'm not getting in any goddam elevator.*

Helen: *Is it an earthquake?*

"No," Kalisha said.

Mindquake. I don't know how—

". . . how they're doing it, but that's what . . ." She took a breath and tasted something acrid. It made her cough. "That's what it is."

Helen: *Something's wrong with the air.*

Nicky said, "I think it's some kind of poison." *Those fuckers, they never stop.*

Kalisha shoved open the door marked STAIRS and they began to climb, all of them coughing now. Between D- and C-Level, the stairs began to shake beneath them. Cracks zig-zagged down the walls. The fluorescents went out and the emergency lights came on, casting a flat yellow glow. Kalisha stopped, bent over, dry-retched, then started up again.

George: *What about Avery and the rest of the kids still down there? They'll strangle!*

Nicky: *And what about Luke? Is he here? Is he still alive?*

Kalisha didn't know. All she knew was they had to get out before they choked. Or before they were crushed, if the Institute were imploding.

A titanic shudder went through the building and the stairway tilted to the right. She thought of what their situation might be right now if they had tried the elevator, and pushed the thought away.

B-Level. Kalisha was gasping for breath, but the air was better here, and she was able to run a little faster. She was glad she hadn't got hooked on the vending machine cigarettes, there was that, at least. The groaning in the walls had become a low scream. She could hear hollow metal crumping sounds, and guessed the piping and electrical conduits were coming apart.

Everything was coming apart. She flashed on a You-Tube video she'd seen once, a horrible thing she hadn't been able to look away from: a dentist using forceps to extract somebody's tooth. The tooth wiggling while blood seeped out around it, trying to stay in the gum but finally pulling free with the roots dangling. This was like that.

She came to the ground level door, but it was slanted now, surreal, drunken. She pushed on it and it wouldn't open. Nicky joined her and they pushed together. No good. The floor rose beneath them, then thudded back down. A piece of the ceiling came free, crashed to the stairs, and slid away, crumbling as it went.

"It's going to squash us if we can't get out!" Kalisha shouted.

Nicky: *George. Helen.*

He held out his hands. The stairwell was narrow, but the four of them somehow crammed together in front of the door, hip to hip and shoulder to shoulder. George's hair was in Kalisha's eyes. Helen's breath, foul with fear, was in her face. They fumbled and joined hands. The dots came and the door screeched open, taking a section of the overhead jamb with it. Beyond was the residence corridor, now canted drunkenly to one side. Kalisha escaped the crooked doorway first, popping free like a cork from a champagne bottle. She went to her knees, cutting one hand on a light fixture that had fallen, spraying glass and metal everywhere. On one wall, askew but still hanging in there, was the poster of the three kids running through a meadow, the one that said it was just another day in paradise.

Kalisha scrambled up, looked around, and saw the other three doing the same. Together they ran for the lounge, past rooms where no stolen children would ever live again. The doors of those rooms were flying open and clapping shut, the sound like lunatics applauding. In the canteen, several of the vending machines had fallen over, spilling snacks. Broken nip bottles filled the air with the pungent aroma of alcohol. The door to the playground was twisted out of shape and jammed shut, but the glass was gone and fine fresh air came in on a late-summer breeze. Kalisha reached the door and froze. For a moment she forgot all about the building that seemed to be tearing itself apart all around them.

Her first thought was that the others had gotten out after all, maybe through the access tunnel's other door, because there they were: Avery, Iris, Hal, Len, Jimmy, Donna, and all the rest of the Ward A kids. Then she realized she wasn't actually seeing them at all. They were projections. Avatars. And so was the huge telephone they were circling. It should have crushed the trampoline and the badminton net, but both were still there, and she could see the chainlink fence not just behind the big phone but *through* it.

Then both the kids and the phone were gone. She realized the floor was rising again, and this time it wasn't thumping back down. She could see a slowly increasing gap between the lounge and the edge of the playground. Only nine inches or so for now, but it was growing. She had to give a little jump to get outside, as if from the second step of a staircase.

"Come on!" she shouted to the others. "Hurry! While you still can!"

25

Stackhouse heard screams from the roof of admin, and the firing from there ceased. He turned and saw something he could not at first credit. Front Half was rising. A swaying figure on the roof stood silhouetted against the moon, arms outstretched in an effort to maintain balance. It had to be Gladys.

This can't be happening, he thought.

But it was. Front Half rose higher, crunching and snapping as it parted company with the earth. It blotted out the moon, then dipped like the nose of a huge and clumsy helicopter. Gladys went flying. Stackhouse heard her scream as she disappeared into the shadows. On the admin building, Zeke and Dr. Richardson dropped their guns and cringed against the parapet, staring up at something out of a dream: a building that was slowly climbing into the sky, shedding glass and chunks of cinderblock. It pulled most of the playground's chainlink fence with it. Water from broken pipes poured from the building's tangled underside.

The cigarette vending machine tumbled from the broken door of the West Wing lounge into the playground. George Iles, gaping at the underside of Front Half as it rose into the sky, would have been crushed by it if Nicky hadn't yanked him out of the way.

Doug the chef and Chad the caretaker came through the screening trees, their necks craned, their mouths open, their guns hanging from their hands. They might have assumed that anyone in the bullet-riddled Suburban was dead; more likely, they had forgotten it entirely in their wonder and dismay.

Now the bottom of Front Half was above the admin building's roof. It came on with the stately, cumbersome grace of an eighteenth-century Royal Navy gunship under sail in a light breeze. Insulation and wires, some still sparking, dangled like broken umbilical cords. A jutting piece of pipe scraped off a ventilation housing. Zeke the Greek and Dr. Felicia Richardson saw it coming and ran for the hatch they had come up through. Zeke made it; Dr. Richardson did not. She put her arms over her head in a gesture of protection that was both instinctive and pitiful.

That was when the access tunnel—weakened by years of neglect and the cataclysmic levitation of Front Half—collapsed, crushing children who were already dying of chlorine poisoning and mental overload. They maintained their circle until the end, and as the roof came down, Avery Dixon had one final thought, both clear and calm: I loved having friends.

26

Tim didn't remember getting out of the Suburban. He was fully occupied with trying to process what he was seeing: a huge building floating in the air and sliding over a smaller building, eclipsing it. He saw a figure on the roof of that smaller building put its hands over its head. Then there was a muffled crumping sound from somewhere behind this incredible David Copperfield illusion, a great cloud of dust arose . . . and the floating building dropped like a rock.

A huge thud shook the ground and made Tim stagger. There was no way the smaller building—offices, Tim supposed—could take the weight. It exploded outward in all directions, spraying wood and concrete and glass. More dust billowed up, enough to obscure the moon. The bus alarm (who knew they had them?) went off, making a *WHOOP-WHOOP-WHOOP* sound. The person who had been on the roof was dead, of course, and anyone who had still been inside was now nothing but jelly.

"Tim!" Luke had grabbed his arm. *"Tim!"* He pointed to the two men who had come out of the trees. One was still staring at the ruins, but the other was raising a large pistol. Very slowly, as if in a dream.

Tim raised his own gun, and a lot faster. "Don't do it. Put them down."

They looked at him, dazed, then did as he said.

"Now walk to the flagpole."

"Is it over?" one of the men asked. "Please tell me it's over."

"I think so," Luke said. "Do what my friend says."

They plodded through the billowing dust toward the flagpole and the bus. Luke picked up their guns, thought about tossing them into the Suburban, then realized they wouldn't be driving that bullet-riddled, blood-spattered vehicle anywhere. He kept one of the automatics. The other he threw into the woods.

27

Stackhouse took a moment to watch Chad and Chef Doug walk toward him, then turned to regard the ruins of his life.

But who could have known? he thought. Who could have known they had access to enough power to levitate a building? Not Mrs. Sigsby, not Evans, not Heckle and Jeckle, not Donkey Kong—wherever he is tonight—and certainly not me. We thought we were working with high voltage, when in fact all we tapped was a trickle current. The joke was on us.

There was a tap on his shoulder. He turned to regard the misguided hero. He was broad-shouldered (as an authentic hero should be), but he was wearing glasses, and that didn't fit the stereotype.

Of course there's always Clark Kent, Stackhouse thought.

"Are you armed?" the man named Tim asked.

Stackhouse shook his head and made a weak gesture with one hand. "They were supposed to take care of that."

"Are you three the last?"

"I don't know." Stackhouse had never felt so weary. He supposed it was shock. That, and the sight of a building rising into the night sky, blotting out the moon. "Maybe some of the staff in Back Half are still alive. And the docs there, Hallas and James. As for the children in Front Half, though . . . I don't see how anyone could have survived *that*." He gestured toward the ruins with an arm that felt like lead.

"The rest of the children, though," Tim said. "What about them? Weren't they in the other building?"

"They were in the tunnel," Luke said. "*He* tried to gas them, but the tunnel collapsed first. It collapsed when Front Half rose up."

Stackhouse thought of denying this, but what good would it do, if the Ellis boy could read his mind? Besides, he was so tired. So completely used up.

"Your friends, too?" Tim asked.

Luke opened his mouth to say he didn't know for sure, but probably. Then his head jerked around, as if he had been called. If so, the call had come inside his head, because Tim only heard the voice a space of seconds later.

"Luke!"

A girl was running across the littered lawn, skirting the rubble that had exploded outward in a kind of corona. Three others were following her, two boys and another girl.

"Lukey!"

Luke ran to meet the girl in the lead and threw his arms around her. The other three joined them, and as they hugged in a group embrace, Tim heard the hum again, but lower now. Some of the rubble stirred, pieces of wood and stone rising into the air, then falling again. And didn't he hear the whisper of their mingled voices in his head? Maybe just his imagination, but . . .

"They're still putting out juice," Stackhouse said. He spoke disinterestedly, like a man passing the time of day. "I hear them. You do, too. Be careful. The effect is cumulative. It turned Hallas and James into Heckle and Jeckle." He gave a single bark of laughter. "Just a couple of cartoon magpies with high-priced medical degrees."

Tim ignored this and let the children have their joyous reunion—who on God's earth deserved one more? He kept an eye on the Institute's three adult survivors. Although they did not, in fact, look as if they were going to give him any trouble.

"What am I going to do with you assholes?" Tim asked. Not really talking to the survivors, just thinking aloud.

"Please don't kill us," Doug said. He pointed to the group hug that was still going on. "I fed those youngsters. I kept them alive."

"I wouldn't try to justify anything you did here if *you* want to stay alive," Tim said. "Shutting up might be the wisest course." He turned his attention to Stackhouse. "Looks like we won't need the bus after all, since you killed most of the kids—"

"*We* didn't—"

"Are you deaf? I said shut it."

Stackhouse saw what was in the man's face. It didn't look like heroism, misguided or otherwise. It looked like murder. He shut it.

"We need a ride out of here," Tim said, "and I really don't want to have to march you happy warriors through the woods to this village Luke says you have. It's been a long, tiring day. Any suggestions?"

Stackhouse seemed not to have heard him. He was looking at the remains of Front Half, and the remains of the admin building squashed beneath it. "All this," he marveled. "All this because of one runaway boy."

Tim kicked him lightly in the ankle. "Pay attention, shithead. How do I get those kids out of here?"

Stackhouse didn't answer, and neither did the man who claimed to have fed the kids. The other one, the guy who looked like a hospital orderly in his tunic top, spoke up. "If I had an idea about that, would you let me go?"

"What's your name?"

"Chad, sir. Chad Greenlee."

"Well, Chad, that would depend on how good your idea was."

28

The last survivors of the Institute hugged and hugged and hugged. Luke felt that he could embrace them like this forever, and feel them embracing him, because he had never expected to see any of them again. For the moment all they needed was inside the huddled circle they made on this littered lawn. All they needed was each other. The world and all its problems could go fuck itself.

Avery?

Kalisha: *Gone. Him and the rest. When the tunnel came down on top of them.*

Nicky: *It's better this way, Luke. He wouldn't have been the same. Not himself. What he did, what they did . . . it would have stripped him, like it did all the others.*

What about the kids in Front Half? Are any of them still alive? If there are, we have to—

It was Kalisha who answered, shaking her head, sending not words but a picture: the late Harry Cross, of Selma, Alabama. The boy who had died in the cafeteria.

Luke took Sha by the arms. *All of them? Are you saying all of them died of seizures even before that came down?*

He pointed to the rubble of Front Half.

"I think when it lifted off," Nicky said. "When Avery answered the big phone." And when it was clear Luke didn't fully understand: *When the other kids joined in.*

"The faraway kids," George added. "At the other Institutes. The Front Half kids were just too . . . I don't know the word."

"Too vulnerable," Luke said. "That's what you mean. They were vulnerable. It was like one of the damn old shots, wasn't it? One of the bad ones."

They nodded.

Helen whispered, "I bet they died seeing the dots. How awful is that?"

Luke's answer was the childish denial grownups smile at cynically and only other children can fully understand: *It's not fair! Not fair!*

No, they agreed. *Not fair.*

They drew apart. Luke looked at them one by one in the dusty moonlight: Helen, George, Nicky . . . and Kalisha. He remembered the day he met her, pretending to smoke a candy cigarette.

George: *What now, Lukey?*

"Tim will know," Luke said, and could only hope it was true.

29

Chad led the way around the destroyed buildings. Stackhouse and Chef Doug trudged behind him, heads down. Tim followed, gun in hand. Luke and his friends walked behind Tim. The crickets, silenced by the destruction, had begun to sing again.

Chad stopped at the edge of an asphalt track along which half a dozen cars and three or four pickup trucks were parked, nose to tail. Among them was a midsized Toyota panel truck with MAINE PAPER INDUSTRIES on the side. He pointed at it. "What about that, sir? Would that do you?"

Tim thought it would, at least for a start. "What about the keys?"

"Everybody uses those maintenance trucks, so they always leave the keys under the visor."

"Luke," Tim said, "would you check on that?"

Luke went; the others went with him, as if they couldn't bear to be separated even for a minute. Luke opened the driver's door and lowered the visor. Something dropped into his hand. He held up the keys.

"Good," Tim said. "Now open up the back. If there's stuff in there, empty it out."

The big one called Nick and the smaller one named

George took care of this chore, tossing out rakes, hoes, a toolbox, and several bags of lawn fertilizer. While they did it, Stackhouse sat down on the grass and put his head on his knees. It was a profound gesture of defeat, but Tim did not feel sorry for him. He tapped Stackhouse on the shoulder.

"We'll be going now."

Stackhouse didn't look up. "Where? I believe the boy said something about Disneyland." He gave a singularly humorless snort of laughter.

"None of your affair. But I'm curious. Where are *you* going to go?"

Stackhouse did not answer.

30

There were no seats in the rear of the panel truck, so the kids took turns sitting up front, starting with Kalisha. Luke squeezed in on the metal floor between her and Tim. Nicky, George, and Helen clustered at the back doors, looking out through the two small dusty windows at a world they had never expected to see again.

Luke: *Why are you crying, Kalisha?*

She told him, then said it aloud, for Tim's benefit. "Because it's all so beautiful. Even in the dark, it's all so beautiful. I only wish Avery was here to see it."

31

Dawn was still just a rumor on the eastern horizon when Tim turned south on Highway 77. The one named Nicky had taken Kalisha's place in the front seat. Luke had gone into the back of the truck with her, and now all four of them were heaped together like a litter of puppies, fast asleep. Nicky also appeared to be asleep, his head thudding against the window every time the truck hit a bump . . . and there were a lot of bumps.

Just after seeing a sign announcing that Millinocket was fifty miles ahead, Tim looked at his cell phone and saw that he had two bars and nine per cent power. He called Wendy, who answered on the first ring. She wanted to know if he was all right. He said he was. She asked if Luke was.

"Yes. He's sleeping. I've got four more kids. There were others—I don't know how many, quite a few—but they're dead."

"Dead? Jesus, Tim, what happened?"

"Can't tell you now. I will when I can, and you might even believe it, but right now I'm in the williwags, I've got maybe thirty bucks in my wallet, and I don't dare use my credit cards. There's a hell of a mess back there, and I don't want to risk leaving a paper trail. Also, I'm tired as hell. The truck's still got half a tank of gas, which is good, but I'm running on fumes. Bitch-bitch-bitch, right?"

"What . . . you . . . have any . . ."

"Wendy, I'm losing you. If you hear me, I'll call back. I love you."

He didn't know if she heard that last or not, or what she'd make of it if she had. He'd never said it to her before. He turned off his phone and put it in the console along with Tag Faraday's gun. All that had happened back in DuPray seemed long ago to him, almost in a life that had been led by another person. What mattered now were these children, and what he was going to do with them.

Also, who might come after them.

"Hey, Tim."

He looked around at Nicky. "I thought you were asleep."

"No, just thinking. Can I tell you something?"

"Sure. Tell me a lot. Keep me awake."

"Just wanted to say thanks. I won't say you redeemed my faith in human nature, but coming with Lukey like you did . . . that took balls."

"Listen, kiddo, are you reading my mind?"

Nick shook his head. "Can't do it just now. Don't think I could even move any of the candy wrappers on the floor of this heap, and that was my thing. If I was linked up with them . . ." He inclined his head toward the sleeping children in the back of the panel truck. "It'd be different. At least for awhile."

"You think you'll revert? Go back to whatever you had before?"

"Dunno. It's not a big deal to me either way. Never was. My big deals were football and street hockey." He peered at Tim. "Man, those aren't bags under your eyes, those are suitcases."

"I could use some sleep," Tim admitted. Yes, like about twelve hours. He found himself remembering Norbert Hollister's ramshackle establishment, where the TV didn't work and the roaches ran free. "I suspect there are independent motels where they wouldn't ask questions if cash was on offer, but cash is a problem, I'm afraid."

Nicky smiled, and Tim saw the fine-looking young man he'd be—if God was good—in a few years. "I think me and my friends might be able to help you out in the cash department. Not entirely sure, but yeah, probably. Got enough gas to make it to the next town?"

"Yes."

"Stop there," Nicky said, and put his head back against the window.

32

Not long before the Millinocket branch of the Seaman's Trust opened at nine o'clock on that day, a teller named Sandra Robichaux summoned the bank manager from his office.

"We have a problem," she said. "Take a look at this."

She seated herself at the ATM video replay. Brian Stearns sat down beside her. The unit's camera slept between transactions, and in the small northern Maine town of Millinocket, that usually meant it slept all night, waking up for its first customers around six o'clock. The time-stamp on the screen they were looking at said 5:18 AM. As Stearns watched, five people walked up to the ATM. Four of them had their shirts pulled up over their mouths and noses, like bandit masks in an old-time Western. The fifth had a gimme cap pulled down low over his eyes. Stearns could see MAINE PAPER INDUSTRIES on the front.

"Those look like kids!"

Sandra nodded. "Unless they're midgets, which doesn't seem very likely. Watch this, Mr. Stearns."

The kids joined hands and formed a circle. A few lines of fuzz ran across the picture, as if from momentary electrical interference. Then money began to spew from the ATM's slot. It was like watching a casino slot machine pay off.

"What the hell?"

Sandra shook her head. "I don't *know* what the hell, but they got over two thousand dollars, and the machine's not supposed to give anybody more than eight hundred. That's the way it's set. I guess we should call somebody about it, but I don't know who."

Stearns didn't reply. He only watched, fascinated, as the little bandits—they looked like middle-schoolers, if that—picked up the money.

Then they were gone.

THE LISPING MAN

1

On a cool October morning some three months later, Tim Jamieson strolled down the driveway from what was known as Catawba Hill Farm to South Carolina State Road 12-A. The walk took awhile; the driveway was almost half a mile long. Any longer, he liked to joke to Wendy, and they could have named it South Carolina State Road 12-B. He was wearing faded jeans, dirty Georgia Giant workshoes, and a sweatshirt so big it came down to his upper thighs. It was a present from Luke, ordered on the Internet. Written across the front were two words in gold: THE AVESTER. Tim had never met Avery Dixon, but he was glad to wear the shirt. His face was deeply tanned. Catawba hadn't been a real farm for ten years, but there was still an acre of garden behind the barn, and this was harvest season.

He reached the mailbox, opened it, started to paw out the usual junk (nobody got real mail these days, it seemed), then froze. His stomach, which had been fine on the walk down here, seemed to contract. A car was coming, slowing down and pulling over. There was nothing special about it, just a Chevy Malibu smudged with reddish dust and with the usual budget of bugs smashed into the grill. It wasn't a neighbor, he knew all their cars, but it could have been a salesman, or somebody lost and needing directions. Only it wasn't. Tim didn't know who the man behind the wheel was, only that he, Tim, had been waiting for him. Now here he was.

Tim closed the mailbox and put one hand behind him, as if to give his belt a tug. His belt was in place and so was the gun, a Glock which had once been the property of a redheaded sheriff's deputy named Taggart Faraday.

The man turned off the engine and got out. He was dressed in jeans much newer than Tim's—they still had the store creases—and a white shirt buttoned to the neck. His face was both handsome and nondescript, a contradiction that might have seemed impossible until you saw a guy like this. His eyes were blue, his hair that Nordic shade of blond that looks almost white. He looked, in fact, much as the late Julia Sigsby had imagined him. He wished Tim a good morning, and Tim returned the greeting with his hand still behind his back.

"You're Tim Jamieson." The visitor held out his hand.

Tim looked at it, but didn't shake it. "I am. And who might you be?"

The blond man smiled. "Let's say I'm William Smith. That's the name on my driver's license." *Smith* was okay, so was *driver's*, but *license* was *lithenth*. A lisp, but a slight one. "Call me Bill."

"What can I do for you, Mr. Smith?"

The man calling himself Bill Smith—a name as anonymous as his sedan—squinted up into the early sunshine, smiling slightly, as if he were debating several possible answers to this question, all of them pleasant. Then he looked back at Tim. The smile was still on his mouth, but his eyes weren't smiling.

"We could dance around this, but I'm sure you've got a busy day ahead of you, so I won't take up any more of your time than I have to. Let me start by assuring you that I'm not here to cause you any trouble, so if it's a gun you've got back there instead of just an itch, you can leave it where it is. I think we can agree there's been enough shooting in this part of the world for one year."

Tim thought of asking how Mr. Smith had found him, but why bother? It couldn't have been hard. Catawba Farm belonged to Harry and Rita Gullickson, now living in Florida. Their daughter had been keeping an eye on the old home place for the last three years. Who better than a sheriff's deputy?

Well, she *had* been a deputy, and still drew a county salary, at least for the time being, but it was hard to tell just what her remit was nowadays. Ronnie Gibson, absent on the night Mrs. Sigsby's posse had invaded, was now the acting Fairlee County Sheriff, but how long that would last was anyone's guess; there was talk of moving the sheriff's station to the nearby town of Dunning. And Wendy had never been cut out for boots-on-the-ground law enforcement in the first place.

"Where is Officer Wendy?" Smith asked. "Up at the house, maybe?"

"Where's Stackhouse?" Tim countered. "You must have got that Officer Wendy thing from him, because the Sigsby woman's dead."

Smith shrugged, stuck his hands in the back pockets

of his new jeans, rocked on his heels, and looked around. "Boy, it's nice here, isn't it?" *Nice* came out *niyth*, but the lisp really was very light, mostly not there at all.

Tim decided not to pursue the Stackhouse question. It was obvious he wouldn't get anywhere with it, and besides, Stackhouse was old news. He might be in Brazil; he might be in Argentina or Australia; he might be dead. It made no difference to Tim where he was. And the man with the lisp was right; there was no point in dancing.

"Deputy Gullickson is in Columbia, at a closed hearing about the shoot-out that happened last summer."

"I assume she has a story those committee folks will buy."

Tim had no interest in confirming this assumption. "She'll also attend some meetings where the future of law enforcement here in Fairlee County will be discussed, since the goons you sent wiped most of it out."

Smith spread his hands. "I and the people I work with had nothing to do with that. Mrs. Sigsby acted entirely on her own."

Maybe true but also not true, Tim could have said. *She acted because she was afraid of you and the people you work with*.

"I understand that George Iles and Helen Simms are gone," Mr. Smith said. *Simms* came out *Simmth*. "Young Mr. Iles to an uncle in California, Miss Simms to her grandparents in Delaware."

Tim didn't know where the lisping man was getting his information—Norbert Hollister was long gone, the DuPray Motel closed with a FOR SALE sign out front that would probably stay there for a long time—but it was good information. Tim had never expected to go unnoticed, that would have been naïve, but he didn't like the depth of Mr. Smith's knowledge about the kids.

"That means that Nicholas Wilholm and Kalisha Benson are still here. And Luke Ellis, of course." The smile reappeared, thinner now. "The author of all our misery."

"What do you want, Mr. Smith?"

"Very little, actually. We'll get to it. Meanwhile, let me compliment you. Not just on your bravery, which was apparent on the night you stormed the Institute pretty much single-handed, but on the care you and Officer Wendy have shown in the aftermath. You've been parceling them out, haven't you? Iles first, about a month after returning to South Carolina. The Simms girl two weeks after him. Both with stories about being kidnapped for unknown reasons, held for an unknown length of time at an unknown location, then set free . . . also for unknown reasons. You and Officer Wendy managed to arrange all that while you must have been under some scrutiny yourselves."

"How do you know all this?"

It was the lisping man's turn not to answer, but that was all right. Tim guessed at least some of his information had come direct from the newspapers and the Internet. The return of kidnapped children was always news. "When do Wilholm and Benson go?"

Tim considered this and decided to answer. "Nicky leaves this Friday. To his uncle and aunt in Nevada. His brother is already there. Nick's not crazy about going, but he understands he can't stay here. Kalisha will stay another week or two. She has a sister, twelve years older, in Houston. Kalisha is eager to reconnect with her." This was both true and not true. Like the others, Kalisha was suffering from PTSD.

"And their stories will also stand up to police scrutiny?"

"Yes. The stories are simple enough, and of course they're all afraid of what might happen to them if they told the truth." Tim paused. "Not that they'd be believed."

"And young Mr. Ellis? What about him?"

"Luke stays with me. He has no close family and nowhere to go. He's already returned to his studies. They soothe him. The boy is grieving, Mr. Smith. Grieving for his parents, grieving for his friends." He paused, looking hard at the blond man. "I suspect he's also grieving for the childhood your people stole from him."

He waited for Smith to respond to this. Smith did not, so Tim went on.

"Eventually, if we can work out a story that's reasonably watertight, he'll pick up where he left off. Double enrollment at Emerson College and MIT. He's a very smart boy." As you well know, he didn't need to add. "Mr. Smith . . . do you even care?"

"Not much," Smith said. He took a pack of American Spirits from his breast pocket. "Smoke?"

Tim shook his head.

"I rarely do myself," Mr. Smith said, "but I've been in speech therapy for my lisp, and I allow myself one as a reward when I am able to control it in conversation, especially a long and rather intense one, such as we are having. Did you notice that I lisp?"

"It's very faint."

Mr. Smith nodded, seemingly pleased, and lit up. The smell on the cool morning air was sweet and fragrant. A smell that seemed made for tobacco country, which this still was . . . although not at Catawba Farm since the nineteen-eighties.

"I hope you're sure they will keep shtum, as the saying is. If any one of them talks, there would be consequences for all five. In spite of the flash drive you supposedly have. Not all of my . . . people . . . believe that actually exists."

Tim smiled without showing his teeth. "It would be unwise for your . . . people . . . to test that idea."

"I take your point. It would still be a very bad idea for those children to talk about their adventures in the Maine woods. If you're in communication with Mr. Iles and Miss Simms, you might want to pass that along. Or perhaps Wilholm, Benson, and Ellis can get in touch with them by other means."

"Are you talking about telepathy? I wouldn't count on that. It's reverting to what it was before your people took them. Same with the telekinesis." He was telling Smith what the children had told him, but Tim wasn't entirely sure he believed it. All he knew for certain was that awful hum had never come back. "How did you cover it up, Smith? I'm curious."

"And so you shall remain," the blond man said. "But I *will* tell you that it wathn't just the installation in Maine that needed our attention. There were twenty other Institutes in other parts of the world, and none remain operational. Two of them—in countries where obedience is inculcated in children almost from birth—hung on for six weeks or so, and then there were mass suicides at both." The word came out *thooithides*.

Mass suicides or mass murder? Tim wondered, but that wasn't a topic he intended to raise. The sooner he was rid of this man, the better.

"The Ellis boy—with your help, very much with your help—has ruined us. That undoubtedly sounds melodramatic, but it's the truth."

"Do you think I care?" Tim asked. "You were killing children. If there's a hell, you'll go there."

"While you, Mr. Jamieson, undoubtedly believe you'll go to heaven, assuming there is such a place. And who knows, you might be right. What God could turn away a man who rides to the rescue of defenseless youngsters? If I may crib from Christ on the cross, you will be forgiven because you know not what you did." He cast his cigarette aside. "But I am going to tell you. It's what I came for, with the consent of my associates. Thanks to you and Ellis, the world is now on suicide watch." This time the word came out clean.

Tim said nothing, just waited.

"The first Institute, although not by that name, was in Nazi Germany."

"Why doesn't that surprise me?" Tim said.

"And why be so judgmental? The Nazis were onto nuclear fission before America. They created antibiotics that are still used today. They more or less invented modern rocketry. And certain German scientists were running ESP experiments, with Hitler's enthusiastic support. They discovered, almost by accident, that groups of gifted children could cause certain troublesome people—roadblocks to progress, you might say—to cease being troublesome. These children were used up by 1944, because there was no sure method, no scientific method, of finding replacements after they became, in Institute argot, gorks. The most useful test for latent psychic ability came later. Do you know what that test was?"

"BDNF. Brain-derived neurotrophic factor. Luke said that was the marker."

"Yes, he's a smart boy, all right. Very smart. Everyone involved now wishes they'd left him alone. His BDNF wasn't even that high."

"I imagine Luke also wishes you'd left him alone. And his parents. Now why don't you go ahead and say your piece."

"All right. There were conferences both before and after the Second World War ended. If you remember any of your twentieth-century history, you'll know about some of them."

"I know about Yalta," Tim said. "Roosevelt, Churchill, and Stalin got together to basically carve up the world."

"Yes, that's the famous one, but the most important meeting took place in Rio de Janeiro, and no government was involved . . . unless you want to call the group that met—and their successors down through the years—a kind of shadow government. They—*we*—knew about the German children, and set about finding more. By 1950 we understood the usefulness of BDNF. Institutes were set up, one by one, in isolated locations. Techniques were refined. They have been in place for over seventy years, and by our count, they have saved the world from nuclear holocaust over five hundred times."

"That's ridiculous," Tim said harshly. "A joke."

"It's not. Let me give you one example. At the time that the children revolted at the Institute in Maine—a revolt that spread like a virus to all the other Institutes—they had begun working to cause the suicide of an evangelist named Paul Westin. Thanks to Luke Ellis, that man still lives. Ten years from now, he will become a close associate of a Christian gentleman who will become America's Secretary of Defense. Westin will convince the Secretary that war is imminent, the Secretary will convince the President, and that will eventually result in a preemptive nuclear strike. Only a single missile, but it could start all the dominoes falling. That part is outside our range of prediction."

"You couldn't possibly know a thing like that."

"How do you think we picked our targets, Mr. Jamieson? Out of a hat?"

"Telepathy, I suppose."

Mr. Smith looked like a patient teacher with a slow pupil. "TKs move objects and TPs read thoughts, but neither of them are able to read the future." He drew out his cigarettes again. "Sure you won't have one?"

Tim shook his head.

Smith lit up. "Children such as Luke Ellis and Kalisha Benson are rare, but there are other people who are rarer still. More precious than the most precious metal. And the best thing about them? Their talents don't fade with age or destroy the minds of the users."

Tim caught movement in the corner of his eye, and turned. Luke had come down the driveway. Further up the hill, Annie Ledoux was standing with a shotgun broken open over her arm. Flanking her were Kalisha and Nicky. Smith didn't see any of them yet; he was gazing out over the hazy distance to the small town of DuPray and the glittering railroad tracks that ran through it.

Annie now spent much of her time at Catawba Hill. She was fascinated by the children, and they seemed to enjoy her. Tim pointed at her, then patted the air with his hand: hold your position. She nodded and stood where she was, watching. Smith was still admiring the view, which really was very fine.

"Let's say there's another Institute—a very small one, a very *special* one, where everything is first class and state of the art. No outdated computers or crumbling infrastructure there. It's located in a completely safe place. Other Institutes exist in what we thought of as hostile territory, but not this one. There are no Tasers, no injections, no punishments. There is no need of subjecting the residents of this special Institute to near-death experiences such as the immersion tank to help open them to their deeper abilities.

"Let's say it's in Switzerland. It might not be, but it will do. It *is* on neutral ground, because many nations have an interest in its upkeep and continued smooth operation. A great many. There are currently six very special guests in this place. They are not children anymore; unlike the TPs and TKs in the various Institutes, their talents do not thin and disappear in their late teens and early twenties. Two of these people are actually quite old. Their BDNF levels do not correlate with their very special talents; they are unique in that way, and thus very hard to find. We were searching constantly for replacements, but now that search has been suspended, because it hardly seems there's any point."

"What are these people?"

"Precogs," Luke said.

Smith wheeled around, startled. "Why, hello, Luke." He smiled, but at the same time drew back a step. Was he afraid? Tim thought he was. "Precogs, that's exactly right."

"What the hell are you talking about?" Tim asked.

"Precognition," Luke said. "People who can see into the future."

"You're kidding, right?"

"I'm not and he's not," Smith said. "You could call those six our DEW line—a defunct Cold War acronym meaning Distant Early Warning. Or, if you'd like to be more up to date, they are our drones, flying into the future and marking out places where great conflagrations will start. We only concentrate on stopping the big ones. The world has survived because we've been able to take these proactive measures. Thousands of children have died in this process, but *billions* of children have been saved." He turned to Luke and smiled. "Of course you understood—it's a simple enough deduction. I understand you're also quite the math whiz, and I'm sure you see the cost-to-benefit ratio. You may not like it, but you see it."

Annie and her two young charges had started down the hill again, but this time Tim didn't bother motioning them back. He was too stunned by what he was hearing.

"I can buy telepathy, and I can buy telekinesis, but precognition? That's not science, that's carnival bullshit!"

"I assure you it's not," Smith said. "Our precogs found the targets. The TKs and TPs, working in groups to increase their power, eliminated them."

"Precognition exists, Tim," Luke said quietly. "I knew even before I escaped the Institute it had to be that. I'm pretty sure Avery did, too. Nothing else made sense. I've been reading up on it since we got here, everything I could find. The stats are pretty much irrefutable."

Kalisha and Nicky joined Luke. They looked curiously at the blond man who called himself Bill Smith, but neither spoke. Annie stood behind them. She was wearing her serape, although the day was warm, and looked more like a Mexican gunslinger than ever. Her eyes were bright and aware. The children had changed her. Tim didn't think it was their power; in the long term, that caused the opposite of improvement. He thought it was just the association, or maybe the fact that the kids accepted her exactly as she was. Whatever the reason, he was happy for her.

"You see?" Smith said. "It's been confirmed by your resident genius. Our six precogs—for awhile there were eight, and once, in the seventies, we were down to just four, a very scary time—constantly search for certain individuals we call *hinges*. They're the pivot-points on which the door of human extinction may turn. Hinges aren't agents of destruction, but *vectors* of destruction. Westin was one such hinge. Once they're discovered, we investigate them, background them, surveil them, video them. Eventually they're turned over to the children of the various Institutes, who eliminate them, one way or another."

Tim was shaking his head. "I don't believe it."

"As Luke has said, the statistics—"

"Statistics can prove anything. Nobody can see the future. If you and your associates really believe that, you're not an organization, you're a cult."

"I had a auntie who could see the future," Annie said suddenly. "She made her boys stay away one night when they wanted to go out to a juke joint, and there was a propane explosion. Twenty people got burnt up like mice in a chimbly, but her boys were safe at home." She paused, then added, as an afterthought, "She also knew Truman was going to get elected president, and nobody believed *that* shit."

"Did she know about Trump?" Kalisha asked.

"Oh, she was long dead before that big city dumb-shit turned up," Annie said, and when Kalisha held up an open palm, Annie slapped it smartly.

Smith ignored the interruption. "The world is still here, Tim. That's not a statistic, it's a fact. Seventy years after Hiroshima and Nagasaki were obliterated by atomic bombs, the world is still here even though many nations have atomic weapons, even though primitive human emotions still hold sway over rational thought and superstition masquerading as religion still guides the course of human politics. Why is that? Because we have protected it, and now that protection is gone. That's what Luke Ellis did, and what you participated in."

Tim looked at Luke. "Are you buying this?"

"No," Luke said. "And neither is he, at least not completely."

Although Tim didn't know it, Luke was thinking of the girl who'd asked him about the SAT math problem, the one having to do with Aaron's hotel room rate. She'd gotten the answer wrong, and this was the same thing, only on a much grander scale; a bad answer derived from a faulty equation.

"I'm sure you'd like to believe that," Smith said.

"Annie's right," Luke said. "There really are people who have precognitive flashes, and her aunt may have been one of them. Despite what this guy says, and may actually believe, they're not even that rare. You may even have had one or two yourself, Tim, but you probably call them something else. Instinct, maybe."

"Or hunches," Nicky said. "On the TV programs, cops are always getting hunches."

"TV shows are not life," Tim said, but he was also thinking of something from the past: suddenly deciding, for no real reason, to get off an airplane and hitchhike north instead.

"Which is too bad," Kalisha said. "I love *Riverdale*."

"The word *flash* is used over and over in the stories about these things," Luke said, "because that seems to be what it is, something like a lightning-strike. I believe in it, and I believe there may be people who can harness it."

Smith raised his hands in a there-you-have-it gesture. "Exactly what I'm saying." Only *saying* came out *thaying*. His lisp had resurfaced. Tim found this interesting.

"Only there's something he's not telling you," Luke said. "Probably because he doesn't like to tell himself. None of them do. The way our generals didn't like to tell themselves there was no way to win the Vietnam War, even after it became apparent."

"I have no idea what you're talking about," Smith said.

"You do," Kalisha said.

"He does," Nicky said.

"You better own up, mister," Orphan Annie said. "These chirrun are reading your mind. Tickles, don't it?"

Luke turned to Tim. "Once I was sure it had to be precognition driving this, and I got access to a real computer—"

"One you didn't need tokens to use is what he means," Kalisha put in.

Luke poked her. "Shut up a minute, will you?"

Nicky grinned. "Watch out, Sha, Lukey's gettin mad."

She laughed. Smith did not. His control over this conversation had been lost with the arrival of Luke and his friends, and his expression—tight mouth, drawn-together brows—said that he wasn't used to it.

"Once I got access to a real computer," Luke resumed, "I did a Bernoulli distribution. Do you know what that is, Mr. Smith?"

The blond man shook his head.

"He does, though," Kalisha said. Her eyes were merry.

"Right," Nicky agreed. "And doesn't like it. The Whatzis distribution is not his friend."

"The Bernoulli is an accurate way of expressing probability," Luke said. "It's based on the idea that there are two possible outcomes to certain empiric events, like coin flips or the winners of football games. The outcomes can be expressed as p for positive result and n for negative result. I won't bore you with the details, but you end up with a boolean-valued outcome that clearly expresses the difference between random and non-random events."

"Yeah, don't bore us with the easy stuff," Nicky said, "just cut to the chase."

"Coin flips are random. Football scores *appear* random if you take a small sample, but if you take a bigger one, it becomes clear that they're not, because other factors come into play. Then it becomes a probability situation, and if the probability of A is greater than the probability of B, then in most cases, A will happen. You know that if you've ever bet on a sporting event, right?"

"Sure," Tim said. "You can find the odds and the likely point-spread in the daily paper."

Luke nodded. "It's pretty simple, really, and when you apply Bernoulli to precognition statistics, an interesting trend emerges. Annie, how soon was the fire after your aunt had her brainwave about keeping her sons home?"

"That very night," Annie said.

Luke looked pleased. "Which makes it a perfect example. The Bernoulli distribution I ran shows that precognitive flashes—or visions, if you like that word better—tend to be most accurate when the predicted event is only hours away. When the time between the prediction and the event predicted becomes longer, the probability of the prediction coming true begins to decline. Once it becomes a matter of weeks, it pretty much falls off the table and p becomes n."

He turned his attention to the blond man.

"You *know* this, and the people you work with know it. They've known it for years. For decades, in fact. They must have. Any math wonk with a computer can run a Bernoulli distribution. It might not have been clear when you started this thing in the late forties or early fifties, but by the eighties you had to know. Probably by the sixties."

Smith shook his head. "You're very bright, Luke, but you're still just a child, and children indulge in magical thinking—they bend the truth until it conforms to what they wish were true. Do you think we haven't run tests to *prove* the precognitive capabilities of our group?"

His lisp was growing steadily worse.

"We run new tests every time we add a new precog. They're tasked with predicting a series of random events such as the late arrivals of certain planes . . . news events such as the death of Tom Petty . . . the Brexit vote . . . vehicles passing through certain intersections, even. This is a record of successes—*recorded* successes—going back almost three quarters of a century!"

Three quarterth of a thentury.

"But your tests always focus on events that are

about to occur *soon*," Kalisha said. "Don't bother to deny it, it's in your head like a neon sign. Also, it's logical. What use is a test when you can't grade the results for five or ten years?"

She took Nicky's hand. Luke stepped back to them and took Kalisha's. And now Tim could hear that humming again. It was low, but it was there.

"Representative Berkowitz was exactly where our precogs said he would be on the day he died," Smith said, "and that prediction was made a full year before."

"Okay," Luke said, "but you've targeted people— Paul Westin, for one—based on predictions about what's going to happen in ten, twenty, even twenty-five years. You know they're unreliable, you know anything can happen to turn people and the events they're part of in a different direction, something as trivial as a missed phone call can do it, but you go on, just the same."

"Let's say you have a point," Smith said. "But isn't it better to be safe rather than sorry?" *Thafe. Thorry.* "Think of the predictions that have proved out, then think of the possible consequences of doing nothing!"

Annie was back a turn, maybe even two. "How can you be sure the predictions will come true if you kill the people they're about? I don't get that."

"He doesn't get it, either," Luke said, "but he can't bear to think that all the killing they've done has been for no good reason. None of them can."

"We had to destroy the village in order to save it," Tim said. "Didn't somebody say that about Vietnam?"

"If you're suggesting that our precogs have been stringing us along, making things up—"

"Can you be sure they haven't?" Luke countered. "Maybe not even consciously, but . . . it's a good life they have there, isn't it? Cushy. Not much like the ones we had in the Institute. And maybe their predictions are genuine at the time they're made. It still doesn't take random factors into consideration."

"Or God," Kalisha said suddenly.

Smith—who had been playing God for God knew how long—raised a sardonic smile at this.

Luke said, "You understand what I'm saying, I know you do. *There are too many variables*."

Smith was silent for a moment, looking out at the view. Then he said, "Yes, we have math guys, and yes, the Bernoulli distribution has come up in reports and discussions. For years now, in fact. So let's say you're right. Let's say our network of Institutes didn't save the world from nuclear destruction five hundred times. Suppose it was only fifty? Or five? Wouldn't it still be worth it?"

Very softly, Tim said, "No."

Smith stared at him as if he were insane. "*No?* You say *no?*"

"Sane people don't sacrifice children on the altar of probability. That's not science, it's superstition. And now I think it's time you left."

"We'll rebuild," Smith said. "If there's time, that is, with the world running downhill like a kid's jalopy with no hand to guide it. I also came to tell you that, and to warn you. No interviews. No articles. No threads posted on Facebook or Twitter. Such stories would be laughed at by most people, anyway, but they would be taken very seriously by us. If you want to insure your survival, *keep quiet*."

The hum was growing louder, and when Smith removed his American Spirits from his shirt pocket, his hand was shaking. The man who had gotten out of the nondescript Chevy had been confident and in charge. Used to giving orders and having them carried out ASAP. The one standing here now, the one with the heavy lisp and the sweat-stains creeping out from the armpits of his shirt, was not that man.

"Think you better go, son," Annie advised him, very softly. Maybe even kindly.

The cigarette pack dropped from Smith's hand. When he bent to pick it up, it skittered away, although there was no wind.

"Smoking's bad for you," Luke said. "You don't need a precog to tell you what'll happen if you don't stop."

The Malibu's windshield wipers started up. The lights came on.

"I'd go," Tim said. "While you still can. You're pissed about the way things have worked out, I get that, but you have no idea how pissed these kids are. They were on ground zero."

Smith went to his car and opened the door. Then he pointed a finger at Luke. "You believe what you want to believe," he said. "We all do, young Mr. Ellis. You'll discover that for yourself in time. And to your sorrow."

He drove away, the car's rear tires throwing up a cloud of dust that rolled toward Tim and the others . . . and then veered away, as if blown by a puff of wind none of them could feel.

Luke smiled, thinking George couldn't have done it better.

"Might have done better to get rid of him," Annie said matter-of-factly. "Plenty of room for a body at t'far end of the garden."

Luke sighed and shook his head. "There are others. He's only the point man."

"Besides," Kalisha said, "then we'd be like *them*."

"Still," Nicky said dreamily. He said no more, but Tim didn't have to be a mind-reader to get the rest of his thought: *It would have been nice.*

2

Tim expected Wendy back from Columbia for supper, but she called and said she had to stay over. Yet another meeting about the future of Fairlee County law enforcement had been scheduled for the following morning.

"Jesus, won't this ever be over?" Tim asked.

"I'm pretty sure this will be the last one. It's a complicated situation, you know, and bureaucracy makes everything worse. All okay there?"

"All fine," Tim said, and hoped it was true.

He made a big pot of spaghetti for supper; Luke threw together a Bolognese sauce; Kalisha and Nicky collaborated on a salad. Annie had disappeared, as she often did.

They ate well. There was good talk, and a fair amount of laughter. Then, as Tim was bringing a Pepperidge Farm cake back from the fridge, holding it high like a comic opera waiter, he saw that Kalisha was crying. Nick and Luke had each put an arm around her, but spoke no comforting words (at least that Tim could hear). They looked thoughtful, introspective. With her, but not perhaps completely with her; perhaps lost in their own concerns.

Tim set the cake down. "What's wrong, K? I'm sure they know, but I don't. So help a brother out."

"What if he's right? What if that man is right and Luke is wrong? What if the world ends in three years . . . or three *months* . . . because we're not there to protect it?"

"I'm not wrong," Luke said. "They've got mathematicians, but I'm better. It's not bragging if it's the truth. And what he said about me? That magical thinking thing? It's true of them, too. They can't bear to think they're wrong."

"You're not sure!" she cried. "I can hear it in your head, Lukey, *you're still not sure!*"

Luke did not deny this, just stared down at his plate.

Kalisha looked up at Tim. "What if they're only right *once*? Then it will be on us!"

Tim hesitated. He didn't want to think that what he said next might have a major influence on how this girl lived the rest of her life, there was no way he wanted that responsibility, but he was afraid he had it, anyway. The boys were listening, too. Listening and waiting. He had no psychic powers, but there was one power he did have: he was the grownup. The adult. They wanted him to tell them there was no monster under the bed.

"It's *not* on you. It's not on any of you. That man didn't come to warn you to be quiet, he came to poison your life. Don't let him do it, Kalisha. Don't any of you let him do it. As a species, we're built to do one thing above all others, and you kids did it."

He reached out with both hands and wiped the tears from Kalisha's cheeks.

"You survived. You used your love and your wits, and you survived. Now let's have some cake."

3

Friday came, and it was Nick's turn to go.

Tim and Wendy stood with Luke, watching as Nicky and Kalisha walked down the driveway with their arms around each other. Wendy would drive him to the bus station in Brunswick, but the three up here understood that those two needed—and deserved— a little time together first. To say goodbye.

"Let's go over it again," Tim had said an hour earlier, after a lunch neither Nicky nor Kalisha did much with. Tim and Nicky had gone out on the back stoop while Luke and Kalisha did up the few dishes.

"No need," Nicky said. "I got it, man. Really."

"Just the same," Tim said. "It's important. Brunswick to Chicago, right?"

"Right. The bus leaves at seven-fifteen tonight."

"Who do you talk to on the bus?"

"Nobody. Draw no attention."

"And when you get there?"

"I call my Uncle Fred from the Navy Pier. Because that's where the kidnappers dropped me off. Same place they dropped George and Helen off."

"But you don't know that."

"No, I don't."

"Do you know George and Helen?"

"Never heard of them."

"And who are the people who took you?"

"Don't know."

"What did they want?"

"Don't know. It's a mystery. They didn't molest me, they didn't ask me questions, I didn't hear any other kids, I don't know jack. When the police question me, I don't add anything."

"That's right."

"Eventually the cops give up and I go on to Nevada and live happily ever after with my aunt and uncle and Bobby." Bobby being Nick's brother, who had been at a sleepover on the night Nick was taken.

"And when you find out your parents are dead?"

"News to me. And don't worry, I'll cry. It won't be hard. And it won't be fake. Trust me on that. Can we be done?"

"Almost. First unball your fists a little. The ones at the ends of your arms and the ones in your head. Give happily ever after a chance."

"Not easy, man." Nicky's eyes gleamed with tears. "Not fucking easy."

"I know," Tim said, and risked a hug.

Nick allowed it passively at first, then hugged back. Hard. Tim thought it was a start, and he thought the boy would be fine no matter how many questions the police threw at him, no matter how many times they told him it didn't make any sense.

George Iles was the one Tim worried about when it came to adding stuff; the kid was an old-school motormouth and a born embellisher. Tim thought, however—*hoped*—that he had finally gotten the point across to George: what you didn't know kept you safe. What you added could trip you up.

Now Nick and Kalisha were embracing by the mailbox at the foot of the driveway, where Mr. Smith had laid blame in his lisping voice, trying to sow guilt in children who had only wanted to stay alive.

"He really loves her," Luke said.

Yes, Tim thought, and so do you.

But Luke wasn't the first boy to find himself odd man out in a lovers' triangle, and he wouldn't be the last. And was *lovers* the right word? Luke was brilliant, but he was also twelve. His feelings for Kalisha would pass like a fever, although it would be useless to tell him that. He would remember, though, just as Tim remembered the girl he'd been crazy about at twelve (she had been sixteen, and light-years beyond him). Just as Kalisha would remember Nicky, the handsome one who had fought.

"She loves you, too," Wendy said softly, and put a light squeeze on the back of Luke's sunburned neck.

"Not the same way," Luke said glumly, but then he smiled. "What the hell, life goes on."

"You better get the car," Tim said to Wendy. "That bus won't wait."

She got the car. Luke rode down to the mailbox with her, then stood with Kalisha. They waved as the car pulled away. Nicky's hand came out the window and waved back. Then they were gone. In Nick's right front pocket—the one that was hardest for some bus station sharpie to pick—was seventy dollars in cash and a phone card. In his shoe was a key.

Luke and Kalisha walked up the driveway together. Halfway there, Kalisha put her hands to her face and started to cry. Tim started to go down, then thought better of it. This was Luke's job. And he did it, putting his arms around her. Because she was taller, she rested her head on his head, rather than on his shoulder.

Tim heard the hum, now nothing but a low whisper. They were talking, but he couldn't hear what they were saying, and that was all right. It wasn't for him.

4

Two weeks later, it was Kalisha's turn to go, not to the bus station in Brunswick but the one in Greenville. She would arrive in Chicago late the following day, and call her sister in Houston from the Navy Pier. Wendy had gifted her with a small beaded purse. In it was seventy dollars and a phone card. There was a key, identical to Nicky's, in one of her sneakers. The money and phone card could be stolen; the key, never.

She hugged Tim hard. "That's not enough thanks for what you did, but I don't have anything else."

"It's enough," Tim said.

"I hope the world doesn't end because of us."

"I'm going to tell you this one last time, Sha—if someone pushes the big red button, it won't be you."

She smiled wanly. "When we were together at the end, we had a big red button to end all big red buttons. And it felt good to push it. That's what haunts me. How good it felt."

"But that's over."

"Yes. It's all going away, and I'm glad. No one should have power like that, especially not kids."

Tim thought that some of the people who could push the big red button *were* kids, in mind if not in body, but didn't say so. She was facing an unknown and uncertain future, and that was scary enough.

Kalisha turned to Luke and reached into her new purse. "I've got something for you. I had it in my pocket when we left the Institute, and didn't realize it. I want you to have it."

What she gave him was a crumpled cigarette box. On the front was a cowboy twirling a lariat. Above him was the brand, ROUND-UP CANDY CIGARETTES. Below him was SMOKE JUST LIKE DADDY!

"There's only some pieces left," she said. "Busted up and probably stale, too, but—"

Luke began to cry. This time it was Kalisha who put her arms around him.

"Don't, honey," she said. "Don't. Please. You want to break my heart?"

5

When Kalisha and Wendy were gone, Tim asked Luke if he wanted to play chess. The boy shook his head. "I think I might just go out back for awhile, and sit under that big tree. I feel empty inside. I never felt so empty."

Tim nodded. "You'll fill up again. Trust me."

"I guess I'll have to. Tim, do you think any of them will have to use those keys?"

"No."

The keys would open a safety deposit box in a Charleston bank. What Maureen Alvorson had given Luke was inside. If anything happened to any of the kids who had now left Catawba Farm—or to Luke, Wendy, or Tim—one of them would come to Charleston and open the box. Maybe all of them would come, if any of the bond forged in the Institute remained.

"Would anyone believe what's on the flash drive?"

"Annie certainly would," Tim said, smiling. "She believes in ghosts, UFOs, walk-ins, you name it."

Luke didn't smile back. "Yeah, but she's a little . . . you know, woo-woo. Although she's better now that she's seeing so much of Mr. Denton."

Tim's eyebrows went up. "Drummer? What are you telling me, that they're *dating*?"

"I guess so, if that's what you still call it when the people doing it are old."

"You read this in her mind?"

Luke smiled a little. "No. I'm back to moving pizza pans and fluttering book pages. She told me." Luke considered. "And I guess it's all right that I told you. It's not like she swore me to secrecy, or anything."

"I'll be damned. As to the flash drive . . . you know how you can pull on a loose thread and unravel an entire sweater? I think the flash drive might be like that. There are kids on it people would recognize. A lot of them. It would start an investigation, and any hopes that lisping guy's organization might have of re-starting their program would go out the window."

"I don't think they can do that, anyway. He might think so, but it's just more magical thinking. The world has changed a lot since the nineteen-fifties. Listen, I'm going to . . ." He gestured vaguely toward the house and the garden.

"Sure, you go on."

Luke started away, not walking, exactly, but trudging with his head down.

Tim almost let him go, then changed his mind. He caught up with Luke and took him by the shoulder. When the boy turned, Tim hugged him. He had hugged Nicky—hell, he had hugged them all, sometimes after they awoke from bad dreams—but this one meant more. This one meant the world, at least to Tim. He wanted to tell Luke that he was brave, maybe the bravest kid ever outside of a boys' adventure book. He wanted to tell Luke that he was strong and decent and his folks would be proud of him. He wanted to tell Luke that he loved him. But there were no words, and maybe no need of them. Or telepathy.

Sometimes a hug was telepathy.

6

Out back, between the stoop and the garden, was a fine old pin oak. Luke Ellis—once of Minneapolis, Minnesota, once loved by Herb and Eileen Ellis, once a friend of Maureen Alvorson, and Kalisha Benson, and Nick Wilholm, and George Iles—sat down beneath it. He put his forearms on his drawn-up knees and looked out toward what Officer Wendy called the Rollercoaster Hills.

Also once a friend of Avery, he thought. Avery was the one who really got them out. If there was a hero, it wasn't me. It was the Avester.

Luke took the crumpled cigarette box from his pocket and fished out one of the pieces. He thought about seeing Kalisha for the first time, sitting on the floor with one of these in her mouth. *Want one?* she had asked. *A little sugar might help your state of mind. It always helps mine.*

"What do you think, Avester? Will it help my state of mind?"

Luke crunched up the piece of candy. It did help, although he had no idea why; there was certainly nothing scientific about it. He peered into the pack and saw two or three more pieces. He could eat them now, but it might be better to wait.

Better to save some for later.

September 23, 2018

AUTHOR'S NOTE

A few words if you please, Constant Reader, about Russ Dorr.

I met him over forty years ago—well over—in the town of Bridgton, Maine, where he was the single physicians' assistant in the three-doc medical center. He saw to most of my family's minor medical problems, everything from stomach flu to the kids' ear infections. His standard witticism for fever was clear liquids—"just gin and vodka." He asked me what I did for a living, and I told him I wrote novels and short stories, mostly scary ones about psychic phenomena, vampires, and other assorted monsters.

"Sorry, I don't read stuff like that," he said, neither of us knowing that he would eventually read everything I wrote, usually in manuscript and often while various works were in progress. Other than my wife, he was the only one who saw my fiction before it was fully dressed and ready for its close-up.

I began to ask him questions, first about medical matters. Russ was the one who told me about how the flu changes from year to year, making each new vaccine obsolete (that was for *The Stand*). He gave me a list of exercises to keep the muscles of comatose patients from wasting away (that was for *The Dead Zone*). He patiently explained how animals contracted rabies, and how the disease progressed (for *Cujo*).

His remit gradually expanded, and when he retired from medicine, he became my full-time research assistant. We visited the Texas School Book Depository together for *11/22/63*—a book I literally could not have written without him—and while I absorbed the gestalt of the place (looking for ghosts . . . and finding them), Russ took pictures and made measurements. When we went to the Texas Theatre, where Lee Harvey Oswald was captured, it was Russ who asked what was playing that day (a double feature consisting of *Cry of Battle* and *War is Hell*).

On *Under the Dome* he gathered reams of information about the micro ecosystem I was trying to create, from the capacity of electricity generators to how long food supplies might last, but the thing he was most proud of came when I asked if he could think of an air supply for my characters—something like SCUBA tanks—that would last for five minutes or so. It was for the climax of the book, and I was stumped. So was Russ, until he was stuck in traffic one day, and took a good look at the cars all around him.

"Tires," he told me. "Tires have air in them. It would be stale and nasty-tasting, but it would be breathable." And so, dear readers, tires it was.

Russ's fingerprints are all over the book you have just read, from the BDNF tests for newborns (yes, it's a real thing, only a bit fictionalized), to how poison gas could be created from common household products (don't try this at home, kids). He vetted every line and fact, helping me toward what has always been my goal: making the impossible plausible. He was a big, blond, broad-shouldered man who loved a joke and a beer and shooting off bottle rockets on the Fourth of July. He raised two wonderful daughters and saw his wife through her final lingering illness. We worked together, but he was also my friend. We were simpatico. Never had a single argument.

Russ died of kidney failure in the fall of 2018, and I miss him like hell. Sure, when I need information (lately it's been elevators and first-generation iPhones), but a lot more when I forget he's gone and think, "Hey, I should give Russ a call or drop him an email, ask what's going on." This book is dedicated to my grandsons, because it's mostly about kids, but it's Russ I'm thinking about as I put it to bed. It's very hard to let old friends go.

I miss you, buddy.

Before I quit, Constant Reader, I should thank the usual suspects: Chuck Verrill, my agent; Chris Lotts, who deals with foreign rights and found a dozen different ways to say *Do you hear me*; Rand Holsten, who does movie deals (lately there's been a lot of them); and Katie Monaghan, who handles publicity for Scribner. And a *huge* thank-you to Nan Graham, who edited a book that's full of many moving parts, parallel timelines, and dozens of characters. She made it a better book. I also need to thank Marsha DeFilippo, Julie Eugley, and Barbara MacIntyre, who take the calls, make the appointments, and give me those vital hours I use each day to write.

Last but hardly least, thanks to my kids—Naomi, Joe, and Owen—and to my wife. If I may borrow from George R. R. Martin, she is my sun and stars.

February 17, 2019

Turn the page for an excerpt from
Stephen King's electrifying thriller

BILLY SUMMERS

Available from Scribner

Billy Summers sits in the hotel lobby, waiting for his ride. It's Friday noon. Although he's reading a digest-sized comic book called *Archie's Pals 'n' Gals*, he's thinking about Émile Zola, and Zola's third novel, his breakthrough, *Thérèse Raquin*. He's thinking it's very much a young man's book. He's thinking that Zola was just beginning to mine what would turn out to be a deep and fabulous vein of ore. He's thinking that Zola was—is—the nightmare version of Charles Dickens. He's thinking that would make a good thesis for an essay. Not that he's ever written one.

At two minutes past twelve the door opens and two men come into the lobby. One is tall with black hair combed in a 50s pompadour. The other is short and bespectacled. Both are wearing suits. All of Nick's men wear suits. Billy knows the tall one from out west. He's been with Nick a long time. His name is Frank Macintosh. Because of the pomp, some of Nick's men call him Frankie Elvis, or—now that he has a tiny bald spot in back—Solar Elvis. But not to his face. Billy doesn't know the other one. He must be local.

Macintosh holds out his hand. Billy rises and shakes it.

"Hey, Billy, been awhile. Good to see you."

"Good to see you too, Frank."

"This is Paulie Logan."

"Hi, Paulie." Billy shakes with the short one.

"Pleased to meet you, Billy."

Macintosh takes the *Archie* digest from Billy's hand. "Still reading the comics, I see."

"Yeah," Billy says. "Yeah. I like them quite a bit. The funny ones. Sometimes the superheroes but I don't like them as much."

Macintosh breezes through the pages and shows something to Paulie Logan. "Look at these chicks. Man, I could jack off to these."

"Betty and Veronica," Billy says, taking the comic back. "Veronica is Archie's girlfriend and Betty wants to be."

"You read books, too?" Logan asks.

"Some, if I'm going on a long trip. And magazines. But mostly comic books."

"Good, good," Logan says, and drops Macintosh a wink. Not very subtle, and Macintosh frowns, but Billy's okay with it.

"You ready to take a ride?" Macintosh asks.

"Sure." Billy tucks his digest into his back pocket. Archie and his bosomy gal pals. There's an essay waiting to be written there, too. About the comfort of haircuts and attitudes that don't change. About Riverdale, and how time stands still there.

"Then let's go," Macintosh says. "Nick's waiting."

2

Macintosh drives. Logan says he'll sit in back because he's short. Billy expects them to go west, because that's where the fancy part of this town is, and Nick Majarian likes to live large whether home or away. And he doesn't do hotels. But they go northeast instead.

Two miles from downtown they enter a neighborhood that looks lower middle-class to Billy. Three or four steps better than the trailer park he grew up in, but far from fancy. No big gated houses, not here. This is a neighborhood of ranch houses with lawn sprinklers twirling on small patches of grass. Most are one-story. Most are well maintained, but a few need paint and there's crabgrass taking over some of the lawns. He sees one house with a piece of cardboard blocking a broken window. In front of another, a fat man in Bermuda shorts and a wifebeater sits in a lawn chair from Costco or Sam's Club, drinking a beer and watching them go by. Times have been good in America for awhile now, but maybe that is going to change. Billy knows neighborhoods like this. They are a barometer, and this one has started to go down. The people who live here are working the kind of jobs where you punch a clock.

Macintosh pulls into the driveway of a two-story with a patchy lawn. It's painted a subdued yellow. It's okay, but doesn't look like a place where Nick Majarian would choose to live, even for a few days. It looks like the kind of place a machinist or lower-echelon airport employee would live with his coupon-clipping wife and two kids, making mortgage payments every month and bowling in a beer league on Thursday nights.

Logan opens Billy's door. Billy puts his *Archie* digest on the dashboard and gets out.

Macintosh leads the way up the porch steps. It's hot outside but inside it's air conditioned. Nick Majarian stands in the short hallway leading down to the kitchen. He's wearing a suit that probably cost almost as much as a monthly mortgage payment on this house. His thinning hair is combed flat, no pompadour for him. His face is round and Vegas tanned. He's heavyset, but when he pulls Billy into a hug, that protruding belly feels as hard as stone.

"Billy!" Nick exclaims, and kisses him on both cheeks. Big hearty smacks. He's wearing a million-dollar grin. "Billy, Billy, man, it's good to see you!"

"Good to see you, too, Nick." He looks around. "You usually stay somewhere fancier than this." He pauses. "If you don't mind me saying."

Nick laughs. He has a beautiful infectious laugh to go with the grin. Macintosh joins in and Logan smiles. "I got a place over on the West Side. Short-term. House-sitting, you could call it. There's a fountain in the front yard. Got a naked little kid in the middle of it, there's a word for that . . ."

Cherub, Billy thinks but doesn't say. He just keeps smiling.

"Anyway, a little kid peeing water. You'll see it, you'll see it. No, this one isn't mine, Billy. It's yours. If you decide to take the job, that is."

Nick shows him around. "Fully furnished," he says, like he's selling it. Maybe he sort of is.

This one has a second floor where there are three bedrooms and two bathrooms, the second small, probably for the kids. On the first floor there's a kitchen, a living room, and a dining room that's so small it's actually a dining nook. Most of the cellar has been converted into a long carpeted room with a big TV at one end and a Ping-Pong table at the other. Track lighting. Nick calls it the rumpus room, and this is where they sit.

Macintosh asks them if they'd like something to drink. He says there's soda, beer, lemonade, and iced tea.

"I want an Arnold Palmer," Nick says. "Half and half. Lots of ice."

Billy says that sounds good. They make small talk until the drinks come. The weather, how hot it is down here in the border south. Nick wants to know how Billy's trip in was. Billy says it was fine but doesn't say where he flew in from and Nick doesn't ask. Nick says how about that fuckin Trump and Billy says how about him. That's about all they've got, but it's okay because by then Macintosh is back with two tall glasses on a tray, and once he leaves, Nick gets down to business.

"When I called your man Bucky, he tells me you're hoping to retire."

"I'm thinking about it. Been at it a long time. Too long."